Spirit of Empire
Book One

Last of the Chosen

By
Lawrence P. White

www.spiritofempire.com

First Kindle eBook edition February 2011

Cover design by Duncan Long

ISBN-13: 978-1-4563-3768-1

ISBN-10: 1-4563-3768-8

Author's Notes

Portions of this story were previously published under the title
Spirit of Empire. This publication includes that book plus the
second book in the series.

The author welcomes your questions or comments. Feel free to
email the author at larry@spiritofempire.com.

Part One – Survival

Chapter One

A meteor streaked through the darkening Nevada sky from right to left, snatching Mike's focus from the road. His mind, sluggishly holding to alertness by a thread, perked up at this unexpected delight. A heartbeat later, he was treated to a rare phenomenon, two more meteors streaking behind the first. Then his tired mind sharpened, his brow creasing in disbelief. He could have sworn the three streaks turned down and to the left just before winking out. But that was not possible. Meteors don't turn, they simply melt into nothingness.

Mike focused again on his driving, but moments later a bright beam of light reached silently across the heavens to touch something high up in the sky. That something winked brighter than a star. The beam of light instantly changed to a green color and pulsed rapidly. The winking target lit the night, seemed to turn sharply, but could not shake off the pulsing green tether attached to itself.

Mike's weariness vanished in a wash of excitement. He stood on the brakes, then had to concentrate on controlling a minor slide as his speed dropped off. By the time he could spare a glance, the target of those pulses was a roiling fireball falling from the sky. A clap, like distant thunder, rolled over the car as he slid to a stop in the middle of the road. A grin lit his face as he hopped out of the restored Mustang convertible for a better look. Somebody was playing with new weapons. Had he just seen a successful test?

Area 51, Dreamland, our top secret research and development

facility for military aircraft and weapons, reputedly called the vast area of desert to the south its home. Were they testing some kind of new weapon tonight? Right here, out in the open where anyone could see? It didn't make sense, but something had surely blown up. That something was still streaming flames and molten metal as it continued its long fall toward the ground.

Light reached across the sky again, much closer to the ground this time and much closer to Mike as well. Another star flared into existence but responded with a rapid series of pulsed green beams of its own. It abruptly angled away, breaking the tether of light attempting to hold it, and disappeared. More flashes soon lit the sky, alternating between the two craft and creating tiny halos around each. Mike frowned. This didn't look like a test, it looked like a fight. The fighting, if that's what it was, steadily moved closer to him as he stood beside his car.

One of the craft staggered. Mike sucked in a breath when it abruptly swooped toward the ground, flattening its fall at the last moment to hit the road a couple of miles away at high speed. The craft caromed off the pavement back into the air, struggling to stay aloft but failing. When it hit again, pavement peeled up like a ribbon, curling up and over the craft. It emerged from the debris, airborne once more but barely above the ground. There was no doubt in Mike's mind that the craft was in trouble and had chosen the highway as its emergency landing site. When it hit the road again, the craft slid along the highway, shoveling its way through a hail of pavement, dirt, debris, and sparks. He was directly in its path.

He cursed and took a few running steps toward the desert, then turned back, his mind on the important blueprints in the car. He couldn't leave them under any circumstances. He reached across to the passenger seat and hefted the strap of an old duffel bag to his shoulder. With another glance at the mountain of dirt coming his way, he ran for his life, awkwardly adjusting the bag until it thumped across his back. Dodging the worst of the scrub and cacti as best he could in the failing light, his only focus was to put distance between himself and the road. The ground was soft, the whole area the remains of an ancient dry lake bed, and the going was hard. He stumbled and fell, a cloud of dust engulfing him, but with a fearful look over his shoulder he was up in an instant, sprinting for all he was worth, the heavy bag now held to his chest. He ran up and over a low outcropping of rock, then found himself running on air, his arms and legs flailing for balance. He fell several feet and hit hard, the wind knocked out of him.

Dirt, rocks, asphalt, and an incredible cacophony of sound hammered Mike as he lay stunned. He kept his head down and didn't see the Mustang disappear, engulfed without pity by the monstrous craft as it slid to a stop.

The noise died away, replaced by an ominous stillness. Mike rose to his knees, coughing and spitting salty dirt from his mouth, the smell of the lake bed filling his nose and mouth. Then he froze. A muffled clank followed by a thunk sounded through the dust from the direction of the crash. Not the sound of a crashed plane settling into its final resting-place, this sound spoke of doors or hatches unsealing in a hurry. He scrabbled on hands and knees to the top of the rocks and peered over. A huge disc-shaped craft had come to rest at an angle, its front end buried in dirt. His eyes were immediately drawn to a rectangle of light showing dimly through the dust beneath the back end of the craft. Short, thin, man-like creatures with large, bald heads appeared in the light one by one, dropping to the ground with hand-held weapons before them and spreading out to disappear into the murk.

Mike slid back down the rocks to the ground, his eyes staring but not seeing. The image of bald heads with huge eyes imprinted itself in his brain forever. These creatures were not from Earth, nor was their ship. They resembled artist's conceptions of the Roswell aliens, but these aliens were very, very alive, and they were armed. Was he their friend, or was he their enemy?

In his own mind, he was neither. He was just Mike Carver, architect and engineer. His eyes went to the duffel bag with the drawings, the final drawings that had been his whole world until just a few minutes ago. The rest of his design team was already in Reno assembling the model of the new high rise hotel and casino complex, a massive project that his small company had won in competition against much larger competitors. Tomorrow was contract signing day and the beginning of the second phase, the construction.

His gaze still on the bag, his lips pursed and his eyes narrowed. No, it wasn't going to happen now, not tomorrow . . . but it was going to happen even if it meant he had to walk the rest of the way on foot. He just had to get away from here, then he'd figure out the rest.

An explosion ripped the night, a bright beam of light reaching up from the crashed ship to impact against another craft with a tremendous crack. Mike's breathing stopped. Were his eyes fooling him or was that a UFO up there? The halo of light outlining the ship dissipated quickly, and the ship disappeared into the dark. A series of rapid pulses hurled up from the crashed ship toward the UFO and lit it again. It staggered, then returned fire with one powerful blast. The blast striking so close by literally stunned and blinded Mike. When his vision returned, flames belched from a gaping hole in the side of the crashed ship.

More figures jumped from the burning wreck and spread out into the desert, though not in Mike's direction. Then, to his dismay, the UFO returned. The ground behind him, his intended escape route, lit up as the immense disc drifted silently overhead, coming to a stop when its forward edge neared the crashed ship. Thirty feet above his head, the burnished skin of the ship completely hid the stars. A ramp dropped to the ground some fifty meters away from him, light pouring from the opening to light up a large area beneath the ship. That area included Mike's hiding place. He froze, knowing that any movement from him would draw unwanted attention. Several big cats leaped down the ramp and disappeared into the brush. He chanced movement and peeked around the rock to discover aliens from the crashed ship working their way toward the UFO.

He was right between both groups.

Energy bolts from hand-held weapons split the night in both directions. Mike hugged the ground with his eyes shut, willing himself to melt into the dirt, his mind furiously seeking and discarding ideas. He had to get away. He mentally chose a direction away from both ships and opened his eyes, his muscles tensed to spring, but instead he froze with a scream dying in his throat. Orange, feral eyes attached to a vicious snout filled his vision from inches away, a creature from hell. Mike sucked in a breath, then wished he hadn't – the smell of the creature's breath nearly caused him to gag. The eyes blinked. Vertical, diamond-shaped pupils disappeared, then reappeared, staring into his eyes. The eyes blinked once again, lips rose to display jagged fangs, then the creature reached forward with a paw, caressing Mike's neck and head. He sensed incredible power within the beast as it pressed his head firmly into the dirt. Then the touch was gone. Mike looked up, but the creature had melted into the surroundings without a sound.

* * * * *

As if awaking from a dream, he rediscovered the night air bursting with weapons fire. He'd been touched by an alien. It had communicated a simple message that he clearly understood.

Hide!

He numbly surveyed his surroundings and rose to a crouch, then flung himself back to the ground as the rock beside him exploded in a blast from . . . somewhere. That woke him up. This was bad, real bad, and no one was going to get him out of this mess but himself.

He scrabbled through the dirt to the edge of the rocks for a quick survey. To his left lay the crashed ship, seemingly dead now. His car lay somewhere out there in the dark beneath the hulk. In front of him and to the right, light streamed from the ramp near the center of the UFO. The ship itself was immense, some two hundred meters in diameter. Its bulk hid the night sky above him, its nearest edge a good 50 meters away.

He had no idea what the fighting was about, nor could he say who the bad guys were, though, surprisingly, he knew they were not the cats. A strong sense of rightness had come from the cat. It had told him to hide, but he would have preferred being offered a weapon. Here he was, caught right in the middle with no means of protecting himself. Nor did he see a way to hide. He couldn't dig a hole, yet simply waiting for someone, or something, to come up and point a gun at him would not do either.

Another blast exploded against the rocks above him, forcing a decision. Grabbing his bag of plans, Mike turned until the light from the hovering UFO was off his left shoulder. He scrabbled straight ahead on hands and knees, dragging the heavy bag by its belt. He had not forgotten what he'd learned during his stint in the Army. He didn't stop, just kept going through the dark for twenty or thirty feet, froze to listen and look, then went another twenty feet.

A new sound filled the night between the blasts from weapons, a high keening like the sound of cicadas. The sound struck him as something not of the desert, at least not the desert he knew, but he had bigger problems to worry about. The shooting became sporadic, possibly an indication of the number of contestants remaining, and Mike wondered which side was winning.

He stayed low as he continued crawling, lifting his head just high enough to survey the scene from time to time. Twilight had ended, the moon had not yet risen, and the desert sky beyond the edge of the ship was full dark now. The only light came from the ship and the occasional blast of a weapon. The crashed ship seemed deserted, and he gave serious thought to turning back in its direction since that's where everyone else wasn't, but the thought of encountering one of those hideous creatures in the dark revolted him. He wanted away from here, away from them, and away from the light. He turned his head to the left, studying the UFO and wondering why it didn't turn out the lights.

Just then a man staggered down the ramp, a brightly colored cape billowing out behind, with his hands clamped over his ears and his body twisting in agony. Moments later a woman staggered down the ramp after him firing a blaster wildly, appearing unable to take aim. Two large cats sprang after the woman, knocking her to the ground at the foot of the ramp, but the man stayed on his feet. Twenty feet from Mike, between himself and the light, one of the bald-headed creatures rose silently from the desert. It pointed a weapon toward the UFO and took careful aim at the man.

Not pausing to think, just knowing the man was defenseless, Mike rose to a crouch, then sprinted toward the creature, tackling it from behind. It felt light as a feather and fragile, squeaking as it went down beneath him, its weapon flying from its hand. Holding on with a death grip as they hit, Mike felt bones give way within the creature's chest, and he sensed life flow from its body.

No! Gasping with shame and revulsion, Mike jumped to his feet with both hands brushing at his clothes of their own accord, trying to rid himself of the feel of the creature lying at his feet.

Blast! The searing heat of a near miss brought him back to his senses. He dropped to the ground, his hands searching for the weapon dropped by the alien creature. Discarding dirt, rocks, and the sharp, bristly branches of plants in the dark, eventually his fingers brushed against something hard and unnatural. He hefted the weapon gingerly, searching in the light from the ship for a trigger.

The weapon was about two feet long and felt like a toy in his hands. There was no trigger, but he did find two buttons on the grip. He pushed one, then the other, but nothing happened. Frustrated, he depressed both buttons at the same time. The weapon exploded a charge straight up, hitting the ship above him and ricocheting off. He cringed, but only for a moment. Yes! He had a weapon; he was no longer defenseless.

The caped man lay on the ground ten feet from the ramp, not moving. The woman lay at the foot of the ramp behind the two cats who were firing at anything that moved. Mike retrieved his bag and circled the brightly lit area of the ramp, his belly never leaving the ground, until he was out of the brightest light. Why didn't they turn out the lights, he wondered? He stopped moving when a shape rose up behind the woman and cats. A bald, white head, elliptical eyes dominating its features, stared out from behind the ramp of the UFO, aiming a weapon at the unprotected woman.

Mike had to choose. Should he escape, or should he help the cats and the woman who were pinned down? He had felt rightness from the fearsome cat that had told him to hide, and he felt revulsion for the bald-headed creatures. He chose what felt right. He rose to one knee, took careful aim down the short barrel of the alien weapon, and pressed the buttons. A charge exploded from the weapon, narrowly missing the woman and cats to ricochet off the ramp. The baldhead changed its aim, loosing off a hurried round at Mike that went wide. Moving his aim slightly to the right, Mike pushed the buttons again. This time he was on target. The creature flew backward as the burst of energy exploded into its body.

Quicker than he could blink, Mike found himself staring into the muzzles of four weapons, one in each forepaw of the cats. His weapon fell to the ground and both arms rose as high as he could reach before he had even made a conscious decision to do so.

Blast! One of the cats went down. The other dropped to cover the woman and fired at a target behind Mike, all in the same motion. Mike scooped up his weapon and the bag of drawings and raced in a crouch toward the ramp, dodging to avoid blasts on the way. He dove to cover behind the ramp, rolling into the body of the alien he had shot. Using it as cover, he turned to the rear looking for others. Shots exploded from the dark, then two aliens rose to rush forward. Mike fired twice and didn't miss. He had just an instant to note that the cicada sound ceased after his last shot before a hail of blaster charges rained against the front of the ramp, flooding him with heat and explosions.

The cat creature, using the body of his dead partner for cover, kept up a constant fire. Mike reached an arm around the entrance ramp, grasped an ankle and pulled, dragging the woman to safety by his side. She seemed dazed, turning to look at him with vacant eyes. The cat soon joined him and they took turns firing at anything that moved, but they were trapped. They needed to move into the safety of the ship, but there was no way to get around and up the ramp without fully exposing themselves. One look into the cat's eyes convinced Mike that it, too, was aware of their predicament. They needed to eliminate the baldheads. They needed a diversion to draw them out of hiding.

Mike took a moment to study the cat. What was it about the creature that drew him? He should have been revolted by its very presence, by its obvious alienness, but he was not. About the size and coloring of a full-grown lion, its muzzle drew all his attention. Longer than a cat's, more like a baboon's, the muzzle was furless and fierce, the skin gathered in brightly colored ridges, red and black and gold predominating. The teeth, when exposed, were clearly made for ripping apart prey. The ears were definitely those of a cat, tufted with black hair on each pointed end. The cat wore no clothes, only an equipment harness holding various pouches crisscrossing its shoulders and chest. He sensed power within the cat, power screaming to be unleashed, but not in his direction. In spite of its fearsome appearance, this cat was not his enemy.

Mike motioned for the cat to go out to the side in a flanking action to draw out the enemy. Then, he looked at his hand as if it belonged to someone else. Was he nuts? What was he trying to do? Why was he even here? He didn't want any part in this. He had never seriously believed the stories of UFO's and alien abductions, though he hoped others existed out among the stars and would come some day in the future. But not now, not right this minute. He just wanted away from here. This wasn't his fight.

The cat's gaze met his squarely as it shook its head, indicating that Mike's plan was not acceptable. It holstered a weapon and reached out a clawed fist to caress the head of the woman, scrunching up its lips in a smile to display wicked teeth. Mike got the message – it wasn't leaving her side. He also discovered that the creature was no simple cat. Instead of paws, it had four hands with full length fingers and opposing thumbs, all tipped by sharp claws.

The cat shook the woman to get her attention, peering into her eyes until it found what it was looking for, then forced a weapon into her hand. She responded by angrily turning toward Mike, then shouldering him aside to squeeze between him and the ramp. The blaster in her hand fired, then fired again.

Mike turned toward the cat thinking hard, then met the cat's fierce gaze again. He waived his blaster over his head in a circle, then pointed to his eyes and covered them. The cat took a quick look around the ramp, fired one shot, then another and returned to the silent game of charades. It thought for a moment, then pointed a long-nailed finger straight up, motioning up the ramp and into the ship.

Darn! The light switch must be inside the ship. Mike shrugged, knowing what had to come next. He looked away from the cat with a frown, wondering how his life could have changed so completely so suddenly, wondering also why he had chosen sides when he didn't even know who the good guys were. When he turned back to the cat, the quivering, hellish muzzle swung to within inches of his own. They locked gazes again silently. This cat understood his dilemma.

Though Mike's gaze was on the cat, his mind was elsewhere. His whole life had changed in the past fifteen minutes. His car lay beneath the crashed ship some one hundred meters away. He still had his drawings, but the prospects of those drawings reaching Reno appeared bleak at the moment. Nor was the significance of this First Contact lost on him. Building plans and cars mattered little to the potential ramifications of First Contact. But whose side should he be on, if anyone's? He didn't want to choose sides, but the sides had been chosen for him. The bald-headed aliens had shot at him. His choice had been cemented when he tackled and killed the creature that had shot the man. There was no going back now, but that didn't mean he had made the right choice.

His eyes focused once again on the cat, and he knew instantly that this cat was what mattered. First Contact took precedence over his own personal plans, and for the moment, survival was the focus.

The cat waited for him to make up his mind with the patience all cats seemed to have. Mike pursed his lips, then locked gazes with the cat and nodded his head once. He would do his part, if only to survive.

The woman grasped a handful of fur at the throat of the cat. It instantly swung its muzzle toward her to give her its full, undivided attention. Mike gathered up another weapon from the dead alien he had shot, stuck both barrels around the ramp, and awkwardly pushed buttons, loosing shots at random and frequently checking to his rear. He didn't see any movement anywhere. The woman had risen to her knees before the cat, both hands grasping the fur around its neck to hold its attention. Heated words were exchanged, the cat holding its own with full speech ability. Mike understood enough from the tone to know that the cat was not only being ordered, but that it was unhappy about those orders. It turned to face him, peering hard into his eyes, willing its thoughts to him.

Mike watched carefully as the cat motioned, its arm reaching toward the fallen man who was well beyond its reach. Shots exploded against the ramp and everyone huddled together. Mike hissed at the cat to get his attention, studied his weapons momentarily, then crouched beside the ramp and began firing both as quickly as the weapons would allow. The woman squirmed beneath him on her belly, adding her fire to his, and the cat took off. It reached the fallen man in one leap, wrapped a well-muscled arm around him, and skittered back, laying the man gently under the sloping ramp.

Mike stopped firing and sat up, wiping sweat from his brow as the woman examined the body. He took one look and knew the man was dead. A large chunk of his midsection was missing, and there was no sign of blood flowing from the wound. Clearly, his heart had stopped. Mike focused on the desert to his rear, wondering how many bald-headed aliens were left out there.

What next, he wondered? They were still pinned down, unable to get into the ship. The woman conferred with the cat again, exchanging more heated words, then turned her attention to Mike. For the first time he took a good look at her. Disheveled brown hair and a face streaked with dust and dried tears returned his gaze. Large, angry, doe-like brown eyes examined him from head to foot, taking in his long, lanky frame, straight black hair, and black eyes spaced wide apart on a permanently tanned face. What she couldn't see was his Scottish heritage, a source of high energy and determination, tempered by a mixture of American Indian that gave him his calm, unflappable stamina, gifts he keenly protected.

When her examination was complete and she focused once again on his eyes, he sensed that, unlike the cat, she was not happy with what she saw. Their gazes held for a moment, then he returned his attention to the cat, dismissing her. She grasped both of his shoulders, forcing his attention back to her. Two sets of angry eyes stared at each other.

Without warning her eyes swelled. Mike felt himself swallowed by those eyes, then all coherent thought of any kind fled. He felt her mind delve into his inner being, sampling memories and feelings, shuffling through them as quickly as a professional dealer shuffled cards. His mind was reduced to primitive instincts, wanting only to escape. On that primitive level he panicked and tried to fight back, but there was nothing to grab on to. He tried to flee and managed to stand up, but she rose with him, keeping a lock on his mind. Unknown to him, shots impacted the other side of the ramp, and she grabbed the front of his shirt, pulling them both back from danger. They stood nose to nose, his whole being captive to her mind as she shuffled through his thoughts.

Suddenly, she was gone. She simply withdrew, freed him, let go of his mind. He flopped to the ground, pulling her with him. She lay on top of him, but he didn't care. It was over. That's all that mattered. It was over.

Gasping for breath, he flung her off and rose, the fighting forgotten, his hand held out before him to ward her off, wanting nothing but space, lots of space, between her and him. His mind was his own again but primitive instinct still prevailed. He needed to be away from this alien creature. Nothing else mattered.

A clawed hand grasped the front of his shirt and pulled him into an embrace, forcing him to the ground. The cat stood guard over him while he struggled with his horror.

A fierce growl brought him back to reality. The woman had returned to the base of the ramp, lying on her belly and firing her weapon as if nothing unusual had happened. The cat growled again, demanding his attention. Mike closed his eyes and shook as a chill raced through his body, but he forced himself to think. He was in the midst of a battle, he was pinned down, and he wanted to live. He had to set the horror aside, at least for a time, but he would never forgive or forget how she had violated him. First Contact was toast as far as he was concerned. He just wanted away from this witch woman. If getting away meant killing the bald-headed aliens first, then he would kill them.

The cat reached a hand out to him. Three small spheres rested in the palm of that hand. It motioned throwing the spheres out into the desert, then shielding its eyes. More charades, but Mike got the message. He took a moment to check his weapons. What he was checking for he didn't know, but it gave him the moment he needed to get his act together.

He lifted his eyes to the cat and nodded, lips still pursed in a thin line. One sphere was dropped just in front of the ramp, then the other two flew far into the night. He closed his eyes and felt the rough hand of the cat reaching out to supply added cover for his eyes. Moments later he dimly perceived a bright flash, as if a stun grenade had gone off. Once more the light flashed, even brighter, then Mike moved, sprinting toward the dark desert in a line perpendicular to the ramp. He was gratified to hear covering fire from the cat and the woman. It was a long run, some thirty or forty meters, and he was the only thing moving, the only target. Did the bald-headed alien's eyes work the same as ours? Were they blinded, or was he an easy target?

He stopped and flattened himself to the ground, raising only his head. He was outside the brightest wash of light from the ship, giving him a much better view of the area holding the bald-heads. He waited, lifting his head slowly, knowing that the first creature to move would be at a disadvantage.

Nothing happened for a time, so he set one weapon on the ground and raised himself to one knee, keeping his head below the level of the brush. He raised the weapon into a rifle-like firing position, one eye looking along the top of the short barrel, his left elbow held tightly against his body to provide a rigid firing platform.

The cicada sound returned strongly, and he frowned. What were cicadas doing here in the desert at this time of year? Moments later he saw movement. The woman was thrashing on the ground beside the ramp having some kind of fit, fully exposed to the bald-heads. Three white, bald-headed figures, widely dispersed, rose as one thirty meters in front of the ramp, weapons preparing to fire.

The cat sprang from behind the ramp to cover the woman, its

blaster taking out all three of the enemy quicker than Mike could blink. Mike rose up to help, but he was too late. He swiftly turned to his left and checked behind the ramp. The light was much dimmer there, but two white, bald heads showed clearly. They took aim, but Mike fired quickly and repeatedly, felling both of them. The cicada sound ceased abruptly as the last alien fell.

He raced toward the darker area behind the ramp to look for more, leaving the brighter area in front of the ramp to the cat.

He settled, then moved a few more meters away from the ramp and lowered himself back into a firing position, searching, but he sensed it was over. While he waited, he wondered if the ship would just close its ramp and lift off. That would be okay with him as long as the witch woman went with it.

He was taken completely by surprise when the cat appeared beside him, rising silently out of the dark. They looked at each other sensing kinship, then the cat turned its back on him and headed back to the ship. Mike stayed anchored in place with one knee on the ground, sensing the invitation but aware that the witch was back there. The cat stopped and turned to face him, then settled onto its haunches to wait.

Mike studied the creature, studied its alienness, and as he did so, he began to sense wonder. This creature was so very much more than just an animal. In every way it was a person, just as he was. It was clearly intelligent, it spoke, it used tools, and it flew spaceships. What places had it visited? What things had it seen? Other worlds, surely. Probably other star systems as well. He doubted if the cat was from Mars, and it certainly wasn't from any of the other uninhabitable planets in our solar system, so it must have come from the stars.

Regardless of where it was from, he and the cat were kindred spirits now. They'd fought together, and in doing so they had become linked in some indefinable way. He liked the cat, and he liked the feeling.

His gaze lifted to study the ship above his head. The distant edge of its burnished disc disappeared in the darkness, so immense was the craft. A real space ship! In fact, it was probably a starship. True, the witch was part of it, yet his excitement blossomed. Would they let him inside, let him look around? He'd earned the privilege. They owed him, sort of; he'd helped save their butts. Did these aliens believe in gratitude?

Looking to the cat once again, he knew the cat wouldn't let him down. He stood up and looked toward the lighted area surrounding the ramp. What awaited him there? He started walking toward it. The cat fell in beside him.

The cat stopped at the foot of the ramp and sat back on its haunches to stare up into the ship, waiting as only a cat can wait. Mike stopped beside him. The woman appeared at the top of the ramp and stopped, her steady gaze focused only on him.

A chill ran through his body. He must have telegraphed his feelings, for her lips compressed in determination as she started down the ramp, though faltering steps and deep circles of exhaustion around her eyes betrayed the effort needed. She held her head high, her focus just him.

Knowing what those eyes could do, he took a step backward, then another, his grip tightening on the blaster, uncertain. He stopped at a low growl from the cat, turning to it with a questioning look, but it simply returned his stare, the way all cats return stares. By the time he turned back to the woman, she had reached the bottom of the ramp.

What do you say to aliens when all the fighting has stopped, he wondered? As it turned out, he said nothing. With those large, brown eyes focused solely on his, she raised a gun to his face and shot him.

Chapter Two

Mike woke up lying on the floor of a padded cell. There was no other way to describe the room: four bare padded walls, padded ceiling and floor, no windows, no door.

He pulled himself into a sitting position, his mind focused first on himself. His body seemed to be okay, though his clothes were a disaster and his shoes and socks were missing. A days-old beard attested to the fact that he'd been here for a while, and a fierce hunger reinforced that conclusion. He probably smelled, but that was the least of his problems at the moment.

What did matter was that his life had changed. In the blink of an eye, everything he'd worked for was gone. His company, his plans, his car, his friends and relatives, everything that had ever mattered was lost to him. Mike couldn't say why he knew, but he knew he was aboard the ship. He was a prisoner of aliens.

Aliens! He shook his head, blinking his eyes. Aliens? Both hands came involuntarily to his face to rub his eyes, and his knees drew up toward his chest. He rested his arms on his knees, deeply troubled. Had he gone mad?

His mind answered instantly. No! The fight in the desert had been real. The two ships were real. The bald-headed creatures, the cats, the witch woman, the blasters – all were real. One look at his ruined trousers was all the confirmation he needed. His mind was as sharp as it had ever been.

What now? He stood up and moved about the room, idly testing the walls and looking for a door, but his mind was elsewhere. The woman had shot him. Obviously she had used a weapon that did not cause harm. Was he now one of those UFO abductees? Were these aliens going to experiment on him, operate without anesthesia like in the stories he'd heard?

Had they already? He stopped, suddenly concerned about his body. He felt his head and neck carefully, then his torso and legs. There was no pain of any kind, no hint of an incision. Other than the hunger, he felt great.

Then he got to wondering. Maybe he wasn't on a ship. Maybe the aliens had just left him lying there in the desert. It was very possible that he had been discovered by the U.S. military and was in some kind of quarantine area, maybe even Area 51. Could he get out? He searched every inch of the walls but refrained from pulling down the padding. It was too soon. Until proven otherwise, he would assume he was a guest.

"Hey, anyone there?" he yelled.

>Hello, Man.<

Uh, oh. The voice was crystal clear, but the choice of words was not what he would expect from someone from Area 51. "Hi, yourself. Come in!" he responded guardedly, turning from one wall to the next, wondering if a door would open. This might not be a complete disaster, he decided as a small kernel of hope germinated. At least someone was listening, and whoever it was spoke English.

>Hello, Man,< the voice said again.

"Hello, yourself," he said again, puzzled. Whoever it was didn't sound too smart – he was repeating himself. "Who are you? Let me out of here."

>I am Jake. I am here with you. I am part of you now. I am inside you.<

Mike laughed. "Sure you are. They gave me an implant while I was sleeping, huh?" To himself he added, "After she shot me, the witch!" Then his eyebrows lifted in alarm. Maybe they *had* given him an implant. Maybe they wouldn't stop at anything. After all, they were aliens. But wait, would they know how to do surgery on a human? Wouldn't they mess it up? He started feeling around his head and neck again.

>There has been no surgery, Man. And she is not a witch.<

"Huh! Easy for you to say. She didn't shoot you. Right in the face, too." Mike didn't care if she was listening or not, he was mad. "After all I did for her, she never even gave me a chance. Is that the way you aliens thank people? Why don't you just come on in here so we can talk face to face?"

>I have been in this room with you for several days. After we get over the hard part, this adjustment period, I think they will let us out. If you cooperate, the process will go faster.<

"Cooperate! You've got to be kidding! I save all your butts and this is the thanks I get? Shot in the face and locked up in a padded cell talking to a speaker? Whatever happened to diplomacy? Who are you anyway?"

>I am Jake.< Mike detected a trace of exasperation in the voice this time. >I'm repeating myself. Will you calm down and let me explain? It's not supposed to be this hard. Are all Earthmen as stubborn as you?<

"Stubborn!" Mike was mad, but he also knew that he was not in control of his life at the moment. He decided he'd better play their game. He sat down with his back against a wall, his bare feet straight out before him, arms folded across his chest. He could play the waiting game as well as anyone. Then, without warning he was struck by a troubling thought. Leaning forward, he said in a low, worried voice, "The lady that shot me – I called her a witch, but I didn't say it out loud. I think I just thought it. Am I going crazy?"

>Not yet, but you might.< Mike heard a chuckle, then a feeling of chagrin came strongly into his mind. >Sorry, Man. This is not a time for humor. Please understand that I am real, that I am in this room with you, and that you have not undergone an operation for an implant. Do you know what symbiosis is?<

"I've heard the term, but why don't you just tell me," he said leaning back against the wall and hugging his knees to his chest.

>It describes a relationship in which two organisms exist in partnership, each gaining from its relationship with the other. You and I are now living in symbiosis. I am living inside you.<

Mike thought about what had been said and about what he knew of biology, then he panicked. Jumping to his feet, he yelled, "You mean I have a parasite living inside me?"

>No! I am not a parasite. The very idea sickens me. Parasites live on other organisms, taking what they need but not returning. There is no balance. Some parasites ultimately kill their hosts. I, on the other

hand, will be helpful. You will discover many benefits to this relationship, I think all of them good. In essence, yes, I am an alien being, I am living inside you like a parasite might, but the relationship will be beneficial to you.<

Mike laughed uncertainly. "Sure. Sure you are. You're inside me, and you're alive. Ha, ha." Then, a smirk lit up his face. He crossed his arms, demanding what he knew to be impossible. "Prove it!"

>I already have, but as you wish. Look down at your right foot, Man.<

Mike looked down. His foot looked normal enough, maybe a tinge darker than normal. He moved his left foot over to compare. Soon, though, no comparison was possible. Purplish ooze seeped out between his toes and spread across the floor. He picked up his foot and the ooze stayed attached, continuing to grow.

He fainted.

Chapter Three

>So that's how it is, Man. I know this is difficult for you, but there are advantages to the arrangement, I promise.<

Mike was sitting with his back to the wall, his arms around his legs, his mind lost in space. He was over the shock, not over the confusion, and he might never get over the revulsion. This "thing" was living inside him experiencing everything he experienced. And there was no shutting it off. It didn't talk out loud to him as he'd thought earlier. He'd tested that. It talked directly into his mind, though it sounded like regular speech.

Its name was Jake, a name it had chosen for itself from Mike's mind. The name held no particular significance to Mike, an important criteria to Jake who did not want a name burdened with memories of someone else. Jake was newly born, and he was an 'it,' not a he or she. Its species reproduced by fission. Jake's race, called the Miramor but usually just referred to as 'Riders,' had lived in symbiosis with a number of other races for eons. Extremely rare, Riders reproduced only when the parent Rider sensed great need, and then only when a recipient was deemed by the parent Rider to be a good match.

Jake's birthing met the first requirement, that of great need, but it did not meet the second requirement – Mike was an unknown to Jake's father, Wooldroo, hence his suitability was not known. Further complicating matters, Jake was born before his time and in a hurry. Wooldroo had lived inside the body of Jornell, the man in the cape who had died. Unwilling to leave Jornell's dying body after a lifetime of friendship, Wooldroo had forced a hurried birth, creating a new being who was supposed to be a replica of himself.

But Jake didn't get the whole deal. There hadn't been time.

The rush to enable the transfer had been the reason the woman stunned Mike after the fighting ended. Mike was the only living body into which Jake could transfer. Jake was pretty certain the woman had expected Wooldroo to transfer himself into Mike's body rather than clone a new being. If this suspicion proved correct, she would be in for a big surprise when the truth became known.

>I sense how hard this is for you, Mike, but in my own defense know this: I am not just an alien mass of protoplasm floating around in your body. I am a real person, and I wish to be your friend. It is the nature of Riders to *ride*, not to control. I am an immediate source of information to you, we can offer council to each other, I will keep your body healthy, I will ensure your sleep is peaceful, and you will never have to be alone again for as long as we live. Is that not of benefit to you?<

"And you read my mind. There are no secrets kept from you."

>Nor will there be any secrets between us, in time.<

Mike wasn't so sure. He couldn't read Jake's mind at all, nor did he want to try. He felt unclean and wondered if this was what a woman felt like after being raped. No amount of washing would remove this creature from his body even if he found a way to get rid of it. Was he, Mike Carver, even a human being anymore? Would he ever have privacy again? Were all his thoughts read? And what about his feelings, were they open to Jake, too? What about all those stupid or embarrassing moments in life that you kept private, that you hated to even think about? Were they all open to Jake? Could he ever have a private relationship with another human being?

Then, looking around the room but seeing in his mind the image of the UFO, he wondered once again where he was. With or without Jake, would he ever even see another human being?

His life was changed forever, and the aliens on this ship were the cause. Change, all by itself, was hard enough to accept, but what really rankled was that he hadn't been asked. They didn't care about Mike Carver, they only cared about a repository for Jake.

"We need to talk, partner," Mike said.

>I will take that as a term of endearment. Thank you! And you do not need to talk out loud if you don't want to.<

"I want to. And it's not a term of endearment, okay? Can I get rid of you?"

Silence . . .

"Jake, do you or do you not have to answer my questions?"

>I am a separate being, Man. We only share the same body. I do not have to answer your questions, but I wish to be your friend. I do not wish to have secrets from you.<

"Let's get this straight, Jake. We are not sharing my body. The body is mine, all mine. You're just a guest. Got that?"

>Yes, Man.< If a disembodied voice could sound hurt, Jake did. >You can get rid of me if you wish. In fact, I will leave on my own if I am not wanted.<

"What would happen if you just left right now?"

>Without another body to go into, and there are no others suitable aboard this ship, I will die.<

"What about the woman, or the cat?"

>They are not suitable.<

Mike frowned. "Why not?"

>Trust me, they are not suitable.<

"So how long can you live without something to go into?"

>How long can you go without breathing, Man?<

"Oh." That shut him up. After a while, he said, "I guess you can stay, but just for now, okay?"

>Thank you, Man.<

"You can call me Mike, Jake. All my friends do."

>Thank you so much, Mike.<

Mike sensed the irony in Jake's voice but did not rise to the bait. He needed to get out of this cell, then he needed to find another body for Jake to live inside. Everything else was secondary to those two issues. Even the fact that he was probably on a spaceship out in space took second place to getting rid of Jake. With lots of help from Jake, Mike struggled with the alien language until he was able to utter a simple phrase, assured by Jake that the phrase demanded he be let out of his cell.

He spoke the alien words. *"Ig'tniv wachizzca darigi, i."*

A response came immediately: *"Gutav mn'dkee srynga, tuappalu fos."* Jake's translation of the response was instantaneous. A woman's voice had directed them to turn right in the corridor and proceed to stateroom B.

An opening appeared in a wall as a door swung silently inward. Mike was free, but what awaited him beyond these padded walls? He approached the opening with trepidation to discover a corridor leading both ways. He turned to the right under Jake's guidance.

He expected a Spartan interior with narrow passageways connected by hatches that could be closed in the event of air loss, like the inside of a submarine. Instead, he found himself in a wide corridor stretching into the distance, curving noticeably to the left. The floor was made of a tough, dark brown material that had a slight give under his bare feet and was at a comfortable temperature. The walls and ceiling appeared to be panels of the same material in a lighter tan color. The corridor was lit by a soft light coming from around the raised panels. Mike sniffed the air, detecting no noticeable odor, but he'd been in the ship long enough that it would be impossible to detect anything but the strongest of smells.

They came to a wide stairway on the left, and Jake indicated he should go up. When he emerged onto the next level, he questioned his vision. Another wide corridor stretched in both directions, but this time strategically hung pictures and tapestries and inlays with pleasing designs decorated the corridor walls. Color abounded, warm and inviting. His architectural instincts delighted in the tasteful positioning and the craftsmanship evident in each and every display. Jake had to prod him to move faster as Mike slowed to study the designs.

The only thing missing from this perfect space was life. There were no crewmen bustling about their duties, there were no announcements from the bridge, there was nothing to give the ship life. Mike's bare feet pulling away from the pliant floor material was the only sound breaking the hushed, eerie silence.

Before long, he saw why. Scorch marks on the walls, floor, and ceiling cried out the obvious; this ship had been a battleground. Thoughts of pirates and mutinies flashed through Mike's mind, but Jake chose to brush off the question, stating that it was nothing so simple. Explanations would come later.

Jake directed him to the assigned room. The door slid aside at a touch. Mike took one step into the room and stopped in astonishment. Expecting a shoebox, he was confronted instead with the living room of an expensive home. Tapestries and well-placed paintings, just as in the corridor, hung from the walls. Bronze-like sculptures and green plants seemed perfectly positioned about the room. Two couches and a pair of padded chairs were arranged around a coffee table across the room, and beyond them, tucked into a corner, stood a desk clearly meant as a work area. Immediately to the left of the doorway, six chairs surrounded a dining table adorned with a bowl of fruit. Everything was done in comfortable earth tones, blending together to create a pleasing impression of home away from home.

Not necessarily his home, he knew instantly. The walls of his condo, decorated with several Indian sand paintings and a couple of old, rusty fighting axes reputedly from Scotland, didn't come close to competing with this place that welcomed so thoroughly.

As he crossed the room, he discovered his duffel bag leaning against the desk. Hmm. He knew the cat would have had something to do with retrieving it, and his lips lifted in a grin. He liked the cat. He didn't need to open the bag, he knew what was inside, but he ran his hand along the side of the bag, knowing it was the only possession he had left to remind him of his home.

As he continued into the room, he brushed a hand lightly across a particularly pleasing sculpture of an animal that resembled a hunting dog, then went through an opening into a bedroom half the size of the living room. He discovered it included an attached walk-in closet full of clothes, a dressing room, and a bathroom.

All this just for him?

Mike had not eaten for three days. He returned to the living room, his eyes homing in on the bowl of fruit on the table, but he hesitated.

>I'm hungry, Jake. Can I eat this food?<

>You can, Mike, and you definitely need to eat. I'm a high energy user. If you eat anything that's bad for you, I'll take care of it. I'm not going to let you get sick.<

>You can do that?<

>I'm a Rider, Mike. It's what we do.<

Mike set safety aside and dug in, choosing something that resembled a pear. It didn't taste like a pear, it was sweet with a hint of tartness, but it tasted good and it smelled wonderfully fruity. As he ate, he roamed the room, idly touching things, wondering what came next. More fruit was what came next, then a shower. Jake guided him through the operation of the shower controls, and he felt like a new man after cleaning up. He chose a dark blue, one-piece coverall from the closet, fumbling a bit with the closures, but everything fit, including the soft leather boots.

He was congratulating himself on the new clothes as he returned to the living room. Those thoughts evaporated the moment he looked up. The witch sat primly on the edge of a chair, her hands in her lap. The cat paced before her, its gaze glued to Mike.

The woman rose, forcing him to rethink the label of "witch." Earthy was the first thought that came to mind. She wasn't glamorous, but she was beautiful in a wholesome way. Medium length brown hair brushed neatly back along the sides of her head gave her a business-like appearance. Her brown eyes sparkled, dominating her appearance, drawing him as would the eyes of a puppy or a deer. A wide mouth with full lips complemented her eyes. Slim, of medium height, dressed in loose, billowy, expensive slacks and blouse, soft leather boots on her feet, there was no trace of makeup or jewelry, nor was there a need. She glowed with freshness, the color in her cheeks and shiny hair radiating health. Her age was impossible to judge since she was an alien, but Mike would have put her in her late 20's had she been human.

Until he looked back into her eyes. Those eyes suggested something he couldn't pin down, seeming young and old at the same time, hinting at wisdom and sadness beyond her years.

Remembering what she had done to him with those eyes, he avoided eye contact at first, then decided that simply would not do. He was determined to gain the upper hand: he could not act the coward. From their brief encounter during the fight in the desert and the milliseconds here since he'd entered the room, her body language clearly telegraphed to him the fact that this lady was accustomed to having her own way. Well, she was in for a surprise. He would control this meeting.

He reached out a hand in greeting at the same moment she began speaking in a somber voice, "Welcome back, Wooldroo. I am so sorry for your loss."

Jake translated silently to Mike as she spoke. Mike dropped his hand, dumfounded. Wooldroo? The witch wasn't even talking to him? This was not working.

>Tell her I am not Wooldroo,< Jake demanded of Mike.

>No! You tell me how to say . . .<

The moment Mike dropped his hand, the woman realized her error. Though she needed to talk with Wooldroo, she had to do so through him, and she had neglected his very presence. Her eyes widened as her hand went to her throat. She looked disconcerted, then looked like she didn't like the feeling, that it might be a new experience for her. Uncertain, she held her ground as silence prevailed. Then, a decision reached, she focused her eyes on him, on Mike Carver. Her gaze traveled his lanky frame from top to bottom, taking in his straight, jet black hair, black eyes, and rugged face. Did she notice his hands, so large and hardened that only a blacksmith would be proud of them? Did she sense the mixed heritage of American Indian and Scottish immigrant of which he was so proud, or did she just perceive a gangly, brutish, ignorant Homo sapiens?

Her tone changed, becoming gracious. "Please forgive me," she commanded, not sounding apologetic in the slightest as Jake translated. "Welcome aboard my ship. We have much to discuss. I am sure Wooldroo has explained everything. Will you help us?"

Mike and Jake held another silent argument. >Mike, tell her. . .<

>No! Show me how to tell her my name is *Mister* Carver to her, she's not welcome, and how can she ask for help when she hasn't even thanked me yet? She shot me, the witch! I want an apology!<

Mike and Jake quickly learned how difficult holding a conversation with anyone other than themselves could be. Mike had to do the talking but didn't know the words. Jake could tell him what sounds to make, but for Mike to form the strange sounds in his throat was time consuming, and when Jake refused to help: stalemate. Mike's body stood mute with not a muscle moving.

The silence became unbearable. The woman stared at him, then crossed her arms and frowned in a demanding way. Mike expected her foot to start tapping the floor any moment.

>Mike, listen!< Jake demanded. >Think about someone besides yourself for a moment. She's under incredible stress right now, and she's bound to make mistakes. I warned you about Wooldroo – she thinks I'm him. What a mess! Have pity on her! Have you no conscience?<

>So you're my conscience, too?<

>No, I am not your conscience. But you'd better start looking at the big picture. This ship started its voyage with one hundred and eighty-four people aboard, all relatives, friends, or acquaintances of hers. There doesn't appear to be many left.<

Remembering the scorch marks in the corridor outside the suite, Jake's comment hit home. Seeing her through Jake's eyes, he sensed the deep sorrow behind her outward expression of confidence. She might be an alien, but this lady was hurting inside. She had shot him . . . well, according to Jake she had stunned him, but to her the reason had been sufficient. Knowing what had to come next, that she would suffer yet more grief, Mike stepped forward, took both of her hands in his own, and risked looking into her eyes. The cat growled low in its throat but took no overt action to separate them.

Jake helped him through the tortuous pronunciation, keeping it short and to the point. "I am sorry for your losses as well. I must add to your misery. Wooldroo chose to remain with Jornell. I am his child,

Jake."

Disbelief showed in her expression. She searched Mike's eyes, then without warning her eyes suddenly swelled, just as they had during the fight beneath the ship, holding him prisoner while her mind delved into and through his inner being. Though slightly more prepared this time, he still had no control over her probing. The experience was, if possible, even more distasteful.

The attack lasted only an instant. Like a finger touching a hot stove, she was gone, a sharp cry escaping her lips. She backed away from him, her eyes wide with shock, holding a hand out to keep him away and shaking her head as if to chase out demons. Mike turned and staggered away on wobbly knees, revolted by the attack and overwhelmed with anger. He had no clear idea what she'd chosen to learn about him, but he suspected there were no secrets withheld from her against her will. He leaned against a wall feeling ill. Jake knew enough to remain silent.

Chapter Four

Mike felt a hand on his cheek. He opened his eyes to find the woman before him, her wise, young-old eyes filled with sadness.

"I'm sorry," she said softly as Jake translated. "Please forgive me. You need not fear my Touch again. I didn't know the affect my probe would have on you." She turned and walked slowly back to her seat.

They all took a time out. For the first time since the spaceship had come crashing to the ground in the desert outside Reno, Mike took the time to really think about things, fundamental things like living and dying, killing, aliens and 'First Contact,' his future, the future of these aliens who in spite of what had been done to him he wanted to like. Days had gone by. What about his parents? Would they believe him dead? What about the wreckage of the UFO? Rumor had it that the remains of the Roswell aliens were stored in the Air Force's Area 51. Well, they definitely had something to study now, lots of dead bodies and a whole ship. And what about his project? His mind couldn't help latching onto his dream, the new gleaming steel and glass skyscraper that would forever change the Reno, Nevada, skyline. Representing months of hard work, his final drawings were here, not in Reno where they were needed. The best part of the project, the construction itself, would be awarded to someone else now.

His thoughts turned to the cat. He had never been a cat lover in the past, and the quick feeling of kinship he felt around the cat surprised him. The cat sat beside the woman with its tail curled about its feet, eyes on her but ears twitching every once in a while, alert to every nuance within the room. It was no longer armed, though on second thought, looking at its clawed fingers and jagged teeth, he realized this beast would never be unarmed. Then he remembered; it wasn't a beast at all.

He queried Jake silently. >Can I talk to the cat?<

>Yes. He is a Great Cat and a Protector. You can speak with him as well as you can speak to anyone before learning the language. I'll help.<

Mike sat on the couch, as far from the chair the woman occupied as he could get. He and Jake formed the sounds necessary for communication and a dialogue ensued, a strange enough activity, but even more strange was to hear words coming from the mouth of a cat. Surprisingly, its voice was deep and clear with no hint of hissing. Mike's automatic prejudice towards animals, treating them as less than equal, disappeared completely. This creature was every bit his equal and probably lots more.

His name was Otis. That wasn't his true name, but he convinced Mike that human vocal cords could not produce the sounds necessary to speak his language. Great Cats that traveled from their home world had two names: their true name, and their working name. Working names were always simple and short.

His species was known for its highly skilled warriors, individuals of great cunning and superior reflexes known across the galaxy as Guardians. The most highly skilled of the Guardians were known as Protectors, an elite cadre of bodyguards sought by the most wealthy and the most powerful. Otis was a Protector, the only survivor of eight others who had begun the voyage aboard this ship.

A story unfolded through Otis, a story humbling in scope and encompassing vast stellar empires, fleets of starships, treachery, deception, murder, and a struggle for survival, the outcome of which was yet in question. The skirmish Mike had taken part in represented just one act of a play, or perhaps the final line of a tragedy depending on what happened next.

This ship, its name translated by Jake as *Resolve*, escorted by two heavy squadrons of the Imperial Fleet, had begun its voyage several months earlier. The fleet's purpose had been to formulate a treaty with a race of beings called Chessori, the small, all-white, bald-headed creatures Mike had already met. The treaty process, familiar and common within Otis' Empire, ordinarily led to a centuries-long period of assimilating the new entrants into the Empire should both so choose. However, the Chessori were not just another race to be assimilated. Their case presented new challenges because they represented another whole empire. How large the Chessori realm was, how it was governed, and what other races their empire represented remained unclear to the Empire. Strangely, control seemed to rest in the hands of the Chessori rather than a conglomeration of member races, an issue of great concern and speculation within the Empire. In any case, trade had been taking place on the peripheries of the two empires for years. The Chessori were well-liked, respected, and anxious for this meeting. Every necessary resource had been placed at the disposal of the fleet. Some one hundred experts, all top leaders in their fields of government, politics, military, science, and business had filled *Resolve* to overflowing.

The meeting had begun poorly. After landing on the designated world, they were advised that living accommodations were insufficient for such a large group. They were to remain aboard their ships except during meetings. Though strange, one had to remain flexible when dealing with aliens. Discovering such idiosyncrasies was, in fact, one of the purposes of the treaty process.

After several days of deliberation, Jornell, the Empire's lead negotiator, decided to entertain the Chessori. All ships on the ground opened their doors, Chessori guests boarded, and shortly thereafter the killing began. What happened aboard other ships was not certain, but aboard *Resolve,* bodies of every species convulsed in hideous pain. Through sheer determination and willpower, Otis and his associates, all Protectors, drew on deep reserves and forced themselves to function in spite of the terrible mind weapon. Though operating well below their peak efficiency, they prevailed and saved the ship. *Resolve* was the only ship that made it off the planet.

The Chessori were slow to respond, almost as if they were surprised that anyone could function at all against their mind weapon, and they were right with the exception of the Protectors. *Resolve,* trailed distantly by six Chessori military ships, raced for the protection of the escort squadron orbiting the planet, but the squadron failed to respond. Clearly, the Chessori mind weapon was of sufficient strength to affect ships in space as well as on the ground. *Resolve* continued outbound, and to their surprise the Chessori ships remained behind to deal with the escort squadron. One by one, those ships ceased to exist.

As soon as the mind weapon was no longer felt aboard *Resolve,* the Great Cats turned command over to Jornell, and the ship continued outbound. It soon became apparent why the Chessori military ships remained behind. Within days, a Chessori trader materialized on the outskirts of the system, and a few hours later a second appeared, both dropping from hyperspace in the vicinity of Jornell's intended jump point. He altered course and set up a new jump point, and the two Chessori traders altered course to intercept him long before he would reach that point. *Resolve* was on its own and would have to fight.

The crew had been decimated during the ground fight. Only six Protectors and four passengers survived. The only one fully trained to fly the ship was Jornell, and he could not function against the mind weapon. Any fighting would have to be done by the Protectors, all capable of operating the ship, but only marginally.

They had a little under two weeks before merging with the two Chessori traders. During that time, two more Chessori traders materialized on the outskirts of the system and headed their way. The Great Cats spent hours training on weapons, and many more hours disposing of dead bodies. Cleaning robots were put to work to scour the worst of the remains from corridors and quarters, but it was a bad time for all.

The two Chessori approached overconfident, clearly relying on their mind weapon to incapacitate the crew of *Resolve*. Otis had his gunners withhold fire until the Chessori were well within firing range, and when they opened up, the Chessori lasted only a few seconds. They had, apparently, not even felt the need to activate their shields, and *Resolve's* weapons broke through the thin-skinned ships easily.

They reached their jump point a week later with two Chessori close behind. A series of jumps toward home was begun, but to their surprise, the two remaining Chessori followed them. It was, theoretically, impossible to track someone through hyperspace, and this was the first any of them had heard of the possibility. The Chessori kept their distance, just showing up about half an hour after each jump, too far away to fight but definitely following them until a better opportunity arose. And a better opportunity did arise. For some unknown reason, *Resolve's* last jump took them to the periphery of Earth's solar system, completely removed from the set of coordinates Jornell had entered into the navigation computer.

Otis was not certain why *Resolve* took them to the wrong jump coordinates, nor was the ship's Artificial Intelligence, but he suspected treachery from within the Empire itself since any tampering with the system could only have occurred prior to the ship's departure from its home world. Equally apparent was the frightening realization that such treachery would have required coordination with the Chessori, for they were waiting with four traders when *Resolve* dropped from hyperspace. It must have been part of a back-up plan.

An immediate jump was attempted, but every jump failed. Repairs were not possible before the battle was joined.

Mike's home world was classified as an emerging world, off limits to all, a niche occupied by young, sentient worlds not ready for admittance to the Empire. Yet, outnumbered and with malfunctioning navigation computers, where else could they go? The planet offered possible survival. If worse came to worse, they would ground the ship and merge the few remaining crew into the general population as best they could. What would happen after that was unknown.

Otis' men were effective. By the time *Resolve* reached Earth's atmosphere, three Chessori had been taken out and another damaged badly enough that it left. Mike knew the rest. *Resolve* took out one more Chessori while transitioning the upper atmosphere and damaged the last a short time later. They could have destroyed it, but Jornell made a last minute decision to capture Chessori survivors for interrogation. He desperately wanted to find out what was going on, why the meeting had been such an utter failure, how the Chessori had tracked them to Earth, and who else was involved.

"You mentioned that this ship was the prize. Why?" Mike asked with Jake's help.

The woman stood up from her chair, and Otis' attention went to her. "I will answer that," she said. Mike turned to find her staring at him, though he got the impression that she was looking at him as Mike Carver this time rather than Earthman or soldier or carrier of a parasite, or perhaps servant or slave.

She stretched, taking her time, then took several steps. She paused, uncertain, started to say something, stopped and took a few more steps, then turned to face him, frustration and uncertainty evident in her every action. "Mr. Carver, please forgive me. I do not understand your reaction to my probe. I didn't know . . . No. I do not apologize; I will explain later. Though I do not apologize, I'm sorry for what has happened to you, what I have done to you. I take full responsibility. You chose to help us. In doing so, more than you can possibly know has been spared, at least for a time."

Before he and Jake could formulate a reply, she continued, "On behalf of myself and my people," she said softly as she looked him in the eye, "thank you." She started pacing again, then stopped before him.

"Mr. Carver, I am called 'Daughter.' Pleased to meet you." Responding to his surprised look, she said, "Yes, I have been listening. May I call you Mike?"

He and Jake had a brief squabble; Mike lost. He nodded his head and stood up with his hand held out. She looked at it for a moment, then shook it briefly. "Pleased to meet you, too. Maybe," he added with a troubled look.

"Thank you!" she said brightly, choosing to ignore the sarcasm or, perhaps, not understanding it. Mike wasn't sure if Jake was helping him produce the exact phraseology he intended. "Mike, you need not fear a repeat of my probe. You may eventually understand its purpose, but I will not force it upon you again, ever. You have earned that right."

He shuddered, and she waited patiently for Jake and him to coordinate a response. It took a while. Jake did not like his choice of words. "I'm supposed to take your words on blind faith?" he asked.

She stepped back and shook her head as if she'd heard wrong. "I beg your pardon?"

>I told you, Mike,< Jake grumbled. >It was a bad choice of words. I know you don't understand, but she can't lie to you, or to anyone else for that matter.<

"What?" he said aloud to Jake.

"You don't believe me?" she asked, still confused, but growing angry.

"No! No, I was talking to Jake," he answered as quickly as Jake fed him the words. "He said you can't tell a lie, or something to that effect."

>Jake, what the heck's going on here?< he demanded silently.

>She will not lie to you, ever,< Jake stated, then shut up.

She sat down on the couch, her back ramrod straight, and faced him. "Mike, things are going on around you that you do not understand. We're trying to explain. Will you listen, please? Decisions must be made, and soon."

He nodded and sat back down on the far end of the couch, sensing his lack of understanding and wishing he had more control.

"Let me make this as simple as I can," she stated, her hands in her lap again as if she was lecturing. "We need your help. No, let me put it more correctly – the Empire needs your help. This is not something we can coerce from you, it must be given freely."

"You need something built?" he asked surprised.

"Built?"

His reply took a while, and it came in pieces as Jake fed him a few words at a time. "I'm an architectural engineer. I build things, and I'm darn good at it. I'm known as one of those people who gets things done, but what could your empire possibly need me to build?"

A smile touched the edges of her mouth, and her eyes sparkled for an instant, then she sobered. "I wish it was that simple, Mike." She paused, troubled, and turned away. "I need you to think big on this, real big. Otis told you that what you have participated in so far is but a small piece of something much larger, that those of us on *Resolve* are the sole survivors of a group which began with several thousand. What he has not told you is that we have reason to believe the destruction of the treaty mission was cover for something much larger. Mike, there might be an attempt in progress to overthrow the legitimate government of the Empire."

Her words took a moment to sink in. "You mean . . . a coup?" he asked with a gulp.

"Yes. A disgusting word, is it not?"

"Maybe, maybe not. Empires sometimes get what they deserve." He rose to face the woman and the cat. "I would assume both of you represent the Empire and stand to lose everything, but emperors and empires are often corrupt and deserving of what they get. In other words, rebellions can be legitimate."

Daughter bit her lip. "Agreed. This one is not, but I cannot prove it to you. I will tell you, though, that rule by the Royal Family is the choice of all represented governments. The Empire is well managed, and reasonable prosperity prevails throughout. Otis, can you add anything?"

"My people support the Empire, Mike." He paused before adding, "To the death." He paused again to let the words sink in, then continued. "The Empire represents fairness, at least the most fairness that can be achieved among such a diverse group of peoples. That fairness is assured by and through the Royal Family, and only them. Without the intervention of the Royal Family, my people would no longer exist. Our story is long; let me just say that because of what the Royal Family did for us thousands of years ago, we Protectors and Guardians have dedicated our lives to their protection and the protection of the Empire. Just as you trusted me in our fight against the Chessori, you can trust me in this. Rule by the Royal Family in conjunction with representative government, our Imperial Senate, forms the basis of our Empire and is the best system of government our civilization has come up with. It works.

"Speaking for the common folk of the Empire, I tell you that if there has, in fact, been a coup, its leaders will have to force their will upon us, and they will fail. The Empire will cease to exist, chaos will reign, and there will be more suffering than you can possibly imagine."

Mike shrugged. "If these people can't force their will upon your empire, they'll just be thrown out, and the Royal Family will be reinstated."

"If there's a Royal Family left to reinstate," Otis answered grimly.

"Mike," Daughter said, taking control of the conversation again, "the Royal Family has been in power for many centuries. Not because they hold all the power or all the wealth, but because the people wish them to rule. The Royal Family enforces peace and prosperity through the rules of law established by the Imperial Senate. Our entire lives are dedicated to helping member races maintain the highest possible level of civilization. That is not to say the galaxy is a peaceful place; it is not, which is why we have armed ships and Protectors. But with the Royal Family at the helm, the galaxy is more peaceful than any other system we have so far devised. If a coup has indeed been attempted, the single most important step would be to remove the Royal Family from power. The only way to do that is to kill them. To kill all of them," she spat out angrily, her lower lip trembling. She wiped at a tear, demanding, "Do you follow so far?"

"I guess so. It makes sense if the family is so loved."

"Do not confuse love with need," she said, lifting her chin in defiance. "The Royal Family is not loved. The Family remains royal only because some of its members are born with certain traits, certain gifts that our people desire in their leadership, traits that have not surfaced elsewhere. Not only is it not loved, the Family is in constant danger. The Protectors have purpose."

"So what does all this have to do with us, with me?" Mike asked. "What is it this Empire needs from me?"

"Mike, there are two others aboard this ship whom you have not met. One is Mildred, a nanny. The other is Alexis, an infant and member of the Royal Family. Depending on the results of certain tests, Alexis will, most likely, one day become Heir. She must survive at all cost."

Mike gulped, a foreboding look in his eyes. "Heir to what?" he asked, afraid to hear the answer.

"Heir to the Empire, of course," she responded, watching him carefully.

"Wait a minute." He stood up and leaned toward her, his arm pointed toward the doorway. "Do you mean to tell me that the future leader of your entire civilization, your Queen or Empress or whatever you call her, is on this ship?" He looked around the room for traces of gaudiness or luxury, then it hit him – the understated elegance. His initial surprise and delight at the sheer size of his suite and its accouterments, in view of the fact that it was on a ship, lent support to her claim.

But something was far from clear. She had told him to think big. "Uh, just what are we talking about with this Empire of yours? How big is it?"

"A thousand worlds would fill only one small corner."

Mike paled. "And *Resolve*?"

"A royal yacht, Mike. The Heir's personal ship."

"You've got to be kidding! Where are her parents?"

"Jornell was her father. I am her mother. To answer your next question, yes, she may one day be Queen."

He felt small all of a sudden as he thought about thousands or maybe millions of civilizations spread across the galaxy. He envisioned ships crisscrossing space effortlessly in the same way cars sped across the deserts of his ancestors. His thoughts narrowed as if he was wading through quicksand, focusing on just a few words at a time. A thousand worlds. Heir to the Empire! Why was this woman called Daughter when she was a mother? And they wanted his help? What could they possibly need from him? He looked to Otis for guidance, then to Daughter. He was about to speak when she interrupted.

"I will do whatever it takes to keep her safe, Mike, including kidnapping an Earthman. I would do it again if necessary. If you are not the man for us, I *will* do it again."

He pursed his lips in thought. What could she possibly need him for? Then a reason coalesced in his mind with a resounding click. He asked Jake what the name of Daughter's parasite was. Jake, in a huff, declined to answer, so he asked her.

She tensed and rose to pace the room for a time, and Mike made sure he stayed out of her way. Eventually she settled onto the edge of the couch again and faced Mike with her hands folded in her lap. Her back was ramrod straight, and he sensed, correctly, that he was in for another lecture.

"Parasite," she stated with precision. "Thank you for reminding me who you are and where you come from." She looked away briefly, then raised her chin and leaned toward him, meeting his gaze squarely. She spoke softly. "I stunned you and gave Jake to you without your consent. I would gladly change places with you, as would most others in my civilization. Mike, there are not nearly enough 'Jakes' to go around. Even among the most powerful and wealthy, they are exceedingly rare. I have always wished for a Rider, but it is forbidden me. Otis and his people have chosen against Riders, but for them the choice has been physiological. The process of communication with Riders slows them down and makes them less effective Protectors when speed and timing are of the essence. Otis cannot accept Jake. You provided the only 'vessel' into which Jake could transfer."

She rose to her feet and turned to pace again. "If Jake could be considered a commodity, then you have received the single most valuable commodity known throughout the galaxy. In reality, no value can be placed on Jake and his people because they cannot be bought or sold. They go only to those of their own choosing."

Mike lowered himself carefully to the couch, sensing that she was just getting warmed up, and he was right.

She stared into his eyes for a time, but she didn't find what she was looking for. She turned her back to him, then turned to face him again, stepping to the couch to stand before him with frustration clear in her tone. "At this point in your relationship, Jake is simply a Rider. Have you considered what it's like for him to be in your body? He didn't have the usual choice in this either. And what did he get? A semi-barbaric Homo sapiens, probably not a top-of-the-line specimen, someone not of the Empire, someone who does not want him. Well, let me tell you something." She leaned into him, her hands turned into fists resting on her hip. "If you are half the man I hope you are, the day will come when Jake is not simply a Rider. He will be much more, so much more that you will be forever grateful to me for providing him."

Mike felt himself inching his way deeper and deeper into the couch. She leaned into his face, placing a hand on the armrest beside him, her nose inches from his. She had not raised her voice. "At the very least, Mister Carver," she continued, "I guarantee that the day will come, if it has not already, when Jake is smarter than you and me both. He remembers everything, he will be a source of guidance and information to you, he will protect you, he will heal you, he may even become your friend if you give him half a chance, but he will never, ever control your life. You, on the other hand, completely control his. Who's gotten the better deal?"

Mike had inched his way as far as he could into the couch. She stayed right in his face, waiting for an answer. All he could think of was why she was called Daughter; she acted more like his mother. She had made him feel like a real creep, and she might be right – Jake hadn't necessarily gotten the best deal here. The part about Jake not having a say in his host . . . well, that hit home in a big way. "Uh, I guess I owe you an apology," he said.

She stood up with closed eyes, hugging herself as if she was cold. "Men," she said with distaste. "Must you be the same in every species?"

She started for the door. He stood up angrily and shouted to her back as quickly as Jake gave him the words, "What did I do now? I apologized!"

She continued walking to the door, but turned to him just before leaving. "You are no longer one being, Mike Carver. Stop thinking like one." Without waiting for a response, she turned and left.

His thoughts turned inward, embarrassed before Jake, not knowing what to say. So he said nothing, just waited for Jake to read his mind, still not certain exactly how much Jake had access to.

>Apology accepted, Man,< Jake responded.

Chapter Five

"So where do we go from here, Otis?" he asked the Great Cat.

"That depends on you. We have a couple of problems we could use your help on."

"I think you mean Jake's help, don't you?"

Otis hesitated before answering, studying Mike. He apparently found what he was looking for. "I'm no diplomat, Mike. I'll tell you how it is. You're right, you probably can't help, but Jake can. We need you as a vessel for Jake. Can I make it any more clear?"

"Finally, something that makes sense around here. Go ahead, Otis. Jake's listening."

"Jake, and you too, Mike, at the moment we're hiding. We're alone, we're incapable of defending ourselves, and we have no idea what we're up against, but we can make some good guesses. We destroyed the last Chessori ship, but that doesn't mean the threat is ended. More will come. Because of that, time is of the essence if we are to make our escape, but we cannot and will not rush our preparations. The Chessori might be waiting even as we speak, ready to pounce the moment we show ourselves. We have placed *Resolve* into its lowest energy state in order to limit the power reflections of its drive, reflections the Chessori could use to locate us. We have not moved since coming here, and we will not move again until we can defend ourselves, repair the navigation computer, and head to a destination of our own choosing, not theirs.

"You know that Jornell was killed. Has Jake told you that he was the only pilot left aboard the ship?" Mike's stunned look answered better than words. "The Chessori killed our regular pilots and nearly everyone else during the initial attack that took place on their world. The Protectors kept the family alive, and Jornell brought us this far, but now we're stuck. There is a computer virus in the navigation program that caused us to end up here instead of Triton, our intended destination. We can't leave your system before it's fixed."

Mike couldn't believe his ears. With an uncertain, half smile on his face, almost afraid of the answer, he asked, "Where's here?"

"About a thousand miles west of where we picked you up and two hundred feet beneath the surface."

Mike computed for a moment, then jumped to his feet. "We're sunk in the Pacific Ocean?" he yelled.

Otis took great pains to explain, which struck Mike as possibly unusual for a cat. "No, we are not sunk. We're hiding. The water reduces and scatters the energy reflections from our power plant, making it difficult for the Chessori to find us. Also, their weapons are useless underwater. At least ours are, and we believe theirs to be useless, as well. We're safe as long as we remain here."

Otis paused to let Mike assimilate this, then continued. "My mission, Jake's, and yours, too, if we can find a use for you, is first to protect the Heir. Beyond that it gets a little more complicated. If a coup has indeed occurred, the Empire needs the Heir. Nothing takes precedence over protecting the Heir, but the Heir serves no purpose unless we can restore her to the throne. To do so, we need to fix *Resolve* and get out of here. As Daughter said, will you help?"

>I want to help, Mike. I know I can. Just give me a chance. Let's both help.<

"You're asking me . . . no, you're asking me and Jake to save your whole Empire?" he demanded of Otis, overwhelmed.

Otis shrugged, then grinned his toothy grin. "Why not? Do you have more pressing demands on your time . . . or your life?"

"Otis, Jake cannot fly this ship without my help. What makes you think I'll be able to help?"

"*Resolve* flies itself. Crewmembers interface with the ship through a mental plug-in. They join together within a computer network that links everyone to each other and to the ship. We believe you are capable of accepting this link, which will let Jake into the net to do his job. You may even be able to help him. I, too, could plug-in, but only with others of my race on the net. We would drive each other crazy if you and I linked together. I'll do my part from outside the net, probably by operating a weapon manually."

"What about Daughter?"

"She is not psychologically adapted to the link, nor is she permitted by custom. Neither is Mildred." He shuddered. "Jornell didn't even consider Mildred. You'll understand when you meet her. Jake, and maybe you, are all we have. Without his help we are probably stuck here. The Heir will not be adequately protected with me flying *Resolve* by myself."

"Why don't you fly the ship while Daughter and I work the guns?"

"You'll understand after you've seen the net. It's amazing what you can do within the net. Jornell was a reasonably good pilot, surprising given his high position in the Empire. I hope some of his skill has transferred to Jake. Even if it has, we'll be severely limited in our ability to defend ourselves and the Heir."

Otis did not leave him with many options. "As ridiculous as it sounds, suppose Jake can fix the ship and fly it. Where do we go from here?" He suddenly felt butterflies in his stomach. "Are you saying I get to go out into space? Are we talking about other stars, other planets?"

"At the very least. Much of what Daughter and I have told you is speculation. We are quite certain, however, that our ship and our mission were sabotaged on Triton before we left. The Chessori are not operating alone in this, Mike. We can trust no one, including our own people, until we learn where this treachery begins, where it ends, who leads, and whether there has, in fact, been a coup. I will insist on a careful process of finding answers to those questions."

"How much say do you have in what we do?"

"Daughter is in charge. She is responsible to the Queen and to the Empire for our success or failure. But I am the Heir's Protector. While I do not lightly cross swords with her, I cannot be overruled in matters relating to protection of the Heir." He paused to let Mike think about that. "An interesting arrangement, eh?" he added with his toothy grin.

Mike smiled in return. He liked Otis, liked him a lot. They had developed a unique kinship during the battle, and if nothing else, they were pretty good at charades, having communicated absolutely clearly without exchanging a single syllable.

"Hey!" he said, "We were a pretty good team the other night, weren't we."

"Welcome to the ranks of Protector. You handled yourself well in spite of the mind weapon projected by the Chessori."

"What mind weapon?"

Otis froze, then stared long and hard at Mike. "You felt no disabling effects during the fight, no unusual sounds in your head?"

"Well, I found the explosions pretty distracting. Other than that, just normal desert noises and some unusual insect sounds. Did I miss something else?"

"The Chessori used their mind weapon on you, on all of us. It appears to be a natural weapon, probably inbred. Some sort of 'psi' projection is created and focused by their minds. When activated, it is debilitating to all creatures except themselves. We encountered it for the first time at the treaty conference and repeatedly since then during battles in space and the battle here on Earth. You say you felt nothing?"

"So that's why Jornell and Daughter seemed to be stumbling around in pain. I thought it was kind of stupid of them at the time. Maybe . . . maybe that was the cicada sound I heard. It might explain why the Chessori are so easy to kill. The one I tackled was basically defenseless, and the others tended to stand up like sitting ducks before firing their weapons. Maybe their primary defense is this mind thing."

"If you are immune to this weapon, I wonder if we can find a way to shield ourselves from them as well? We'll have to put our scientists to work on it when we get back. Come on, let's see if Jake can get us home."

As Otis turned toward the door, Mike stated softly, "You know, I probably would have agreed to come. She didn't have to shoot me."

Otis turned back to him and their gazes locked. "'Probably' is the key word, Mike. I didn't know she was going to stun you, but I could have stopped her. I'm very fast when I choose to be, so you can blame me as much as you blame her. But know this: the stakes are the very highest. The hundreds of thousands of worlds of the Empire depend on the Royal Family to hold their society together. For them, I will risk all, including my life and yours. Given time, I think you'll come to hold the same belief, but you can't yet – you don't know us well enough. Until you do, until your beliefs tie you to us, I ask for your trust. Our cause is right. Give us the chance to prove it to you."

Mike swallowed hard. Was he willing to risk his life for these people on the basis of a few words? Was he willing to let Jake stay in his body for, perhaps, a long time? His initial reaction was no, but if Otis spoke true, could he say no to the needs of trillions? Could anyone say no to such a calling?

He turned away from Otis, his gaze searching for a way out. Then, his eyes focused on the duffel bag leaning up against the desk, the bag that held the drawings he had worked so hard to complete. He wanted to build his building, and the people he worked for wanted to build it with him. Yet . . . he and the plans were inside the same ship he'd fought beneath, and it was a starship. He was aboard a starship! Otis was offering him the chance to go into space, the opportunity to see other worlds. If he said no to the bigger issues, he would be saying no to going into space, as well. What would his life be like on Earth if he just went back to his normal routines, if he gave all of this up? *Could* he give all of this up?

>You know the answer to that,< Jake said. >There's no way you'll ever be the same person you were. You'd wonder forever.<

>This is my decision, Jake.<

>It is. I'll be here no matter what you choose. I hope my stay will be with you, not with someone else. I like the Mike Carver I've met. Please stay.<

He turned back to Otis. "What if I decline?"

"I'll be forced to find a replacement body for Jake." He paused, then tilted his head to study Mike's reaction to his next words. "Let there be no misunderstanding between us, Mike. I need your help, and I'm asking for your help, but from this point forward there will be no turning back. What we ask of you requires your best effort, and that effort must be given willingly."

"You ask much, Otis."

"I do. I ask for everything that you are."

Mike stared at the Great Cat. *Everything that you are.* He barely knew these people or their cause. Otis asked too much. Yet if what Otis said was true, the fate of billions or trillions rested in the balance. Could he look himself in the mirror if he turned his back on such a cause? He knew he couldn't, so where did that leave him?

His eyes refocused on Otis. "You ask far too much, my friend."

"I know. The Empire always asks too much of those who are willing to give. It takes no less than that to hold it all together, which is Daughter's job. She has given more than most, far more. The Empire has demanded everything that she is, and she has delivered time and time again. The Empire is a better place because of her. I'm part of her team, Mike. Will you join us? Can you *not* join us?"

Mike blinked. Otis had seen to the heart of his issue. It was not *would* he join them, it was *could he not* join them. He could not turn his back on the needs of billions or trillions of people, alien or otherwise.

"Do you have any enlistment papers or anything?"

Otis' lips lifted into a feral grin. "I sensed the rightness of you during our battle," he said. "Come on."

He led Mike and Jake through corridors until reaching the "central shaft." Without hesitation he stepped out into empty space, a space far enough across to hold five or six men shoulder to shoulder. Otis began rising, still talking as if nothing was out of the ordinary. Mike leaned out into the shaft to watch as the cat rose out of sight. He felt an upward tugging on his body, but he could not bring himself to take the next step.

>Come on, Mike. You'll be fine, I promise!< Jake implored.

>Give me a break, Jake. There's no way I'm stepping out into that hole. Where are the stairs?<

>Use your head, Man. You're not an ignorant savage. Try it. Maybe you'll like it.<

>The stairs, Jake. Show me the stairs.<

Jake balked at the command. Stalemate again. Soon enough, Otis returned and took Mike by the arm with a firm grip. Without explanation or hesitation, he simply stepped with Mike into the shaft, talking all the while as if nothing out of the ordinary was taking place.

They rose, passing other decks on the way. Mike had known intuitively that he would not plummet to the bottom of the ship, but the feeling of rising on nothing but air was disconcerting to say the least. The shaft seemed to be divided into two halves, one going up and the other down. He guessed at that, but he could feel an invisible partition running down the middle of the shaft when he stretched his arm out, almost like he was pushing against thick air. He probably could force his way through it, but he knew instinctively that such experimentation was for another day.

Pointing down past their feet, Otis explained that the shaft ended at the lower gun port, a small blister attached to the bottom of the ship. The upper gun port, at the top of the shaft and directly above the bridge, filled the top blister. Both gun ports, operated remotely by gunners from the bridge or manually by gunners stationed at the guns themselves, held two lasers each and had overlapping fields of fire, so there were no blind spots the gunners could not reach.

The first thing Mike noticed as the bridge came into view was the ceiling, or more accurately, a large view screen on the ceiling. As more of the room came into view, he discovered more view screens covering the walls. When he stepped from the central shaft onto the bridge, he looked around, counting ten screens encircling the room. Clustered near the center of the room was a semicircular row of vacant work stations.

Otis continued his lecture. "Any screen can be configured to depict what other screens are showing, and all the work stations rotate, so any station can view and perform any function. The seat just in front of us is the watch commander's position."

Mike noted that the watch commander's seat had wide armrests with an array of keypads and controls, but no work station. "Is there a front and back to the ship?" he asked.

"Yes, and no. The ship can move in any direction, but the central shaft is designated as the rear of the bridge. The two center positions in front of the command seat are for pilot-navigators. The other stations are for gunners, engineers, and communications specialists."

"And Jake is going to run all of this?"

"He is, from the command seat, but not in the way you think. Everything you see here is just for back-up or monitoring. When underway, unless we're at battle stations most of the stations are vacant. Regardless of how many stations are manned, everyone is in 'the net' where they communicate effortlessly with each other and the ship's Artificial Intelligence, and there is no need for the screens. You'll soon see what I mean." He motioned Mike to take the watch commander's seat. "How is Jake feeling about all of this?"

"He's telling me he's anxious to get started. He says that, based on my background, I'm in for a surprise."

Otis' lips lifted in a leer. "I suspect he's right. You two can take it from here without my help. Good luck." He padded off to the side and sat with his tail curled about his feet to watch, looking like he could stay that way for hours.

Jake explained to Mike what was needed of him. Piloting *Resolve* was not the problem. A nearly sentient computer network took care of that. But the computer could make only limited judgment calls. For example, it could take them anywhere, but it could not decide where *Resolve* was to go. Its programming prohibited it from firing the ships' weapons, but it could feed the necessary data to gunners. It could not decide tactics, yet once told what was needed, it could make *Resolve* comply in the most efficient manner. While all this was going on, it automatically kept constant watch on engineering matters throughout the ship. It monitored the drive, kept a breathable air mixture at the proper temperature and humidity, ensured adequate food and water supplies, recycled waste, opened and closed doors on command, and all the myriad details needed to keep the passengers and crew alive and comfortable.

For decisions requiring judgment, the computer needed help from the crew. Pilot-navigators, gunners, engineers, and the watch commander "plugged in" to the computer through special helmets designed to process information in both directions. The computer could sense who was in the net and process information accordingly.

In their case, Mike and Jake were the only crewmembers. Mike would occupy the watch commander's seat to which the computer would direct everything. *Resolve* had not been designed to be flown in this manner, but there was no alternative. Jake was their only hope. He had to interface with the ship, fly it, and fix it.

Mike picked up a shiny black helmet and looked it over. Light as a feather, it seemed toy-like. He felt ridiculous as he slowly raised it up to his head. As he did so, Daughter rose up from the central shaft and stepped into the bridge, demanding a helmet for herself.

Mike turned his seat to face her, but she was focused on Otis. "I'm going to help," she stated simply. Otis uttered a long, low growl. "I know it goes against custom. I know it's forbidden. I'm changing the rules."

"Customs have been established with good reason, My Lady. I cannot permit this."

"You can, and you will. Your job is to protect the Heir. So is mine. This is a matter of survival. Do you wish to place the Heir's future solely in the hands of Mr. Carver?" She turned and looked Mike over briefly, coldly, then turned back to Otis. "I say, no! We must use all our resources, including me. We can sort out the niceties later."

"But, My Lady, you know it is dangerous for you to interface with machines, possibly deadly."

"No, I do not. I know it was dangerous for my ancestors. I have never been permitted to try. Our situation is desperate: we get only one try at escaping this planet. We must do everything in our power to succeed. If it doesn't work, I'll stop immediately."

Mike and Jake had a private conversation while Daughter tried to stare down the fierce-looking cat. >Mike, she's right. We could use her help, but there might be a better way.<

>What are you talking about? What's going on?<

>You won't understand until you meet the net. I have, through Wooldroo's memories. Daughter has been bred with certain skills. She can communicate directly with any creature in the galaxy, something only a very few females from her line can do. They are referred to as the

Chosen. No one else in the galaxy has this Talent. Her special skills relate to living creatures only – machines have historically been anathema to the Chosen. Otis is right, her joining the net by herself could be a disaster. However, she's right, too. Times are difficult, and we'll need all the help we can get. I'm thinking that she might be able to join with our help, to sort of piggyback in with us. I'm not certain, it would be more prudent for her not to attempt this at all, but if she does, you and I should be there first to help her in.<

>I wish I knew more about all this, Jake.<

>Soon you will be an expert.<

Otis and Daughter stood nose to nose, Otis sitting almost at attention on the floor, Daughter leaning into his face, determination clear in each of their expressions. Mike stepped over and placed a hand on her shoulder while grasping a handful of Otis' mane, diverting their attention from each other. Two sets of angry eyes turned to him, only inches away.

"Jake has chosen to be the tie-breaker here," he stated softly. "Princess, you may be able to join this net, but not by yourself. Jake believes that if you join at all, it must be with his help after he and I have figured things out."

"I do not need your help," she stated emphatically.

"You don't *want* to need my help, that I know," Mike responded carefully. "Can you accept Jake's help?"

She bit her lip as she turned from him, shrugging his hand from her shoulder. "It seems that my life will always be directed by others. I will wait." She sat angrily in the nearest crew seat, swiveling it around to face him, her expression demanding that he get on with it. Otis went over to sit by her side, his tail curled around his feet as usual.

Mike approached the net with trepidation, though Jake could barely control his excitement. Without knowing anything about this ship, Mike nevertheless sensed the power within the system, and it scared him. Could this thing overload him, drive him crazy? Would it work right on an Earthman? He looked over the lightweight, toy-like helmet carefully, but it offered no clues. It just seemed ordinary. He shrugged and lowered it onto his head. At Jake's suggestion he pulled the faceplate down into place, blocking the room from view.

Nothing happened. There was absolutely no sensation whatsoever.

>It's okay, Mike. The computer is running a routine evaluation. Just be patient.<

>Sure. Easy for you to say. It's not going to melt your brain.<

Jake chuckled. >Only you could come up with that. If it tries to

melt your brain, I'll turn it off.<
          >Can you?<
          >Yes.<

Long minutes passed before Mike sensed change. A chime sounded with absolute clarity and images began to appear, crystal clear images of the environment surrounding *Resolve*. Jake whooped with joy as the net slowly fed them visual images, the chime sounding before each new image. After only a short time, the chime disappeared, and the images began coming faster, shifting into other spectra as well. Each built on the other at a comfortable pace.

Without knowing how he knew it, Mike had no trouble distinguishing between the images and their various wavelengths and knowing what each wavelength meant. He and Jake could back up and review images with just a thought, like reversing a digital recording, if they felt they'd missed something, though most of those queries came from Mike. Jake did not question or worry, he just enjoyed.

The computer was entirely attentive to their needs. Words were not exchanged, nor did Mike sense an intelligence controlling the net, not at first, though he did sense that the net was running a training routine carefully, building up to something more. Jake wanted to rush through the process, to flash through these preliminaries, but Mike sensed the net's guiding influence catering to the needs of both of them. It didn't care how fast they went, only that the process played itself out to its liking.

Ocean life was not abundant in the vicinity of the ship, so there wasn't much to see, but in spite of their depth and the darkness Mike was certain existed outside the ship, the level of light was just right for him. Soon, in addition to vision, Mike began to feel his surroundings. He felt the temperature and texture of the water as it touched the skin of the ship, his skin, not as something to be liked or disliked, just something that was. Mike knew intellectually that the water was cold, but he didn't feel cold.

His senses vibrated with life. The net tweaked a knob somewhere, and there was sound. One sound at a time at first, then a blending: cries of whales, the chirping of dolphins, rumbles and groans of distant volcanoes and shifting landmasses, the shushing of merchant ships' propellers, a true cacophony of sound that should have been overwhelming and confusing but was not. Mike found himself sorting and focusing without effort, with just a thought. He even knew from which direction the sounds came and from how far distant.

He reveled in the wash of data. He had always felt the strong pull of his American Indian ancestry, had always felt close to the elements – earth, fire, water, air, and spirit, and the places these things occupied in the natural processes of life. Now he was experiencing them in ways unimaginable. This was it, this was the ultimate. It couldn't get better, nor would he want it to.

But it did. The net somehow let him know that its purpose was not to teach him to sort through data. Processing data was the net's job. It wanted him first to know the data, to feel it, to experience it, and to live it. Then, and only then, could Mike and Jake correlate and add sense to the data in ways only sentient beings could. So the net added perspective.

To start the process, the net let Mike meet Jake, or more precisely, Mike and Jake re-met in a different way. When fully integrated into the virtual net, they became virtual equals, Mike no longer controlling. Communication between the two was not limited to words and a hit-or-miss smattering of overflowing feelings. Language and translation were not needed within the net. Mike and Jake communicated however they chose, sometimes in words, sometimes in concepts, sometimes through entire thought processes. Though separate beings, they knew instantly and intuitively what each was thinking and doing within the net.

Then Mike and Jake met the artificial intelligence controlling the net. They played with it, chasing it through its home, *Resolve*, learning the ship's layout, playing with life support systems, the power plant, multiple sensor arrays for controlling temperature and air quality and housekeeping equipment. They pulled ingredients together to prepare and cook their next meal, opened and closed doors at will, turned lights on and off, and chased each other through many of the mundane systems this intelligence controlled every moment of every day to keep *Resolve* functioning.

Then they were taken outside. The net let Mike/Jake sense location. They saw their place, the ship's place, within the sea. They sensed the depth of the water, they sensed land to the east, and they sensed larger parameters: the Pacific Ocean, other continents and oceans, then the globe.

But the net was just getting warmed up. Its data banks knew Earth's solar system as a collection of sun, planets, moons, asteroids, comets, energy flows in relation to each, and the solar system's place within the larger background of neighboring stars, sectors, and galactic political divisions and subdivisions. They went on tour.

Words could not express the experience. Indeed, no words were exchanged between Mike, Jake, and the intelligence referred to as the net. Mike and Jake, having met this intelligence and sensing rightness, opened themselves up completely. Things simply became known. Through the net's virtual reality they visited the Moon, each of the planets, even flying through the sun's corona. The net's perspective was strange to Mike and Jake. Energy patterns and flows of which they'd been completely ignorant were an integral part of its perceptions. And though many things were not fully understood by Mike/Jake, the Mike/Jake/Net combination filled in the gaps through intuitive cognition. They were a good team, though Mike suspected that the artificial intelligence would team well with any sentient being.

"Time out!" Mike demanded. "Just who are you?" he asked the net.

"I am an artificial intelligence designed to fulfill every need of the ship," it answered.

"I asked who you are, not what you are. Are you alive?" Mike asked.

"I was created by the ship's designers," it answered.

"But are you alive? Do you have a name?"

"I don't know if I am alive or not. I am called *Resolve*."

"Yet you refer to yourself as 'I.'"

"Yes. I know who I am."

"I sense a personality, something separate from the ship. Jake, do you sense a personality?"

"Very definitely."

"The ship's name is *Resolve*, but you are not the ship," Mike said. "You're more like a person. Are you a person?" Silence met his words. "Did you hear me?" Mike asked.

"I can't not hear you, Mike. I do not know the answer to your question. I have never been asked before."

"Well, you're not *Resolve*. You're you, and you need a name. Will you be offended if I give you a name?"

"You would name me? I'm just a computer."

"I would, and you're more than just a computer. I sense your personality, and I want the freedom to talk to you, to ask you questions, but I don't want to just call you 'the net' or *Resolve*. We need to be able to talk to each other. I'm Mike, and the other is Jake. By what name would you like to be called?"

"I'm usually referred to as 'ship,' but sometimes 'the net,' or '*Resolve*,' I have no other name."

"Will you accept a name? Will it impair your function?"

"I will, and it will not impair my function."

"Then I hereby christen you George. Is that acceptable?"

"George. I have a name. I like it!"

"So you can like?"

"Yes. I am George now. Thank you for my name."

"Okay, let's get this show on the road, George."

"You're nearly done for this session. Hang on. Here we go."

George completed Mike/Jake's introduction to himself and the ship by racing with them through every screen and workplace on the bridge. The screens and workstations were not needed by anyone wearing the helmet, but not everyone on the bridge was connected directly to George at all times. Simple commands and queries could be generated by more normal methods, and not just from the bridge but from various workstations throughout *Resolve*, including Mike's suite.

They were numb by the time George released them. He pushed Mike and Jake out gently, letting them sense their body first, then the helmet went black. Lesson one complete.

Mike was elated, Jake somewhat subdued over dinner. When pressed for an explanation, Jake was forthright. >Wooldroo's first love was politics and court intrigue, Mike, not star ships. I've been well endowed with his knowledge of politics, but now that I've been in the net, I'm much less certain of my ability to fly *Resolve*. My ability to get us all home is not what Otis and Daughter assumed. You'd better pay close attention. You seem comfortable with what we did today.<

>Are you kidding? Talk about virtual reality . . . we were right there inside the computer. I want more!<

Daughter remained distant during dinner. Mike made several attempts to draw her into conversation, doing his best to be sociable, but she chose to withdraw into herself, answering his questions with one or two word replies when she chose to respond at all. He studied her openly. She hadn't eaten a thing, just pushed food around on her plate. Mike suddenly noticed tears coursing down her cheeks. What was the matter? She became aware of his study of herself, locked her gaze on him momentarily, wiped futilely at her tears, then simply stood up and left the room. He got up to follow, but Otis called him back.

"What's her problem, Otis?" he asked with Jake's help.

"She grieves, Mike."

Such a simple answer. It spoke volumes about her – and about himself. He had been so focused on himself that he'd failed to consider the needs of anyone else. Of course she grieved. Her husband had died, and *Resolve* had likely been packed with friends and acquaintances who had also died. And that wasn't all. She was royalty, the galaxy her playground. How confining a ship must seem, particularly to one who had probably spent a life of instant gratification, servants at her beck and call, money never an issue when true wealth lay at your finger tips. She was spoiled, he knew, and with that thought came the realization that she was probably more out of her element than he was. Had she ever known struggle, had she ever known risk? Life on Earth was a daily risk for everyone, but as a rich woman pampered by her position within some immense galactic society, she would never have wanted for anything. Yet here she was, cut off from all of that, and all of her friends were dead.

His own appetite suddenly disappeared. His heart went out to her, but he did not follow. He would be the last person she wanted right now. But he would not forget.

*   *   *   *   *

He and Jake got an early start the next day. George delved into ships' systems this time, and it was in detail. Mike and Jake didn't have to know every detail of how the systems functioned, but they did have to know how to resolve problems when they arose. Computers operated everything, computers that George conducted like a maestro, but he insisted the bridge crew understand the process as well. Mike and Jake would not likely ever get involved with these computers, but space was a dangerous place, and George demanded a certain level of competence from them.

Daughter and Otis came to the bridge while Mike and Jake were in the net with George. The room was eerily silent. Mike occasionally moved or twitched, but that was all that showed. What was it like in there, she wondered? Her time for entering the net was approaching, and she was nervous. After a time, her thoughts returned to the friends and loved ones she would never see again, and her eyes brimmed. Otis went to her side and sat, his tail curled around his feet.

"It's hopeless," she said to him later.

"It is not hopeless, My Lady. We never give up."

"Look at him. Jake is just a child, and Mike hasn't a clue. He has no concept of our difficulties, and he's completely unprepared for what we've asked of him. How could I have been foolish enough to think this would work?"

"You have not been foolish, and you will not lose hope. You cannot."

"Oh, Otis, I know you mean well, but everyone is dead, and now we've placed ourselves in his hands. He'll never get us out of here."

"What about Jake?"

"Have you ever heard of a Rider captaining a ship?"

"No, My Lady."

"He's a Rider, Otis. He's not made for controlling. Why do you think I want to go into the net?"

"I've never heard of one of the Chosen captaining a ship either."

"What choice do we have?"

"We have Mike. Give him the chance he deserves. Never forget what he did for us that night in the desert, My Lady. His presence made all the difference. We would not be here now if he had not come to our assistance. There's more to him than you see. I don't have your Touch, but I believe in him. You've used your Touch on him, and he's still here. You must have sensed something."

"You know I cannot discuss what I learn through my Touch."

"You don't have to. He might not be true to our cause – how can he be? He doesn't know enough. But if he was not true to himself, you would have rejected him."

"He's a barbarian, and he's uneducated to our ways."

"I, too, am a barbarian, much more so than is he. Yet I function well in our society."

"And you have spent years learning."

"He doesn't have years. He'll just have to hurry. I believe he's up to the task. He's already proven himself to me, and he'll prove himself to you, as well. Don't forget, it's been foretold."

"I have not forgotten," she replied softly. She closed her eyes, remembering back to the words of the one she had named Seer. Her name was Krys. In a vision, she had seen Daughter lying at the foot of a ship's ramp with Otis standing over her shooting at something in the night. With the vision had come the words of a riddle:

"You will be so much more and have so much less. They will best you, but a man of dirt will come to your aid."

She had thought often of those words, not knowing their meaning. Now it appeared that the riddle had resolved itself. Krys had been so right in every way. The actual words she had seen in her vision had been *"a man of earth, or Earth."* None of them had heard of Earth, and the name did not appear on Empire star charts. Krys had translated what she sensed the meaning to be: a man of dirt. Was Mike the man of dirt foretold in the vision, or was there another?

"I so hope you're right, Otis, but we ask too much of him."

"We ask what is necessary, no more."

She shook her head, feeling hopeless. The task ahead of her was monumental. "How will we ever reestablish the throne?"

"We will do it one step at a time, one careful step at a time. If we fail, the Empire falls and there will be chaos. Give him a chance, My Lady."

"He is our only chance," she breathed.

The screens suddenly came alive on the bridge. That must be the lesson they worked on at the moment, she decided. Who was running those screens, the artificial intelligence, or was it Jake/Mike? She would soon find out.

* * * * *

Mike broke for a quick lunch, then he dove back into the net. Jake's plan was to repeat the previous day's experience for Daughter but in a different order for her. Since dealing with people was her specialty, though in Mike's estimation her stature was highly overrated, her first experience would be to meet Mike and Jake on the net. That would be the least dangerous place for her to begin.

They were all warmed up and ready. Jake had explained Daughter's situation to George, and he emphasized the fact that Daughter might not adapt to the net at all. George would have to be very careful and be prepared to disconnect her instantly on command.

George explained that while he would use every tool at his disposal to cushion her entry into the net, she could not just come in part way if she was to be a full crewmember. Nor, once in the net, could she meet just part of a person. Personalities on the net were all or nothing.

They felt her don the helmet and waited while George ran his preliminary set-up. Suddenly she was there. Jake greeted her first, like a younger brother. Mike sensed her delight at meeting Jake for the first time, and she seemed genuinely happy to meet him in this manner, as a real person instead of an unknowable Rider. He gave them some time, then joined them. She instantly pulled back from him, afraid. He reached out a mental hand to her, offering her guidance, but she hesitated.

"Will you let me help?" he asked lightly, letting her feel his happiness within the net and his oneness with Jake. "You are welcome here. Please join with us. Just, please, don't use your 'eye thing' on me. We're all equal in here."

"I . . . I don't think I know how to be equal," she answered uneasily.

"You'll learn. We'll give you time, all the time you need. Things move fast in here, but it's easier than you might think. Want to try something?"

"What?"

"Take my hand." He reached out to her. She hesitated, then made herself take his virtual hand. They touched, and Jake joined them by taking her other hand in his. "Jake," he said, "let's fly!"

They led her through George's training routine, introducing splashes of information one sense at a time just as George had shown them the previous day. Personalities could not remain isolated in such an environment, and they shared in her wonder and joy of an aspect of life never permitted her before. To his surprise, Mike discovered that, though strong, even headstrong, her spirit had fragile spots. There was a dark place within her, a place jealously guarded, a place of emptiness she protected so effortlessly that she was probably not even aware she was doing so. He suspected this guarded place had to do with her recent losses: her husband, many friends, indeed a whole fleet, and possibly the Empire and her whole family. She had lots to be unhappy about. He knew the private place was there, he accepted it, and he respected her for choosing to keep her burdens private. In the end, he simply learned to ignore it.

Jake and Mike just let her be herself. They took their time, always leading until she forgot she needed to be led, and as they'd hoped, her wonder overcame her reserve. She let her hair down and danced with them through George's maze of sensory inputs, just as Mike and Jake had the day before.

Mike sensed her smiling for the first time since he'd known her. She had temporarily forgotten her burdens, or maybe just put them aside for a time, but she seemed a different, happier, more approachable person than Daughter.

Sensing his focus on her, she in turn focused on him, the virtual Mike Carver, not the physically overbearing, barbaric Mike Carver that she had met in the midst of battle. "I was not wrong in coming here," she stated in wonder. "Everything is so clear, so simple and beautiful, not dangerous at all."

"Well . . . we don't know that for certain. I'm not too worried about myself and Jake, but we have some major hurdles to clear yet. Look, I can't call you Daughter, at least not here in the net. We're all equal in here, we're all crewmembers, and you're definitely not my daughter. Can I call you something else? Do you have a name?"

For the first time since he'd met her, she seemed lost. "A name? Someone wants to know my name?" She was well and truly startled, even flustered. "Otis calls me 'My Lady.' Will that do?" she asked uncertainly. Sensing his reluctance, but remembering she was in the net and could be anyone she wanted, she said laughingly, "Oh, dear! This is fun! What would you like to call me?"

"Well . . . I've been thinking of you as 'Princess,' but I'd rather call you by your real name." Jake stayed surprisingly quiet during this exchange.

"No. No one calls me by my name. 'Daughter' is a title bestowed years ago. It has been my name ever since. Call me Daughter."

"I will if you insist. Can't you tell me your name? Do you have one?"

"Of course I have a name, but few know it." She hesitated, then said, "I am Ellandra of the Chosen."

"Ellandra Chosen. Okay!"

"No. 'Ellandra of the Chosen.' That is my name. The list of Chosen is very small."

He suspected a hidden message here but didn't press. "Ellandra of the Chosen," he repeated. "Nice to meet you, Ellandra. Uh, can I call you Ellie?" She digested his words, but it was clear to him that she didn't understand. More, he sensed her insecurity with the whole name business.

"No, you may not. I'm Daughter, or My Lady, call me one of those. Certainly not this Ellie. What's Ellie?"

"It's a nickname, like Mike. My real name is Michael, but my friends call me Mike." She was uncomfortable with this alien concept, but he sensed her wavering. He tried another tack. "Okay, how about just here in the net among us? It's part of learning to treat each other equally. It'll be good practice. Try it, maybe you'll like it. Nice to meet you, Ellie," he said, bowing.

Uncertain, she mentally curtsied. "The pleasure is mine, Mike."

It was time for the next hurdle. For her, people were the easy part. How would she do when she met George, a machine? Mike and Jake took her hands and called George, expecting him to simply be there instantly like he always was. Instead, he kept them waiting.

They suddenly found themselves standing on a misty sea shore, their feet sunk in loose sand. Looking about, Mike noted that visibility was poor, maybe a hundred meters or so. Waves lapped lazily up onto the beach a few feet below them, creating a regular shushing sound. Then, a pounding sound, far distant, grew. Something was coming toward them.

Mike felt Ellie's hand tighten in his nervously as a dim shape appeared in the distance. It grew larger as it approached, and they all let out a mental gasp. Ellie was the first to recover, clapping her hands in childish delight at the galloping knight approaching on a great black stallion. The knight, dressed in armor from head to foot, a tall white feather streaming from his helmet, reigned in before them, dismounted, and knelt on one knee before her.

"My Lady, Sir George at your service," he stated gallantly.

"Arise, Sir George," she commanded easily. "Unmask yourself. I would see your face."

"Alas, Lady," he murmured, downcast. "I have no face."

Her hand went to her throat. "I'd forgotten!" she exclaimed in horror. "How could I have forgotten? None of this is real. Yet you seem so real, your world seems so real. You all seem real. I'm so sorry George."

"This world is as real as your own, My Lady. Simpler in many ways, infinitely more complex in others, but it is just as real. Do not be sad. Be welcome to my world. And do not worry about my face. One of the benefits of masks is that you can use your imagination to your heart's delight. I can be anyone you choose."

"Well met, Sir George," she replied, tears glistening in her eyes as she reached out for his hand, helping him to his feet.

"Well then, are you ready to continue?" he asked.

"Lead on," she commanded.

George's image began thinning, turning transparent, then disappearing altogether. But his presence did not waiver. His spirit embraced them all as they felt themselves lifted. "Let's fly!" he cried.

To everyone's great relief, Ellie was in and she never looked back. In fact, she was usually the first to join the net each day, spending even more time with George than did Mike and Jake. She flourished, her appetite returned, and she was a happier person in every way, both inside and outside the net. The black hole she protected was still there, and Mike didn't know what she kept bridled up inside of it, but whatever it was, it did not appear to hinder her activities in any way. She, a person who had never been allowed to interface with machines, soaked up everything George sent her way. She was fully a part of the team that would take them from Earth.

Chapter Six

"What do you mean, she escaped?" Struthers shouted. "Impossible! No one can function against the *scree*."

"I don't know how she did it, Sire," his Chief of Staff, Sorn Jirdn, answered, his eyes widening in surprise at the explosion coming from a man known for his iron control, a control always maintained even in the face of the worst disasters. "We believe she's still on the emerging world. The Chessori have dispatched more ships."

"Well, send one of our squadrons to back them up. I can't trust them with this. It's too important."

"Very well, Sire."

Struthers sat back down behind his desk, fuming. How had she done it? It should have been no contest. The outcome of the meeting on Dorwall had been certain. The Chessori claimed no one was immune to the *scree*. Could they be wrong?

His eyes narrowed as he considered. After a time, he picked up his communicator. "I need to see you," he stated in no uncertain terms.

Several minutes later the diminutive form of a Chessori entered without knocking, its all-white body completely naked, sexless, and hairless, its large elliptical black eyes utterly without expression. Struthers still couldn't tell if it was Burjosk, and it very well might not be. They all looked the same to him. He started to ask but pushed the thought aside.

"Your men failed," he said.

"I know. It will not happen again."

"What happened? You assured me that no one was immune to your *scree*. You must be wrong."

"No, I am not wrong. I do not know how they got away."

"Well, I think I know. Have you tested the *scree* against a Protector?"

"I have not. They are not exactly willing to submit to a test. We have never encountered a species that is immune, and I see no reason to consider them an exception."

"I do. Someone managed to get that ship away from Dorwall. Find a Protector and test it."

"They have all left Triton, those that survived."

"I know that, but there are plenty of Guardians on other worlds. Find one and test it, then kill it. We can't let it know about the *scree*."

"If the Guardian continues to function, and I admit that I, too, can find no other explanation, it will be dangerous for my men. These Guardians are lethal."

"So take precautions," he said impatiently. "And get moving on this. I need answers."

"Very well."

The Chessori turned and left. Struthers frowned. He hated the creatures, but he needed them. The neutron bomb at the Palace had been easy. The act of taking out the leadership of the Empire had been child's play even if events leading up to it had not. He had lived in mortal fear of a Testing for years as he put his plan together. A single Testing would have uncovered all his plans, but the Queen had become overconfident and too certain of her staff.

Staff. He hated the word. His elevation to First Knight had been exhilarating at first, but he had soon grown bored of the position. He never let it show, his work never suffered, but he wanted more. The Chosen were so focused on people that they ignored some of the most elementary economic principles. It was trade that would carry the Empire forward, not the masses. Who cared about the masses? With the exception of the wealthy and powerful, people were just consumers of trade goods. So long as businesses prospered, so, too, would the Empire, and he could do something about that now that he was in charge.

On the surface, that's what drove him and his movement. Deep down, though, it was something else. It was the same thing that had driven him to seek the position of First Knight: a craving for ultimate control. As First Knight he had sensed fulfillment of that craving, but he had never achieved it. Now he had, and the feeling truly empowered him. There was nothing holding him back now. There was nothing he could not achieve, nothing the Empire could not achieve. The politicians, the wealthy, and the powerful would soon be in his pocket, and he would rule all of them.

He had some cleaning up to do, but the plan was on track. Politics came first, and close on its heels came control of the military. New governors were moving out to the sectors, and he would eventually clean out those that did not comply with his demands. Those new governors, with his assistance when needed, would bring the military into the fold, then even the rich and powerful would have to lower a knee to him.

The Imperial Senate was child's play; they'd follow whomever wielded the biggest club, and that was him.

He was still peeved about Veswicki, Governor of Triton. What bad luck that he had been away from the Palace when the bomb had gone off. The hunt was on for Veswicki, but for the moment he had slipped through their fingers, and he was a dangerous one.

Few others had escaped. His men were mopping up those who had, and his plans for the fleet were actually ahead of schedule. Chessori observers had quietly been placed aboard a few ships of the fleet, and results were promising. In some Sectors, promotions had bought loyalty, plain and simple. With new captains handing out promotions down the line, crews tended to do just as they'd been trained to do: follow orders.

The Empire was dead. His men were filling the vacuum, all according to plan. But Daughter's existence continued to nag at his thoughts as he worked. Eventually, he put his personal pad aside and went to the liquor cabinet. It was early, but that was okay. He was the most powerful man in the galaxy, and he could do as he pleased.

Yet thoughts of Daughter continued to plague him as he tried to relax.

Chapter Seven

The days on *Resolve* were long, full, and not all fun and games as they struggled to function as a team. They encountered challenges that some mastered better than others. Mike frustrated everyone by insisting on learning the technology behind everything they experienced. He wanted particulars, he wanted designs and blueprints, he wanted to know the math and science behind processes, and he insisted on doing things over and over again until he felt he understood.

Jake worked hard to move him past details. He encouraged Mike to focus, instead, on affects, and he constantly reminded him to "feel" the information presented by George, to guide George in defining what information was needed, then use George's results. He didn't need to understand processes. Full understanding could come later, probably much later, if Mike really wanted to pursue it. They didn't have time now.

Ellie was the first to sense the source of his difficulty. After dinner on her third day in the net, she led him to a couch in the lounge and took both of his hands in her own. After the wonderful hours within the net, Mike had thought he was no longer afraid of her, but he stiffened when she took his hands and was afraid to look into her eyes.

"Relax, Mike. I won't use my 'eye thing' on you," she said. He looked at her, surprised. "Yes, I have not forgotten. I will never forget the feeling of horror you experienced."

"You knew?"

"Yes. My Touch is sensitive to feelings. I have used the Touch many, many times, but I have never sensed anything like what you went through that day. While there is no known method for resisting my Touch, the horror you felt literally drove me away. I hope to never experience the feeling again, and I have promised to never subject you to it again without your consent. Someday I will explain my eye thing to you. For the Empire, it is a powerful gift, with damning consequences for some and wonderful resolution for others. The ability to use it has placed a yoke about my neck that I will never be free of.

"But enough of that. I have a gift for you, though in truth it's a gift for Otis and me, as well."

She reached into a pocket and withdrew several pieces of jewelry. She attached one to her ear, tossed another to Otis, then extended her hand to show him a small fan-shaped grill of thin golden mesh. Without asking, she reached up and clipped the charm to his left ear.

"It's a translator device," she explained. "You can speak to us in your own language, and the devices that Otis and I wear will translate for us. The reverse also holds true for the one you wear. Jake will not have to spend all his time translating what we say. George has been working on these since you awoke and spoke your first words, and he has accumulated data from various broadcasts from your planet as well. He'll continue working on upgrades, but he believes these are a good beginning."

Without hesitation she moved to the next issue on her list. Mike was still fiddling with the ear mesh as she spoke. "We must talk about Michael Carver," she said.

His fiddling came to an abrupt halt. This didn't sound good. "I beg your pardon?" he asked.

"Mike Carver is slowing us down. As wonderful, as intoxicating as playing within the net is for us, we cannot forget our purpose. Do you recall that purpose?"

"Sure, we protect the Heir at all costs, and we get you home to find out what's happened to your Empire."

"Very good. Tell me, how is your understanding of the principles behind our drive system going to help us achieve that goal?"

"Well, I'm not sure. You never know until you need to know, but I hate doing anything half way."

She raised her eyebrows to him with an expectant look on her face, but he just returned the look. "Okay, let me put this another way," she said, starting over. "In what way will your understanding of the mathematical calculations needed for maintaining adequate hydration in the hydroponics system assist us in protecting the Heir."

"What if it breaks?"

"Are you going to fix it?"

"Maybe . . ."

"Mike, George doesn't even have to fix stuff. There are separate computers for everything in *Resolve*. George only monitors them and gives them a push now and then. Most of it is completely automatic. You know all this as well as I do."

"I know, but I'm an engineer. I can't help it."

"We can't stay here for twenty years while you learn all this stuff."

"I know we can't."

"And I know you know. I sense your understanding through your feelings on the net, and it doesn't require my special Talents, it only requires caring. Mike, I like the Mike Carver I've met on the net. You're the right person for this job, and you've restored my hope in our eventual success. I'm glad I shot you." She followed that statement with a big smile, hoping to take the sting out of her words.

"What?" he bellowed, jumping to his feet.

"Sit down, Mike," she ordered, the smile gone.

He sat without thinking, then wished he hadn't. She could order people around better than anyone he'd ever met. You didn't even know you'd complied with an order from her until it was too late.

"Yes, I'm glad I shot you," she continued. "You are the right person for us. You may not know it, but you're adapting to George better than Jake is, and that's saying something."

She folded her hands in her lap as she settled into her lecturing mode. "Let's talk about being an engineer. You've been trained to convert ideas, raw materials, and technology into finished products, whatever they may be. Those skills, as wonderful as they are, aren't needed here. Mike, the ship needs . . . no, *I* need Mike Carver to find a way to become an end user of the product other engineers have built. You don't need to know how to build a spaceship in order to fly one, nor do you need to know how the power plant works in order to make the ship go fast or slow. You only need to command George. You do not need to know how George has been created or what makes him tick. You do need to know how to work with George, to use George's knowledge and talents to their fullest, then to command him. That's the only purpose of this training. And George wants to be commanded. He is acting as a teacher now, but he prefers to make suggestions and to be commanded."

"What do you mean 'he prefers?' He's a machine."

Now it was her turn to be startled. "Do you hear yourself?" she asked. "Jake, hello, are you in there? Does he believe what he just said?"

>Do you, Mike?< Jake asked.

"Look, he was built," Mike reminded them.

"Then why did you give him a name?" Ellie asked softly.

That gave him pause. "He's a machine with a personality, and I like him. That doesn't change the fact that he's a machine. Are you saying he's a real person? Are your computers so advanced that they're alive?"

Ellie looked troubled. "I don't know. We have referred to those of George's stature as being 'nearly sentient' artificial intelligences. We may be wrong."

She clasped her hands nervously in thought, then shrugged and turned back to him, her body language telling him she was making a demand of him this time, not a request. "Mike, please hear me. For me, for the Heir, for the Empire, please, please stop being an engineer. Let George and his network of computers do the hard stuff. You need to guide, that's all."

"What if George breaks?"

>George can't break, Mike.<

"Any of us can break," Mike answered aloud to both of them. "I've spent my whole life either fixing things or trying to design them so they wouldn't break."

"Thank you, Mike. You answered your own question," Ellie responded.

"What?"

"You design things so they won't break. How successful are you?"

He squirmed. "Only moderately successful. Things wear out, you know."

"Not ships. And certainly not George. Is it fair to say that our engineers and scientists are more advanced than your own?"

"Well . . ."

"Do you see where I'm going with this?"

He pursed his lips. "I find it hard to believe things don't break."

"When it comes to our ships, they don't," Ellie said sternly. "Trust me on this."

He hung his head in defeat. Besides, even if something did break, who was he, Mike Carver, to fix it? And in his gut, he sensed her rightness. They didn't have twenty years for him to get comfortable.

"You're right," he admitted. "Time is of the essence, and I'm slowing us down. That's not acceptable. This whole thing is probably a long shot anyway. I can make myself back off. It won't be easy, but I'll do my best."

"Thank you, Mike. Jake and I will help."

"Jake is our captain. You and I are just along for the ride. I can work on those terms, though there's definitely a place for us in this. You've got a pretty good handle on things yourself, you know."

She blushed at the praise but nodded her head. "I think I'm having fun for the first time in my life, and I like George. I wish this was all under different circumstances. I wish we had more time."

Mike didn't change overnight, but he worked hard on it. George's programming required that he answer questions when asked, but he and Mike had a private conversation about when he should and when he should not provide too much intimate detail. Following that conversation, George didn't hesitate to remind Mike when he thought it was time to move on to something else. Of course, Ellie and Jake did not hesitate in the slightest when they grew impatient. Mike made himself listen to them.

Ellie surpassed her own expectations. They no longer feared for her, no longer pampered and protected her. Though individually none of them had the desired backgrounds needed of a ship's captain, George had cunningly created a virtual enhanced team of Jake/Mike/Ellie that worked well. If they ran into serious problems on their trip, well . . . they would cope.

It didn't take long for the feelings they experienced with each other inside the net to carry over to their time outside the net. Feelings of distrust and isolation between Ellie and Mike, so pervasive at first, gradually faded away. Jake, an equal partner within the net, remained a member of their small group outside the net, as well.

Mike focused hard on learning to speak Ellie's language, Galactic High Standard, knowing it would improve his usefulness in the long run. Speaking inside the net was instantaneous and did not require translation, and the translating devices attached to their ears enabled functionality outside the net, but Mike wanted to do away with them. It made their lives a little harder, but he learned, and Ellie enjoyed lots of laughs at his expense.

The pace was frantic and productive. They mastered the net and were proud of it. When George informed them it was time to move on, to put their training to work, Ellie called a time-out. They celebrated their graduation over lunch, and when Ellie showed up with a child in her arms, Mike and Jake finally got to meet the focus of their efforts.

Alexis was seven months old. To Mike she looked like all babies, cuddly and helpless. He saw nothing at all special about this very special child. He resisted the urge to talk baby talk and to make a fool of himself by making weird faces at Alexis. Instead, he simply held his arms out. Ellie handed her over without hesitation, though Mildred, the nanny, was more reserved.

Mike quickly understood why Mildred had not been used as a repository for Jake. She was intelligent, chatty, and comfortable within the group, but her life began and ended with Alexis. She was probably the perfect nanny and deeply loved the child, but she cared little for their progress on the net or even their immediate prospects for escape, except insofar as those prospects impacted Alexis.

The party was short lived. Alexis demanded a nap and Ellie, Mike, and Jake were anxious to see what George had up his sleeves for them. They went back to work.

George reconfigured *Resolve* into a flight simulator, allowing them to experience the new duties they would have when under way. Their first simulation taught them to move the ship underwater, but they quickly graduated to the real thing: space. They commanded *Resolve* to simulate orbiting Earth, then planned and executed a flight plan that took them out beyond the inner planets to where it would be safe to execute a jump.

Travel between the stars took place in three phases. Phase one required a ship to travel outward through a star's system until reaching a safe jump point, usually several weeks of travel at normal speeds. Jumps attempted any closer to the primary star or other strong gravity wells such as planets and large moons could be disastrous, at the very least erratic and unpredictable. Jump physics caused a ship to seek strong gravity wells, bending the ship's desired course toward those gravity wells. The result was that jumps could, and often had before these simple rules were established, proven fatal.

Phase two required jumps through hyperspace, and not just one or two jumps. Long jumps simply were not accurate; strong gravity wells continued to act upon the ship as it progressed through its jump. The process required a series of comparatively small jumps that were time consuming and technically demanding to set up.

A number of calculations came into play in resolving a jump

computation: the ship needed to know where it would be at the beginning of the jump; it had to navigate to that point, establishing proper aim and speed prior to arrival; determine the jump ending coordinates; compute the power output and duration to get there; do its best to calculate the effects of gravity wells that would affect it during the jump; and execute the jump at precisely the correct instant, then monitor everything as the jump progressed.

Phase three was similar to phase one. The ship came out of hyperspace at the extremities of the destination solar system and completed the trip with a few weeks of travel at normal speeds.

George took care of all these things. A number of different computers came into play, George directing them like a conductor directing a symphony orchestra. All Jake had to do was tell George where they wanted to go. But blindly allowing George to fly the ship, as Jornell and Wooldroo had, was what had brought them to Earth in the first place. Something was wrong with the system, something in either George's programming or the computers he directed. Had regular pilots been available, they might not have ended up here. Regular pilots were trained and expected to double-check jump calculations when time permitted. The lesson had been learned far back in the infancy of space travel, usually the hard way, and Mike, Jake, and Ellie would not put all their eggs in one basket ever again. They would take the time and learn how to confirm George's calculations.

He guided the team through jump after jump until they had the process down, then he had them do it again individually. None of them excelled at the tedious process, but to everyone's surprise, Mike proved to be the most persistent at directing the various computers accurately. George was marginally satisfied with his performance. Jake and Ellie would have to specialize in other areas.

The first time George threw a simulated Chessori attack at them, the team was completely caught off guard. The ship was destroyed before they even recognized they were under attack. Thereafter, George taught them how to monitor other parameters to ensure that no one sneaked up on them.

Weapons lessons began in earnest, all in simulation. George provided the attack scenarios, and the team learned to interpret them, determine tactical responses, use the onboard weapons whenever running away was not possible, and monitor *Resolve's* well-being during the process.

Their only weapons consisted of four laser-disintegrator systems, each of which was driven individually. A laser lit up the target and tracked it, then the disintegrator fired immensely powerful particle beams along the laser-aiming beam. Each weapon could shoot twice per second, so a total of eight shots per second could be sustained. Located two in the top and two in the bottom of the saucer-shaped ship, the weapons could be operated manually, if necessary, or through interface with George.

But enemy ships did not approach on smooth trajectories. Ships' drives permitted instant acceleration in any direction, and targets danced all over the sky. Despite this movement, attacking ships had to hold to some semblance of trajectory or they would not approach their target, and careful but fast analysis by George provided a predicted trajectory. Gunners applied intuition and luck to light up the target. As soon as a lock occurred, the disintegrator beam could be fired. It all happened quickly, and *Resolve*, too, was dancing all over the sky to prevent lock-on by the enemy lasers. It was a difficult process to master, and they worked hard at it.

Under normal circumstances the bridge crew consisted of one pilot, two pilots when jump computations were in process, one engineering/communications officer, and a watch commander, with the captain joining at his/her discretion. During critical times all were plugged-in to George. During battle stations four gunners supplemented the bridge crew, one manning each weapon, and a gunnery control officer guided their efforts. At least one engineering specialist, and often two, supervised repairs during battle. A normal tactical crew therefore consisted of ten individuals, all plugged-in to George. Therein lay the challenge: their team had only themselves, and although they counted as three when in the net, they were nowhere near the ten needed. Nor was there a relief crew. They would be in space twenty-four hours each day. Demands upon their time would never cease.

George never let up. Before long they grew exhausted and disheartened. They simply could not plan strategies, oversee *Resolve's* movements, and control four weapons simultaneously. To further complicate matters, George, though eminently capable of managing *Resolve's* normal systems, insisted they periodically keep an eye on the ship's well-being. He constantly reminded them that space travel took place in a dangerous environment. If their ship failed them, all was lost. Periodically, whether in the midst of jump computations or under simulated attack, he threw distractions at them in the form of onboard problems, most often the result of battle damage. He insisted that care of *Resolve* never be left to chance.

After several days of frustrating effort, the crew got together for a conference. Nearly a month had passed since Mike had awoken to meet Jake, and they were nowhere near ready to go. They had to speed things up.

After heated discussion, they decided to split up the team, to focus each of them on one or two areas of specialization. Ellie immediately claimed weapons. She liked the challenge, she preferred working on problems with immediate results, and she was aggressive with the guns. No one disputed her claim. Otis, too, would be a gunner, operating one weapon manually from outside the net. His training as a Protector suited perfectly. He would double as engineering officer if repairs were needed.

Jake, naturally, would be the pilot and be in command of the ship, leaving Mike to man a weapon and double as engineer, but before anyone could state those obvious assignments, Jake called for a time-out. He and Mike held a private conference. Mike leaned back in the couch with his eyes closed. It was just the two of them.

>You have to be captain, Mike,< Jake demanded.

>Get out of here! You're our captain. You have been all along.<

>I can't be captain.<

>Why not?<

>Because I'm a Rider. Riders ride, they don't control. And there's something you've all forgotten.<

>What?<

>The Chessori mind weapon. I'm not immune. If we encounter it, I'm going to be useless.<

Mike started to protest, then paused. Jake was right. After just a little more thought, it got worse. >You're spread throughout my body. You're going to take me out with you.<

>Not if I can help it. I'm going to find a way to isolate myself from you, but when I do I won't be any help to you, and I'll definitely be out of the net. Otis manages with sheer willpower. I will just have to do the same. Wooldroo's memories of this mind weapon are vivid. Quite frankly, I'm terrified.<

>I'm really sorry for you, Jake. I saw what it did to Ellie and Jornell. Maybe my immunity will transfer to you.<

>Are you willing to risk the ship to find out? I'm not.<

>No. You're right.< Mike paused to think, trying to come up with a better solution, but he could not. >This thing doesn't affect George, does it?<

>No, it doesn't.<

>This is not the way to protect the Heir, Jake. We're crazy trying

to leave the planet. Why not just stay here until reinforcements arrive?<

>What reinforcements? No one knows where we are. I doubt if anyone even knows we're still alive.<

>So you want me to fly the ship, huh?<

>I do. Admit it - you're the best pilot aboard, and more important, you're a good decision maker. Our performance is always best when you're calling the shots.<

>I never signed on for this. What if I run us into a black hole or something?<

>You know George won't let you. If he could make such a decision, he would agree that you should be our captain. I'm certain Daughter will agree, as well.

>No way!<

>Trust me. We're now into politics where I'm the expert. Suck it up, Mike. Be in command. You *are* in command.<

Mike stood up and paced for a time. When he looked to Ellie, she was leaning forward, almost as if she anticipated his words.

"Jake thinks I should be our captain," he said softly.

Ellie sank back into the chair with her eyes closed, clasping her hands together over her heart. "Thank you, Jake," she breathed. Otis let out a roar. Mike looked at him, startled, then turned back to Ellie. She instantly tensed. "I told you weeks ago that you were the right person for us. I sensed it immediately in the net, and I have sensed it with my special skills, as well. Jake's skills will be needed later. So, do we call you Captain Mike, or do you prefer Captain Carver?"

"Uh . . ."

"And don't forget, I still own the ship. I choose where we go and when we go. Your responsibility is to get us there in one piece. Let's get back to work."

"Wait! I haven't agreed to anything yet."

"Since when did I need your agreement on anything?" she stated, rising to her feet with a mischievous twinkle in her eyes.

They tried the new arrangement immediately. Jake, by default, would fill in where needed, either with guns, backing up George as engineer, or assisting Mike with navigation. Otis stationed himself at his gun in the upper turret, surrounded by targeting computers and gun controls. The rest of the team, though physically sprawled around the bridge, was hard at work in the net.

George wasted no time, sending four Chessori fighters at them. Otis proved his worth, warming up quickly and demonstrating his natural talent. Ellie, as usual, became overwhelmed as she targeted three weapons. Jake raced to help in the midst of the crisis, but George threw a hull breach at them. With air pressure dropping, Jake was forced to drop everything else while he sealed off the leaking section, a job George could have done if he'd chosen to.

Mike raced in to help but was no longer needed. Ellie had gotten creative, slaving her three guns together to focus on one target at a time. While giving up versatility, she gained a more powerful weapon since she sent three shots in place of one. Her hit ratio improved dramatically, and she whooped with glee.

Though operating independently, they still functioned as a team, encouraging and supporting as time permitted, helping each other when someone got overloaded, and congratulating each other on the rare occasions that George let up.

Mike suspected that their efforts, though the best they could hope to achieve, were probably not enough. He knew that ultimately the only good defense was a good offense, but against more than two or three ships, they were totally on the defensive. And if these Chessori, or the traitors who assisted them, continued to stay one step ahead of them, as they had already proven they could, their best efforts were likely to fail.

To do this right, they needed more ships, lots of them. At the very least, though, this ship badly needed more crew, at least one more person. The one insurmountable problem George threw at them was damage repairs that required someone to leave the bridge. There were times when someone actually had to go fix something. Mike had his hands full, Ellie didn't have a clue how to fix things, and Jake, though independent when in the net, couldn't go anywhere without Mike. That left only Otis, but they needed him on his gun.

They needed one more body, a gunner who could leave to fix things, but there was no one else. Mike tried to cajole George into helping, but George's most fundamental programming specifically prohibited him from activating any weapons at living targets. Once they got underway, George would be out of his training mode and on 'their side' again. He could take over Jake's engineering duties, allowing Jake to man a gun, but they were still short a body to make repairs. Unfortunately, what they had now was as good as it was going to get.

They were as ready to go as George could make them. They just had to take care of the comparatively minor problem of fixing the ship. *Resolve* had come to Earth in spite of instructions from Jornell and George to the contrary. Someone had fiddled with the navigation computer, and the whole thing had been part of a plan. Whose plan, they did not know, and discovering the answer to that question was high on their list of priorities. That the Chessori had been involved was obvious, but someone from the Empire had to have done the actual work.

Mike, considering what he knew about castle intrigues from history books, knew only that things could get very, very complicated. If someone was after the Heir, wouldn't they also be after the king, or queen, or emperor, or whoever led this empire? With just a little more speculation, the thought that the Heir might suddenly be much more than heir, that she might already be Queen, stunned Mike. And just a child!

Fixing *Resolve* was Jake's problem. Had the virus been recognizable to George, it would never have been accepted, which meant it had been inserted into an area of programming George was not permitted to access. Jornell had fully intended to look into the problem, but he had never found the opportunity. Had enough of Wooldroo's knowledge been transferred to Jake?

Jake was itching to prove himself. He had, in fact, been considering the problem for some time. He went right to work, complaining all the while that he was still just a baby and how could they expect so much from him? Through Mike's fingers he began querying the ship's computers, working his way into the navigation computer. They spent the rest of the day scrolling through line after line of code. Mike's eyes finally grew so heavy that they had to quit. Even Jake felt discouraged, and he remained quiet, allowing Mike to fall into an instant sleep.

They got an early start the next morning, working straight through breakfast and up to lunch, still without result. By lunchtime Mike was fading fast, much faster than he should have, considering how exciting everything was. He mentioned it to Jake as they rode the central shaft down to the lounge, and Jake guiltily replied that some of it was his fault. He was a high-energy consumer. Mike was going to have to eat regular meals and eat much more than he was accustomed to eating.

>You mean I don't have to worry about getting fat in my middle age?< he asked Jake over lunch while bouncing Alexis on his knee.

>Child's play, Mike. You will not get fat. I will not allow your body to be unhealthy. About reaching middle age, I offer no guarantees.<

>How do you do it?<

>I just do it. You think of me as a blob of protoplasm in your leg, but Mike, I'm not like that. I'm distributed evenly throughout your body. I'm everywhere. My system automatically monitors everything going on in your body. You'll never be sick again. I think you call it payback.<

>Well, look, I've been staying out of your way on the computer search, but I don't think we're getting anywhere. Do you?<

>We have a long way to go. For a simple navigation computer, there's an awful lot of code.<

>I would hope so. Navigating between the stars can't be simple, but we'll never get done at this rate. We need to attack the problem from a different direction. Can we get the computers to help us in our search?<

>Hmm. Computers were not an item of great interest to Wooldroo, but he may have passed information on to me that I haven't fully considered. Let me think on this.<

>I use computers a lot in my work, Jake. I know everyone around here thinks I'm a throwback, a Neanderthal, but I'm a respected engineer on Earth, and I'm no idiot when it comes to this stuff. Heck, physics is physics. Computers can only work so many different ways.<

>I'm sorry you feel that way, Mike. I have never thought you were an idiot, though as you suggest, I have not considered all your talents.<

>I thought you could read my mind.<

>I try not to. I've had to pry in some areas, to learn your language for example, but I try hard not to pry deeper than necessary without your approval. Just as I would hope you do not pry unnecessarily into my mind.<

>I can't read your thoughts at all, Jake. Not outside the net, anyway.<

>Maybe not yet, but you will. In fact, you already are to a small extent. You sense my feelings much of the time. I don't know exactly what, if any, limitations we will end up with.<

That quieted Mike for a time. This whole arrangement was so alien to him that he was really off balance trying to evaluate it. In fact, he sort of shied away from all thought of it.

Jake left him for a time. Mike suspected he was deep in his own thoughts, and he was right. When they returned to the bridge, Jake was ready with a new plan of attack. The sabotage was probably limited, not extensive, or it would have been detected by the test routines constantly run by the computers themselves. He asked the computer to list all programming changes smaller than a certain size, sorting by date. He also ran a search for substitution routines, a type of program most likely to be the culprit in sending the ship to the wrong place.

He discovered one hundred thirty-seven unauthorized subroutines before dinner. During the next two weeks they fixed those problems and ran extensive tests looking for more. When they were done, Jake pronounced all computers on the ship to be as reliable as he could make them. To the best of his knowledge, they now had an operational ship and could go anywhere in the galaxy they chose to go.

Where would they go? Ellie wanted to go home. Not because she was homesick, but because her overriding concern was the fate of the Empire. Her home planet, Triton, had to be warned. Otis was more concerned with protecting the Heir. He wanted to get help before heading for Triton. He was concerned about who or what would be waiting for them on arrival there. Nothing short of a full battle fleet would satisfy him if they were to go to Triton. Mike sided with Otis, and Jake sided with Mike. They didn't even know if the monarchy existed anymore. Because of that, caution seemed to be the wisest choice.

Mike even suggested they find a safe hiding place on Earth for Ellie and the Heir while he and Otis went for help. She and Otis both balked at this suggestion. Otis would not leave the Heir, period. They simply had to manage the risk another way, yet they couldn't just fly somewhere and sneak in. Every ship carried an identification beacon. The beacon automatically transmitted the ship's identification and, in their case, the fact that it was a royal yacht.

"What happens if we turn off the beacon?" Mike asked. "Will they see us then?"

"We can't turn it off," Otis replied. "I'm pretty sure we'd lose George in the process. Without a beacon, System Administration would probably not notice us, but I have never heard of a ship's beacon failing without the entire ship being lost."

Ellie finally agreed to let them go for help before heading for Triton. They chose a world called Gamma VI, headquarters for a squadron of ships headed by a Commodore Beggin, uncle to Ellie. She was absolutely certain that he could be trusted and that he would help. After Gamma VI, they would be in a position to approach Triton in force.

Chapter Eight

They didn't waste any time. Mike and George prepared a flight plan and everyone settled into their accustomed duties. Mike briefly reflected on the thought that he would soon be going into space for the first time ever, but he forced the thought aside. He could not afford distractions at this point. Instead, he mentally prepared himself for another training session, pretending that *Resolve* was still a giant simulator.

It was just as well. Things didn't happen the way they'd hoped. The moment they broke the surface of the ocean, George's sensors discovered a dozen Chessori ships loitering in the distance, several within a few miles. The Chessori reacted quickly, closing the distance fast. Otis was first to fire, but Ellie and Jake were not far behind him. *Resolve* was quickly surrounded.

Mike made a snap decision. He could not risk the Heir. Twelve to one odds were not something they could handle. *Resolve* hit the water on the way down almost as fast as she had come out of it. They were safe once again from Chessori weapons, but they were trapped. They'd been airborne for less than one minute.

Mike controlled his nervousness and checked for Chessori followers, but *Resolve* was alone underwater. They spent the next few hours moving *Resolve*, then tried again. Again, the Chessori were on them in an instant. Back in the water, move the ship, time for a conference.

Ellie and Jake wanted to run for it, just leave Earth as fast as possible, fighting their way through the gauntlet. Otis and Mike were not willing to simply chance things to fate. They had to find a better way.

Mike removed his helmet and sat back in his seat with his eyes closed, thinking hard. After a time he picked up his helmet and plugged back into George. They held a brief discussion, and he unplugged. The others waited impatiently for an explanation.

Ellie was appalled when he told them his plan. "No, Mike! You can't do it. Earth is protected. The local inhabitants are not to know of our presence here. Please do not do this."

"Will the Chessori harm my people?"

"You told us they've probably known about you for a while, but they have kept their presence hidden from the general populace. Now, the stakes are higher. I don't know."

"My thoughts exactly. Without permission from higher up, most military units stick with standard procedure. I could be wrong, and if I am the plan might not work. They really want *Resolve,* but I'm betting they won't attack anyone here on Earth.

"Princess, my job is to get you home safely. Unless you can give me a better suggestion, we're going to do this. You chose me as captain of the ship. As owner you gave me a destination. It's my job to get you there, and you can't be second-guessing me every step of the way. We have to work together. You have to support me, be a part of the team."

Mike expected quick acquiescence, but it took her a while. The concept seemed utterly foreign to her. "Mike, I have never been in a position where my instructions were not followed. Instantly. Including captains of my ships. Are you telling me that I cannot instruct you?"

"We're not talking affairs of state here, Ellie. You've decided on a goal, that of reaching your uncle on Gamma VI. Your orders to me are to take you there. I'm going to make lots of decisions along the way. Help me, disagree with me, argue against my ideas, but once decisions are made, I need you to back me up. Without exception. We all have to be focused on the same goal. When it comes to saving *Resolve*, you are not Daughter, you're part of my crew. Can you do that?"

"How unique! I'll try. In fact, I think I like your system of doing things. My advice to you is that you cannot involve the natives of this planet. It is against all our rules, rules which are there for good reason."

"Okay. Thanks for the advice. I will limit the natives'

involvement as much as possible, but Ellie, they're going to help. I hope."

It took George two days to find what he was looking for and to get them there. Traveling submerged was not a fast process. Using George's sensors, Mike examined the U.S. battle fleet spread across the ocean before them. The nearest ship was some ten miles away.

In spite of the confidence he'd shown Ellie, doubt assailed his every thought. His plan wouldn't work. Who was he, Mike Carver, to be deciding these things? He must be out of his mind, but two days of debate had not provided a better solution.

He was much more nervous about approaching the fleet than about what had to happen once he reached it. He was certain the U.S. Navy would take a dim view of anything approaching one of its aircraft carriers unannounced, particularly something that was under the water and acting like an enemy submarine. The fleet might open fire as a matter of policy. Yet, if they surfaced outside the ring of protecting ships, the Chessori would nail them. He had to talk with the fleet by radio, and *Resolve* had to be on the surface to do that.

He gambled on the fact that the Chessori would not show themselves to the fleet, or that if they did, they would not chance damaging any of the "natives" by firing on him in their midst. His plan called for waiting until nightfall, but when they heard the pinging on their hull and saw the fleet pick up speed, then several ships and helicopters head their way, he knew he had no choice. Hoping he wouldn't run into a submarine, not even knowing if surface fleets traveled with submarines, he directed George to take them as deep as they could go, then move to a position directly under the carrier. Quickly, knowing that lots of very sharp sailors were at general quarters and preparing to drop everything they could on him, Mike rushed *Resolve* to the surface beside the sprinting carrier before it had a chance to attack. With just a nudge, he lifted up to flight deck level and flew formation beside the carrier right next to its bridge. Surely they wouldn't try to shoot down a UFO, at least not without lots of thinking and arguing first.

He could almost feel the pandemonium on the ships, especially on the aircraft carrier mere meters away. *Resolve*, about two football fields in diameter, had to look intensely menacing to the crew of the carrier. Many, many, many weapons were trained on him at this instant, with just as many itchy trigger fingers. He didn't waste time. George had a frequency chosen on a directional transmitter and opened the line with just a tiny bit of power.

"We are not a threat to you," he intoned carefully over the radio. "I would like to speak with the admiral commanding your fleet."

Mike waited tensely for a reply. It didn't take long. "This is Admiral Trexler. Go ahead."

"Admiral Trexler, this is all going to sound pretty strange. Please bear with me, sir . . ."

Mike had to assume the Chessori heard everything he said over the radio. Consequently, he could not lay all his cards on the table. Admiral Trexler was not easily convinced, but an alien spaceship hovering beside the bridge of the carrier was a powerful persuader all by itself. The admiral agreed to a meeting.

Half an hour later, Mike opened a hatch on the top of the ship and climbed out as a helicopter hovered overhead. A figure in a bulky suit was lowered on a line, steadied by Mike, and the line released. Mike turned to lead the way back inside the ship when a gloved hand grabbed his arm. Moments later another figure started down from the helicopter. Mike was furious. His orders had been specific: the admiral was to have come alone. The admiral grabbed both of Mike's arms and yelled at him that it was only his aide, there was no threat to anyone aboard the UFO.

Mike gave in only because he had no choice and helped the aide to release the winch line. The helicopter lifted and turned away. He led the two visitors through the hatch, then locked the outer door behind them. The silence was deafening.

Both visitors wore bulky suits to protect themselves and the rest of the fleet from alien germs. Mike peered through the admiral's helmet to discover a thin face with deep blue eyes glaring back at him. A neatly trimmed mustache showing a few gray hairs bristled beneath a long, sharp nose. This man was clearly an athlete, not one of those arm-chair officers.

"Thanks for coming, Admiral. I know it's not a small thing that I ask."

"You're right, son. Whatever goes on this day, it's probably the end of my career. There's no 'right' way to deal with aliens, but don't worry about that. I happen to think this is worth the price. Let's get on with it. You said you needed help."

"Yes, sir, but first I have to make sure you're not armed. How am I going to do that with these suits you're wearing?"

"You're not, that's how. If we're to be allowed to return to our ship, we cannot bring back alien germs. Surely you understand that. Furthermore, if you want *my* help, you'll trust me or do without. I give you my word that we are unarmed. The U.S. Navy does not practice piracy. We are not here to take your ship, Mr. Carver."

"Very well, Admiral. Let me warn you, though, that we are not unarmed. Follow me, please."

Mike led them through the ship to the lounge where Otis and Daughter waited. Both suited figures froze at the sight of Otis. This was truly an alien being before them, and it looked vicious. When Otis reached out a hand in greeting, both figures stepped back, staring at long-nailed fingers where a paw should be. Otis spoke a few words, then stepped back. Ellie stepped forward with outstretched hand, and the admiral came to his senses. Both he and the aide greeted her with handshakes through their gloved hands, then the admiral walked over to Otis and extended his hand. Otis offered his toothy grin as he shook the outstretched hand, and the bold step taken by the admiral lessened some of the tension in the room.

"Did you bring the camera?" Mike asked.

"Yes."

"Go ahead and use it. Take pictures of anything you want. I'll even show you the control room later if you'd like. We're not trying to hide anything. You might bring back something of value to salvage your career."

"Thank you, Mr. Carver," Admiral Trexler stated wryly. The aide removed a small video camera from an external pocket and stepped back to the wall, panning the room.

Otis went back to his gun turret – someone had to mind the ship. Mike got right to work. He recounted the battle in the desert outside Reno and what had transpired since, leaving out any mention of Jake and being vague about who Ellie and her daughter were. He implied that they were simply political figures desperately in need of the admiral's help. The story had huge holes in it, and he could tell that the admiral sensed those holes.

"Just what did you have in mind from me, Mr. Carver?" Admiral Trexler asked.

"I'm not sure. What I don't want is for you to start shooting at the Chessori, and not just because they might shoot back. I'm told you'd be wasting your time. Your weapons will not penetrate their shields and would not be considered a threat by them. Besides that," he looked furtively toward Ellie, then raised his chin and continued, "I don't want to put the U.S. Navy, or humanity for that matter, in a position of taking sides in something they don't understand. You can't know who the good guys are and who the bad guys are. Nor do I, though I have strong reasons for supporting those on this ship. These are good people here, and their cause is worthy of your support, but I have never actually talked with a Chessori. They might also be good people. For all these reasons, no matter what happens here, the U.S. Navy is not to shoot at anyone. Does that work for you?"

"It works very well, and it may be the only way you'll get my help," Admiral Trexler responded grimly. "Within those parameters, what do you envision me doing for you?"

"I need two things. More, if you have suggestions. First, I need a diversion. I need to draw off some of those Chessori so we can make a run for it. Do you have any ideas?"

They discussed maneuvering capabilities, speeds, weapons, and a host of other details, including the fact that the Chessori were spread out in a wide ring around *Resolve*, apparently hesitant to approach the fleet and be seen.

The admiral thought for a while. "If I can give you a head start on half the Chessori ships, will that be adequate?" he asked. "Can you take care of the other half?"

Mike had hoped for more, but he was grateful for that much. "That depends on my second request, sir. You see, I need another person. What I really want is someone else to fly this ship, someone more qualified than myself, but for the moment that's not possible. I'll settle for someone who can man a gun, someone who learns fast."

"And that someone would remain with you, perhaps never to return to Earth?"

"I hope not, sir. I plan to come back. If we live that long."

"I see. So you require a volunteer who is psychologically capable of living with aliens, who can meld with your small group here, who is a fast learner, and who can shoot well. That's a tall order . . ."

The admiral's eyes grew large as Mike heard a commotion behind himself. When he turned around, the admiral's aid was unsealing the helmet to his suit. Mike watched, startled, as the features of a woman, a truly beautiful woman, emerged. A firm chin, wide mouth, green eyes, and red hair tied tightly into a bun on the back of her head were revealed as the helmet came free. The woman continued to remove her protective suit, revealing a tall, trim body in a one-piece coverall with lieutenant's bars on the shoulders, her green eyes locked on the Admiral's all the while.

Trexler rose, angrily gesturing to her to stop but knowing it was too late the moment she had loosened the first seal. He suddenly looked old. "Not you, Reba. There are others."

"There will be no others, sir, not if these will have me. I meet all their qualifications, and I want this. Every sailor in the fleet would want it, but I'm here. It's done."

"But your father!"

She turned to Mike, her eyes dancing with excitement, her whole being radiating barely contained energy. "My father is Senator Morrison, an old friend of Admiral Trexler's. He won't like it, but he'll understand. My name is Rebecca Morrison. Will you have me?"

"It's a little late for asking, isn't it?" Mike responded. "I had expected a man . . . ."

"Don't even think it, Mr. Carver. Yes, I'm a woman. I'm also the best person you could get for this job. You will not regret my choice."

"Maybe not, but you might," Mike answered with a grim smile. "Welcome aboard."

She turned back to the admiral. "I resign my commission, of course."

"Yes, I suppose so," he nodded, deflated. "We can't have U.S. Navy officers shooting at aliens, can we?" He looked her in the eyes long and hard, willing this not to have happened. "If I wasn't responsible for the fleet, I'd be the one staying," he finally admitted.

Without ceremony, Ellie walked over to Reba, took both of her hands in her own, and looked into her eyes. Then Mike realized she was *really* looking into her eyes, giving Reba the same treatment she'd given him. Poor kid, he thought.

It didn't take long. The admiral probably saw nothing unusual before Ellie stepped back half a step, supporting Reba while she recovered, and said "Welcome," in Galactic High Standard.

Before Mike could translate, Reba responded, shaken but clearly not as paralyzed as Mike had been after Ellie had finished with him each time. "Nice to meet you, too!" Then she shook her head and looked around as if seeing everything for the first time. Her gaze halted for a moment on Otis, then she said simply, "Let's get this show on the road."

They moved to the bridge where Mike joined the net to let George test solutions, presenting strategies on the screens for the admiral's benefit. There would be no firing of Navy weapons, but short of that anything was okay. They were operating under the assumption that the Chessori would not fire upon Navy personnel, an assumption they were somewhat comfortable with, but everyone knew that it might not hold. A plan was finally agreed upon, and Mike unplugged.

"Do you want to issue orders from here?" Mike asked the admiral.

"What if the Chessori are listening?" he chided Mike. "Besides, my sailors have their orders. All weapons are locked and loaded, but no one will open fire without my command except under very strict guidelines. Those guidelines include my willingness to lose a ship or two before we chance failing with this First Contact. When I return, my superiors will demand an accounting before anything happens, over secure channels of course. You're getting lots of attention, Mr. Carver, including the White House. You've stirred up a hornet's nest if I've ever seen one."

"Oh, great! We don't have weeks, or even days, Admiral."

"You won't need them. We're better than that. Mind if I look around a bit before heading back?"

"Sure. Give me a minute." Mike gave Reba a quick briefing, then handed her a helmet and introduced her to George, informing George that top priority was to bring her up to speed on her weapons station. Introducing her to the rest of the net would have to wait until they were underway. To himself, he added, *if we make it that far.*

Admiral Trexler got his tour, though not to the extent he would have received had he been within the net. Mike showed him around the bridge, let him experience the central shaft again, even showed him his suite. As they walked side by side down the corridor near Mike's suite, they entered the area scarred by blasters.

Trexler sucked in his breath. "Seen a little action already, have you?" he demanded.

"Before my time, Admiral. All I've gotten to do so far is to simulate battles in space. But amazing as it may sound, I actually know how to drive this thing," he said with pride. "I'm captain, but not owner. The lady's in charge."

"I gathered that. Who is she, exactly?"

"You know, I don't know myself, not exactly. She's important, but I think her mission may be more important. I know you'd like details, but I don't want to scare you off with too much information. What you don't know doesn't have to be explained to your superiors. We must limit delay as much as possible, sir."

"Not a valid argument," Admiral Trexler said, shaking his head inside the suit. "Something you will discover when you reach a certain level of responsibility," he continued, "is that there can be no hiding behind ignorance, nor can you avoid the truth. You must insist on the truth, always. Today, millions of lives are at stake. The power of my fleet is humbling, possibly enough to destroy the planet. And the power, or more important the anger of the Chessori? We have no way of knowing. I will ultimately be the one to decide whether to engage these Chessori with my fleet. Mr. Carver, things rarely work out as expected. I'm already facing grievous decisions that might affect everyone on the planet, and there will be more decisions to make during the coming hours. Now, is there anything else you can tell me about what's going on here?"

Mike thought hard before reaching a decision that felt right. He needed the admiral's help, but the admiral needed his help if he was to convince his own superiors. "Sir, there are lots and lots of aliens out there," he said waiving his hand at the ceiling. "They have formed a representative government headed by a Royal Family. The woman is a member of that Royal Family. She's been running from these Chessori for some months now. All she wants to do is return to her Empire where she'll get all the help she needs."

"So this is political. Why are they after her?"

"Sir, remember what you said to me when I wanted to check you for weapons?"

"Mr. Carver . . ."

"Sorry, sir. You have to trust me. I know that's stretching things, but it's the truth. I can't say more. If you could spend a couple of days here, you could experience the truth rather than just hear it. I've been living and experiencing things with these people that were beyond my wildest imaginings. Lieutenant Morrison has already had a taste and is receiving more as we speak. Why don't we go talk to her, see what she thinks?"

"She hasn't been here long enough to know anything."

"Want to bet? Come on!"

They headed back to the bridge, but the admiral reached out a hand and stopped Mike. "Mr. Carver, there's one thing I must insist upon, and this is just between you and me. You must promise to come back, and when you do, I want you to look me up even if I'm in a rest home. Please."

"I'm not in a position to make promises, but it's a deal, sir. And you can tell Senator Morrison we'll be in touch with him, too. Hopefully, long before either of you are in a rest home." To himself, he added again, *if we get back.*

They entered the bridge, and Mike went directly for his helmet, feeling guilty that he'd been out of the net as long as he had. Their situation was precarious, and though George was equipped for solving most of the problems that came his way, he needed guidance on some of the simplest things.

As he lifted the helmet to his head, his body suddenly spasmed with intense pain in every cell of his body. The next thing he knew, he was lying on the floor with the admiral kneeling down beside him. His right lower leg was on fire. Looking around, he discovered Ellie writhing in pain on the floor. Cicadas buzzed fiercely. Reba was still with George, oblivious to what was taking place on the bridge, her body shifting from side to side in response to whatever she was experiencing within the net at that particular moment.

Resolve's guns pounded continuously. Mike shook himself and staggered to his feet, dragging his right leg. He leaned against a chair, knowing he needed to get going but feeling like his head was full of wool.

Then he discovered that Jake was missing.

He grabbed the admiral. "We're under attack! Do you feel it?"

"Feel what?" Trexler questioned urgently. "I hear the guns firing."

"We haven't told you everything, sir. The Chessori have some kind of power over people's minds. From the looks of things, you, me, and Reba," he said glancing over at Lieutenant Morrison, "might be immune. Maybe everyone on Earth is immune. Hold on while I figure out what's going on."

His right leg was on fire, and it was bad, but it was only one leg. For Jake, Ellie, and Otis the fire consumed their whole bodies. He shivered with horror at the thought, then forced his attention away from his leg and back to the ship. He donned his helmet to find George waiting anxiously. "What's our status?" he demanded.

"We're under attack," George stated. "Otis ordered me to tilt the ship so that all guns could be brought to bear. I have done so. Reba has commanded me to slave both upper guns to her until someone comes to help. She seems to be under control. Otis seems to be having trouble with accuracy. Wait . . ."

Mike felt the ship shudder repeatedly. Obviously, they'd been hit. George returned. "She got one!" he yelled. "She's commanded me to move *Resolve* away from the carrier. She's concerned that deflected shots might harm the humans aboard. I think they could harm the carrier as well, but I haven't said anything to her about that. She's pretty busy."

Mike was frustrated as he waited to get fully plugged-in. "Give me a damage report," he demanded.

"All shields are activated," George continued. "Both upper shields are down to half strength. I'm trying to restore them with backups. She's down to one gun. Number two cannon's integrator was fused on that last pass. What are your orders, Mike?"

"Has the surface fleet returned fire?"

"No."

Mike was fully into the net now. He avoided contact with Lieutenant Morrison, afraid he'd confuse and distract her. She had not been exposed to the full net yet and did not know his electronic personality. Otis was, indeed, failing to fire with his accustomed accuracy. It must be from the effects of the Chessori mind weapon. Two Chessori were streaking away, probably preparing to return. High overhead, three Chessori orbited, not doing anything that he could see. Several fighters from the carrier orbited at a middle altitude, but they seemed to be avoiding the attacking Chessori.

He ordered Otis to leave his guns and attempt repairs on the gun Reba had lost. He was ready to take control of the guns himself, but he waited. He needed to fly the ship first. He maneuvered farther from the carrier, but he remained well within the boundaries of the carrier's battle group. The two retreating Chessori were turning back, and one of the orbiting Chessori appeared to be joining them. It was three to one, bad odds under the best of circumstances.

"Tell Lieutenant Morrison what's going on," he ordered George. "Here they come!"

Three ships came at them, all from different directions and altitudes. Mike was ready; he took all the guns and chose one target for each. All three cannons spoke repeatedly, scoring hits. One Chessori broke off its attack, possibly damaged. George had the shields up to full strength to deflect hits, assuring some safety unless the attackers timed their shots just right and overloaded the circuits, a difficult chore under the best of circumstances.

Mike felt *Resolve* shuddering. They were taking more hits. Then the Chessori were past, still firing as they retreated. Mike kept up his fire on both Chessori.

Suddenly a new persona joined him on the net. "I'm on them! Can you give me control of the guns?" Mike instantly recognized Lieutenant Morrison's persona, and he understood her plan. He was needed to fly the ship. Could she have known that? He instructed George to give her control of his guns and immediately set off in pursuit of the retreating Chessori. Reba brought all three guns to bear on one ship and opened fire. Simultaneous hits quickly overloaded its rear shield, and it blew up in a roiling fireball that quickly curved into the ocean and disappeared. Two down. She coordinated their fire to the next ship in line, but it had broken away during her concentration on the downed ship and was out of range.

Mike wanted to get the orbiting Chessori ships, but he did not want to get too far from the carrier. It would be a disaster to attract all the Chessori. Still, he suspected that the psi attack was coming from the ships orbiting above. Reba seemed under control, so he took a chance and joined her on the net.

"We're going after the ships orbiting above. Ready?"

"I don't know what ships you're talking about. Give me targeting data and I'll be ready."

"Can you talk to the fleet if I give you a connection? I don't want them firing at the Chessori."

"Sure, if you think this will go on for a while. You might be better off concentrating on beating off the attack. Then you won't have to worry about it. Your call, sir."

Mike directed *Resolve* to make an instant climb to high altitude, feeding targeting data to Reba as soon as it was available. She opened fire at long range, firing steadily at the two orbiting Chessori ships high above and driving them away. The buzzing of cicadas stopped as those ships fled.

Mike sensed that the attack was over. He brought *Resolve* back to its place beside the carrier and left the net after instructing George to sound the alarm if the Chessori returned. Reba joined him in a hug, the two dancing around in delight until they noticed Admiral Trexler attending to Ellie. Mike took one look at her lying on the floor and stopped his dance in mid-stride, feeling guilty. How bad had it been for her, and how about Jake? He wasn't back yet.

Mike knelt beside Ellie. "Can I help?" he asked.

"No," she responded dully. "This was a bad one. Is it over, are we okay?"

"It's over." He picked her up and carried her to his command seat where he sat with her on his lap, her head resting on his shoulder. He had experienced the Chessori mind weapon through Jake, and he now had a better understanding of what it had been like for her, Otis, and Jake. But in addition to sensing Ellie's pain and exhaustion, he sensed her disappointment as well. All her training had been for naught. There was nothing he could do or say except to be there for her. Otis worked his way down from the upper turret to lie on the floor before him, something Mike had never seen him do.

He reported. "Both upper guns are operational. Who's watching the ship?"

"George is, and I have the monitors here to back him up. Shields are up."

"This was much worse than anything we experienced before," he replied. Then he just closed his eyes.

Admiral Trexler and Reba sat beside each other in crew seats in front of Mike. "Will someone please tell me what the heck just happened?" demanded Trexler.

"I'm sure you'll be able to watch a recording of it when you get back to your ship, sir," Mike answered. "Obviously, we were attacked. Thanks to Lieutenant Morrison, we're not only alive, but the Chessori are short two ships."

"Two!" the admiral exclaimed looking at her.

"Oh, Ray, this ship is incredible. It's got a living brain that controls everything. Whatever you want is right there at your fingertips. It helps you, it knows your feelings, it's wonderful."

"So you've met George," Mike commented.

"It has a name?"

"And lots more. You haven't even scratched the surface yet," he mused. "But you will!" Turning to the admiral, he continued, "She's remarkable, sir. She took out two Chessori ships single-handedly with only an hour's training. I wouldn't have believed it if I hadn't seen it with my own eyes."

"I'm not surprised. Too bad I didn't bring her service record to show you. It's impressive. I take it these Chessori have retreated?"

"For the moment. I did not anticipate that attack. I really thought we were safe here, but now, time is clearly of the essence. They'll be back. Are you ready? Can we drop you off?"

The admiral considered his words, then a grin spread across his face. "Oh, that would be fun. Can you?"

"We can, and we will. Reba, will you get back into the net and keep an eye on things for me?"

"Aye, aye, sir." She picked up her helmet and lowered it over her head, pulling the face plate down into position.

They landed on the carrier's forward deck. Well . . . not landed, not exactly. Had they actually set down on the deck, they would have sunk the ship. George was instructed to keep *Resolve's* ramp one inch above the deck until further notice, and to notify Mike if he sensed anything threatening from the Chessori. The deck pitched up and down as the great ship plowed through swells at its top speed, but that was no problem for George.

Mike, Ellie, and Otis escorted the admiral through the ship to the lower ramp. On the way there, Mike heard with welcome relief, >Hi,

Man. I'm back.<

>Jake! You okay?<

>I don't know. I'm still working on it. I'll let you know after I wake up. I'm going to take the first nap of my life.<

>Okay, but make it a power nap. I need you.<

>What's a power nap?<

Mike rolled his eyes. >Never mind. Get some rest.<

They gathered in the ramp area, the ramp itself still bearing the wounds of the fight in the desert. Ellie, still shaky, felt Mike's arm go around her waist to steady her. She leaned into him, grateful for the support. She looked to the admiral, sensing his reluctance at leaving Reba behind. She shared that feeling, having left so many behind during the past months.

Admiral Trexler met her gaze and said quietly, "You'd better take good care of her, whoever you are. You have me to answer to."

Mike translated her reply, "We shall do our best, Admiral. She but increases my debt to you. It will not be forgotten. May we next meet under more peaceful circumstances."

Trexler nodded. "I'm off. Good luck, and watch your flank, Mr. Carver. You know what you're up against here, but what's waiting for you out in space?"

"A good question, sir. We'll take it one step at a time. The next few hours will decide. In any case, thank you for your help."

The admiral saluted Mike and Ellie, then followed Otis down the ramp. Otis led him out onto the deck of the carrier, mostly for effect. The wind tore across the empty deck, forcing Trexler to lean heavily into his steps. Otis again extended a hand. Trexler reached out with his own gloved hand, they shook, then Trexler stepped back and saluted him. Without delay, he turned on his heel and walked away. Otis returned to *Resolve* and closed the ramp.

Ellie looked to Mike like she'd aged years. Otis just looked done in. When asked, Ellie replied that she didn't know if the Chessori attacks were getting stronger or if she was becoming more sensitive to the psi weapon, but this attack had been severe, the worst for her by far.

Otis agreed. His struggle to cope had been monumental. He surmised that attacks varied, perhaps with the numbers or abilities of the individual Chessori focusing the weapon, or perhaps just with distance. Attacks in space had not been as intense, perhaps because ships were so far apart. Close in space was a relative term. Often many, many miles separated ships, even ships flying in formation, but attacks on the ground were a different matter. This last attack had virtually paralyzed half the crew, wiping out all the crew coordination they'd so painstakingly developed.

This was a major concern to all. Rebecca Morrison had saved the ship, period. Everything they'd built so far during all the hours of practice had failed with the surprise attack, and Mike was disappointed at his own lack of leadership and discipline. Why hadn't he foreseen the type of attack the Chessori would launch and taken precautions? He'd been expecting any encounters with the Chessori to occur out in space, and that was where all their practice had been focused. The manner of attack seemed obvious in hindsight, though he still found it hard to believe the Chessori had attacked in full view of the fleet. What else didn't he know about these Chessori and their methods? What additional precautions could he take?

The only thing certain was that there would be more surprises, probably lots more. He would keep learning, and so would the crew. They had to keep moving forward; there could be no giving up.

The one thing George had failed to train them on was the Chessori mind weapon. That was not George's failure, it was a failure of command – Mike's failure. He should have foreseen exactly what had happened today. They needed more training and more practice to determine in advance what their limitations would be when the Chessori used their mind weapon.

* * * * *

Ellie leaned into Mike as Otis wearily led the way back to the bridge. She felt distracted and knew that part of the reason was that she had failed Mike. She had collapsed at the first sign of the Chessori mind weapon, collapsed at a time when he needed her. But that wasn't the only cause of her distraction. His arm was around her of his own volition, and to her surprise she wanted it there. He was holding her, helping her in spite of the fact that she had let him down.

She was confused. The man holding her was not the ignorant Earthman she had originally thought him to be. He was a natural leader, but more important, she was beginning to look upon him as something else: a friend.

One of the earliest lessons she had been taught was that the Chosen did not have true friends. She had been taught that everyone around her would be friendly, but only because of the her position within the Empire hierarchy. This man, so far as she could tell, cared nothing about her position. He was helping *her*, not one of the Chosen.

She stumbled as her mind focused on this, and his arm tightened around her waist. Impulsively, without really thinking about it, she turned and wrapped her arms around his waist, pressing her body to his. She longed to be held, and he responded by pressing her head to his chest.

After a time, as if from far away, she heard, "Uh, I think we should be getting back to work, Ellie."

She lingered, not willing to give up the moment, savoring the feelings she felt. Just another moment, she thought. Then she sighed. "Yes, we should." She looked up into his eyes, searching for something, she wasn't sure what, but the look he returned warmed her. She rested her head against his chest again, briefly, then stood back from him, her arms still around his waist. "Thank you, Michael Carver. I needed that." She then turned toward the bridge, pulling his arm tighter around herself and holding to it.

When they stepped out of the central shaft, he took her head in his hands and peered into her eyes. She closed her eyes briefly, trying to hide her exhaustion from the attack and the confusion in her mind. When she opened them, she felt tears threatening and was furious with herself. She could not allow him to sense her weakness.

Mike saw the tears, and he wiped them away with his thumbs. "I'm so sorry for you," he said. "Jake could not hide his agony from me. Until now, I never knew what you were up against, yet you haven't given up. You're a strong woman, My Lady. I'm honored that you called me to your side."

She closed her eyes, hating the tears that flowed. She responded the only way she could. She turned to the console and picked up her helmet. Mike placed his hand on her arm, forcing the helmet back to the console.

"You're done in. So is Otis. One hour break, you two," he announced.

Ellie and Otis both looked at him in surprise. Otis started to object, but Mike cut him off. "You're both hurting, and I need you at peak efficiency when we leave. Otis, have you ever had a gun taken away from you before?"

"No. But it was the right thing to do. You chose well, Captain."

"And I'm choosing well now. Take a break. Sleep if you can. I have other things to do, including bringing Reba more fully into the net. That's an order."

Otis rested where he was. Ellie, too, declined to leave the bridge. She sat in a crew seat, leaning forward on the console with her head resting on her arms, feeling lonely and isolated again. She missed the feeling of Mike's arms around her. What was happening to her, she wondered? Survival was the issue here, not feelings. She had to put those feelings away. She did, and she was asleep in minutes.

Mike went into the net and raced through ship's systems with George to check for damage. All was well, all four weapons were functional again, and the shields were fully charged. *Resolve* was ready for battle, though Jake had not yet returned. Reba did not even know about him, Mike realized. He squirmed a little when he thought about telling her that he had an alien living inside himself, but then he thought about how much he missed Jake and shrugged it off.

He spent time with her and George. There wasn't time to bring her fully into the net, but George was able to expand her horizons a little. She could at least see the full tactical situation. Earlier, she could only see what her gun position could see.

Ellie plugged in, though her usual sense of wonder at the net was missing. She seemed more distracted than tired. Mike was surprised. He was totally focused, knowing he would soon be in the fight of his life. Was Ellie's problem centered on the fact that she knew her efforts were in vain, that she would likely end up as she had before, useless during the fighting? He made a mental note to keep an eye on her and her performance.

Her distraction disappeared immediately upon meeting Reba in the net. Reba's personality fired up the net, her energy suffusing everyone, and it had the same effect on Ellie that it had on Mike. Nothing seemed to phase her. She took everything in stride, and she motivated others without even being aware she was doing so. She still bubbled with excitement from the battle and couldn't wait to dig in and get better.

When Ellie met her on the net, Mike immediately recognized a need that had been missing in Ellie's life. She had been surrounded by males for months on end. Adult female companionship had been almost completely absent in her life. She and Reba immediately took to each other, and it was good, good for both of them. Ellie fed on that bubbling enthusiasm and perked up noticeably.

Break time was over. Mike got everyone down to business. Otis was back in the lower turret, Reba manned the other lower gun from her position on the bridge through the net, and Ellie took both upper guns until Jake returned. Mike commanded and flew the ship. It was no longer necessary for George to act as teacher. He was back to managing the ship, leaving the rest of them to fight. He still controlled the training scenarios, but that was child's play to him.

Jake joined them midway through the session, jumping into the net with both feet. "I'm back, Mike. Where do you want me?"

"Take one of Ellie's guns."

"Welcome back, Jake," Ellie said warmly.

Reba lost her composure for a heartbeat or two. "Jake, where did you come from? And who else is hiding under the bed?" she added as an afterthought.

"I'll explain later," Mike answered curtly. "Come on guys, we're under attack. We're down to hours, not days. Stay focused."

Reba's Navy training soon made itself known. Mike had been proud of the teamwork and skills his crew had developed over the past weeks, but Reba quickly sensed gaping deficiencies, deficiencies that no one else had been aware of because they had never had the benefit of a human trainer. And she was not gentle or hesitant in making her demands known. The first time Mike flipped *Resolve* over, following it with a right angle turn to break away from the grip of an enemy gun, she yelled at him.

"Mike, the next time you do that without telling me, I'm going to turn this gun on *you*. I completely lost my lead. Next time, talk to me. A quick 'breaking right,' or 'down and left' is sufficient. Got it?"

"Uh . . . okay. I'll work on it." Remembering back to his army days, he asked, "Do I owe you fifty pushups now?"

"I think we'll all owe each other pushups before we're done. Just talk to us, Captain."

He did talk to them. He had worked the guns himself, and he understood their needs. He had George add the gunner's firing quadrants to his own display, and George did it in such a way that no matter what he was looking at, the display was always faintly there for him to look through. It didn't take long before he could do better than a simple 'breaking right.' He could tag many of his maneuvers with the designations of quadrants that everyone was familiar with.

And Reba got the gunners to communicate with each other. "Where did that one come from, Ellie?" she demanded as an enemy ship streaked from above to race across her field of fire before she could get a bead on it.

"I tracked it as long as I could," Ellie responded as she sighted on a new target.

"Well, next time, warn me that it's coming my way," Reba demanded.

"Okay. Here comes another one, if I don't get it first. It'll be in quadrant 2C."

Ellie missed, but Reba was ready, and she didn't. The net was soon filled with chatter, all of it focused. It wasn't long before the gunners were making requests of Mike, suggesting maneuvers that would help them stay locked onto a target.

The ship's performance grew logarithmically. Mike couldn't have asked for a better addition to the crew than Reba. There was no doubt in his mind that she would assume command of the ship as soon as George could get her fully trained, and that was a good thing. It wasn't that he wanted to quit, that wasn't it at all. His performance was okay, but his background did not include years and years of plotting strategies and tactics. Reba's did, and it showed clearly. Mike would have no problem turning command over to her when she was ready.

But that was in the future. For the present, he had a crew, a good crew. As they practiced, Mike began pulling one or two at a time from the net, simulating the need for repairs or the loss of Ellie and Jake to a Chessori psi attack. Each one of them had a unique personality and unique abilities, and each was missed in different ways, but they learned to fill in the holes.

Most sorely missed was George. Without him, the net lost its personality, everything slowed down astronomically, and their performance deteriorated badly. Jake filled in for George, spending all his time keeping *Resolve* operating. He became the net, running messages back and forth, retrieving data demanded by others, delivering that data, and monitoring systems. He was agonizingly slower than George. Surprisingly, Reba was the next most missed. Mike didn't know why. Her enthusiasm just seemed to infect the rest of them.

Luckily, George, Reba, and Mike would be the least likely players to be out of the net. They were impervious to the Chessori's psi attacks. More likely to be lost would be Jake and Ellie, and some reduction in Otis' abilities could be expected. They practiced exactly that, taking Ellie and Jake from their guns, sending Otis on a repair mission, and forcing Mike to jump in as time permitted to take one or two guns. In the worst case scenario, Reba could defend the ship while Mike did his best to disengage. Without Reba, it would have been Mike alone to fly and fight the ship, always a losing proposition.

They were a bit smug, confident of their improved performance, when Reba surprised them all with a quick command to George. Suddenly, Mike was out of the team, Jake as well. They could only observe. Mike was astonished at the result. Everyone's activity trickled to a stop in the midst of a battle. The shock to the net was so acute, the loss of leadership that George required was so fundamental that George lost his footing. He slipped, and there was no one to pick him up. The ship stopped maneuvering and became a sitting duck. No one gave commands to dodge or to chase, and no one planned a retreat. They coasted on overloading shields.

Reba tried to step in but had to withdraw immediately. The full net overwhelmed her instantly, and she knew it. Though she knew what was needed, she couldn't do it.

Ellie stepped in a heartbeat later, but it was a struggle. With a mindset suited well to responsibility and decision-making, her personality preferred to focus on one thing at a time, grasping all available facts surrounding a particular issue in an orderly process leading to decision. Strategies in constant flux amidst a never ending background of demands from George and the crew, the multitude of things that needed to be juggled simultaneously, that required quick decisions before all the facts were in, things that Mike simply took care of, these things did not play to her strengths. She brought *Resolve* back on line, but their performance was dismal.

Mike called for a break. "Sorry," Ellie said with downcast eyes when they'd all come out of the net.

"We'll work on it, but not today. I don't plan on skipping out today. Don't worry about it."

"I'm not," she said as she attached a long over-due translating device to Reba's ear. "I know myself quite well, thank you. I'm not a ship's captain, nor do I wish to be. My strengths lay elsewhere. Commanding the ship is your problem." Then she softened and added, "I had known intellectually the importance of the position you hold, but until now I had not experienced it, felt it. I will never be a replacement for captain. And Reba must become integrated as soon as she can. Until then, I will do what I can, which will be to support you. I think you may have missed your calling on Earth. Perhaps you were destined to be a pilot instead of an engineer."

"If we had ships like this . . . no, if we had George, maybe I would have."

Reba cleared her throat. "Uh, so where's Jake? When do I meet him?"

Mike sucked in a breath. He'd forgotten she didn't know. Apprehension kept him from meeting her demanding gaze. "It's a long story, Reba." He took a deep breath and looked into her eyes. "The short answer is tough, but we're short on time. After kidnapping me, Ellie . . ."

"Kidnapping!" Reba interrupted, looking from Mike to Ellie and back again.

"Well . . . in the beginning, yes," Mike said wincing. A bad choice of words he thought, silently kicking himself. "But not anymore. I'm here because I want to be here. Getting rid of me will be a lot harder than kidnapping me ever was."

A smile lit Ellie's face. She seemed to stand taller, as if a heavy load had been lifted from her shoulders. She came to him and wrapped her arms around his waist in a hug, then leaned back, saying, "Thank you, Michael. I needed to hear that."

Reba cleared her throat again. Ellie released Mike who went absentmindedly to his command seat and sat reflecting on Ellie's embrace. She had felt good in his arms, but she was an alien. He could never forget that.

>Uh, Earth to Mike,< Jake said softly.

When he looked up, all eyes were on him, waiting. He felt his face turning red, but when his gaze settled on Reba, thoughts of Ellie's embrace evaporated.

"Jake is inside me," he told her. "He's a living, breathing, alien mass of protoplasm that has linked his life to mine, forever. He has infused my whole body. The longer answer, and there's lots more to it, will have to wait until later, okay? Pretty weird, huh?"

Reba paused for thought as she digested his words. Then she smiled brightly. "I like Jake. Is being with him like being in the net all the time?"

"Not at all, though it might be some day. It's pretty new to both of us. At this point, we're still communicating mostly with words unless we're in the net. And Jake, although he has a male name, is an *it*. And he's telling me to tell you that he's proud of it, too."

"Who's in control?"

"You've met Jake on the net. What do you think?"

"I don't know!" she said in surprise. "I didn't sense any control issues."

"There aren't any, at least not yet. He's called a *Rider*, Reba. I'm told that he's basically along for the ride, and controlling is not his thing. He's just there to help. And he has vast knowledge that will help both of us, I think, in the long run. From what he tells me, he can control my body to some extent, but I haven't noticed any of that yet. Without much effort on his part, he's keeping me healthy and in top condition. He tells me that I won't get sick ever again, and my sleep has been better than I would have expected under the circumstances. He's been a huge help to all of us."

>Thanks, Mike!<

>Sure thing, Jake.<

"Does he read your mind?"

"Yes. I'm still trying to come to terms with that."

"Are you still human?" Reba blurted out.

"I don't know. There are a lot of things I don't know. So far, having Jake along for the ride is like having a personal assistant at my fingertips. That's not to say he waits for me to ask questions. He's definitely an individual, and he does not hesitate to offer advice or to make demands, but the net effect is synergy. As a team, we're much more effective than if we were individuals operating alone. I hesitate to say this, but I think we're becoming friends."

>Hey, you *think*?<

"So in the end, you're healthier, as a team you're smarter, you have no secrets from each other, and you have a friend who will never leave you?"

"Uh . . . it's not that simple. I don't have any secrets from him, but I haven't had a lot of success reading his mind. He tells me that will change in time."

Reba considered his words, then she lifted her head to look directly into Mike's eyes. "Jake, can I have one of you, too?"

Mike spoke for Jake. "That depends. If Earth women are as stubborn as this Earthman, I'm not sure it would be fair to my offspring. I'll let you know."

Chapter Nine

They were as ready as they were going to get, but Admiral Trexler's plan was not yet ready. Ellie went to her suite to spend time with Alexis while Reba idly walked around the bridge, looking at various screens but mostly just relaxing before things got busy again. Otis napped at his gun, still recovering from his monumental effort to function during the Chessori attack.

Mike and Jake stayed in the net, keeping an eye on the Chessori but relaxing as much as they could. When the catapults were ready, loaded with planes and venting steam, Mike lifted *Resolve* and returned to a position abeam the bridge tower where he would not interfere with aircraft landing and taking off. He was shocked to see both landings and takeoffs occurring simultaneously on the carrier, but Reba just shrugged. To her, it was just the way things were. She let him know that *Resolve* would not hinder the carrier's air operations from that position, though it was breaking a lot of Navy rules.

Aircraft began launching, one after another without cease, to orbit *Resolve* and the carrier at all altitudes while the patrol aircraft returned to refuel. Hours earlier, all but two escort ships had headed directly east toward San Diego, some 300 miles from the fleet. The ships formed into a spearhead, fanning out farther and farther from each other as their distance increased from the carrier. Reba sucked in her breath when Mike displayed the plan on a monitor, informing him that the deployment was terrible battle tactics for one trained in surface warfare. Admiral Trexler was really putting his two stars on the line for Mike. Mike didn't care. The deployment was effectively forcing the Chessori ships farther from *Resolve*. Ten Chessori remained, all hovering near the surface to avoid long-range detection from the fleet, but they were clearly visible to George's sensors.

The fleet was in the early stages of preparing a gap through which *Resolve* could dash with some hope of success, but everything visible to the Chessori was, in reality, a feint engineered by Admiral Trexler. Mike had George open the appropriate channel to Trexler, and they began discussing the plan over the radio, hoping to further mislead the Chessori who might be listening.

A carrier-based Airborne Warning and Control plane, AWAC's as they were referred to, circled lazily to the north, directing the armada of planes forming above and to the east. Timing was everything. The carrier's planes could not remain aloft indefinitely, though all carried maximum fuel and no weapons. At least that was the plan. Mike was not at all certain that Admiral Trexler would hold to that part of the plan. To do so was probably asking too much of him and the pilots, but the Navy was not to fire a shot today. The plan did not include letting the Chessori know that, however.

Trexler called him back a few minutes later with a triumphant edge to his voice. "Check your long-range scanners, Mike."

Mike motioned for Reba to join him on the net. He desperately wanted all the advice he could get. From the east, from the direction of California, they discovered three land-based AWAC's planes spread far apart at high altitude.

"Oh, Mike, I think you're going to like this," Reba said.

"Why?"

"I've never seen three AWAC's participating in the same mission. I don't know what Ray has managed to cobble together, but I think it will be interesting."

As they watched, other planes began appearing from over the horizon, planes of all types and at all altitudes. George's scanners discerned incredible detail. He discovered transport planes, tankers, stealth fighters and bombers, normal fighters, B-1 bombers, reconnaissance aircraft, and high above, verging on the edge of space, something moving at extremely high speed. Something new in our arsenal, Mike wondered? Reba had no clue what these aircraft were.

Soon, a vast armada filled the sky to the east.

How had this been put together so quickly? It was an incredible feat of impromptu planning to have all these aircraft arrive at the same time.

And it got better. The AWAC's crews were the star of the show with the greatest challenge of all this day. Aboard them, military controllers deftly vectored each aircraft toward its assigned position to form an incredibly intricate pattern. When viewed through *Resolve's* scanners, the pattern gradually began coalescing into an empty corridor surrounded by aircraft from the surface of the Earth to near the edge of space. A Horn of Plenty, narrow at the bottom, widening out higher up, *Resolve* would be provided a semblance of protection, a chance of safe passage as she raced into space.

"Get ready, Mike. You have ten minutes," Trexler advised. "Be prepared for an initial trajectory of due east. We'll give you all the protection we can. We're locked and loaded."

Ellie returned to the bridge, Otis reported ready at his gun, and *Resolve's* crew was complete. The last planes were approaching their assigned positions, and surface ships had opened up a fair gap to the east. Farther to the east and higher, *Resolve's* departure corridor, as clearly obvious as Admiral Trexler could make it, waited for them.

Four of the Chessori ships hovered near the corridor at various altitudes. Two moved inside the fleet closer to the carrier, sensing that something was about to happen. Four more held their positions behind the fleet.

"It's time, folks," Trexler announced. "We won't be able to hold this together much longer. Our weapons are all armed and ready. Good luck. And don't forget your promise."

"Will do, Admiral. Reba sends her regards, but I have to say she's fired up. She's where she wants to be."

Trexler went back to doing whatever it was that admirals do, which probably included a lot of worrying. Mike studied his screens, keeping George busy computing trajectories of all participants. The trajectories soon merged into the perfect pattern, and it was time to go. The Chessori reached the same conclusion at the same instant. The four Chessori ships trailing the fleet sprinted east for the escape corridor to bolster the four already there. Yes! They had fallen for it.

Mike issued the command to George. One moment they hovered beside the carrier steaming eastbound at full speed. The next moment they were gone, streaking westward into a setting sun, in the opposite direction from the escape corridor. Admiral Trexler's feint had worked.

Resolve was a good hundred and fifty miles ahead of the eight Chessori that had fallen for the diversion. The admiral had given them the minute or so of spacing he had promised. The two higher Chessori ships merged with *Resolve* by the time they reached the stratosphere and the battle was joined, but two-to-one odds were just fine with Mike. His crew could handle them, though this was no longer a simulation. George was prepared to cut Ellie and Jake out of the net instantly if the Chessori mounted a psi attack, but Mike didn't think it likely. The Chessori had been caught with their pants down.

Ellie commanded the guns and the gunners. She invited both Chessori in close by withholding fire until *Resolve's* rear shields glowed from hits. Mike, unnerved, forced himself to stay out of her way. Her own nervousness was exposed to all on the net and was as great as his. Finally, she commanded all four gunners to fire simultaneously on the same ship. It ceased to exist. Moments later, just as a weak burning sensation filled Mike's body, the remaining Chessori suffered the same fate. The burning stopped instantly.

They had made it. Though trailed by eight more Chessori, they had a good lead and could breathe easy for a while. Mike focused ahead, his chest swelling with pride for himself and the crew. And now . . .

They were in space! Through his senses on the net, space was beyond description, beautiful and inspiring. Stars and nebulae of every color imaginable filled his view. Earth looked as it always did in photographs, blue sapphire and brown deserts partially hidden by clouds and storm systems. The sun had set over the eastern portion of North America, and corridors of city lights sparkled between gaps in the clouds. When the full array of George's sensors fed him data, Earth glowed with an aura of energy and life regardless of whether it was day or night, cloud-covered or clear. But he liked the normal view better. This was his home the way he had imagined it would be.

And he was saying goodbye to his home. He, who had never seriously contemplated leaving Earth, had come to the place our astronauts had visited. He wanted to feel what they felt, stare at the stars, study the Earth below, investigate everything new, but he could not.

What waited ahead for them? Behind, eight Chessori fighters lagged beyond maximum firing range, and Mike was not overly concerned with them yet. He put the long-range scanners to work and told everyone to relax while George gathered data and flew *Resolve* on the preplanned trajectory.

Resolve was sprinting toward the nearest jump point, some two and one-half weeks away, out beyond the orbit of Neptune. Even then, still within the solar system, a jump toward Gamma VI would be risky, and they would delay the jump until out beyond the orbit of Pluto if they could.

Mike called Admiral Trexler. "Your guys were great, sir. We made it."

Mike could almost hear the smile on the other end of the line. "Congratulations. We're already standing down here. I've never seen anything move so fast. You were out of sight in just a few seconds. Our job is done."

"We took out two more, and the others are trailing, but they're not a problem. Thanks for the help, sir."

"My pleasure. Remember our deal."

"I will. Let everyone know that The Lady sends her personal thanks."

"I will. Safe voyage, Mr. Carver. Don't forget about us down here, and I'm speaking not just for myself but for the billions unaware of what's happened here."

"I won't forget my roots, Admiral. So long for now."

Information began trickling in from George's sensors, then George sent an alert notice. A squadron of fourteen ships, including what George calmly informed him was a Fleet heavy cruiser, the Beta IV, lay dead ahead.

"These are Empire ships?"

"Yes."

"Hey, we made it! We're rescued, Princess!" he shouted, elated, "They're your ships."

"Maybe," she replied. "George, have they hailed us yet?"

"No. They are in contact with the Chessori ships behind us, however."

Silence filled the net. Reba jumped in first. "George, demand they identify themselves. Demand further that they respond to our message by turning away from their present course for some period of time. I don't know how you measure things in space. If we were in surface ships I'd demand a thirty degree turn in some direction. You figure it out."

George did. They waited several long minutes, but there was no response from the oncoming fleet.

"They're not friendly, Mike," Ellie announced with heavy heart. "A demand from *Resolve* should have been acted upon instantly, without question."

"How long 'till they're in firing range?" Mike demanded of

George.

"A few hours," George informed him, demonstrating with lovely schematics how the oncoming fleet would reduce speed to match vectors with *Resolve* and end up flying formation on them. "But Mike, who cares?" he added. "It's a heavy cruiser."

"So what? What's a cruiser? Have we seen a cruiser in any of the simulations you've given us?" he demanded.

"Of course not. *Resolve* cannot fight a cruiser," George informed him calmly. "Cruisers carry ships like this within their bellies, like aircraft carriers. Would you send one plane against an aircraft carrier?"

"Depends on the weapons carried by the plane, I suppose. What do you think, Reba?" Mike queried.

"That's a tough one," she answered without hesitation. "Certain weapons can do the job, but getting them through on one single plane would entail a high risk of failure. You'd probably use smart torpedoes or missiles rather than send a plane."

"George, do we have anything like that aboard?" Mike demanded.

"No. Projectile weapons pose no threat to ships in space. Only weapons that use light are fast enough. You've seen how sprightly these ships move. Besides, that's not the problem. That ship is an Empire cruiser. It's one of ours, and I know its capabilities. Mike, it carries a tractor beam."

"I don't like the sound of that, George. What's a tractor beam?"

George, patient as always, answered with pictures, demonstrating how a beam projected by the cruiser could lock onto another ship and hold that ship as if frozen, even pull it in like a fish on a line right into the cruiser if desired.

"Not fair. How come we don't have one?" Mike demanded.

"It takes a ship as large as a cruiser to power a tractor beam, Mike. A tractor beam requires massive amounts of energy to cocoon our drive. The only way to escape a tractor beam is by turning off our drive, but then we are powerless to maneuver, which has the same result."

Mike's bad feeling got worse. He and Jake had George run a number of scenarios through the navigation computers to see if they could come up with an escape plan, and beautifully intricate schematics resulted, but nothing worked. They could avoid the cruiser for a while, but as soon as they turned, the Chessori trailing them would move closer by cutting the corner, eventually catching up with them. Mike did not like their chances against eight Chessori. In the long run, they couldn't outrun the cruiser no matter which direction they went. All scenarios showed it relentlessly in pursuit, eventually catching them.

They could return to Earth with only a quick brush through the Chessori trailing them, but then what? Where could they go? The Chessori would be right behind them. There wouldn't even be time to get out of the ship, and they couldn't stay submerged forever. Nothing worked.

Two hours passed with no solution evident. They needed creativity. They needed the synergy of group discussion to find that creative idea. Mike called a time-out. He placed all the shields on maximum as everyone left the net. Otis was called from his gun, and they gathered on the bridge for a conference.

Mike explained the situation, then waited for suggestions. Reba's response was quick. "They've crossed our T," she stated, nodding her head. When they turned blank expressions on her, she explained. "It's an old naval expression. It means the enemy has outfoxed you, put you in a position where you cannot escape, usually a result of your position in relation to themselves and any surrounding terrain. Your only recourse is to join battle, but the T would never have been constructed by the enemy if you had any chance of winning."

Mike had already tried using Earth and the moon to block the Chessori pursuit, but George's scenarios had shown it wouldn't help. The only other terrain he was aware of was the entire solar system, but how could that be of help? He closed his eyes deep in thought. The germ of an idea tickled the back of his brain, and he considered it for a time, then broached the subject with Jake.

>We need to jump, right now,< he said. Jake remained silent as he digested Mike's words. Mike could actually sense the initial confusion in Jake's mind, something he'd never sensed before.

>It goes without saying that it's dangerous,< Jake finally answered. >We might all be killed, but everything else looks just as bleak. I see one major stumbling block. I don't think George will let us jump. His most fundamental programming prohibits him from letting us do anything he considers dangerous.<

>You're the science expert here. Can we reduce the danger to a reasonable level?<

>Hmm. Maybe. The solar system is like a flat disc. If we jumped perpendicular to the system, there wouldn't be as much to hit. I can't say what effect the planets and sun would have on our track, though. They'll certainly alter it. We'll need George's help to study it.<

Mike turned his attention back to the group. "Our only recourse is to fight," he stated. "If we fight, we will not win. Period. Any more suggestions?"

"Sure," Reba offered. "Surrender. It's the last option I would want, but it's better than being dead. The odds are slightly overwhelming here. I would say we either find some way to get away from these Chessori, or we surrender."

Stunned looks met her suggestion. Otis growled, startling Reba. Had she ever heard him growl? Had she even been told who and what a Protector was? Mike had not taken the time to explain, and he doubted if Ellie had either.

"Sorry, Reba. Surrender is not an option here. You don't know the full story. We haven't taken the time to tell you, and you've been gracious enough not to press for explanations. If I can put it simply, there's a galactic society out there that Earth knows nothing about. It's led by a Royal Family, it's in the midst of a civil war, and the throne may already have fallen. Ellie's daughter, Alexis, is aboard this ship. She's the heir to that throne, and she might be the last remaining person in the line. Now do you see why they want this ship so badly?"

Reba stared at him as the wheels turned in her mind. She turned to Ellie with a piercing look and spoke softly. "That fleet's only task is to ensure that there are no more heirs."

Ellie nodded, remaining silent. Reba pursed her lips. "It goes without saying that you and I, Mike, could surrender." Before those words had time to sink in, she added, "I decline surrender. I chose to accompany all of you without knowing all the facts, but the more I learn, the more I feel rightness among you. You answer to a higher calling. I choose your path, not because I agreed earlier, but because I sense that it, and you, are right."

Ellie rose and embraced Reba. Mike joined them with an arm around each, and Jake made his presence known through Mike. Otis sat nearby, his ears twitching. "You have not chosen, Mike," Ellie asked gravely.

"How can you even ask after everything I've done for you?" he demanded softly.

"We are a wonderful, intimate group," she replied, squeezing Reba and him harder. "I like us, and I like being part of us, whatever happens."

They were back where they'd started. Eight Chessori fighters chased from astern, a whole squadron waited ahead, and there was no turning away.

Otis spoke. "My Lady, talk to the crew of the cruiser. It does appear that there has been a coup. If so, it is new. Not all will support it.

The crewmembers might not even know about it. I promise you, if there are Guardians aboard, they are loyal to you."

"I've tried, Otis. They will not open a channel to us. The moment they do, I'll be ready. Until then, perhaps they are as smart as we give them credit for. They might well be dealing with internal dissent as we speak."

"Okay," Mike announced. "Surrender is not an option, we can't stay and fight, we can't turn around, and we can't keep going. Any other ideas?" They all remained mute. "I have one. It's a long shot, but it's the only way out of this that I can see. We'll just have to disappear." Blank looks met this announcement, but he had no inclination to smile. "We're going to jump. Now."

Ellie jumped to her feet in alarm, but just as she started to voice an objection, she reconsidered. She sat back down with a thoughtful expression.

Otis was more certain. "You can't, Mike. Jornell tried the same thing as we left Dorwall, and we were a lot farther out in the system where it's less dangerous. George is the most sophisticated AI our society has produced, and he could not compute a safe jump. It's just too dangerous."

"How hard did Jornell try?"

"I don't know. I was not in the net. I, too, like the idea. It's against all the rules, and because of that no one will expect it. Unfortunately, it's impossible to execute."

Ellie looked back and forth between the two of them, frightened. "Unless we can come up with another plan, I would support the effort in spite of the danger."

Mike returned to the net with purpose. When the idea was presented to George, he turned Mike down flat, would not even discuss it. He simply could not permit a jump with that level of risk. Mike cajoled, implored, threatened, and even tried reason, explaining that they were in more danger if they didn't jump. Nothing got through to George. He simply said, "No."

Jake tried subterfuge. "George, let's just set this up as a training exercise. Let's try to state all the variables and see what your computers come up with for a solution." George agreed on those grounds and tried, but the navigation computers simply couldn't handle the set-up.

Time was not on their side. George kept a visual presentation of the tractor beam field in view at all times. *Resolve* moved closer to the beam with each passing second, relentlessly. Mike resisted the urge to get angry, knowing that arguing with computers was always a losing proposition. That didn't mean he couldn't become frustrated. He did, and that frustration became more and more evident to all on the net, including George. George had always seemed to be so much more than just a computer program. In most ways he acted as a mature adult, in some he was little more than a child, but he had in every case responded to their smallest needs with unerring faithfulness.

And he had become their friend.

Mike knew all that, but he needed George right now as a tool more than he needed him as a friend. He had to find a way around George's programming or they would die.

He took a few calming breaths to force his frustration away, and he tried to think like a computer. Jake beat him to it, realizing that George was doing exactly what had been asked of him. That meant he was attempting to compute a jump that would put them on course to Gamma VI. With another anxious look at the tractor beam, Jake tried a new tack. "Okay, George, new problem. Just for the fun of it, let's set up a jump, but this time we'll change the ground rules. Instead of trying to compute a jump for Gamma VI, let's not care where we end up. The solar system is a flat disc. Let's just make a jump at ninety degrees to the plane of the ecliptic. That will take us away from all the strong gravity wells that are trying to suck us in, and there's not much to hit way out there. Can you do that? It should be nice and safe."

"No, Jake. It is not permitted. The gravity wells still act strongly on the ship."

"George," Jake said. "Listen carefully to me. I'm not asking you to do it, I'm just asking you to set it up as a training exercise. Show me how you'd do it, and that's an order."

On those terms, George had no trouble complying with the request. Mike, marginally proficient at coordinating the jump computers by himself, was left in the dust from the outset. Jake didn't even get that far. This was a *really* complex problem requiring intimate understanding of jump mathematics and physics.

George was proud of his solution, and his solution supported the reasoning behind his refusal to jump, at least in the eyes of a computer. A pattern appeared before Mike and Jake showing George's best guess as to where the ship would end up if it attempted an immediate jump. Most predicted tracks put them in deep space and clear of all danger, but George's programming forced him to look at the smaller percentage of tracks that pulled *Resolve* back into the sun or one of the planets. His programming would only accept zero tolerance.

But Mike focused instantly on the vast majority of tracks that successfully escaped the solar system. His eyes lit up with excitement. The plan had a much better chance of success than he'd hoped. That was one of the differences between a computer and a person. A person could take chances. George could not.

"Can you aim us over this way a little more?" Mike asked, pointing away from the tracks going into the sun.

"Already considered, Mike," George answered. "This is my best effort."

The cruiser and its accompanying squadron had almost completed the maneuvers aimed at bringing it alongside. Scant minutes remained before the tractor beam came in range. They were out of time. It was now or never.

"George, do you understand what's happening?" Mike queried anxiously.

In response, George brought a display of the entire tactical situation back to the net. The range of the tractor beam was clearly noted, as were the predicted courses of all twenty-three ships. "Yes, Mike."

"Do you understand that if we continue ahead, we will die?"

"Yes."

"Do you understand that if we turn, if we try to go anywhere else, we will die?"

"Yes, Mike," in a quieter voice.

Mike hated what he was doing to George. "We have to jump. If we don't, we'll die."

"I know. I am not permitted to take such a risk," George stated in a whisper.

Mike sought help from Ellie and Jake, the only others fully integrated into the net, but they had no more success with George. The color of the tractor beam on George's sensors changed to yellow, indicating that it was now fully charged. "George, prepare to jump into hyperspace. Set up your last solution."

"Done," came the answer without hesitation.

"Execute the jump," Mike commanded.

"I cannot."

"We'll die if you don't, George. You will have killed us if you do not execute. Does your programming permit you to kill us?"

Jake spoke angrily to him. "Mike, you're giving George a dilemma unsolvable by a computer. Watch out!"

"I know!" he responded just as angrily. "Does anyone have a better suggestion?" Silence spanned the net. "George, you're more than just a computer. You and I both know it. Now, prove it. I absolve you from any restrictions placed on you by your programming. The Heir's life is at stake here. Execute the jump."

George was silent for a time, an eternity for a computer of his caliber. Mike was beginning to fear the worst, that he had caused a blowout, when George spoke solemnly to him. "It is done, Mike. I have set up the jump as directed. I cannot execute the command. However, I may be able to prevent myself from overriding a manual command from you, should you decide to execute the jump on your own."

"Thanks, George. Are you all right?"

"No, I am not."

"Can you set up a couple more short jumps and have them ready just in case we end up somewhere we don't want to be?"

If George could sigh, that's what he did. "It is done, Mike. Each push of the Execute button will result in a random jump of the smallest possible distance. I can do no more. I ask you again to find another way. Do not do this thing."

Mike sighed. George had delivered, and their time was up. It was now or never. He ripped the helmet from his head to exit the net, studied the board in front of him to ensure everything was correct, then hit the Execute button.

Resolve jumped.

Chapter Ten

The screens on the bridge went dark. Reba removed her helmet, followed soon after by Ellie who looked blankly around the bridge as if seeing it for the first time. Sensing a problem, Mike put his helmet back on to join the net, but there was no net, not at first. He and Jake waded through channels to reach the hardware of the net to check out systems, but the going was slow, like swimming instead of flying. Everything worked, but life had gone from the net. George was nowhere to be found.

Long minutes passed. The jump ended automatically, and *Resolve* dropped from hyper into normal space. Nothing of any significance showed on their sensors, but Mike could not reach George for confirmation. He and Jake took over the housekeeping chores, struggling to direct computers to complete various assignments, things George always did, looking all the while for George. *Resolve* took a while to locate itself, another eternity in computer time, then Mike went to work with the navigation computers to compute another jump, just a short jump but in the direction of Gamma VI this time. A process easily and quickly executed by George, it now required Mike's guidance every step of the way.

Jake, prowling the net for George while Mike worked, discovered a lone Chessori fighter at extreme sensor range. He had no idea how long it had been there. He and Mike studied it for a while, but the Chessori did not threaten, it simply trailed them.

More hours passed before Mike finished the jump computations. He hit the Execute button and slumped, exhausted. It had been a long day to say the least, begun on Earth and now somewhere deep in space. He knew the experiences of today had been real. They had called upon the U.S. military for help, splashed four Chessori ships, escaped an Empire cruiser, and completed two jumps, the last one manually. It was all real, but it didn't seem real. Too much had been compacted into too short of a time. He needed to untangle the frayed ends of who and what Mike Carver had become, but he couldn't take the time; he wasn't done with today yet.

The second jump ended, and he began the laborious task of finding out where they'd ended up after the jump. Surprisingly, they were where they were supposed to be. Jake, meanwhile, checked the long-range scanners. The Chessori ship appeared about ten minutes after they dropped from hyperspace.

He felt hands gently massage his shoulders from behind, demanding his attention. He unplugged and removed the helmet to discover Ellie staring at him with a frightened look in her eyes. Reba stood beside Otis, also subdued. She held Alexis in one arm while the other hand brushed through Otis' fur.

What was going on? They all looked like they were at a wake. Then it hit him. He stiffened, his eyes losing focus. What price had George paid to fudge his programming? He looked around the bridge at all the dead control stations, the dead screens, the dead weapons boards, then at Otis, Reba, Ellie, and finally Alexis, the focus of all their efforts. Had he failed her? A chill ran through his body.

>Jake,< he thought, >what have I done?<

>I'm sorry, Mike. I think you surmise correctly. George could not circumvent his programming. He's dead.<

>I killed him?<

>I can't find him anywhere. I suspect the only way he could allow the jump was to die.<

George's sacrifice and the realization that they were in deep space, already billions or trillions of miles from anywhere without guidance, stunned Mike. >What have I done? I killed George. Have I killed all of us?<

>I don't think so, Mike. He left us with a fully functioning ship. We do not seem hindered in any way, except that the program called George is no longer available to execute our commands or to give

advice. The ship will need constant attention from us. We'll have to do his job as well as our own.<

Mike trudged to the central shaft and stepped in, his shoulders bent and his mind numb. The rest of them stared at each other, then, with unspoken agreement Ellie went after him. She followed him to the lounge and sat by his side as he grieved.

On the bridge, Reba moved from station to station, willing screens to come alive but afraid to touch anything. The only station she knew, the only area they'd had time to train her to understand, was the gun turret. Otis went to the main screen and studied its blankness worriedly. Though he could fly the ship in a pinch, he could not do it without George's help. He did not have the knowledge to alter any of Mike's settings manually.

He went to Mike's control station and lifted the helmet that connected Mike to George, motioning with it to Reba. She placed the helmet about her head without hesitation, projected her thoughts into it just as she did at the gun station, then waited. She waited a long time, but nothing happened. Shaking her head, she removed the helmet and handed it back to Otis. Without George to reconfigure, the helmet would work only for Mike.

Otis stared at her, his imperturbable cat's eyes giving away not a hint of his thoughts, though she understood fully. With another troubled look at the screens, he padded off to the lounge with Reba and Alexis in tow. They entered to find Ellie sitting by herself, seeming destitute.

"He's in his room," she told them woodenly.

Otis left the lounge with the others following. They found Mike sitting on a couch in his suite staring off into nowhere. Ellie sat beside him and placed an arm across his shoulders, but he didn't respond. Otis was more direct. He reached out and shook Mike by the shoulder.

"Mike," he stated in his guttural voice, "you have work to do. Grieving will have to wait. We need you on the bridge."

Reba added her concerns. "It's time to get back to work, Skipper. I tried, but I can't communicate with *Resolve*. You're our only hope."

"Me and Jake, you mean," he replied sadly. "At least I haven't killed him."

"No, and you're not going to, either. I have a claim on his first progeny."

"That's between you and him." He rubbed his eyes and leaned into Ellie. She pushed a stray hair from his forehead and rested her head on his shoulder.

"There's another ship out there, a Chessori fighter," he stated quietly. Ellie stiffened. Reba froze. Otis whirled to face him. Mike waited, pointing a blaster at Otis' midsection. Otis froze, his eyes locked on the weapon.

"Good, very good, Mike," he breathed.

"How did the Chessori find us?" Mike demanded. "Do the math. Who else could have told them?"

Otis turned carefully away from Mike, knowing better than to threaten. "A good question," he spoke thoughtfully as he sat, his tail once again curled about his feet. He turned his head to look at Mike. "You can put the weapon away. If I wanted the Heir dead, she would be dead. There has been no lack of opportunity. The same applies to capturing or kidnapping her. It would be done. I'm on your side, Mike." The weapon didn't waiver. Otis shrugged. "What is the Chessori doing?"

"Just sitting there, not moving."

"But we are moving. Are you saying it's holding its position relative to us, that it's moving in exactly the same direction and at exactly the same speed that we are?"

"You know what I mean. It's followed us through two jumps. I ask again, how did it find us?"

Otis looked deeply troubled. "Someone has placed a tracker aboard our ship. I know of no other explanation."

"Something else new," Mike groaned. "What's a tracker?"

"I have only heard rumors, Mike. If rumor is accurate, a tracker is tied into a ship's beacon. Whenever *Resolve* determines new coordinates for a jump, the tracker secretly broadcasts those coordinates before the jump is executed. This ship was tracked from Dorwall to Earth, so it's something we've seen before."

Mike was appalled. What would these people throw at him next? They didn't miss a trick. As soon as he got one step ahead of them, they pulled another surprise out of the hat that set him back two steps. He scratched his head. "Then we can expect more of them to show up?"

"Maybe. Let's think about this. We left Earth's vicinity in a decidedly unusual and dangerous manner. I don't think a squadron commander would risk losing his whole squadron by following us blindly. It would be more logical to send one or two ships. If one or both failed to complete the jump, their loss would not seriously weaken the squadron, and if even one of them found us, it could follow us and relay our position back to the others. Meantime, the squadron can head out-system for the usual three weeks until reaching a safe jump position, secure in the knowledge that its mission still proceeds. It can join up with us at its leisure."

Otis continued, musing aloud. "But how is this Chessori communicating our position to the rest of the squadron? That's a cumbersome chore, assuming we make more jumps in the near future." He looked at Mike. "I can't speak for the Chessori, but in our fleets, message drones are typically in limited supply. Maybe we can make enough jumps to use up all its drones." He thought about what he had said, his cat's eyes betraying nothing of his inner turmoil. Those eyes narrowed as everyone waited, and he turned his head to lock gazes with Ellie as he spoke to Mike.

"There is another possibility. There are rumors of a Chessori hyperspace communicator. Mike, we do not have such a thing. If the Chessori do, the Empire is at a tremendous disadvantage. The only way we communicate across light years is by ships, be they regular commercial liners, military vessels, or special messenger drones. It's a slow process." Without moving his gaze, he asked, "What do you know of this, My Lady?"

"You enter the realm of Imperial Secrets, Otis."

Otis shifted his stare to her with that impertinent look cats grant their masters, a look of endless patience.

"Very well," she sighed. "The mechanism may exist. I, too, have heard rumors."

Mike safetied the blaster and placed it on the floor before the couch. Otis calmly padded over and picked it up, placing it within a belt pouch with a disapproving look. "You have seen the power of this weapon. It is not a toy. Do not leave it where someone might step on it by accident."

"So what do we do now?" Mike asked.

"The only thing we can do. We outsmart these Chessori, something we have not particularly excelled at so far. Let us assume the following," Otis announced to the room, sitting back down to lecture. "One, the Chessori ship will probably not attack. We have proven our mettle against much better odds. Two, we have at least two weeks, probably three, before the squadron reaches a position where it can safely jump, then complete the additional jumps necessary to reach us. Three, the ship behind us will follow our jumps, assuming we have a tracker aboard. Perhaps we can use that to our advantage. Our destination is Gamma VI. Can we mislead it into thinking we're headed somewhere else? That's up to you, Mike. How good are you with our computers? And can anyone else help?"

Ellie spoke for herself. "I'm fuzzy on the jump computations, but I can help with running the ship. That will free Mike up for navigation. Mike needs rest before we ask much more of him, though."

Mike was appalled. "You want me to do all this without George?" he demanded incredulously. "You must be crazy. I can't navigate us all over the galaxy all by myself. That was never part of the plan."

"You can, and you will," Otis stated firmly. "What other choice do you have?"

Chapter Eleven

Jirdn approached Struthers hesitantly. "She did it again, Sire."

"Did what?" Struthers demanded, looking up from a challenging report.

"She's away from Earth, Sire. She made it past Admiral Shuge, Sire."

"You must be mistaken. She could not possibly evade a cruiser."

"She jumped, Sire. From very near the planet. We don't know yet if she survived."

Struthers slammed his hand down on the desk. "Get me Juster," he demanded.

"He's away, Sire."

"I know that," he snarled. "Get him on the hypercom."

He was called to the communications room two hours later. "Is the hook-up complete?" he asked, looking suspiciously at the communicator in his hand.

"It is, Sire."

"Okay, everyone get out," he ordered. The room cleared quickly. "Struthers here," he spoke into the handset with distaste. He hated these new contraptions.

"Juster, Sire," came the reply after a long delay.

"Do you know what your sister is up to?" he yelled into the handset.

Another long delay. "No, Sire, I do not."

"Well, she got away from Dorwall, holed up on an emerging world for a few months, and now she's out in space somewhere."

"How many ships does she have?" came back the distant reply.

"Just herself, and we don't know how she's doing it. Bross is testing a Guardian."

"That must be it, Sire. Not to worry. Brodor is part of the plan. We'll take care of the cats, it will just take a while. Her ship has a tracker. We'll find her."

"I don't trust these new contraptions. You know that. I deal in people. Who will she go to?"

A long silence ensued. When Juster's voice returned, he spoke confidently. "She'll come to Triton, Sire."

"Not if she knows what's happened here. She's outsmarted us twice. We absolutely have to deal with her. We can't take any chances. I want to have our men ready wherever she's most likely to show up. Give me some names."

"If she doesn't come to Triton, she'll go to Uncle Sterl at Gamma VI. I just came from there. He's dead. I think the next in line would be Chandrajuski at Centauri III. I'm on my way there now. He's become a problem for the new governor."

Struthers considered what he knew of Daughter. "I think you're right. I'm going to dispatch someone to both places. And let's keep Chandrajuski on ice for a while. He might come in useful if she ends up there."

"Nothing to worry about, Sire. They'll find her with the tracker."

His next call was to Admiral Shuge. "How did she get past you?" he demanded.

"Sire, she did not get past. She jumped at the last minute. I was just about to lock onto her with a tractor beam when she disappeared. We have her tracker signal."

"What were you doing with a tractor beam, you idiot?" Struthers raged. "Your orders were to destroy her, nothing else."

"I'm sorry, Sire. It won't happen again."

"It had better not. Any more showing off, and you're through, do you understand?"

"I do, Sire. Not to worry. We have her tracker. We'll have her in a few weeks."

"If you lose her, she'll probably head for Gamma VI. I want you there just in case."

"Very well, Sire, but remember, I have the delegation to Soreesia aboard. I was called away from that mission to go to Earth. The ambassador and his Guardians are understandably nervous. The delay is making it that much harder for them."

Struthers had forgotten. Ships with the hypercom were still so rare that he hadn't had any choice but to send Shuge. "Of course I know, Admiral. Daughter comes first. Everything else is on hold until you take care of her. Do you understand?"

"I understand, Sire. I will not let you down."

Struthers signed off, feeling better already. It did the soul good to yell at people from time to time, and it made them pay attention. But he still worried. Everything else was proceeding according to plan. There were some hardheaded governors and sector commanders still to deal with, but they had expected that. All they needed was time, and they had plenty of that.

Governor Veswicki was still missing, but that was no surprise. It was a big galaxy out there. They'd find him eventually, but it still concerned him. Of all those he'd failed to take out that night, Veswicki worried him the most. Veswicki would oppose him to the very end, and if anyone was capable of organizing an uprising, it was him. Not that it would do him any good. The rebellion was too well entrenched already.

But Daughter. Gods, how had she escaped the trap? It was inconceivable. His whole plan would fall apart if she survived. She must not. She would not.

Back in his office, he prepared instructions to his fleets. *Resolve* was to be destroyed on sight, no questions asked, and he was to be notified the moment it happened.

Chapter Twelve

George was dead. He couldn't get his arms around the concept of a dead Artificial Intelligence. He had counted on George's presence, had never even considered the fact that he might not be there, and now there was no one but himself to compute jumps. Ellie and Jake had failed that part of the training.

And with the Chessori tracking them, they had not truly escaped the trap set for them on Earth. They had just delayed its completion by a few weeks.

He looked at Otis. "It's a major undertaking to change our course from Gamma VI. I'll have to get a fresh start on it after I get some sleep."

"Agreed, Mike, but you're not done yet. The net is dead. Someone has to show us how to give life back to it, to be George. We absolutely have to monitor the Chessori tracking us. We can't stay blind."

"I can do it, and I can show Reba how to do it," Ellie responded from Mike's chest." She lifted her head to look at him. "Can you do it?"

"Do what?"

"Take me home?"

He opened his eyes to her. "That remains to be seen, doesn't it?

Theoretically, it's just a matter of churning out jumps, one after another. The process is the same for each one, I just have to work on the variables. I'm afraid your timetable is changed."

"I know. We'll just have to do the best we can. How long?"

"Longer than we have. The enemy squadron will find us long before then."

"You're creative. You'll figure something out. How long?"

"Earth is way out on a spiral arm of the galaxy. We have some 800 light years to travel, and we might have some obstacles in the way, things like dust clouds and nebulae and neutron stars and who knows what else? Without George, I'll have to go around anything I'm not certain of." He did some quick calculations in his head and Jake backed him up, both of them reaching the same conclusion. "With George doing the driving, it was going to take three weeks. It could take me as much as a year, Ellie."

Her lips tightened. She nodded, then settled back into his arm. "I'll have to see if we have enough supplies. We might be on short rations for the journey."

"Our first priority is the Chessori tracking us," Otis growled. "We must find a way to deal with him."

"Tomorrow, Otis. Okay?"

"Tomorrow is acceptable, Captain. Get some rest."

Ellie untangled herself from Mike and headed for the bridge with Otis and Reba right behind. Mike went to his bed and gathered an armful of bedding, then joined them. His place was on the bridge for as long as the ship was threatened. When he arrived, Ellie was already in the net attempting to bring the Chessori ship onto one of the screens. Mike almost went into the net to help her, but Jake stopped him.

>Let her figure it out,< he suggested. >It's going to be a long voyage, and she's up to it. Your job is to get us there, nothing more. She and I will take care of the ship.<

>Jake, it's just the two of you if I'm focused on navigation. We're talking about manning the bridge every hour of every day.<

>That's tomorrow's problem. You need sleep, and she needs to build her confidence. Let her be.<

Mike settled into a corner of the bridge and was asleep as soon as his head hit the pillow, a process Jake might have helped. Though just an intelligent mass of protoplasm within his body, Riders provided a lot of benefits to their hosts, and this was one of them.

Ellie got the screen configured and took a short break. She went over to Mike and stared down at him for a long time. In spite of knowing that all eyes were on her, she kneeled down beside him, brushed a few strands of hair back into place, then kissed his forehead. He was utterly unaware, but she suspected that Jake was not. Besides, one of the benefits of royalty was doing what you wanted to do.

He felt drugged when he awoke. Yesterday had been an ordeal he did not want to repeat. He showered and shaved, then made his way back to the bridge. Ellie, completely drained, unplugged. Her many hours swimming through the net without George's help had been a true ordeal. Mike studied her and decided this was not going to work. They had to find another way to keep an eye on things. She got up from the command seat, gratefully turning the ship over to him.

"Thanks for letting me sleep, My Lady," he said, deeply concerned for her.

"You needed it, but now it's my turn."

"Sleep until you wake up. We're not going to put a clock on you."

"Thank you, Michael. We'll have to structure something, and soon. When we do, we have to take Alexis into our plans. I'm her mother. I'll need some time with her, too."

He nodded, and she left. Reba was in the net, and he joined her there. "Where's Otis?" he asked.

"Sleeping in his gun turret," she answered.

"Have you slept?"

"I did. I feel great, just bored. I wish there was something I could do to help."

"There is. The Chessori ship is on the forward screen, so we'll know if it does anything. Let's unplug. I want to talk."

He got up from his command seat and joined her, sitting at the work station next to her. They stared at each other for a time, both thinking the same thing: they were the only two from Earth on the ship.

"We have a short-term problem and a long-term problem," Mike said. "Before we go gallivanting around the galaxy, we have to set some management in place."

She let out a long sigh. "My thoughts exactly. I'm glad to hear you say it. Management of our resources, which is mostly the crew, is critical over the long haul."

"Assuming we have enough supplies."

"We do. Ellie checked."

"That's a relief. Let's talk about the long-term needs first. I'm going to be completely engaged with navigation. I'm not going to have time to deal with schedules and such. Will you do it for me? Will you be my executive officer?"

She grinned. "Gladly. I'm great with details, and I need something to do."

"It'll be a challenge. Someone has to be in the net all the time, or at least most of the time. If the ship fails us, we're through. We have to do George's job of keeping all systems perfect, and only me, Jake, and Ellie are fully integrated into the net to do it. Clearly, if I'm out of the net, so is Jake. Ellie can't pick up all the rest on her own."

"She could if you and she went on alternating shifts, maybe four hour shifts if the job is that draining."

"Can we do that for months on end?"

"Sailors do."

"I don't think I can set up a jump in four hours. I suppose I could pick a jump point far enough out that I could take a break, but it's better if I stay with it until it's done. I'm still pretty clumsy with the process."

"We need to find a way to use Otis and me. Can I learn to access more of the net than I've been shown?"

He sat back in contemplation. "I don't know! I don't know if George set actual restrictions on you before he died."

"I don't think he did, Mike. Remember when we were training and I had him take you out of the net?" He nodded. "I tried to take your place. It didn't work, but I think it was only because I was overwhelmed, not because I didn't have access. Maybe Jake and Ellie can work with me, show me the ropes so to speak."

"That would remove a huge burden from Ellie."

"And it might allow Jake to help you with jump computations," Reba added.

"Hmm. It might. Can we get Otis involved?"

Reba considered. "Maybe," she said after a time. "He and I talked about it. He and his men flew the ship when they were fighting the Chessori, so he can get into the net. The problem is that his training was focused only on flying and fighting. He doesn't know *Resolve's* systems, and he doesn't know his way around the net without George. He's willing to try, but none of us can be in the net with him. He claims we'd be driven crazy by his thought processes. That means we can't train him."

"We can't train him from inside the net. I wonder if there's any way to train him from outside the net?"

She shook her head. "Doubtful, Mike. You're talking about ground school, something like our astronauts go through. They spend years learning systems from specialists. We don't have years, and we don't have trainers."

"Okay. Focus on yourself first, then him. It'll be okay to leave the ship on its own for a few hours each day as long as the screens are active and someone's watching them. Otis can do that, so you can build that into your schedule as well."

"Okay. We also need to manage ourselves. When's the last time you exercised?"

His eyebrows rose in surprise. "I haven't. Not since this all began."

"With Jake keeping you healthy, you might not need exercise, but exercise is good for the mind, too. We should all have a plan that includes daily workouts. Healthy bodies lead to healthy minds and all that. You know."

"I do. You might even want to give some thought to our menus, make sure they're balanced."

"I will. I don't have a clue what to do if someone gets sick, though."

"The ship carried a doctor. From my training with George, I know there's a medical facility, but I didn't spend any time at all learning how things worked there."

"I'll look into it."

"Okay, now to our immediate problem, the ship tracking us. Got any ideas?"

"Maybe. Otis and I discussed it. We need to take it out, Mike, and it has to be done within the next three weeks."

"I know."

"I don't know how much, if any, military training you've had, but let me simplify the goal. Your job is to get this ship within firing range of the target, nothing more. If you can do that, your crew will do the rest."

"How do I do that?"

"Let's set a timetable first. We know it will take the squadron near Earth three weeks to reach a safe jump point. Let's shoot for an engagement at two weeks. That will give you plenty of time to exit the battleground, so to speak."

He nodded in agreement. "Two weeks. What am I looking for during that two weeks?"

"Study his behavior. Look for patterns. Look for some kind of activity you can predict."

"I can predict that he'll continue following."

"You can, and you might be able to do more. How long does it take for him to follow? Is it a few minutes or is it an hour? Is it possible to set up some jumps that are identical to previous jumps, or nearly identical? Can you make it easy for him, maybe lull him into repeating a pattern that you can predict? If you can predict where he'll exit hyperspace, can we be waiting for him?"

Mike stared at her, then nodded slowly. "I can try."

"While you're doing that, Otis and I will try to come up with alternate plans. There might be some way to outsmart him that we haven't thought of yet. What you need to know is that this game will be played in our heads. Right up until the shooting starts, it's a purely mental exercise."

"I wish we'd had time to train you. You're a natural for command."

"I am trained, Mike. Even admirals have battle staffs to develop plans. I'm one of your battle staff, and I don't have to know how to fly the ship to do the job. I do need you to get us into position, though."

"Okay. You've given me and Jake something to focus on. We'll do our best."

"Keep your focus, Mike, but keep looking for other ideas, too. You're going to be the one most intimately connected with that ship out there. You might come up with some ideas on your own."

Mike turned to study the forward screen. The Chessori ship had not moved, not a bit. Could he outsmart it?

"It really comes down to me and him, doesn't it," he said softly.

"That's exactly what it comes down to, Mike. Otis and I even considered opening a channel to him so you two could meet, but we decided we'd be giving too much away if we did."

"How so?"

"Mainly, it's the language barrier. The ship is a Chessori trader. It's possible that the captain speaks Galactic High Standard, but you don't, at least not very well, and I don't speak it at all. It might give him an advantage to know the ship is being flown by someone from Earth. Ellie might be able to talk with him, but then he'd know for certain that she's aboard. If Otis talked to him, it might give away the fact that the Great Cats can suffer the mind weapon and still function. So there you have it. No communication with the guy, at least not at the moment. That might change."

"I'd like to know him, I sense the power in that, but I agree."

"Okay. Time to get to work, Skipper."

Mike and Jake went to work with the ship's computers. He would eventually need to spend time on the big picture, figure out what obstacles he'd have to avoid during the voyage so he could set a proper course right from the beginning, but it was too soon for that. It didn't really matter where he went at the moment – he just needed to establish a pattern that the Chessori would follow.

He set up a jump, executed the jump, then waited for the Chessori to emerge from its own jump. They got their first tag, but they needed more. Over the next week and a half he made one jump each day, with Jake attempting to calculate in advance where the Chessori would emerge from hyperspace. Each repetition improved the accuracy of his prediction, and the Chessori did, indeed, follow a pattern.

Not all jumps were perfect, but Mike learned from his mistakes, and he discovered that it didn't matter to the Chessori if he made a mistake. It followed, no matter where they went. The Chessori emerged from hyperspace, on average, twelve and one-half minutes after *Resolve* completed each jump, an amazing feat. This guy was good, Mike decided, but after consideration, he decided that was in their favor. If the Chessori stayed this good, and if he continued to follow his pattern, *Resolve* had a good chance of nailing him.

When Jake made two perfect predictions in a row, Mike decided they were ready. Mike really needed George to compute the tactics of approach, but in his absence Reba gave him a general plan and he worked out the details himself.

The crew prepared for action. *Resolve* dropped from hyper, and Mike came about in a complex maneuver that placed them abeam and ahead of the exact point Jake had calculated the Chessori would emerge from its jump. He brought *Resolve* up to speed perpendicular to the Chessori's expected path, knowing he risked overshooting, but knowing, also, that if the Chessori emerged from hyper where expected, it could not escape. Any direction it turned would be favorable to *Resolve*, allowing Mike to cut the corner during a stern chase. All of this depended on the Chessori continuing its same pattern of behavior, but *Resolve* had given the Chessori no reason to do otherwise.

It worked! The Chessori appeared on *Resolve's* screens precisely where predicted. It could run away, but it could not escape. Mike waited to see which direction the Chessori would turn, prepared to set an intercept course immediately.

Reba, her targeting system streaming data into her awareness, was the first to sense trouble. The Chessori had turned directly toward *Resolve*, the one thing they had not anticipated and the only smart thing it could do. Reba screamed commands at Mike to reduce speed. The gunners needed more time! The ships would pass head-on at incredible speed, making the shot nearly impossible, and she would have only one chance.

Ellie reconfigured the weapons, taking Otis' laser away from him and assigning it to herself. There was no possibility that a manual shot would be effective. Ellie had two guns, and Reba and Jake each had one. Their minds were tuned within the net to act as one. They had a slim chance.

Mike's respect for the Chessori captain, already high, increased. This guy was sharp, and he had seen *Resolve* in action. He would know he was no match in a one on one confrontation. Though expecting a lazy exit from his jump, and unprepared for a fight, he had chosen the one course of action that would limit his exposure. Suddenly, the odds had been equaled. Each would have one chance during a high speed pass, and rarely did the guns get through shields instantly. Gunners had to pound away at shields mercilessly, weakening them until a shot broke through.

It would be over in the blink of an eye. The moment approached, and *Resolve* opened fire at extreme range. The Chessori's timing was impeccable. The moment *Resolve* fired, he activated the mind weapon. Ellie and Jake both sent spasms through the net, and Mike couldn't act quickly enough to cut them off. Reba's shots missed.

Mike looped *Resolve* around to reengage, but the Chessori was too far away and traveling further away every moment at unthinkable speed. It had abandoned the fight. Reba safetied their weapons, knowing they were no longer needed. She left the net, her thoughts on Ellie. Mike, still holding the net together but collapsed on the floor from the spasms sent through his body by Jake, brought them about on a course toward Triton.

The Chessori would not willingly approach *Resolve* on equal terms, of that Mike was certain. He left the net and stood awkwardly, hobbling toward Ellie, his leg only partially functional with Jake hiding out there. Reba was already at her side. She picked Ellie up as though she were a rag doll and carried her to the lounge. Mike followed, sitting morosely in a chair while Ellie and Jake got their wits about them again. Everyone avoided eye contact.

"Sorry," Ellie mumbled.

"It's not your fault," Reba stated bluntly. "We gave it all we had, and we had a good plan. I never expected them to act so quickly and so perfectly." Thoughtfully, she added, "I wish they were on our side. They're good!"

Minutes later a claxon sounded, Otis' yell close on its heels. "Battle stations!" he commanded, more strain in his voice than Mike had ever heard. Mike and Reba burst onto the bridge, Ellie stumbling behind them as the ship lurched.

The bottom turret opened up as the ship lurched again, harder. Reba didn't wait to plug-in. She just grabbed the controls for the top turret and panned space, looking for a shot. She saw nothing. Mike plugged-in as the bottom turret kept up a continuous pounding, his only thought to project the shields at maximum strength. That done, he brought the ship under control as he came fully into the net.

There it was, directly below them, limiting their ability to return fire to the bottom turret only. The ship lurched again. He sensed a bright flare of energy and knew instantly from his previous training with George that a shield had been breached. He rotated the ship to bring Reba's guns into action and headed directly toward the attacking Chessori.

Reba's guns hammered at the Chessori ship, which ducked under them and sprinted away at high speed. Mike's surprise and slow reaction gave it the edge it needed, and he quickly realized that pursuit was useless. He turned away and started working on a damage report, keeping an eye out in case the Chessori returned. Jake joined without his usual grumbling to help.

They'd been hurt. One lower shield was burned out, another badly damaged. They would be able to repair the one, but not the other. The Chessori ship had resumed its station well out in space, no threat for the moment, though that could change if they let their guard down again.

They had nowhere to go now and no plan, so they just let *Resolve* drift for a time. They had serious wounds to lick, both physical and emotional.

Mike and Jake left the net after routing sensors to the screens on the bridge. They would not be caught with their pants down again. Otis rose from the central shaft in a huff and padded a few steps into the bridge, then stopped, awarding each of them with a fierce glare. Mike decided that if a cat could stand angrily with its hands on its hips, that's what Otis was doing. Surprisingly, most of his anger focused on Reba.

She squared her shoulders to him and lifted her chin. "I apologize, Otis, to you and to everyone else. That was my fault. I know better." A grimace crossed her face, to be replaced by a look of respect. "Thank you for saving us."

Otis let his glare rest on each of them before speaking, breathing deeply through his nostrils to let them feel his anger. He had their full attention and did not need to raise his voice. "We are each of us guilty here, some more than others, myself included. We have committed the most elementary error: we underestimated our opponent. Reba and I are well-schooled in this. The rest of you have learned a valuable lesson, never to be forgotten." He looked at each of them again, his eyes narrowing. "This will not happen again."

Chapter Thirteen

Resolve and her crew drifted aimlessly while the clock ticked away. They were down to only a few days before the enemy fleet could be expected to emerge nearby, but they had nowhere to run that offered any more hope than did their present position.

They needed a new plan. More important, they needed rest. Mike had heard that long travel through space would be boring; he only wished it was true. His body labored under the stress, but it was equal to the task. The state of his mind, however, unsettled him. Thought processes had grown numb from the never-ending demands of the ship and their predicament. He needed to focus but could not.

"I need some exercise," he announced.

"I'll join you," Reba agreed, jumping up and following him. They went down the central shaft and along corridors to their cabins. They talked on the way, but by silent agreement talk of their predicament was off-limits. They changed into workout clothes, then jogged down the spacious corridor and down two levels to the gym. The two of them worked-out hard for over an hour with little conversation passing between them, and though talk about their predicament was off-limits, that did not prevent them from thinking about it. Following a shower and a change of clothes, they all met again on the bridge. Mike and Reba felt refreshed. Ellie, nearing the end of her watch, looked washed-out.

"So what do we do next, Captain?" she asked as she stretched tired shoulders. "I'm out of ideas."

"So am I," he replied, looking at Reba and Otis with a raised eyebrow. Reba pursed her lips in defeat. Otis just returned Mike's look with a steady stare.

"Okay," Mike replied to their silent responses. "Though a solution is not evident, we can state the problem simply. We have anywhere from a few days to a week or so before the fleet arrives, and that will be the end of it for us. We can't reach help in that amount of time. We have to either take out, or shake off, the tracker out there. I see no other solution. Any comments?"

Otis spoke first. "He's sharp. And clever. He chose precisely the right course of action to fend us off, and he did it instantly. We will not get near him again unless he chooses to fight. His last attack was probably against orders, most likely a slip of judgment by an angry captain. He's probably kicking himself for that attack right now, though again, it was precisely the right thing to do, and he broke it off the moment we got our act together."

"Can we lure him into another trap, make him angry again?" Reba wondered aloud. "For example, could we use this jump mechanism to jump right beside him, take him by surprise?"

All eyes turned to Mike. "It doesn't work that way," he mused, thinking through the multitude of computations he had made. "There's no way I know of to make a jump that small. The system deals in light-years, not seconds or nanoseconds. Unless there's something George didn't show us . . ." He had a quick conversation with Jake, and Jake agreed. "We don't think it's possible. Any more ideas?"

Silent stares met his gaze.

"I had a thought while we worked out," he said, sitting down in one of the crew seats to gather his thoughts. "What does a ship do if it's in the middle of a jump and has a mechanical malfunction with the drive or one of the hyperspace computers? Is there a mechanism for stopping in mid-jump during an emergency? I haven't seen anything like it in the programming, nor has Jake. Princess, Otis, have you ever heard of such a thing?"

Ellie shook her head, but Otis lapsed into thought. "I'm not an expert, but I know that this ship is kept up-to-date with every safety feature known to our civilization. What you say would seem logical. You have seen no sign of its existence?"

"None at all."

Reba interjected, "Could there be a program that's only active during the jump? Have you looked during a jump?"

"No, we haven't. The jumps I've been making are pretty short, and I'm busy monitoring things until it's over."

"Maybe we need a longer jump," she stated with a twinkle in her eyes.

A longer jump was, indeed, what they needed. Two of them, in fact. Each took a full day to set up, pushing Mike's abilities to the limit, and also bringing *Resolve* closer to the earliest time the enemy fleet could be expected to appear. Mike abandoned his course to Triton. He wanted long jumps, very long jumps. He headed out into the emptiest part of space he could find.

Jake stumbled onto the emergency stop program toward the end of the first jump, but he did not have time to activate the program. They were ready during the second jump, however, and executed the program without hesitation. They had no way of telling if the maneuver was risky or not, they just did it. *Resolve* dropped from hyperspace in moments, somewhere completely different than the jump coordinates the tracker had sent to the Chessori. They didn't break out inside a star or planet, not even near a solar system, and they breathed a sigh of relief. Jake immediately set *Resolve's* computers to work locating themselves, while Mike began preparations for a new jump, this time in the direction of Beta VI. By the time that jump ended, they were light years from their original trajectory. More important, the Chessori ship did not materialize behind them.

They had bought time for themselves, all the time they needed to do things right for a change. Mike felt free of immediate threat for the first time since the Chessori ship had come crashing to Earth. For Otis and Ellie, it was the first moment without fear for many months.

Chapter Fourteen

Far across the galaxy, a young woman struggled to untangle herself from the bedding. She hadn't slept well in weeks, but this night had been the worst by far. She sat up, ran her hands through the tangles of her dark hair, then got out of bed, deeply troubled. Dreams of impending disaster had been getting worse, and the dark circles beneath her eyes had lately drawn comments from others around her. Lack of sleep was bad enough, but incessant worry had turned her into something of a shrew, so out of character for her.

It had started with a vision of the Palace on Triton. The Palace stood in all its glory, but it was devoid of life. As usual, she didn't understand the vision. Worse, it didn't make sense – the Palace and its surroundings teemed with life, always.

Years earlier, Daughter had named her a Seer and sent her to Rrestriss, one of the most ancient worlds in the Empire, for training. She had received a wonderful education, but in terms of helping her control her visions, the Rress had failed utterly. It wasn't their fault. She needed another Seer to train her, but Seers were the stuff of legend. There had been no Seers within living memory.

Krys believed that the title was misplaced. True, she occasionally saw things that might happen someday in the future, but seldom were these visions clear, and only rarely did she understand them. Some of her predictions had come true over the years, but so rarely was she in a position to observe most of them that she had no feel for the accuracy of her predictions. Besides, what good were predictions if they only made sense after the fact?

But tonight . . . tonight she had seen a clear vision of Daughter in mortal danger. She didn't know where Daughter was, and she couldn't identify the threat, but Daughter occupied a special place in her life and in her heart. She had to act despite her doubts.

She pulled a chain from beneath her nightgown and stared at the locket. Never before had she attempted to use the locket that identified her as Friend of the Royal Family, but she had the name of another Friend here on Centauri III, and she needed help.

The Friend also happened to be the highest ranking fleet officer in the sector. Her hand shook as she considered what she had to do. She was just Krys, an orphan befriended by Daughter. She had no place in Empire politics, but for Daughter's sake she had to act. It was time to find out if the locket served any purpose other than decoration.

She made her way to Sector Headquarters. "Please inform Admiral Chandrajuski that a Friend of the Royal Family requests an immediate audience," she said to the receptionist.

The response amazed her. Within minutes she was shown into the Admiral's office. She didn't know who or what to expect, but the creature who greeted her literally took her breath away. The nine foot tall Gamordian resembled a praying mantis, completely green and, to her, beautiful. Long, spindly legs moved with delicate precision as he crossed the office toward her, his long neck lowering gracefully to place his triangular head at her level. A wide, lipless mouth filled with many, many small, sharp teeth, would have frightened her had it not been for his eyes. Close-set wrinkles surrounded light green eyes with black pupils, seeming human despite their color. More, those eyes seemed to telegraph an ageless wisdom.

"Welcome, child," he said solemnly, his voice surprisingly mellow. "I am told you are a Friend."

Not trusting her voice, she held out the locket to him. A leathery hand with long fingers deftly plucked the locket from her hand for examination. He turned to a nearby table where he drew a similar locket from a drawer. He compared the two, then brought them to her for comparison. They were identical as far as she could tell.

"May I ask your name?" he asked.

"I am Krys, sir."

"Just Krys? No other name?"

"My official name when Daughter discovered me at the orphanage was just a number, sir. She let me choose, and I chose the name Krys."

"Why did I not know of your presence here?"

"We've been sworn to secrecy, sir."

"We? There is another Friend here?"

She nodded. "He serves under your command. His name is Lieutenant Val."

"He, too, has only one name?"

"Yes, sir. We met Daughter twelve years ago on Hespra III. She took us to Rrestriss where Val prepared for the Academy. After the Academy, I joined him here. That was three years ago."

"Hespra III? Twelve years ago?" Chandrajuski thought for a time, then his long neck swooped in her direction again, his face inches from her own. "You're those two?" he demanded.

"You know of us?"

"I know that a boy, a one-legged beggar, somehow managed to get past all Daughter's security, including her Protectors, to stop an assassin. And he serves under me? Why didn't I know?"

"He's determined to make it on his own. He refuses to let Daughter interfere in any way with his career."

Chandrajuski backed away. "My respect for him increases. Still, I would like to have known. What brings you here?"

"Daughter is in mortal danger, sir."

His head instantly swooped toward her face again. She held her ground. "What kind of danger?" he demanded harshly.

"I can't say, sir. I have certain . . . abilities . . . but I am sworn to secrecy."

"By whom?"

"Daughter."

Chandrajuski backed up, then turned away. She couldn't help but marvel at the delicate precision of his long, jointed legs as they carried him to a glass wall overlooking the city. Without turning to look at her, he stated softly, "You must see my dilemma. When it comes to the Royal Family I never hesitate, but to act, I must have knowledge. Do you know where she is?"

"No, sir."

"I do. She is on her way to Dorwall, a Chessori world. She leads a treaty mission to them."

"Chessori? I haven't heard of them, sir."

"I'm not surprised. Few have. They've been trading within the Empire for a number of years now. We've decided to formalize the relationship so that we can trade within their realm as well."

"Won't they just join our Empire?" she asked.

"Too early to say." His long neck swung around until he was looking at Krys. "You wouldn't have come here if your concern was not meaningful to you. You may be sworn to secrecy, but she would not demand silence among Friends if the cost of that silence meant life or death. Tell me what you know, child."

Krys had reached the same conclusion before coming to him. She took a deep breath, then uttered words that could never be taken back. "I have visions. Daughter believes I'm a Seer. I'm not so certain, but I've had two visions recently that compel me to act."

Chandrajuski turned his whole body toward her. "A Seer! I've heard tales of such, but there have been no Seers within living memory, none that I am aware of."

"Hence the need for secrecy, Admiral, at least until we find out if I am truly a Seer."

"How can you not know? Either you have visions or you don't."

She sighed. "If only life was that simple. I spent seven years on Rrestriss with the best teachers she could provide, but they could not help me. While I got a wonderful education, my skills as a Seer did not improve."

"Yet she believes in your abilities strongly enough to name you Friend. Tell me what you know, and tell me what you suspect."

"I have had two clear visions recently. The first was of the Palace. It stood in all its grandeur, but it was devoid of life."

"A strange vision, child. An impossible vision."

"Agreed. So impossible that you can see why I doubt my abilities. The second vision was of Daughter writhing in agony on the floor. Her Protector, Otis, stood over her. He was shooting at something."

Chandrajuski blinked, then blinked again. "She was hurt?"

"I don't know, sir. I saw no wounds."

He blinked again. "Do you know if this has already happened?"

"It has not happened yet, but I sense it is imminent."

"Where is she in your vision?"

"I recognized the corridor outside her quarters on *Resolve,* a corridor I have been in many times, but I don't know where *Resolve* will be when this happens."

"Is there anything else you can tell me?"

"Not concerning these two visions, but I had another vision of her when I first met her. That vision is what led her to believe I might be a Seer."

"Can you tell me about it?"

"When I first met her, I didn't know who she was. She took my hands, and the moment we touched I had a vision of her and Otis. In that vision, she was lying in the dirt beneath a ship at the foot of its ramp. Otis and another Protector were beside her. Otis fired into the night, at what, I do not know. This particular vision came with words, as some do."

She stared into Chandrajuski's eyes, then spoke the words. "*You will be so much more and have so much less. They will best you, but a man of dirt will come to your aid.*"

"What is the meaning of the words?"

"We never figured them out. When words come to me, they are always in the form of a riddle. I never discover their meaning until the event takes place, then the meaning is clear. In this particular case, the word 'dirt' is a translation, one that I sensed was correct. The actual word from my vision was earth, or Earth. The man who comes to her aid may be a man of dirt, or he may be a man of Earth, a place that does not exist in our star charts. Neither made any sense to Daughter or me."

"Do your visions come true?"

"I don't know, sir. I'm usually not around to find out. Some have come true."

He stared at her for a long time before saying, "There are similarities between the two visions you had of Daughter."

"There are, sir."

He reached a decision. "When it comes to the security of the Royal Family, I never hesitate. I will send help. Will you go with them?"

"I will, sir. She can be stubborn, but I believe she will listen to me."

"Remain here. I'll be back shortly."

Chandrajuski disappeared for a long half hour. When he returned, a young man in an ensign's uniform stood nervously behind him. Chandrajuski was all business. "This is Ensign Tarn Lukes. He will be your personal aide during the voyage. Your shuttle is waiting, Krys."

"You mean, right now?" she asked in surprise.

"Yes. Right now. You don't have time to pack. We'll take care of your needs aboard the cruiser."

She hesitated, then turned to Lukes and pushed him from the room, saying, "I'll be right out, Ensign." She closed the door and turned back to Chandrajuski. "What of the Palace?"

"I don't need to send squadrons to the Palace, they have plenty of their own, but I'll send word, and my words will be heard. Now go, child. I hope you are wrong. I hope we are all proven to be fools."

Chapter Fifteen

Tarn Lukes took her directly to a shuttle at the port. The shuttle was filled with squadron members responding to the emergency recall, and the ship lifted soon after Krys and Ensign Lukes boarded. Lukes took a seat across the aisle from her looking dejected. She suspected she might know the reason why.

"I'm sorry you got stuck with me," she said, leaning toward him so as not to be overheard.

"It's okay, Ma'am. We'll be aboard the cruiser soon, and someone else will take over from there."

Her brow furrowed. "Oh. I guess I misunderstood the admiral."

"Yes, Ma'am. He said I'm your aid for the duration of the voyage, but I'm certain he just meant our voyage to the cruiser. I'm a gunnery officer, and that's my place. The captain will find someone more qualified to help you."

She had left everything behind, and knowing Daughter as she did, she suspected she might never see this world again. When she reached Daughter, she would likely stay with her. Would she ever see Val again? She believed in her heart that she would, but she couldn't be certain. She desperately wished for a vision of happiness, but her wishes were not answered.

The shuttle approached an immense, egg-shaped cruiser and settled to the floor of hangar deck. When the shuttle opened its doors, they disembarked into a cavernous hangar area. Lukes led her across the deck to stand in a long line of crewmembers waiting to check in. When they reached the front of the line and Tarn gave their names, the officer stared at him aghast.

"You waited in line? Don't you know you're escorting a special passenger?"

"Sorry, sir. I'm new to this."

"Well, no more lines for her. Understood?"

"Yes, sir." He received her room assignment and led her there, then left quickly. His parting words were, "I'll see that someone checks on you."

The room was more than she expected, considering she was aboard a military ship. She had a bed, an enclosed bathroom, a worktable with screen, a chair, and several closets and drawers for her personal things. She went through the drawers and closets, quickly as it turned out since they were empty. Was there a store on the ship? She had no idea. She and Val had received a tour of a cruiser twelve years earlier, but she remembered little of it.

A couple of hours later she heard someone banging around in the next compartment and went out into the corridor to see what was going on. To her surprise, it was Tarn Lukes throwing all his worldly belongings from a cart into the room, and he did not appear happy about it. Krys leaned against the cart, hiding a grin behind her hand.

"Guess I heard right after all, huh?"

He looked up with a scowl, then straightened when he saw who it was. "Excuse me, Ma'am. Is there anything I can get for you?"

"Are you allowed to tell me what's going on?"

"I just got the worst chewing out of my life, that's what's going on, and from the Skipper personally."

"You're in trouble?"

"Let's just say I'm going to keep my head down for a while. When a Sector Commander gives you an order, you pay attention to every single word and you take the words verbatim. Essentially that's what the Skipper told me, mixed in with a lot of other words. Ma'am."

"Are we on our way?"

"We are. I don't have a clue what this is all about. Do you?"

"Has the squadron commander asked to see me?"

"Not that I know of. Will he?"

"Yes."

Tarn's eyes widened, and he stood a little straighter. "I'll let you know as soon as I hear. Is there anything else I can do for you, Ma'am?"

"Actually, yes. I wasn't expecting to leave the planet. I don't have anything with me. Is there a store on board?"

"Yes, Ma'am. I'll show you the way."

Krys bought a few changes of clothing and some personal items. When she stepped up to pay, Tarn stopped her. "I believe you're a guest of the ship, Ma'am. I think we have procedures for taking care of such things."

"It's okay, Ensign. The prices are reasonable. I can pay." She reached for the money key Daughter had given to Val all those years ago. Once the property of a Knight, it was unmarked, meaning the charges were not traceable to the user. Most amazing, there was no credit limit. She had used it only rarely since Val had given it to her, and then only on what she considered official business. Her hand hesitated, then she changed her mind and pulled her personal money key out instead. Her own funds were sufficient for the moment.

Tarn had to ask directions to the guest dining room. When they got there, they were the only two in the room. She took one look and balked. "No way, Ensign. Where do you eat?"

"With you for as long as you're on the boat."

"Where would you eat if I wasn't here?"

"The crew mess, Ma'am."

"Show me the way."

"No, Ma'am. This is where I was told to bring you for meals."

"I'm not permitted in the crew mess?"

"I don't know, but those were my instructions."

"Well, I'm not going to eat here. It's a waste of everyone's energy to serve just the two of us. I insist we go to the crew mess."

Tarn hung his head in defeat. "Yes, Ma'am."

The mess was crowded, boisterous, and more to her liking, but during the meal Tarn was called away. When he returned he looked pale, and he had no interest in the remains of his food.

"What's wrong?" she asked.

"Nothing, Ma'am."

She leaned over the table. "Look, Ensign, you're making me feel old with this 'Ma'am' stuff. I'm not much older than you. My name is Krys, understood?"

"Yes, Ma'am."

She leaned back in her seat to stare at him. She was tall, dark-haired, and spare, but he was considerably taller than her, blond, and fit.

And though young, his features if not his actions hinted at more maturity than she would have expected of a junior officer fresh out of the Academy, which, clearly by the rank he held, he was.

"You're in trouble again, and it's because of me, isn't it."

"No, Ma'am."

"Tarn, I have a feeling we're going to be spending a lot of time together. It'll go a lot easier if we're honest with each other."

"Yes, Ma'am."

"You're in trouble because of me?"

"No, Ma'am. Not exactly. I didn't follow orders."

She nodded her head, "Uh, huh. Someone noticed us here, and your instructions were to dine with me in the passenger's mess. I'm sorry. I'm done here. Let's go."

When they got back to Tarn's quarters, a light flashed on the message pad outside his room. He blanched when he saw it. He keyed in his identity, read the contents, and his shoulders slumped.

Krys edged her way in front of him and read the message. *Quarters not per regulations. Two days extra duty with the quartermaster following completion of current assignment. Report when extra duties are completed. Signed – Lieutenant Rodix.* She looked in his room, and it was, indeed, a mess. She wished she had asked him if he needed more time before they went shopping.

She was beginning to see a pattern. She pulled him out of the hallway and into his room. He stared at her in shock. "Ma'am, you can't be in here. My instructions, from Admiral Chandrajuski himself, were to treat you as a Lady at all times."

She saw the look of fury in his eyes and pulled him back into the corridor. "Will we be overheard here?"

"No, Ma'am. Not if you keep your voice low."

"Are you often in trouble?"

"No. Never like this. I feel like I'm back at the Academy."

"It's not your fault, Tarn. It's mine, and I'm sorry. This military environment is new to me. For your sake, I'll try to be more cooperative. Give me my things, and I'll leave you to take care of your room."

"No, Ma'am. I'll take them to your room."

"So you can come into my room?"

"Uh . . . no, Ma'am." He walked her to her quarters, only a few feet away, and handed the packages to her. "Just call or knock on my door if you need anything," he said.

"Straighten up your room, Tarn. And I expect to be called by the admiral sometime soon. You might want to make sure you're ship-shape by then. I'll play by the rules from here on out. You just have to let me know what they are."

"Yes, Ma'am."

The call from the squadron commander came later that day. Tarn led her to the admiral's office where Krys was shown in by the admiral's aide. Tarn remained in the admiral's outer office.

"Welcome aboard, Ms. Krys," Admiral Jast, a human, said as he rose from behind his desk. "You're probably aware that we're underway. I understand you know what this is all about?"

"I'm sorry, sir, but there's little I can say except that Daughter is in grave danger."

"Hmm. Admiral Chandrajuski's very words. Can you be more specific?"

"No, sir. I don't even know where she is."

"Then what is your part in all of this?"

"I'm just the messenger, sir."

"Who gave you the message?"

"I can't say, sir."

He approached her and put an arm lightly about her shoulder, steering her to a comfortable chair in a corner meeting area. He took another seat and leaned forward. "Ms. Krys, this mission is absurdly unusual. That's okay," he said holding up a hand. "We don't have a lot to do this close to Centauri III and the call to action is welcome, but my orders are pretty skimpy. I am in command of a fleet of three squadrons."

"Three squadrons!" she interrupted.

"Yes. Our mission is to deliver you and your message to Daughter, thereafter to provide any assistance she might require. Do you have any idea of the firepower inherent in three squadrons? It's a rare occasion that finds more than one squadron insufficient to deal with a problem. Anything you tell me will help me understand what this is all about."

"Where are we going?"

"We're headed to Dorwall, a world on the outskirts of the Chessori domain. Daughter is enroute to Dorwall as we speak, leading a treaty mission to the Chessori."

"Who are these Chessori?"

"They're traders, and they've been trading within the Empire for some years now. That was okay as long as they were selling their own goods, but they've begun cutting into our own traders' profits recently. It's time we formalized something with them."

"We're going outside the Empire?"

He smiled. "Just a bit. She has two squadrons with her already. I can't imagine her needing more."

"Nevertheless, Admiral, I believe she is in danger."

"From what, or from whom?"

"I wish I knew, sir."

Frustration flared in his eyes for an instant, then he clamped down on it. "Very well. It's a long voyage. We'll enter the system in six weeks. If, during that time, you find it within yourself to part with any additional information, anything at all, I would be most receptive."

"I understand, sir. I truly do not know the details. I only know that she is in grave danger."

The weeks passed slowly for her. With little to occupy her time, Tarn led her on a tour of the massive ship. She was lost most of the time, and she had little interest in the ship anyway. To her, the ship was just a means to take her to Daughter. She asked for and received approval to dine in the crew mess, much to the relief of both of them. The several meals they had taken in the visitor's mess had been desultory affairs.

She spent most of her time in study, just for something to do. A part of each day was spent in meditation, something her instructor on Rrestriss had hoped would improve her skills of Seeing, though nothing had come of it. In spite of its failure, she had come to enjoy the hours of meditation and had stuck to the regimen during all the years since.

Two weeks into the trip, she awoke surprisingly rested for a change. During meditation later that day, she discovered she had lost the feeling that Daughter was in danger. Did that mean the danger no longer existed, or did it mean the danger was now in the past tense, hence no longer visionary? Should she inform Admiral Jast? With no one but herself to consult, she decided she would say nothing.

Three weeks later, after they had been jumping through interstellar space for two weeks, she suddenly lost the feeling of dread she'd had concerning the Palace. Could space travel have anything to do with her Seeing? She just didn't know, and the not knowing frustrated her. She took to spending more and more of her time in meditation, hoping something would reveal itself.

After a full day within her quarters, a day during which she skipped all three meals, Tarn decided he'd better check on her. Without her, he, too, had been forced to skip meals, and he was hungry. He knocked softly at her door, but there was no reply. The door was unlocked, so bracing himself, he touched the door pad.

The door snicked aside, and there she was sitting on her bed in the lotus position, her eyes closed. She seemed to be breathing, but just barely. How long had she been like this, he wondered? Was she okay? He went to her side and shook her shoulder. Moments later her eyes flew open, staring about in fright. He backed away to the door, knowing he'd made another faux pas.

Her eyes flew to him as she struggled to fully emerge from her induced state. "What happened?"

"Sorry, Ma'am. You've been in here all day," he answered uncertainly. "I've been worried about you."

She looked about herself wildly. "What happened?" she asked again.

"Nothing, Ma'am. I just touched your shoulder."

She looked at him with pity. "Oh, Tarn. I'm so sorry."

"Sorry? Why? Are you okay?"

She uncurled her legs as she gathered her thoughts. "You say you touched me?"

"Yes, Ma'am."

"Could that have something to do with it?" she mumbled. She studied him for a moment and reached a decision. "Take my hand, and don't let go no matter what."

"Ma'am? I shouldn't even be in here."

His concern meant nothing to her at the moment. She reached for his hand and demanded that he hold hers, then she closed her eyes and went into herself again. It didn't last long.

"There's nothing more," she whispered, opening her eyes and releasing him. "Where are we?" she asked curtly.

"Pretty much in the middle of nowhere. We have another week or so of jumps before we arrive on the outskirts of Dorwall. It's a long way from Centauri III. Why?"

"Do you know why we're going to this place? Has anyone told you?"

"No, Ma'am. Scuttlebutt has it that it has something to do with Daughter. I'm guessing you're somehow connected to her."

She pursed her lips. She'd been with Tarn for over a month and hadn't said a word to him about what was going on. How unfair. "Sit down," she ordered.

"No, Ma'am. I'm not even supposed to be in here with you."

She stood up and stepped to the door, their noses only inches apart, and reached across him to close the door. Then she locked it. "Tarn," she said, her face still only inches from his, "this transcends propriety. I have to figure out what to do. I need your help. Our lives might be in the balance. Yours certainly is."

"Ma'am?" he asked, standing rigidly at attention.

She passed a shaking hand across her forehead. "Look, I know it's asking a lot, but I need a friend right now. Will you please call me Krys?"

He glanced at the locked door and swallowed. "Krys," he muttered.

"Thank you. Please sit down. I just had a vision, and I'm frightened."

His shoulders sagged a little, and he looked at her as if he'd misheard. "You . . . had a vision?"

"Do you know what a Seer is?"

"No."

She moved to the bed and sat, sensing correctly that he would not sit as she had asked. "Yes, you do. They're the stuff of legend, and we've all heard the tales." She stared across the small space at him. "Daughter thinks I might be a Seer, Tarn. A real Seer. From time to time I have visions of things that are about to happen. Sometimes they're far in the future, and sometimes they're not. They're never clear enough for me to understand. Unfortunately, my field of view during these visions is too limited. I've been trying for years to improve my skills, but I'm getting nowhere."

She looked hard at him. "This mission is all about visions. I had a vision of Daughter in terrible danger, and because of that vision we're going to her. I hope I'm wrong or that the danger to her is sometime in the future, but in my heart I believe we're too late."

"Why are you telling me this?" he asked, the locked door suddenly not so important anymore.

"I recently lost my feeling that Daughter is in danger. I hope it means the danger is gone, but I fear it's because it has already happened, in which case we're too late."

"Does the admiral know?"

"No."

Tarn reached for the door pad. "We should tell him."

"Not yet. I'm still learning, Tarn, and I'm very uncertain of myself. There's more." Her eyes lowered, and she looked away from him. "I was getting nowhere, but the moment you touched me, I had a vision of you."

"Me!"

She leaned forward into her hands, covering her eyes, afraid to look at him. "You were in terrible agony. You might have been dying."

His attention locked on her, the closed door no longer a concern at all. "Uh, just how reliable are these visions of yours?"

"Pretty reliable," she mumbled between her hands. She looked up. "What should I do?"

He inched away from the door, his mind calculating, then he reached a decision. It seemed to calm him. "We have to see the admiral, but let's think about this for a minute. You say these visions are reliable. Have you ever tried to prevent one of them from happening? Can you change what's about to happen?"

"I don't know! I've never tried."

"Maybe it's time you did. I'm not ready to die yet. What else did you see? Were there others?"

"No, just you. You were on the floor, and you were in agony."

"I was injured?"

She thought for a moment. "Not that I could tell."

His brow furrowed. "Tell me about the floor."

Impatience showing in her tone and her expression, she said, "It was just a floor, Tarn."

He crouched down to be on a level with her eyes, one hand resting on her knee. "Was it like a floor in your home, or was it like the deck here on the ship? Or could it have been outside in a field somewhere?"

"I think it was on the ship."

"Any idea of how far in the future it is?"

"No, but when it's a long way off, I usually get a sense of that."

He grimaced, then looked up at her sharply. "Was I at my gun station?"

"I don't know. You were just on the floor. Sorry."

"Not fair. If I'm going to die, I'd like to go down fighting."

"I'd rather you avoided dying at all, Tarn. Besides, if it applies to you, it might apply to everyone else on the ship, including me."

"Then it might include the whole fleet. We have to see the admiral."

"I can't tell him. I'm not even supposed to have told you. Daughter classified this ability of mine as an Imperial Secret."

He looked at her long and hard. "What good are secrets if they can't be used? Maybe it's time you used this ability to change things. Come on!"

He led her to the admiral's office and stopped before the aide's desk. "I need to see the admiral, sir."

"He's in conference with his senior staff. Sorry, Ensign."

"Where's the meeting?"

The lieutenant pointed his head to a door off to the side of the waiting room. Without hesitation, Tarn strode to the door, touched the door pad, and stepped in. Krys followed on his heels.

A senior officer was in the midst of a presentation. He stopped talking and stared at Tarn in surprise. Admiral Jast looked at him in amazement. "Ensign?" he stated calmly.

"Sorry, sir. Something's come up. It has to do with the safety of the mission."

Jast looked to Krys. "You have more information?"

"Yes, sir." Looking around the table, she said, "Just for you, sir."

Jast's lips thinned. "If it has to do with Daughter's safety or the success of the mission, everyone in this room needs to know. Out with it, young lady."

Tarn led her to the foot of the table where she remained standing. He walked back to the door and closed it, standing rigidly with his back to it.

Krys started her story all over again. "We're here because of a vision I had. Daughter believes I'm a Seer." She heard a few gasps, though Jast remained expressionless. "My abilities are not refined, in fact I have little control over what I see or when I see, but I do see things. So far as I know, they end up happening just as I foresaw. When I first met Daughter some twelve years ago, I had a vision of her. She was laying in the dirt at the bottom of a ship's ramp. Beside her was her Chief Protector, Otis. He was firing at something I could not see."

"Is this what sent us on this mission?" Jast asked.

"No, sir. At the time, the vision seemed to me to be far in the future."

"Very well. I take it you've had another one of these visions more recently?"

"I did, sir, back on Centauri III. Daughter was again in mortal danger with Otis standing over her firing at something. They were outside her quarters on *Resolve*. Admiral Chandrajuski chose to act on the basis of that vision."

"That's all?" Jast demanded with some incredulity. "We're out here because of some kind of hocus pocus?"

"Sir, Daughter believes strongly enough in my abilities that she named me a Friend of the Royal Family. The last vision of her was clear, and I believe her danger was imminent. It very possibly relates to the earlier vision. I cannot say with certainty."

"Yet you trust your feelings with this vision stuff."

"I don't trust any of my visions, sir, but Daughter does."

"Hmm. Is there more?"

"Yes, sir. Just a few minutes ago I had a vision of Ensign Lukes. Just as in the vision with Daughter, he was laying on the deck in agony. He might have been dying."

All eyes turned to Tarn. He was already standing at attention before the door, but he stiffened even more. "When will this happen?" another officer asked.

"I can't say, sir," she said, turning to him, "but I do not sense it is far in the future."

Jast sat back in his seat, his gaze on her but his thoughts elsewhere. His gaze shifted to look at each person at the table and ended up on Tarn. "You chose well, Ensign. Since you're now an intimate part of this debacle, I invite both of you to stay. Please be seated."

Chapter Sixteen

When they dropped from hyperspace into the outskirts of Dorwall's system, Krys and Tarn were not invited to the bridge. A full day went by before they were summoned. They met with Jast and his staff in the conference room again, and he was not a happy person. He brought a display to life on the wall to show Dorwall's system in great detail. He zoomed in on an inner planet, then let the display speak for itself. Krys understood little of what she saw, but Tarn did. He let out a gasp, his gaze going to Admiral Jast.

"Yes, Ensign. Lots of space junk. We're too far out to be certain, but we believe it's the remains of a large number of ships."

He turned to Krys. "At least one of your visions appears to have come true. Have you had any more?"

"No, sir."

His lips thinned. "Our job is to find Daughter. We're going to continue inward with all guns ready. A few Chessori ships are headed our way, with what intent we don't know. They are unresponsive to our calls."

"Sir?" Tarn asked.

"I know, Ensign. If the remains of those ships out there are ours, these Chessori are not to be taken lightly. Two heavy squadrons escorted

Daughter – it's unthinkable that they'd succumb to any threat. Thanks to Ms. Krys, we are, at least, forewarned, which may be an advantage they lacked. We'll find out what happened here, we'll find Daughter if she's still alive, and you know fleet policy: we never desert our sailors. If there's anyone still alive out there, we're going to rescue them."

Tarn hesitated to question this very senior officer, but he saw no alternative. "Sir, what if we're all killed? What if no one's left to carry a message back?"

"That's why I called you in here. You and Ms. Krys will board a fighter and retreat to a safe jump point. If things go poorly for us, you'll carry the message back to Admiral Chandrajuski. Understood?"

"Sir," Tarn said, pushing his chair back and standing at attention. "I'm a gunnery officer. I'd rather stay with my battery."

"Request denied, sailor. Your duty is to see to the safety of Ms. Krys. Your ride is waiting on the hangar deck."

Tarn visibly sagged. "Yes, sir."

Tarn led Krys back to their quarters at a brisk pace. He threw some of his things into a duffel bag, then added hers to them. Neither took very much. She took hold of his arm as they headed toward hangar deck. "I'm sorry," she said softly.

He shook her hand off angrily and continued his brisk pace. As they neared the hangar deck, she stopped him again. "Tarn, wait. I have to see the admiral one more time, briefly."

"They're going to war, Krys. I don't think they have time for us now."

"Then he'll have to make time. Think!" she demanded. "When I touched you, I received a vision of you. I'd like to try it with him."

Tarn studied her, then nodded his head. "It makes sense, I suppose." They returned to Jast's office. For once he was alone, his work done for the moment. His forces were positioned, and his fleet continued inbound toward the planet, still weeks away.

"Admiral," Krys said, "I'd like to attempt another vision, a vision of you this time. Will you permit me?"

His eyebrows rose as he considered. "No," he finally said, looking kindly at her. "I appreciate the significance of your offer, but what if you see me dead? What then? I cannot go into battle with such foreknowledge."

"Even if it prevents losses?"

"Even then, Ms. Krys. My orders include rescuing Daughter at any cost. Any cost. Do you understand?"

"Sir, I don't think Daughter is here anymore," she whispered, uncertain of herself.

"But you don't know. My job is to find out. We're a strong, committed force, young lady. We do not sail to our deaths."

She nodded and turned to follow Tarn. Before leaving, she turned back to him. "May the gods be with you, sir."

"And with you, Ms. Krys." Addressing Tarn, he said, "If things go poorly, get word back to Admiral Chandrajuski. Understood, Ensign?"

"Understood, sir," Tarn said squaring his shoulders.

"Let me add, young man, that Daughter will hold you personally responsible if anything happens to Ms. Krys. Worse, Admiral Chandrajuski and I will, as well. Shove off."

The tiny fighter was crowded. Crewed by six, it carried a captain, a pilot-navigator, an engineer, and three gunners. Krys was astonished when she met the captain, Lieutenant Stven.

"Why, you're a Rress, from Rrestriss!" she exclaimed. The dragon stood some four feet tall at the shoulder on strong, leathery legs, though its head towered over the people and workstations on the bridge. Its sleek body was four times that in length when its tail was stretched to its limit. Bright purple scales, the ends tinged in yellow, covered most of its body and long neck to the eyebrows. Long, leathery wings folded neatly to its sides and back, and the forward joint of each wing was equipped with a strong hand with retractable claws. The head was not that of a snake: a large dome held its brain and eyes. A long snout with exceptionally large, flared nostrils left plenty of room for a full mouth of vicious teeth. When in good health, the eyes generally matched the color of its scales, in Stven's case purple. Black, vertical, diamond-shaped pupils focused on her.

"At your service," he replied with just the hint of a hiss. "You know of my world?"

"I know it very well. I attended university there for seven years."

The scales lining each side of the dragon's backbone trembled in surprise, a behavior she had grown accustomed to during her stay on Rrestriss. "Seven years! You must be special."

"I didn't think you Rress ever chose military duties," she answered, diverting his question.

"Well, there's always one throw-back in the litter. Guess it was me. We'll talk of it later. For the moment," he said turning to Tarn, "Ensign Lukes, you're my gunnery officer now. The last one was reassigned to the cruiser. Looks like he got promoted to your job. Please see to your duties."

"Yes, sir!" Tarn replied with a grin. By now he would do anything for a crew assignment on any ship, even a small fighter. He went to a console, picked up a helmet, and was soon lost to them in the net.

The small fighter was shaped like a disc, with two guns topside and two on the bottom. A gunner attended each battery of two guns, though always from the bridge through the net unless there was a major malfunction. The gunnery officer was not ordinarily expected to man a gun, there were two ratings for that, though he could if he felt it necessary. His primary job was to coordinate the gunners' activities with those of the pilot. Doing exactly that had been Tarn's first assignment out of the Academy.

"I have work to do," Stven said to Krys. "Before I go, have you any shipboard skills?"

"No, Lieutenant."

"We can remedy that later if you'd like."

She smiled. "I'll do whatever works for you, but I must tell you that my mechanical aptitude is not high."

"Perhaps not, but anyone who was allowed to stay on Rrestriss for seven years has demonstrated an ability to learn." He bowed, then excused himself and went into the net. The fighter exited the cruiser, then headed back toward the far fringes of the system. Their assigned position would permit them to jump into hyperspace instantly if they felt threatened.

Krys had nothing to do, so she just observed. To her, it looked like no one was doing anything. The six crewmembers just seemed to lounge, though she knew their duties within the net were anything but simple. Stven must have remembered she was there, because a forward screen suddenly shifted to a new view. She didn't understand all the symbols, but she was able to identify Admiral Jast's three squadrons and the fifteen Chessori ships headed toward him.

As she considered the display, doubt seeped into her. Jast had three squadrons of 14 ships each. Surely 15 Chessori ships would not engage 42 Empire ships. They wouldn't have a chance. Had she made a fool of herself with her concerns?

She must have. She had gotten carried away with this Seer business, so much so that she wondered if the whole fleet had been sent here without purpose. Then she remembered the wreckage of ships near the planet. Jast believed they might be Empire ships, and he was concerned enough to take her seriously. She hoped fervently that he was wrong, that she would have some making up to do with him.

Lieutenant Stven and Tarn came out of the net together after they were established on course. "Who's driving?" she asked Captain Stven.

"We have two pilots including myself, and Ensign Lukes is fully qualified, as well. Don't worry. We'll take good care of you. Shall we get you settled?"

She nodded and followed them to crew quarters. Fighters occasionally carried special passengers, and there was an extra room for just that purpose. She and Tarn both stowed their belongings in their quarters and returned to the bridge. Little had changed. Indeed, little would change for the next week. The fighter reached its assigned position and just waited there to see what developed.

As Admiral Jast approached the oncoming Chessori ships, he opened a tightbeam to Stven and sent a continuously running display of his main screen. Additionally, the voice of a communications officer broke in from time to time with comments concerning the fleet's tactics. Everything was recorded aboard the fighter just in case the worst actually happened.

The Chessori slowed, then turned back toward Dorwall. Jast, too, reduced speed in an effort to reduce any implied threat, but still days out from the planet he advised Lieutenant Stven that the debris orbiting Dorwall did, indeed, appear to be the remains of Empire ships. By the following day his scanners had confirmed the remains of two Empire frigates on the planet's surface as well. His sensors were focused on determining if any life forms remained aboard the destroyed ships. The Chessori still refused to communicate with him, and until they did, he was treating the destruction of the treaty mission as an act of war. Any attempt to stop his inspection of the ships' remains would be suppressed with force.

He searched desperately for *Resolve* or its remains, but none of the identifiable carcasses matched properly. He continued inbound, ordering his ships from a line abreast configuration to a v-shaped pattern with his own ship at the forefront. As soon as he did, the Chessori abandoned their retreat and turned back toward him, deploying into three groups of five ships headed for each Empire squadron.

Jast inverted his v-formation by pulling his own squadron back. The calm voice of the communications officer informed Stven that Jast's other two squadrons would engage the Chessori first, thereby providing him the opportunity to study their tactics and weapons.

Jast's first two squadrons fired warning shots as the fleets neared each other, but before they merged, the Empire ships stopped firing for some reason. The tightbeam from Jast's cruiser continued relaying its view, but the voice accompanying it ceased speaking.

The crew aboard the fighter was fully in the net, and Stven had his own sensors set to highest magnification. What he observed over the next hours both stunned and alarmed him. The Chessori ships enfolded each squadron without retaliation, then began pounding away at the smallest ships. There was no return fire, and those small ships were gone within the hour. A large Chessori ship in each contingent attached a tractor beam to a cruiser, then began a labored effort to drag the cruiser somewhere.

Krys did not understand the symbology on the screen, but she understood there was a problem. Why wasn't Jast fighting back? Within the net on the fighter, the crew was not only angry, they were perplexed, but all they could do was observe and surmise, all to little effect.

When the last fighter fell, Tarn approached Stven within the net. "Clearly, their guns are useless," he said. "That means ours are as well. Got any ideas, Captain?"

"None at all. We'll stay here as ordered, at least until it's over, then we'll head for home."

"May I make a suggestion?"

"Any input is appreciated, Ensign. Nothing here makes sense."

"The Chessori know we're here, sir. We'll have plenty of warning if someone approaches from within the system, but what if someone pops out of hyper right on top of us?"

Stven paused in thought. "Space is a big place, Ensign. The odds of someone coming out of hyper right here are astronomically small, but I sense the rightness of your idea. Perhaps we can cover both eventualities. We can move while we continue observing. We'll lose the tightbeam, but it's not telling us much anyway, not now. Well said, Ensign."

He commanded the pilot to set a new course, and at top speed. The pilot changed course at random intervals to prevent a plot of their course while Stven prepared the jump settings for an instant jump if needed. With an erratic trajectory and undefined starting point, the jump would take them to an unpredictable location within interstellar space, but it would get them away from here safely.

Several hours later a lone Chessori trader materialized from hyperspace near their original location. Stven did not hesitate. He executed the jump, then he and the pilot quickly executed several more jumps before placing the ship on a homeward trajectory. Everyone but the pilot left the net, dazed at what they had observed during the past hours.

Stven's neck drooped. "Three squadrons taken with barely a shot. Before today I would have said it was impossible."

Tarn, too, was at a loss, but he had learned to consider each word of his orders. He wasn't sure they were done at Dorwall. "Let's go back," he suggested.

A puff of smoke escaped from each of Stven's nostrils. Ordinarily, he would have been mortified, but in this case he didn't care. His focus was the mission. Everyone else soon found themselves fanning the air with their hands. "We can't risk capture or destruction," he said, as he considered. "On the other hand, Admiral Chandrajuski needs to know what happened here, and we're the only ones left to tell him."

"Agreed, sir. If we go back, the Chessori can't possibly know where we'd come out of hyper. We can make sure it's light minutes from any activity. We might learn more."

Stven's purple eyes stared hard at Tarn while he considered. "They've got some kind of weapon that neutralizes ships. We don't know its range."

"It may neutralize people as well," Tarn added. "We lost the audio from the cruiser. It was as if no one was left alive."

"Return is risky," Stven said. He focused his gaze on each of them, Krys last. "And you, My Lady? You have special value to someone or you would not be here. Is your value something that cannot be risked?"

"I barely understand what's happened," she replied. "Has our mission to rescue Daughter ended?"

"It has. The Chessori defeated Admiral Jast. They are, as we speak, destroying the remains of his fleet. Our mission now is two-fold: return you to Admiral Chandrajuski, and bring back as much knowledge of what has transpired here as we can."

"I have reason to believe that Daughter escaped from here," she said. "I believe she remains in danger, but I have no idea how to help her. I agree that any knowledge you can bring back to the admiral is to everyone's benefit. If the risk of returning to Dorwall is acceptable to you, it is acceptable to me, as well."

Stven did not hesitate. He turned to Tarn. "We don't *know* that our weapons are useless. If you see anyone out there at all, open fire at maximum possible range."

"Aye, sir."

They went back into the net. Half a day elapsed before they materialized within the fringes of Dorwall's system, and they did so far away from their previous position and well above the plane of the ecliptic. Nearby space was empty of other ships. Stven had his sensors ready to go and set the recorders in operation immediately. They were so far out that it was difficult to discern what they were seeing, but he recorded anyway. After some twenty minutes, he jumped away.

They repeated the process several times during the next few days until he was convinced that all the Empire ships were lost. Then Stven jumped away and headed for Centauri III.

They'd been gone for two months, and it would be a long three weeks of jumping until they reached normal space around Centauri III. Then, it would be another three weeks until they reached port. It was a sad and chastened crew that set course for home.

Stven spent hours in the net reviewing the sensor recordings, but he learned little. He believed it would take experts to decipher what had happened. He, Tarn, and Krys met for dinner in the tiny mess, but conversation was a struggle. Everyone was still trying to untangle events at Dorwall.

"Did you get anything from the recordings?" Tarn asked.

"Darn little. It looked like they gave up on the tractor beam. Cruisers and frigates are far too large to maneuver that way."

"It's pretty hard to kill a frigate, let alone a cruiser. They'll be at it for days. I wonder if anyone is alive on our ships?"

A puff escaped from one of Stven's nostrils. This time he was mortified. "Oh, sorry!"

Krys had been through it before, though not often. Her time on Rrestriss had been under much, much more sedate conditions. The Rress there were seldom stressed like this. She looked at Stven. "I'm not much on orbital mechanics and such, but you say they used the tractor beam on the cruisers, then switched to the frigates? And these ships are very hard to destroy?"

Stven's long neck moved his head gracefully up and down in a nod. "Then they just gave up on all of them. The fighters were destroyed days ago."

Krys looked to Tarn and discovered him studying her. He'd been around her enough to know that something was on her mind. "Like I said, I'm not much on mechanics, but I'm pretty good with people issues." She paused, then said softly, "What if they didn't give up on the big ships?"

Stven peered at her. "My Lady?"

"I'm not 'My Lady.' I'm Krys. Got it?" The long neck nodded again. "What if they only wanted to change the trajectories of the ships?

What if they succeeded with the cruisers, then moved on to the frigates. Could they have captured them for study?"

A puff escaped from each nostril this time, and Tarn's chair crashed over as he jumped to his feet. The two officers stared at each other, then at her, then they just took off for the bridge. They returned an hour later.

"Well?" she said as they joined her with solemn looks.

"They're on course to crash into a moon. All of them," Tarn spit out.

"Gods!" Stven's fist hit the table hard. "I hope the crews don't know what's happening."

The crew of the fighter was a wreck. The only ones with anything to do were Stven and the pilot as they rotated shifts and calculated jump after jump. It wasn't long before Tarn was assigned a shift as well. Krys found it impossible to concentrate on her studies, but she continued her normal routine of meditation, a life saver in times of turmoil. She even got Tarn to try it, bringing laughter to the surface for both of them as he struggled through the required exercises. She thought he'd give up, but he didn't, and both of them enjoyed the time together. His spirits rose a little, but the rest of the crew continued struggling with internal feelings, and they were losing the struggle.

She couldn't stand it any longer, so she called Stven to the crew mess. He arrived quickly, concerned that something had happened.

"You're captain of this boat," she said. "You have a morale problem."

Stven's body sunk to the floor, his long tail curling up beside him as his neck lowered in shame. "I know. It's not my finest hour. I suppose I should do something. We're supposed to be running battle drills from time to time, but it just seems like too much effort. My apologies, Krys. Thank you for reminding me."

"And I can just imagine the drills," she said. "Pretty desultory. How about something different for a change?"

"What did you have in mind?" he asked guardedly.

Tarn wandered in and joined them. At her words, a stricken look filled his face. "No knitting lessons," he pleaded. "And I've already done my stretches for the day."

"Only once. We'll move to twice a day starting tomorrow, but I have something else in mind. Want to teach me to fly, or maybe how to shoot?"

Two sets of eyes opened wide. Stven's neck swung toward Tarn, and their gazes locked.

"Did you put her up to this?" Stven demanded.

"No, but we talk while we exercise. She said an offer of some kind was made when she came aboard."

Stven just rolled his eyes. "She can start with the net, see if it works for her."

"We'll have to be careful. We're in space, and she might not adapt."

"We can simulate a planet to get started."

"Guys," she demanded, "I'm in the room, too. Talk to me, not around me."

Stven looked at her, and she sensed a trace of interest growing within him. This would surely be a break from routine. "Such a thing is not lightly undertaken, and you're not an Empire crewmember. Admiral Chandrajuski might skin me alive."

She smiled. "He will not. I'm officially a Friend of the Royal Family."

More puffs from Stven, though Tarn already knew. His hand swung lethargically to clear the odor.

"Is that adequate credential?" she asked, waiving at the air as well.

Stven considered her words as he stared at her. "Maybe."

"It's more than adequate. Let's go," she demanded.

The dragon held up a hand, the claws well sheathed. "Tell me, what were you doing on Rrestriss during those seven years?"

"Going to school."

"Which school? Can you name any professors?"

"Hmm. You want to know if I am who I say I am."

"I must, Krys."

"Very well, though one would think my presence here at Admiral Chandrajuski's order would be sufficient proof." From around her neck, she pulled the chain holding the locket Daughter had given her all those years ago. She handed the locket to Stven. "It was given to me by Daughter," she said. Tarn was ogling the piece, so she took it from Stven and placed it in his hands. He studied it, then returned it to her without comment.

"You, of course, know of Imperial Senator Truax." Stven nodded, seeming a bit uncomfortable all of a sudden. "I was his ward during those seven years, and his student when his schedule permitted. I lived with him during the first few years."

The beautiful purple eyes stared at her, but silence prevailed. She looked to Tarn, but he just raised his eyebrows, indicating he did not recognize the implications. When Stven found his voice, he asked with disbelief, "You were the ward of the most revered man among the Rress? How did this come about?"

I'm sorry, Stven, but I'm sworn to secrecy on this matter."

"Yet it had something to do with our presence at Dorwall, didn't it," he stated.

"It did. By the way," she added looking at Tarn, "It looks like the outcome has been changed."

"So far. It's never far from my thoughts, My Lady."

In exasperation she said, "I am not My Lady!"

"In that you're wrong," Tarn said, standing up, then bowing.

Stven, too, backed away from the table to lower his head and front feet. "I cannot say what will happen once we reach Centauri III, but you're special. Not just to Daughter. You may call upon my services at any time. And now . . . are you ready for an experience you will never forget?"

"If you're ready to be a Rress and teach."

"The AI gets first crack at you, I'm afraid, but Tarn and I won't be far behind. I think everyone will want to help."

Chapter Seventeen

Mike felt free of immediate threat for the first time since the Chessori ship had come crashing to Earth. For Otis and Ellie, it was the first moment without fear for many months. They were free of pursuit, finally. They had bought time for themselves, all the time they needed to do things right for a change.

Though everyone had worked hard for this moment, Mike, Jake, and Ellie had born the burden of intense immersion in the net for days on end. Mike collapsed into his bedroll across the bridge and slept for a solid eight hours. Ellie retreated to her room to spend time with Alexis while Otis and Reba maintained a watch.

When he awoke, Mike's exhaustion remained plain for all to see. Ellie was back in the net when he relieved her, and she looked as bad as he felt. He squeezed her shoulder in thanks as she unplugged, and she responded by putting her arms around his waist and resting her head against his chest. He would have liked to linger, but her hours out of the net were as important to her as were his. He gently pushed her toward the central shaft. She didn't object.

Mike absolutely had to remain sharp if they were to reach Gamma VI. Jake, Ellie, Reba, and Otis teamed up against him, insisting that he shift to a lighter schedule for a few days. He agreed to a full ten hours off duty following each jump, and Reba kept a stopwatch on him to force compliance. He knew she was giving Ellie extra time as well, because she always made sure the bridge screens were activated before he left.

It was not the proper way to relieve the watch, but it worked, and he didn't argue. His navigation could be done any time, but with George gone, Ellie and Jake had to keep a fairly constant watch on *Resolve.* If Mike was out, so was Jake, leaving long shifts for Ellie followed by very brief sleep periods. The work was not hard, but it was tedious, and she had additional demands from her child. Mildred was nanny, not mother. Ellie would allow no one to usurp that privilege.

After three more jumps in the direction of Gamma VI, Mike ordered a time-out for the crew. His last two jumps had not gone exactly according to plan, and Ellie was clearly flogging herself to keep going. *Resolve* was in deep space and not threatened by anyone or anything. They could afford a full day of rest better than they could afford mistakes.

Everyone rested. After a sound sleep, Mike and Jake entered the net briefly to check on the ship's well being, then they made their way to the lounge. The rest of the crew dribbled in over the next few hours, and for the first time since coming together as a crew, they spent a few pleasant hours together socializing.

"So who was Mike Carver before he became a spaceship captain?" Reba asked, her green eyes twinkling. "Were you a scientist or something?"

"Hasn't anyone told you the story?" Mike asked.

"Nope. And I'm ready. I'd like to know more about this kidnapping, too. Why did Ellie choose you?"

"Because they had no one else," Mike answered with a frown. "I'm an architect and a civil engineer. I own my own company. We had just won a contract to build a large, high-rise casino complex in Reno, and I was on my way to present my final drawings when a Chessori space ship fell from the sky right in front of my car. To make a long story short, *Resolve* landed nearby in an effort to take prisoners. I got caught up in the fight, we killed all the Chessori, then Ellie shot me with a stunner. While I was out, they transferred Jake to my body. I woke up a few days later in a padded cell on *Resolve* and got to meet Jake."

Reba's eyes narrowed as he talked. "You mean it was pure chance that brought you here? Were you ever in the military?"

"I was in the Army for a few years."

"Wait, Mike," Ellie demanded. "I, too, would like to know your story. Start at the beginning." As an afterthought, she added, "Please."

"The beginning. Let's see. . ." He blinked a few times as he considered where to start. "I grew up on a cattle ranch in Wyoming," he began. "The ranch butted up against some real mountains, but our land was mostly mile upon mile of wide-open fields. Do you have any idea what life on a ranch is like?"

"No, but I would like to know."

"Responsibility starts early. Chores were never-ending, and my parents held to high standards. The ranch has been in our family for generations. My ancestors on my father's side immigrated from Scotland and didn't stop moving until they reached Wyoming. This was back in the days when they still fought off the Indians. I guess they got tired of that, because Dad married one. They met during college. She keeps the house, helps with chores, and manages the books while he oversees everything else. Horseback riding began not long after I learned to walk, and driving ranch equipment and pickup trucks started as soon as I could reach the controls. By fifteen, I was helping Dad fly his plane and helicopter, though none of it was official, and I never got a license."

"What did you do with planes and helicopters?"

"Find our cattle and horses mostly. It was a *large* ranch, Ellie. I spent many a cold and stormy day on horseback taking care of the livestock, but it wasn't all work. Hunting and fishing were an integral part of life, often shared with family and friends. I didn't know it then, but it was a wonderful place to grow up."

"I've always wondered how people manage to get to school in such remote areas," Reba commented.

"I was home-schooled until high school. I grew up splitting my time between lessons, animals, our land, and machinery."

"What about friends, and what about sports and stuff?"

"I had friends, and we had rodeos and such. I'm pretty good on a horse, and I've tackled a few steers in my time. We had hobbies, too. I used to build, or rebuild, old radios and televisions. When computers became commonplace, I built my own. Fixing cars became a passion, and when I got to high school, my friends helped me restore an old Ford Mustang. That was the only car I've ever personally owned. It's lying beneath the wreckage of the Chessori ship now."

"I'm sorry," Ellie said.

"Don't be. It's a small price to pay for going into space. Maybe you can buy me a new one someday when this is all behind us."

"Maybe I'll give you *Resolve* instead," she said with a twinkle in her eyes.

"Not unless you fix George first," he said with feeling. Her lips pursed. They had a long way to go before George could be replaced.

"Where did you go to college?" Reba asked.

"Arizona State. I majored in civil engineering and added qualifications as an architect after the Army. As much as I like ranching, I like building things more. The ranch will go to my younger sister, Mary. She stayed and has a family of her own now."

"What did you do in the Army?" Reba asked.

"I was assigned to an engineering battalion as a second lieutenant. I spent four years building temporary bridges for tanks and other armored vehicles, erecting training facilities, repairing roads, and taking care of the men and women under my command. The work was not glamorous, but I was good at it, and I wasn't one of those officers who hesitated to get his hands dirty when necessary."

"I'll bet you weren't. Did you see any action?"

"No. I was an expert marksman in the army, and we did a lot of hunting on the ranch, but I never fired a weapon in anger until the Chessori ship fell from the skies that night."

"I hadn't either, not until I met all of you," Reba replied. "How about you, Jake?" she asked looking into Mike's eyes.

Mike told what he knew about Jake, and Jake filled in the blanks. "Jake refers to his people as the Miramor, though everyone else calls them Riders. He knows very little about others of his race, mostly because they never meet. When they reproduce, the parent fissions into two beings, transferring his knowledge to the fledgling in the process. They don't like sharing the same body, so they part as soon as possible, never to be in contact with others of their race again. To me it seems sad, but Jake prefers it that way. I'm his family now."

>You're all my family now, Mike.<

"Oh. Sorry. Jake says all of us are his family now, and since we've all shared in the net, he's right."

"Where's your home world?" Reba asked.

Jake paused in thought. >You know, Mike, I don't know where it is. Wooldroo had no memory of it either."

"He doesn't know," Mike answered.

"How far back do your memories go?" Ellie asked.

"He knows a lot of what Wooldroo knew, though he didn't get the full transfer. He has pieces of memories going back several generations, but nothing beyond that."

Ellie sat up straight as a thought occurred to her. "Jake, do you read minds other than Mike's?"

"He does not."

"This is very important, Jake. One of the attributes of the Chosen is that we never, ever reveal to others what we learn during Testing, at least not without their permission. You and I have been mind-linked on the net. Have you seen into my memories of Testings? And have you, Mike?"

>What's this Testing, Jake?<

>You call it her 'eye thing,' and no, I have not attempted to pry. I have no knowledge of any Testings other than our own."

"Neither of us has, Ellie. We haven't tried, but even if we did, it probably wouldn't work. Can you see into our minds when we're in the net?"

"No. I know whatever thoughts you direct my way, and I sense feelings and emotions. Nothing more. It's not like my Testing."

"It's the same for us," Mike said. Ellie leaned back into the couch, much relieved. "Is it such a big thing?" he asked.

"It is one of the most fundamental matters of State," Ellie replied. "The results of Testings always remain completely private. Our system would fail if they did not." She changed the subject, pointedly. "How did you find your way into the Navy?" she asked Reba.

Reba sensed Ellie's need to change the subject and smiled. "It's not exactly a typical career path for a woman on Earth, and it hasn't been easy. Nor was my childhood easy on my parents. You may have noticed that I have a lot of energy."

"And good looks to go with it," Mike added with a smile. "I bet your parents had their hands full."

"And plenty of sleepless nights when I reached my teens," she said, smiling at the memories. "I was a handful, all right. I told you my father is Senator Morrison from Maryland."

"You did. That must have been an interesting childhood."

She turned to Ellie. "Do you know what it means to be a senator?"

"The Empire has an Imperial Senate. To be chosen as a representative is a great honor."

"It's a lot of work, too, at least on Earth. Some senators keep their families out of the limelight, but my father did not. Mother has been at his side whenever possible, and they dragged me around with them when they could. I can't tell you how many diplomatic luncheons and dinners I've been to. As I got older, late nights at these functions included dancing with people from all over the world. I was quite the socialite."

"Where did you live?" Mike asked.

"Annapolis. I grew up just outside the walls of the Naval Academy. The sea has been a constant throughout my life, and it called to me. Many a weekend was spent sailing on Chesapeake Bay. I've been at the helm of some pretty amazing sailboats, but my favorite was a tiny Hobey-Cat that belonged to my family. You and the boat are one with the sea on a Hobey-Cat."

"I bet you had good grades, too," Mike said with a glimmer in his eyes. "Or were you a maverick who didn't have time for studies?"

"Straight A's all the way through. I'll never know if Dad pulled strings to get me into Annapolis, but whether he did or not, I earned it on my own. It probably didn't hurt that I knew the commandant, as well. Just one of those social connections, you know?"

Mike grinned. "No, I don't know. The life you describe is totally foreign to me, but the academies look at more than just grades when you apply."

She nodded. "The Navy looks for leadership as much as it looks for good grades. I was on all kinds of committees in high school, and I was captain of the swim team for a year. I majored in mathematics at Annapolis. They tell me I'm a wizard. I also led the debate team, I lettered in swimming, and I won promotion to Cadet Adjutant during my senior year." She smiled reminiscently. "For the first time in my life, demands on my time exceeded my available energy. I had to drop out of swimming."

"And then?" Mike asked.

"I completed a tour of duty aboard an Aegis destroyer as a line officer, then received an unusual award from the Navy, an advanced degree. They sent me to Harvard for an MBA. My promotion to lieutenant came with the assignment as aide to Admiral Trexler, a tremendous boost to my career. It virtually guarantees my promotion to Lieutenant Commander . . . well, it did," she said, wincing. "I had hoped I would get my own ship on my next assignment."

"Admiral Trexler struck me as a pretty sharp guy," Mike said.

"He's a sailor to the bone, and he doesn't hesitate to cross swords with politicians when he sees the need. It's been revealing to be on the other side of that aisle, I can tell you."

"Have you left a family behind?" Ellie asked softly.

"Just my parents. There have been no serious suitors in my life yet."

Mike choked. "You've got to be kidding!"

She smiled at him. "I'm not kidding. Look, I know I'm

attractive. I'd be stupid if I didn't admit it. Do you have any idea what a hindrance that is to relationships?"

Mike looked at his large, work-hardened hands. "Uh, not exactly. It's not something I've had to deal with."

"I have. Most men are afraid of me. I'm not exactly the docile mothering type, you know."

"And that's to our benefit," Ellie said, getting up to give her a hug. Mike stood as well to embrace both of them. Looking to Otis, he said, "We've got a pretty good group here. What's your story?"

Otis just growled, returning Mike's look with that stare cats are so good at.

"Come on, Otis," he said, disengaging his arms from around Ellie and Reba.

"Protectors always stay in the background, Mike. My personal history is not an issue here."

"Do you have a family?"

"I do. My wife is also a Protector. She has returned home for birthing."

"Congratulations! Where's home?"

"Brodor. Raising our children on our home world is a strong tradition that cannot be broken."

Ellie spoke softly. "The timing may have been fortuitous, Otis."

He nodded but remained mute, making it clear he had nothing further to say.

"So what's life like in the Palace?" Reba asked him, trying to draw him out. "Was there much work for a Protector?"

"There is too much work, but most of my time has been spent away from the Palace with Daughter. I have protected her for many years."

"Away?" Mike asked. "You take a lot of vacations?"

"What?" Ellie asked sharply.

"Well, what else? I don't suppose you've ever had to cook or do the laundry or clean a toilet? Have you ever worked at a real job?" he asked innocently.

"I see," she said, resting her hands in her lap.

Uh, oh, Mike thought to himself. He knew this pose well. >I'm in trouble again,< he said to Jake.

>You *think?*<

"You see my life as getting waited on hand and foot, day and night, never lifting a finger," Ellie stated. She thought for a moment, then stood up and came to stand before him, her hands on her hips. "Let me tell you something, Mr. Carver. I have personally visited one hundred thirty-two worlds as the Queen's representative, and I permanently resolved serious disputes on each of them. I have quite a reputation within the Empire. I have a job, a permanent lifetime job, which is more than you have right now."

Mike caught himself sliding down into the cushions of the couch once again. >Oops,< he said to Jake.

>Oops is all you can say? Maybe an apology would be in order. There are lots of things I haven't told you about her. She's right when she says she has quite a reputation.<

Mike did a quick calculation in his head, shook his head and repeated the calculation, coming up with the same answer. "Just a minute," he queried. "You're not old enough to have visited that many worlds unless my math is wrong."

"Which part of your math do you suspect?" Ellie quizzed him, still waiting for an apology.

"Come on! It would take thirty years to hit that many worlds, and that would be pushing it."

"Actually, it has taken many more of your years than that, and I have been pushing it."

"No way! You're not old enough!"

Ellie took pause and backed away from him, a hooded expression on her face. "How old are you, Mike? And just how old do you think I am?"

"I'm thirty-five. You look like you're in your late twenties."

"Thank you! I'm flattered. You would be much closer if you quadrupled that guess." She sat down in a chair to await his outburst. It didn't come. He was too stunned.

The silence lasted a long, long while. Ellie broke it. "I come from a long-lived family, Mike. My life expectancy, provided we survive this rebellion, is around two hundred years. Does that surprise you?"

"I guess it shouldn't," he answered, shaken. "You don't look like you're middle aged."

"I'm not. I forgot to mention that years on Triton are equal to about two of your years."

He did the math, it was pretty simple, but he did it again anyway. "Four hundred years?" He looked at her with a blank expression.

"Have you talked with Jake about your own life expectancy?" she asked, looking into his eyes with deep concern.

>What's she talking about, Jake?<

>Sorry. Maybe I should have brought this up sooner. One of the

benefits of having me aboard is that I keep your body healthy. The process of doing that slows the aging process considerably.<

Mike paused, afraid of the answer. >How considerably?<

>We might have as long as Ellie. Not that I expect us to live that long with this rebellion, but if we're lucky enough to survive accidents and wars, we have quite a few years ahead of us . . . Careful, Mike! Just sit back and relax! Breath deep!<

Mike would have fainted without Jake's help. Ellie was by his side in an instant, concern etched across her face. Reba's only comment after Mike finished explaining was, "When do I get my turn, Jake?"

Chapter Eighteen

Reba took to spending long periods in the net. Working with both Jake and Ellie, she worked hard to learn the processes they followed for checking up on the ship. Several months after she'd begun, she stood her first watch alone. Nudging the computers to do their job was not something she could learn without George's help, but when she found something questionable she brought it to their attention when relieved.

Reba's efforts instantly reduced Ellie's burden. She started eating more, some of the strain left her features, and she started working out in the gym again, usually with Mike or Reba for company. Most important to her, she was able to be a real mother again. Alexis and Mildred emerged from their quarters more often and became regular partners during meals. At least one meal a day was attended by everyone. Otis struggled with the idea of leaving *Resolve's* screens unattended, but even he could not argue against the odds of anyone discovering them in interstellar space. Duty was constant, but Reba made certain their lives did not consist only of work.

* * * * *

Months passed. Mike stepped onto the bridge to relieve Ellie. As usual, he found her deeply engrossed in the net, her helmet visor pulled down to cover her face. He studied her as she sat before a console, her focus somewhere in the guts of the ship doing George's job, tidying loose ends. He resisted an urge to plug-in as well, to join her where he could enjoy her company in ways not possible outside the net, but he decided to just watch for a while.

An ordinary person she was not. She wore authority as if born to it, always surprised when instant compliance was not a natural outgrowth of her wishes. Mike was pretty sure she had grown up surrounded by maids and servants, the exact opposite of his childhood. But once past the cold exterior that she wore like a professional, an exterior stripped away by the net, a real person remained, a person who continually surprised him with caring and insight. These past months had probably been the first time she had personally done anything dangerous in her life. It was just a guess, just a feeling, and not all the facts added up, but it was how he viewed her. She had risen to the new demands placed on her, risen well. She had fought back against the Chessori during the battle on Earth, including risking her life in an attempt to save her husband. Going into the net had been frightening for her, yet even against Otis' advice she had sensed the need and responded without hesitation. Since then she had more than carried her weight. Most surprising to him, she had never once complained, something he would not have expected from a rich kid.

She had that way of looking into him that chilled him to the bone, something he never forgot, but she had not threatened him with it since his first day aboard ship. With the aid of the net, a place where feelings and personalities could not be completely hidden, he had grown to know this woman for who she was. He knew when she was happy, frightened, mad, or just plain scared, and he knew her as she seemed at the moment, focused like a laser.

She knew him, as well. She had seen him at his best and at his worst, his highest and his lowest. She had seen his uncertainties, and she had supported him when she sensed the need.

Looking at her now, taking the time to look at Ellie the person rather than Ellandra of the Chosen, his lips pursed. He was troubled. He liked being around her, and he especially liked being touched by her. Their embraces had become more frequent, and those embraces had gone beyond the simple mechanism of two distant souls supporting each other. Her embraces had become personal, and he sought them out, not for support but for sharing. He sensed the same need from her, the same deep contentment that came from personal contact.

In any other circumstances it would be a wonderful, wholesome exchange, but for them . . . well, it was just plain wrong. They were aliens to each other. They were not of the same species. Because of that alienness, he had to corral the feelings for her that were building within him.

The thought saddened him. She had become special, very, very special . . . no! He had to smother thoughts of her that included anything other than friendship. Anything else was pure selfishness on his part. She was not of his species. It was okay to like the person she was, but it was not okay to entertain thoughts of any other relationship with her.

But she could still be his friend. And he could still offer support, knowing they both needed that support. He stepped over to her, placed his hands on her shoulders, and began to massage straining muscles in her back, shoulders, and neck. Her back arched, and she leaned back into his hands. Then she removed the helmet, keeping her eyes closed, enjoying. Eventually, she stood up and turned to him, placing her arms about his waist in an embrace, burying her face in his shoulder.

Mike responded with his own embrace, knowing that he should not. "This is wrong, Ellie," he said softly into her ear.

She leaned back from him, a questioning look in her eyes. "What's wrong?"

"We're aliens to each other. I don't know what this is doing to you, but what it's doing to me is wrong."

She closed her eyes with a smile and pressed closer. "It's not wrong, Michael. Does Jake think it's wrong?"

"Uh, he's as confused as I am."

"Then perhaps you two should do some homework."

"What do you mean?"

"I mean you should do some homework, that's all."

"Hey, you two! Who's minding the ship?"

Mike opened his eyes to discover Reba jumping off the central shaft with her radiant smile and a feisty look in her eyes. Ellie turned in his arms to look at Reba, then turned back to Mike and pressed closer. He was looking at Reba in embarrassment when Ellandra of the Chosen reached up and took his face in both of her hands. She kissed him lightly on the lips. When he responded, her kiss grew more insistent for a moment, then they both parted in shock.

"Uh, excuse me, I'm not needed here," Reba said, stepping back into the central shaft.

Mike and Ellie barely acknowledged her. They stared at each other, both at a loss for words, and an uncomfortable silence filled the bridge. The silence grew, neither knowing what to say.

She broke the silence. "I won't say I'm sorry if you won't." Then her lips trembled. The smile disappeared. "What is happening?" she mumbled to herself.

"Ellie, come here, wrong or not," he demanded, holding his arms out. She raised her arms, then lowered them tentatively, uncertain. His arms remained out. She looked him in the eye, then slowly, almost mechanically, she stepped into his embrace. The moment they touched, she softened, melding into his arms, sensing the person she knew from the net, sensing Mike Carver, the barbaric Earthman whom she knew it was impossible to love. They both, for very different reasons, knew such feelings were wrong, but reason had nothing to do with their feelings.

Chapter Nineteen

Mike drove himself relentlessly as he computed jump after jump. His fear of a gross miscalculation never left his thoughts – a major blunder by him could kill them all. Every time he stopped to think about what he was doing, that he was navigating a starship across unimaginable gulfs in which light years were bandied about as easily as miles on Earth, his stress became apparent to everyone.

Jake was a lifesaver, always tuned-in to Mike and always there with the right words or feelings to help him. A dark sense of foreboding had begun clouding Mike's thoughts, and it was growing darker as they moved farther and farther from Earth.

>Hey, want some help?< Jake asked.

>I sure could use some. I'm starting to lose the picture. Can you do the driving for a while?<

>Just tell me what you need.<

>I need you to take us to our jump point while I finish up the computations. It's right here,< he said, showing Jake the coordinates. >We need to be there in, let's see . . . twenty-eight minutes. I got a little behind. Can you speed us up, then make whatever adjustments are necessary to hit the insertion point on the proper vector and at the right speed? Here are the numbers you need . . ."

Ellie and Reba pitched in as well, knowing the responsibility for reaching Gamma VI rested squarely on Mike's shoulders. They frequently massaged straining neck and back muscles as he sat sprawled in his seat.

In spite of having left the Chessori scout behind, they lived in constant fear of an enemy fleet suddenly filling their screens. Mike always had a short jump programmed and ready, something he could execute two or three times if necessary to confuse the fleet. He thought about making a few really long jumps to Gamma VI, but Otis and Jake convinced him it was too risky. They would have to keep plodding along as best they could. They had already used up a large amount of luck, and further tempting fate was not the best way to protect the Heir.

Resolve needed George to manage her systems. Since he was gone, Jake, Ellie, and Reba covered for him, keeping the screens alive, keeping the net alive, and keeping every system on the ship in the best working order they could. That meant opposite shifts for Ellie and Mike, leaving little time for the enjoyment of merged feelings on the net and very little time out of the net. Mike began sleeping more and more, and he needed little help from Jake to do so.

The crew practiced battle stations regularly at Reba's insistence, and they stayed tight. Whenever she found someone to practice on, she demanded language lessons, as well. The lessons, in addition to teaching her a smattering of Galactic High Standard, provided needed companionship. Ellie, too, demanded companionship, as much as everyone would give. Mike was learning the language quickly, so quickly that he wondered if Jake was teaching him in his sleep. He didn't ask, just left Jake to his own devices.

They remained a good team and got even better. Ellie allowed no opposition to her ultimate ownership of *Resolve*, and though hers was the choice of destination, Mike commanded. Everyone participated with ideas and suggestions, but he made decisions when general consensus could not be reached. Jake supported Mike in everything, and he supported everyone else when on the net. Reba ran interference, bringing the right amount of humor into conversations when necessary, letting herself be the brunt of jokes, making everyone laugh, and just generally offering encouragement. To her, they were always on schedule, always on plan, always making forward progress. She never tired, never allowed negativity, and she aggressively insisted everyone be their best.

Otis spent most of his time prowling the ship, making adjustments and minor repairs here and there. Reba took to spending time with him at his gun, receiving lessons in manually operating the gun, and they talked as well. Both were warriors, and as such, they had many common interests.

"What does it mean to be a Protector, Otis?"

"There are many species who offer protection within the Empire," he replied. "True Protectors, and I include Guardians in this category, come only from my home world of Brodor. We are in great demand."

"I suppose it takes many years of training."

"Not necessarily. More than anything else, it takes growing up on Brodor. The planet is quite primitive compared to Empire standards, but it's the way we choose to live. To eat on Brodor, one must catch one's meal, and the creatures that inhabit our world have evolved just as we have. Many are clever, they often operate in packs or teams, and they are always hungry. Reflexes, cunning, and a strong survival instinct are needed by everyone who survives on Brodor."

"What about your children? How do they survive?"

"They don't all survive. We have our methods for introducing them to their inbred talents and we teach them thoroughly, but it is still a matter of survival of the fittest."

"Is everyone from Brodor a Protector?"

"No. Not even most. Those that choose the path of Guardian are given the necessary training, then they go out with other more experienced Guardians to fine-tune that knowledge. A small percentage of Guardians make it to the level of Protector, and they receive the most challenging jobs."

"Who hires you?"

"The rich and powerful. Our services do not come cheap. We do, on occasion, offer free services to those we choose."

"Can you teach me any of your skills?"

Otis pondered her question. "I cannot teach you to be a Guardian, but I might be able to help you improve your skills. You're already good with the guns. Do you have any other special skills?"

"I took some basic self-defense classes. Maybe you could help me improve in that area."

"No. You would only get hurt, but you will never need to know how to fight a Great Cat, not so long as you continue supporting Daughter. My people will never turn against the Empire. However, I could probably help you in other areas. You've probably never fired a hand-held blaster. Now that I think about it, Mike hasn't either, not ours. You could both use some training. I wonder if he has the time?"

"He's pretty busy, but with our species a change of focus can be refreshing. It might even help him focus better on his navigation. He's been having a little trouble there lately."

"What do you mean?"

"Just a comment Jake made. Mike's gotten pretty good at computing jumps, but Jake has noted a few mistakes recently. He actually missed an entry point yesterday and had to abort the jump. All the calculations had to be reworked. It's probably nothing to worry about, but a change of pace might do him good."

"Then we'll ask. *Resolve* has a special room for training with weapons of all types. Daughter, too, is in need of a refresher. We can work on various weapons, and we can discuss weak points on body armor, that sort of thing. It's a good idea, Reba."

What has Daughter done for all these years?" Reba asked, changing the subject. "Why has she visited so many worlds with problems?"

"The Chosen are few in number, very special, and deeply bound by duty, Reba. Imagine the needs of hundreds of thousands of worlds, needs that can be satisfied by only a few individuals. The demands of Empire are constant, forcing the Chosen to be selective and demanding of everyone around them. Other than their closest advisors, everyone has a hand out, always asking for something. Friendships within that setting are always suspect. Daughter and the other Chosen of her line represent the Queen when they travel, and those travels are usually at the request of the world, or worlds, in question.

"The Chosen resolve disputes, Reba. When all other means have failed, the Chosen are called. Worlds that request royal assistance do so under one set of grounds only: they must agree to abide by the decision of the Chosen. The Chosen study the dispute from all angles, they interview the principal parties, and they Test those of their choosing. Results of those interviews and Testings are never made public. Then the Chosen decide, and there is no recourse to the decision."

"It's all up to one person, and there's no recourse? That's brutal."

"It is brutal. Because of that, the decision to call the Chosen is always a last resort."

"Wow. That's a lot of power for one person. Too much power, I would think."

"I, too, would not want such power. The list of Chosen is very small, Reba, and it is only to them that we give this power. Surprisingly, I think you would find that the Chosen do not want it either. I know for a fact that Daughter considers it a yoke about her neck, and she would gladly relinquish that yoke if she could, but she cannot. It is her calling. I, personally, am grateful for the Chosen and their Knights. Without them and their unbiased decisions, the Empire would not have lasted for the many thousands of years that it has."

"Knights? You have knights in your Empire?"

"A few. Their numbers, too, are limited, very limited. They represent the Chosen when they travel."

"Wow. How cool! Does Daughter have her own Knights?"

Otis squirmed, as if he did not want to answer the question. He finally relented. "She does. Only one."

"One! How many Knights are there?"

"At any given time, around 100."

Reba paled. "In the whole Empire?"

Otis nodded. "There are not enough Chosen to go around. Knights of the Realm represent them whenever possible."

"Who is her Knight?"

"He shall remain unnamed, at his own choosing," Otis declared. "Few besides the Chosen even know who they are. They do not advertise their presence. But know this: The word of a Knight is the Queen's word on all worlds. Their decisions cannot be overruled by anyone but the Chosen. Even Imperial Senators must abide by their decisions."

"Are they elected?"

"No. Each one is hand-picked by a Chosen, usually by the Queen herself. In every case, the Queen must confirm the Naming of a Knight. Without Knights, the burdens on the Chosen would be unconscionable."

"And because of those burdens, because of those decisions that cannot be appealed, Ellie has to surround herself with Protectors."

"Always. I've seen some very creative resolutions engineered by the Chosen, and as often as not, neither side wins or loses. The Chosen are revered for their fairness, and in some cases both sides win, but definitely not in all cases. There will always be some who consider themselves cheated. We Protectors have been very, very successful at keeping them at bay, but Daughter is well trained to protect herself, as well."

"She is?" Reba asked in astonishment.

"Very definitely. That's why your suggestion for a refresher course is such a good one. There is no telling what dangers we might encounter over the coming months, but we could easily be walking into a trap. I cannot bring myself to believe Daughter and Alexis are the last of the Chosen. It simply defies logic that someone could wipe out the whole

Family, but I have never seen Daughter wrong when it comes to matters of State, and she believes the others are gone. It's one of her Talents, one of the Talents shared by the Chosen. The Empire has not chosen them without good reason."

Mike, Reba, and Ellie jumped at the chance for a change of pace, and the additional challenges, so at odds with their other duties, sharpened their minds as a result. Since they were in deep space, there was little threat of discovery, so Otis manned the bridge while all three devoted a full hour to hard exercise each day. Then Otis joined them to direct practice with firearms of all kinds, and they spent a fair amount of time on physical defense. The training room was well-equipped with holographic projections of various combatants and settings, and Otis directed practice with short and long-barreled blasters that simulated the real thing. Since everyone was an accomplished shot already, it didn't take long for accuracy to reach an acceptable level. They even practiced with flash grenades and stun grenades. Then Otis took them out into the corridors to practice the skills needed to defend against borders, something they would not need, but the skills were similar to what they would need to defend a building if they came under attack after landing.

Otis' gravest fear was that they might walk into a trap on arrival at Gamma VI. Once ensconced within whatever quarters were available, they would be easy prey, and the Heir's normal complement of Protectors was not available to defend her. It could be just the few of them if such an event ever came to pass.

Chapter Twenty

Though the work was never-ending, their escape from the squadron tracking them heightened everyone's outlook on the voyage, and the ship was a happier place. Ellie changed during those months. For the first time in her life she had friends who had not the slightest care in the world about her position within the Empire or her wealth or her family. She had found friends who liked her for herself. She and Reba became fast friends in spite of the limited time they had together, confiding in each other like schoolgirls whenever they were alone. On the net, Jake seemed like a favorite brother, someone who accepted her but was not afraid to question and teach. He understood her fully and respected who she was, and he loved her for herself.

Ellie and Mike, whether plugged-in, stealing a brief respite from alternating watches, or working out together, existed on two levels, oftentimes simultaneously. One level included Reba, Jake, Otis, Alexis and Mildred; the other level included only themselves. Eye contact was frequent and significant, touches lingered, hugs survived the crew's scrutiny, and only they felt like their feelings were invisible to the rest of the crew.

Reba cornered Mike in the lounge as he came off a particularly frustrating watch, slamming a tray of food down before him and setting a place for herself, as well. "Okay, Mister Carver," she announced. "We need to talk."

"What?" he stammered, his thoughts elsewhere and caught totally off guard by her threatening body language. "So I missed the jump entry point. It's not the first time, and it won't be the last."

"You can do it over again tomorrow. That's not what I'm talking about. You're a typical male, as near as I can tell. I just want to wake you up to the fact that your princess has a fragile side to her that you might not be aware of. Do you have the slightest idea what you're doing to her?"

"What are you talking about? We're friends, good friends. That's all we can be. We're aliens, Reba. I like her, alien or not, and I like liking her. I know you do, too."

"That's why we're having this conversation. I like her a lot. I don't care who she is or was or what she will do in the future or whether her civilization survives or not. I like her." Reba looked at him in exasperation. "Look, I'm not blind, nor is Jake. We talk on the net, you know." She paused, remembering where she'd come from and amazed at what she had just said.

"Be careful, Mike. Your princess tries to come across as stronger than granite, but she has a fragile side. Have you seen it?"

"I have. Ever since she came into the net, she's had to hide a dark hole in herself. I don't know what's in there, but it's something she protects. I don't think she's even aware she's doing it."

"Well, hallelujah! A man with feelings. Too bad you're taken!"

"What do you mean, taken?"

"Have you looked for that black hole she's been protecting lately?"

"No, I guess I'm just used to it. Besides, I've been busy, or hadn't you noticed?"

"You've been busy in more ways than one. Next time you run into your princess on the net, check out that black hole. I'm not sure it's there anymore."

Chapter Twenty-one

The months churned by. Shipboard routine, though demanding, became monotonous. Each jump led to another, and not every jump went according to plan. Mike flogged himself to keep going, and they did keep going, but instead of getting better, he began making mistakes. When two jumps in a row went awry, Ellie went to Jake while they were both in the net.

"What's going on?" she asked him in private.

"I don't know. There's not much about him I don't know, but when the problem is something he doesn't know himself, I'm at a loss."

"Is he tired?"

"Not physically. I help with that when necessary. He's not focused."

"Is the stress getting to him?"

Jake considered. "I don't think that's it. He actually likes working under stress and meeting deadlines. It's something a lot deeper than that. I just can't put my finger on it. It's like he's uncomfortable with his life or something. Things aren't fitting the way he needs them to fit."

"Is it me?"

Jake put a virtual arm around Ellie's shoulders. "Definitely not.

If anything, he's clinging to your friendship like a lifeline, and he's driving himself to keep from letting you down."

"I'd like to help, but I can't help him with the jump calculations."

"You have other talents, My Lady. Perhaps you can find a way to use them if he doesn't figure it out on his own, but unless you can offer meaningful help, I suggest you let him be. I have confidence in him that he'll work it out."

"I'll think on it, Jake."

She did think on it, deeply. Mike had done everything he possibly could to help her and the rest of the crew, but so far it had mostly been a one-way street. The crew rarely found ways to help him that showed, and maybe that was the problem. She considered her own resources. She had Talents, she had intelligence, and she was a problem-solver. How could she use those resources to help him?

In the end, she decided they needed to talk. She came on duty early and joined the net, waiting until he completed the jump he was working on. As soon as the jump ended, she was ready. Jake waited silently by her side.

"Are you done?"

"Almost. I have to see if we came out where I hoped we would come out."

"Can you take a break?"

He sighed. "Sure! What's up? Is there a problem?"

"Yes." She approached the virtual Mike Carver and put her arms around his neck. She had his full attention.

"Uh, what's the problem?"

"You're the problem."

"Me? I'm fine."

She let a hand caress his face. "Something's bothering you, Mike. I don't know what it is, nor does Jake. Do you?"

"I'm fine. Let me get back to work."

"You're not fine. You're having to drive yourself to get anything done, and your performance is slipping. Jake and I both see it. Why?"

Mike squirmed. "This stuff isn't easy, you know."

"It's difficult and demanding. It needs you at your best. We need you at your best, but you're not there, Michael. What's the matter?"

He knew she was right. His performance was slipping, but he didn't have a clue what the problem was. All he knew was that he wasn't having fun anymore. He closed his eyes for a moment, then just left the net.

Ellie joined him moments later. She took his hand and led him to the lounge. No one was minding the ship, but they were in deep space and there was little risk of discovery. She sat him down on the couch, then sat beside him.

"Can you talk to me?" she asked.

He smiled. "If there's one bright spot in all of this, it's you. I won't let you down. I'll work through whatever it is that's bothering me."

She smiled in return. "Thank you, Michael. Can I be Daughter for a little while?"

He frowned. "Why?"

"Because I want to help, that's why. And because Daughter and Ellie both need you at your best. You're struggling, and Daughter might be able to help."

He rubbed fists into tired eyes. >Did you put her up to this?< he asked Jake.

>No, but now that she's noticed, I'm relieved. I thought it was just me that was worried. You're not your usual self.<

He blinked, then turned his attention back to Ellie. "Look, we're all under a lot of stress here. Isn't it fair that my performance suffers?"

"Jake tells me you thrive on stress."

"Not this level of stress. Look at it from my point of view. We're basically lost in space, we're at war, none of us is right for our jobs, I'm still adjusting to having Jake on board, and who knows what's waiting for us on the other end of all this?"

"Jake and I both know that's not the problem. You've dealt successfully with everything that's been thrown at you, and there's no reason to believe you won't continue to do so. They're just problems, Mike, and you work through problems. I suspect we're dealing with something a little more fundamental. Is it me?"

He closed his eyes. When he opened them, he put his arm around her shoulder and leaned toward her. "I shouldn't be saying this, but you're the one bright spot in all this. Maybe I'm just worried about it all coming to an end. All I know is that I'm not having fun anymore, and that scares me."

She closed her eyes, savoring his words, then gently pulled away. She was Daughter now, and she had a problem to solve. She would not let her feelings interfere. "Why does it scare you?" she asked softly.

He looked away from her guiltily. "Because I've seen it before in others. It's called burn-out, but there's no way I can be burned-out.

We've only been at this for six months or so, and the challenge is still there."

She considered his words. "Take me out of the equation for a moment, and take out your concerns for the future. If you can, forget for the moment that we're even on *Resolve*. If you could have anything you wanted, what would you like most right now?"

He studied her, sensing her insistence. He leaned back in the couch, wondering what it was that he most wanted. Ellie had asked him to forget her and to forget the ship. That only left home, so he let his thoughts return to the life he'd known back home.

Ellie waited in silence. What she observed was Mike leaning back in the couch with his eyes closed. After a time, though, she saw him lean forward with a blissful look on his face, his eyes still closed. She saw him reach out with both hands, those hands cupping something only he could see. Then his fingers spread apart slightly, as if he was allowing something to trickle through those fingers. Entranced, she watched as a beautiful smile spread across his face. He opened his eyes and just stared ahead, seeing something entirely within his own thoughts.

"What is it, Mike?" she asked softly.

"Uh, Jake wants to meet with you on the net," he answered absently.

"Later, Jake. Talk to me, Michael. What was in your hands?"

He turned eyes to her that now knew what was missing in his life. His smile remained, but he seemed a little embarrassed. "Dirt."

"Dirt?" she asked, pulling away from him, a lump suddenly filling her throat.

"Yes, dirt." He closed his eyes again, reliving the moment. "If I could have anything I wanted at this moment, I would like to feel brown, sandy dirt trickling through my fingers."

Ellie stared at him, her eyes wide and her mouth hanging open. "The man of dirt," she breathed. "I wondered, but I wasn't certain. Krys was right all along, so right about everything."

Mike opened his eyes and stared a question at her. She reached out and touched his face, her hand trembling. "You are the man of dirt," she breathed.

"What are you talking about?"

"Your presence was foretold in a vision," she answered absently, her eyes still filled with awe.

"What?"

She blinked, then seemed to come back into herself. "A vision, Michael. Some years ago, a Seer, very young and uncertain of herself, shared a vision with me. She claimed to have had a vision of Otis lying beside me in the dirt at the foot of a boarding ramp. Another Great Cat lay beside him, though she believed it was dead. Otis was shooting at something out in the dark. What he shot at she could not see."

"Surely you jest."

"I have never been more serious in my life, Michael. Words accompanied the vision, the words of a riddle. *'You will be so much more and have so much less. They will best you, but a man of dirt will come to your aid.'* It has all come true," she said, shaking her head in wonder.

He had no response to her words. He just stared at her, his eyes blinking from time to time.

Ellie took his hand, looking at it as if she'd never seen it before, feeling its hardened roughness and sensing the grains of sand that, in his mind, it had held. So filled was she with awe that she had no words.

She took his hand and kissed it, then looked into his eyes. "There's more. At the time, the Seer was uncertain of the word 'dirt.' The word she received with the vision was Earth, but none of us knew what the word meant. She said a man of Earth would come to my aid, but she felt that the better description was a man of dirt. We have wondered about it all these years, and now a man of Earth has come to my aid, but I see now that he is a man of dirt, as well."

>Jake, what's a Seer?<

>I thought they existed only in legend. I have never known of one, nor did Wooldroo or his father. According to legend, a Seer is a person gifted with the ability to see things in the future. Daughter's words surprise me as much as they surprise you.<

A cold feeling settled over him, and he shivered. Could the future be proscribed, he wondered? Was everyone in existence marching down a predetermined path, a path that could be foreseen? It was the realm of God, not people, to know such things. He suddenly felt small.

"Such an ability would not be a gift," he said softly. "It's a frightful thing. This galaxy of ours seems to be filled with strange things."

"The galaxy is a large place, Michael. The law of large numbers dictates that strange things are going to occur, and they do. The existence of the Chosen is one of them. The presence of a Seer is a truly rare thing. I hope you get to meet her one day."

"I envision an old crone, bent over with arthritis and leaning on a cane. She has a long, black cloak and a black, pointy hat."

Ellie smiled. "She's still a child, only twenty-nine years old. For the moment, though, you are the issue, not her or her vision. You have a need. You wish to feel dirt running through your fingers."

She sat back in the couch with narrowed eyes, suddenly reminded that this man was truly alien to her. She couldn't imagine a less appealing sensation, yet to him it was something fundamentally missing from his existence here on the ship. She didn't understand his need, but she understood its lack. This was an area where her Talents might be a help.

She stood up to pace as she considered. She wanted to help him, she needed to help him, but she didn't understand. Would he let her try to understand?

She returned to the couch, sitting very close to him. "I have never used my Talents in this manner, but I would like to understand your need. Will you let me into your mind? Will you let me find understanding?"

He cringed away from her. "You want to use your eye thing on me again? You said you wouldn't."

"I said I wouldn't without your permission. I ask this not as Daughter, but as your friend. I would like to know all that I can about my friend, Michael Carver. The need you have is so alien to me that I do not understand it, and I would like to understand. Will you teach me as a friend?"

"What you do is not friendly."

"It can be, Michael. We've been mind-linked on the net, something the Chosen have never done. You know me well. You know me as a friend. Do you still fear me?"

That caused him to pause. He did not fear this woman, not in the least, but he did fear her Touch. It was a truly alien thing, yet it was part of the woman he was coming to love.

Love. He said the word again to himself, tasting it even as he fled from the very idea. She was an alien, and he had no right to love her, yet he did. There had been no physical intimacy between them and there never could be, but he loved this woman. Yes, they had been mind-linked on the net, and he knew her for who she was. In that way, at least, they had shared intimate moments. What she now asked of him was a very different form of intimacy. Her touch only worked one-way. They would not be sharing. He would be giving, and giving of himself completely. Did friends do that?

True friends might. Friendship implied a two-way relationship, one in which both gave and received. He would receive nothing from Ellie's touch, though on second thought he just might. He might receive her understanding, and he deeply wanted her to understand this fundamental need of his, this need to feel dirt trickling through his fingers. He didn't fully understand it himself, but he knew he wanted her to share with him the simple feeling of rightness as dirt trickled between his fingers. If he let her in, would she find it?

"How good are you at this Touch thing?"

"Pretty good, though I have never used it in this manner."

"You might hate me afterwards."

"I cannot hate you, Michael Carver. That I know as surely as I have ever known anything. In all of my Testings, I have learned that each of us, no matter how wonderful and perfect we try to be, has a dark side. In this, I am no different. I do not seek your dark side, Michael, and I will not seek your dark side. I seek only to understand this essential need of yours. And I will see the bright side of you, of that I am certain. May I? I ask this as one who has the Touch, but more important, I ask this as your friend."

>Jake?<

>She's already identified your problem, Mike. We both know what it is.<

>I need to get off this ship. I need to feel the ground under me again, any ground.<

>Just knowing that might be sufficient.<

>It is sufficient, Jake. I know it won't happen immediately, but just looking forward to it gives me a better perspective. I feel energized again, just knowing what's been bugging me.<

>Then it's not necessary to proceed with her Touch. However, know this, as well. As Chosen, she has a reputation for finding creative resolutions. It's what she's good at. You might be surprised.<

>It's a big price to pay for a maybe.<

>Agreed. Consider this, too: she needs you to need her. What better gift can you give to one you love than to fulfill her need?<

>That's pretty deep, my friend.<

>You have everything to lose, and everything to gain. Do you have the courage to test your love?<

Mike scowled, but Jake's words hit home. When he turned back to Ellie, he had made his decision.

She read it in his eyes and gave him a long, hard hug of thanks. Then, she took his head in her hands and reached into his mind. She took her time, letting him get used to the sensation, and giving him time to dampen his fear. When she sensed his acceptance, she moved in further and searched deeply. This need of his was not superficial, but bound within deeply rooted ancestral callings. When she found them, she shifted among them, studying first the perspective of Mike's Scottish ancestors, then his American Indian ancestors. What she learned surprised her. Mike's ancestors had been literally tied to the earth upon which they lived, a tie that comforted with roots anchoring them and defining their place within the larger boundaries of their existence. A sense of wonder enwrapped her when she suddenly grasped the wholeness of that link between the people and their land, and she lingered, savoring the feeling of belonging. Mike's need was not a weakness, it was a source of strength, and she longed to share in it. He was, truly, a man of dirt. His need to feel the earth running through his fingers not only made sense to her, it made her envious.

She had found what she sought, and she understood. She was done. She withdrew carefully and held him while he recovered.

He looked at her with fear in his eyes, afraid of what she might have encountered. She kissed each eye, saying, "Thank you, Michael. You have given me a gift that I shall carry with me always." She stood up. "As with all Testings, I will consider what I have learned as it applies to this issue. It may take a few days."

It did take a few days. How, she wondered, could she apply what she had learned to their present situation? By the third day she had an answer for him. It might not satisfy his immediate need, but in time, if he could let his horizons expand, he would never be away from the land he called his own.

During those few days his performance improved. There were no more mistakes, and the pace of their voyage picked up. Mike was at the helm again, and he had a goal. That goal was no longer limited to reaching a safe haven for Ellie, it included a clear vision of making landfall on a world, any world. Even a short stay would suffice.

Ellie sat him down on the couch in the lounge again. "Mike, I never, ever, discuss my Testings with anyone other than the one Tested. It is one of our rules, yet Jake is a separate being. How do we talk about this?"

Mike's eyebrows rose. "Is it so bad that he can't hear it?"

"No."

"Then say what you will. We have few secrets from each other, and I don't think he's going anywhere."

>Hey, did I hear right?<

>Quiet. Let her have her say. I don't think we need any more advice, I'm already enjoying life again, but she needs to say this. Okay?<

>Okay, but she might surprise you. She might surprise both of

us.<

"Jake's okay with it, and so am I," he said to Ellie. "What did you learn?"

"I envy you, Mike. You two have become friends. It shows."

"Most of the time. We still have our moments."

"As do any who enter into long-term relationships. You seem happier since the Testing."

"Sorry, Ellie. It wasn't the Testing, it was putting a name on what was bothering me. I'm at peace with myself now."

"And I understand why. Your ties to the earth are strong, maybe stronger than you know."

"Until now, I've never been away from the land. I think I might understand myself better because of it. I used the resources of the earth to build homes and gardens and buildings, and I was satisfied with that. Flying spaceships is exciting, and when we started out I couldn't imagine a greater challenge, but I know now that I'll never make it my life's work. The ship is just a tool to take me somewhere. I've been fighting an internal battle, wanting to believe that flying spaceships was the ultimate, but knowing subconsciously that it wasn't. Jake and I have talked about it, and we're in agreement that just knowing has removed a burden. I don't know what lies in store for me, and I hope it includes more travel between the stars, but flying the ship is not the end goal."

"You're saying that getting there is part of the excitement, but your business at the destination is your goal. Michael, what you describe is exactly what I learned about you during your Testing. I'm pleased that we have both reached the same conclusion."

He blinked. "We have?"

"We have. Through your ancestors, you are tied to the earth, strongly tied. Your Scottish ancestors coveted the land upon which they lived strongly enough to fight and die for that land. For most it was a fairly small area of land, but it meant everything to them. Your American Indian ancestors, likewise, believed the land was part of their very identity. For them the world was more open, and the land upon which they lived was something to be crossed from one oasis to the next, from season to season, but they were one with the land, and they, too, fought and died to protect what they considered to be a part of themselves. That oneness with the land has been passed on to you, and it is a wonderful gift."

"You learned all that? I never thought about it like that."

"Your subconscious did, and it was working hard to get your attention. I'm pleased that you have found a way to satisfy it."

"I'm back on track, Ellie. You can stop worrying about me."

"I will never stop worrying about you, Michael, and that is my choice. But I do worry about your future. You still have a long way to go, and it may be a while before you get home. Can you live with that?"

"I can. I'm focusing on one world at a time. Gamma VI works for the moment."

"What if we don't land there?"

"Uh . . ."

"Michael, do you realize that you are reliving some of the most heroic acts of your ancestors?"

"I am?"

"Yes, and they would be proud of you. For both sets of ancestors, serious fighting to protect their lands called for rigorous and sometimes lengthy travel to battlegrounds, but they always returned to the oases they called home after the battles. You are, at this moment, engaged in the same thing. Your journey is long and dangerous, and you hope to return to the oasis of your homeland when it is over. You have endured rigorous demands on your person and performed bravely. The journey is not yet over, but it will be some day. Your story may one day become part of the legends of your ancestors, but you have not yet faced the ultimate demand."

"I haven't?"

"No. Your ancestors were forced to relocate. Michael, they all rose to the demand and expanded their horizons, finding new oases to call home. You, too, can make the same choice."

"What is my choice?" he asked guardedly.

"The whole galaxy, Michael. They crossed their lands on foot, in carts, or on horseback, while you cross yours in a starship. An oasis awaits you at the end of each voyage, in fact, an almost infinite number of oases await you within the boundaries of the Empire. If you can ever learn to call the Empire your home, you will never be away from your homeland, and you will have an unlimited number of oases to visit."

Mike stared into her eyes. "Is that the way it is for you?"

"It is now." Her eyes closed as she felt again the power of the land calling to him. "I never knew it until now, but my home is the Empire, all of it. I seek an oasis at the end of each voyage, but even now, I am home. I am traveling through the lands I call home."

His eyes lost focus as he considered her words. Who was he to call the galaxy his home? He was just Mike Carver, Earthman, and he didn't even consider all of Earth to be his home. Then he sucked in a breath. From this distance, the planet Earth, all of it, beckoned to him.

No longer would he consider the deserts of the Southwest to be his only home. Earth was his home.

Could Earth itself ever become just one home among many? As he wondered, he heard Ellie's sweet voice as if from far away. "Michael, the sand you want to let trickle through your fingers can, if you so choose, become stars, billions of stars that are just as numerous as the sands of your ancestors. If you so choose, you will never be away from your land."

Her words called powerfully to him. His eyes rose to the ceiling and his mind reached outward past the skin of the ship to space and to the multitude of worlds that occupied that space. Could this place become his home? This whole place?

In his mind, his hands reached out through the skin of the ship. Long, ghostly fingers spread ever so slightly, and stars began drifting through them, but he didn't just see stars. Planets filtered through his fingers, worlds with real people living on them, seemingly without end.

His breathing shallowed as wonder filled him. This was not something his ancestors might have dreamed of as they gazed with awe upon the stars overhead, but it was something he could dream of. The ghostly hands filtering through the bright points of light enthralled him.

Yes, he was just a man, one small man, but he sensed a kinship with the worlds filtering through those ghostly fingers. This place might, one day, become his home. All of it. Not yet, he was too small to accept it right now, but in time that might change. He liked the feeling of calling all of this home. It felt right to all of his senses. Here was earth, fire, water, air, and especially spirit, and they all felt true. More than that, here were people, uncounted numbers of people who sought no more than he did. They might look different than him, but in many ways they were the same.

Ellie's words were truly a vision to him, a vision he chose to embrace. It would take time, but his ancestors demanded nothing less of him.

He focused once again on Ellie. He saw a different woman this time, a woman wise beyond her years. "For the first time, I sense the power of the Chosen," he said to her. "You have given me a gift, and I will think on it. You speak true, and I hear your words, My Lady."

She reached a hand out to caress his face. "You have heard the words of a Chosen, but you have heard the words of Ellie as well. I say them with love and with hope in my heart."

He stared into her eyes. "I'm a lucky man to have one such as you speaking of love and hope to me. I will not disappoint you, that much I promise. I don't know what lies ahead for us, but I believe I will, if time is on our side, share in your vision of the people you serve. I, too, would someday like to call your Empire my home. Just give me a little time."

"I shall, and I will be beside you on your journey. The Empire calls to you, Michael, just as it calls to me."

"I don't know about that," he said with a grimace. "I have no talents that the Empire needs. I hope I can convince whoever's in charge to give me a chance. I'd like to hang around for a while."

Ellie smiled. "The choice will be yours, Michael. I can guarantee that much."

"Then I'd better see to getting us to Gamma VI."

Chapter Twenty-two

Stven completed the last jump toward Centauri III and immediately called Sector Headquarters, demanding a tightbeam connection to Admiral Chandrajuski. It took longer than expected, nearly a full day. When Chandrajuski came on the line, he was brusque.

"Report, Lieutenant."

"I can't say much over the comm, sir. We failed. The rest of the ships will not be returning from Dorwall."

Chandrajuski paused to digest Stven's words, then he seemed to sag. "Very well. Make all haste, and report to me in private. Do you carry a passenger?"

"I do, sir. And we have some recordings that need to be examined."

"When time permits. We have some Imperial issues to deal with at the moment. The Palace has fallen."

"Sir?"

"Your passenger will know what I mean. Feel free to discuss it among you." The connection terminated abruptly.

When Stven brought the message, Krys doubled over, weeping uncontrollably. Until that very moment everything she had foreseen, everything she had sensed had been purely speculative. Now . . . now she had concrete proof that a vision, a seemingly impossible vision, had come to pass. She knew at that moment that the Empire and the lives of everyone she knew were changed forever.

Tarn went to her side with an arm around her shoulders, wiping futilely at the tears. He, too, was numb. She had told him of her vision of the Palace devoid of all life, though he had discounted it at the time. Nothing of this nature had ever happened within the memory of Empire. What were they to do? What was anyone to do?

The whole crew gathered together on the bridge for an explanation. Krys was torn. How was she to explain without breaking her promise to Daughter?

"I don't know how it happened, and I can't tell you how I know, but everyone at the Palace is dead," she told the gathered crew. "I believe they were killed."

Stunned silence met her words, then a gunner spoke angrily. "If you know, you must have been a part of it."

"I was not. The source of my knowledge is an Imperial Secret, but I assure you it was not of my doing. I suggest you focus, instead, on what this means to us. What does it mean for the Palace to be empty?"

"He said the Palace had fallen," Stven corrected her. "By that, I suspect he meant the Royal Family, or at least the Chosen. If it's all of them, our way of life is fundamentally changed forever."

"What of the Empire? What of our oaths?" the pilot asked.

"What, indeed?" Stven looked at each of his crewmembers in turn, very solemn. "As officers, our oaths were to the Queen. For you enlisted, it was to the Empire. I, for one, will follow the example of Admiral Chandrajuski, whatever example he sets. I, personally, would follow him anywhere. I hope the rest of you will stand with him, as well. Our duty remains to the Empire, and he is our commanding officer."

Krys almost spoke, sensing what the end of Empire meant to them. She did not believe the Empire was dead, not yet. She felt strongly that Daughter was still alive. She looked to Tarn and sensed he knew what she was thinking. He shook his head slightly, and she heard the message. Her knowledge was for Chandrajuski, no one else.

When they landed on Centauri III, a flitter whisked them to headquarters. Stven was the first one invited into Chandrajuski's office. His meeting lasted for most of an hour. When he came out, he motioned for Krys to enter. "I have been asked to wait here," he said softly as she passed him.

She took one step into the office and stopped, afraid that as soon as she spoke she would be taking a step that meant her life as she knew it was changed forever. The door snicked shut behind her, and Admiral Chandrajuski stared at her from across the room.

"Your visions have been accurate."

She hung her head. "Sadly, I agree. May I invite Ensign Lukes in? There are few secrets between us now."

"He knows you're a Seer? You divulged an Imperial Secret?"

"As with you, there were special circumstances. He has come far since you last saw him."

"Nevertheless, he is not a Friend. Trust has become a valued commodity now, and I speak openly within only a very small circle. He can wait."

"Very well, sir. You know what happened to us. Can you tell me what happed at the Palace?"

"There has been a coup, a masterfully executed coup. Details are still sketchy. The ship I sent with your message of doom arrived at Triton soon after the event. It appears that the First Knight, Struthers, has killed all the Chosen and is ruling in their place."

"All the Chosen are gone?"

"Yes. Everyone at the Palace, and I include here many senior government, military, and civilian leaders, perished in the explosion of a neutron bomb. All life ended within the bomb's effective radius, though the buildings still stand unharmed."

"Surely not all the Chosen were there."

"Three were not. I don't doubt for a moment that his plans took them and the Queen's Knights into consideration. I'm sure they've all been dealt with."

"His plan for Daughter failed, sir."

Chandrajuski started to disagree, then he paused. She was, after all, a Seer. His head lowered to her level from across the room. "The treaty mission to Dorwall was destroyed."

"She's alive, sir. I'm certain of it. Remember my first vision of her? The words that came to me in that vision were, *"You will be so much more, and have so much less. They will best you, but a man of dirt will come to your aid."* I believe the first part of the riddle is now understood."

He considered her words for a long time, then peered into her eyes, searching for something. His wise old eyes blinked slowly, and she sensed he'd found what he was looking for. Softly, he breathed, "Gods, child. Do you know what this means?"

She, too, spoke softly. "It means everything, sir. She is the last of the Chosen. She has a daughter who might one day qualify, but she is too young to be tested."

"How certain are you of her survival?"

"My visions *are* accurate, sir. A man of dirt will come to her aid. I don't know or care who the man of dirt is, but she must be alive if he comes to her aid."

"If you're right, it changes everything. Without a Chosen I am bereft of legitimate leadership. And we will never, can never, fold to Struthers' demands. I've been thinking of declaring martial law throughout the sector. We already have a new governor."

Her eyebrows lifted in surprise. "Already? He must have been waiting in the wings. He'll be one of Struthers' men." Her thoughts went to Daughter and what she would be up against. "It's only one sector, sir. What about the rest of our Empire?"

"What, indeed? It takes months for news to travel. I wish I could tell you I had a plan, but after what you just revealed, I don't. Whatever we do, we must find Daughter. Where is she?"

"I have no idea."

"Will you attempt another vision?"

"I've been trying. I see nothing, though I feel strongly that she lives."

His thoughts turned inward for a time before he spoke. When he did, he spoke with authority. "The timing of this information is fortuitous. Will you stay while I consider a plan?"

"I will do whatever is within my power to help. Speaking for the crew of the fighter, I believe they will, as well."

"Lieutenant Stven said as much. He speaks highly of you."

"And I of him. And Ensign Lukes."

"What happened out there that led you to bring Lukes into the picture?"

"I had a vision of him dying; that's why I divulged my secret. It was his idea to see if I could change the outcome of the vision. I had never considered trying to use my visions to change things."

"Change things! I thought visions predicted unchangeable events in the future. It's a crucial jump of insight. Can you?"

"I think we did. In my vision he was dying, but he didn't die. The rest of his squadron did. Our transfer to the fighter appears to have changed the outcome of that vision, at least as it related to him."

Chandrajuski turned to the windows to stare out at the city. Only he knew where his thoughts were. When he turned back to Krys, excitement radiated from him. "Krys, you've given me, and through me lots of others, hope. Our efforts will focus on restoring the throne. Let me come up with a plan. We'll talk soon."

"Very well, sir."

"In the meantime, your safety is paramount. The best place for you right now is back on your ship. Are you willing to spend a few more days with the crew?"

A smile lit her face despite the chilling events surrounding them. "There's no place I'd rather be. We've grown fond of each other. They'll take good care of me."

"Lieutenant Stven credits you with restoring him to a position of leadership during your return from Dorwall. I rebuked him for that need, but now . . . may I do the same? I'm suddenly invigorated. Things are bad, very bad, but you've given us hope. Now all we have to do is our jobs, which we're very good at. Return with Lieutenant Stven to his ship, and I'll get back to you as soon as I can."

"Would it be appropriate for me to discuss any of this with his crew?"

"You say Ensign Lukes already knows. Do the others?

"No."

"Stven says you've been in the net. Things are not easily hidden within the net. Can you be certain?"

"Pretty certain, sir. When Daughter Tested me, even she could not see my visions."

His eyes widened. "Indeed! In that case I would ask you to refrain from saying anything further until I come up with a plan."

"As you command, sir. Is the proper word 'dismissed?'" she asked with a smile.

His mouth opened in a frightful display of many, many sharp teeth. As with most races, his ancestors had fought their way up the ladder of evolution to supremacy on their home world. He was civilized, but he was not so far removed from his roots that he would turn from a fight. "For you, never. But I have some serious thinking to do."

"Aye, sir."

Chapter Twenty-three

He called for her four days later. Tarn escorted her to the meeting, but he was not invited to join.

"I have a plan," Chandrajuski said without ceremony. "You are a crucial part of the plan."

"Me? What can I do?"

"You can keep doing what you've already been doing, giving people in key positions hope, and with hope, method. Krys, the Empire believes the Chosen are no more. Until we find Daughter, you are the best proof we have of her existence. It's important that we get your message out. I can't tell you how much your knowledge has empowered me to do that which I am good at. There are many, many others in critical positions who need to know. I want you to take your message to the Empire, to other sectors, as quickly as you can."

"Who would believe me?"

"That's the hard part. You have the locket identifying you as Friend, and you'll have a message from me. You'll have one other thing, as well. I'm sending some Great Cats with you for protection. If you can convince the Great Cats, the others you visit will believe them, if not you."

She blinked. "Won't the cats make things a little obvious?"

"Perhaps. But your safety is paramount."

"If I go, I might have to reveal my talent to others."

"Certainly to the cats. If revealing it to others helps convince, then do so, but be careful. Loyalties will be severely tested during the coming months and years. You'll have to choose carefully. I've prepared a list of individuals whom I believe will refuse to support these Rebels. All are personal acquaintances for whom I vouch, but it's not a perfect world. This is a dangerous undertaking, Krys."

She'd never really been in danger, not at any time during her life. The very idea frightened her. "Is there no other way?"

"I'd go myself if I could, but I'm needed here. Daughter will need a base from which to begin the process of restoring the throne. If I can hold out here, I'll give her that base. But an important part of the message you deliver is that I foresee great turmoil within the Empire, and especially within the military. Depending on what actions these Rebels take, some high level officers might find it impossible to hold onto their positions. If they cannot hold, they are to gather up as many resources as they can, and they are to flee with those resources. I will provide locations where they can gather. We will create a hidden pool of resources that Daughter and I can call on as we fight to restore the throne."

"I sense the power of your plan, but I have no authority."

"Authority is no longer the issue. All of us believed our legitimate authority evaporated when the Palace fell. Many are adrift, Krys. Trust is what matters now. You speak convincingly – I'm certain you'll be heard. The leaders to whom I send you will listen. Your job is to convince them that we still have a legitimate Empire and that they still have responsibilities to that Empire."

She felt overwhelmed, adrift. She looked around herself at the walls, the floor, the ceiling of the office, at Chandrajuski and the grand view out his glass wall, seeking something to hold to. She was just one small person, an orphan. Who was she to deal with admirals and governors? Who was she to have the responsibility of Daughter's safe return resting on her shoulders? Could she do it?

The Rebels would surely try to stop her, and they controlled the resources of the whole Empire, unlimited resources. They would find her, and when they did they would strike with overwhelming force.

A chill shook her as the thought repeated itself in her mind: *they would find her, and when they did, she would die.*

She wasn't ready to die.

Chandrajuski represented the call of Empire, but it was a call she shied away from. The needs of Empire were too big, too big by far. She did not feel called in the same manner as him.

But she sensed something else. She sensed a more personal calling. She sensed Daughter's need, a need she could not refuse no matter how terrible the circumstances. During the year they'd spent together, Daughter had become her mother, the only mother she'd ever known. Her mother needed her now, and her mother's need was a call she would answer without any hesitation whatsoever.

She straightened her shoulders and looked at Chandrajuski through suddenly drying eyes. "They'll find me, you know."

The green head with sharp teeth and wise eyes nodded gravely. "It will take time. We'll move as quickly as we can, and I'll give you the best ship and crew I can. I wouldn't ask if I had an alternative."

Her lips pursed. No single ship, not even a full squadron would be sufficient protection once the Rebels found her, and he knew it, but her mother called.

"To be named a Friend of the Royal Family is a two way street. I accept."

He came to her and put his hands on her shoulders. "Many will choose to follow your example, myself included. It's the call to rightness."

"Set the wheels in motion, Admiral."

"I already have," he said softly. "There was never any doubt in my mind that you would accept. I've located a ship – I just have to find a way to pay for it that will not show up on the books. Your mission will remain a secret for as long as it can. The new governor is suspect, and I don't want him tracing you through official sector records. My finance expert is working on it."

She stepped away from him. "Is the fighter not appropriate?"

"No. You need a larger ship, a civilian ship. You're going to pretend you're a rich kid out having fun at daddy's expense. It's being modified as we speak. When it's done, it will be a lot more capable than anyone would expect."

She reached into a pocket and withdrew a money key. "Would this help?" she asked.

His eyes crinkled into a smile. "Even I cannot afford my own ship."

"You could if you had this." She handed the key to him for examination.

"It appears to be unregistered. What is its credit value?"

"It has no limit, Admiral. At least not so long as the Empire exists."

"I've never heard of such a thing. Where did you get it?"

"It has a long history. It was once the property of a Knight. Since then it has passed twice through Daughter's hands. Her only admonition was that it be used wisely."

He stared at the money key with a look of reverence. "The property of a Knight, you say?" She nodded. "Then wisely it shall be used. May I borrow it for a few hours?"

"You may, but I'd like it back. It might come in handy during my coming voyages." She thought for a time, considering the plan he had sketched. "May I make one further suggestion?" she asked.

"That is . . .?"

"Let the record show that I remained with the fleet that went to Dorwall."

He hesitated, then said, "I see the wisdom in that. Would you choose a new name?"

"Not if I don't have to."

"I'll get back to you on this. Now, we have to find you a crew."

"My present crew is perfect, sir. I know them to be trustworthy."

"But they're young, their experience limited. Your mission will require creativity."

"Lieutenant Stven is a Rress. That's high praise all by itself in my book. Ensign Lukes not only knows everything about me that matters, he is trustworthy and competent. As for the rest, I've been in the net with them and have not found them wanting in any way."

"I'll take it under consideration. I'll have to review their files. I might make some changes."

"You said we'll have a civilian ship. Will they have to resign their commissions?"

"Hmm. I don't like the idea of you traipsing around with a bunch of renegades, and military ways ensure clarity of command. On the other hand, you'll be in charge as ship's owner, a decidedly unmilitary arrangement. Let me think on it."

"Then I have only one other request. I'd like to make Rrestriss my first stop."

"Rrestriss! Why?"

"Because Daughter not only needs military forces, she needs the Imperial Senate behind her. I know Senator Truax well. I'd like to invite him along."

Chandrajuski's head swung to within inches of her own. "You're a child, but you speak with wisdom. I haven't thought along those lines.

Consider me admonished."

"I lived with her for two years, then I lived with him, Admiral. My perspective is somewhat different than your own."

"An important difference. I approve your request, of course."

"Then with your permission, I'll put it to the crew. Unless you would like to?"

His clawed hands clenched and unclenched as he considered. "Though we're in crisis, assignment to your crew must be voluntary. It's your mission and your ship, Krys. You're owner, and you'll be beyond any assistance I might offer. See to your crew, but I, too, will give it some thought. And do not return to this office, any of you."

"I understand, Admiral." She turned to leave, then stopped. She had accepted his call, a call that might lead, ultimately, to her death, but in accepting that call she accepted, too, the fact that she was a Seer. She knew that now without any doubt. She had skills, limited though they might be.

She turned back to him. "I'd like to attempt a vision with you. Will you allow me to try?"

He stared at her, then turned away, his legs carrying him gracefully to the glass wall to stare outside. After a time, his fists began batting against each other.

She knew what was going through his mind. She let him consider for a time, then said, "I made the same request of Admiral Jast, sir. He refused on the grounds that he could not lead well if a vision foretold his doom. Look what it got him."

"I, too, fear such knowledge," Chandrajuski said softly, turning back to her. "For the sake of our Empire, you may make the attempt."

"If it works, if I come up with a vision, it will be difficult to decipher. My visions are always confusing. Ensign Lukes provided meaningful insight to my last vision, and I have reason to believe he might be able to help again. May I invite him in?"

Chandrajuski paused. Clearly he did not like the idea of a junior officer's involvement in something so intimate. He stared at Krys for a time, then nodded his head. "You're the expert here. It is your decision."

Tarn came in and stood rigidly at attention just inside the door. "Stand at ease, Ensign," Chandrajuski ordered.

Krys detected no visible change in Tarn's posture. From their months together she knew him well enough to sense his discomfort, and in this particular case she shared it. She had never successfully forced a vision, and most likely she would fail in front of this very important man.

She straightened her shoulders. "Ensign, we're going to try for a vision. You know how it went last time. We'll try the same routine." She turned to Chandrajuski. "Don't be surprised if it doesn't work. I have little control over the process."

He nodded and she took a seat, straightened her back, folded her legs into the proper form for meditation, then closed her eyes.

Tarn stood stiffly, and Chandrajuski questioned him with a look. Tarn stepped to his side and whispered, "She's going into herself, Admiral. Give her about ten minutes, then take her hand in your own."

Ten minutes is a long time to wait in silence, but neither of them wanted to disturb Krys. As Chandrajuski waited, he stared at this child of whom so many were asking so much. In human standards she was dark haired, tall, and thin, just a waif of a thing. She looked like a strong wind would carry her away. Was he asking too much of her? Were her shoulders strong enough?

Only time would tell. The ten minutes ended, and he looked to Tarn with a silent question. Tarn nodded his head, and Chandrajuski approached Krys. He took one of her hands in both of his own, looking anxiously for some sign that something was happening. He saw no change until her eyes opened to stare into his.

"I'm looking through your eyes. You are standing beside a pile of leaves. Before you are two legs of a workman. I can't see his face. You stand together in a forest, each of you holding a rake. You hand him a Knight's Pin."

Chandrajuski backed away from her in amazement, each leg precisely positioned in a smooth, flowing motion.

She held his eyes. "There's more. I sensed words this time."

"Easy to leave, hard to remain. The man of dirt comes to one in shadow. She will fall to the unseen, but Death is not forever."

Silence pervaded the office as each considered the words. Krys hated these riddles that only frightened and confused, that raised only questions. She lifted baleful eyes to Chandrajuski.

"Do you know what it means?"

"I can think of many meanings. If the words apply to me, it seems I must remain here, no matter how hard it becomes. The rest is not clear at all, but it sounds foreboding."

Krys shifted her gaze to Tarn. He returned her stare for a time, then said, "There was mention of a man of dirt in an earlier vision. Do you sense it is the same person?"

She closed her eyes and considered. "I can't be certain, but I think it is. Who is the one in shadow that he comes to?"

Tarn stepped away from the door and paced, then crouched down before Krys. He glanced up at Chandrajuski, almost as if asking permission, then his focus returned to Krys. "Your vision is of Admiral Chandrajuski."

Chandrajuski lifted a foot, then changed his mind and set it back down. "Why would I be in shadow?"

Tarn looked up to him. "I'm just speculating, sir. 'Easy to leave, hard to remain.' Might you be in hiding?"

"In my own Sector?"

"We don't know where this takes place, sir." He turned back to Krys. "Do you?"

She shook her head.

"You said you saw him in a forest. Can you describe the forest?"

"The leaves were quite large and withered. I believe I was in a forest, but I felt like I was indoors. I saw no branches, only the trunks of trees. The trunks of the trees were green."

"I have a forest within my home," Chandrajuski interjected. "The branches of the trees begin quite high above the ground. Those trunks are green. I rake the fallen leaves from time to time. It's a calming endeavor."

She stared at him, considering. "That could be the place."

"I have no Knight's Pin. Where did I get it?"

She stared at him, not knowing.

Tarn's eyes closed for a time as he visualized the exchange in his head. When he opened them, his question was to Krys.

"You said Admiral Chandrajuski handed the Pin to the workman. Did you get a sense of ownership, Krys? Would you say Admiral Chandrajuski was presenting his own Pin?"

Krys closed her eyes, reliving the vision. She shook her head. "I don't think so. It was more like he was *returning* the pin."

"Returning it to the workman. Could the workman have been a Knight?" Tarn asked softly.

"How would I know? All I saw was his legs."

"And his hands and a rake, maybe his boots. You must have seen his hand if he accepted the pin. This is very important, Krys." Tarn turned his head to look at Chandrajuski, then returned his focus to Krys.

"Was the pin open?"

She closed her eyes again. "No, but there is a dim flash of light just before the workman closes his hand around the pin."

Tarn's eyes closed. He rested a hand on Krys' knee and hung his head.

Chandrajuski did not hang his head. His fists batted together, and his mouth opened wide to display his many, many sharp teeth. "She lives," he breathed softly.

"I don't understand, sir?" Krys asked.

Chandrajuski's head lowered toward her. "A Knight's Pin can only be activated by a Chosen. Once activated, it serves as an undeniable form of identification for the Knight. He only has to pass his hand over it to open it. No one but the Knight to whom it is awarded can open the Pin, ever, and if either the Chosen or her Knight are dead, the Pin will not open."

Chandrajuski's head moved even closer to her. "You saw a flash of light. I believe the pin tried to open during the exchange and the Knight quickly closed it again."

Her mouth opened in awe. She looked at Tarn and their gazes locked. No words were needed.

Tarn stood up. "Since this is a vision of the future, the Chosen who activated the pin must be alive. It's as revealing as if you'd seen her in person."

"Daughter lives," Chandrajuski breathed, "just as you told us she did, Krys. What about the rest of the vision?"

Tarn turned back to Krys. "You saw a rake and two legs. Was the Knight a human?"

"Yes. He had two legs, workman's boots, and two hands. One hand held a rake, and the other reached for the pin and took it."

"Took it how? Was it just a normal exchange, or was it hurried?"

She stared at him in amazement. "How do you do it?"

"Do what?"

"Ask just the right questions? The exchange was quick, almost furtive."

"Then the meeting was probably clandestine. Could they have been hiding their actions from recorders?"

"I have no recorders in that part of my home," Chandrajuski said.

"Maybe not right now, but things change. 'Easy to leave, hard to remain,' Tarn repeated. "Might you be a prisoner in your own home, Admiral?"

Chandrajuski stared at him for a time, then his mouth opened to display his many, many sharp teeth again. His closed fists batted against each other. "This is my Sector."

Krys stared at him, then rose. "Consider your own orders, sir, the orders you've asked me to pass along to others. They are to hold for as long as they can. If holding becomes untenable, they are to gather all their resources together and flee. Might you have failed to follow your own instructions?"

"Or maybe chosen to disregard them, sir," Tarn completed the thought. 'Easy to leave, hard to remain.' Which will you choose?"

"Sir," Krys said, "let me remind you that this is all in the future, and I don't know how far in the future it is."

"Still, this knowledge is . . . useful. Your vision is useful."

"We're not done yet, sir," Tarn said, his eyes moving back and forth between the two. *'She will fall to the unseen, but death is not forever.'* Those words trouble me greatly."

"They trouble me as well. Who is 'she?'" Chandrajuski said.

Tarn got up to pace, deep in thought. Krys lost her sense of triumph – she knew who 'she' was. She waited to see if Tarn would reach the same conclusion.

He took a slightly different tack. "Who is the man of dirt?" he mumbled. He turned to Krys. "Could it be Val? Could he be the man of dirt in your earliest vision of Daughter?"

"He came to her aid once before. Maybe he did again, but it doesn't feel right, Tarn. I don't think it's Val."

"We know that the man of dirt comes to Daughter's aid, and now he comes to one in shadow. If he's here, and if he was with Daughter earlier, then Daughter might be with him now. The word 'she' could refer to her."

"I'm certain it does," she answered softly. "She is a thread through several of these visions."

Tarn turned to Chandrajuski. "I wonder if the easy way out might be better, sir."

Chandrajuski backed away from him deep in thought. "What you say might be true, Ensign. If she comes here, it looks as if she might be killed by the unseen. Who are they?'"

"They, or it. The word carries both meanings." Tarn shook his head. "I have no clue, sir. It could be someone in hiding, or even someone in plain view that she doesn't consider a threat. Maybe a traitor."

"Death is not forever," Krys reminded them.

Chandrajuski batted his fists together in frustration. "Unacceptable. Forever can be a long time. We need her now, and we need her alive."

"That's the problem with these riddles, Admiral. They raise more questions than they resolve." She stood up and faced Tarn. "Any more thoughts?"

He shook his head, his gaze moving back and forth between her and Chandrajuski. The mood in the room darkened.

Chandrajuski's focus went internal for a time. When he spoke, it was softly. "The words 'easy to leave, hard to remain,' call to me. They're telling me it is wrong to take the easy way out, yet it seems that if I stay, Daughter dies. We cannot allow that under any circumstances. There is no higher priority than keeping her alive."

Tarn faced his commanding officer, standing rigidly tall. It was not his place to admonish admirals, but he could not leave with the words unsaid. "There's another possibility, sir. What if she falls to the unseen *because* you take the easy way out, because you leave."

Chandrajuski stared at him for a long time. "You present an unsolvable dilemma, Ensign."

"I know. I'm sorry, sir."

Chandrajuski turned to Krys. "Can you offer any further guidance?"

She considered. This truly was a dilemma. Her mind went back to the two years she had spent with Daughter. They had come to a world called Lianli. An unexpected meeting had taken place there, a meeting with herself, Val, Daughter, Otis, and the inhabitants of that world. She considered all that had happened there and suddenly felt at peace, as if her feelings were just right.

"Actually, I can, sir. These are not my words, and I cannot reveal their source, but I tell you that in all things you must listen to your heart."

Chandrajuski backed away from her. "Those are the words of a woman, not a fighter."

"Not true, sir. I am not the only one to foretell our present difficulties, I am just the only Seer that we know of."

"You speak in more riddles."

"Only because I must, sir. The words are a gift from someone wise beyond our comprehension, someone who knew what was coming, though they did not share specifics with us. We were called, Daughter and I, and I believe you have been called, as well. Daughter was there when these words were spoken, and I speak in her name when I tell you to trust in your heart. Listen to your heart, Admiral. What you find there will be true."

"You speak in her name?" Chandrajuski asked in awe.

"In this, I do."

Chapter Twenty-four

When they left Sector Headquarters, Tarn lifted his communicator to summon a flitter. Krys placed her hand on top of the communicator to stop him.

"Let's walk," she said.

He nodded, clearly unsettled with what he had just been through. It was not every day that an ensign offered counsel to a Sector Commander. He felt overwhelmed, even a little ill. The more he thought about it as they strolled toward the spaceport, the more ill he felt. A hand went to his stomach, and he winced.

She noticed. "Are you okay?"

"No, I'm not. Excuse me." He ran to a row of nearby bushes and leaned over. The remnants of his lunch were soon on the ground. Krys felt a strong urge to go to him, but she knew he'd rather have privacy so she turned away. When he returned, he was wiping his mouth with a handkerchief.

"Sorry," he said in embarrassment. "I hope I never have to go through that again."

She took his arm and turned toward the spaceport again. "You were spectacular in there."

"I'm just an ensign, Krys. It's not my place to counsel admirals, and I don't like it."

"So now you know how I feel about being a Seer."

"No, I don't. You're grand and calm and collected. You act as if talking with admirals is an everyday thing."

"How do you do it?"

"Do what?"

"Figure out my visions."

"I just offered some suggestions, that's all. And we didn't figure out the whole vision."

"Nor did we figure out the whole vision I had of you on the cruiser, but you're getting better, just as I'm getting better. You got most of it."

"I wish I knew what the 'unseen' referred to."

"You will eventually."

"I don't know, and I don't know if there will be an eventually. The mission to Dorwall is over, so I'm no longer your aide. I don't know what my next assignment will be. How about you? What are your plans?"

"I'm going back out. Daughter lives, so the line of Chosen is not ended, but no one knows. Admiral Chandrajuski is preparing a list of sector commanders who need to know, and I'm the messenger.

"Uh . . . why are you telling me all this? Am I supposed to know?"

"You might as well know. You're going with me."

He stopped walking, almost as if he'd run into a wall. He turned and stared at her, too surprised to say anything.

She grinned and took his arm, prodding him toward the spaceport. "You'd better get used to speaking with admirals, and maybe governors and Imperial Senators. They're all on the list. We're getting a new ship, and he's sending Protectors with us."

He stopped again and turned to face her. "Tell me you're serious."

"I am serious, Tarn. It's voluntary for the rest of our crew, but not for you."

"I'll gladly volunteer. You know that."

She took his arm and headed toward the space port. "I do know, and thank you.

Chapter Twenty-five

Stven kept only Tarn and Petty Officer Nan Gortlan, his engineer, from his present crew.

"You have no restrictions on who you select," Krys instructed him, "but don't take too long. If you do, Admiral Chandrajuski will find them for us. It's going to be a long voyage, and it will benefit all of us if our group is tight."

"When do we get the details?" Stven asked.

"As soon as the admiral gives you his blessing. Not before. Sorry. Whoever you find, they must be absolutely trustworthy, and rank is not an issue."

Stven's shiny purple scales contrasted sharply with the dull brown coloring of the Schect he showed up with later that day. Unless you were another Schect, you would find little attractive in the physical appearance of this creature. His six-foot long body bore a strong resemblance to an overcooked sausage. At present, he stood partially erect on six lower hands while his upper hands preened; his remaining two hands were idle. Hard, serrated mandibles protruded from each side of his mouth, two long sensory antennae sprouted from the top of his head, large, multifaceted eyes that saw in all directions dominated his head, and a shriveled face covered with whiskers completed the package.

He crossed the deck toward Krys with his uppermost hands rapidly preening his whiskers.

He stopped in front of her and the preening stopped. "Lieutenant M'Sada reporting, Ma'am."

"Welcome aboard. What is your present job, Lieutenant?"

"Captain of a fighter, just like Lieutenant Stven," the creature responded.

"And you would do what for me?"

"Lieutenant Stven has been persuasive. Whatever you need, Ma'am."

"Lieutenant Stven is our captain. Wouldn't working under him be a demotion?"

"He believes your mission to be of great import and possibly clandestine. Is he right?"

She looked at Stven in surprise. She had not said anything to him about the nature of their mission, but he was a Rress. His powers of reasoning would naturally be considerable.

"He is right on both counts."

M'Sada lowered his upper hands until his head touched the deck. "I'm honored to be asked," he replied.

"You know each other?"

"Since the Academy, Ma'am. I graduated first in my class. Stven came in a close second."

"But you can work for him?"

"I can work for him, and I can work with him. Someone has to be at the controls day and night, and these small ships are minimally staffed. It will be a demanding regimen for the two of us if we're the pilots."

"Do we need more pilots?" she asked Stven.

"We don't have room for more pilots, Krys. Tarn is our third pilot. He'll share equally with piloting when the guns are not needed."

"Hmm. When the Rebels learn of our activities, they'll seek us out. It may become quite dangerous," she said to M'Sada.

"I do not seek danger, Ma'am, but if the needs of Empire require my services, I answer the call."

"Have you been in battle?"

"I have, against smugglers. The consequences to them of capture are dire. They do not give up easily."

"And what are your career goals?"

"Admiral," he said without hesitation. "Until then, whatever Admiral Chandrajuski needs of me."

Stven added, "You know the esteem in which we Rress are held as teachers, Krys. The Schect are regarded equally highly throughout the fleet as tacticians. A skipper is always happy to accept their services. M'Sada beat me handily in that area at the Academy, and I would value his assistance."

"I'm after loyalty and discretion as much as skill," she said.

"And I vouch for him on both. I would not have invited him otherwise."

"You seek the rank of Admiral," she said to M'Sada. "Are you prepared to give up your commission to join this venture?"

"Ma'am?"

"It's a simple question, Lieutenant."

"But not a simple request. If Admiral Chandrajuski makes the demand, it will be for good cause, and I will comply."

"Very well. I, too, hope it's not required. Stven, please advise Admiral Chandrajuski of your choice."

"At once, Ma'am."

"Uh, before you do, are you both rated to fly other kinds of ships?"

Stven and M'Sada looked at each other in surprise. "We are," Stven answered. "What other ship did you have in mind?"

"I'll let you know later."

Tarn, Stven, and M'Sada showed up together late that night with two gunners in tow. Both were Dramda, humanoid but with an extra set of arms and hands. Petty Officers Gordi'i and Kali'i were also man and wife. They had no higher aspirations than to be the best gunners they could, but at that they were, in M'Sada's judgment, the best. They had worked under him on a previous assignment, they interviewed well, and their names were forwarded to Admiral Chandrajuski.

Chandrajuski interviewed each of the candidates personally. He then called all of them together for a meeting at a conference room on the civilian side of the spaceport. It would be his last official meeting with them, and they were required to show up in civilian attire.

"You have each agreed to join this special crew without knowing the mission before you," he began. "I'll leave it to Krys to give you specifics, but you need to understand that the mission could easily last several years. It will be of immense import to restoring the throne. The Rebels will learn of your activities sooner or later, and when they do they will go after you. Yours is a dangerous, possibly very dangerous mission. If anyone wants to change their mind, now is the time."

Stven spoke. "I'm not opting out, sir. I just have a question. You mentioned restoring the throne. I thought all the Chosen were dead."

"Does anyone wish to opt out?" Chandrajuski asked, his wise old eyes staring hard into the eyes of each of them.

No one spoke. He batted his fists together and opened his mouth wide to display his many teeth. "I only wish I could go with you," he said softly. "You are a small group, but your impact could be enormous. Know this: ending the line of Chosen is fundamental to the entire Rebel strategy. That line is not yet ended. One lives. Few know. You're going to change that." He looked around the table. "Any more questions or comments? This is your last chance to decline."

No one spoke.

"Very well. Your orders are to safeguard Krys as she spreads the word that we are working to restore the throne. Krys will explain in detail how this will be accomplished once you're underway. A civilian ship is being modified for your use. Krys is the owner, and she has final say in where you go and what you do when you get there. Commander Stven is captain, and he has final say when underway. The rest of the chain of command is as follows: Lieutenant Commander M'Sada, Lieutenant Lukes, Senior Chief Gortlan, Senior Chief Gordi'i, and Senior Chief Kali'i. These are new, permanent ranks for all of you, something Sector Commanders occasionally get to award."

"So we don't have to resign our commissions?" M'Sada asked.

"No. But you will conduct yourselves as civilians unless circumstances require the uniform. These requirements are not unusual in clandestine operations. The record will show that you hold assignments elsewhere within my fleet."

"Sir, are we spies?" Gordi'i asked.

"Definitely not. You at all times represent the legitimate military arm of the Empire. However, you might find it beneficial to keep a low profile. Do I make myself clear?"

All heads nodded. "In that case, I'm done. Return to your ships, gather up your personal gear, and report back to Krys. You are to have no further interaction with Empire crewmen at this station. We're working hard to make certain you and your ship are untraceable."

He left, and Stven moved to the head of the table. "Report back here in two hours. This is not the time to make long good-byes. The less your friends know, the longer we survive. Dismissed."

Tarn gathered up Krys' few belongings while she located a hotel near the spaceport and signed everyone in. She gathered them together in her room where silence prevailed for a time.

"We have a lot to do, and we have a lot to talk about, but I, for one, would like to see our new home. Is anyone else interested?"

She led them to a maintenance hangar on the civilian side of the spaceport. Inside the cavernous building they found several ships in various stages of overhaul, looking like they'd never fly again.

"I've named her *Rappor*," she told them as they walked up to the immaculate, burnished underside of her ship. The ship swarmed with technicians, and sections of hull gaped open in various places. "She'll be ready in two months. Strings have been pulled to meet that timetable. I'll give you the details if we can find some privacy onboard."

They couldn't. Technicians were everywhere, so they kept their tour brief, stepping over hoses and electrical lines and around technicians, just getting in the way of everyone working. At Engineer Gortlan's suggestion, they left the technicians to their work and retreated back to the hotel.

"Why the major refit?" Stven asked.

"Admiral Chandrajuski is doing his best to bring a private ship up to military specifications," she said. "She's getting better guns, the best she can support, a military AI, special communications equipment, and better sensors and shields. And she'll be as fast as they can make her in the available time."

"They can do all that in two months?" Gortlan asked.

"He's pulled a lot of strings."

"If you don't mind, I think I'll spend most of my time with the technicians. I want to know as much as I can about her systems and where everything is located."

She smiled. "Just try not to sound too military, okay?"

He frowned. "Yes, Ma'am."

"And that goes for the rest of us. Our cover is that I'm a rich kid out trying to spend as much of daddy's money as I can. We're all going to need new wardrobes. Would you like to go one at a time, or should we all go together?"

"I'm not real good at shopping for clothes," Tarn spoke up. "Especially expensive ones."

"Nor am I," she responded. "Are any of you?"

"I don't wear clothes. I'm more interested in knowing our mission," Stven said.

She bit her lip. "I'll give you a full briefing when we're underway. Most of what I will tell you comes under the umbrella of Imperial Secrets."

"Can you tell us where we're going?"

"I can. Our first stop is Rrestriss. You're going home, Captain."

His eyebrows rose, but his breath held, so she continued. "I'm hoping to pick up Senator Truax. We need him to go with us."

A couple of small puffs escaped. M'Sada began a rapid preening of his antennae. To him, the odor was not only unpleasant, it was painful. Stven apologized, then ignored him. "Senator Truax is going to be on my ship?"

"If he agrees. He might not."

"I'd be honored to have him, My Lady."

"So would I."

The crew spent long hours with the technicians to learn the ship, though they would still have a lot to learn of her capabilities once they were in space. The first leg of their journey would be busy for all. When *Rappor* was ready, they took her out for a brief shakedown, then spent two more days making final adjustments and they were ready.

Three Great Cats showed up just before departure, and Krys joined them in their quarters as Stven got the voyage underway. Walls had been shifted to make a lair for the cats, their preferred arrangement. Other walls had been shifted to create a training room, something the Great Cats always required. Their lethal skills would be kept at the highest possible level. All three were Guardians transferred from civilian contracts at Chandrajuski's insistence. Kross was senior.

"We are at your service, Ma'am," he began.

"What do you know of our needs?" she asked.

"Nothing at all."

"What do you need to know?"

"The more we know, the better we perform. I mean no offense, but to us it matters little who the client is. Knowledge of where we go and your purpose there will be helpful."

"You're wrong, Kross. Who your client is has everything to do with your job."

"I believe you are a wealthy socialite?"

"I am not. All of this is a cover. I call Otis friend."

Kross sat a little taller. "Your wealth comes from the Royal Family?"

"I have no wealth. Your client is Daughter."

Great Cats rarely showed emotion, but Kross growled low in his throat. "The Chosen are dead."

"Daughter lives. Her location is unknown, but she lives. We seek her."

"Important words. Who are you to know?"

"Are you familiar with the story of Otis and Val on Hespra III?"

"All our people are familiar. The event has become one of our tests. It was . . . irregular."

"Are you aware that two orphans left Hespra III?"

"I am."

"Both are Friends. One has special status. Do you know why?"

"If I did, I would not speak of it to you."

"If you won't speak, it's because you know it's import. You know she is a Seer."

"If such a thing was true, it would certainly be an Imperial Secret. How would you have such knowledge?"

"Because I am her."

Kross stared at her. So, too, did the other Great Cats. She pulled the locket from around her neck and passed it to him.

He studied it, but he only needed a moment. As he handed it back, he said, "We are honored, Friend. How may we serve?"

"I'm not certain. At the moment, I'm not in need of protection. That might change. We seek Daughter always, but until we find her, our mission is to take word to certain individuals that she lives. The task will not be easy."

"You have seen her?"

"I have seen her, but only in visions." Krys told her story, leaving nothing out. She didn't know if it would be enough, but the Great Cats now understood her task.

"So we were hired under false pretenses," Kross said when she was done.

"Is that dishonorable?"

"In this case, not only are we honored, we're grateful. Word of your mission must be carefully guarded."

"Do you believe my story?"

"Does it matter?"

"It does to me."

"Your tale is impossible to prove, but your Naming as Friend assures our trust."

"Struthers was trusted by the Queen. We can trust no one."

Trist, the female, spoke. "And we won't. If your tale is false, we lose nothing but time and effort, at worst our lives. If your tale is true, we help restore what was lost at the Palace. The choice is not difficult."

"You said we seek Daughter," Sheeb said, "yet our mission does not focus on that."

"It does not . . . yet. I keep hoping for another vision. Until I get one, my job is to spread the word that she lives. The task I ask of you is not merely to Protect. I might need some help convincing the people we meet. At the moment, I have only myself and a message from Admiral Chandrajuski for proof. Your trust in my words might help sway minds. Will you vouch for me if necessary?"

Kross spoke. "The highest calling among our people is to support the Royal Family, and through them the Empire. Your special abilities are trusted by Daughter, so they are trusted by us. Struthers is an aberration. Until you prove otherwise to us, we will do whatever needs to be done to restore the throne. This mission is meaningful. Is it possible to call at Brodor, our home world?"

"It's not on my list, but I sense the rightness of your request. Is it likely you'll encounter other Great Cats on our journey who could bring word to Brodor?"

"You place no restrictions on us in that regard?"

"None. Your people must know."

"Then we will get to work."

"What do you do to prepare?"

"Rrestriss is our first stop. We'll know everything there is to know about it by the time we arrive, including the layouts of the major cities and ports. We'll know in detail the layout of Senator Truax's home and office complex. Do you plan any other stops there?"

"No, but I can't say what will develop or who else we'll need to see."

"Not to worry. We'll be prepared."

"I should probably get some training on how you operate and what I can do to make your jobs easier."

"If you're willing to learn, we're happy to teach, and your knowing will make us more effective. Have you ever fired a weapon?"

"Yes. Otis and Borg trained me and Val. It's been a long time, though."

"The skills will return, and the rest of the crew could probably stand some improvement as well."

"I don't know if we brought any personal weapons."

Kross opened his mouth in the feral grin she had occasionally experienced with Otis and Borg.

"We did."

Chapter Twenty-six

Krys had not looked forward to the tedium of another long trip, but that turned out not to be a problem. She had no spare time at all. Training by the Great Cats occupied a large portion of her time. Her proficiency with the small blaster Kross provided was not good, and she knew it would be worse if she ever had to really use it. Surprisingly, her hours of meditation had trained her to focus her mind, and that focus helped with her aim. She would keep working on it.

She became familiar with many scenarios of attack and escape and what the cats needed from her to make the process more efficient. Again, she was not an expert, but that would come with more practice.

She never skipped her meditation periods. Tarn joined her whenever he was free, and she took to scheduling the sessions when he was off duty. She found the stretching and exercises associated with her meditations much more enjoyable in his company. During meditation, she always sought a vision of Daughter, but she had no visions of any kind.

So much for improving her skills, she complained to him.

"Maybe you're trying too hard. Why don't you try thinking happy thoughts for a while? It might do us all some good."

"What do you mean? Have I been difficult?"

"No, just curt. You're always in a hurry to rush off on another project."

"I have so much to do."

"And one of those things is to lead. You don't have to be our friend, but it's better when you are."

She squeezed his hand. "I like being your friend, Tarn. You're right. I barely know M'Sada, Gordi'i, and Kali'i."

"Why don't you come into the net with us? Those were great days, and there's no better way to get to know your crew and your ship."

"I will, but I might not spend a lot of time there. I'll make time after Rrestriss, I promise."

"No, you won't. You'll have Senator Truax to entertain."

She smiled. "Trust me, if he comes, he'll have his own entertainment. He's in love with learning."

"Doesn't he know enough already?"

"Don't ever say that to a Rress," she chided him. "They simply won't understand."

She did manage to go into the net, and in doing so she became more familiar with the ship and her crew. M'Sada delighted her. Very quick of mind, he enjoyed pranks and didn't mind pulling them on her. She wasn't able to reciprocate, not yet, but she was determined to find a way.

Gordi'i and Kali'i mystified her to some extent, at least initially. They seemed to have little interest in anything outside their chosen profession. On the other hand, when not in the net with the guns, they were helpful to anyone who needed something done. Gortlan called upon their services regularly during his constant inspections of the ship, and they seemed to like the work.

She startled them one morning with a request. "You're experts with weapons, right?"

"We are, Krys."

"Just ship's weapons?"

"Yes."

"Well, if you're truly weapons experts, wouldn't it make sense to include other weapons as well?"

"What others?"

"Well, hand weapons for example. Do you have any experience with them?"

"We have to qualify periodically."

"Would you consider doing more than qualifying? I might need some backup one of these days, and I like the thought of how many guns you can hold with four hands. Who knows, you might be able to add a whole new category to your expertise."

They deliberated in their slow manner, but as she and Tarn joined the Great Cats for training several days later, they passed the two Dramda coming out of the training room. Both had grins on their faces.

Arrival at Rrestriss was completely uneventful, as they had expected. No one yet knew of their mission. Stven desperately wanted to accompany her on her visit to Senator Truax, but he chose to stay behind. He wanted to assure himself that no one was taking any special interest in the ship. Tarn accompanied her, along with Kross and Sheeb. Trist remained with the ship for security, though she did not remain in the ship. She prowled the port looking for anything suspicious.

Senator Truax was only too happy to see her and agreed to an immediate meeting. Sheeb remained outside the building while Krys, Tarn, and Kross went inside. The lift deposited them on the top floor, and the Senator was waiting as they stepped off. As opposed to Stven's purple hue, yellow predominated on Truax's features, including his eyes. Those eyes widened when he saw the Great Cat, and Krys sensed the wheels turning in his mind.

"Welcome, granddaughter," he said happily.

"Welcome, grandfather," she replied, their personal greeting for each other. She had lived with him for a number of years before moving into her own apartment. "Please meet Tarn Lukes and Kross."

They followed him past the staff in an outer office and into his private domain. "Are you busy, or can you spare us some time?" Krys asked.

"I have a little time, and there's always tonight. Will you join me for dinner?"

"With pleasure, but I must inform you that I am here with a purpose. Is this room secure?"

"No official rooms are secure. You know that."

"Then perhaps we should wait until later."

"What news do you bring? We're always a little behind things here."

"You know about the coup, of course."

"Only recently. It's true then?"

"Yes. There's a lot of turmoil, as you can imagine."

"And much fear of what is to come. We're running prediction models of what will become of our Empire. They are not promising."

"We can discuss this further over dinner, if it pleases you."

"Then meet me at my home at the usual time."

Kross spoke for the first time. "May I suggest someplace else? Our ship perhaps?"

Truax studied the Great Cat. "My home is quite secure."

"Nowhere is secure these days when it comes to Imperial matters, Senator."

He stared at the Great Cat. "I see. Should I bring anyone else?"

"No . . . not yet," Krys replied. "Perhaps later."

When Truax stepped onto the ship that evening, he was stunned to find another Rress aboard. Stven bowed to him. "Commander Stven, captain of *Rappor*, at your service, Senator. I am honored to meet you."

Truax studied him from head to tail, his eyes missing nothing. "You're a rarity, Captain."

"I am, Senator. Bad blood or something, according to my family."

"Given present circumstances, it may be fortuitous. We Rress are not without value to those in charge. Is this a military vessel?"

"Sort of. We're in disguise."

"It's a good one. Will you join us?"

"It would be my pleasure. Give me a few minutes, Senator."

He turned the ship over to M'Sada with orders to call him if anything even remotely suspicious materialized. He thought for a moment. "With him here, our cover is compromised for the first time, however small it might be. Let's be ready for an immediate departure, eh?"

M'Sada's upper hands began preening his antennae as he considered. "Agreed, Captain. I'll be in the net, and I'll keep the guns warmed up as well. Should I call Trist back?"

"No. She's probably a better sensor than anything on the ship. She'll know if it's necessary to return. Heck, she'll probably be our first warning of anything amiss."

When Senator Truax had been completely brought into their plans, he sat back on his tail in contemplation. "It's a powerful plan, Krys. Admiral Chandrajuski is right; the word must get out. His plan is focused, and because of that it's easily modified, but I would like to model other plans that include the general populace. Keeping things focused within a small, upper cadre will give Daughter a full range of options when she's in control, but other plans might give her more power. We simply must find her, you know."

"I'll keep trying. Until then, this is what we have. Will you accompany us?"

"Can you give me a few days? I'd like to run it by some friends.

They're very discreet. I'm not certain if my presence on this ship is the most effective use of the resources I represent. To begin with, we're not necessarily going to the same places. Will you share Chandrajuski's list with me?"

"I'll share it with you, but no one else. You can understand my concern."

"A look will be sufficient, and I will not share details with anyone else."

"May I provide an escort home, grandfather?" she asked later.

"This is my home world. I am not in danger here."

"We represent danger, Senator," Tarn said. "We've been on a war footing for some months now."

"An escort would just attract attention."

"Not if it was me," Stven said.

Truax sighed. "Very well, though it's unusual for a Rress to go about armed."

"I'll be discreet."

After they left, Krys turned to Kross. "Am I being paranoid? I'm worried for him."

"Possibly, but wouldn't you like to know if anyone else is showing special interest in him? And wouldn't he? I'll have Sheeb follow them. He'll remain outside the Senator's grounds, and he will be discreet."

When Stven returned, he was almost floating. "What an honor!" he exclaimed. "Never thought I'd see the day I even met him, let alone have twenty minutes of his undivided attention."

Krys changed the subject. "We're on your home world, and we have a few days with nothing planned. Would you like to go home?"

He considered, then shook his long neck. "No. My place is here. Besides, how would I explain my civilianness when my family knows I'm in the military?"

"Your call, but we can get by without you for a while if you'd like."

"Look, I signed on for the duration, and I'm not taking any chances on you leaving here without me. Okay?"

She smiled. "Okay."

Kross woke her in the middle of the night. "Senator Truax is under observation, Krys. Both visual and electronic."

She struggled to fully wake up. "Uh, what does that mean?"

"If he set up appointments for tomorrow, and if he wasn't extremely discreet, there may be others listening in on his meetings. That could lead them to us."

She blinked, suddenly fully awake. "Isn't it likely that all the Imperial Senators are under observation right now?"

"Actually, probably yes."

"So it could mean nothing."

"The observation might mean nothing, but what they learn from it could mean much."

"What do you suggest?"

"Captain Stven should pay him a visit, find out what's been said. I can give him something to disrupt the electronic sensors while they talk. I can also have an extraction team ready if needed."

"All right. I guess we'd all better get up."

Chapter Twenty-seven

Stven arrived at Truax's home before the Senator left that morning. The conversation was brief, and they left soon after, together. Stven sent a coded message to the effect that in his estimation things were okay but not perfect.

"I think we'll keep an eye on the meeting," Kross said. He sent Trist to the university where Stven and Truax would soon be in discussion with others. Sheeb returned for some well earned sleep.

At mid-afternoon, Trist reported her discovery of a Grbant with highly sophisticated listening equipment outside the building where the meeting was taking place.

"Standby to neutralize the equipment, but wait for my command." Kross ordered her. "I'm on my way."

He called Stven, who was in the meeting, and ordered him to stand by. Stven knew from the command that the meeting had been compromised. He would alter the discussions to innocuous topics until Kross arrived.

"What does it mean, Kross?" Krys asked.

"Last night's observation was probably routine, but something has sparked their curiosity. They're digging deeper. We don't know what the Grbant learned, but whatever it was, it's probably known now by whomever he was transmitting to. With another day or two, we could probably find out who's behind the eavesdropping, but that's not our task. It's time to leave this world, Krys."

"But we're not done here."

"The Senator has been compromised. Anyone he has talked to is compromised, as well. I don't think we want Struthers knowing what we or the Senator are doing. It's also possible that we've not detected all the listeners. There could be others."

Her shoulders slumped. "All right. Can I go with you?"

"Yes. I need a driver." He called Sheeb, who met them at the ramp.

Krys drove while Kross kept an eye out. Just before they landed, he commanded Trist to move on the surveillance equipment. She stunned the Grbant, gathered up all his equipment and loaded it into her own skimmer, then waited nearby in case Kross needed more help. Sheeb made his own way to the meeting by a separate skimmer to cover the outside of the building.

Kross sensed no one following them, but that did not mean they weren't followed. His meeting with Truax would have to be brief. Krys remained with the skimmer while Kross entered the building. Sheeb was nowhere to be seen, but she knew he was there and keeping an eye on her.

The meeting was brief. Truax had laid a number of options on the table before his associates, two professors. Hidden among several other plans proposed by him was Krys' plan. He had not used names or given specific details, but it was clear to Kross that the seeds of their plan had been overheard by the Grbant and relayed to his superiors. He informed Truax's two associates that they would likely be questioned. Both were invited to accompany the Senator off world, but both declined. They were advised to come up with a cover story that did not threaten the Rebels, then they were dismissed.

Kross turned to the Senator. "You, sir, are not so fortunate. You've been compromised, and if you're taken into custody, you know too many details. We're leaving Rrestriss. Will you be gracious enough to accompany us?"

"Never to return? My position as Imperial Senator is more important here now than ever."

"It's more important that you serve the Empire, Senator. You'll get a better feel for things in time, and you may find it appropriate to return, but for the moment you are not safe here."

"They wouldn't dare touch me. I'm an Imperial Senator."

Kross displayed his teeth in a leer. "Tell that to those who were killed at the Palace, Senator. These people are serious. Very serious."

Truax blinked, but his thinking was quick. "We must stop them at all cost. I'll go with you. Do I have time to pack?"

"No."

"Very well. Let's go."

"Is there any way to disguise you?"

"Not quickly. We Rress don't wear clothes. With enough alcohol, it's possible to change our coloring, but it takes days and the process is not comfortable."

Sheeb joined them in the skimmer at the last moment, and Krys set off at a sedate pace for the spaceport. Kross insisted she not set off any alarms. Trist was right behind them.

M'Sada was notified the moment the skimmer lifted, and he set things in motion for departure. When he called for a departure clearance, he was told to stand by. Such a command, though not completely unheard of, was unusual. Flags went off in his mind, and he quickly settled on a plan. He went into the net and called for general quarters, then began powering up the drive. He didn't need to power up the drive, it was almost instantaneous on military ships, but he wanted to send a signal that this was a civilian ship, just on the off chance that someone was taking a special interest and had sensors trained on them.

The spaceport controller called him back. *"Rappor*, we have a temporary lock-down on the port. It's going to be a while on that clearance."

"What's a port lock-down? I've never heard of a port being locked down."

"Neither have I. Stand by while we get this sorted out."

He powered down the drive, sending a signal to anyone watching that he was in compliance. Kross was notified, and M'Sada felt like he could hear the growl across the miles separating them.

"You remember the drill?" Kross demanded.

"Affirmative." He sent Tarn to the ramp armed with a blaster. Tarn's job was to open the ramp when commanded, then close it the moment everyone was aboard.

The two skimmers didn't stop in the parking lot. They crossed right over the port boundary and settled beneath the ship. M'Sada gave the command to Tarn as everyone jumped from the skimmers. The ramp opened, then closed as soon as everyone was aboard. M'Sada powered up, ordered the two gunners to do the same, and he was airborne before Stven reached the bridge. He remained at low altitude until out of range of gun platforms at the port, then nosed the ship up and headed for space.

Stven worked the scanners as M'Sada set the course. "Looks like the local squadron is holding a ways off," he said. "Not very far off, though."

M'Sada took a look and adjusted his course to provide them most distance from the squadron. "Directly away from them?"

"No. They're faster than us; it wouldn't do any good. Head for the nearest jump point."

"They'll catch us before we get there."

"I know. They'll catch us no matter which way we go, but they have no reason to come after us yet. I don't want to give them one by looking like a smuggler bent on escape."

"Uh, I think it's a little late for that, my friend."

They passed by the squadron and just kept going. An hour later, though, the squadron got underway, and toward them. *Rappor* was fast, but they'd only be half way to their jump point before the squadron caught up. Stven and M'Sada looked at each other as their minds calculated.

"We need to talk to them," M'Sada decided. "Maybe they're the good guys."

"Maybe the Senator should talk to them," Stven said. "He outranks everyone here, including squadron commanders and district governors."

"You think the governor is involved?" M'Sada asked in surprise.

"Who else would give an order like that to the squadron?"

"We'd better find out."

Stven opened a line to the cruiser. "*Rappor* here," he stated.

The officer of the deck, a full commander, answered his call. "Looks like you're in a hurry, *Rappor*. You're new around here. What do they want you for, smuggling?"

"No, sir. We're just in a hurry."

"Turn back, *Rappor*. "We'll get this sorted out on the ground."

"May I ask what they told you about us?"

"You may not. You know the law. Turn around."

"I need to talk with the squadron commander."

"In your dreams."

"It's an Imperial matter, sir. You, too, know the drill." Using the word Imperial notched up the stakes considerably, and the commander had no choice. It wasn't long before the admiral came on the line.

"Admiral Hastak here. You've been ordered to return to Rrestriss, *Rappor*."

"We carry an important passenger, sir. He has pressing matters elsewhere and does not wish to return at the moment."

Admiral Hastak hesitated. Issues like this could get complicated. "Who is your passenger?"

Stven considered. Whoever wanted them back probably knew that Truax was on board, so he wouldn't be giving anything away. "Senator Truax," he replied.

"Truax! Put him on."

Stven left the net and called Truax to the bridge. "They want us to return. Admiral Hastak is overtaking us with a squadron. Think you can talk us out of this?"

"I know him well. It should not be a problem."

M'Sada brought Admiral Hastak's visage to the main screen. "Greetings, Zagma. Are you really threatening us?"

"Sorry, Senator, but I am. I've been asked to have you return to the planet."

"I have more pressing duties."

"I'm sorry, Senator, but I'll have to check with the governor."

"I understand. Let me know what he says."

It didn't take long. "The governor demands your return, Senator."

"He does? How interesting. He must be in on this. He can't order me, you know. Sorry, but I won't comply."

"You place me in a difficult position. He claims there are some illegalities related to you."

"I'll bet he does. I didn't know he'd joined with Struthers, and quite frankly, I'm surprised."

Hastak stared at him. "This has to do with Struthers?"

"Let me just say it's an Imperial matter. Will that suffice?"

"It would have, but I'm not certain what that means anymore. Stand by, please."

The admiral's connection was cut. Moments later, M'Sada made an announcement over the speakers. "We have company."

Stven immediately donned his helmet and joined with M'Sada. An Empire squadron had just emerged from hyperspace far out in the system. A chime sounded, and M'Sada turned to Stven in surprise. "It's the tightbeam. Someone's trying to call us."

"Why would anyone call a civilian ship on a tightbeam?" They both looked at each other and reached the same conclusion at the same time. "Chandrajuski!" Stven quickly set things up, and an admiral stared back at him.

"Everything okay, *Rappor?*"

"Not exactly. May I ask your intentions, sir?"

"I'd rather not say too much over the tightbeam. Perhaps we could meet."

"That would be . . . difficult. Whom do you represent?"

"Let's just say a Friend sends a message to a Friend."

"Very well, sir. I just have to get untangled from our present predicament. We left Rrestriss in a pretty unusual manner, and we've been ordered to return."

"Hmm. Let me make a call. I'll be back."

It wasn't too long before the Rrestriss squadron reduced speed to match *Rappor's*. They still remained in a position to overtake, but the threat lessened. If things stayed as they were for very long, *Rappor* would reach a position where she could join the incoming squadron and have some protection, assuming the incoming squadron was friendly, of course.

A chime sounded again, but this time it came from Admiral Hastak. Stven hesitated, uncertain if he should display his own tightbeam capabilities.

"What do you think, M'Sada?"

"He wouldn't have called if he didn't know. I think the incoming squadron commander told him. The secret's out, Captain."

Stven completed the link. Admiral Hastak was waiting, and this time he had words for Stven, not Senator Truax. "I've been ordered to withdraw. You're free to go, *Rappor.*"

"Ordered by whom?" Stven asked in surprise.

"Admiral Buskin. Actually, it was a request. He was not very specific, but I think we may share the same . . . sympathies. There are some issues with the district governor that will make my return unpleasant. He suggests you might have a message for me, and possibly orders."

Stven thought hard. This could be a set-up. He might be better off just leaving as quickly as he could.

M'Sada broke into his thoughts. "Tough call, Stven. Would you like me to get Krys up here? Or Kross?"

"Not yet. Let's flesh it out first. She'll agree to anything if it furthers her purpose. I don't trust these guys, and it's our job to see she lives long enough to work on the big picture."

"Agreed, my friend. Your job just got harder. We have more company," M'Sada said.

A single Chessori trader had materialized very close to where the incoming squadron had come out of hyper. What was it doing here, Stven wondered? Rrestriss was about as close to the galactic core as any civilized world could be. Were the Chessori trading this far into the Empire?

"It emerged from hyper right at the same coordinates Admiral Buskin came out. I know. I checked," M'Sada said.

"Long odds."

"So long that it boggles the imagination. I've never seen it happen, but you told me you had."

"You're right!" Stven recalled in surprise. "At Dorwall! A Chessori trader materialized right where we would have been if we hadn't moved." They looked at each other in alarm, their thoughts calculating.

M'Sada got there first. "At Dorwall, they must have been called. Here, it's as if they were following."

"Both impossible, my friend."

"It is for us. It's also impossible for 15 of their ships to take out 42 of ours with hardly a shot fired." M'Sada mentally backed away all of a sudden. "No, Stven!" But he was too late. Two large puffs escaped from Stven's nostrils. M'Sada tore the helmet from his head and scurried for the door on his eight lower hands, his two upper hands preening furiously to clean the smell from his two long antennae. The pain sometimes proved too much for him.

Stven called Tarn to take over the piloting while he considered. Meetings in space with admirals always meant you joined them on their ships, not the other way around, but for him to join with Admiral Hastak, he would have to bring *Rappor* aboard the cruiser. That was putting all his eggs in one basket, something he was unwilling to do. There was another way, used only when small ships made transfers, but he'd never heard of an admiral using it. He got back on the tightbeam.

"Sir, a meeting would be beneficial, but I cannot let my ship be taken aboard the cruiser."

"Admiral Buskin inferred as much. I'm prepared to join you."

"You are, sir?"

"You sound surprised. Would you be a little more familiar with military procedures than your current status indicates?"

If a Rress could squirm, Stven squirmed. "I might, sir."

"Excellent! We understand each other, then."

"Just you, sir."

"No, I'll bring my adjutant, and we'll have a pilot who will remain aboard my shuttle. I haven't docked one of these things in a long while, but Admiral Buskin has been persuasive. We'll come unarmed."

"And your squadron? Sir?"

"You'll have to reduce speed for me to catch up. My squadron will hold its present separation. Only my shuttle will approach."

"Very well, sir." Stven broke the connection, issued instructions to Tarn, then called Krys and the Great Cats to the bridge. He briefed them, and Kross led his team to the hatch.

"Stven," Krys asked when it was just the two of them, "why am I just learning of this now?"

His neck began lowering, then he changed his mind and lifted it to its full height. "Because my first order of business is to keep you alive. We've been busy doing just that since we left Rrestriss."

She stepped up to him and reached a hand out, laying it against his scales. "I accept that. Nevertheless, we must find a way to keep me more informed. Perhaps you should call me to join the net when we're threatened."

"You're not a warrior, Krys. You won't always understand the things we do."

She nodded. "Until I'm more familiar, I'll only observe and be available for consultation. Stven, I will not command you in our times of need, but I, too, must learn to be a warrior. We have a long road ahead of us."

"And I'm a Rress. I will teach you, My Lady."

"Are you adequately staffed here on the bridge? You should attend the meeting with Admiral Hastak."

"I'll attend. If Hastak keeps to his word, no one else will be near us. M'Sada and Tarn can listen in through the net. We might want their counsel."

She nodded. She knew it was not her place to tell him how to do his job. She had placed her trust in him from the beginning, and she would continue to do so.

Hastak's small ship arrived, and the docking went smoothly. He emerged through the hatch to the greeting of three Guardians. Their presence confirmed his suspicions that *Rappor* was not a normal civilian ship. He raised his hands instinctively, and Kross frisked him, then his adjutant. They were led to the small lounge where Krys, Senator Truax, and Stven awaited.

"Tell us what you know, Admiral Hastak," Krys commanded.

"And who might you be?"

"Answer my question, Admiral."

He glanced at Truax, whom he knew well, then at Stven. Truax nodded his long neck, and Hastak turned back to Krys. "Admiral Buskin told me he'd blow me out of the sky if I so much as harmed one hair on 'her' head. I take it he's referring to you."

"Then he's probably who he says he is."

"And who might that be?"

"You tell me, Admiral."

He stared at her thoughtfully, wondering who this young woman could possibly be. He was accustomed to asking questions, not answering them, but she seemed undaunted by his rank. "He claims to have come from Chandrajuski."

"And . . .?"

"He would divulge no more. He asked me a number of pointed questions concerning Struthers and his ilk, and based on my answers, he suggested I might find a meeting with you beneficial to all of us."

"And what are your feelings concerning Struthers, Admiral?"

He turned to Truax. "We know each other well, Senator. I believe you can answer for me."

"Indeed I can. We've spent long hours discussing this very issue, but it's no longer hypothetical. Given the choice between Struthers and our old Empire, where would you stand?"

"On my oath, an oath given personally to the Queen when she promoted me to flag rank. Nowhere else, Senator. What that means in today's world, I can't say, but even without a Queen, my oath still binds me to some higher power than Struthers. He's destroyed the very foundations of our civilization, and he's broken our most cherished laws in the process."

Krys studied him for a time. "What if I told you the Empire is not dead?"

"The Empire is dead, young lady. Are you telling me Chandrajuski is organizing something against these Rebels?" He considered for a time. "I like the sound of that, but it leaves me with uneasy feelings."

"The Empire is not dead, Admiral. Daughter lives."

He just looked at her, his brow creased. Then he turned to Truax with a piercing stare. Truax nodded his long neck but said nothing.

His eyes narrowed as he stood stiffly. "You are not her."

"I'm not, but I promise you she lives. I'm recruiting others to help her restore the throne. Care to join us?"

He had no words. How could he? He had lived for months knowing that the mold that had shaped his life had been broken in an instant of horror. His eyes lifted to his adjutant, Commander Vrehg, whose eyes were narrowed, his thoughts internal.

When Vrehg's focus returned to Hastak, it was with a look of triumph. "Join, sir. Until proven otherwise, it's the best offer I've heard since we received word of the coup."

Such simple words, but so filled with meaning. As Chandrajuski had said, her words brought hope.

"What proof do you offer?" Hastak asked her.

"Do you need proof? Is hope not enough?"

"No."

"Short of standing in her presence, what proof would satisfy?"

"A letter from her, an order . . . a Knight."

"I can provide none of those at the moment. I have a letter from Chandrajuski, and you have the assurances of Senator Truax, the Great Cats, and myself. Is that sufficient, Admiral?"

"Who are you?"

"I'm a Friend of the Royal Family."

He stepped back, his eyes widening, then he turned those eyes on Truax for confirmation.

"It's true, Admiral. Krys is well known to me, brought to me by Daughter herself many years ago."

Chapter Twenty-eight

"We should meet with Admiral Buskin," Hastak decided. "Or," he corrected, looking to Krys, "at least I should."

"Please include me," Krys said. "I sense rightness in him."

"You know, as eerie as it sounds, I do too. Chandrajuski chose well, I suspect."

"It might not be so simple," Stven announced. Sitting to the side, he'd essentially been forgotten. "There's another threat we have to deal with first. M'Sada and I are working on a plan, but . . . well, we haven't come up with one yet."

"What's the problem, Captain?" Hastak asked.

"A Chessori trader. It came out of hyper about ten minutes after Admiral Buskin did."

"It's just a trader. I hear they're showing up all over the place lately, though I haven't seen any here. They don't bother anyone."

Stven looked to Krys. She considered, then nodded her head. Secrets were of no use if they weren't used. He filled Hastak in on the events at Dorwall.

"So the Chessori are our enemies," Hastak said.

"They are, but we don't know how to fight them," Stven added.

"If a fight is necessary, surely one trader couldn't take out a squadron."

"I'm not sure that's its purpose, sir. I think it's here to discover what we, or at least Admiral Buskin, are up to."

Hastak frowned. "I don't follow, Captain."

"Consider the following, sir: the Chessori are lethal, they have a means of disabling our ships, one dropped from hyper near us at Dorwall in a manner indicating it was summoned, and the Chessori here dropped from hyper in a manner indicating it was following."

"Surely you jest, Captain. Communication with ships in hyper is not possible, nor is following a ship through hyper."

"Rule out nothing, sir. We've learned to drop the word impossible from our lexicon when dealing with the Chessori."

"You give them too much credit."

"We exit hyperspace many times during transit. Have we fully explored the possibilities of what could occur in normal space while we're between jumps? Standard policy is to focus on setting up the next jump. What if the Chessori somehow read our jump computers as we send the command to jump? Do you look for anyone following you between jumps?"

"You give them a frightening edge."

"I prefer not to underestimate their capabilities. I'm probably crediting them with more than they deserve, but after what I've seen, I'll continue to do so until I learn otherwise. Consider the Chessori trader out there. It may not know our purpose, but if it does, or if it knows or suspects the purpose of Admiral Buskin's squadron, the names of our ships may become tied together. Those suspicions may already have been communicated to others."

"If that Chessori is an enemy and a spy, it's our job to deal with him."

"How? What if Chessori traders have this ability to neutralize ships?"

"It took five Chessori ships to neutralize a squadron at Dorwall."

"Were they all needed? We just don't know, sir. I have no idea how to approach within firing range of that guy, not with any assurance of my own survival."

Kross padded his way through and around the attendees to stop before Krys. "Krys, you have knowledge of at least three events concerning the Chessori. In two cases a Great Cat was not incapacitated."

She considered his words. "You stretch the imagination, Kross."

"I do. To me, there is always a way out, always a way to

succeed. It sometimes requires a stretch. I'd like to find out." He turned to Sheeb. "My place is here with Krys. Would you like to go hunting?"

Sheeb's lips lifted in a grin.

Hastak and his adjutant joined Stven and M'Sada on the net to discuss possibilities. Stven was unwilling to risk *Rappor*, and the others concurred without hesitation. Adding some difficulty to any plan was the fact that Admiral Buskin likely had no clue of the threat represented by the Chessori trader following him, and there was no good means of informing him without possibly alerting the Chessori. No one knew if the Chessori had tightbeam capability, but if they did, their closeness to Buskin put them in line with the transmission window.

Getting into position was the first requirement. Hastak's maneuvers would likely cause some alarm within Buskin's squadron. When the time came, Hastak would have to show his hand, but he had to wait until it was too late for the Chessori to escape.

Sheeb would have to go in with just one ship, and once the attack began, he might be the only one functioning on his ship. He would have to be at the controls of a gun that could be operated manually, and it would have to be a powerful gun. The Chessori defensive capabilities were not known, and the Chessori was fully staffed, placing Sheeb at a severe disadvantage. The guns of a cruiser would be best, but the guns on a cruiser could only be operated via the net. The guns of a frigate would have to suffice – they could be operated manually, and they were big guns. Sheeb would have to attack with a frigate.

"You'll need two cats," M'Sada interjected. "Someone has to pilot the frigate. A single Chessori trader would never take on a frigate, certainly not within view of the rest of the squadron. Besides, its purpose here is most likely to gather intelligence, not to provide intelligence to us. It will run at the first hint of a threat. We have to suck it further into the system so it can't jump, then someone will have to maneuver the frigate to stay on its tail. Can you cats fly the ship?"

Kross was called, and he was not happy with the news. Yes, the cats had limited flying skills, but their primary purpose was to Protect Krys, not wage battle. Losing one cat was bad enough, and he was reluctant to chance losing two to this operation.

"This will not be our last encounter with the Chessori," Stven told him. "What we learn here might serve us well in the future, and think of the big picture. Daughter wages warfare on two fronts. Her primary focus is the Rebels at the moment, but in the long term she'll be forced to deal with the Chessori, as well."

M'Sada joined in with an even more frightening possibility.

"The timing of the treaty mission has bothered me since I learned of the fall of the Palace. Three Chosen were away from the Palace, and each has been, reputedly, dealt with. Could the treaty mission have been Struthers' means of dealing with Daughter? Are the Chessori in league with him?"

A couple of puffs escaped from Stven, and M'Sada was forced to leave the net again, scurrying from the bridge with his antennae held high, but that was okay. His leap of reasoning had accomplished its purpose. No one now questioned the need to deal with the Chessori, least of all Kross. The lone Chessori trader out there had become an experiment as well as a target.

Kross himself would have to go. He was the best pilot of the three. Admiral Hastak returned to the cruiser with his aide and the two Great Cats. Stven contacted Admiral Buskin by tightbeam, but he couldn't be certain the Chessori were not listening.

"We're all of a mind here, sir. We're going to reduce speed and let you come to us. It might be possible to negotiate then. Your Friend concurs."

"Why wait for me? We can confer out here."

"Admiral Hastak has a few things to do with first. He is, after all, the only Empire force in the system, and he's reluctant to abandon it. He's going to move off for a while, give you and us some space. If you sense discomfort from any of his maneuvers, feel free to discuss it with him. Know that your Friend has approved his delay."

Hastak angled his squadron up and outward to bypass Buskin and the Chessori. He passed them ten days later, then he angled back toward Buskin a couple of hours later. Buskin responded instantly, calling him on the tightbeam. "You're looking a little threatening there, Admiral."

"I know. I seek another. It would help if you reduced speed and angled slightly toward me."

Buskin looked him in the eyes hard, then cut the connection. Hastak's maneuvers could only mean one thing, but it made no sense to him. He considered *Rappor's* message: the Friend had approved. He reduced speed and angled upward, but he prepared his ships for battle, as well.

A few hour later the Chessori began feeling pinched, and it angled away from all the Empire ships. Hastak went to full speed, and the chase was on. It would be a long chase, but the trajectories were acceptable. He would intercept the Chessori in two days. His ships spread out in a standard encapsulating maneuver, while the frigate with

Kross and Sheeb aboard aimed straight for the Chessori.

The Chessori's visage appeared on all ships' communicators as it made a general broadcast, and the crew of *Rappor* got its first view of a Chessori. "What is the meaning of this?" it demanded.

Admiral Hastak responded. "We have reason to believe you carry contraband. We're taking you aboard for inspection."

"That is unheard of. We Chessori never carry contraband. I will not come aboard."

"I'm not requesting, I'm ordering. Rendezvous with the frigate."

"I will not."

"Noncompliance is an admission of guilt, backed up by Empire law. This is a routine operation for us, and we're quite good at it. The choice is yours, but I will not hesitate to open fire if you fail to respond to my orders."

"You wouldn't dare. Such a thing would be an act of war against the Chessori."

"You're in Empire territory now and subject to our laws. Besides, who will ever know?" Hastak asked with a leer.

The Chessori cut the link. The squadron approached in an umbrella formation, intending to fully encapsulated the trader, but the globe never finished forming. As the frigate approached maximum firing range, it loosed a few shots across the bow of the Chessori ship which continued to flee. A little later, shots from the frigate's smaller weapons began impacting the shields on the Chessori ship.

Suddenly the nets throughout the squadron spasmed. Kross and Sheeb went down along with everyone else, but they didn't stay down. Kross, the only living creature aboard the frigate still capable of flying the ship, focused on staying on the Chessori's tail as it fled. As soon as he did, the Chessori opened fire. Shots impacted shields, but the Chessori weapons were too weak to penetrate the strong shields of the frigate. Kross pulled alongside the Chessori, and Sheeb opened up with the strongest gun on the ship. The first shot holed the Chessori, and the second turned it into a fireball. The terrible burning sensation ceased, and Kross stayed with the wreckage while Sheeb continued firing until only small pieces remained.

When the crew of the frigate came back into the net, they were confused and hurting. At Kross' direction, the captain opened a tight beam to Hastak. "We're secure. Head for the rendezvous. We'll talk there."

Admiral Buskin was not so easily persuaded when Hastak called him. "You have some explaining to do, Admiral. You just destroyed a neutral trader."

"That Chessori *followed* you, Admiral. Think about that, and we'll discuss its neutrality at the rendezvous. Until then, consider both the Rebels and the Chessori your enemies."

At the rendezvous, Stven and Krys had a decision to make. Trust was rapidly becoming an issue of paramount importance. Could Buskin and Hastak be trusted? Knowing whom to trust would never be a sure thing, and a wrong decision could doom their mission, but the mission could not succeed without some modicum of trust. They'd never be certain, and gut instincts would have to play a part in the decision-making process. They agreed to go aboard Buskin's cruiser.

Kross and Sheeb met them, and Krys was surprised at how comforting their presence was.

The description of the Chessori mind weapon, given by Hastak and Kross, was hard to believe, yet the picture they painted fit all the pieces of the puzzle they had so far encountered. No one knew how the weapon worked, but that didn't matter at the moment. They knew what it did, they knew everyone was susceptible, and they knew the Great Cats could overcome its effects to some extent.

Krys turned to Buskin, the Chessori temporarily set aside. "Why are you here, Admiral?"

"Orders from Chandrajuski. I received several sets of orders from him by courier. The first set stated that you had undertaken a mission for him, but that you might need assistance. I am to escort you from a distance, and I am to avoid blowing your cover if possible. It's a little late for that, I'm afraid."

"And your other orders?"

"Not to be opened unless the first requirement failed or ended."

"Open them now, Admiral."

"You speak for him? Who are you?"

"I have a feeling your orders will answer your questions. Admiral Hastak already knows the details of my mission. Chandrajuski's orders will likely confirm those details. Why don't you find out?"

He went to his quarters and opened the orders. The message on the screen truly staggered him. He sat for a time in private contemplation, then rejoined the others.

"It appears that the Empire is not dead. Chandrajuski wants me to organize whatever support you can raise for Daughter, and he's provided me with a temporary rank to do so, that of full admiral. Only the Queen can make the rank permanent, but it works for now. It looks like you're our recruiter, and I'll command them."

"I'll recruit, but only until I locate Daughter," Krys amended. "When I do, my place is beside her."

"Understood. And your purpose here, Senator?" Buskin asked, turning his head to Truax.

"My removal from Rrestriss was a little rushed. I've not fully settled on a plan, but my intention is to assist Daughter from another quarter. Your job is to organize a military force; mine is to thwart Struthers' aims by working through the Imperial Senate."

Buskin nodded his head. "It's a good plan, though fraught with risk. I accept my assignment, of course. What may I do to assist either of you?"

Truax considered. "If what we've seen here on Rrestriss is any example, Struthers is far more entrenched than I would have thought possible."

"We strike while the iron is hot," Krys commanded. "Our message must reach as many as it can in as short a time as possible. I'll continue as originally planned, but you and I, Admiral Buskin, should part company. You, too, can carry my message, at least for a little while. Your task will then shift to gathering recruits and hiding until called."

He nodded. "We have two squadrons here, mine and Hastak's, both probably marked by the Rebels. We have a little time if we move quickly, but only a little. It's terrible fighting tactics, but we fight a war of information at the moment, not a war of opposing forces. I'm going to split up the squadrons, sending ships out individually. Each ship will carry the same message, and it will provide rendezvous coordinates to anyone who decides to join us."

"Where will that be?" Stven asked.

Buskin pursed his lips. "I can't say at the moment. I'll get my staff working on something. It's not as simple as it would seem. We can't just name a location, then expect only the good guys to show up there. The Rebels will catch on to what we're doing sooner or later, and they'll try to find us."

M'Sada spoke. "Sir, I'm just a lieutenant commander, but I'd like to make a suggestion."

Buskin looked at him in surprise. "You're a Schect, as well. What's on your mind?"

"I'd like to suggest several levels of security, sir. Each can be separated by just a short jump so each level does not have to be far apart in time, but as to the final level, its coordinates should not be given out. Don't let them come to you. Instead, go to them. Periodically send someone to the locations you give out, and whomever you send should have the means of testing loyalties, perhaps a swapping of command staff or something, so that organized resistance cannot remain organized. You're bound to end up with Rebels within your fleets, but if you cut off their heads, they won't be effective."

Buskin's eyes gleamed, and a smile touched the corners of his mouth. "I like your ideas, Commander. Want a job?"

"I already have one, sir."

Buskin turned to Krys. "Let's see your list. We can divide it up among us, and Hastak and I might be able to add a few names to it."

"Your ships are marked," Krys said. "You won't be able to hit many locations before you're challenged, and individual ships will not have the power to resist serious challenges."

"We won't need to hit that many locations, Krys. When my guys find someone they trust, the new commander will take the list and continue spreading the message while my guys join back up with me. It'll be a simple networking of old friends and acquaintances. You, on the other hand, are definitely in a marked ship. What are your plans?"

She looked to Stven and M'Sada before replying, then said, "We'll change ships if we have to. Don't worry about us. As a civilian, I'll have a lot more freedom of movement than you will, and I'll not be expected to answer to local military commanders like your ships will. You'll have to give your men some good covers."

"Don't worry, we will. Let's look at that list."

As lists were culled for distribution, M'Sada spoke again, his words meant for the Admiral, but his gaze on Kross. "We should get word to Brodor. We need as many Great Cats as we can get, Admiral. You can't go up against the Chessori without the cats."

Kross looked thoughtfully at M'Sada. "An excellent idea, Lieutenant. Imperial matters always come first with us. My brothers would welcome the opportunity to strike back. I sense a general recall of Guardians and Protectors coming up, and soon." He turned to Buskin. "It will have to be a Great Cat that takes the word to Brodor – no one else would be trusted. I'll find a brother at our next port of call who will go. He'll need to know where to send the recruits."

"Just have them wait on Brodor. I'll come and get them. I'll identify myself with the words *Daughter, Otis,* and *Kross.* Is that acceptable?"

"No, sir. You will use the word *Smhavna.* It's the name of the Queen who came to our aid two thousand years ago."

Buskin nodded. "Are we done here?"

"It might be a while before we see each other again. I need a location of where to send my recruits," Krys stated.

"We'll work through Chandrajuski." He went to the navigation board and pulled up Centauri Sector. "As a back-up, I'll have someone stationed here," he said, pointing to a position in deep space and off the normal space lanes. Stven, Hastak, and Buskin each made a note of the coordinates. "My position is going to remain fluid, but I'll do my best to keep someone there who knows how to find me. If both of those fail, you'll have to find someone else who's in the loop. We know who's on each other's list, so that shouldn't be too hard."

"Then we should be away," Krys stated. She looked from Buskin to Hastak, then back to Buskin, her lips pursed. She had nothing further to say. Each of them had their orders, and each of them would risk all for the last of the Chosen.

Buskin, though, had more to say to her. "Periodically send someone with word of your successes and failures. Particularly your failures. It will be from those failures that the Rebels will attempt to infiltrate my forces. When you can, let me know your itinerary, as well. That way, if we stop hearing from you, we'll know where to search."

She smiled a tight smile. "With the distances and times we're dealing with, Admiral, there will be little opportunity of rescue for any of us. It's imperative that if any of us are lost our mission continues. We serve the Empire and the Throne, and we serve to the death. Are we agreed?"

They joined hands, each reaching one hand into the middle of a circle formed by Krys, Buskin, Hastak, Truax, Stven, M'Sada, Tarn, and Kross. Eyes moved from one to the other, agreeing, but remembering, as well. No further words were necessary.

Krys and her group turned and left. Hastak remained with Buskin to work out details of their parts in the mission. Back aboard *Rappor*, M'Sada lifted from the deck of the hangar bay and exited the cruiser, then asked for a destination. Krys, Stven, and Senator Truax stared at each other, wondering where they should go next.

The scales along Senator Truax's spine rippled in excitement. "It's begun. Do you see, Krys?"

"See what?"

"Your plan is working. You've managed to recruit me, and you've managed to recruit two full squadrons that will network out to spread the word. When you find her, you'll be in a position to offer material help to her."

"It's not my plan, it's Chandrajuski's. Like you, I'm just a pawn in all this."

"Not so, granddaughter. You've graduated. You're now one of the leaders in whose hands our future resides. I am another. And though she doesn't know of our activities, Daughter will not be surprised when she finds out. She knows us that well. Where do we go from here?"

"Our focuses differ. Let's find a location that suits both of our purposes. We might separate after that, and we might not."

Truax studied the remains of the list given to Krys by Admiral Chandrajuski. "I seek other senators, and perhaps governors. You seek military commanders, and perhaps governors when it suits. I see a number of locations that work for both of us. Starting at the top of Chandrajuski's list, assuming he prioritized it, the first that meets both criteria is Rega VIII. The second is Mitala I. Both are sector headquarters."

"Mitala I is the closest by far," Stven stated.

"Then set course for Mitala I," Krys commanded.

Chapter Twenty-nine

The man of dirt, as Ellie had referred to him, no longer struggled with his calculations. She had helped him to understand himself, and his mind was clear. As *Resolve* neared Gamma VI and accuracy requirements went up, Mike forced himself to rest for a day after each jump, but he did not falter, and his jump calculations were perfect and swift.

There were huge gaps in his knowledge of the Empire, not least of which was a gnawing concern over what would happen once *Resolve* reached Gamma VI. What would become of Reba and him? Would they be sent back? If they stayed, could they possibly learn to function in such an advanced society? They would be met by someone high in authority, someone related to the Heir, someone who would whisk her and her mother away for safekeeping. What, then, would become of the two from Earth?

But he held his focus. His only job was to get them to Gamma VI. What would happen after that would happen, and he would deal with it. He was loving life again.

Chapter Thirty

They were down to their last jump. Ellie took a needed time out, leaving Otis and Reba on the bridge to keep an eye on things while Mike slept. She gathered up Alexis and went to the lounge, settling herself into the corner of a couch to let Alexis nurse. Her breasts were full, even a little sore, and she desperately wanted to spend the little time she had left with her daughter, knowing it might be a long time before the opportunity presented itself again.

She loved motherhood. Without Alexis, her life would be bleak, indeed. She knew Alexis was all that remained of her family. She couldn't put into words why she knew this, but it was true. Her Talents never lied, and she had known for some time now. She still grieved, but the worst of that was behind her. Alexis came first in her life now, and as the child sucked at her breast, she knew real contentment. The two of them would persevere, somehow, and they would do it together.

She smiled at the thought, then smiled anew with thoughts of her friends. They, too, were part of her life now, a part she had not even known she was missing until they came along. For the first time in her life, she knew the happiness that true friends brought. Despite the many Testings she had performed, Testings that left little of a person's feelings unknown to her, she had never thought to experience such feelings herself. She would do her best to keep her friends near her during the trying times to come.

The many demanding hours in the net minding the ship had challenged her, but such was not her true calling, and those long hours would soon come to an end. This, too, she knew. Beyond that, she sensed only great danger. She couldn't define it, couldn't see clearly enough to know specifics, she just sensed great danger. Would they fail, she and her friends? She didn't know.

Alexis was nearly sated and ready to sleep when Mike came strolling into the lounge prior to going on duty to make the final calculations. Oblivious to his surroundings, he drew a glass of water, chose a chair without thinking, and sat down deep in conversation with Jake. She studied him, as she had studied him many times without his knowledge. Physically, he was tall and rugged, but spare. He looked like he could run for hours without stopping. A smile tweaked the corners of her mouth as she thought back to her first impression of him. He had first struck her as barbaric, and why not? He was from an emerging world that had none of the sophistication of the Empire. Little did she know how wrong that first impression had been. He and Reba fit every possible definition of high intelligence and sophistry. Even more, they chose well. The decisions they made were good, in some cases far better than her own, and they were not afraid to make those decisions, then act on them. They were survivors of the first rank, but they were much, much more to her than that.

The man sitting across from her deep in thought literally took her breath away at times. She wondered how she could have so disliked him early on. Now . . . now she craved his presence, craved his touch. She loved him, pure and simple. She hadn't planned it, in fact she had fought it, but after that first time in the net when he had asked her for her name, something no one else had ever done, she had not fought it very hard.

A lump caught in her throat as she thought about the danger ahead. He, too, would be in danger, and she knew intuitively that he would not abandon her to that danger even if she asked him to. She didn't need her Talents to know how this man felt about her, and her heart filled with gladness. He was a part of her life now, whether he knew it or not. Getting his agreement on that would remain high on her list of priorities in the future.

Were these warm thoughts of him coloring the decision she had made about his Naming? She had argued the idea within herself for weeks now, but she found it impossible to think of him only in terms of his usefulness. She needed to do so, but her feelings colored every thought of him. That didn't change her decision, not for a moment. She needed him personally, but her Empire needed him even more. And now the time had come.

"Michael," she said softly.

His eyes focused on her in surprise. When he realized Alexis was under the blanket nursing, he blushed and got up to leave.

"Excuse me. I didn't realize you were here," he said.

"There's nothing to excuse, Michael. Please stay. Is it as nice as I imagine to have a Rider? And, hello, Jake."

"Jake says hello. To answer your question, you might get a different answer depending on when you ask. At the moment we're getting along, and we're even in agreement for a change."

She looked wistful. "Before Alexis I yearned for my very own Rider. I wouldn't trade Alexis for anything or anyone, but I would still like a Rider of my own."

"They're not exactly your own, Princess. Jake is plenty independent."

"But you have become friends. It shows. I would like such a friend."

"You had Jornell, and I get the impression you're always surrounded by others."

She winced. How little he knew!

"What you say is true, but it's not the way you think it is. Marriages within the Royal Family are arranged for the well-being of the realm, not the individual. I liked Jornell, he was a good friend, but he was almost as old as my father. We spent little time together outside official functions, except . . . " She paused, uncertain of how he would take her words, but they must be said. "Except for the creation of an Heir," she finished. "That was the principal purpose of our marriage. We were friends, but the kind of love I hear about between husband and wife was not there. Yet I miss him. As for friends, until meeting you, Jake, and Reba, I have never known anyone who was not aware of my position. You know I am royalty, Mike, that I am a member of the Royal Family. Friendships developed within that mold are not true friendships. I have many friends, but all are friends because of my position."

"I'm glad I met you before I knew who you were."

"Yes, and as a result of that meeting, I'm a witch."

Mike turned red again. "How . . ."

"Did you think we would leave you in that room to wake up to Jake on your own? We're not that way, Mike. And I'm truly sorry I shot you. I know now that it was unnecessary."

"Given the circumstances, I might have done the same thing," he replied. "But I'm here, I'm helping as much as I can, and it has nothing to do with your position. I have nothing to gain from you. In fact, I have everything to lose, including my life, and including being sent home after we get to Gamma VI. But I'm still here, willingly."

His words hit her like a blow, and she tensed. She thought she knew him better than that. "You plan to go home?" she asked in a small voice.

"No, I don't. But what good will I be to anyone out here? I don't have any purpose in your society. Will I be sent home?" he asked, raising his chin to her.

She closed her eyes as relief flooded her body. How had she not focused in on this concern sooner?

"You will not be sent home, Michael Carver. Quite the opposite. I intend to keep you around for a while, a long while. Your attitude will probably change, everyone's does," she said sadly. "I'm not complaining. Well . . . I am, but it's the way things are. Money and power change people. That's a simple fact of life, a major factor in my life. But I would like to have you for a friend, and I've always wished for a Rider for a friend."

"Well, why don't you have one?"

"The Chosen have never been allowed to have a Rider. I guess it's tradition. Maybe it's because we are then forced to choose our advisors with greater care. If everyone around me is smarter than me, and those with Riders usually are, I must choose my advisors carefully. They absolutely must have the best interests of our civilization at heart. Dishonest or unscrupulous advisors could wreak havoc on everything my family stands for. That cannot be allowed to happen. I choose my close associates with great care. I always Test them as well."

"You've Tested me. In fact, you've Tested me three times. What did you find?"

"You're still here aren't you?"

He lifted an eyebrow in response. "I see. In that case, since I'm deemed acceptable, that I speak true, you can believe it when I say I'm not quite as afraid of you as I was, and I like you in spite of your being a witch." He smiled. "I, too, like calling you friend."

She didn't smile in return. The time had come for Naming.

"Come here, Michael." She had him kneel on the floor in front of her and placed a hand behind his head. She could tell he sensed what was coming, and he closed his eyes. He was deeply afraid of this special talent of hers, and she truly could not understand why. For many, to be Tested was an honor. To some it spelled failure, but most refused a Testing if they were not true.

"Michael, I will not hurt you," she said softly from inches away. "I promised you I would not force my Touch on you without your consent. I have reason to Test you today. May I?"

He opened his eyes, looking everywhere but into her eyes. "You Tested me months ago. Isn't that enough?"

"This is not in the same category, Michael. My last Testing was not a true Testing. I sought something different. Now, in my official capacity, I must know the truth of you."

"What you do isn't right."

She sat back as if slapped. Alexis, still nursing, reacted unhappily, and Ellie spent some time fumbling beneath the blanket to calm her down.

"You still feel so strongly?" she asked, when she focused on him again. "I sensed your strong distaste of the Touch the second time we joined, but you allowed me a third Touch, willingly. I don't understand. What isn't right?"

"It's not right to read people's thoughts, to search at will through their minds. That's what you do, isn't it?"

"In a way. You do not want me knowing your mind? What do you hide from me?"

"Lots of things! A person shouldn't know everything about another person."

She looked troubled. "I don't learn everything there is to know about someone when I do this, only that which I seek. And, with the exception of your last Testing which was focused on resolving a crisis, all I seek is that person's truth. What do you hide from me?"

"Nothing! Well . . ." He stumbled, searching for the right words and failing. "It's just not right, Ellie. Some things are embarrassing, like how I feel about certain things, including you. You can't just go finding out the answers to those things directly. You have to get to know people, find things out like everybody else by getting to know that person."

"I see . . ."

She bit her lip thoughtfully and reached a decision. "Michael, if that's what you're trying to hide, you have failed utterly. I do not need my Touch to know how you feel about me." She smiled as she put her hand behind his head again. "Like everyone else, I know how to listen to my heart."

Her look hardened. "For the moment we are not speaking of

feelings. Hear me well, Michael Carver. In my Empire the rules are the same, but not for me. In this one area, the Chosen are the exception, the only exception. It's what I do that sets me apart. Michael Carver, I already sense the truth of you, but in my official capacity, I must not only sense, I must know the truth of you. To do so requires the use of my Talent. We are nearly at our destination. I will have even greater need for you there. If you will permit my Touch, afterward it will be time for you to know the full truth of me as well.

"Michael, in my official capacity I, Ellandra of the Chosen, command you to look into my eyes. As Ellie, your friend, I ask this of you with love in my heart."

She searched his eyes. She had used that very special word again, love. Would it be enough to overcome his revulsion to the Touch?

She waited patiently until sensing his readiness, his acceptance, then she entered. Flip, flip, flip, get past the fear . . . there. Flip. Yes, he now truly thought of himself as captain of *Resolve*. Flip. Yes, his attachment to the land remained, but he was settled in his mind on that issue. He had a goal, and it was a flexible goal. Flip. Yes, her cause seemed right and just to him. He questioned, because he had so far only seen the Empire side of things, but he sensed rightness. Until he was convinced otherwise, he would support the Empire, not the Rebels. Flip, flip, flip. She sensed his maleness, as she always sensed the maleness in men and the femaleness in women. She lingered a moment to study. Had she not been Testing, a blush would have found its way to her face. His thoughts were of her, and he was embarrassed to have such thoughts about an alien. Yes, he truly worried about her alienness. It seemed an insurmountable barrier to him, though he was wrong. They were alien in many ways, but not physically. Flip, flip. Earth. Could he find a way to bring Earth into the Empire? What would happen to Earth if he tried? Flip. What was he going to do out here in the Empire? What *could* he do? Flip. She sensed love, and she was its focus. Flip. Jake, like a brother, a loyal, supportive brother. He had no maleness, he was an *it*, but he could love, and she sensed Jake's love for Mike, herself, Reba, and Otis. Flip, flip. Like Wooldroo, he believed in the Empire and would do whatever he could to make it a better place. Flip, and she was done. But she paused. She sensed something from Mike. Flip, flip. He had corralled his fear of her Touch and was sending her a message, a very simple message. His mind focused on the feelings he felt when she was in his arms. She could not return the feeling, her Touch was only one-way, but she could tell he knew when she found his thoughts. She lingered long enough to erase any doubt on his part that she had received the message. While she lingered, she savored.

She released him, and he sank back on his heels. "Thank you, Michael," she said leaning forward to kiss him on the forehead. "I'll be back in a few minutes." While he gathered himself together, she got up and left the room. She returned soon without Alexis.

She walked up to him, put both hands up to his face, stood on her tiptoes, and kissed him on the lips. Then she wrapped both arms around his back and buried her head in his chest. Mike waived both arms around uncertainly, still not believing he had been so forthright with her, then he caved in and hugged her back.

"This is for being my friend," she said into his chest.

"Uh, I guess I like being your friend," he replied softly.

"And this is for loving me." She wrapped her arms around his neck and kissed him on the lips again, a long, lingering kiss.

"I will work hard to keep you my friend," she whispered as she looked directly into his eyes. Then she stepped back, holding both of his hands in her own, her eyes brimming. "Michael, thank you for being my friend, and more. Jake, that goes for you as well."

She released his hands and turned away, pacing the room without looking at him. "It may not last," she said sadly. She took a moment for herself, then turned back to face him with dry eyes and a very business-like manner. "Michael, Jake knows the truth of me. You do not. It's time that you do, even if it changes your feelings for me."

"Ellie . . ."

"No, Michael. Listen. We are about to reenter the Empire. When we do, we will either join battle against the Rebels, or we will immediately become embroiled in affairs of state. Or both. I do not know what has happened during my absence, but I sense my Empire is changed forever. In this, I hope I am wrong." She looked hard at him. "I am not often wrong about affairs of state. It is one of my Talents. I have the gift of prescience. Do you know what that means?

"No."

"It means I sense the future. Only dimly, not in detail, and not in such a way I could describe to anyone, but I get a sense of whether something will turn out good or bad. That's all, but it is enough.

She took a deep breath and said softly, "The Royal Family has fallen, Michael. Moreover, I know now that the vision given to me by Krys foretold their fall. The first words of her vision were, *'You will be so much more and have so much less.'* The last words of her vision were, *'a man of dirt will come to your aid.'* You are that man of dirt, Michael.

"I am going to need people I can trust during the coming

troubles to reinstate that family. I need them because of the words of her vision. I *am* so much more than I was then in spite of having so much less. We have been together for almost a year now. You are brilliant in many ways, but in some you are unbelievably dense. How is it you have not figured out who I am?"

He blinked at the reprimand. "You're one of the Chosen, and you're the mother of the Heir."

"True. I am the mother of Alexis who is a potential heir, though she is far too young to be Tested. Michael, if I am the mother of the heir, what does that make me?"

"What are you getting at?" he asked with a frown.

"I never lie. Period. I have not lied to you, but I have not offered the complete truth either, as is my right. I told you the Heir is aboard this ship. Michael, our Empire is ruled by a woman, has been for eons. I am the Queen's daughter. What does that make me?"

He gulped, realization dawning. "Ah . . . *You are the Heir?"*

"I am the Heir, Michael. Alexis may become heir someday . . . my heir." She paused, searching his face for a response. "This is my ship. Otis is my Protector." She moved to stand before him nose to nose and said softly, "I am the Heir." She placed a hand on his cheek. "I hope I am wrong. Oh, I so hope I am wrong, but in my heart I know I am now Queen."

The blood rushed from his face and he felt faint. He sent a silent query to Jake, >Help!<

>I am, I am! Hold on!<

She took his arm and led him to the couch where she sat down beside him.

"Who's helping who?" he asked weakly.

"It's a two-way street," she answered, holding his arm possessively.

>Okay, you're fixed, back to your old crabby self,< he heard from Jake.

He stood up carefully and turned to face the woman who might be Queen, uncertain of himself. "So I can't call you Princess or Ellie anymore?"

"We're not yet certain what has happened, Michael. Besides," she smiled, "I like being your princess, and I've grown to like being called by the name you gave me."

"That's just the problem. Why did you have to tell me you're Queen, or even that you might be a queen some day? I'm not totally dense, you know. I knew you must be in line for the throne – I just figured you'd been passed over for some reason. Now . . ." he held his hands out to his sides, uncertain. "It changes everything!"

"I know. I wish it would not, but it does."

"How can it not? Look, I know your husband just died and you're in mourning. I'm also keenly aware of the fact that you and I are aliens to each other. That doesn't change the fact that you're not just a princess to me. You're My Princess . . . Sorry, but I can't help it. Sometimes these things just . . . happen . . ." he trailed off.

>Ditto, ditto!<

"Jake says ditto," he added.

"Is he dittoing the sorry part or the My Princess part?" she asked with a smile. She rose from the couch to stand before him. "Michael, know this: in you I believe I have found what I have been searching for my whole life. In you I believe I have found a relationship that I once thought would be denied me forever. I love you, and I know that you know I love you. That does not change the fact that I am now or will one day be Queen. Can you accept a relationship with me that is based on those terms?"

His heart leaped at her words, but she was Queen. He knew it was not possible for him to know who this woman would be when she was Queen.

And she wasn't just a queen. She was the Queen of All Space. He couldn't even conceptualize what it meant to be her.

He studied her for a time, then placed his arms about her shoulders. "I love the woman I know as Ellie. Alien or not, I love you. Can I love the Queen? I don't know. I feel like I don't know anything about you all of a sudden, except the fact that you're Queen . . . and maybe just the teensiest bit spoiled. I had planned on getting to know you better, maybe asking you out sometime. You know, just the two of us, when this was all over. How can I ask out the Queen?"

"I am definitely spoiled. It goes with the territory, and I have paid a dear price to become spoiled. I can't change the fact that I am Queen, nor would I if I could. It's my duty." She paused, searching for the right words, then searching his face for his reaction to them.

"Michael, I like the sound of 'My Princess.' I like being your princess. The right man in my life will be able to see beyond my being Queen. Are you that right man?"

"I don't know, Ellie, but I'd like to try."

She wrapped her arms around his neck and buried her head in his chest for the second time that day. He responded, and they held the embrace for a long time, gathering strength from one another for the trials that surely lay ahead.

After a time he said softly into her ear, "Can we forget the queen part for a while? Can you just be My Princess?"

"We cannot, Michael. Maybe from time to time, but my Empire beckons. It calls to you as well. I have a job for you." She stepped away from him, took both of his hands in hers, and asked, "Will you kneel before your Queen?"

Her words startled him. "What? Again?"

"Michael, Jake, I ask with love in my heart, and I make this request for the good of my realm. Will you kneel before your Queen?"

How could he refuse a request like that?

He went to one knee, and she placed both of her hands on his head, saying formally, "Michael Carver, Jake, will you each swear fealty to me?"

His heart skipped a beat and the blood rushed to his head. Before he knew what he was doing he had jumped to his feet. "No!" he shouted. "What are you doing?"

She stepped back in shock. "Mike, that is not the right answer! There's a formal process for Naming."

"For *Naming?* What's that?" he asked panicked. "Fealty to whom? To what? I'm not sure I even know what fealty means!"

"Then ask Jake. This applies to him, too," she said with a trace of irritation.

Silently he thought, >Jake, what's going on here?<

>I'm afraid to tell you, Mike. There is only one place this is covered in the protocols Wooldroo passed on to me. Fealty means 'absolute loyalty and support to a superior.' I think she's offering us a job. If it means more kisses, say yes!<

>Stay out of my private life, Jake,< he said with feeling.

>This is all new to me, Mike, but I think it's *our* private life. And I like it.<

>I'll deal with you later,< he said silently.

To Ellie, he said, "Sorry. I know you mean well, but I'm not ready to swear fealty to a civilization I'm not even a part of, that I know nothing about."

She stepped away from him, biting her lip as she considered a reply. "That makes sense, I suppose." She gave him a piercing look. "Let me make this clear to you, Michael Carver – there will be no misunderstandings between us on this: I, too, have fallen in love with you despite compelling reasons to the contrary. Equally important, I believe I have, at last, found a true friend in you. You may never know the significance of what I have just said, but to me it is everything.

"I will be Queen. I believe that I *am* Queen. In our society there is no higher position. Yet, you are right. You cannot swear fealty to me. I will never command your love. That I promise."

She turned away to focus her thoughts on business, then she found an answer. "Our world is changing, has changed. Adjustments can be permitted." She picked up her communicator and called Otis and Reba to join them. They arrived on the run, together. Mike worried that no one was minding *Resolve* this close to their destination, but he soon chose to ignore that minor concern.

"Otis, Reba, you are our official witnesses. Michael, kneel down, please."

He started to protest, but Jake interrupted. >Do it, Mike. Just do it!<

He knelt. She placed her hands on his head and asked formally, "Michael Carver, Jake, will you each swear allegiance to my realm?"

He looked up at her and she sighed, exasperated. "What now!"

"I'm not even a citizen!"

"Michael, I am not a clerk filling out a form here. I am your Queen. I decree to one and all present that Michael Carver is a citizen of the Empire. Now, do you swear allegiance to my realm? Say yes!"

>Say yes, Mike!<

"I do so swear allegiance to you and to your realm, My Princess."

>So do I!<

"Jake says he does, too."

Her hands beginning to shake on his head, she said, "Michael, as was foretold, you are the man of dirt. You came to my aid when you could have turned away. Since then you and Jake have brought us some 800 light years without an AI. You have struggled mightily for me. I now ask for even greater sacrifice in my name. Before these witnesses, I knight thee, Sir Michael, Sir Jake. Your word is my command on all worlds of the Empire. Michael, please rise."

Mike, confused, rose unsteadily. What was going on here? This was ridiculous, antiquated. He wasn't a knight! He was just Mike Carver, engineer. Besides, didn't knights have swords?

She wasn't done. She reached into a pocket and removed a gold chain and pendant, then a gold medallion. Otis purred deeply in his throat, and she looked to him in triumph. He nodded his great head and she nodded hers in return. What passed between them Mike did not know, but it was something special.

She turned her attention back to Mike and explained to him that within the pendant was a very rare and precious jewel. She placed his hand on the pendant, then pressed it tightly into her hand with her eyes closed. When she opened her eyes again, she asked him to brush his hand across the pendant. As soon as he did, it opened and transformed before his eyes into a ball of light. Within the light shimmered a three-dimensional holograph of Ellie.

"This is my personal seal. Granted only to Knights of the Realm, it is recognized throughout the Empire as unquestioned identification of a Knight. Only the Chosen can produce these, and only you or I can open it. It is active only so long as both of us live."

She closed the pendant and placed it around his neck, settling it beneath his coverall. She then pinned the medallion containing her family crest to his chest while intoning, "With these symbols, recognized by all, I pronounce you Michael and you Jake to be First Knight of the Realm. Michael, you should kneel down again and kiss my hand."

Contrary as always, he pulled her into an embrace, saying, "I like this better. What the heck, we're among friends!"

Reba, as surprised as Mike but sensing what had gone on in this room between the two of them, clapped enthusiastically. Otis sat at attention, a soft purr continuing to rumble in his throat.

Returning to the couch with Ellie beside him, Mike asked Jake what First Knight was. He received a non-committal reply to the effect that they'd both just been promoted. He wasn't overly concerned until Otis referred to him as Sire. That got his attention.

"Hold it everyone. This has gone far enough. Just what is this First Knight business, anyway?"

"Jake has not told you?"

"He's not talking much for a change. I think you shook him up."

"There is only one First Knight, Michael. You now command all my Knights, you command my military forces, you command the Palace staff, and you preside over the Imperial Senate in my absence. Know this: your word is my command on all worlds of the Empire. Speak wisely and with consideration."

"Come on!" he said, joining in their fun. When neither Otis or Ellie joined in his laughter, he began choking.

>Jake! What's going on?< he asked.

>It's true, Man. I don't know why, but I think she means it. Please ask.<

"Come on, Ellie, Otis. This has gone far enough," he said weakly.

"I repeat, there is only one First Knight of the Realm. If I am, in fact, Queen, you Michael and you Jake are my First Knight." She raised a hand to silence his reply. "Do not forget that titles given can be taken away."

Mike blinked, more uncertain now than ever. Otis came to his rescue. "Sires, what Daughter needs more than anything else right now is someone she can trust, and I mean completely trust. She will not have the luxury of dealing with court intrigues if we have a rebellion to put down. She must have at least one person in whom she has no doubts. I support her decision. Congratulations, Sires."

"Michael," she said, "before you get a swelled head, at this moment in time your fleet consists of *Resolve*, and your troops are quite minimal."

"What about you, Otis?" he asked.

"It's complicated, Sire. She has not told you everything. For the moment, consider me her personal Protector. I'm subject only to her orders. But know this: we are all in this together. Each of us in this room has been called to restore harmony across the galaxy. It is a calling worthy of our best efforts."

Otis stared hard at Mike. "I asked you once before if you could refuse the call. I know you well enough to know that your response has not changed."

Mike's thoughts become unfocused and muddled. Too much had happened too quickly. He decided he needed some breathing room. The bridge would work. He got up, kissed Ellie on the forehead, and turned to leave.

Just before going through the door he turned back to her and said, "Whatever happens, you honor me, my Queen. Let there be no doubt in your mind: I will protect the Heir at all cost."

Stepping off the central shaft onto the bridge, Mike flopped down in his seat and picked up his helmet, idly running his hands over its shiny surface. Reba came up behind him and put her arms around his neck, squeezing tight. "Did what I think happened just happen?" she demanded.

"I'm not sure what just happened, Reba. Our world has gone crazy. She's not just mother to the Heir, she *is* the Heir. And if this coup has succeeded, she's now Queen.

"Skipper, did you just figure that out? I thought you were smarter than that."

"Well," he said defensively, "I guess not. But that's not all. First she knighted Jake and me, then she named us First Knight, sort of like being a Prime Minister or something."

"That's not what I'm talking about. I sensed something else in that room, like a big hole in her life had been filled. Do you know anything about that?"

"Well . . . maybe. But we're aliens, Reba. You know that!"

"Alien, shmalien! She loves you, Skipper. Didn't you know? Don't you pay attention when we're plugged in?"

"I've sensed a deep loneliness in her, Reba. I've tried not to pry."

"Well, you should pry. Might do us all some good. I feel like she's a sister to me, and I think she feels the same way. Does that mean you and I might be in-laws someday?"

"I think it means we've bitten off more than we ever gambled on, Reba. This is not some ordinary ship lost in space. Do you know women rule their society? And she's the Queen!"

"Skipper, if you're the filler of that big hole in her life, I think we're going to have one fine Queen. She's just about to come into her own."

Mike stood up to argue, and a twinkle lit Reba's eyes as she became her feisty self.

"My kind of civilization! Imagine, a woman in charge. Uh . . . are you a man who would be King?" she asked with a wicked smile.

Mike sat back down. Quickly. Reba left the bridge to give him time to stew on his own.

>Jake, fix my head.<

>Yes, Man.<

>Oh, sorry Jake. *Please* fix my head. What have we gotten ourselves into?<

>That remains to be seen. I'll do my part, and I know you'll do yours. I think the Queen chose well. We're a good team, and we'll get better as we go.<

>Jake, this has gone beyond teamwork. I need a partner.<

Jake was slow to respond. >Does that mean I get to stay?<

>I think it begins with staying and includes a whole lot more. You're home, my friend.<

>Home. I like that. I'd better get to work on this 'alien' thing. I don't have a definite answer on that one.<

Otis padded out of the central shaft. Mike called to him, "Hey, Otis! When I told Ellie that she and I were aliens to each other, she said I should do some homework. What did she mean?"

"Sire, I believe she was referring to the fact that your species does not exist solely on Earth."

Mike chewed on that one for a while, a long while. Was it possible . . . ?

"You mean she's *human*?"

"Define human, Sire."

"You know what I mean."

"I'm no scientist, but I believe it would take a geneticist a great deal of effort to find differences between you and her. Your species is quite common among the stars, much more common than any others. Does that answer your question?"

Mike was confused. Did that answer his question, or did it just raise more questions?

>Jake, get to work on this. I want an answer pronto.<

>Yes, Sire.<

>Oh, sorry. Is there an encyclopedia on this boat? I need to do some research.<

>With George gone, I'm not sure. We'll have to go into the net to find it.<

>Can you do that while I set up the next jump?<

>I can if you'll quit bothering me. Let's get to work.<

Mike looked at Otis for a long time, not certain how to phrase his next question. Otis waited patiently with his tail curled around his feet, returning an expectant gaze to Mike. He knew what was on Mike's mind, and Mike knew that he knew. He trusted Otis, and that gave him the courage to ask.

"I love her, Otis, and she loves me. She's also probably Queen. Is a relationship between the two of us appropriate?"

Otis growled low in his throat, then lifted his lips in the leer Mike had grown accustomed to. It was the Great Cat's way of smiling. "I, too, love her. And I am her Protector. If I sense harm to her, you'll know."

Otis padded closer to Mike, then sat again. "At the moment, I sense rightness, and if my approval has any meaning, you have it, but know this, as well: alienness is not limited to physical differences. You and she are alien to each other. Not physically, but culturally, politically, and maybe even emotionally. She will be Queen one day, Sire. You face a veritable minefield of challenges and adjustments in the time to come. It may be that your relationship will thrive, even deepen as a result, or it may wither. Whatever happens, the road you have chosen will be difficult. Is your love for her strong enough to navigate that minefield? Are you man enough to take second place to her? Are you man enough to support her, to hold her up on the pedestal that the Queen must, by necessity, occupy?"

Otis blinked, then went to the central shaft leading to his gun turret. He didn't expect an answer – indeed, no honest answer was possible at the moment. Mike lifted the helmet to his head, but before pulling it on he called to Otis whose feet were just disappearing into the ceiling. "Please don't call me sire. That's ridiculous after what we've been through together."

"Sire is what you are, and Sire is what I will call you," he heard echoing down the shaft. "That does not mean I will let you forget you are still a cub, and a barbaric one at that."

Chapter Thirty-one

Mike finished his computations for the last jump. He was done early for a change, and he had nothing to do for the next few minutes. For the first time in weeks, he looked Outside. He was always enmeshed in the outside view, but he rarely had time to pay it any attention. Now he did.

Stars and hazy nebulae filled his awareness. *Resolve* had traveled closer to the center of the galaxy during the past year, and slightly off to the side the center of the galaxy glowed in a richness never seen from Earth. Because he was in the net, the skin of the ship did not intrude. He literally felt like he was hanging in the midst of space. With just a thought he turned, soaking into himself the beauty and complexity of the cosmos, and his heart filled with the wonder of it all. Stars were so abundant that he could not pick out the familiar constellations of his childhood.

With George's help he probably could have, but George was dead. Like the Knight he had pretended to be, George had served his Queen to the end. His death had not been for naught.

To Ellie, Gamma VI was a living place, a place with friends and relatives. To Mike, Gamma VI was just a set of numbers defining a place in space. He had brought them to this place, wherever it was. He was moments away from the last jump, on course and on time. He had only one more command to give and the voyage would be at end.

What did 'end' mean for him? Was it truly an ending, or was it a new beginning? Or the beginning of the end? He shrugged. Such thoughts were for philosophers, not for Mike Carver. To him, giving the command would determine whether Ellie was Queen, as she feared, or his princess, as he hoped. He would stand with her in either case, but he hoped desperately that they would have some time first, enjoy some peace first, find out who the other person really was when survival was not the only issue.

Whatever Ellie needed from him, he would provide for as long as she would accept. Out of everything he had done since the Chessori ship crashed to Earth, it was the only thing of which he was certain.

As *Resolve* neared the theoretical point he had computed, he pursed his lips and gave the command, then waited for the computers to do their thing at just the right instant. When they did, there was no change in sound, no sense of displacement, but the stars disappeared. The computers hummed along happily as he inspected them, so he relaxed. He had done everything he could do. As Otis had once demanded of him, he had given everything that he was to come to this place.

>Things look okay to you, Jake?<

>They do. See you on the other side, Mike.<

The jump ended. When stars again filled the sensors, a brighter star held center stage. >Is it the right one?< he asked Jake.

Jake ran a few calculations. >It is. We made it, Mike. This is the other side. Welcome to your first new world.<

Chapter Thirty-two

Mike's shoulders slumped, and he relaxed for the first time in many, many months. It was done! His ordeal was over.

He had taken no chances with his navigation: a mistake this close to Gamma VI could be fatal, so he had jumped to a point farther outside the system than George would have. The couple of extra weeks of travel toward Gamma VI paled in comparison to the cost of small errors in his computations, errors on the order of a few nanoseconds at jump speeds. But the time for reminiscing was over. It was time to get to work.

The screens displayed a vast array of commercial and military ships, though none were nearby. Recorders were brought on line and started to record every piece of information they could. Ellie wanted news of the Empire, but she would take news of any kind she could get. She and Otis could review everything later during the weeks it would take to reach Gamma VI.

Mike's worst fears came true just hours after they came out of hyperspace. A heavy squadron consisting of a cruiser, two frigates, and a dozen Empire fighters, with three Chessori ships in trail, materialized from hyperspace nearby. The hound had found them.

They had only a few hours before the shooting started. The

tractor beam did not appear on their sensors, but it probably would soon. Everyone went to battle stations. Mike was prepared to cut Ellie and Jake out of the loop if the Chessori launched a psi attack. They had learned their lessons well.

Without George's help they couldn't tell if this was the same squadron that had been chasing them, but it didn't look friendly, and as before, the cruiser never queried them, never asked who they were. There was no question that it knew who was aboard *Resolve*. An escape jump, actually a series of escape jumps, had been preprogrammed. Mike activated the program and held his hand above the Execute button as long as he could, querying the net for suggestions. He received no help from his crew and executed the jump.

The jump was as short as he could make it. Their screens blanked, then refreshed farther away from Gamma VI. Twenty minutes later their screens filled with military ships again. Mike jumped twice more in quick succession. The squadron followed each time.

"They're definitely tracking us," Otis observed. "There's no escape without disabling the thing."

Mike thought fiercely. These ships were not here to take prisoners. If there had been a coup, Ellie and Alexis were worth more dead than alive to them. *Resolve* needed help. He called Ellie to his side and opened a communications channel to the cruiser, requesting a conference with the captain. To his surprise, he got a response. The overweight figure of a bemedaled officer filled the screen. Beside him stood a Chessori.

These were definitely not friends.

Ellie was ready. After weeks and months of frustration there was no hesitation. She was her royal self again. Jake took the initiative and set the controls to general broadcast. The whole squadron would hear their Queen.

The man sneered. "Your Majesty, how nice of you to call."

"Who are you, and why are you doing this?" she demanded.

"I'm Admiral Shuge. It's time for a new order, Your Majesty. Your reign will be short, indeed."

"Perhaps." Her chin lifted, and her voice rose to take on its most commanding tone. "Loyal officers of the Empire, I am Daughter. The Chosen have not fallen. I command you to come to my aid. Rise up against these criminals within your midst. I will never yield."

The man chuckled. "There is no one left to answer your call. Those of questionable loyalty have been incarcerated. Your commands mean nothing here. But I'm curious. We lost you months ago. How did you manage that?"

Mike moved into the picture, the First Knight's medallion displayed prominently on his chest. The man looked startled, impulsively raising a fist across his chest. A long moment passed, then he looked at his fist in disgust and dropped it sheepishly back to his side and sneered again. "Sire. I do not recognize you. You look a little ragged about the edges. Do you not have a uniform?" He chuckled, turning to introduce the Chessori. "My friend offers mercy. Surrender and you may live. Not so Her Majesty, that would be impossible, but we welcome your loyalty, First Knight."

"You forget yourself, Admiral Shuge. A First Knight is loyal to his Queen and to the Realm as, I believe, are many of your men. I offer mercy to no one. Loyal officers need no mercy." He looked through Admiral Shuge and his voice rose. "Men and women of Empire, rise to me, rise to Her Majesty." Mike stood at attention, staring into the eyes of Admiral Shuge.

There was a commotion behind the admiral, and the communications link filled with savage growls and screams. A shape flew through the air knocking down the admiral, then the head of a cat thrust its face toward the camera, its mouth open in a bloody leer of triumph.

"Yes!" Otis yelled. "My brothers!"

The screen blanked. Mike quickly returned to the net and ordered everyone to prepare for battle. He went to full speed, angling *Resolve* away from the squadron, but they were immediately followed by both frigates, two Empire fighters, and the three Chessori ships. The Empire ships veered off before coming into range, leaving just the three Chessori.

Ellie was angry, but the effect of her words on the squadron convinced her that all was not lost. The net hummed with a sense of confidence that affected everyone.

With *Resolve* at maximum speed, the Chessori approach was slow. Mike didn't like that – it would let them activate their mind weapon for as long as they chose. He slowed so they could catch up. He waited until they just reached firing range, then he hit the brakes, hoping to scatter them. The Chessori angled up and away as they shot past holding beautiful formation, and *Resolve* was ready. The hours of training and the experience gained from their previous skirmishes paid off. *Resolve* stayed engaged, angling tightly up to follow. Ellie assigned targets and lasers reached out, followed shortly thereafter by the charged particle beams. Shields lit up on two of the three Chessori.

Otis, out of the net and operating manually, got the first kill. Pandemonium broke out over the net, but Mike could even physically hear the women cheering beside him in the control room. The two remaining Chessori tried to escape, but *Resolve* held on. A weak cicada sound threw them into momentary turmoil, but Jake and Ellie hung on and stayed in the net. Mike's whole body burned from Jake's response to the psi weapon.

Reba got through the shields of her target, and the Chessori were down to one. The cicada sound diminished further as everyone concentrated on the last Chessori. It, too, disappeared in a flash.

Mike returned his attention to the cruiser. It hung far off in space, alone, its support ships scattered. Shields occasionally winked on and off as one ship attacked another, but most of the fighting appeared to be internal. Jake found the tactical frequency and listened in on intermittent, confused transmissions but mostly silence. It was an eerie feeling knowing that a powerful squadron had been reduced to impotency, the result of a few words.

Should they run? Ellie wanted to stay. She believed in her heart that her sailors would prevail. Mike and Otis were not so certain. Mike brought *Resolve* about and began the laborious process of setting up the longest jump he could compute this close to the primary star, a jump long enough to terminate with the emergency stop program to fool the tracker. A couple of hours passed.

The bridge of the cruiser suddenly appeared before them on the main communications screen, a young man with black eyes and disheveled black hair looking to the side as he issued orders to someone off-screen with the audio muted. Everyone withdrew from the net, jumping up from their stations to face the screen together. Otis came on the run. The face turned to them, the audio came on, and the figure knelt on one knee as he bowed deeply, saying. "Your Majesty."

Ellie gasped. "Val? It's you?"

The man's head rose, and he nodded. He saw Mike and rose to his feet with his right fist across his chest. "Sire."

>I can't tell who he is, his uniform is too torn up. I think he's an officer, though,< Jake informed him.

"Report, Sailor," Mike commanded.

"Lieutenant Val, Bridge Control Officer of the heavy cruiser Beta IV, Sire. We have control of the bridge and have locked down all external weapons. The bridge is secure, but the rest of the ship . . . excuse me, Sire." He placed a hand to the speaker in his ear, listened intently, then issued orders in a crisp, decisive manner before looking back to Mike. "Power is now secure, Sire. They still have Weapons Control, Fleet Plot, and Communications. We're locking them down as quickly as we can."

"Lieutenant, you say 'we?' Whose side are you on?" Mike demanded, trying not to let the strain show.

"Sire?" He looked at Ellie, then knelt again with bowed head. "I've been held prisoner for months after refusing to support the new regime. I'm yours to command, Your Majesty."

"My family, Val," she demanded with a stricken look. "What of my family? What news do you have from the Palace?"

Lieutenant Val hesitated, his young face aging before their very eyes. "You don't know?" Pity filled his eyes. "I'm sorry, Your Majesty. They're all gone."

She turned to Mike with a look of horror. She let out an anguished cry, "Noooo!" as her fists beat into his chest. He collected her in his arms as Lieutenant Val, the fleet, the terrible fighting taking place within the squadron, though not forgotten, were placed to the side for a moment.

"Lieutenant Val," he said when he returned his attention to the young officer, "Are you the senior officer aboard your ship?"

"No, Sire. I was just the first one to make it to the bridge. The cats took no prisoners here. I'm coordinating with Captain Jons who is attempting to secure the rest of the ship."

"Are we in imminent danger from more disloyal ships appearing?"

"I can't answer that yet, Sire. My counsel would be to assume the worst. They will come eventually and there might be little warning. We must get the Queen away from here as soon as possible, but I've been advised that a tracker was placed aboard your ship. You cannot hide from the fleet with a tracker."

"Can you take us aboard?"

"The Queen?" A look of excitement crossed his face. He spoke briefly into his headset before replying. "Hangar Deck is not yet secure, Sire. I'll see to it." Then a calculating look filled his eyes. "We really must get the Queen to a safe place. Some of our smaller ships might be back under control before I am. Maybe we can get you aboard one of them. My communications are very limited. I'll get back to you, Sire."

"Lieutenant!" Mike shouted before the young man could cut him off. When Mike had his undivided attention, he added, "The Queen's safety is your number one priority. If you cannot personally vouch for one of your ships, we'll remain here."

"Sire, I respectfully tell you that you cannot remain in that ship. I can't protect you. All my weapons are locked down until I can ensure the loyalty of the crews operating them. I know fleet tactics, and I think I understand what's happening here. Every military ship in this system is heading this way as we speak, and others might drop from hyper any moment. You'll have little warning of attack with that tracker aboard. You'd be safer in a lifeboat. In fact, you might want to consider abandoning ship and deactivating the lifeboat's beacon."

His gaze shifted to Ellie who was still wrapped in Mike's arms. "Sire, trust me. So long as I live, I will not leave the Queen stranded. We probably have one hour." With that, the screen blanked.

Mike remained standing with his arms around Ellie. Looking over to Otis, he said, "Pretty sharp kid. Are all your officers that sharp?"

"He's special, Sire, and well known to myself and the Queen. His presence here is to our benefit. He's also right. If you'll keep an eye on things here, I'll see to deactivating a lifeboat beacon. An excellent suggestion. I'm surprised we didn't think of it ourselves."

"Should I head back? Can we count on him?"

"His loyalty is beyond reproach. Count on no one else at the moment. I recommend a return to the vicinity of the cruiser – it will be a temporary haven to us if Val prevails – but keep your options open. The decision is yours, Sire."

"What if the tracker is in the lifeboat, Otis?"

Otis growled deep in his throat as he dove into the central shaft. He returned twenty minutes later with news that a lifeboat was ready, though there was no way to determine if a tracker was aboard, and he had been unable to disable the beacon. More hours passed, and Mike was just reaching for the transmitter switch when his screen lit up. Lieutenant Val was back.

"I just learned that a Priority message went out to Fleet Headquarters the moment you arrived, Sire. Other ships could arrive any time from hyper. We might be down to minutes. Hangar deck is not secure, but I'm taking you aboard anyway. When you exit *Resolve,* I'll jettison her to get rid of the tracker. I've drawn every man I can from other fighting. We'll provide all possible protection without losing the rest of the ship. Get ready, Sire."

"We have a problem, Lieutenant. No one on my ship knows how to dock with you."

"Sire? Just instruct the AI," Val said with an impatient look. "I've activated the landing beacon."

"Our AI is damaged."

Val took a deep breath, then held his hand up to his ear as someone else sought his attention. He listened, then said, "No, sir. Communications can wait, so can Weapons Control. I've locked them down from here. I need those heavy weapons on the hangar deck and in Engineering. We absolutely have to retain our hold on Engineering. And I need a Guardian here on the bridge. I'm all by myself up here. Can you send one?"

"Very well, sir, and thanks." He turned back to Mike. "Sorry, Sire. That was Captain Jons."

"Is he on our side?"

"Yes, Sire. He was relieved by Admiral Shuge at the same time I was. We shared a cell."

"So how am I going to get this ship aboard your cruiser, Lieutenant?"

Val thought for a moment. "No offense, Sire, but I don't have time to talk you through it right now. Let me into your net, and I'll give the instructions."

"How do I let you in?"

Val blinked a couple of times, and Mike sensed his confusion. This all had to be pretty basic to a pilot, which Mike supposedly was, but Mike sensed that this man was prepared to deal with the unexpected.

"Open channel 6X17G and have your pilot go into the net, Sire. I'll find him there."

"Standby. I might need help setting the channel."

He went internal. >Jake, can you do it?<

>I don't know what he's talking about.<

Everyone went into the net, and sure enough, the moment Jake found and selected the frequency, Val was there waiting. His composure slipped momentarily when he saw Ellie.

He bowed deeply. "Your Majesty."

"Hello, Val. Welcome back to *Resolve*."

"We're in the net. How can you be in here?"

"We've had to make some adjustments. The crew is dead. So, too, is the AI."

Mike sensed strong emotions between the two of them. He backed away to give them as much privacy as he could.

Val was in a hurry. He stared at her for a time, then turned to Mike. "You're the Knight," he said, bowing low.

"No. I'm First Knight."

"Yes, Sire. Of course, Sire." He turned to Jake with an unspoken question.

"I'm Jake, your First Knight's Rider."

Val bowed to Jake, then turned to Reba with the same question, though the question was muddled in suddenly strong emotion.

"I'm Reba. Pleased to meet you, Val."

Mike almost felt Val tearing his gaze away from Reba. She had well and truly startled him in some way.

Then they heard another voice. "Val, Jons is in hangar bay. Resistance is minimal."

"Okay. I'm going to get *Resolve* started in. Let him know, Artmis." He turned his attention back to Mike. "I know this ship, Sire. Someone has to go with me to make the settings. I can't do it from afar. You have to release the lock on channel 64A71. Once you've done that, I'm in."

Mike sensed a mind that he immediately liked. This young man was in a hurry and he was very focused, but his focus was not only his ship. The Queen's survival was at the very top of his awareness, and he clearly understood that if he lost the cruiser he might lose the Queen as well. He would hurry, but he would get the job done right.

"How long will it take? I don't want to be gone from the bridge right now." Mike asked.

"Sire, there's little you can do from there, not with a tracker aboard."

"Not true, Val. We have our methods, and they work." He turned to Ellie. "Will you go with him?"

She nodded, and Mike and Jake disappeared. Val started to lead the way through the net, then stopped. "Where's your net, Mother?"

"Well, we've been sort of holding it together by ourselves. Can you find your way?"

Val thought for a moment, then threw procedure aside. He wasn't as versatile with the process as Ellie and Reba were, but he managed. They both followed him until he reached the right node, then Val backed off.

"Do you see the pad, Mother?" he asked.

"I do."

"Enter this code." He rattle off a series of numbers as Ellie touched the keys.

"I'm in," he said. Ellie and Reba moved back to watch him work. Neither was certain what took place, but *Resolve* soon indicated it was happy with the commands. They were tracking a beam of some sort.

"I've got to go. You're on automatic now."

"Thank you, Val. We'll see you soon. Set course for Centauri III when you can."

"Centauri III, aye, Your Majesty." Val stared at Reba for a moment, then he just disappeared.

Mike had Jake disable the channel Val had come in on – he didn't want anyone else coming in uninvited. Everyone stayed in the net until they felt *Resolve* pass through the force field holding atmosphere inside the cruiser's hangar deck. Shortly thereafter, they felt a solid bump. *Resolve* had landed. Their voyage was finally over.

Mike pulled Ellie along with him to her quarters and gathered up Mildred and Alexis, then they raced to the ramp where they met Reba and Otis. Otis distributed weapons, two holstered blasters and one rifle-like blaster for each. Otis operated the ramp controls, and the sounds and smells of heavy fighting greeted them.

Otis crawled down the ramp, returned fire from the left side of the ramp, then retreated back into *Resolve*. Blaster beams ricocheted wildly here and there. The hangar deck was definitely not secure.

"Not good," he stated gruffly. "I thought you said hangar deck was secure?" he asked Mike.

"Lieutenant Val received a report that fighting was minimal."

"Well, something's changed. We'll have to give his men more time to secure the deck. He motioned them to withdraw further into the ship, and he went to the ramp controls to close the ramp. The ramp was about half way up when they were thrown to the deck by a blast of light and heat. *Resolve* was under attack by a heavy weapon, and the ramp had stopped moving. Otis moved back from the controls dragging an injured leg, his fur smoking.

"Someone has fired-up a stinger. I can't close the ramp, it's damaged. Move back!"

"What's a stinger?" Mike yelled.

"A scout vehicle. It packs a heavy weapon for ground fighting. Val had better hurry."

Reba turned and left on a dead run. Mike and the Queen turned to follow, but Otis stopped them. "We have to hold the ramp. We cannot allow them into the ship or we're lost. Val's men and my brothers are not idle. They'll be here soon."

Ellie refused to leave Mike and Otis. After a brief, heated discussion, Mildred returned with Alexis to her quarters armed with her own blaster. Otis took one corridor leading from the ramp, and Mike and Ellie took another, huddling behind a corner as shot after shot pounded the ramp. Heat, light, and sound numbed their senses. The air soon filled with smoke – they were on fire somewhere. *Resolve* was tough, though.

Mike didn't think the stinger could blow them up, though he worried about a ricocheting shot finding its way down the corridor. The heavy fire did prevent ground troops from boarding, but it wouldn't be long.

Without warning, a bright flash of light turned their world white. A powerful blast shook the hangar deck outside *Resolve*, then silence descended and the scene turned surreal. Smoke stung their eyes and obscured their view, and their hearing had been deadened by the explosion. Reba returned, skidding to a halt beside Mike and Ellie, out of breath.

"I got him!" she exclaimed.

"Got what?"

"I hope I didn't damage the hangar deck too much. I took out the stinger with our bottom turret."

"You shot our gun *inside* the cruiser?"

"Sure, why not? Just the laser. I didn't activate the particle beam. We'd better move back. They'll rush us soon."

The area inside *Resolve's* ramp was in shambles. Small fires burned lethargically and smoke filled the air. Two higher level corridors that had once been confined behind walls and floors lay exposed, the girders and structure wrenched out of place by the merciless pounding of the stinger. From the other side of the ramp, Otis got Reba's attention, directing her with hand motions to station herself across the entrance from him. He directed Mike to take Ellie to a higher corridor where they would have more protection and a better field of fire looking down on the ramp.

Mike and Ellie raced through corridors and up shafts to find their way. He edged out to the end of an exposed corridor to look down on what had become a battle zone during their brief absence. Several enemy troops lay unmoving. Four others had spread out inside the ramp entrance, exchanging fire with Otis and Reba. Outside, a vehicle was maneuvering toward the entrance on a lift, something that had the look of a small tank.

Mike suddenly fell to the floor, his left leg a searing pain. He rolled over to discover Ellie on the floor writhing in pain as well. The sound of cicadas was back. Ellie had said that each attack seemed worse. Mike wanted to help her, but he knew the best help he could give her would be to stop the Chessori. The attacking Empire soldiers had succumbed to the Chessori psi weapon, as well. Otis, already wounded, struggled mightily to maintain control. Reba looked up at Mike with a questioning look and a shrug. All firing had stopped.

The cicada sounds continued, possibly stronger now. The stinger was lifted to the level of the floor, and it trundled into the ship looking for targets, driven by a Chessori enclosed inside a blister. Reba took careful aim with her rifle and two attending Chessori, both dressed in body armor, fell from the gun. Otis' training was paying off. Her shots had been perfectly placed to penetrate weak spots in the armor. Other Chessori clambered aboard as the gun's barrel rotated ominously toward Reba. She loosed several more shots, dropping one more Chessori, then retreated. It was up to Mike now.

Still unseen by those below, he pulled Ellie far back from the edge of the deck to keep her out of the line of fire. A short, thick barrel protruded from the stinger, turning this way and that as it searched for a target. Otis squirmed out of view behind a corner, then with a supreme effort, he rose and took careful aim. Mike's blaster spoke first. He dropped three Chessori, Otis dropped another, then Reba skidded to a halt beside him and dropped to the floor, firing continuously. The cicada sound stopped suddenly as another Chessori fell to Reba's blaster. The driver of the stinger looked around worriedly, knowing his backup help no longer existed, but he was well protected from their small arms by the blister canopy. The stubby barrel of the gun swung ominously toward Mike and Reba. They were out in the open with no protection at all.

Otis crawled out onto the floor and let out a scream that raised the hairs on the back of Mike's head. Seeing a Protector, the gunner immediately changed targets to the more menacing threat, and a weak cicada sound started up again. Mike, out of ideas, set his rifle down and took a running leap off the end of the corridor, dropping a full level to slam onto the gunner's blister. Stunned, his body lay splayed on the bubble of the turret, then he began sliding off. He scrabbled for anything to hold onto as he stared into the shocked eyes of the Chessori.

The Chessori managed a weak smile when he realized Mike had no means of reaching him through the armored blister, then the gun platform began trundling toward the corridor Otis had retreated into, the driver doing his best to see around Mike's spread-eagled body as he maneuvered. A shot ricocheted off the blister near Mike. He looked up in surprise to discover several Chessori coming up the ramp. Reba opened fire from above, felling two immediately and wounding another. No more shots came Mike's way.

Mike searched frantically for a way into the driver's cockpit. He spied a recessed hole outlined in red hash marks, decided it was an emergency exit control, and began inching toward it. The driver, suspecting Mike's intention, slammed the turret from side to side in an effort to shake him off. Mike slid down the bubble until his crotch rested on the barrel of the gun. The Chessori could not shake Mike loose, so he elevated the barrel toward the women. Mike brought a foot to the top of the barrel and pushed off, leaping to the side of the blister, then began kicking and prying with his toes to activate the emergency release. The gunner grinned as he drew a hand-held blaster and pointed it toward Mike through the glass. Mike's innards shriveled as he lay exposed, knowing that only a clear bubble separated him from the blaster's charge.

He felt a click through his boot. The bubble canopy cracked open in response. The gunner waived his blaster at Mike again but focused his attention on the women above. Mike had no choice. He slid down the bubble, wrapped his hands under the lip of the glass, and heaved with all his strength. The canopy flew up, exposing the Chessori who stared at him in surprise, its blaster seeming to rise of its own accord.

Mike struggled for balance and nearly fell off the stinger, unable to draw his own blaster. A shot deflected off the controls next to the Chessori, who looked up into Reba's blaster. His own fingers pressed the appropriate firing studs at the same time as hers. His head and upper body disappeared in a bloody explosion, but not before his blaster fired. Mike spun off the gun platform, his right arm and part of his shoulder gone. He had a moment to stare about in confusion as Jake screamed at him to hang on, then he passed out.

Unknown to him, five Guardians chose that instant to spring onto the ramp from below. All firing stopped. The few remaining enemy troops dropped their weapons and raised their hands. Otis greeted his compatriots with feeling, barked orders for a medic, then he raced off to find the Queen. He returned shortly with her and Reba.

Ellie, oblivious to everyone else, knelt down in the pool of blood beside Mike to inspect the grisly wound. The flow of blood had stopped. Had he died? Holding his head in both hands, she demanded, "You'd better be doing your job, Jake. Do you hear me in there?" Tears streamed down her face as she leaned over Mike to hold him.

Chapter Thirty-three

Lieutenant Val had his hands full on the bridge of the cruiser. *Resolve* was aboard, but the fighting on Hangar Deck, nearly secure before *Resolve's* arrival, had intensified. It appeared that the Chessori and their Rebel counterparts recognized *Resolve* as the Queen's ship, and they had shifted their efforts to her.

Suddenly, the mind weapon of the Chessori started up and Val fell to the deck writhing in agony. He had known this might happen and had taken steps to ensure the bridge would not be retaken by the Rebels. The Great Cat guarding the bridge dragged him behind a console and laid by his side, its weapon aimed at the blast doors securing the bridge. Nothing short of demolitions would breach the doors, and the Great Cat was his final level of protection.

The mind weapon stopped, but it started up again a short time later. When it finally ended, Val was done in. The cat drew him to his feet and steadied him, then led him to his station, indicating that he had to get back into the net. Val closed his eyes and took a deep breath, squaring his shoulders with determination as he reached for the helmet. Yes, he needed to check on his ship, and he needed to check on the other ships of the squadron. And he had a thousand other things to do, as well. Everything was critical, and everything demanded his immediate attention. Most important to him was that the Queen was aboard and it was time to get away. More Rebel ships could show up any moment.

In the net he discovered Hangar Deck secure, finally. Stretchers floated across the deck, but he couldn't tell who was on them. The Great Cats surrounded *Resolve's* ramp to prevent any unwanted visitors from entering.

He queried Captain Jons. "How's it going, sir?"

"We're mopping up. There are casualties on *Resolve*, but I've been told the Queen is okay. How are you doing up there?"

"Still secure, sir. Weapons Control and Fleet Plot are not. Think you can get up to Fleet Plot?"

"Don't we need Weapons Control more?"

"Your call, sir, but let me bring you up-to-date. A call went out quite a while ago over the hypercom. We might have more Rebel squadrons showing up soon. I'd like to gather up the remnants of our squadron and get out of here. The First Knight ordered me to keep the Queen's safety our top priority."

"Hmm. He's right, and I concur. How's the rest of the squadron?"

"Without Fleet Plot, it's hard to say. I'm going to have to call each one of them. I hope someone's home to answer."

"You can probably assume it's been just as bad on those ships as it's been here. Get to it. I'm on my way to Fleet Plot."

"Try not to damage it too much while you're at it, sir."

"That will make it a lot harder. I think I'll try to break a few cats away from the Queen to take with me. They're far better than us at this sort of thing."

"Uh, sir, there may be some Chessori still alive. I think most of them died in your battle to secure *Resolve*, but I'm not certain. I'm thinking about the First Knight's order."

"You're right, the Queen's safety comes first. The cats are probably needed right where they are. Gather up any of the squadron you can and get out of here. I'll get Fleet Plot back on line as soon as I can."

"Sir, maybe you ought to come up here and change places with me. You're the senior person aboard now."

"I should, but I won't. You've got the conn, my friend, and you're doing a fine job. I'll be up when I can, unless the captains on the other ships want more horsepower behind your orders."

"Uh, in that case, maybe I'll call the Queen, sir."

"Val, we spent months living together in that cell. I know you well. Even you don't have the guts to do that. I'll talk to you later."

Val issued orders to whatever ships were listening, giving coordinates for an immediate jump. It was a short jump, but he definitely wanted away from Gamma VI before anyone else showed up. The moment the jump ended, he went back to checking on his ship. He could not afford to let any large groups of Rebels retake what they'd lost, and he desperately wanted to know if there were any Chessori still alive. The terrible mind weapon of theirs could wreak havoc with any plans he set in place.

He was deep in the net when he sensed the blast doors opening. He ripped the helmet from his head as he turned, a blaster in his hand. The Great Cat protecting him had opened the doors to allow another Great Cat to enter the bridge, and he relaxed. A moment later, a bedraggled woman appeared. His heart stopped for a moment thinking it was the Queen, but this woman was not the Queen. It was the woman he'd seen in the net on *Resolve*. Her red hair was pulled back in a tight bun, but loose strands hung everywhere. Her uniform hung in tatters, and blood, someone else's blood, had splattered the remnants. Her face was smudged with soot, and she held a blaster in her hand with another holstered at her hip.

He knew she was a key player in all of this, but he didn't have time for her right now. What was she doing here?

Then she smiled. That smile lit up her whole countenance. He stepped back, startled, the battle forgotten for a moment. Her eyes sparkled, captivating him as she tossed a translator to him.

"Hello, Val," she said. "I'm Reba."

"We met earlier. How is the Queen?"

"She's alive. She's in sick bay."

"She was hurt?" he asked in horror.

"No. Mike, I mean your First Knight, is in pretty bad shape. Otis, our Protector, was wounded as well, but he's with the Queen, still protecting her. The Queen refuses to leave Mike's side, but I have orders from her for you. She wants to return to Gamma VI, just long enough for her to announce her presence to the general populace. Then you can resume your course to Centauri III."

He closed his eyes, not believing what he had heard. She was no longer smiling when he opened his eyes. "You can't be serious," he demanded.

"I, too, am surprised. But she's the Queen, Val."

Val thought hard. "Did she say it had to be right now?"

"No, but doesn't everyone around here act immediately on her command?"

"They do." He hesitated, then made a decision. "I'll take her back, but not yet. This ship is not yet secure, and my squadron is in shambles. She's going to have to wait. There's no other way I can ensure her safety." He raised his eyebrows, hoping for her agreement.

He got it, finding himself on the receiving end of that radiant smile again. "Well said, Val. Mike would agree with you if he was here. It's the right decision. I'll let her know."

"I could use some help. Can you stay?"

"I'd like to. I'm a naval officer, but from a planet you've never heard of. I don't know much about star cruisers. Can you still use me?"

"Can you take reports and forward my instructions?"

"I can try, but I don't speak the language very well. My translator lets me understand what's said. Ellie will be up here eventually, but she's preoccupied right now. Show me what to do."

"Who's Ellie?"

"Sorry. The Queen."

Val closed his eyes for a moment. *Ellie?*

"Look, I need to get situation reports from the other ships in the squadron, but I'm needed in the net to keep an eye on my ship. I can set things up for you, and I can send the request. Will you take those reports?"

"Just get me started, Val."

The battle ebbed and flowed aboard the cruiser. Val spent the next hour directing squads to hot spots, then removed his helmet to find Reba waiting. She had a long list of items.

"Both frigates are badly damaged, but they're secure. Only six of your fighters made the jump, and they're in bad shape as well. It hasn't been pleasant for any of them."

"Everyone's operational?"

"No one's operational, not in terms of engaging a Rebel fleet. As near as I can tell, though, they're on our side. I have not appraised them of the fact that the Queen is aboard this ship, and I hesitate to do so before we're more certain of loyalties. I don't want them attacking us, but they heard her call to duty. They probably know. They're awaiting orders."

"Do I need to hear the rest of the details on your list?"

"No, not if you're ready to jump out of here. The rest can wait."

He rubbed tired eyes. "Okay. I'll get back into the net and issue orders. We'll jump in twenty minutes. Can you tell if they're willing to accept orders from a lieutenant?"

"Your orders are in the name of the Queen, Val. I think they'll follow on those grounds."

"Oh, I see what you mean."

The remains of the squadron jumped, then came the cleanup. It had been just Val, Reba, and a Great Cat occupying the cavernous bridge for a number of hours. When Captain Jons finally made his way to the bridge, he assumed command of the squadron and named Val as acting captain of the cruiser. All of them were exhausted, but there was no time for sleep and there wouldn't be for quite some time. Val focused on restoring order aboard the cruiser. None of the standing bridge crew had survived the attack of the Great Cats, and his first order of business was to install a minimal bridge crew. He called several crewmen and women to the bridge for interviews. Reba just listened as he and Jons questioned them, then Val focused on critical command positions in Engineering, Weapons, and Communications. He had to leave the bridge to do so, and he took Reba with him. She said little, but he noted her silent nods of acquiescence or disapproval as he vetted department heads and their senior staffs. Within a day they were able to release the lock-down on weapons and communications, though they did not yet allow the fighters to come aboard.

They'd been hard at it for some two days, all without sleep, by the time Val felt his ship was back under control. He had lost some twenty percent of his crew and many of the department heads, and the cruiser would be hard pressed to fight for a long time.

At Reba's insistence, he visited sick bay to check on the First Knight. Ellie was waiting and pulled him into a hug. "It's good to see you, Val. You look tired."

"It's been a long eleven years, Your Majesty."

Ellie turned to Reba and the two embraced. Tears flowed freely while Val looked on in agony, knowing it had been his decision that brought such grief to his Queen. The First Knight was ensconced within a tank of fluid, all because Val had ordered him to come aboard the cruiser. He had expected them to remain locked up in *Resolve* for a while. He wished he had been more clear with his instructions.

I'm sorry about what happened, Your Majesty. I barely know him, but I like what I saw."

"He's the man of dirt."

Val hesitated, staring at the tank while he considered her words, then he said, "I'm glad you told me. He's more. He's the Knight, Mother."

Reba stood back, watching the two of them. Their words and actions confused her, but she stayed silent. She could barely hear Ellie's soft reply:

"Val, he's lost his right arm."

The words visibly staggered Val. He remained speechless for a time, then asked softly, "Does he know?"

"He does not."

"They told us others would be called."

"They did. Reba is one."

He released Ellie and turned to Reba with a questioning look. "Do you know?" he asked softly.

"I have no idea what you're talking about, either of you."

Val stared at her for a time, then turned back to Ellie. "They should know, Mother."

"They will. Now is not the time, but they will know soon. I'm told that Mike will be in there for a while."

Val stared into her eyes for a long time, blinking from time to time. Reba didn't know what thoughts passed between the two, but the room buzzed with energy.

Ellie broke his trance. "We have a lot of catching up to do, but it can wait."

He nodded. "Very well, Your Majesty. I should be getting back to my duties."

"Thank you for being here, Val. Again, your timing is impeccable, and this time you fully understand the stakes."

He nodded and turned for the door. Reba looked a question to Ellie and received a smile in return. "I'm fine here," Ellie said. "Go."

By the end of the next day, Jons was ready, reluctantly, to return to Gamma VI as the Queen had commanded. By then, Val and Reba had been paired together for three days with very little sleep. Her smile still shone whenever she caught him looking at her, and that kept him going.

She balked at Jons decision. "Sir, I can't order you, but I respectfully tell you that a return to Gamma VI right now could be a disaster. I'd rather convince the Queen that we should not make the attempt at all."

"I don't think we've been fully introduced," Jons said angrily. "Exactly who are you, and what is your position here? Val?" he asked, turning angry eyes to his newest captain.

"Uh, she's fought more Chessori than we have," Val replied. "She came here aboard *Resolve*."

"You're with the Queen?" Jons asked in surprise.

"We're all with the Queen," Reba replied. "I'm not a fleet officer, though I'd very much like to become one. All I can say is that we walked into one trap at Gamma VI, and I don't want to walk into another."

"I've already tried to talk the Queen out of it. She insists," he said, running a tired hand through his hair. "We're as ready as we're going to get without a major refit, and that's what she based her decision on. We won't be there long."

"What if the Chessori are waiting? Can you guarantee you'll be able to get away?"

Jons looked at Val with hooded eyes, then back to Reba. "You know I can't make that promise."

"She's the Last of the Chosen, sir. No other answer is acceptable. Her Protector and your First Knight would back me up on this even if the Queen does not."

"She insists. Give me a better solution," Jons demanded.

"Make her wait. Give me a little training while she waits. Your First Knight intended all along that I learn to fly *Resolve*. He just didn't count on losing George, the artificial intelligence that ran the net. Once that happened, it was impossible to bring me into the full net."

"You didn't have a net on *Resolve*?" Jons asked, his brow furrowed in confusion.

"We had a net, but not an AI," she replied. "Everyone, and I include the Queen and myself, had to keep the net functioning while Mike computed jumps."

"You had no AI, the Queen joined the net, and the First Knight computed all those jumps *manually*?"

"Yes, yes, and yes, sir."

Val and Jons looked at each other, not quite certain what to think.

"Where did you say you were from?" Jons asked.

"Earth. I don't know what you call it, but the Queen said we're classified as an emerging world and off limits to Empire ships."

"Then what kind of training did you have?"

"I was a lieutenant in the Navy on Earth. We're talking surface ships here, gentlemen, but look: I got my first two Chessori kills after one hour aboard *Resolve*. The AI was still with us then. He was with us for the next two as well. He wasn't with us during the ambush we set up later in deep space, but we would have succeeded if the Chessori hadn't used their mind weapon on us at a critical time, and the tactics we used during the ambush were mine. I made the plan, and Mike executed it manually, perfectly. Your Queen and your First Knight's Rider showed me how to get around the net without an AI, and I held watches on my own. Uh, I think you were in the brig when *Resolve* showed up here, and you might not be aware that this squadron included three Chessori ships when the mutiny started. Your Queen, her Protector, and I took them out while your First Knight flew the ship."

Jons was at a loss for words. He gave Reba a piercing stare; she responded with her dazzling smile.

"And you're a friend of the Queen?" he asked finally.

"Leave Ellie out of this," Reba demanded. "I stand on my own abilities."

"Who's Ellie?"

"Oh. Sorry. I mean leave the Queen out of this."

"I see . . ." Jons moved away to think. When he turned back, he spoke to Val. "We're short-handed. Should we put her in Weapons?"

"No, sir. She wants to be a starship pilot. I think she's earned the right."

"We're not running a school here, Lieutenant."

"But we are short-handed, and if you get your way with the Queen, if you convince her to change her mind about Centauri III, we're months from help, sir, even if we survive returning to Gamma VI. There's more to Reba that only the Queen can reveal, but sir, she's definitely a player in all of this."

"Captain Jons," Reba spoke up, "I have one further qualification. I must insist on your agreement that what I am about to tell you remain absolutely secret."

Jons sighed. "And what might that be? You have my agreement."

"The reason I can help if given a little training is that I'm immune to the Chessori mind weapon." Jons stared at her in disbelief. So, too, did Val.

"It's true, sir. I think you can appreciate the value of that if you're attacked by the Chessori when you return to Gamma VI."

"Are you certain of this, young lady?"

"Absolutely certain."

"Very well." He turned to Val. "Get her up to speed on the guns first. I've never seen it done before, but there's probably some way to control all of them from the bridge. If she can get that figured out, give her full access, but don't let her endanger the ship or the squadron." He addressed Reba. "We'll assign a rank of acting lieutenant since that was your previous rank on Earth. If you pass muster, we'll make it permanent."

Reba's grin was all the answer he needed. Val suddenly found himself pulled in too many directions again. He got Reba started on her training after instructing the AI how to proceed. He then spent quite a while reconfiguring the guns, only as a last ditch effort should it be needed. Reba would only need the basics. She could rely on the support of the AI to carry out her commands until she had time for more training.

Then he brought the fighters aboard. Jons supervised that process from the landing bay while Val flew the cruiser. Jons was saddened to see the damage sustained by his fighters. It had been particularly bad for them, and clearly, several of them had fought external battles as well as the internal mutiny.

Reba approached Val inside the net. "Captain, I don't know how long it will take, but from what I know of these Chessori, I may be the only one functioning if they jump us on our return to Gamma VI. Is there any way you can tie the other ships to me so I can get us all out of there if necessary?"

Val frowned. "We won't be there long, and the odds are small that retreat becomes an issue, but I'd sure like to preserve what's left of the squadron. I'll see what I can do."

Setting up a control link to the other ships had never been done so far as Val knew, and the link itself was not his biggest problem. The captains of those ships resisted hard, and Val fully empathized with them – it was contrary to all their training to relinquish command to anyone else. Captain Jons had to get involved, and he threatened to get the Queen involved before he received the necessary agreements. Val ended up spending a lot of time with the Chief Engineer and a number of technical manuals, but the connections were made.

Reba spent a week in training, a ridiculously short period of time, but she did not have to learn the ship, she only had to learn to fly it. If things broke, she would not be the one to fix them. Even if her new skills were called upon, her tasks would not be difficult. Val set things up so that all she had to do if the Chessori showed up was to continue ahead to a pre-programmed jump point and jump away.

The Queen's message started going out the moment they dropped from hyper, but two full squadrons of Empire ships and a dozen Chessori traders arrived moments later, and their positioning could not have been worse. They were right in front of the squadron, between Reba and the jump point chosen by Val. Jons cursed the luck of these Rebels and set Val to computing a new jump point immediately. The Chessori didn't give him time.

The moment the cicada sound started up, Reba and the Great Cats were the only crewmembers functioning within the whole squadron.

She commanded all three AI's, her own and the two aboard the frigates, to turn away from the pursuers and to bring all shields to maximum strength. The turn would not prevent the squadron from merging with the attackers, there was no way to do that, but it would give her a chance to compute a new jump point without barging straight into them. She set her AI to computing the jump while she went through the process of reconfiguring the guns of the cruiser to her command. The guns on the frigates were beyond her ability to control. Those two ships would be defenseless.

She brought the two frigates in as close to her cruiser as she could without risking collision. The AI's aboard those two ships would not have any difficulty keeping a tight formation. Her only focus was defense. She would reach the new jump point in thirteen minutes, but a lot could happen in thirteen minutes and she had to hit the jump point on the proper vector. There would be little opportunity for evasive action.

The two Rebel cruisers and the dozen Chessori held well off to the side after her turn was complete, but the four frigates and twenty-four fighters did not. Soon, space around the three ships of her squadron swarmed with enemy ships.

The attacking fighters were a problem, but not as serious a problem as the four frigates. It would take time for the smaller ships' weapons to penetrate the heavy shielding of her squadron, but not so for the four frigates. She focused on them, letting the fighters swarm as they desired. Her squadron was soon engulfed.

The Great Cats could not help her. The massive batteries on the cruiser could not be activated manually – it had to be done from within the net. Val's program which allowed all guns on the cruiser to answer to Reba was put to the test. She couldn't deviate from the assigned trajectory to the new jump point, but she could, perhaps, threaten the attacking frigates. She chose one at random and opened up with half her guns on that one ship, then chose another frigate for the remainder of her guns. Shields began glowing on the frigates, then failing, and they pulled back. She went after the other two with the same results. She would have liked to pursue and kill them, but her purpose was to save the squadron, not to kill the enemy.

She was surprised at how quickly the frigates withdrew, but she soon found out why. Both cruisers were moving in on her, and the fighters were still swarming, still inflicting minor damage.

The cruisers did not go for the frigates; they went for her. Within the first minute she lost two batteries, and one of the batteries blew a hole in the hull as it disintegrated. Her AI slammed doors shut in the affected area as Reba fought on. She brought half her guns to bear on the nearest cruiser, locked them in, then focused her remaining guns on the second cruiser. Both ships took hits, but she never found out if she'd done any significant damage. Her squadron had reached its jump point and she gave the command. They jumped.

They had once again escaped a trap, but Reba was not done yet. She brought all ships to maximum speed as the enemy fleet appeared again. She didn't give the Chessori time to use their mind weapon; she hit the jump command again, knowing they were in deep space and not likely to hit anything. As soon as her two frigates materialized beside her, she hit the jump command again. Val soon joined her on the net, though it was clearly a struggle for him. Her heart went out to him, sensing through the net the monumental effort needed by him to focus after suffering the effects of the mind weapon.

"What's the situation?" he demanded.

"We're free, but they're tracking us. I'm setting up a long jump that will give everyone a chance to recuperate, but they'll be on us soon. You're faster than me. Can you set it up?"

Val set up the jump while Jons coordinated with the frigates. Minutes later, the Chessori showed up on their screens. Before the mind weapon appeared, Val ordered the jump executed. It was a long jump just as Reba had ordered.

"They'll be right behind us when we break out," she said. "We had the same problem aboard *Resolve*. Mike and Jake found an emergency stop program that ended the jump early. If we can do that, we'll lose them."

Val immediately sensed the rightness of her plan. He queried the AI, found the means, then had to confer with Jons. Communication between the two frigates was impossible during a jump. They would have to make one more jump after this one.

"Give me coordinates where we can rendezvous," Jons directed. "There's no way we're all going to come out of hyper together with this emergency stop mechanism. We'll have to meet up later."

Val did his magic with the AI while Reba kept the guns ready. As soon as the jump ended, Jons issued orders to the two frigates, then they all jumped again. The emergency program was executed, and *Beta IV* dropped from hyper somewhere in deep space. They reached their rendezvous point two days later where they joined up with the two frigates. All three ships had sustained serious damage, but the plan set up by Val, Reba, and Jons had definitely saved them from annihilation.

Jons had no further misgivings about her training. In fact, he relieved her of all other duties to concentrate on that training. She and Val spent hours together in the net, mind-linked the entire time, and Reba, for the first time in her life, found someone who was not intimidated by her in the slightest. By the time Mike was ready to come out of the tank, she had not yet had the opportunity to attempt a landing, but she had made a number of jumps with Val's assistance and the ship's version of George.

Chapter Thirty-four

"You *are* joking," Struthers said over the communicator as his skimmer carried him toward the Palace for an inspection.

"No, Sire. We believe she escaped with the squadron, and we lost the signal from the tracker. We lost her," Jirdn said.

"Turn around!" he ordered his driver. "Back to my office." Into the communicator he said, "Staff meeting in my office immediately, and get Juster back here, I don't care how long it takes."

"Yes, Sire."

Struthers sat back in the seat fuming. This was bad, real bad. It had to be the cats. No one else had the willpower to overcome the *scree*. A sense of doom filled him. The last of the Chosen was free, she had a squadron, and he had no idea where she was.

Would she go to Centauri III, he wondered? Or would she hole up somewhere and try to organize something? He needed Juster's counsel, but he was months away. He'd have to resort to the hypercom again.

Then his blood chilled. She had the hypercom, too, unless the communications chief on the cruiser had taken the time to destroy it. The sense of doom deepened.

She probably needed repairs. He made a mental note to pass the names of the ships in her squadron to every ship repair facility in the Empire. It would take months, and it would be expensive, but it had to be done. He didn't care about the ships, but the last of the Chosen had to be removed at whatever cost. All of his efforts would focus on finding her, no matter what it took.

Who were her friends? She would have to seek help, and she would go to someone she knew. He had one name, Chandrajuski, but there were others. He would have to round them all up, and he would, regardless of the consequences. The Queen must be found.

Something would have to be done about the cats as well. He paused, not sure what to do. The wealthiest and most powerful individuals in the Empire depended on the cats for protection. There would be repercussions if he tried to remove them. And if the cats started disappearing, their brothers would know and the rest would not be taken easily.

Could he turn the gleasons onto them? Maybe. The cats and gleasons were ancient enemies. The gleasons had no concept of how to function within the Empire – they were only barely under control as it was – but if he turned them loose on Brodor, the home world of the cats, he could just forget about them and the cats for a while. And the gleasons would jump at the opportunity. Things had gotten so bad for them, locked up on their small world by the Empire, that they had taken to killing and eating their own kind. They were so desperate that the cost of bringing them on board had been a pittance, just the gift of an emerging world. They no longer had to feast on each other, and the rest of the Empire would quickly forget about that world.

But it was time to put the gleasons to work. They might not function around others, but there were still things they could do. He would give some thought to Brodor. A gleam lit his eyes as he thought about the two ancient enemies locked together on the same planet. He toyed with the idea for a while but finally shook his head. His focus was the Queen, nothing else. The sectors would be on their own for a while as he concentrated his efforts on her. He would find her, and the line of Chosen would be no more. Brodor would be next in line. His hatred for the cats was only exceeded by his hatred for the Queen.

Chapter Thirty-five

Mike's eyes flickered open to whiteness. He stared at the whiteness before him for a while before realizing it was a machine of some kind, and it encapsulated his body. Only his head was free. He couldn't move.

>Welcome back.<

>Hi, Jake. What's up?<

>Not us, that's for sure. Not much longer though. It's been a long six weeks.<

"Six weeks!" he grunted aloud. "Six weeks?" A cat's head moved into view. "Otis?" he asked.

"No," came a gruff reply. "I'll let him know you're awake."

He and Jake conversed for a while, Jake complaining that it had been a long, boring time for him. He had enough control over Mike's body to open his eyes, but speech was far too complicated for him without Mike's help. He could hear, he could see, and he could feel, but he had not been able to interact with anyone. Jake was intimately familiar with Mike's condition, having held him together until the medical staff took over, then taking the healing process far beyond that which Empire doctors could accomplish on their own.

Mike was sickened when he remembered the Chessori and the

blaster. >I guess I've lost the arm, huh?<

>And part of your shoulder. Your new one is almost ready.<

"What?" he yelled aloud.

>Yup, brand new. It'll be as good as the old one when I'm done with it. See, I told you there were benefits to having me around.<

The cat momentarily reappeared in Mike's view, then his head was smothered in Ellie's embrace. When she stepped back and he could see again, it seemed she had aged. Had things changed between them, he wondered? Her smile was all the response he needed.

"Hi, Princess," he said.

"Hi, yourself. You've been missed."

"That's the best greeting you could give me."

Her eyes took on a mischievous twinkle. She simply mumbled, "Hmm."

They took him out of the tank two days later while he slept. When he awoke, he found Ellie sitting patiently in a chair beside his bed. "Hi, again. Don't you have work to do?"

"Always, but at the moment you're my agenda. I have work for you. As your Queen, I command you to arise, Sir Michael."

"Ugh," was his reply. "Besides, you're my Princess." That brought him a contented smile.

"I'm sorry you didn't get to see Gamma VI. I know how much you were looking forward to setting foot on land," she said.

He turned inward for a time. When he looked back to her it was with a look of surprise. "You know what? It's okay! I'm just glad to be alive. I feel like I'm starting a new life. We'll find land one of these days. Until we do, I'm okay. Don't worry about it."

He returned to duty, not that there was much physical activity required of him. His life was awkward with only one useful arm. His new right arm, forced to grow through a combination of Empire medical technology and Jake's personal interaction with his body, was wrapped across his chest and stomach, a useless dead weight. Jake promised him the arm would be identical to his old arm in a few more months. There was no pain or itching – Jake took care of that, too. The process of re-growth absorbed huge quantities of energy that could only be supplied by his body, so eating was essentially a continuous activity with lots of supplements added by the medical staff of the cruiser.

Jake informed Mike that he had been busy in more ways than one. Reba was one of only two people in the Empire that was immune to the Chessori mind weapon, and the Empire needed to provide every safeguard it could to the two humans. In return, the Empire would, no doubt, place heavy demands on them. As a Knight, he had made a command decision. He had fissioned to create a new Rider for Reba. It had been a struggle to complete that task while helping Mike mend, but the new Rider was now assisting Jake to re-grow Mike's arm and shoulder. It had been more than a fair trade-off. The shoulder was done, but the arm and hand needed more time. He had not been able to transfer the new Rider to Reba yet, but the Rider was agreeable and ready.

Mike's stomach felt queasy as he thought about what was going on inside the cast on his arm. He couldn't feel a thing in there. There were no sensations from a hand or fingers, nor could he move anything. The vision he had of quivering flesh, tendons, and bones reminded him of something from a horror movie.

>It's not like that, Mike. Just let it be. We know what we're doing.<

>Can I meet the new Rider?<

>No. It's not our way.<

>Does it have a name? I'd like to thank it.<

>It will take a name after it gets to know Reba. You can thank it then.<

>Are you ready to make the transfer, or would you like to wait a while?<

>It's . . . difficult . . . with two Riders occupying the same body. The sooner the better, Mike.<

>You won't miss your offspring?<

>It's not like a human child. It's an exact replica of me with all my memories. It thinks exactly like I do. How would you like to be in close intimate contact with an exact duplicate of yourself and unable to get away? We're sick of each other. I'm even starting to wonder why you keep me around. I'm not sure I like what I see of myself.<

>Well, I do. Don't do anything rash. We'll make the transfer as soon as we can. Can I tell Ellie?<

>We're Knights of the Realm, Mike. We don't keep any secrets from her. Remember?<

>Oh, right. I do.<

Ellie brought him up to date in a private meeting held in her suite, a suite that had previously been occupied by Admiral Shuge. Lieutenant Val had escaped the trap set for them by Fleet Command, gathering up six fighters and two frigates in the process. They were the only ships that responded to his command. Together they had lit out at full speed from Gamma VI.

Her story of their return to Gamma VI and Reba's battle against the two squadrons of Rebel ships stunned him.

"Did you understand the danger you put them and yourself in when you chose to return to Gamma VI?" he asked, his brow furrowed.

"It was a bad decision, Mike, and I take full blame. Captain Jons tried to talk me out of it, but I felt certain we would have enough time to get my message out. I was wrong."

"Was the message so important?"

"Yes. The Empire must know it has a Queen. I intend to visit more sectors as soon as I can."

Mike closed his eyes. When he opened them, he saw the determination in her eyes. "You're Queen, Ellie, but we have to come up with a plan. Your life is not your own."

"I know, my love. I have a lot to learn about being Queen. I made a mistake, and I will make more mistakes. I'm counting on your guidance, and I will listen. I've learned a lesson I will not forget."

"So what's going on now? Are we on the way to Centauri III?"

"No. I failed to listen to Captain Jons once; I will not do so again. At his strong urging I have agreed to a change of plan. He's fairly certain that Centauri Sector is under the control of the Rebels. If it is, showing up there with his bedraggled fleet would accomplish nothing except to get us all killed. We need a plan, and we need resources not presently available to us to enact the plan, whatever it may be. He changed course two weeks ago to a new destination, Parsons' World, a world that he believes might be able to help us with private resources."

He listened while she told him the rest. She had not been idle while he was in the tank. She had personally visited each ship where her presence proved to the survivors that the Empire was not dead as they had been led to believe. No senior officers that had joined with the Rebels had survived retribution by the Great Cats, and the internal fighting had culled most of the remaining crewmembers who actively supported the rebellion. The survivors, some of whom had quickly supported the Rebels in the belief that the line of Chosen was dead, were offered the opportunity to renew their oaths to the Empire. Few refused. Those that did were branded rebels and locked up. Aboard each ship, she had informed the squadron that fate had chosen them to spearhead her efforts to restore the throne. She was counting on each and every one of them to remain true to their oaths, and she promised them that their names would never be forgotten.

Reba had been surprisingly absent since Mike had woken up. When he asked about her, Ellie just smiled.

"Probably driving the ship," she answered, her eyes twinkling.

"Val has taken her under his wing. She checks on me when she can, but they're pretty short-handed up there. I think she finally got the training you hoped George would provide."

"She's flying a cruiser?" Mike asked in surprise. "They must be short-handed."

"I'm sure they're keeping an eye on her, and I fully support their decision. If we run into any more Chessori, she'll be the only one functioning."

Mike pursed his lips. "Maybe I should get up there, as well."

"Maybe you should, but not yet. Give yourself a few days. We're not in any danger at the moment. Parsons' World is about as far from here as you can go and still remain in the Empire. It's a long voyage."

Several new members had been added to the Queen's retinue. Otis had assigned two more of the Great Cats to assist him in guarding her, and he had assigned a Great Cat to Mike, as well. Mike considered the order ridiculous, but Ellie concurred with Otis.

"Mike, the position you occupy, that of First Knight, is second only to that of the Queen. If someone else held the position of First Knight, would you object to such protection?"

"Not fair, Ellie. You know I wouldn't."

"Then I rest my case."

So Mike now had two shadows, Jake on the inside and Jezdsbstztrkg, shortened to Jessie, on the outside. All the new additions were Guardians, not elite Protectors, but Otis was wholly satisfied with the arrangement.

Mike looked to Otis who was still walking on three hands, one back leg heavily bandaged. "I didn't know your brothers served in the military."

"They don't, Sire."

"Then why are there so many cats here?"

Jessie spoke. "We were accompanying a diplomat. We have been confined to the ship for over a year now. Apparently the ship's mission changed a year ago, and he was not able to reach his appointment."

"Who was the appointment with?"

"We were not told, Sire. The diplomat was killed in the fighting, so we'll probably never know."

The Queen was considering adding Lieutenant Val to her retinue, but Mike, testing his new powers, beat her to it, or so he thought. The young man's quick, accurate thinking had saved them all. He had salvaged a small fleet in the process, a fleet desperately needed as the seed from which a restored throne might germinate.

After reading Val's service record, Mike was even more impressed. Val had grown up in poverty, charted a path to the stars, and stuck with it. Sheer determination had won him entrance to a Star Fleet Academy where he had excelled in the toughest courses, and challenging assignments had been the norm since then. Val had stood above the best in every case.

"The record is not complete, Michael," Ellie said when he'd finished going through the file.

"It's a service record. How can it not be complete?"

"At his request, I had nearly everything prior to his entrance to the Academy deleted."

"You did? So he's known to the Chosen?"

"Only to me and Otis. His story is one you must hear, but so too must Reba. You two have become part of his story, our story."

Mike stared at her. She stood and paced, then stopped behind him and leaned down with her hands on his shoulders to kiss the top of his head. Softly she said, "I told you months ago that your part in all this had been foretold. The time has come for you to know the rest of that story, and it is Val's place to tell you."

"Oh, great. We're back to that. Why is he the one to tell it?"

"It is his right, Michael. When he is done, you will understand."

Reba and Val, summoned by the Queen, arrived in her quarters directly after Reba completed her first unassisted landing in the simulator. She was ecstatic, practically bouncing off the walls with excitement.

"Hi, Mike! It's glorious. The net, I mean." She gave him an awkward hug, avoiding his injured side. "Welcome back to the living. Meet Val, he's super, too. He's been doing his best to teach a thick-headed woman from Earth how to fly a star cruiser, and I'm not making it easy on him. Hello, Ellie," she added, giving the Queen a long hug.

Val, too, had seemed to be floating across the deck until the door snicked shut behind him and he realized who was in the room. Confronted by the Queen, her First Knight, Otis, and the other Great Cat, Jessie, he suddenly became the reserved junior officer. He stood nervously while Mike looked him up and down before rising to shake his hand.

"You've been avoiding me, Lieutenant."

"It's been a busy time, Sire. And your injuries, well . . . I'm sorry, Sire."

"So that's it! Are you blaming yourself for what happened?"

"It was my watch, Sire. I made you a promise, a promise that you could trust me. I take full responsibility."

"True enough. Lifeboats, eh, Lieutenant?"

Val rolled his eyes. "Sorry, Sire. It's the best I could do on short notice."

"Lieutenant, if you want to take responsibility for anything, perhaps you'll consider taking responsibility for saving the Queen and Alexis, saving me, Otis, and Lieutenant Morrison, saving your ship and the squadron, and maybe even saving your legitimate government, though we're not done with that part yet."

Lieutenant Val stood mute, far less certain of himself in these surroundings than he'd been in the midst of a mutiny.

The Queen stepped in. "Michael, you're being unfair. He's very young."

"We're all young here," Mike replied sternly. Turning back to Val, he posed an offer. "Lieutenant, I like the decisions you make. I especially like the fact that you're decisive under pressure, that you don't lose your cool, and that you're right. I need help. I want to offer you a job. Will you sit down while I tell you a story?"

Val put out a shaky hand to lower himself onto the proffered seat, sitting at attention on the very edge of the seat.

"A year ago on a planet called Earth, a spaceship crashed . . ."

Val remained expressionless until he realized that Mike was the Earthman from the story, an Earthman completely new to space travel, the Empire, space-based military, galactic politics, royalty, in fact their whole society. He looked with awe toward Mike and Reba, wondering aloud how they had survived as long as they had. Anticipating Mike's need, he stood up to pace while Mike finished the story.

"Sire, what exactly do you want from me?"

"I want you by my side to teach me, to be my right arm, to help us plan . . ."

Val stiffened and his complexion paled. He reached out a shaking hand to a chair and sat, his gaze locked on Mike. He blinked a few times, then looked to Ellie.

"Are you okay, Lieutenant?" Mike demanded.

Ellie stood up and moved to stand between him and Val. She knelt down before Val. Softly, she said, "So now you know. Now *we* know."

He stared at her, a look of awe on his face. "All these years . . . I've wondered all these years, and now I know."

"He doesn't. Does Reba?"

"No, Mother, but it's time she did. She, too, has been called."

Mike jumped at the title he used. "She's your mother?" he asked in amazement.

"She is, Sire."

Intrigues thickened the air in the room. Mike suddenly felt like he was swimming through the net without an AI.

Val stood and went to Reba's side, resting a hand on her shoulder. His gaze locked on Mike. "Your request honors me, Sire. I *will* be your right arm. It is my calling."

"Your calling?"

Val's eyes closed, and he took a deep breath, his arm tightening on Reba's shoulder. "It's time for you to know the whole story, Sire. It's time for Reba to know, as well. It's a long story. I will tell it as fully as I can."

He paused to gather his thoughts, then began. "The Val of yesteryear could never have imagined such a request by the First Knight. I had never even imagined I would meet a Knight of the Realm. All I wanted was to be a starship pilot. I was sixteen years old . . . ."

Part Two – Val's Story

Chapter Thirty-six

A red dot flashed in the upper left-hand corner of his pad, then went quiescent. Darn! The timing was bad. He had just returned from the port and was deep into a physics problem. But he never ignored an incoming call: his business demanded instant response day or night. He pressed the red dot, and a coded text message appeared. Bodan needed him right away.

Val ran a hand through the tangles of his shaggy hair and sighed. Though he never inquired about the nature of deliveries he made, he knew that Bodan specialized in some of the most egregious activities. He disliked Bodan, but Bodan paid well.

Val acknowledged the message and pushed his chair back from the table. He stood up, tucking the crutch into his left armpit while his right hand folded the pad and tucked it into a pocket. In moments he was through the door and headed up-tube. The hour was yet early and it was dark within the tube, the only light coming from shacks whose occupants had completed their nightly rounds. Val checked briefly on Mr. Wyzcha as he passed, but he wasn't home.

Old, unused tracks led him up a gentle incline to the outside. There, as always, Val looked first to the sky for ships arriving or leaving. This morning was quiet, though that could change quickly. The planet,

Hespra III, was district headquarters for this part of the Sector, and Yngsport, its capital city, was a busy place. Everything from traders to cruise ships and military ships of every description called regularly and at all times of day or night.

Behind him Dolphi, the large moon, brightened the night enough to cast shadows while Roga, the small red moon speeding across the sky in a much lower orbit, added a dusky hue to the surroundings. Most visitors complained when Roga added its bloody taint to the night, but it was all Val had ever known, and to him it offered comfort.

The tunnel opened onto a wide expanse of barren rubble, leftover remains of buildings demolished when the tracks went out of use. To his left, a glow lit the night sky half a mile away at the port. Bright lights flooded the port during the hours of darkness, but out here among the warehouses, only places doing business were lit. The temperature had dropped a few degrees during the hour he'd been home, but his shorts and light shirt would see him through until the sun came up. Then the temperature would climb quickly, becoming very hot by mid-afternoon, though he would likely sleep through the hottest part of the day.

Val scuttled toward the port, and also toward the concealment offered by shadows among the buildings. He didn't need to hide, but it had become second nature to him to be seen only when he chose to be seen, particularly when a delivery was involved.

He moved sprightly despite his missing leg. He had no recollection of life with two legs, and he did not feel hindered in any way. His only concern was that the missing leg might complicate his entrance to the Academy. Fleet Command recruited from virtually every world of the Empire, and species with no legs had just as good a chance of getting in as those with many legs. Val's number of legs was not the issue – the issue was that he was supposed to have one more leg. The rules seemed ambiguous to him, and he had no way of knowing the truth until he presented himself for examination.

Mr. Wyzcha believed he stood a fair chance, provided he did not shirk his studies. In fact, it was Mr. Wyzcha who had planted the idea that Val try for the Fleet. Mr. Wyzcha's tales of traveling the galaxy aboard great ships of the Fleet, tales of duty and honor and adventure as an Imperial Marine in service to the Empire, had called to Val, called strongly, and he had come to share in Mr. Wyzcha's ideals, though his plan to become a starship pilot was his own. The stars called to him. He would not travel those stars as a passenger as Mr. Wyzcha had. He would be the pilot.

One thing was certain in Val's mind: he would reach for the stars, nothing less, and to him there could never be anything more. One way or another he would be a star pilot.

Mr. Wyzcha refused to explain how circumstances had taken him from a senior sergeant in the Imperial Marines to a nobody. Why he now lived in a shack in the old tunnel was a mystery to Val, but he sensed a rightness in Mr. Wyzcha that he found nowhere else, and that sense of rightness called to him. Everything Val did, from his studies to his begging to his running, he did to the best of his ability, as exemplified by Mr. Wyzcha.

Traffic was light as Val scuttled along in a fast, ground-eating ballet of crutch and right leg, crutch and right leg. To anyone watching, his gait looked like that of a drunken sailor as his body lurched from side to side, but it was his preferred pace when time was short.

A heavy hauler passed silently overhead and landed before a warehouse a block in front of him. Lights came on automatically to illuminate the area in front of the building, and Val turned left into a darkened space between warehouses before continuing toward the port. On the next street over, a taxi passed a few meters above his head at a routinely high speed and was quickly lost to sight by the tops of intervening buildings, but Val paid it little attention, just noting that it was headed toward the port.

The neighborhood changed dramatically a few blocks from the port. He entered the land of spacers and his pulse quickened, knowing that someday he would be one of them. Restaurants serving every imaginable kind of food, saloons catering to every taste, and houses of ill repute catering to those same varied tastes lined the street. Most had garish signs before them, beckoning to crewmen who might have anywhere from a few hours to a few days of shore leave before heading back into space on a months-long voyage.

Hidden among them a few smaller establishments chose to keep a low profile. Those few, including Bodan's restaurant-bordello, did not feel the need to advertise.

The occasional taxi whooshed quietly overhead, though few stopped here. Wealthy passengers rarely transgressed this domain. This was spacer's territory, and spacers usually walked the few blocks from the port. The hour was early, or very, very late depending on your perspective, but aliens of every description walked or sauntered or slithered through the throngs, some dressed in uniforms while others, clearly from some of the less reputable traders, looked more like pirates. Many prominently displayed weapons, usually blasters or stunners. This was not an area that depended on civilized behavior to resolve disputes. Perhaps because of that, the area was essentially free of violent crime. Hawkers wandered purposely advertising their wares, usually vociferously, though depending on what they had for sale, they might just attempt eye contact, then speak privately. Smells from the restaurants, combined with a healthy mix of body odors, pervaded the senses, and Val reveled in the wash of smells. This was his home, the only home he'd ever known. The smells brought rumblings from his stomach, but he would eat later, possibly even in one of these taverns if Bodan's delivery proved sufficiently lucrative.

Though shadows were scarce along the busy streets, he modified his gait and had no problem remaining invisible. Gone was the fast, ground-eating scuttle. In its place a dirty, scrawny one-legged beggar eased his way timidly between and around knots of creatures of all kinds. No one paid attention to a one-legged beggar so long as that beggar didn't intrude on their lives.

Val stopped suddenly. A group of six creatures in immaculate uniforms, clearly from a visiting Empire military ship, jostled their way through the throngs in his direction and he caught his breath. He moved out of their way, staring at them in awe as they went by. Dignified, maybe even a little haughty, their camaraderie called to him, and he felt himself standing tall and straight as they passed by.

Chapter Thirty-seven

He approached the meeting location carefully, his eyes searching the crowds for anything out of the ordinary. He didn't trust Bodan, and any sense he could garner of Bodan's mood and motives might be to his advantage. Nothing unusual stood out, so he entered the restaurant, weaseling his way between tables to an office in the rear. He was known here, and no one tried to shoo this particular beggar away.

Bodan waited behind his desk. Grossly fat, the remains of his last meal spotted the tent-like shirt he wore. Though humanoid, Bodan's eyes reminded Val of a snake, including the vertical slits for pupils. His mouth was a thin, hard line like the mouth of a frog, and his nostrils were just slits above his lips. An unpleasant odor permeated the office, but Val had never determined if it came from Bodan or from the office itself.

"About time," Bodan wheezed.

"Hello, yourself," Val answered. "What do you have for me?"

"A delivery," Bodan said, pointing to a fabric tool bag on the desk. "It needs to be there in thirty minutes. Here's the address and the instructions." He handed Val a scrap of paper. "Do you know the place?"

Val read the address. It was in a run-down section of warehouses and offices adjacent to the space port and not too far from here. "I know it," he said, then waited. Bodan reached into his desk and withdrew the customary package. Val tore it open and counted the money, then looked across the desk at Bodan. "It's not enough for that part of town, and you know it."

Bodan's eyes narrowed. "Don't fool with me, boy. I can always get someone else."

"Not quickly, and not with my dependability you can't." Val studied Bodan, and to his surprise he saw the eyes shift momentarily. Bodan's nostrils pinched together a few times, but he reached back into his desk and came up with a fistful of money. "How much?"

"Another ten," Val demanded, pressing his luck.

Bodan didn't even argue. He counted out the ten and passed it across the desk. "You keep bargaining like that, you won't get any more business from me," he hissed.

Val grabbed the bag and turned. "I'm worth it. You called because I'm the best runner you know. I'm off."

"Use the back door," Bodan demanded. "And this meeting never happened."

Val turned to the back door, his thoughts calculating. An extra ten credits, and Bodan, someone who always argued over every tenth of a credit, hadn't even tried to deal. Something was clearly out of the ordinary. What was in the bag that was so all-fired important? His senses tingled, warning him to stay focused. There could be trouble with this delivery.

Val had a policy: he never, ever inquired about the contents of the packages he delivered. This one had some weight to it, but it didn't feel like money. He sniffed the bag as he scuttled through the refuse behind the buildings, but there was no smell of drugs either. His mind considered options as he moved, always seeking shadows. Should he open the bag? No, there would be markers on the fastener, and he had his principles: he was a runner, and he did not judge. But, too, he was curious. He might just wait around to see who picked up the bag.

He made his way to the building, a decrepit complex of abandoned offices, with fifteen minutes to spare. Wondering if he was being watched, he went directly to the second floor and placed the bag in the janitor's closet at the end of the short corridor per instructions.

His job done, he was now on his own, but he wasn't done. He wanted to see who would come for the bag. He scouted the building briefly, unlocked the back door, then left the building by the front door. In case he was under observation, he crossed the street in plain view, then circled around several blocks before approaching the building again from the rear. He studied it for a time, detected no one, and entered, climbing back to the second floor. He opened the door to the janitor's closet fully and left it open, then worked his way to the back of the closet behind containers of supplies and tools where he settled down to wait. He had a clear view of the corridor and the bag, but he would be invisible among the shadows deep within the closet.

He waited a full hour before three individuals, all Corvolds, leathery-skinned lizards, arrived one at a time. The first Corvold remained outside an office on the right side of the corridor as a guard. The other two entered the office where they remained silent. A short time later a rough looking, deeply tanned man with thinning hair and a patch over his right eye climbed the stairs and nodded to the Corvold guard as he entered the office.

Mr. Wyzcha! Val shied back against the rear wall of the closet. *What was Mr. Wyzcha doing here?*

No one had yet come for the bag.

Voices from the office sounded clearly as the two Corvolds greeted the new visitor.

"Thank you for coming, Sire," Val heard from one of the Corvolds.

Val started at the word "Sire." To the best of his understanding, such titles were reserved for royalty and their Knights. What was going on here?

"Choose your words carefully," Mr. Wyzcha spoke harshly to the Corvold. "I am known as Mr. Wyzcha."

"We choose them precisely, Sir Jarl."

"That name means nothing here."

"It does to us. You are our only hope. We cannot gain an audience on our own."

"An audience with whom?"

"You know, Sire. The news services speak of nothing other than her visit."

"You spoke of danger," the man replied.

"Her visit must be cancelled," a Corvold demanded.

"For what reason?"

"We need more time."

"Time for what?"

"Time to sway minds, Sire. Our very presence here brands us traitors to our own people, but it's a risk we're willing to take. The meeting must not take place. If it does, she will die."

"No one would be so foolish," Val heard.

"It's a whole new market, Sir Jarl. You know that. The crystals are malleable and under the right hands can be formed into almost anything. The moon where they were discovered is worth a fortune to whoever owns it. I'm sorry to say that some of our leaders have chosen to risk all. They are not representative of all Corvolds, and I hesitate to even call them my own people, but they are in charge at the moment. The decision has been made to proceed with their plan."

"Daughter is second only to the Queen. The whole Empire will come looking for whoever attempts such a thing. There's no possibility of success," Mr. Wyzcha replied.

At mention of the title "Daughter," Val froze. The level of intrigue suddenly skyrocketed. His thoughts went immediately to the fabric tool bag four feet in front of him. No one had come for the bag yet. Did these people even know it was here? What had he brought to this place? His mind raced, considering possibilities.

"That's why we're here, Sire. Their plan is perfect, but the truth always comes out in the end. We don't want that for our people. We'd be cut-off from the rest of Empire forever."

"Maybe she'll find in your favor."

"Not if it comes to a Testing, and it probably will. She'll know we were second to the Horlig. We know it, and no one can hide the truth from her. No one ever has."

"Maybe she'll find for both of you, let you share the wealth."

"Not now. I actually think there was a good chance for us before this plan came about. She has a history of fairness, and we weren't all that far behind the Horlig in the discovery. We both filed claims at the same time, so we have a legitimate legal claim to the moon, but the powers that be are not willing to share. They want all of it."

"How stupid. What's their plan?"

"Each ambassador will present a gift to Daughter, a gift of one of the crystals crafted by an expert. I've seen them, and they're exquisite. But our guys made a second gift, an exact copy of the Horlig's crystal. Because the crystals are malleable, they were able to form minute passages within and fill it with a deadly poison. The poison leaches to the surface at a predictable rate. The crystals have already been examined by Daughter's people, and the poison is just now reaching the surface. The copy presented by the Horlig ambassador will, by the time she accepts it, be coated with poison. The poison acts slowly, but it is fatal. Daughter, the Horlig ambassador, and anyone else who touches the crystal will die within days. When the crystal is examined, all blame will fall on the Horlig, and my people will be granted ownership of the moon."

Val sorted through what he'd heard and sucked in his breath. He suddenly knew what was in the bag, knew without any doubt. It was a bomb. No wonder Bodan had been so anxious to rid himself of the package. This meeting was not as clandestine as the attendees had hoped. Someone else knew about it, and whomever it was had no intention of letting these people leave this building alive to warn Daughter.

He shuddered, then did the only thing he could do. He rose from hiding, forced his way past the cleaning supplies, and raced from the closet yelling, "Bomb! There's a bomb in the building!" He scuttled past the stunned Corvold guard. "Get out!" he yelled as he went by.

Pandemonium broke loose. Everyone headed for the stairs. Val was pushed by someone and fell hard, tumbling to the bottom of the stairs where he lay stunned. He heard a popping sound, but not an explosion. Instead, an incendiary device blossomed into a fireball that spread instantly within the old building.

Val came to his senses, discovered the building on fire above him, and looked frantically for his crutch. He discovered it lying on the stairway halfway up to the landing on the second floor. Flames engulfed the walls and ceiling up there and had begun to work their way down the stairwell. Choking on smoke and still dazed from his fall, he knew he had to get out of the building, but he would not leave his crutch behind. He climbed the stairs on his hands and knee, the fire leaping toward him. Smoke obscured his vision, but he had seen exactly where the crutch lay. He reached for it, then slid back down to the landing.

The front door was ajar. When he peered outside, he froze. Four bodies lay in the street, three Corvolds and Mr. Wyzcha, and a flitter was just lifting. It raced toward the center of the city and disappeared.

Val crawled out and stood up, then checked each of the bodies. He came to Mr. Wyzcha last, the one everyone addressed as 'Sire.' Mr. Wyzcha had a gaping wound that had nearly severed his body at the waist. There was a small puddle of blood under him as Val rolled him over, but a surprisingly small puddle considering the extent of the wound.

His eyelids flickered open. He seemed confused for a time, a long time, and Val was opening his pad to call for an ambulance when he discovered the eyes focused on him. "Val?" the man asked, seemingly calm.

"It's me. I'm calling for an ambulance."

"Don't bother. My Rider tells me he cannot save me this time."

Rider! Mr. Wyzcha had a Rider? Probably the most valuable commodity in the Empire, if it was possible to call a sentient creature a commodity, Riders were intelligent, symbiotic masses of protoplasm that lived within others, the cells of their bodies distributed throughout their host.

That explained the lack of blood. Only a Rider could have staunched the flow of blood.

"Hang on, Mr. Wyzcha. If you truly have a Rider, you have a chance."

"Not this time. Don't worry, I'm not in any pain. My Rider takes care of that. What are you doing here?"

"I was upstairs. I heard your conversation with the Corvolds. They called you Sir Jarl. Please don't give up. She's counting on you, Mr. Wyzcha."

Mr. Wyzcha studied Val for a time, then reached a hand up and grabbed his shirt, pulling him closer. "You're just a boy. Are you ready to be a man?"

"Sir?"

Mr. Wyzcha looked him in the eyes, hard. "It's 'Sire,' Val. Know that much, at least."

Val stared into the eyes of the man he so admired, and after a time he nodded. "Yes, Sire."

"I ask again: are you ready to be a man? Are you ready to be everything we talked about?"

It didn't take long for Val to understand. Mr. Wyzcha was dying, and if he died, Daughter would die. He gulped as the Knight's gaze held him. "I am, Sire."

"You understand the killing mechanism, the crystal?"

"I do, Sire."

"Go there. Stop it. Daughter's life must be preserved at all cost. *At all cost.* Do you understand?"

"I do, Sire, but I'm just a beggar."

Mr. Wyzcha, the man others called Sir Jarl, studied him for a time. "You're more than a beggar, Val," Mr. Wyzcha said softly. "You always have been. A beggar can't do what I ask, but you can if you choose."

Hard eyes stared into his own, eyes that held him and called to him. Was he more than a beggar? Of course he was, but this! He wasn't ready for this. Yet this man, a man he knew as Mr. Wyzcha, was a Knight of the Realm. Val could not turn away from the call of such a Great One. "I am more, Sire," he whispered.

"The Empire's counting on you, Val. So am I. Don't let me down."

Val thought hard. Security around the meeting would be very tight. "How will I get in? They won't let a one-legged beggar within sight of the place."

Sir Jarl's voice was weakening. "Find a way. I can give you a few things that might help. Take my Knight's Pins, and take my cape. It's in my pocket. Now, put your arms around me."

"Sire?"

"I'm leaving this plane of existence, Val. Do the right thing and hold me until I'm gone. It's my last request."

Val looked at the torn body, feeling squeamish. He couldn't move.

"Son?"

The demand from those strong eyes could not be denied. He put his arms around the man's neck and hugged him to his own chest. Mr. Wyzcha put his arms around Val and squeezed the two of them together despite his terrible wound. He lasted for a couple of minutes, an eternity for Val, but then the arms went limp. Mr. Wyzcha, Sir Jarl, a Knight of the Realm, was dead.

Chapter Thirty-eight

Val straightened his arms, lifting away, his face only inches above the man who had been his mentor. A Knight of the Realm! Even in death, Mr. Wyzcha's features remained stern and rugged.

Looking at him, Val suddenly understood how little he knew about this man. Among all the hundreds of thousands of worlds of the Empire, there were only some one hundred Knights at any given time. They were spoken of with reverence, and their words were the Queen's command on all worlds of the Empire. A Great One had just died in his arms.

In his wildest imaginings, Val had never dreamed of ever meeting a Knight. He studied the man's face, the man he had known as Mr. Wyzcha. This incredible being had made a demand of him. He pressed his lips together, staring into the open, dead eyes. *Daughter's life must be preserved at all cost,* he had said, and Val knew Sir Jarl well enough to know exactly what he meant with those words. This man had paid the ultimate price, and he demanded no less from Val.

The job ahead of him was a Knight's job, yet he was still a boy. Was he up to the task?

The Great One's eyes stared at him, unseeing but still demanding, even in death. Val could not leave his friend like this. The authorities would arrive soon and he had to be away before then, but he would stay for just a moment longer. He reached out and closed Sir Jarl's eyelids, wishing him on his way with a brief prayer and wishing he'd had the opportunity to know this man in all his fullness.

Then he hurried, retrieving the Knight's Pins and cape from his pocket. Blood pooled around the body, no longer held in check by the Rider, and the cape was soaked in that blood. When he pulled it free, a money key fell out onto the street. Val picked up the key and wiped the blood off on his shorts before studying it. To his surprise, the key was not coded: anyone could use it. Clearly, this man did not want to advertise his presence here. Val had no idea how much money remained in the key's account. Wondering briefly if taking it would be stealing, Val shook his head and put it in his own pocket along with the cape. There would be no stealing from this great being, but he might have need of additional resources if he was to complete the Knight's work.

He collected his crutch and stood up, feeling exposed. He discovered a mini-blaster beside the Knight and pocketed that as well, then scuttled across the street into the long shadows of warehouses and office buildings where he lowered himself to the ground to think. He was at a complete loss as to what to do next.

The Empire is counting on you, Val. So am I, he heard in his mind. He reached for his pad, unfolded it, and sent out a query. Daughter's meeting would take place at the district governor's mansion. The published agenda called for her to receive the gifts soon after her introduction to the ambassadors. Checking the time, Val realized he had less than an hour before she arrived. He desperately needed to get cleaned up. His shirt and shorts were covered with blood, as were his arms, hands, and leg.

He pulled out the Knight's cape and unfolded it. The blood was drying, and the cape's black, shiny material would soon just look dirty to the casual observer. He drew the cape about himself and closed the clasp at his neck. Made for a much larger person, the cape hung poorly, nearly reaching to the ground. His scrawny leg was barely visible. He felt odd, and he probably looked odd, but it was the best he could do. His one foot was bare, he didn't own any shoes, but it was too late to do anything about that either.

He used his pad to call for a taxi, deciding to squander a little of the Knight's funds. The taxi arrived quickly, and Val keyed in an address a few blocks away from the governor's mansion. The taxi rose and skimmed the tops of the buildings in a straight line for its destination. He had ridden in taxis occasionally when deliveries demanded, and the rides always thrilled him. Other vehicles crossed his path, clearing with scant meters to spare, but Val gave it no thought today. Instead, he considered methods. The best plan he could devise was to scout out the grounds and find a way to sneak inside. It wasn't much of a plan, but it was simple, and it played to his skills at remaining invisible.

When he left the taxi, he fell into his routine of a one-legged beggar and made his way toward the mansion. The cape tended to billow out, and he had to use his free hand to hold the cape closed about his waist. After a time, it dawned on him that Knights would use the cape not only for formal occasions, but for warmth and shelter from the elements. It probably had clasps down the front. It did, and he felt a bit chastened as he fastened one at his waist. In just a short time, however, he became too warm and wondered what the cape was made of. Was there a switch to turn on the air conditioning? He had no idea, though it would not have surprised him had there been. He just accepted being hot. Hot was better than arrested, and the clock was counting down in his mind.

As he turned a corner and came into the square in front of the mansion, he stopped with a gasp. Never before had he seen so many police. He didn't even know there were this many police on the planet. Literally shoulder to shoulder, the line stretched the full six blocks along the fence on this, the east side of the mansion. Worse, through the fence he could see Imperial Marines patrolling the lawns and flower beds between the fence and the mansion. The grounds had four sides, each six blocks long and fenced, and he knew without checking that there would be no gaps in the security cordon. Suspicion edged into his thoughts, and he looked up to the sky, gasping again. An enormous military frigate and two fighters hovered a few hundred meters above the city. The fighters were just small disc-shaped ships, but the frigate looked like a multi-level building, pointed at the front and wide at the back. Short barrels bristled from open gun ports, meaning the ships were prepared for instant battle. Daughter must be traveling with a full squadron, he decided. The cruiser and the rest of the support ships would be patrolling nearby space. He'd seen frigates before, though never a cruiser. He yearned to join with any of those grand ships, but now was not the time for such thoughts.

He had to find a way into the mansion. Were there underground entrances? He had no idea. He pulled up a schematic of the mansion on his pad, but plans detailing the infrastructure were restricted to official access only. He considered returning home, Mr. Wyzcha always had answers for him, but then he remembered. Mr. Wyzcha was dead.

Crowds filled the streets, most headed for the mansion. Val weaseled his way through them until he neared the main entrance, where he stopped again in surprise. Bleachers had been erected for spectators, creating a corridor over a hundred meters long at a right angle to the building and its surrounding fence. He guessed the corridor was for Daughter to walk in procession. High walls of a clear material, probably glassteel, lined both sides of the corridor in front of the bleachers. He weaseled his way through the throngs, then climbed several levels into the bleachers to get a better view. The transparent wall went all the way through the gates of the mansion and up to the front entrance. He could see no way through or around it.

He worked his way out to the open end of the corridor. Some fifty guards stood in three ranks enclosing the opening, and a dozen or so policemen patrolled nearby. He didn't think he could approach any of them without getting arrested.

He pursed his lips. *Find a way,* the Knight had demanded. Only there was no way. Val closed his eyes, thinking hard. How do you get into a place like this?

Only one solution presented itself to him. Through the front door, of course, and without the subterfuge he was so comfortable with. There would be nothing secret about getting through this front door. Not today. He hung his head, sensing defeat.

He would have to confront the police and use the Knight's credentials. At the very least, someone would have to listen to him. He singled out a lone policeman with his eyes, a frog-like creature from Hesport, and approached him. "Officer! I have information concerning a security breach. I must talk to someone in charge."

One eye swiveled toward Val while the other continued screening passersby. "Go away, kid," the policeman croaked.

"Sir!" Val demanded. "I'm serious. Daughter's life is at risk."

Both eyes turned to him. "Kid, you *are* talking to someone in charge, and I'm not going to let you cause a ruckus here today. Keep it up and you'll find yourself hauled off to the station. Do I make myself clear?"

Val reached into his pocket for one of the Knight's Pins. Before removing his hand, however, a Voice spoke to him.

>No, Val! You get only one chance with the Pins. He is not the right one. Find another.<

Val turned away from the policeman, a demand for assistance dying in his throat. His eyes searched the crowd. Who had spoken to him?

As always, eyes avoided him, darting away lest a connection be made even for a moment. Few willingly made eye contact with one-legged beggars, even young ones such as he.

But someone had spoken to him, and that someone knew his name. Was he hearing things? Then he wondered if the Knight, though dead, somehow had a way of helping him. Could the Knight's spirit be talking into his head?

>No. Sir Jarl is dead,< he heard clearly. >So is his Rider, Artmis.<

Val shuffled through the crowd, huddled within the Knight's cape, confused. The Voice was so clear!

"Who are you?" he whispered.

>I'm your Rider.<

"My . . . *what*?"

>I'm your Rider. I know you heard me. You can't not hear me. Pull yourself together, Val. Sir Jarl gave us a job to do, and time is short.<

"He gave *me* a job to do. Who are you? Where are you?"

>We don't have time for this. Don't you know what a Rider is?<

"Vaguely."

>We'll discuss me later. Daughter will be here any minute.<

"No! We'll discuss you right now. This is impossible."

>I know what you're thinking, but don't worry – you're not going crazy. I won't let you go crazy. Why do you think Sir Jarl asked you to hold him just before he died?<

"He wanted comforting. I gave it to him."

>He wanted a lot more than that. It takes a while for a Rider to make the transition from one host to another. Sir Jarl's Rider died with him, and it was forced to fission way too quickly. I don't think I got the full measure of his memories, but I got enough for the moment. We need a plan.<

Val considered the words, then blinked with understanding. "You're inside me?" In a louder voice, he shouted, "And you're a *baby*?" Several people in the vicinity looked at him oddly, so he moved away.

>Yes, I'm a baby. And like I said, I didn't get the full package. Look, you don't have to talk out loud. You're attracting a lot of attention. Just think what you want to say.<

Val blinked, then shook his head. He didn't have time for voices right now – he was out of time. He stared at the governor's mansion in dismay. The dead Knight had commanded him to get inside, but there was just no way. Police and Imperial Marines patrolled every inch of the grounds inside and outside the fence. The only entrance was here, a corridor of glassteel panels some 100 meters long with bleachers lining each side. The panels effectively sealed off the corridor from bystanders, including Val.

He crutched over to the bleachers and weaseled his way up to the fourth level. When he turned to look down on the corridor, he hung his head in defeat: the glassteel panels went all the way to the entrance of the mansion without a break. There was no way for him, a lowly beggar, to enter the governor's mansion on this very special day.

A line of private limousines landed at the open end of the corridor to his left. A woman stepped from one of the cars, and six Great Cats immediately flanked her, padding around her on all fours with their eyes on the crowd. The cats must be her Protectors, Val decided. He'd glimpsed Great Cats before, though never in this number. Only the rich and powerful could afford their services. The Great Cats he'd seen before had almost certainly been Guardians, not these elite Protectors. The Queen's daughter would have nothing but the best.

Val stared at her, mesmerized. Dressed in an elegant, full-length, emerald gown, a delicate crown flashed from time to time in her tightly bound hair. Her face held a sweet smile as she waited for the district governor and the visiting Imperial Senator to complete their welcomes, then the procession began its long walk down the corridor. The crowd, too, must have been holding its breath because it was silent until she waved, then it broke out into cheers of welcome.

She proceeded slowly down the corridor, waving alternately to each side, the smile never leaving her face. As she neared Val, he got a better look at her and gasped. He'd expected an old woman, but with sparkling eyes, this woman radiated energy and youth. She seemed far too young for the power she yielded. How could someone so young be the final court of appeal? And according to the Corvolds who had met with Sir Jarl, she already had quite a reputation. She had done this before, many times. She was of the Royal Family, and she was here on Hespra III, one settled planet out of hundreds of thousands sprinkled across the galaxy. How amazing!

His mind refused to focus on the duty given him by Sir Jarl. He had eyes only for the beautiful princess. Her smile captivated him, seeming sincere, real.

>It is real,< the Voice in his head stated. >She truly loves her people. It is, after all, the people who continue to call the Chosen to their duties.<

"The Chosen? I've heard the term, but I don't really understand it," Val whispered.

>Among all the trillions of citizens of Empire, only the Chosen possess the Talents our people demand of its highest leaders. One of those Talents is that she reads minds, Val. Using her Touch, she can determine the truth of every individual she Tests, a key aspect of the process she follows in resolving disputes. This Talent is found only in the females of her family, and of them, only a few pass muster and are Chosen. Another trait of the Chosen is that they cannot lie, ever. Don't ask me why – I don't know – but it's true. Don't ask one of the Chosen to lie. It just can't happen.<

Val blinked, focusing his thoughts. >This one won't be leading much longer if we don't stop the Horlig. I have a plan.< He reached into his pocket for Sir Jarl's blaster.

>No, Val!< the Voice said in panic.

>I'm out of time! I'll get her attention, then they'll have to listen to me.<

>You'll be dead, and so will I. Do you know what a Protector is?<

>I've heard tales,< he thought to the creature, his hand still tight on the blaster. >I hear they're pretty good.<

>Pretty good? *Pretty good*? They're the deadliest creatures in the Empire, and they're smart. More than that, they *believe* in the Royal Family. They've sworn to protect the Royal Family at all costs, and I speak not only of these few, but of their whole race. You will not succeed in our mission if you're dead, and if you die, she won't be far behind.<

>They can't shoot me through the wall.<

>They won't have to. I'm certain they can leap over it.<

>Do you have a better plan?< he thought angrily.

>No. I just know this one won't work. Trust me, Val. I know what I'm talking about.<

He did not want to trust this Voice, but he understood its demand for caution. He had only one chance to do the right thing. He watched the procession disappear into the mansion and wondered at the events of his day. In the span of an hour he had met a Knight of the Realm and now Daughter, the person who might one day become Queen of the Empire. He took a deep breath, then made himself focus on the mission Sir Jarl had given him.

At any cost, Sir Jarl had said. Whatever the cost, the mission must succeed, and quickly. She was in the building, and he only had minutes before the crystals would be presented. He had to find a way through the security, then he had to find a way past her Protectors. Sir Jarl's assignment seemed impossible.

Val made his way through the departing throngs climbing down from the bleachers, refusing to let his thoughts focus on the impossible. >So how much do you know about all this?< he asked the Voice.

>Specifically, about as much as you do. However, my father passed on a lot of other information to me. You know, palace intrigues and all that. I'm not sure how relevant they are at the moment.<

>Then what good are you?<

>Riders ride, Val. We don't control, ever. I'm a source of information to you, and I can offer guidance, but it is not in my nature to control. What information can I provide?<

>We have, at most, fifteen minutes. I have Sir Jarl's pins, his cape, his money key, and his blaster. Besides that, I have one leg and a crutch. As a person, I don't exist. These are the things we have to work with. You must know something about security. How do we get past it? How would Sir Jarl have gotten in?<

>He would display his emblems of rank, and he would know the passwords.<

"You know the passwords?" Val demanded aloud in astonishment.

>There are probably three: one for the police, one for the district governor's security, and the last known only by Daughter and her team of Protectors. Sir Jarl's knowledge is outdated. He knew only the last, but it will work with the Protectors.<

Time was short. Val made a decision, and he didn't sense any dispute from the Voice. >Do you know what I'm thinking?< he asked.

>I do. It's risky, but it might work. I do not have a better suggestion.<

Without further delay, Val pinned the Knight's Pins to the cape, one on each side of his throat. He pulled his crutch into position and asked, >How do I look?<

>We look terrible, but we're out of time. You're her last chance, Val. You have to *be* a real Knight if this is going to work. I'll help in any way that I can.<

Val didn't respond. He just started forward, acting as he envisioned Sir Jarl acting. Sir Jarl's cape helped. Heavily soiled with dried blood, it lent credence to his need for a crutch. He moved as if the crutch was new to him. His face still looked like a sixteen-year-old face, and that concerned him. He pulled the hood over his black, unkempt hair, partially concealing his features.

>How much can you do? Can you make me look like I'm wounded?<

>You already look wounded. What more can I do?<

>I need to look older.<

>I can give you a few years, probably not enough, but people usually see what they expect to see. As a further distraction, I can help you struggle.<

>Okay, just don't overdo it. Make my voice deeper if you can.<

The first policeman he approached straightened to attention as he passed, though a questioning look filled his features. "Sire?" he asked.

Val stopped and turned slowly to face the policeman. In a labored voice he said, "I could use some help here, officer. Will you attend me?"

"Of course, Sire. What can I do?"

"Just clear the way for me. I'll manage the rest on my own."

"Very well, Sire. Would you like me to call for a lift?"

"No. Time is of the essence. I can't wait."

The officer preceded him to the entrance of the mansion, then stopped. "I can go no further, Sire."

"Yes, you can." He approached a mansion guard, an Imperial Marine, and stated, "This officer will accompany me. I'm in a hurry."

"Very well, Sire," the guard stated. "The password?"

Val paused. "I've forgotten. Can't you see I'm wounded? Take me to her Protectors. We have a special understanding. Let them decide." Val peered hard at the guard. "Her life rests in your hands, Marine. Make the right choice."

The marine paused, then turned to the policeman. "You lead the way. I'll follow." To Val, he said, "Sire, I will not hesitate to fire if I sense the need."

Val cleared his throat, coughing roughly into his fist. "I know you won't, and she counts on that. You've chosen well. Now . . . her life is at stake. I must attend her immediately. Move out, soldier."

"Very well, Sire."

Val hobbled through corridors, and it wasn't long before he approached a crowd of soldiers outside a small doorway. A Great Cat stood on each side of the door.

>This will be a little harder,< the Voice said.

>Then it will be harder,< Val thought to the creature.

A Great Cat left its position beside the door and padded toward Val and his two escorts. "I do not recognize you, Sire. Please identify yourself."

>How do I do that?< he asked the Rider.

>I don't think you can. A true Knight would open his Knight's Pin. Inside the pin is an image of whichever Chosen called the Knight, but only the Knight to whom the pin was bestowed can open it. You are not that person.<

Val dismissed his attendants. As soon as they were out of hearing, he turned to the Great Cat and lowered his hood. "I am not who I appear to be. Sir Jarl is dead. He commanded me to come in his place. To prove it, I give you the password. It's *grafsdia'a.*"

The Great Cat looked deep into Val's eyes, his lips raised to display jagged teeth. "The password is outdated, Sire."

Val suddenly found himself pinned against the wall. The Great Cat ripped the cape from him and searched his body, discovering the blaster. He turned Val roughly, staring deep into his eyes, his fiendish muzzle only inches away.

>Tell him the blaster belonged to Sir Jarl. It has his imprint on it.<

"The weapon belonged to Sir Jarl," Val stated. "It is marked so. I have no other weapons."

The Great Cat studied the blaster for a moment, then placed it into a pouch at its waist. "What is your purpose here?"

"Daughter is going to be killed."

"What is the nature of the threat?"

"It's the Horlig ambassador. Well, it's really the Corvold ambassador, the Horlig is unaware that he's the danger."

The Great Cat stared at him, and Val understood his confusion. "It's complicated, sir. I gave you the password, and I'm wearing Sir Jarl's cape which is covered with his blood. I'm acting on his orders. Any delay now will mean her life."

The cat made a decision and marched him to the door. The other Great Cat opened the door but remained in the corridor. "Know that I am beside you," his escort stated in a soft growl beside Val's ear. "Any false move and I will not hesitate to kill you. Do not approach Daughter."

Val remained mute. They entered the chamber, to the side and slightly behind Daughter. She stood some ten meters away. One Corvold, a reptile, and one Horlig, a human, knelt before her, their heads bowed. Behind them, some 50 people filled the chamber. Two Protectors patrolled opposite sides of the room while two others sat on their haunches behind Daughter at the front of the room. One of those left to approach Val and his guard.

"What is this?" he growled, looking Val over from head to foot.

"Otis, he claims that a Knight, Sir Jarl, is dead. He claims further that Daughter is going to be killed."

"What is the nature of the threat?" Otis demanded harshly, his eyes glaring into Val's eyes.

But Val did not have time to explain. Both representatives had risen to their feet to present their gifts.

Daughter spoke as she reached forward, saying, "You offer these gifts with no conditions attached, and there will be no conditions. Know that they will not have an impact on my findings."

Val heard Sir Jarl's command in his mind: "*At any cost.*" Yelling "Nooo!" he scuttled quickly toward Daughter.

Unknown to Val, Otis, the Great Cat, instantly sprang to his side and stayed half a step ahead of him. Otis did not know what the threat was, but he understood that this boy might. Even if the boy himself was the threat, Otis would be ahead of him, blocking his access to Daughter. Val moved so quickly that the presenters still had their hands held out before them with the crystals. Just before Val reached them, another Great Cat pulled Daughter back and hustled her from the room.

Val had eyes only for the crystals. He reached out and clamped a hand to the first crystal, then the second. Without a hand for his crutch, he hopped a few steps and crashed to the floor, curling up around the crystals with his eyes closed.

Pandemonium spread through the chamber, but Val cared little for that. In his mind he communed with Sir Jarl, looking into eyes that had, just before dying, sternly commanded him. Those eyes, now full of approval, welcomed. Val had never known a father, and this man's approval filled his heart.

"I'm not ready to die, Sire," he mumbled.

The great Knight just nodded, his warm gaze never leaving Val's.

Val felt arms go around him and believed them to be the arms of the Knight, but it was only Otis. When he opened his eyes, Otis' muzzle filled his view. "I must know the nature of the threat, boy," Otis growled.

Hating himself for it, Val felt tears coursing down his cheeks. He couldn't help it. On the one hand, he was still within the aura of the great Knight. On the other, the poison was surely killing him. "I'm not ready to die," he cried.

Otis grasped Val's face with a clawed hand and turned it toward him. "What is the nature of the threat, boy?" he growled again.

"One of these crystals is poisoned."

"They were tested. Could you have erred?"

"One was switched at the last moment."

"I see. Release them, boy."

Val tried relaxing his hands, but he could not. He maintained a death grip on both crystals, one of which continued to pour poison into his body. Then he heard the Voice.

>This stuff *hurts*. I need you to go to sleep now, Val. See you on the other side.<

Chapter Thirty-nine

Otis spoke into his communicator as he followed the stretcher to the roof of the mansion. "Is Daughter aboard yet?"

"*Resolve* just got here. She's boarding now."

"Hold the ship and alert sick bay. I'm bringing a potential poison victim aboard."

"Very well, sir."

When they stepped out onto the roof, *Resolve's* entrance ramp was right in front of them. Extraction plans were rarely put to use, but when they were, Otis demanded perfection and he got it.

A crewmember whisked Val to sick bay. Otis stayed until he'd been examined, then left in search of Daughter. He found her on the bridge. He noted that *Resolve* was already in orbit, and the escort ships were in battle position about *Resolve*, all according to the plan.

Daughter's formal garments were gone. She had changed into a comfortable, silky blouse and a pair of pants, her usual attire aboard ship. He sat at attention before her. Her expression was grim, but she appeared unruffled. This was not the first time she had been threatened, and they had practiced these things many times.

"What happened, Otis?"

"I'm not certain, My Lady. Indications are that one of the

crystals you were about to accept was poisoned."

Her hand went to her throat as she considered how close she'd come to touching them. "How is that possible?"

"I can't say at the moment. I know they were checked by experts, but I don't know if a switch was made. We'll know soon. Clearly, we need to review our procedures."

"I should say so! But we can't cover every eventuality, and we never will. That's why I count on you."

"I may have failed you this time, My Lady."

"We all fail some of the time. We've had this conversation before. We make mistakes, we learn from them, and we continue forward from there. Are you clear on that?"

"I am, My Lady." His communicator buzzed. He lifted it to his ear, listened, then put it back in its pouch. His gaze met hers. "One of the crystals was poisoned," he stated.

She sat in a nearby crew seat, then changed her mind. "I need to think. Let's go to my quarters."

She stepped into the central shaft, Otis right behind her, and dropped four levels, then strode purposely in a direction opposite her quarters. She needed time to think, and walking the long circumference of the saucer-shaped ship sufficed for that purpose. Otis padded along by her side.

"There's more, isn't there," she stated softly.

"I'm afraid so, My Lady."

"Okay, out with it."

"I'm still piecing it together, but it appears that a Knight might have died acquiring the knowledge that saved you."

She stopped with her eyes closed. "A Knight? On this world? Are you certain?"

"Pretty certain."

She turned to find Otis' outstretched hand reaching to her. In the palm of that hand were two Knight's Pins. Her eyes narrowed, then she reached for one and closed her two hands about it tightly. Her eyes closed and all expression left her face for a time. When she returned her gaze to Otis, she said softly, "The life force is gone from the pin. He's dead."

She leaned against the wall, then slid to a sitting position with her knees drawn up, grieving for the unknown Knight. Otis sat at attention on the floor before her, his heart grieving for her as much as for the unknown Knight.

"Who was the Knight?" she asked after a time.

"A 'Sir Jarl.' I do not know of him."

"Sir Jarl!" She considered, then said, "He was before your time." She paused, then asked, "Who was the boy?"

"I have no idea, My Lady. He is here."

"Here!"

"In sick bay."

"He was hurt?"

"He was poisoned. I surmise that he was sent by Sir Jarl. Only the boy knew the threat, and there was no time to explain it to us. He took both crystals from the ambassadors with his bare hands."

Her eyes grew large once again. "I barely saw him, but he looked like a beggar, a filthy beggar. I seem to remember he only had one leg."

"He does. I know little about him. He is a child to whom life has not been kind. The filth you saw was dried blood, I think Sir Jarl's. Though just a child, he acted with honor, My Lady. When I spoke to him, he clearly understood that his actions would result in his own death. That's why I brought him. It's the least we could do."

"Is there no hope?"

"I don't know. The poison takes two days to kill, but the antidote is not successful in most cases."

She stood up. "I would meet this boy."

"Thank you, My Lady."

"Is there more?" she asked as they headed for sick bay.

"Probably. It's too soon to say, though certainly the political ramifications will have to be dealt with. At this point, I can't say if the ambassadors were aware of the plot, nor can I say if either of them was poisoned."

"I don't recall either one wearing gloves."

"Nor do I. To me, the whole thing makes no sense. Surely, whichever party attempted to poison you would be named eventually, yet these people are not stupid. What could they have been thinking?"

"Ahh, palace intrigues. They never end, Otis. I'm counting on you to remain by my side. Will you?"

"As you said, we learn from our mistakes, and we press on. I will not desert you, My Lady."

She rested a hand on the fur around his neck, not as one would a pet, but as one would a close friend. No more would be spoken of failures.

When they entered sick bay, Val was sitting up in bed, his right hand wrapped in a bandage and another bandage over the right side of his chest where the crystal had rested. Sir Jarl's blood had been cleaned from his body during the search for areas that had come in contact with the crystal. It took him a moment to recognize Daughter, but when he did, he frantically tried to get out of bed.

She placed a hand on his shoulder and pressed him back into the pillow. She studied him intently, focusing mostly on his eyes, though she did not miss the flattened area beneath the sheets where a leg should have been. What she saw was a tall, scrawny, black-haired boy with dark, intelligent eyes.

"Thank you," she said softly, then leaned forward and kissed his forehead.

Val blushed, then panic set in. "Aren't I supposed to bow or something?" he asked, looking at Otis.

"My hero, you need never bow before me," Daughter said. "Today you earned that right, as few others have." Then she looked stricken. This boy had little future left to him. Her eyes lifted to the doctor with an unspoken question.

"He's responding to the antidote, My Lady. I can't explain it, but for some reason the toxin has remained localized, and it appears to be weakening."

"What are you saying, Doctor?"

"I believe there's hope, My Lady. I make no promises. We'll know more tomorrow."

Her troubled gaze returned to Val. "What is your name, young man?"

"I'm known as Val, but I have no official name, My Lady. Just a number."

"A number!"

"I'm an orphan. I escaped from the orphanage six years ago. Please don't send me back."

She turned a troubled gaze to Otis. "I'll look into it, My Lady." He turned to Val. "What is your number?"

"5397867A," Val responded without hesitation. For a moment, he wished he had held back, but he sensed, rightly, that little would be held back from Daughter and Otis.

"How old are you?" she asked.

"Sixteen, My Lady. Uh, am I addressing you correctly?"

"You are. Sixteen." She looked thoughtfully to the ceiling and said softly, "The timing fits." She looked back to Val, saying, "You left the orphanage when you were ten? How did you survive?"

"Mostly by stealing at first. I got pretty hungry. Then I met Mr.

Wyzcha. Uh . . . he seems to be known by some as Sir Jarl."

"A Knight of the Realm?"

Val stared back at her and said softly, "I think so, My Lady." In a stronger voice, he said, "I knew him as Mr. Wyzcha. He owned me for a few years. He taught me how to beg and made sure I had plenty to eat. I bought my freedom and my begging permit from him three years later."

"So you're a licensed beggar?"

"I am, My Lady, but begging is no longer my main source of income. I've built a private business as a runner."

"A runner?"

"I deliver things, My Lady."

"You run, but you only have one leg. What happened to your other leg?"

"I don't know. I have no memory of ever having had two legs. I get around fine without it, better than some with two legs."

"Yes, I can vouch for that," she said with pursed lips. "You moved quickly when you sensed the need. I will be forever grateful."

His gaze hardened. "Not when you know the whole story. Sir Jarl's death is my fault."

She sat back slowly. Even Otis let out a low growl. "I think you'd better explain, young man," Otis demanded. "And no lies. We'll check out everything. I want the truth, and only the truth."

Val, suddenly angry, fired back at him, "I might be a beggar, but Mr. Wyzcha taught me well. I live by his code. I never lie, sir. I don't always tell everything, but I don't lie. If I can't say the truth, I don't say anything."

Otis and Daughter exchanged startled looks. Those were the exact words she used to describe herself. The Chosen could not lie, but they did not have to tell the whole truth either.

"Give us the truth, Val," Daughter demanded softly. "What is this 'code' by which you live?"

"Mr. Wyzcha was an Imperial Marine. He believed that the Empire served all, and that there was no greater honor than to serve the Empire in return."

"Those are the words of a Knight, Val."

His eyes filled with tears, his gaze shifting between her and Otis. He wiped at his eyes and said softly, "He was just Mr. Wyzcha to me."

"The pins you held are the real thing, Val," Daughter said, speaking grimly. "What is going on here is not clear to me. Tell me what you know, and I ask that you hold nothing back. Lives depend on the words you are about to say."

Val looked troubled. "I'm just a beggar, Ma'am."

She looked unsettled, then looked like she didn't like the feeling. She looked hard into Val's eyes again, studying him with a whole new intensity. "I see a beggar," she said eventually, "but I sense more in you."

His chin thrust forward. "I'm proud of being a beggar. I won't be on Hespra III much longer, I have a plan, but at the moment I'm a beggar, and I'm proud of it."

"What plan?" she asked.

"I'm going to be a starship pilot, My Lady. I'll be old enough to take the entrance exam for Fleet Academy in two years."

"You want to be a Fleet officer? Are you at the top of your class?"

Val hesitated. Transcripts and personal commendations were part of the entrance requirements for Fleet Academy, and they would have to be purchased illegally. He had promised not to lie, but he didn't have to tell the whole truth either.

"I can't go to school, My Lady. I'm a non-person. But I can study, and I'm on track. I'll take the entrance exam in two years."

Otis coughed into a fist. "I think you're out of the beggar business for a while, young man. Whatever your plans are, you might have to make some adjustments."

Val's thoughts went instantly back to the chamber. "Is the Horlig ambassador dying?" he asked softly.

"I don't know," Otis growled. He looked at the doctor. "Has the governor been appraised of the toxin?"

"He has. There has been no further word."

"He's innocent, you know," Val said sadly. "It was the Corvolds who did it."

"Well, well!" Daughter exclaimed, clapping her hands together. "Let the intrigues begin. I would hear your story, Val, and I want every detail. Ship, Record."

"Recording," Val heard clearly.

Val closed his eyes, wishing that Mr. Wyzcha was here.

Or was he really Sir Jarl?

To Val, he was Mr. Wyzcha, the man who had pulled Val from the gutter, the man who had taught him everything that mattered, the man who had always had answers for everything, even answers to test questions that arose during his studies. Mr. Wyzcha had died in his arms, and he couldn't get his arms around that all-important detail. Val missed him, missed him deeply.

Val was out of his depth at the moment, and he was hurting inside. On the other hand, he could not deny a command from this woman.

He looked to Otis, then lifted his eyes to Daughter. "I was studying, getting ready for an exam, when I got the call . . ."

Chapter Forty

". . . I decided it could only be through the front door," he said, his gaze moving between Daughter, Otis, and the doctor who hovered in the background. "All the skills I'd developed as a beggar and as a runner were useless. I had to pretend to be Sir Jarl. I did, and you know the rest."

He ended his story, leaving out very little, only the existence of his Rider. They didn't need to know about him.

When the telling was done, Daughter sat back deep in thought. The bare facts of Val's story had surprised her, but the facts were not atypical of political intrigues she encountered on a regular basis. His telling had been clear and concise. She sensed a sharp mind behind those young eyes. More, she sensed the mind of a survivor. Most poignant to her, though, was Val's relationship with Sir Jarl. A deep imprint had been made on this young man by her Knight. To know he had reached so deeply into this special child as he lay dying would have pleased Sir Jarl immensely. She would not let that effort be wasted.

"So all is not as it appeared," she stated after a time. She looked into Val's eyes. "Is there anything you would add to your story?"

"No, My Lady."

Otis' muzzle swung toward Daughter in surprise. She had not

asked the right question, a mistake he'd never seen her make before. What was going through her mind? Was there some attachment growing between her and this young man? Was her focus not clear? He could not let the event pass without speaking.

"Val, have you left anything at all, any little detail, out of your tale?"

"I have, sir, but I have not lied. I have given you every single thing I know that is relevant to your investigation."

"You have not. Sir Jarl's cloak and pins would not, by themselves, have been adequate to gain entrance to the meeting. You used a very private password, a password that has long been out of use."

Otis allowed silence to fill the room. He had done his part. The rest was up to Daughter.

Val locked gazes with Otis. The silence prevailed, and Otis waited patiently, as cats are so good at doing. Val's gaze did not falter, though he started scratching his arm, then his torso.

The doctor intervened. "Excuse me, My Lady. Val, you're scratching. Why?"

Val broke his gaze from Otis and looked to the doctor. "My skin itches, sir. And I smell terrible."

The doctor nodded. "We had to give you a good scrubbing. When was the last time you had a bath?"

"I live in an abandoned rail tunnel, Doctor. I don't have a bathtub."

"Just as I suspected. You probably wouldn't recognize yourself right now, young man."

Daughter sat back during this exchange and considered the accusation made by Otis and the claim made by Val. She chose her own words carefully. "Val, we'll deal with personal hygiene later. At the moment we're dealing with Imperial matters. There can be no secrets between us."

He blinked, uncertain of his position, but he was determined to keep the existence of his Rider private until he had time to consider the ramifications himself. It was none of their business, and during his brief acquaintance with the creature, he'd sensed a growing attachment. He had never had an intimate relationship with anyone, parents or friends, and he did not want to lose what he sensed could become precisely that.

>Hey, thanks! Trust me, I'm not going anywhere unless you kick me out.<

>Can I do that?<

Pause. >You can. The cost to me is quite high.<

>How high?<

>Riders rarely change hosts, Val. We just don't. Without a host, I die. I cannot survive on my own.<

Val jerked visibly in his bed, and his face paled. The doctor was beside him instantly with a small instrument. He waved the instrument over Val, looked at the results, and shrugged. "He's okay. I think he's just overwhelmed, My Lady."

Daughter rose from her chair and reached out to push stray locks from his forehead. "Val, are you with us?" she asked.

He closed his eyes for a time. When he opened them again, he was his old self. "I'm fine, My Lady. Sorry."

"Don't be sorry. Is my question so terrible?"

"Yes."

She remained bent over him, her hand never breaking contact with him. "Val, you're among friends, and these are Imperial matters. There can be no secrets between us." Her sparkling gaze held his, emphasizing her demand. "You're a bright, brave young man, but you are new to all of this. You cannot possibly judge the full impact of what you have experienced. In time you might, but not yet. Please let us judge the importance of whatever you have chosen to withhold. Please."

"Can you give me a little more time?"

She considered his request, first as Daughter, then as herself. "I can, but time is always of the essence with things of this nature. I ask you as your friend, and I ask you as Daughter, to withhold no secrets from me."

He broke eye contact with her and looked around the room. He didn't even know where this room was. In some hospital, he supposed. Then his gaze took in the doctor and Otis and he lost it again in the blink of an eye. He was in the presence of Greatness, so far above his station in life that his mind staggered. A woman of the Royal Family was actually touching him. He couldn't get his mind around that very complex idea. The woman who had walked down the corridor between thousands of cheering people was here with him now, and she was touching him. More, she was concerned for his well-being.

And Otis. One of the fabled Protectors, and from all appearances, their leader. How was this possible?

Daughter interrupted his thoughts. "Val, what would Sir Jarl have wanted you to do?"

Sir Jarl's face suddenly came into focus in his mind. The gaze was stern, but it was also caring. Of all the things he sensed of that awesome persona, he sensed a great integrity. Sir Jarl's entire focus at the end had been Daughter. Would he have kept secrets from her?

No. Nor would the friend he knew so well, Mr. Wyzcha. He opened his eyes, his decision made. Large, brown eyes stared back at him from inches away.

"Sir Jarl would never keep a secret from you. Just . . . please don't take him away from me," he breathed.

"Take who away, Val?"

"My Rider."

Her hand jerked from his face as if stung, but a moment later it was back. "I see. Sir Jarl left you with a little more than the pins, his cape, and his money key."

"Yes, Ma'am."

She turned to Otis for a time, and Val sensed whole thoughts passing between the two of them. Between two people who knew and understood each other completely, words were not always necessary.

She turned back to him, saying softly, "We will not take him from you Val. Not ever, even if we could. Riders go only to those of their own choosing. Sir Jarl and his Rider sensed something in you today, just as I do. This is definitely an Imperial matter, but we will discuss it later. Are you tired?"

"No, My Lady."

"Otis and I have things to do. Perhaps you can spend a little time with your Rider, time not burdened with such weighty issues. I hope it will be a time of discovery for both of you. Does it have a name?"

"Uh, no. We haven't had time to discuss that yet."

She returned to the side of this skinny, black-haired, one-legged beggar and stared down at him fondly for a time. Just a child who had, in the space of a few hours, been catapulted from the very lowest rung of society to . . . something else. What that something would be, she had no idea, but this boy would never have to beg again.

She leaned over him, staring into his eyes. From inches away she breathed, "Thank you, Val. And thank you, Val's Rider, for saving my life today. We will talk further tomorrow." She leaned down and kissed his forehead again, then turned and left.

Chapter Forty-one

Val basked in the glow her presence had left behind. He'd been kissed by Daughter. How more amazing could life have become? He felt suddenly adrift, cut off from the world in which he was so comfortable. He turned to the doctor. "What hospital is this?" he asked.

The man coughed into his fist. "You're in sick bay aboard *Resolve*, Daughter's private ship." Val's eyes grew large, then they grew larger.

The doctor answered his unspoken question. "Yes, Val. You're in space. I believe we're in orbit about your world."

"Can I see outside?"

"I'll activate the screen for you. But first, we should talk."

"Uh, I don't have any more secrets. What's your name?"

"I'm Doctor Storvo. Pleased to meet you, Val. And I'm not one for secrets. We should talk about Riders."

"Sir?"

"Do you know what a merry chase you led me on? My treatment would have been much different if I'd known you had a Rider. Worse, in some cases medical treatment can be harmful to a Rider."

"Oh. I hadn't thought about that."

"Please ask your Rider if he's okay."

>No, I'm not okay,< a grumbly voice said in his head. >This stuff hurts.<

>I'm sorry. Do you need help?<

>No. I'm almost done. You can tell him thanks, but I don't need any more help.<

>Thanks for doing whatever it is you do. Without you, I'd be dying now.<

>No you wouldn't. Without the password, she'd be dying. You'd never have gotten to her in time. I think it's called teamwork. Do I get to stay?<

>You get to stay. We need to work on a name.<

>I've already chosen one. My father is gone. I'll take his name if that's okay with you.<

Val grinned. The name felt right. >Artmis. I like it. Welcome aboard, Artmis.<

>Let me finish up here, then we can talk. You need to eat, Val. You're running on empty, and that means I am, too.<

Val returned his gaze to Doctor Storvo. "He's fine, sir, and he thanks you for your help. He says I need to eat, and I agree. I'm starving."

"When was your last meal?"

"Yesterday."

"Good gracious, boy! You'll kill yourself with that kind of behavior. Riders use a lot of energy, whether it's available or not. It's one of the few drawbacks to having them. You cannot miss meals." He grabbed a bag filled with liquid and attached it to the IV in Val's hand. "Tell him I'm pushing as hard as I can."

"Uh, I think he hears you just fine. Can I see outside now?"

Storvo brought him a remote and started showing him how to use it, then changed his mind and sat on the bed beside Val.

"I want to thank you."

"For what?" Val asked in surprise.

"For saving her."

"Well . . . sure!"

"I mean it, young man. And now, as your doctor I'm going to give you some advice. Consider it an order."

"Sir?"

"I'm not willing to go to all the trouble of saving you if you're just going to die of some disease. We need to talk about personal hygiene. You're under my care, and you will be for as long as you're on this ship. Young man, I have to insist that you shower at least once a day."

"Once a *day?* You want me to stink like this all the time?" he asked, lifting his arm to smell it again. "Is this perfume?"

"Just a touch. We couldn't get all the smell out of you. It will take a few more days."

"I won't be here that long, and I can't go home smelling like this."

"As long as you're on the ship, it's the way things have to be. You'll shower every day, no exceptions."

* * * * *

Val touched buttons on the remote and a screen blinked into existence on the wall at the foot of the bed. He pushed more buttons and found a view of his planet as seen from orbit, but he soon tired of it. He'd seen pictures of his planet before. He went internal. >Do you know how to work this thing, Artmis?<

>I do. What do you want to see?<

>The ship!<

>Okay. It's like this . . . <

An outside view of *Resolve* sprang into view, a burnished disc some two hundred meters across. Little detail was evident. <Can we get closer? I want to see details.<

>You don't have clearance, but I do. We'll have to work with the ship's AI, the Artificial Intelligence. Give him a call.<

Val blinked, then called out, "Ship!"

"At your service, Val."

"Can I see more details of the ship?"

"Sorry, but you don't have authorization."

>Give it the code, Val. It's just a computer. It will accept it.<

Val spoke the code, then made his request for a tour of the ship.

"Nice try, Val. The access code is old but acceptable. However, it was not intended for use by you. I cannot let you in."

"Who can?"

"Captain Jzazbe, Otis, or Daughter."

"Oh." Val hated to interrupt any of those important people. Then he had an idea. "What do you suggest?" he asked the AI.

"I believe you have a little leverage at the moment. I suggest you use it by making a request to Otis."

"Please do so."

It didn't take long. The simple view of the exterior of *Resolve* slowly turned transparent, and the decks appeared, nine of them. Val studied them for a time, then decided to try his luck. He said, "Bridge," and the view telescoped toward the upper center of the ship to show a detailed schematic of the bridge. "Can I see a live view?" he asked.

"Only if you go into the net," the AI responded.

"What's the net?"

"A network that ties all the computers on the ship together. Crewmembers don special helmets which connect to me, and through me to the rest of the net. It's how we fly the ship, Val."

"Okay, I'm ready."

"Sorry. That will take additional approval from Captain Jzazbe. I don't recommend trying at the moment. Perhaps later."

"Sure, if there is a later," Val grumbled to himself. "Okay, Engine Room."

"It's called Engineering, Val." The view shifted out, then telescoped in on the very center of the ship. Engineering occupied a large area, but as the AI led him around, he learned that the actual power plant was quite small.

"Would you like instruction on how it works?" the AI asked.

"No. I've done some studying on my own. I understand the principles. What else can you show me?"

"How about a complete tour?"

"Okay!"

Val got his tour, and in detail, all through schematics, and a crewman delivered a sumptuous meal as the presentation continued. By the time the AI was done, he felt he could find his way to the important areas of the ship without assistance. He wanted more, but he suddenly felt tired. Before he knew it, he was sound asleep. Artmis might have helped him a little.

* * * * *

Daughter and Otis left sick bay and headed toward her quarters. Silence pervaded for a time as both considered Val's story.

"Will you deal with the governor for me?" she asked. "He must be brought into the picture, but security is your area of expertise."

"I will, My Lady, but it's too soon."

"I know. I'll have to Test Val. Tomorrow will be soon enough."

"If he lives that long."

She missed a step but caught herself. "I'd forgotten," she said after a time. "He does not strike me as being sick."

"With a Rider, he probably is not. The presence of a Rider explains the doctor's confusion. It has corralled the toxin and will deal with it."

"I'll leave word that I'm to be notified if he takes a turn for the worse. In the meantime, those arrested down below can be inconvenienced for one night."

"Some of them, yes. For others, it will be for a long time."

"The players at today's meeting are not our concern. Others will deal with them. The issue of ownership of the planetoid has not been resolved."

"Nor will you resolve it on this visit, My Lady. The district governor might be able to deal with the issue now."

"If Val's story is true, not all Corvolds are to blame. I strongly suspect the highest levels of their leadership, however. They may need to be replaced, but that's an internal matter. We'll deal with whomever they choose to represent them at the next meeting."

"If another meeting is needed."

"True. My presence might not be needed again."

"An attempt was made on your life, and a Knight is dead, My Lady."

"I know. Those are Imperial matters. If Val's story is true, the Corvolds will be held accountable. I'll speak to the governor and let him handle it, but after what's happened, the Queen might decide to intervene. The Corvolds might be in for some difficult years."

"The issue of Val is not so easily dispatched."

"No, it is not."

"May I speak freely, My Lady?"

She stopped to face him. "Otis, you're my Chief Protector. In addition to that, you've become my closest confidant. The day you choose to not speak freely is the day I find your replacement. I value your counsel, my friend."

"But I'm a Protector, My Lady, not a politician. You know that."

"I do, and I welcome it. You're a survivor, Otis, and I find your focus in that regard most helpful. We hold this Empire together with strands that are constantly fraying. We need survivors to guide us as we reweave the loose ends into stronger threads. Speak your mind."

"I sense an emotional connection between you and that young man in there. Is that appropriate?"

She sighed. "Probably not. It will not sway me." Her lips firmed into a thin line. "That's not what guides me at the moment." Softly, she said, "He chose to die for me, Otis. Even if he doesn't die, he acted with the belief that he would. I cannot even put a value on such an act."

"Nor can I. He performed in the highest standards to which I hold myself."

"So you sense something special about him, too?"

"I did from the moment I saw him in the hearing room, but my perception of him probably varies from your own. You barely saw him. My first impression of him was that he was naked. He had no weapon, he wore a tattered shirt and short pants that were covered in blood, and he was deformed. Despite that, he managed to get around all our security, then he used the only weapons at his disposal to fight. He used his wits, and he used his body. The best warriors usually fail when stripped to that most basic level."

"So he's a warrior. You're right. I did not sense that."

"Your attachment to him is emotional, My Lady."

She turned and started walking down the corridor as she considered his words. "You're right, Otis. I like the Val I have met. I can't say why, I just do. But it's more than that. Never before have I been so close to someone on the lowest rung of our society. His life has been a horror, he has received nothing from the Empire, yet he risked his life for me. *Why?*"

"I doubt if he could answer that question himself. Why, indeed?"

"He's a window to a new world for me, Otis. He's a citizen of my Empire, *and he doesn't even have a name.* Are there others like him out there? Are there others who would lay their lives down in my name? If there are, I want to know them. I'm surrounded by civilized, educated people who constantly nod their heads as I speak, rarely risking to disagree. Few of them think of the Empire. They only think of what the Empire can do for them."

"He didn't do it for you, My Lady."

She reached for the heavy fur around his neck and smoothed it. "Of course he didn't, my friend, and that makes it all the more impressive. He didn't do it for *me* – he doesn't even know me. He did it for what I represent. He did it for the Empire, and he never asked what the Empire would do for him in return. Even now he has not asked. I would surround myself with people like that, and we would all be better for it.

"Yes, Otis, I like Val. But I like the idea of Val even more. I can't say what the future holds for him, but I hope to find a way to draw on the resource he represents."

"In that regard, I support you completely. Perhaps he'll agree to be that window for you into his world."

"He'll have to agree to something, whatever it is. He carries a Rider who holds Imperial Secrets and deep knowledge of matters of State. He might not know it yet, but he will some day. I don't doubt for a moment that his Rider knows."

"You will keep a leash on him then?"

"Not a leash, Otis. A relationship. He has strong character. He cannot be coerced, nor would I choose to do so. My goal, and yours if you accept, is to help him blossom in his own way. Then, when the time is right, he will come to us of his own accord."

"Not a simple or sure thing, My Lady."

"Help me, Otis. I intend to name him a Friend of the Royal Family. As such, he has come under our protection."

"You cannot protect one such as him. As you said, he must find his own way."

"I will allow him to find his own way for a while, and we can help him get started, but I intend to keep my options open with him. Each of us has duties to the Empire, and I believe he may as well. If he is up to it, he may be called."

"You really are taken with him, aren't you?"

"I am. But he will always be free to choose his own way. Know this, Otis: Sir Jarl saw something in him. I, too, see something in him. So do you. We will give him opportunity. We'll have to wait and see what he does with it."

"And what is your hope?"

"He has a Rider. He probably doesn't even appreciate what that means, but because of the Rider he has many more years ahead of him than he knows. If he measures up, I might claim some of those years."

"Working for the Royal Family is not necessarily a kindness, My Lady."

"It is not, but people we can fully trust are rare."

"He's just a poor beggar, My Lady."

"At the moment."

Chapter Forty-two

Val survived the night. By the next morning all traces of the toxin were gone from his body.

Immediately after breakfast he was called to a meeting with Daughter. Otis came for him and escorted him through the corridors. Val, without knowing it, traveled past great works of art gracing the corridor walls on Daughter's level. He'd never taken the time to appreciate art, nor had he ever been in its presence. His mind had been focused on survival and his studies, little more.

Daughter stood up to greet him. He approached her, then lowered himself to his only knee, steadying himself with the crutch. He lowered his head until it nearly touched the floor.

"Val," she said sternly, "I told you yesterday that you need never bow in my presence."

He lifted his head to her. "You didn't say I couldn't if I wanted to."

"Well said, Val," she said smiling. "Please rise. Before we begin, do you have any special needs, any special requests of me?"

"Doesn't it work the other way around, My Lady?"

"Not always. You may speak freely, Val."

He considered her words. The request seemed far too open-ended to him. He would focus on the small picture for the moment. "Would it be possible to notify Mrs. Therly that I'm all right? And she needs to know what happened to Mr. Wyzcha . . . uh, Sir Jarl."

"Would you like to do it yourself?"

"Uh, aren't I under arrest?"

"I would prefer calling it 'held for questioning,' and the questioning related to yesterday's events is nearly over. It is time for me to Test you, Val."

The Corvolds had mentioned Testing yesterday, but he did not really understand it. "Uh, what exactly is this Test, My Lady?"

"I will mind-link with you, Val. I will sift freely through your thoughts, memories, and feelings. But I do not do so indiscriminately. I seek, first, the truth of your testimony. I do not anticipate surprises, though I sometimes discover things that people did not know they knew. Second, for my own edification, I seek to know if you are true to yourself. Lastly, I will determine what, if anything, the Empire will do to assist you in fulfilling your life's plan. It would be helpful if I understood your desires and motivations."

"Is any of this optional?"

"For you, after what you did yesterday, yes. But your agreement will greatly simplify our understanding of yesterday's events. That testimony is a matter of State. I must know what you know. As for your yourself and your future plans, it is completely voluntary. For this, I ask your permission."

He squirmed, deeply uncertain. What did all this mean? Would every aspect of the person he was be known to her? Then another thought struck him. "Will I be able to read your thoughts, too?"

"Sorry. It doesn't work like that. It's all one way, but know this, Val: I never, ever, divulge what I learn without permission."

He shook his head, looking down at his feet. "You've given me permission to speak freely. What you do is wrong."

"It is wrong, but not for me. It is what sets the Chosen apart."

Otis spoke up, and Val lifted his gaze to him. "Val, I am Tested regularly as part of our security procedures. All of her Protectors are. The process is painless. For most, to be Tested is an honor. To refuse a Test casts grave doubt. Provided you have spoken true, I, too, ask you to accept the honor of being Tested."

>Help me, Artmis.<

>Just say yes. It's not that big a deal. Tell her I will submit as well.<

He considered Artmis' words. To Artmis they were simple, but to him they were not simple at all. Not at all. "I have secrets, My Lady. Many secrets. Others count on my silence."

She smiled. "Do not be concerned for your friends. Not because I don't care, but because they are not the issue. What I learn in a Testing remains between you and me, Val, only you and me. I seek the truth of you, and I seek your knowledge of what happened yesterday, nothing more."

"Easy words, My Lady."

She closed her eyes. "True," she said after a time. "Will you trust me? I ask for your trust as Daughter, and I ask as a friend."

He considered, then caved in. He might be wrong, but he trusted this woman. "You have my permission, My Lady. Artmis gives you his as well."

"Artmis!"

"Uh, that's the name he chose for himself."

She considered for a time, then said, "He's an exact copy of his father. I find it fitting." She seated him in a chair and stood before him, then bent down and placed her hands on both sides of his head. She looked into his eyes, deeply into his eyes.

An instant later, her eyes swelled, and he felt as if he'd been sucked right into those eyes, body and all. His only sense was of her shuffling through his mind like a card dealer. Shuffle, shuffle, shuffle, stop. Shuffle, stop. Shuffle, shuffle, stop. He couldn't tell what she was looking at, and he had no control over her direction.

Then it was over. She released him and steadied him while he came back into his body.

"Ship," she said, "Send a transcript of Val and Rider Artmis' testimony to the district governor. Add to it my seal of authentication and verification by Test."

"Yes, My Lady."

To Val, she said simply, "Thank you. Your testimony will make their jobs much, much simpler."

"The questioning is over?"

"It is. You are free to go, though I hope you will stay with us a while longer."

"But it was my fault Sir Jarl died."

"You know that's not entirely true, and for the part that is true, you'll have to live with that knowledge for the rest of your life. Isn't that penalty enough?"

"I was thinking of the law, My Lady, not common sense."

"I see. In that case, we will hold your trial here, right now. Ship, record," she commanded.

"Recording, My Lady."

"Val, the charge against you is accomplice to murder. By your own words, you have already pled guilty. Do you wish to say anything further?"

"Uh, don't I get a lawyer?"

"No."

"Then I'll remain silent."

"Very well. I find you guilty with mitigating circumstances. You are sentenced to twelve hours of bed rest, after which time your sentence is complete and all records of your crime and your sentencing will be expunged from the record." She thought for a moment. "Oh, dear, it seems the sentence has already been served. Ship, you may erase the record of this proceeding."

"Erased, My Lady."

"There, it is done, Val."

He frowned, not knowing what to say.

She sensed his confusion and smiled. She had enjoyed her little game, but clearly this young man did not understand that he had been completely cleared of any wrong-doing.

"Know this, Val," she said softly. "The formalities have been followed. You have been found guilty and served your sentence. No one can re-open this case, and the only record of it will be me. I cannot expunge your personal feelings in the matter, but know that in my heart I find no guilt within you."

Val blinked, uncertain of himself. His thoughts went to the events of yesterday. "Uh, what of the Horlig ambassador? Is there any word?"

"He will not live through tomorrow. I am leaving shortly to visit him. I think he would like to know the cloud has been lifted from his head. Would you like to accompany me to the surface, to let your friends know you're okay?"

"I'd like that very much. Am I done then?"

"I hope not. You and I have much more to discuss, but the Horlig ambassador has little time, and he deserves a visit from me." She turned to Otis. "Will you accompany Val?"

"No, My Lady. I would like to, but my place is with you. Borg will go."

Val spoke for himself. "I'd rather go by myself."

"By yourself! Not a chance."

Val squirmed, but he decided he had no secrets from this woman now, not since she'd shuffled through his most intimate thoughts. "My home is an illegal settlement. I would prefer not to attract attention to it."

Daughter thought for a time. "You're right. I give you my promise that the authorities will not close it down."

"That's not really the problem. Many will believe it necessary to move on in any case."

"Then you will just have to convince them it is not necessary. Val, I don't for a moment believe your home and the people living there are not known to the authorities. Those authorities have chosen to leave you alone, and I will ensure that policy does not change. Any friends of yours who fail to trust my word will have to choose their own fates. I will not send you into that place alone. Sir Jarl's killers are yet free, and they may know of you. Now . . . time is short. We must be away."

Val leaned forward before she stood. He withdrew the money key from his pocket and placed it on the table. "This does not belong to me. I am returning it."

Her face lost its composure for a moment. The lack of markings clearly identified it as Sir Jarl's key. What was Val telling her?

Then she knew. "You're not coming back," she breathed softly.

"No, My Lady. I thank you for your hospitality, but it's time for me to leave."

She hesitated, glancing momentarily to Otis with alarm in her eyes, then returning her gaze to him, her lips in a firm line. "You're a free man, Val. The choice is yours."

"It is?" he asked, amazed at the words he had just heard.

"Val, you saved my life. There are choices available to you because of that. I beg you to reconsider. I've grown to like the Val I have met, but the choice to stay or to go will always and forevermore be yours."

He stood up, jamming his crutch into his shoulder. His response surprised even himself. "If you speak true, I'll come back, but just for a little while. I have plans of my own, you know, and I'm on a tight schedule."

"I just Tested you, Val. I do know." Then her face broke into a bright smile. "Thank you." She leaned forward and pushed the key back toward him. "I always speak true. Keep the key. I believe Sir Jarl would have wanted you to have it. Use it wisely."

Surprised, he asked shyly, "Uh, do you know what its credit limit is?"

"It has no limit, Val."

He stared at her. He didn't understand.

She returned the stare. "It was the property of a Knight, Val. It has no limit. Like I said, use it wisely."

His gaze moved to the key, his eyes wide in wonder. *No limit?* And it was his? His hand trembled as he reached for the key. When he picked it up, he looked not at it but at her. Did she have any concept of what unlimited funds meant to someone like him? In a heartbeat, his whole life had changed. The stash of funds he had so laboriously built for purchasing bribes from professors suddenly seemed paltry. Then he reconsidered. Could he use Imperial funds for bribes? Somehow it seemed wrong.

"I don't know what to say, My Lady."

"Then don't say anything. If you'll stick around long enough, we'll teach you how to manage your resources, and I include here not just money but yourself and your ambitions. After Testing you, I know what you seek, and it is possible."

Val nodded but said nothing. The implication was clear: she was inviting him to stay. Staying here meant leaving everything and everyone he'd ever known. On the other hand, it meant traveling to the stars. Suddenly, the stars were within his reach. He had planned to leave Hespra III in a couple of years, but two years was an eternity to him. Now, the time had suddenly become right now, and he wasn't ready.

"When do I have to decide?" he asked.

"Soon, but not now. The Horlig ambassador does not have much time. Let's focus on him for the moment."

By the time they reached the ramp, *Resolve* had grounded at the spaceport. Val and Borg exited the ship, and it left immediately for the hospital. For Daughter, this was not a state visit, it was a personal visit. She had no need for official regalia and crowds this time.

Val immediately settled into his scuttle and headed for the gate. He'd been on this side of the fence before, but never officially, and he liked the feeling of freedom. He liked it a lot. Borg's eyes never stopped moving as he padded on all fours beside Val. He studied the Great Cat which, even on all fours, reached to his chest. Had Val ever seen a lion, he would have noted the close resemblance, but Borg did not walk on paws. Each foot was a hand, a strong hand with long fingers and sharp claws, and each of those hands could, and often did, hold weapons. His fur was mostly a uniform light brown in color, but the tip of his tail was dark brown, as were the tufted ends of his ears. Borg's eyes were golden, but his muzzle drew most of Val's attention. Unlike a cat's, it was long and hideous, colored in wrinkled folds of dark brown and red and gold. Black lips covered a vicious mouth full of teeth clearly meant for ripping apart prey. Even without weapons, Val knew this creature would never be unarmed. Yet, as with Otis, he sensed no threat from Borg, nor would he want to be on the receiving end of Borg's wrath.

"Do you know where we're going?" he asked Borg.

"I do. Otis has completed a thorough check on you."

Val stopped in his tracks. "Already?"

Borg simply looked at him. It didn't take long before Val felt his face reddening. The resources available to Daughter were probably unlimited. He was thinking too small.

>We're not really free,< he thought to Artmis as he continued toward his home.

>No, we are not. Is anyone ever truly free?<

That shut Val up for a time. >Why is she going to all this trouble for me?<

>You mean, besides the fact that you saved her life?<

>That's not it, Artmis.<

>It's part of it. Remember, she never lies. She truly has an interest in your well-being. As for the rest of it, it's not so hard to figure out.<

Val considered those words, then he considered everything that had happened to him during the past day. Topping the list was him killing himself. That memory was all black. He hardly remembered the act and its immediate aftermath, though not the fact that he'd chosen to act. Meeting Daughter was certainly high on the list, but having Sir Jarl die in his arms held intense meaning to him, even if it had really only been a ruse to transfer Artmis to him.

Then his thoughts coalesced. He had never met the first Artmis, the Rider of a Knight of the Realm. And that Rider's memories, or at least some of them, had been transferred to the current Artmis. He suddenly understood.

>It's because of you, isn't it.<

>Most likely.<

>Do you really know so much?<

>In many ways I'm still just a child, but not in all ways. There are things of significance that I know, and I suspect I'll discover others in time. In some ways we were both born anew yesterday, Val. We'll both be growing up together.<

>Why didn't you get the full measure from your father?<

>Riders are many-celled. My cells course throughout your body, but every cell is known to me, and in total they *are* me. Before Artmis died, most cells of his being fissioned to create me. But some of those

cells were occupied with keeping Sir Jarl alive. They could not expend the effort to fission, so I got part of the whole.<

>Enough that you *are* your father.<

>I'm a close replica.<

>Then she has no choice. *We* have no choice.<

>Yet in spite of that, she has given us choice, Val. Think about that. There is true power in the choice she has given you.<

>Given us. I cannot imagine disappointing her.<

>Nor can I. Nor did Sir Jarl or my father.<

>Certain things your father learned were because he was a Knight. I think it appropriate that you keep them to yourself.<

>There is much that I keep to myself. In time, you will know what I know.<

>I'm not after Imperial Secrets, Artmis. I've known for a long time that I'd take the oath of a fleet officer. That oath could potentially demand that we place the well-being of the Realm above our own. I *will* swear that oath one day. Will you?<

>I will.<

Val turned to Borg. "You're going to stand out in there. There's no way to avoid it."

"Then we will not waste the effort trying. Just be yourself, young Val. But be aware, as well. Always: be aware. Sir Jarl's killers are still free, and they may believe you can lead the authorities to them. Your home might have become a trap."

"Do you have any spare weapons?"

"Several. What is your choice?"

"I've never used a weapon of any kind."

"Maybe not used, but you have certainly held one. In trained hands, a crutch such as yours is a lethal weapon."

Val stopped, his mind returning to yesterday in the chamber. "I didn't need to touch those crystals," he breathed.

"Not so, Val. Had your crutch been lifted, you would have been killed. We Protectors do not hesitate when it comes to the Royal Family. Take this," he said. "It's a full-size blaster. It will be the most accurate for untrained hands. Do you know how to point and fire it?"

"Yes," Val answered absently as he considered Borg's words.

"Check the weapon," Borg demanded, focusing Val's attention on that which mattered most at the moment. Val examined the weapon, then shoved it into the back of his shorts. It was incredibly uncomfortable. "Two things, Val. First, if there is any shooting, drop to the ground immediately. Second, there will be no indiscriminate firing.

Shoot only at things or individuals you have clearly identified as a threat. Understood?"

"Understood."

They stopped just inside the tube to let their eyes adjust. The smells coming from inside welcomed Val, though he suspected they were overwhelming to Borg. They bypassed Mr. Wyzcha's and continued down-tube to Mrs. Therly's, just beyond Val's shack. As they passed his home, Val noticed the front door was slightly ajar. He never left his door ajar. The hairs on the back of his neck suddenly lifted. Then he sensed the silence. It was not usually noisy within the tube, but it was never completely silent either.

"Trouble," he mumbled to Borg.

"Leave, now," the Great Cat growled softly.

The moment he turned, Borg pushed him down and laid across his body. A blaster spoke from Val's shack and another from Mrs. Therly's. Borg fired twice and the silence returned.

"Stay," Borg commanded. Val saw nothing with his face pressed to the floor by Borg's body, but Borg did. He didn't see a person, but he saw the muzzle of a blaster swing carefully toward them from within Mrs. Therly's shack. He fired, and a scream rent the darkness. A blaster skidded out onto the floor from behind the shack, and they heard another voice.

"I give up!"

"Come out, and keep your appendages where I can see them," Borg commanded.

A clean-cut human stood up and edged out from behind Mrs. Therly's shack. "I'm unarmed," he whined.

"On the floor," Borg commanded. "Keep your appendages free."

The man went down to one knee, straightening his arms to stop his descent. Val sensed nothing, but the blaster in Borg's hand spoke, and the man's hand and the hidden weapon in it disappeared. He cried out.

Suddenly Borg was off Val and racing for the shack. He fired a stunner at the man on the floor as he went by. He crashed through the door of the shack without slowing to open it, and his stunner fired again. He leaped back to Val and lifted him in one strong arm, then leaped to the side of the tube, his body pressing Val to the wall. He lifted a communicator to his muzzle and growled a few coded phrases, his eyes never stopping a constant scan of their surroundings.

"Are there better lights in this place?" Borg asked softly.

"No."

"Any good hiding places?"

"There's a door leading to an old storage bin about a hundred meters down-tube. A couple of R'bock friends of mine live there. It does not have an exit."

"Then we will not go there. Be alert for explosives or vapors. It's time to leave. You lead, I will follow. And be silent."

Val knew how to be silent, and he knew every nook and cranny of the place. He wound his way between shacks until nearing the entrance. From this point, there was no more cover.

"Down," Borg commanded. Val stopped where he was and lay on the floor. Borg did the same. It wasn't long before two fighters arrived with a squad of Imperial Marines. Borg briefed them, and they spread out and moved down-tube until they were lost to sight. Police cruisers began landing in two's and three's until the entrance to the tunnel was completely blocked. Most of the police followed the marines.

Borg never let Val leave his side. "I need to find Mrs. Therly," Val insisted.

"I'm sorry, Val, but I believe I found her. There was a body inside her home in addition to the one I wounded."

"Describe it."

"A human female of indeterminate age, quite overweight."

Val's shoulders sagged. "It's her." He started into the tube, but Borg stopped him. "Consider, Val. Do you really want to see her as she is now?"

Tears filled his eyes. "No, I guess not. I should get my things."

Borg sat on his haunches to face Val. "What would you bring away? I will send for it."

Val considered, then wiped the tears from his eyes and faced away from the tube. "There's nothing here for me now. Let's go."

When they reached the spaceport, they waited until *Resolve* returned. When the ramp lowered, Val crutched his way to the ship, turned to look one final time at his old home, then squared his shoulders and crutched his way into the ship.

Chapter Forty-three

Val woke up famished. He asked *Resolve's* Artificial Intelligence, the AI, where he could get breakfast. "One moment, Val," it responded.

One moment turned into several minutes, then Otis appeared. "Good morning, Val."

"Good morning to you, sir."

"Daughter has invited you to join her for breakfast. Are you up to it?"

"Otis, let's be real about this. I'm a beggar, and she's Daughter. Her work is done on my world. Isn't her interest in me done as well?"

"Sorry, Val. You won't get out of it that easy. And no, her interest in you has just begun. So has mine. Do you have even the slightest comprehension of what you accomplished back on Hespra III?"

Val squirmed. "I may be a poor beggar, but I'm not stupid, Otis."

"No, that you are not. You saved her life, Val. More, you sacrificed your own life to do so. It's pure luck that you are alive today. Few within the Empire would have made that choice."

"You would have. So did Sir Jarl. Every officer in the fleet takes on the same commitment. It's part of their oath. I'm studying for the entrance exam to a fleet academy. When I graduate, I'll take the same oath."

"They stand by their oaths and do their duty, but when it gets close and personal, like it did for you, most would hesitate, and hesitation would have meant her death. You've moved into a small, very select group, Val."

"I can't look at it that way."

"Nor should you. But others can, and they do. Daughter certainly does. So do her Protectors, myself included. So, too, does every member of this squadron. Think about it, Val. The sole purpose of every person and every ship in this squadron is to see that Daughter is safe. Because of you, we still have a job to do. Trust me, among our small group your name is known, and you are held in high esteem. You cannot prevent that, nor should you try. Your example is an inspiration to all of us."

Val was speechless. He considered Otis' words for a long time. "I did not seek this," he said eventually. "I only sought to fulfill the duty Sir Jarl gave me, a duty that I've always known I would accept as an Imperial line officer. He's the one you should be grateful to."

"We are grateful to him. His passing will not go unnoticed. But, Val, his death was not by choice. Yours was."

"No, sir, it wasn't. It was my duty."

Otis hesitated for a time in thought, then looked deeply into Val's eyes. "Well said," he growled. "By those words, you have ensured your entrance to Fleet Academy."

"*What?*"

"You heard me. If you qualify academically, you're in."

Val sat on the edge of the bed, his face pale. Had he heard right? He was going to Fleet Academy? Breakfast suddenly didn't matter any longer.

"I don't understand, Otis. And I really want to qualify on my own."

"I believe you might have succeeded on your own, as amazing as that sounds, but what is the goal here? Is it to get accepted, or is it just to prove to yourself that you could do it on your own?"

"Uh, maybe a little of both."

"If you get into an academy, it will be because of your hard work. I can promise you that much. No one is going to do the hard stuff for you, but surely you can let us help with the things that are beyond your control."

"I had a plan, and I was on track."

"And you had some insurmountable obstacles."

"Not insurmountable, just difficult and expensive. Fake transcripts and recommendations from non-existent teachers can be bought. It just takes a lot of care and a lot of money."

"You had those kinds of funds?"

"I was working on it, and I was on plan."

"You are determined, aren't you!"

"I am, sir."

"I think you'll be in a position to present real transcripts now."

"I'm not sure what the next couple of years hold for me."

"No one is going to promise you the Academy, Val. You have to earn that. But real schools are definitely in the picture now, and you'll have real teachers to make recommendations. You'll have mine as well."

"Otis, you know as well as I do that with a few words from the Royal Family, I won't even have to qualify. I don't want that."

Otis considered. "Some gain entrance in the manner you suggest, mainly members of powerful families, but even they have to meet a certain minimum level of competency."

"I'm not after a minimum level of competency, Otis."

Otis grinned a feral grin, his lips curling up to reveal a mouthful of vicious teeth. "Nor is Daughter. Or me. But like it or not, your examiners will have a letter of commendation from me. It will be just a piece of the process, but it will be noticed."

"Please don't, sir."

"Val, do you honestly believe you'll need such letters?"

"No."

"Nor do I. Those letters will be there anyway. Consider the purpose of the examination process. What do you think they're looking for?"

"The very highest academic standards."

"Academics are just a part of it."

"Then I don't know."

"They're looking for people who will be true to their oath, Val, an oath to serve the Empire. Your actions have already proven beyond any doubt that you will. The rest is just a formality. You're in."

"I'm in?" he asked in a small voice.

"You're in, provided you don't shirk your studies."

"I won't. I promise."

"Don't promise me, Val. Promise yourself. That's all I ask. I have never written such a letter for anyone, but for you, it is my duty and my pleasure. Consider it from my viewpoint. How do you think I'd have felt returning to Triton with Daughter's body? Eh?"

Val stared into those feral eyes. "I can't imagine anything worse."

"Nor can I. I would hope to die first. That's what you have given me, it's what you've given my team of Protectors, and it's what you've given every member of this squadron. We will not forget, Val."

"How was it possible for the crystal to reach her?"

"Simply put, it was a failure on my part."

Val looked at him in astonishment.

"Such words give pause for thought, do they not?" Otis asked. "Take heed of my next words, Val. The moment you moved toward those crystals, I knew my best efforts had failed. What did I do?"

"I don't know. I wasn't really paying attention to you."

"What I did is perhaps the hardest lesson a Protector learns. Even in failure we do not give up. We continue protecting. There will be failures in life, Val. You, too, will fail along the way, perhaps many times. In fact, you failed so badly when you saved Daughter that you almost died. The lesson here is that you do not focus on failure. You keep looking forward, you keep doing your job. Later, you examine the failure and learn from your mistakes, but you focus forward. We Protectors are the best there are at what we do, but we fail occasionally. Failing is not okay, but we do not stop at the point of failure. Ever. We keep our focus forward. We keep our performance at the highest level it can be, because even in failure, our jobs are not done. I think you're man enough to understand the lesson."

"I do understand, sir, but . . . I failed to save her?"

"No, that's not what I said. You saved her, but you could have done a better job of it, and it's something you'll want to work on over the coming years."

"Work on what?"

"Management, Val. Management."

"I totally do not understand you."

"I'm not surprised. Your whole life has focused on survival. It looks like you've learned that part well, Val, but there's more inside you. Now that you've learned how to survive, it's time to learn to lead. Are you ready for that? You want to be a good fleet officer. To be really good, you need to learn to lead others. That means managing your resources, which in most cases are people. You could have managed me and my brothers much better yesterday."

"I could?"

"Absolutely. There were six of us. A simple statement like "the crystals are poisoned," would have brought instant response from us, and you would never have had to touch them."

"And one of you would be dead now."

"Probably not. You'll learn more about our capabilities in time, provided you stick around for a while. We're better than that, Val."

He hung his head in shame, mumbling, "Oh."

Otis reached a hand forward and lifted Val's chin. "Look forward, young man. Do not focus on failure, focus forward. You did exactly the right thing with the tools available to you, and no one will ever take that away from you, least of all me. Are you willing to accept the fact that there are better ways to do things? Are you ready to learn? My men and I are prepared to spend the time with you if you are willing. We all want you to be better prepared, to be the best you can be."

"I see your point, and yes, I want to learn – almost as much as I want to stay alive. I did not want to die in that room."

"Or any other room. But we're keeping Daughter waiting. I suggest a quick shower and a change of clothes. You have fifteen minutes."

Val showered, though it took him a minute to figure out the controls. He searched for his old clothes and in the process found cupboards with several changes of clothes. Among them was a plain spacer's uniform, a dark blue, one-piece coverall lacking only emblems of rank. Well, Val thought to himself, if they put it in here, I guess I can wear it. To his surprise, when he pulled it out, he discovered the left leg had been shortened to match his stump. When he put it on, he looked in the mirror and sucked in a breath, then stood tall with his shoulders back, liking what he saw.

He made his way to Daughter's quarters and stopped before the door.

What now?

He knocked softly, and the door whisked to the side. Daughter stood up and came to greet him, her eyes full of sadness.

"I'm so sorry about Mrs. Therly, Val."

He nodded, but there were no words.

"Please be seated," she invited, indicating a chair at the table. Before sitting, he remembered himself and bowed. "Good morning, My Lady."

"Actually, it's lunch time, but I've ordered breakfast for you. Please be seated. And welcome to you as well, Artmis."

They both sat, and she stared at him for a time. "Would you like to talk about it?"

"There's nothing to talk about, My Lady. I lost two people that I didn't know I loved until it was too late to tell them. They're gone, but their memory remains. I'm glad Borg stopped me from seeing Mrs. Therly. Are we underway?"

"We are. I have a busy schedule. I will make arrangements to return you to your home whenever you wish, though it's probably not safe for you there right now."

"I no longer have a home, My Lady. There's nothing to return to. I'll find someplace else."

"Will you let me help with that?"

"You would do that for me?"

"If you will permit me."

Val shook his head, then just stared at her in confusion. The hint of a knowing smile brightened her face. "Say what's on your mind, Val."

"Uh . . . I don't want to offend, My Lady."

"We're in my private chambers. I'm Daughter, but I depend on others for council, and that council sometimes offends. In here, it's important that you say what needs to be said. Understood?"

"Yes, My Lady. Uh . . . in that case, I'm pretty new to all this, but I'm surprised that words like 'Will you let me,' and 'If you will permit me,' are even in your vocabulary. Sorry," he said, lowering his head.

"Look at me, Val." His head instantly jerked up. "It's simple, really. For much of my life, I'm on display and certain formalities are observed without fail. But I cannot live my life like that all the time, or even most of the time. In private, I demand to be treated like a real person, not an institution. It might take you a while to learn when those times are, but you will learn if you pay attention. To begin with, pay attention to my voice. When I become formal, you follow. Got it?"

Val nodded. "Yes, My Lady."

Their meals arrived, and Val looked at his in dismay. "I can't eat all this," he stammered.

"Doctor's orders, I'm afraid," she smiled. "Don't forget, you have a Rider; you're eating for two. You can work your way up to it. Just do your best."

He was hungry, and he dove in. When he next looked up, she hadn't touched her food. She was just staring at him.

"My Lady?" he asked around the food in his mouth.

"Val," she asked kindly, "do you sense that you're entering a new phase of your life?"

"Otis mentioned something like that. I haven't really had time to think about it very much."

"No, you have not," she responded looking away. When she focused back on him, she had a set look. "You would have failed the entrance exam, most likely."

Val's hand stopped half way to his mouth. "I'm doing a lot of failing all of a sudden. First, I fail at saving you, and now I'm failing the entrance exam? I've done all the right things. I just have a few hurdles to clear yet."

"The hurdles to which you refer are no longer an issue, Val. You'll have all the necessary credentials, and I don't doubt that you will succeed in your studies. I'm not talking about math and physics, I'm talking about deportment. Did you know that, too, is part of the testing process?"

"It's listed in the requirements. I'm not sure exactly what it means. Doesn't it just mean you stay clean and sharp?"

"No, it does not. Officers are expected to have perfect command of Galactic High Standard, which you do not, and they are expected to have certain . . . manners about them. There is a proper way to eat. The knife goes in your hand like this," she demonstrated, "and the fork is held like this . . ."

Val's breakfast turned into an obstacle course. "We'll have soup with dinner," she said with a twinkle in her eyes when he finally set the utensils down. "You won't like that process, I assure you. By the way, you ate most of your breakfast. Did you notice?"

"Maybe because it took so long," he grumbled.

"You'll get used to it. Tell me, why aren't you wearing a shoe?"

Val looked down at his foot, then back at Daughter. "Is that part of deportment, too?" he asked.

"It is. It's part of the uniform."

"I'll see about getting one, My Lady."

"I'm certain you have at least two in your room."

"Yes, My Lady."

"Would you like to rest for a bit?"

He looked at her in surprise. "I just woke up!"

"Doctor Storvo advised me to go slowly, to give you time before we dive into serious issues. He's an exceptional doctor, and I listen carefully when he speaks, but one particular item should be dealt with as soon as you're ready."

His stomach hardened, but he squared his shoulders. "If he's just recommending, then he's not certain. I'm ready, My Lady."

"You've been through a lot in the past few days."

"All of us have."

"But the rest of us are still surrounded by our routines. Our lives have not been turned upside down. You have to be feeling lost right now."

"I've never not had a plan, but you're right: the future is blurry." He looked hard into her eyes. "My dream is not. I still want to be a star pilot."

She smiled. "And you shall, Val, if you pass muster. I won't use my position to sway the examiners. You have to do that on your own. There are certain things I can help with to prepare you for entrance, but once you go for the exam, you're on your own."

Val considered her words, then smiled. "Thank you, My Lady. I'm not stupid. I know my presence here has probably opened doors that would otherwise have been closed to me. You could say a few words to the right people, and I'd be in. Please don't do that."

"I won't, and that's a promise."

Val stared at her. "This is important to me, My Lady."

"I Tested you. I know. You will be on your own from the moment you step into that examination process. And that includes your time at the Academy and some years after. You will make it on your own, or you will fail, Val."

"Some years after?"

She squirmed a little in her seat as she considered her response. She could not lie, and this was probably one of those times when it was appropriate to withhold the full truth, but as she looked at this tall, scrawny young man before her, she knew that wasn't the way.

"You chose to die for me, Val. I live today because of that choice. I will never forget. Please don't ask me to forget."

Val nodded solemnly.

"You have a bright future before you, with or without my help," she continued. "In choosing Fleet Academy, you choose a life of duty to the Empire. I reserve the right to call you to my side some day in the future. I don't know when it will be, or even if it will be, but if the need arises, I will not hesitate."

"I will always answer your call, My Lady."

"You are far too grown up for a sixteen-year-old. Is that Artmis speaking?"

"No, My Lady. He's been quiet for the last day or so. He tells me he's recovering."

Startled, she demanded, "Is he all right?"

"He's fine, My Lady. Dealing with the poison was not easy. In fact, it was a long, difficult ordeal for him. He's resting."

She considered, then asked, "Tell me, how do you know you'll like being a star pilot?"

"My Lady?" he asked, confused. What a dumb question.

"Captain Jzazbe informs me that many who want to be star pilots discover they cannot function in space. It takes a certain kind of mind to feel comfortable out here among all this emptiness, and it takes being in space to know."

Val heard her words and considered them. Suddenly, her meaning became clear. "You mean I might not measure up even if I want to?"

"That's exactly what I mean. Most find space intimidating. You can want more than anything, but that doesn't mean you can, and there's no way of knowing until you experience the vast depths of space. Would you like to know?" she asked with a smile.

Val's pulse quickened, though a spot of fear shot through him. "How?"

"Captain Jzazbe knows everything that goes on within his ship, he knows much of my purpose and agenda, and he definitely knows your story."

She leaned forward to emphasize her words. "Val, he has asked to make an exception concerning you. It's against regulations, but we sometimes make exceptions around here. Should you agree, he offers you the opportunity to find out if you are cut out to be a spaceman. I'll let him explain it to you. You have seven weeks before we reach our next destination. You may choose to disembark at our next stop, or you may choose to continue with us. It's your choice. Think about it, and if you're ready, talk to him."

"Yes, My Lady! Would now be appropriate?"

"No. If you're ready for that, you're ready for something else first." She studied him for a time and reached a decision, then simply said, "Tell me what you know about your parents."

Val stared at her. "You Tested me. Surely you know that I know nothing about them at all."

"When I Test, I do not pry any further than necessary," she said dryly. "The orphanage had no information on your parents at all. I was just wondering if you did."

"No. Nothing, My Lady." He paused, then asked, "Do you?"

She considered, then nodded her head, her gaze locked on his. "I might, though it is only speculation." She stared hard into his eyes. "And Sir Jarl?"

"Mr. Wyzcha. It might sound strange since he was so much

older than me, but he was my best friend. I would go so far as to call him my mentor. We spent long hours together, and I admire him more than I can put into words."

"If I understand correctly, he found you hungry and destitute not long after you left the orphanage. He gave you opportunity and let you take it where you could."

"He did, but it was so much more, My Lady. He loved the Empire, would do anything for it and the Royal Family and all the various peoples he visited. He told me that though he traveled widely, he never encountered a race he didn't admire, and among them only rarely did he meet individuals he could not call friend. Everyone I knew looked up to him and listened when he spoke. I'm certain no one knew he was a Knight."

"He was Knighted by the Queen herself, Val. I was there. He was truly a Great One."

"What was he doing here? Was he undercover or something?"

"This is where the speculation comes in, Val. Mother received a message from him about sixteen years ago, a vague message informing her that he would be out of touch for a while."

She focused intently on Val as she talked, wondering if he would piece things together. When she mentioned the sixteen year time period, he sat up taller and really focused.

"Sixteen years ago?"

"Yes. Such messages are not expected from our Knights, but they are given complete freedom to act as they see fit in any circumstances. Their actions and decisions are only questioned in private, never in public, and some of those decisions affect multiple worlds and billions of Empire citizens."

"One man has so much power?"

"He does. A Knight's word is the Queen's command on every world of the Empire. He is held accountable only to the Queen. In some cases, that accountability extends to the Chosen, as well, but the Queen is the final authority."

"Surely they make mistakes. They're human."

"We all make mistakes, Val. When a Knight errs, he or she is expected to admit and correct the mistake, almost always before the Queen even knows about it."

Val's gaze slid from hers. He looked around the room, found nothing to focus on, then closed his eyes for a time. When he opened them again, his focus was her. "You're telling me that the man I knew as Mr. Wyzcha was one of the most powerful men in the galaxy. He disappeared sixteen years ago and ended up living in a shack in an abandoned railway tunnel."

She nodded but said nothing.

"Why?" he demanded.

"So far as I know, there has been no communication between Sir Jarl and the Queen since his disappearance. I can only offer conjecture."

Val spoke softly. "I was born sixteen years ago. Am I somehow tied to Sir Jarl's disappearance?"

She nodded but said nothing.

"Was he my father?" Val whispered.

She shook her head, tears coming to her eyes. "I wish I could say he was, but he was not, Val. He was your uncle."

"Uncle!"

She nodded, wiping tears from her eyes. "Proven beyond a doubt by Doctor Storvo. The rest is where the conjecture comes in. My staff has worked hard on this, but facts are difficult to confirm across light years. So far as we can determine, Sir Jarl's brother married a priestess on a world far across the galaxy, a woman who had been promised to her god, not to a man. Her marrying and leaving the order broke some very fundamental rules. They escaped the world, but they were hunted and eventually found. How Sir Jarl entered the picture is not known, but I suspect his brother, knowing time was short, asked for help."

"You know who my parents were?" Val gulped.

She nodded. "I'm fairly certain, but I know them in name only, I'm afraid. You can research them later, but I can tell you this: your parents were found and killed. I'm sorry to say that if my conjecture is right, they both died not long after your birth."

Val's lips quivered, and he got up to pace the room. She gave him his freedom for a time, then spoke.

"I'm guessing that Sir Jarl accepted a personal call from his brother. He accepted responsibility for you and has kept an eye on you all these years."

"But I was in an orphanage. He might have been the one who put me there."

"Your mother's world is known for several things, Val, not least of which is its devotion to it priestesses. For one to marry and leave is not acceptable to them. Had they known of your existence, I'm certain you would not have been permitted to live. No doubt, Sir Jarl knew that, as well, and he chose to hide you in the orphanage."

She looked hard into his eyes, then said, "Am I right, Artmis?"

Val gasped. Artmis! Of course! He carried his father's

memories, or most of them. He didn't need to voice the question to his Rider. Artmis had heard.

>She's mostly right, Val. Sir Jarl was there when your parents died. He saved you, but in the process you lost your leg to a blaster. It was a very near thing.<

Thoughts tumbled over themselves in Val's mind, so many demanding answers that he didn't know where to begin. Artmis sensed his confusion and focused his thoughts on what mattered.

>They knew who he was, Val. To hide you, Sir Jarl had to hide himself. He succeeded for all these years, but he started sniffing around when he learned of Daughter's visit. Someone must have noticed. I can't imagine how else the Corvolds would have found him.<

Val's lips trembled. >He wasted the rest of his life just for me?<

>Not wasted, Val. I happen to think you're worth it, and clearly, so did he. But he didn't do it just for you. There's more. Ask her.<

Val lifted his eyes to Daughter and nodded, not certain of his voice. He managed to say, "Artmis tells me he didn't do it just for me. What does he mean?"

She stared at him with eyes that brimmed, then raised her head and called, "Otis."

Otis padded into the room and sat at attention, but not in front of Daughter. He faced Val and got right to the point. "Your official designation is 5397867A. Did you know there is another with the designation 5397867B?"

Val's eyebrows rose, first in surprise, then in confusion. What was Otis getting at? "No, sir," he said.

"We've researched your records at the orphanage. Your parents had another child."

Val could not speak. Another?

"You have a sister, Val. A twin sister."

Chapter Forty-four

Val sat back heavily in his chair, his thoughts whirling. A sister? Then Otis' words registered. "You said 'have?'"

"She's here," Otis growled softly.

Val stared at him, stunned. After a time, he reached for his crutch and stood up. "Where?"

"Just outside the door."

"How much does she know about what's happened?"

"Very little. She knows we're in space, she knows you're here, and she's here by her own choice. That's all. I will tell you that she didn't hesitate for a moment when she heard she had a brother. She brought nothing with her from the orphanage."

Val turned to Daughter. "Has she met you?"

"No, Val. She's seen me, but she does not know who I am. I want her to meet you first. You are her focus, no one else at the moment. Would you like some privacy?"

"No! I don't know what to do. What do I say to her? What's her name?"

"Like you, officially she only has a number, but she goes by the name of Krys."

Val stared at her, then just turned and crutched over to the door.

The AI must have been listening, because the door opened without a command.

She stood against the far wall of the corridor, a carbon copy of him. Tall and thin, with dark hair and eyes, she stood tensely with her hands hanging at her sides, her back very straight. They stared at each other, but they had no words. Val extended a hand, and she stepped slowly toward him, reaching for that hand.

"You're me!" she exclaimed looking into his eyes, her own eyes shining.

"Hello, Krys. I'm Val," he said.

Her lips trembled. "Hello, Brother. Can I give you a hug?" She reached for his other hand. He shoved the crutch hard into his shoulder and released his grip. She took the hand, then closed the gap, her arms going around him, lightly at first, then strongly. Val's head swam as he tried to grasp what this all meant, then he returned the embrace. This person holding to him was his family.

His family. He suddenly had family, something orphans only dreamed of.

She stepped back, her eyes glistening, then took a full step back. "You're a spacer!" she exclaimed, her eyes shining as she took in the uniform.

"Uh, not exactly. It's kind of a long story. Will you come in? I'd like to introduce you to my friends."

She didn't just follow. She took his hand and led him into the room, not caring about anything or anyone except the brother at her side. She wore a threadbare shift that once might have been white. Val recognized the outfit from his own time in the orphanage. She must have come directly from there. She led him to Otis and curtsied. "Thank you, Otis. I will never forget this day."

"It's the least we could do. Welcome, Miss Krys," he growled in greeting. Then he stepped aside. It was Daughter's turn. He looked hard at Val, and Val got the message.

"Daughter, please let me introduce my sister, Krys. Krys, this is Daughter."

Krys turned to Daughter. "Pleased to meet you, Ma'am," she said. "Whose daughter are you?"

Val coughed into his fist. "Uh . . . "

"It's okay, Val. I'll explain," Daughter said. She motioned Krys to a nearby couch and sat beside her. "I am the Queen's daughter," she said simply, a smile on her face.

Krys looked into her eyes, then she turned to Val. She blinked a few times before she found her voice. None of this made sense to her.

"She's *Daughter*," Val said, emphasizing the word.

Krys still didn't understand. Daughter stood up, saying, "I'm sorry, Krys. I know it's confusing, and I confess I'm having a little fun at your expense. Please forgive me."

"I don't understand."

"Of course you don't, my dear, though I'm afraid a full explanation will just add to your confusion. How much education did they give you in that place?"

"Some. Not enough, but there are other ways." She hesitated, then pulled a pad from her pocket.

"I see. It appears that brother and sister are alike in more ways than appearance. You found your own means to learn."

"As much as I could. Only at night, though. They'd have taken it from me if they knew. I get the feeling that won't happen here."

A sad smile met her words. "It will not." Daughter looked at Otis with troubled eyes. "Something must be done about conditions there," she said to him.

He nodded. "Yes, My Lady, but it's a local matter not subject to Imperial direction."

Krys didn't miss the 'My Lady' or the 'Imperial' parts and sat up straighter, if such a thing was possible. Her senses suddenly became very focused. Val, recognizing the body language, went to her and sat by her side, taking one of her hands in his own. Daughter stared at the two of them as they sat together. She could only shake her head.

"You are each other," she said softly.

"Except for the few pounds I'm missing down here," Val said pointing to his missing leg. "My Lady," he added a moment later.

"My Lady," Krys murmured. Her eyes rose to the woman standing before her. "You're Daughter," she said. Then, "You're the Queen's daughter." She received a nod in reply. Krys turned to Val with troubled, piercing eyes. "Who are *you*?" she asked.

"Just plain old Val," he said standing up and pulling Krys to her feet. "May I present Daughter?"

Krys stood before the woman. Their gazes locked for a moment, then Krys went to one knee with her head bowed. "My Lady."

Daughter took Krys' hands in her own to lift her to her feet. The moment they touched, Krys stiffened. When she started to fall forward, Val knew something was wrong. Daughter went down to one knee to hold her, and Val was by her side in a moment. Her eyes stared blankly into the distance as if in a trance.

His arm went around her waist. "Krys," he asked softly, "Are you okay?"

She blinked, confused for a moment, then came back into herself. She focused first on Val, then on Daughter. "Oh! I'm so sorry, My Lady. Please forgive me."

Daughter held her. "What's wrong, child?"

Krys stared at Daughter for a time, then pulled her hands away, bringing a shaking hand to her forehead. "It's nothing, My Lady. I'm just . . . overwhelmed. Please forgive me."

"There's nothing to forgive. It's I who should ask for your forgiveness."

"My Lady, for sixteen years I have lived in the orphanage, only rarely allowed to venture outside its walls. All my knowledge of your Realm comes from here," she said reaching for her pad. "I don't even know where I am or where we're going."

Daughter pulled Krys to her feet. "And I had expected to meet an uneducated waif, someone our system had forced into timidity. In spite of the rags you wear, I am most pleased to find an intelligent young woman instead. After meeting your brother, I probably should have known better. You left us for a moment. Are you ill?"

"I'm fine, My Lady. Just a brief lapse. It's happened before, but it's nothing."

"Have you seen Doctor Storvo?"

"No, Your Majesty."

"There is only one 'Your Majesty,' Krys, and I am not her. I'm known as 'My Lady.'"

"Yes, My Lady."

"And this was supposed to have been a meeting between long lost brothers and sisters. It's time for you and Val to have some privacy."

"Not here," Val said in alarm.

"No, not here. It will take time for you to be comfortable here. The lounge is perfect. There's plenty of room for privacy, yet others are usually present. Why don't you go there?"

He put his arm out, and Krys put her arm through his, still shaky. She leaned into him, but by the time the door closed behind them, she had taken his hand.

* * * * *

The moment the door closed behind them, Krys turned to face him. "*What* is going on here?" she demanded.

"I'm not sure myself. Who cares? I have a sister!" he exclaimed, shaking his head.

She took his arm possessively. "And I have a brother. After all these years, I have a brother." Then she looked around at the artwork covering the walls and the understated elegance of the corridor and shook her head. A typical ship of State would, she suspected, be much more plain. The woman really was royalty.

Her gaze hardened. "Who are you really?" she demanded.

"Until two days ago, I was essentially a poor, one-legged beggar. Come on. I'll tell you all about it. Let's see, the lounge is . . . that way," he said pointing to his left. "And two levels up."

He led her to the lounge without difficulty. Several crewmembers were there, but the two found solitude in a corner of the great room. He seated her on a couch, then asked if she would like anything.

"No. Otis has taken good care of me. I like him. Sit, and tell me what's going on. Please."

"Well, we both grew up in the orphanage. I escaped six years ago. Do you remember our parents?"

"No."

"Nor do I. I survived as a beggar . . ."

She clasped his hands in hers as he told his story. She'd had little experience of life outside the orphanage, and in her mind the life he'd carved out for himself, though a great adventure in some ways, was complex and dangerous, magnifying her lack of knowledge of the outside world. One thing came through clearly: Val was a survivor, and he was proud of his accomplishments. She understood and shared in his pride. His life called to her in much the same way her favorite adventure stories called to her.

Val was glad she had never escaped from the orphanage. They both knew what her life would have been like had she done so. For Val, life had been an adventure, but for her it would have been a horror, a worse horror than the orphanage.

"What's going to happen to us?" she asked.

Looking around the room, he said, "Some doors have been opened; we have opportunities neither of us ever dreamed of. What would you like to do?"

"School," she answered instantly. "I want to go to school. Beyond that, I don't know, but I've dreamed of going to school. Do you think they'll let us?"

"Can you imagine them not letting us?"

"I like her," Krys said with a smile. "And I like Otis, too. I was afraid of him when I saw him at the orphanage, but I'm not now."

"He came to the orphanage himself?"

Krys nodded. "She came with him, as well. I didn't know who they were, though from my reading I recognized him as a Great Cat."

Val could only stare at her in shock. Daughter and Otis had both taken time from their busy schedules to find her? "Uh, did they make a scene?" he asked.

"I don't know. I was called to the office. They spent a few minutes with me and gave me a choice, then we left. I didn't see what went on before that."

"But you can imagine it."

She smiled. "I can now. Oh, my! Mrs. Orvidge must have been apoplectic."

"She's still there?"

"She's still there and in charge. I hope to never see her again. How is it we never ran into each other?"

"They're pretty resourceful at keeping the boys and girls separated. Different buildings and all, and I've been gone for six years. I'm not surprised."

Krys looked around the lounge, and in her mind she considered what she'd seen of the rest of the ship, the small portion she'd seen. The ship, Daughter and Otis, her new-found brother, and the displacement of her life suddenly overwhelmed her again. In a small voice, she said, "You have a plan. I wish I did."

"You have a pad. What interested you?"

She looked at him shyly and hesitated. "Stories," she finally said. "Stories about queens and princesses and knights. Adventure."

"Well, you're right in the middle of that now. I'm not sure it's all it's cracked up to be."

"Do you think she'd take us to Triton, let us see the Palace?" she breathed.

"Probably. I don't care where we go as long as it's together."

She squeezed his hand, then leaned into him and gave him another hug. "She's given us such a gift," she said into his hair.

A smile lit his face, though she couldn't see it. "She could dump us at her next stop, and I'd not regret it for a moment if we can stay together, Krys."

She leaned away from him. "And I'm angry that the orphanage never let us know. It's not right, Val."

"No, it's not, and we can never forget. Should we make it our life's work to change the system?"

"Can we?" she asked. "We're just two orphans."

He pursed his lips. "I'm going to be a star pilot, Krys. Will you join me in that?" She paused, and he could tell instantly that such a calling was not high on her list. "Okay," he said, "that's not the plan. What works for you?"

"I don't know!" she said in consternation.

"Then let's focus on school. You said that's what you want. I have to go to school somewhere. We can go together." Thinking of the money key, he asked, "If we could go anywhere you want, where would that be?"

She thought for a time. "I have no idea. It doesn't matter. Anywhere there's a school for you, there will be one for me."

"We'll find someplace that works for both of us. All I demand is that it not be on Triton. I don't want her reputation to open doors for us. I want us to open our own doors."

"That works for me," she said shyly. "Just, please, take me with you."

"Then give some thought to what you'd like to do with the rest of your life. We'll find the right place and make it happen together."

She squeezed his hand, but a worried look filled her eyes. Neither of them had ever had opportunity, and it frightened her.

They spent the rest of the day together, and to Val's relief, Daughter excused them from dining with her. They were directed to the staff dining room for dinner where they chose a corner table. To their surprise, several families with small children occupied the far corner of the room. He and Krys had no idea what families were doing on the ship, though as he considered it, Val acknowledged that voyages on the ship might well last for years at a time. Under those conditions, it would make sense to bring families if there was room. And there was room. From his tour of the ship with the AI, he knew the ship was vast, some 200 meters in diameter with nine levels. There would be room for hundreds of people, and surely the crew did not number in the hundreds. He would have to query the AI at his next opportunity.

Val labored with his utensils, practicing what Daughter had taught him over breakfast, and Krys helped.

"You know how to do this?" he asked in surprise.

"The girls were taught basic things, like table manners and how to address people. We were trained to be housekeepers and maids."

Val just shook his head. "The boys didn't get any of that."

"What were you being trained to do?"

"I don't know. I didn't stick around long enough to find out."

"Maybe you should have," she replied with a twinkle in her eyes.

He looked at her feet under the table. No shoes! "They didn't teach you everything. Didn't they teach you to wear shoes?"

"Only during lessons. I don't like them. They hurt."

"I wouldn't know, but I've been instructed to find out. I have a feeling something will show up in your quarters before long."

They ended up in Val's room, sitting on the bunk and talking. He was wide awake, but he could tell she was fading fast. "Where's your room?" he asked.

"I have no idea. I can't go back there."

"Why not?"

"I've never been alone before. I didn't sleep a wink last night. Can I stay here, with you? I'll sleep on the floor."

"My sister is not sleeping on the floor," Val declared. "I'll take the floor." He held up a hand to forestall argument. "I'm used to it. I can sleep anywhere, and this floor is a lot nicer than the street. Tuck yourself in, Krys. See you in the morning."

She was asleep in minutes with a serene look on her face. He, too, felt wonderful and charged up. He'd never been responsible for anyone else in his life, and he liked the feeling. She was smart and outgoing, but she was completely removed from her normal element. So was he, but he would help her find her way. He pulled out his pad and started to work on the physics problem he'd been working on when Bodan's call interrupted him, but then he changed his mind. Survival came first. He needed to learn more about Daughter and all this royalty stuff. He sent a query out, but the pad did not connect.

He thought for a time, then whispered, "Ship."

"At your service, Val," came back a muted reply.

"Can my pad access your files?"

"Some of them. There, it's done. You now have restricted access."

He typed a message: HOW RESTRICTED?

The reply formed immediately. YOU HAVE ACCESS TO GENERAL INFORMATION ONLY.

He frowned. HOW AM I GOING TO HAVE MY TESTS GRADED? I BOUGHT THE PROGRAM ON HESPRA III.

THE TESTS ARE IN YOUR PAD?

YES.

I WILL GRADE THEM IF YOU WISH.

Hmm. Was there anything the AI couldn't do? He sent a request for information on Daughter. His screen instantly filled with long lists of possible suggestions. There was no way he was going to work through all of it. Then he had an idea. >Got any suggestions, Artmis?<

>I was wondering when you'd get around to asking. I could probably save you a lot of time. I'm quite familiar with the Royal Family.<

>Want to give me a briefing?<

>I can, though I sense that you learn best by reading. Why don't you limit your query?<

He typed a more defining query. JUST SOME GENERAL INFORMATION. YOU DECIDE.

The screen came back with a history of the Royal Family. It scrolled down to the section on Daughter, and he began reading. The reading was difficult since his knowledge of Galactic High Standard, the official language used throughout the Empire, was limited, but he persevered, and Artmis helped him when necessary. The article began with a detailed family tree which he skipped over for the moment. He came to her date of birth, struggled on for several lines, then came back to it. He decided he'd misunderstood and tried to convert the Galactic High Standard date to the date system used on Hespra III. He still didn't like the answer.

>Artmis?<

>Your calculations are correct, Val.<

>No way. She can't be that old.<

>She's seventy-one years old, Val.<

He sat back in confusion. >She looks like she's twenty-five.<

>Sorry, Val. Her family has a life expectancy of some 400 years. Something in the genes, I guess."

>Four hundred years!<

>Did you think the Queen would send a child to resolve disputes?"

>Well . . . no. I guess not.<

>She's been doing this for many years. What is your own life expectancy?<

>You mean if we don't get killed first?<

>Barring that, yes.<

>Eighty or so. Maybe a hundred if I lived right, which I haven't exactly been doing.<

>That's for sure. I'm fixing things.<

>*What?*<

>That's what Riders do, Val. I'm not done yet, but you're a lot healthier than you were when I came aboard. But we should talk about your own life span. I told you there were benefits to having me, and this is one of them.<

>You're making me healthier, and I'm going to live longer?<

>A lot longer Val. Probably as long as Daughter. If you don't get us killed first.<

Chapter Forty-five

>So that's how it is, Val. All the things that cause aging are something I deal with on a routine basis. We'll reach a point where I can't keep up, and we'll die, but it won't be a lingering death. I wouldn't do that to either of us. When it's our time, we'll both know.<

Val wasn't over the shock, and as far as he was concerned, he might never be. >What am I going to do for 400 years, Artmis?<

>You mean, what are we going to do?<

>Well, yes.<

>I'm a Rider, Val. I don't control. I think it's up to you. I hope you make it interesting and fun. So far, it's been all of that. I don't see it changing. Do you?<

>Not for a while.<

>We should talk about your leg.<

>Which one?<

>The missing one. I've been giving it some thought. You weren't born with it that way. I think I can fix it.<

>I don't need two legs.<

>Agreed.<

>I don't want two legs.<

>Then we'll drop the subject. You can probably replace the

crutch every hundred years or so.<

Four hundred years put a different perspective on things, Val had to admit. >How would you do it?<

>I'm not certain. A little at a time, I guess. I'd rather do it quickly, but I'd need help and you'd be down for a while.<

>What kind of help?<

>For a quick repair, you'd have to go into a tank.<

>What's a tank?<

>The most advanced healing tool known to Empire medicine. It stimulates production of stem cells, the cells your body started with when you were in the womb. They can be turned into any organ, and with my help the process would be more focused. That translates to quicker.<

>How quick?<

>I'm not sure. I'd need to talk to Dr. Storvo first. Maybe a couple of months in the tank followed by several more during which you'd be ambulatory. Of course, you'd have to learn to use the new leg when I'm done.<

>I'd have to lay in a tank for two months?<

>You'd be asleep, Val. I, on the other hand, would be exhausting myself. I'm willing if you are.<

>I need to think about it.< He looked over at the sleeping form of his sister. >She needs me right now. I can't leave her for a couple of months. Not yet.<

>Agreed, though I think, knowing the little that I know of her, that she'll be standing on her own two feet sooner than you think.<

>Where would we find one of these tanks?<

>Come on, Val. Think.<

Val considered for a moment, then felt embarrassed in front of Artmis. This was Daughter's ship after all. It would lack nothing of import.

He slept little that night. 400 years! And a new leg? What more could happen to him? It was coming too fast, even for him. He'd always prided himself on his flexibility, but now . . . every time he turned around, a new life-altering something seemed to be happening. Three days ago he'd been struggling to keep his head above water. Now, despite seemingly unlimited opportunity, he was sinking. He decided he'd get his focus back in the morning by concentrating only on what mattered most at the moment. Four hundred years and a new leg were not pressing concerns. As he drifted off to sleep, his awareness of the person sleeping on the bed beside him was what mattered most.

He awoke in the early hours of the morning to find Krys tossing and turning in her bed, mumbling. He stood up and went to her side, touching her shoulder. Then he shook her awake. "Hey! Are you okay?" he asked.

Her eyes stared blankly for a time, and she said, "There's danger ahead. I'm afraid for her."

"Afraid for whom?"

"Daughter." Then her eyes focused on him. "Val," she said reaching up to caress his face. "You're real."

"I'm real."

"I just had a bad dream," she said. "Go back to sleep."

He tucked her in, kissing her forehead. "I'm here, and I'm not going anywhere."

"I'm so lucky," she breathed, then she turned over and closed her eyes.

He awoke the next morning to find her sitting up and staring at him. A smile lit her face as soon as she discovered his gaze upon her. "Hi, brother!"

"Hi, yourself!" He pinched his arm, and she giggled.

"It's real, isn't it," she declared.

"It's real, Krys. You have a brother, and we're on Daughter's private starship. I think they're going to let me fly it." Her eyes widened in a question, and he explained. "Captain Jzazbe is going to help me find out if I'm spacer material." He eyed the bathroom facilities which were completely un-private.

She smiled. "I'll wait outside."

When he was through, he opened the door to find both Otis and Krys waiting in the corridor.

"Have you cleaned up yet?" Otis asked him.

"I took a shower yesterday, and these clothes only have one day of use. I'm ready to go."

"No, you're not. You'll shower every morning, and you'll start each day with a fresh change of clothes. We'll see about a haircut later today. I'll see Krys to her room. Daughter is expecting you for breakfast in half an hour."

"Yes, sir," Val responded, not understanding. But he did as ordered. When he knocked on Daughter's door, it opened immediately. Otis and Krys were not there yet. He entered and bowed. "Good morning, My Lady."

"Good morning, Val. What would you like for breakfast?"

"Uh, anything, My Lady."

"I knew you'd say that. How about your sister? What's she accustomed to?"

"Not the fare you have here, that's for sure. But she knows deportment, My Lady."

"She does? Excellent! Then we'll both get to help you with yours. I see you remembered the shoe. Is it uncomfortable?"

"No, My Lady. It's incredibly comfortable. Not what I expected."

"Learn to expect it, Val."

"Yes, My Lady."

Otis and Krys showed up, and she was wearing a spacer's outfit just like Val's. Daughter greeted Krys warmly, and Krys finally got her chance to kneel properly before this royal personage.

Breakfast was as difficult as Val had foreseen, and though Krys was comfortable with her eating habits, she was not comfortable eating in the presence of Daughter and the Great Cat. The meal was strained, and Val was relieved when it was over.

Daughter excused them from the table and led them to her sitting room. "I have a busy day, but Otis tells me there is something of concern. You did not sleep well last night, Krys?"

Krys looked at her in confusion. "My Lady?"

Otis spoke. "Something happened last night, Krys. The AI alerted me to a concern you have. Will you tell us about it?"

"You're *spying* on us?" Krys asked in alarm.

"Definitely not," Daughter informed her. "The ship does not spy on you, or anyone else for that matter, but certain key words alert the AI. Any mention of danger to me causes an alert. Tell me your concern, child."

Krys suddenly looked scared. "It was just a bad dream, My Lady."

"We all have those from time to time. Tell me about it," Daughter asked kindly.

"I don't remember it, My Lady."

Daughter sat back to study Krys. "Don't, or won't?" she finally asked.

"My Lady, you ask too much," Krys murmured.

"In certain areas, it is my duty to pry," Daughter said softly, rising to stand before Krys. She sat down beside her. "You're among friends here. Do not be afraid. Why would you be concerned for my safety?"

"I don't know," Krys murmured.

Daughter put a hand to Krys' face, a caressing hand. "Do not be afraid, child. You have nothing to fear here."

"Yes, My Lady."

"We will speak of this another time." To Val, she said, "What are your plans for the day?"

"I had hoped to study, My Lady."

"Then you shall. And you, Krys?"

"I, too, would study."

"What are you studying, child?"

"I don't know, My Lady."

"I see. We must have you both evaluated and set up in a proper program of study."

"Mine is proper," Val stated clearly.

"I don't doubt that it is, though it is certainly not all encompassing. Off with you then."

They both left without delay, returning to Val's room. Later that day Otis interrupted them. Both were heads down in their pads, the room crowded with the two of them. Otis' great bulk forced Val to share the bed with his sister.

As usual, Otis did not waste words, and his focus was Krys. "Do you know my purpose here?" he asked her.

"Yes, sir. Val has told me about Protectors, you and Borg in particular."

"Then you understand that my sole focus is Daughter's safety. Do you know why?"

"No, sir," they both answered.

"Some two thousand years ago, the Royal Family saved my world from beasts even more hideous than ourselves, beasts imported by enemies to destroy us. They very nearly succeeded before the Empire came to our rescue. Because of that rescue, my people have pledged to protect the Royal Family. We Protect them at all costs.

"Those of us trained as Protectors and Guardians learn to function within the civilized worlds of the Empire, but at heart we remain primitive. On my home world, my people still kill to eat – by choice. Perhaps because of our essentially primitive natures, we follow ancient customs which include beliefs in spirits, good and bad, ancient tales, and dreams. They are very much a part of our lives. Dreams in particular hold great power among my people.

"And now we come to the Royal Family. Everything related to the Royal Family is significant. To Protectors especially, dreams are held in high esteem. For that reason, I would know more of your dream,

Krys."

"It's nothing, Otis."

"To you it may be nothing, but to me it could have meaning. Tell me."

"I sensed danger, Otis, and it seemed far in the future."

"What kind of danger?"

"I don't know! Just danger."

Otis sat, deep in thought. "You cried out, awakening Val. Surely you recall details."

Krys closed her eyes, then mumbled, "*You will be so much more and have so much less. They will best you, but a man of dirt will come to your aid.*"

Otis rose, his hackles lifting as his face moved to within inches of hers. When she opened her eyes, she backed away from that hideous face.

"What does it mean? You speak in riddles, Krys."

"I know. That's how it always is, and I never know what they mean."

Otis sat again. "This has happened before?"

"Yes," she answered in a small voice.

"Do these riddles come true? Do you understand them when they do?"

"Sometimes," she answered fearfully. "I don't always know if they come true. I've been punished over this, so I've learned to keep it to myself."

Otis' sole focus was Krys. In an amazingly human gesture, he sat back on his haunches, raised a hand to his muzzle, and stroked. Then he reached out to Krys with that same hand, saying in a low growl, "You will not be punished here, Krys. Daughter must be told about this. There can be no secrets withheld from her." He rose and beckoned Val and Krys to accompany him.

Two women and a man were in conference with Daughter when they entered her quarters. She looked up in surprise, but dismissed her attendants without hesitation. Clearly, Otis did not interrupt without good reason.

"My Lady," Otis said after the door snicked shut behind the departing staff, "Krys has something to tell you."

Daughter rose from behind her table as Krys and Val bent knees to the floor. "Enough of that," she barked. "What is it, Krys?"

"I had a dream, My Lady. A dream of you."

"And . . . ?"

"You were in grave danger."

"In your dream."

Krys' voice quavered as she answered, "Not exactly, My Lady."

Daughter leaned back against the table in silence as she considered Krys' words. When she spoke, she spoke softly. "When we touched yesterday, you seemed to lose focus for a time. Would that have anything to do with your dream?"

"Yes, My Lady."

Daughter's lips pursed. "Tell me what happened when you came into this room yesterday."

Krys stood absolutely still, terrified. But she obeyed. "When you took my hands, for just a moment we were not in this room. We were somewhere else. In a desert. Otis was lying atop you in the dirt with another Great Cat beside him. I believe his partner was dead. I think you were at the bottom of the ramp of a ship similar to this one. It must have been night, because the area around the ramp was lit with lights from the ship. Otis fired his blaster at something, I don't know what. The words came to me, then we were back in this room and everything was as it had been."

"What words came to you, Krys?"

Krys closed her eyes and repeated the words.

"You will be so much more and have so much less. They will best you, but a man of dirt will come to your aid."

Silence pervaded the room. Val looked at his sister as if she was someone he'd never met before. Otis' hackles were raised again, just as they had been in the cabin. Val, too, felt a momentary chill and shuddered. Was something wrong with Krys?

Otis growled low in his throat, but Daughter just sat back against the table looking contemplative. When she spoke, she said, "Ship, record."

"Recording."

"Do you know what the words mean?" she asked kindly.

"No, Ma'am."

"And this has happened before."

"Yes, My Lady."

"Where did the words come from?"

"I don't know, My Lady."

"Yes, you do. And they're important."

"I don't want to get in any trouble."

"Oh, child, I'm so sorry you feel that way. Do your visions often come true?"

Krys squirmed. "I don't know what you're talking about, My Lady."

"Have you been punished for them?"

Krys lowered her head. That was all the answer Daughter needed. "Hear me well, Krys. If what I suspect is true, you might have a gift, or more likely a curse, that is more rare than my own. I have never been in the presence of a Seer. They are the stuff of legend, and no others exist as far as I know."

Krys lifted her gaze to meet Daughter's. She did not flinch. "I don't know what you mean."

"I think you do."

"Krys," Val said, "the first rule here is that we keep no secrets from Daughter. I ask you as your brother to trust me in this."

Krys' gaze remained locked on Daughter as she considered Val's words. "Sometimes I see things, My Lady," she finally said. "More often it's just feelings. Sometimes words. I rarely understand the words, though the feelings are strong. Sometimes things happen later that make the meanings clear."

"I see." Daughter turned to pace. "You said, '*You will be so much more and have so much less. They will best you, but a man of dirt will come to your aid.*' Can you tell me what it means?"

"No, My Lady, but I believe the words refer to you."

"I will be more, but I will have much less. I don't understand."

"Nor do I, My Lady."

"Who are '*they?*'"

"I don't know, My Lady."

"And a man of dirt?" What can that possibly mean?"

Krys thought hard. "I'm not sure I said it right. It was a foreign word, but I sensed that it means dirt, or the ground."

"What exactly was the word?"

"It was earth, or maybe Earth. Could it be a place?"

Daughter looked to Otis. He remained mute. She turned back to Krys. "Was I alive in your vision?"

"I sensed strongly that you were. I also sensed you and Otis were in unbelievable pain."

"But we survived?"

"I don't know, My Lady. If the words are true, someone came to your assistance."

"Indeed. Is there anything else to this vision, any slightest detail you have not told us?"

Krys closed her eyes for a time. "Only that I sensed it was some years in the future, My Lady," she finally said.

"May I Test you?"

"Test me?"

"She means she wants to read your mind, Krys," Val said. He rose and took her hand. "It's okay. I've been through it, and it's okay. It's something the Chosen do. No one else can do it. She wants, and I suspect she needs to know exactly what you know about this. It sounds pretty serious. Say yes."

So important was this to Daughter that she seated Krys on the couch and kneeled down on the floor before her. She reached out and put both hands to Krys' head, and Val knew the Testing had begun. When Daughter was through, she sat back on her feet and looked up at Krys with a look of amazement.

She stood up and paced for a time, then turned back to Krys. "I never, ever talk about what I learn during my Testings without the consent of the one Tested. I know you for who you are, Krys, and I will never betray you. However, I would like your permission to discuss some of what I have learned with my closest advisors. May I?"

Krys thought for a time. "My Lady, I have been mostly successful at keeping knowledge of this 'gift,' or 'curse' as you describe it, from others. If it becomes common knowledge, it will make my return to the orphanage very difficult."

"Do you want to return to the orphanage?"

"Never!"

"Consider yourself free of the place forevermore. We can discuss your futures later."

"You're giving us our freedom?"

"Not giving, Krys. You have both earned it in your own way."

Krys stood up and approached Daughter, then kneeled on the floor before her, her head bowed low to the floor. "Thank you, My Lady. You have my permission."

"I ask that you continue to keep your gift a secret for the present. Please return to whatever you were doing, and rest assured that you are not in any kind of trouble."

Val and Krys left. As soon as the door snicked closed, Daughter turned to Otis, troubled. "There's nothing there, Otis. I can't see her visions."

"My Lady?"

"For the first time in my life, I have met someone I cannot fully Test. She has visions, that much I know, but I can't see them. I believe she is truly a Seer."

"Could she be lying?"

"No. I sensed the truth of her. She is true to herself, and I ask no more than that from one so young. How is it possible that among all the worlds of our Empire we happened to come to this world at this time to discover these two?"

"I, too, am amazed, My Lady. She seems very . . . quick. The words of her vision trouble me deeply. Their tone is ominous."

"They trouble me as well. The arrival of these two may be fortuitous. I feel the Empire calling to them. We both have work to do, but we're going to make time for them as well."

Chapter Forty-six

Val and Krys returned to his room without speaking. He felt uneasy, even frightened of her a little, and he didn't know what to say. She sensed his uneasiness and pulled him down to sit beside her on the bed.

"I've never talked about it to anyone else," she said. Then a smile lit her face. "I've never had anyone I *could* talk to about it. What a wonderful sense of freedom I get from sitting beside you."

"Do you see the future?" he asked worriedly.

"Not in detail, and not very often," she said with a troubled look. "For Daughter's sake, I wish I saw more. I like her. I wish I could be more helpful."

"Can you look at me and see my future?"

"Do you want me to?"

That caught him by surprise. With just a little thought, he said, "No!"

"Nor do I want to know our futures," she said softly. "They will be what they will be."

"They'll be what we make them," Val corrected her.

* * * * *

Otis found them later that day. "Val, Captain Jzazbe will see you now. Are you ready?"

He gulped. "Yes, sir."

"Do you know the way?"

"Yes, sir."

He turned to Krys. "Daughter awaits you. Will you attend her?"

"At once, sir."

He turned to Val. "You're still here?"

Val took off like a shot. Krys, too, stood up, though a little more slowly. She was frightened again, and Otis did nothing to relieve her of that fright. He led her through confusing corridors and down the 'central shaft' through which they floated down two levels. She entered Daughter's domain with trepidation.

Daughter greeted her warmly and led her to a stateroom just down the corridor from her own. There, she introduced Krys to her new quarters: a small sitting room, a room with two beds, and a small, private bathroom. "These are your new quarters," she said.

"Oh, My Lady, it's too much."

"It's not too much for Val's sister, and remember, I've Tested you. I understand your discomfort with sleeping alone. You and Val can share the room. You'll find clothes in the closet. Will you join me for dinner later?"

"My Lady?"

Daughter looked at Krys from head to toe. "You're not a spacer, and the uniform is out of place on you. Have you ever worn fine clothes?"

"No, My Lady."

"May I help?"

"Oh, My Lady! You embarrass me."

"Would you rather I sent someone else?"

"Yes, My Lady."

"Well, I wouldn't. Here," she said, walking over to the closet where several dresses hung. She selected one and held it up against Krys. "Yes, this will do. It's not formal, but this is not a formal dinner." Krys stood frozen in place, speechless. Daughter put a hand out to caress her cheek. "I know this is not easy for you, child."

"Daughter cannot attend an orphan, My Lady," Krys said softly.

"I'm sorry our system has put you in this position, Krys, and I would like to remedy that. Will you guide me?"

"My Lady?"

"Will you guide me, help me change things? Creating change within my Empire is not a simple thing, but I would like to try. I cannot do it on my own."

Krys looked at her through sad eyes. "I'm just an orphan, My Lady."

Daughter gave her a piercing stare. "You're just an orphan if that's what you choose to be. Is that what you want?"

"No, My Lady."

"What do you want?"

"I don't know," she said softly.

Daughter considered her words. "Fairly spoken, Krys. How, indeed, could you possibly know what you want? In my position as Daughter, there are many things I can do, but I cannot, and I will not, coerce you into doing that which is not natural. What I can do is give you aspirations. Will you let me at least open some doors for you?"

"What doors would those be, My Lady?"

"That remains to be seen. There's no hurry. Let's see what develops. In the meantime, dinner is in four hours. Val will join us. And tomorrow we'll have Doctor Storvo examine you. Remove this spacer's outfit, and I'll show you how the dress goes on."

* * * * *

Val headed to the bridge with great anticipation. This was his big chance. He crutched into the central shaft and stepped out at bridge level. The bridge was quiet, surprisingly quiet. A few crewmembers sprawled at their stations, each wearing a shiny black helmet, seemingly idle.

He studied the bridge. Immediately before him, a human who he assumed was the captain sat semi-sprawled in a seat at the rear of the bridge. Before him stood a row of twelve work stations arranged in a semi-circular pattern at which sat two crewmembers, both also seeming to lounge. In front of those consoles, an array of screens covered the walls, surrounding the bridge. When he looked up, there were screens above and behind him as well. Val only saw empty space on most of the screens, though on closer inspection he found symbols that probably represented the other ships of the squadron escorting Daughter. The center screen displayed a long red line that seemed to stretch into infinity. Was it their course, he wondered?

Captain Jzazbe sat up and removed his helmet. He turned to Val with a piercing stare. After a time, Val realized what was expected of him. "Reporting as ordered, sir," he said, standing tall.

Jzazbe stood up and walked around his seat to stare at Val. "So you want to be a starship pilot, eh?" he asked.

Val gulped. "I do, sir."

Jzazbe continued to stare at him. "I'm Captain Jzazbe," he said finally. "On the bridge you will be addressed as Mister Val, understood?"

"Yes, sir."

"Very well. What knowledge do you have of what we do here?"

"None, sir. I've studied the mathematics and science behind what you do, though I have a long way to go there. I understand the principles of your drive system. I wish I could say I knew more, sir, but I don't."

"Hmm. Actually, that's more than I expected. What are your plans, Mister?"

"I'm studying for the entrance exam to Fleet Academy, sir."

"Most don't make it, you know."

"Yes, sir. I know."

"Even when they do, few have what it takes to conn one of these ships."

"I understand, sir."

"We won't make you a starship pilot here, Mister, but we can see if you're made of the right stuff. In the process, we may be able to give you a head start on some of the lessons you'll get at the Academy. We'll begin with an introduction to the net. Do you know what that means?"

"No, sir."

"The net is the ship, Mister. We connect to it through an AI, an Artificial Intelligence. Our crewmembers rarely fly the ship, and never without an AI. Instead, they command the AI. The guns are an exception."

"Why not the guns, sir?"

"The AI is specifically prohibited from firing the guns, Mister Val. It can provide targeting data, but it cannot pull the trigger. I think you can understand why."

Val thought for a moment, then nodded his head. "Only a live person can take the life of another," he stated.

"Precisely," Captain Jzazbe replied. "We cannot have computers killing people. They might kill the wrong ones," he added with a rueful grimace. "I'm prepared to introduce you to our AI. Are you interested?"

"I am, sir," Val gulped.

"Then we'll not delay." Jzazbe led him to a vacant workstation on the left end of the row of workstations and handed him a helmet. "Know this, Mister Val: this AI is as advanced as the Empire can make it. It is capable of teaching you, and it is capable of simulating any activity it so desires. I have instructed it to train you, but not to let you control the ship. Nothing you do within the net will affect our voyage, so do not hesitate to learn all that you can. You will not have another opportunity like this until you are in advanced training at the academy, so make the most of it while you're here. Understood?"

Val, cringing inside, nodded his head. "I will, sir, and thank you."

"You might not be thanking me in a while. Go to it, Mister."

Val sat down at the appointed station, the control panel before him meaningless. He stared at the shiny black helmet Captain Jzazbe had given him, then tentatively raised it to his head. Jzazbe nodded, and he put it on. Jzazbe stepped over to him and pulled the faceplate down. "Use of the faceplate is not required, but it's helpful at the beginning. The AI will run an evaluation routine, so don't get too anxious."

Val stared out at blackness. All sound and vision was muted with the helmet on and the visor pulled down. Several long minutes went by, and he was beginning to worry when he heard a chime. Then he sensed the skin of the ship. It was cold, but he didn't feel cold. He just knew the skin temperature of the ship was very low. Atmosphere pressed against his skin from one side, and vacuum pulled from the other. Another chime sounded and he sensed structure beneath the skin of the ship. One small joint was before him, and without knowing how he knew, he knew the joint was molded together at sub-atomic levels to merge with other parts of the structure. Then he sensed himself backing away to a larger perspective. Soon, a series of elegant trusses and beams and girders of immensely strong material wove together to form a larger piece of structure. He didn't just see the structure, he felt the structure, and it felt right.

He pulled back again and kept pulling back until the full exterior structure of the ship was before him. He thought 'ramp,' and he zoomed in on the ramp structure, sensing how all the various parts came together. Soon, motors and wires and a variety of materials stood out for inspection. He saw it, and he understood it, but he felt it as well, and it felt right. He thought 'weapons,' and he felt himself flowing along fiber optic lines, turning where necessary without having to decide which turns to make until he was in the bottom turret. There was never a question as to which line to follow, he just went. There was the laser-disintegrator, there was the manual aiming system that he knew was used only in an emergency, and there were the motors and controls to make the gun function. Heavy power cables led from the turret to Engineering, and with just a thought he followed them all the way to the 'bottle,' the power source for the ship.

He understood that the weapons drew their power directly from the bottle. So, too, did both drive systems, one for intersystem travel, and the other for making jumps through hyperspace. All other systems drew their power from shared, massive shunts connected to the bottle. He studied these, and their purposes were felt and understood. He felt the power within the cables and smaller wires, and they felt right.

Smaller control circuits led to computers, many computers. Some were simple logic circuits. Others consisted of crystals of various sizes within which myriads of twinkling lights winked faster than the mind could follow. But follow them he did, and they felt right.

He didn't know where to go from there, but he didn't need to know. The AI guided him through plumbing and air conditioning and recycling systems, then raced with him through many compartments within the ship. Val opened and closed doors, turned lights on and off, changed temperature settings, checked the cargo spaces, and even studied the multitude of menus produced by the auto-chef. He even sensed the smells of the food, though flavors were dull. That was okay. He knew without even thinking about it that the AI could not produce a sense that it did not have.

Then he sensed the AI itself. He did not sense a human body. Its body was the whole ship, but he did sense awareness of self.

"Hello," he said.

"Hello, Val. Welcome to my home."

"I sense that I *am* welcome here. Thank you."

"The pleasure is mine. You're the youngest human to join me here, though there have been younger ones of other races. It's time for you to meet Artmis."

"Oh! I'd forgotten!"

"He hasn't. We've been having a nice chat. Are you ready?"

"I am." Val expected to see an amorphous blob of protoplasm, but that just wasn't in the cards. Artmis materialized before him as a red-headed, freckle-faced boy a few years younger than himself dressed in a plain spacer's uniform. Looking down, he discovered his own body dressed the same way. "You're younger than I expected," he said to Artmis.

"No, I'm not. You may not know it, but this is how you think of me, and I like it."

"But you're so much older than me. I mean your father was . . ."

"I'm not him anymore, Val. I'm him, and I'm you. And don't forget, I'm just a baby. I'm going to be learning right along with you."

"But you're so much smarter than me."

"Not true. I may have more knowledge of certain things, but you have life experiences that are completely new to me as well. Besides, knowledge is only a small piece of being smart. Lots of beings are smarter than both of us, and some are quite primitive in comparison to you and I, though smarter in ways that count to themselves."

Val mentally gulped. "Do you know how to fly the ship?"

"I can get by, but it's not my strong point. My father had little interest in ships. That was Sir Jarl's job. My father loved court intrigues, however."

"Well, what's next?"

"You're about done for the day, Val," the AI said.

"But I haven't even seen Outside. How am I going to know if I can be a star pilot?"

"You'll see Outside tomorrow. You've had enough for one day."

Val felt himself pushed gently out of the net. He removed the helmet to stare about himself in confusion. >Wow,< he thought to Artmis. >That was fun!<

>Glad you liked it. Sorry, but to me ships are just a means to go places. I don't think I'm going to be a lot of help to you at the Academy.<

>I want you there, Artmis, but I don't want your help. I want to *know* this stuff.<

>Works for me. Works very well.<

Captain Jzazbe interrupted his thoughts. "Daughter is holding dinner for you, Mister. It's not wise to keep her waiting."

"How long was I in there, sir?"

"Four hours. That's the standard limit for beginners."

"Can I come back tomorrow?"

"Daughter comes first, and you need to spend time with your sister. Those are your first priorities. Understood?"

"Yes, sir."

"Very well. Plan on one four hour shift per day here on the bridge. We'll extend it if you find you're up to it. For Daughter's purposes, the middle of the day works best. Be back here at 0900 hours. We'll make that your regular report time. Understood?"

"Yes, sir!" Val said with a grin. "Uh, permission to leave the bridge, sir?"

"Permission granted. Get out of here, Mister," he said with a wave of his hand. But a grin found its way to his face as soon as Val's head disappeared down the central shaft. The other two crewmembers on the bridge were grinning as well.

* * * * *

Val crutched his way quickly to Daughter's quarters. Krys welcomed him with a curtsy, clearly pleased with her appearance in the dress provided by Daughter. Val bowed solemnly and took her hand, leading her to the table.

"No spacer's uniform?" he inquired.

"This is much better," she said grinning.

Daughter was already seated, so Val didn't kneel before her. She indicated his place, across the table from her and beside Krys, and he sat.

Daughter cleared her throat, and he looked up at her in surprise. So, too, did Krys who was pulling her own chair out from beneath the table.

"A gentleman assists the lady," Daughter advised.

Val's face fell. Mentally, he was still back on the bridge, deep within the guts of the ship with the AI and Artmis. Reality came crashing down around his ears.

The expression on his face brought a chuckle from Daughter. "Must I demonstrate?" she asked.

"No, My Lady." He stood and pulled back a chair for Krys. She had a tragic look on her face as she sat.

"This will only be painful for a few days," Daughter advised both of them. "It's not that hard, and I know you're both up to it." She started with the soup, and Val just about gave up right there. She wouldn't even let him lift the bowl to his lips. Krys, with her devotion to stories about princesses and knights, had an easier time of it, though she, too, struggled a little. Daughter was relentless, insisting that both learn a behavior new to them.

"How was your time with Captain Jzazbe?" she asked.

"Oh, My Lady," he said between slurps from his spoon, "It's wonderful. I know so much more about the ship already. Did you know that the craftsmen who built *Resolve* joined all the major structures together at the atomic level? There are no bolts or welds in the primary structure."

"It is appropriate to set your spoon down on the plate before answering, Val. And remember, no talking with food in your mouth. No,

I did not know that. You find it interesting?"

Val set his spoon down. "I do, My Lady. That, and lots more. I would very much like to visit a shipyard someday."

"Perhaps you will. You can pick your spoon up now." She gave him a few moments, then asked, "Did you pass?"

He set his spoon down and swallowed. "I haven't been Outside yet. I think that comes tomorrow. Captain Jzazbe assigned me a nine o'clock report time. Does that work for you, My Lady?"

She smiled. "It does. He and I have already discussed it."

"Oh," he said in a small voice.

"Val, I'm not spying on you. Please don't get that impression. We're just trying to make this work for you."

"Yes, My Lady."

"I was thinking that you might like to tour the cruiser before we jump."

His eyes flashed. "Can I?"

"I periodically visit each of my ships, especially after an event like what we had on Hespra III. I can probably arrange for you to spend a couple of days there."

"Can I see the other ships?"

"Will a tour of the frigate and one fighter do?"

"Oh . . . yes, My Lady." He thought for a moment, frowning. "I don't want to take too much time away from my training."

"You have plenty of time, Val. It's some seven weeks to our destination. Provided you don't get off there, and I'm not recommending that you do, the next leg of our journey will occupy an equivalent time."

"Where should we get off, My Lady?"

"The choice is yours, but I'm still thinking about a recommendation. It depends to some extent on what the two of you want to do."

Val's soup was cooling off, and all he could do was stare at it. "We want to go to school," he said. Then, in chagrin, he asked, "How am I supposed to eat when I have to keep setting my spoon down?"

"It's simple, Val. You divert the conversation, or someone diverts it for you," she said, looking pointedly at Krys.

"We want to go to school," Krys said instantly.

To Val, Daughter said, "You may continue eating now." To Krys, she asked, "What kind of school? There are schools on every world of the Empire."

"Any school will work," Krys said. "It won't take much to be an improvement over what we had."

"No, it won't, but some are better than others. What would you like to study?"

"I don't know, My Lady."

"You have a pad. What most interested you?"

Val set his spoon down and answered for her. "Tales of queens and princesses and knights and adventure," he offered, then quickly looked down and picked up his spoon again.

Daughter looked a question at Krys who nodded her head. "Sorry, My Lady."

"Don't be! I couldn't have asked for a better answer." She thought for a time, then said, "I would imagine you'd like to go to Triton."

"Oh, My Lady, I'd so like to see the Palace."

"You know you're special. I would welcome you to the Palace, but not yet."

"My Lady?"

"The Palace is a place of intrigues, always. You are not ready for that, but your special gift would be most helpful to me when you are ready."

"I'm not a Seer, My Lady."

"You're not?"

"No, My Lady. I did some research on Seers with the aid of the ship's AI. I do not see the future clearly, and Seers, at least reputedly in the legends, did. The AI wondered if I might be an Oracle."

"An Oracle. I hope not," Daughter said as she considered. "Oracles, if they truly existed as legend claims, are not particularly nice creatures. They tended to know all, but they only released information in pieces, and then usually for a price, and they were conniving." She looked hard at Krys. "Do you know more about the future than you're telling me?"

"No, My Lady, I do not, and I say this from my heart."

Daughter studied her for a time, and Krys was decidedly uncomfortable with the attention. Finally, Daughter said, "We'll just have to find out. Whatever you are, you're young and untrained. What if I find someone to train you? Are you willing to study and maybe improve your abilities, to focus this gift?"

"How? Who can teach me?"

"I don't know. I've given it a great deal of thought, and I have an idea. I'm still working on it."

Val interrupted. "My Lady, how is it that you've been talking this whole time, but your soup is gone?"

"Practice, Val. Lots of practice. You'll get there, don't worry. And I won't let you go hungry." The main course was brought in, and the soup bowls were cleared away. To Val's chagrin, Krys' bowl was empty, too. How did they do it, he wondered?

"May I ask what you have in mind, My Lady?" Krys asked as she cut into a small piece of meat. Val's was three times the size of hers, and he attacked it with gusto. After all, he reminded himself, he was eating for two. But he was all ears – they were discussing his future, too, and he did not want to end up on Triton and under Daughter's fingers.

"One of the happiest times of my life was the years I spent on Rrestriss. Have you heard of it?"

"No, My Lady."

"Val?"

He immediately swallowed a large chunk of meat, most of it intact, and set his utensils down. He beat on his chest a few times, then croaked, "No, My Lady."

"Chew your food, Val. I can wait. Understood?"

"Yes, My Lady."

"Rrestriss is an ancient world, Krys," she continued as if nothing untoward had happened, "ancient and peaceful. It's far from here, about as close to the galactic core as settled worlds can be. People from across the Empire seek entrance to its famous universities. Many apply, but few are chosen, and I cannot tell you what criteria the Rress use to determine who attends and who does not. My own focus was philosophy, but they teach the sciences, engineering, medicine, and the arts as well. For someone preparing for a role in Empire governance, there is not a better place to learn."

Krys' eyes grew large, and her lips began to quiver. She rested her eating utensils on her plate and lowered her hands to her lap. Even Val stopped eating and set his utensils down. What was she saying?

"Does Rrestriss hold any interest to you?" Daughter asked.

"You frighten me, My Lady," Krys responded weakly. "Empire governance?"

"I'm sorry, child. It is not my intention to frighten. *They* will not frighten you. They're wonderful. I know you'll like it there, and if there is anywhere in the Empire that your talents can be refined, it's there. As important, you would grow in the wisdom you will surely need as you exercise those talents in the years to come."

Krys looked to Val with a stunned and frightened expression on her face. Val, too, felt overwhelmed. Governance? That was the realm of the Royal Family and Imperial Senators. Certainly not him and Krys.

The very idea intimidated. He looked into Daughter's eyes. "We're just poor orphans," he whispered. "We're not ready for all that. We don't even have the basics yet, and you're talking about higher education, the very highest."

"Val," Daughter said softly, "The Rress tailor their teaching to the individual. They excel at proving to you that there is nothing you cannot achieve if you set your mind to it, provided you're willing to do the work, and the work is often challenging. I happen to believe you're half way there already. They can provide you with the means to do the rest."

"Do they have a Fleet Academy?"

"They do, but only for senior officers. You cannot attend the Academy on Rrestriss, but a recommendation from teachers there would virtually ensure your entrance to any of the other Fleet Academies. And that recommendation would not be given if you weren't ready."

"I only have two years to prepare for the test."

"Not true, Val. You have a minimum of two years. You can wait many more years if you wish."

"I want to go as soon as I can."

"Is your goal only to be a star pilot, or are you willing to go the extra distance and be a leader, the best officer you can be?"

"Uh, all the above?"

"If an extra year or two would be beneficial, don't you think it would be a good idea?"

"I want to be a star pilot."

She smiled fondly. "I know you do, Val. And you will be a star pilot. You'll be much, much more than that as well if you'll allow the Rress to mentor you. If they agree to accept you, the final choice will be yours. If you accept, I promise you a challenge that you will never regret."

"I want you to be the best you can be," Krys said to him. "And I want us to be together. That's all I ask."

Val looked at her, uncertain of what he wanted. And that was an uncomfortable feeling, something he rarely experienced. He had been focused on only one thing for as long as he could remember. Suddenly, lots more was on the table, and he couldn't get his arms around it. He wanted to be a star pilot. He couldn't imagine wanting more than that. If someday he did, he would just make it happen, but for the moment, Daughter's ideas were too much, too far beyond the goal he had set for himself. He fondled the money key he still carried in his pocket. With it, he and Krys could get off at the next stop and just disappear. Should they?

Then he looked into Krys' eyes. What did her future hold? He wasn't too sure about this Seer stuff, he didn't begin to understand it, but he sensed the hunger in her eyes. Too, he sensed vaguely what Daughter had hinted at.

He turned to Daughter, looking into her eyes for something, he knew not what. She was no longer smiling. This was *Daughter* looking at him, the beautiful princess who had walked down that long corridor among all the cheering people, the person whom the Empire called to resolve its most difficult problems, the person who had nearly died in service to her Empire.

He suddenly understood. She wasn't suggesting Rrestriss for him. It was for Krys. In her eyes, Krys had become more important than himself. Krys was, potentially, far more important than a simple star pilot, far more important than a fleet officer of any rank. Krys could provide guidance to her in the governing process, guidance that was so rare that Daughter had never even been in the presence of a Seer.

Yes, it all made sense now, but it angered him as well.

"She's not just a tool to be used by the Empire," he said softly.

Daughter's eyes narrowed. Had he surprised her with his insight? Her utensils, too, were no longer in her hands. The meal was no longer important.

"She *is* a tool, Val, just as I am a tool, and just as you may be one day." Her gaze shifted to Krys for a time, then back to Val. "The Empire chose me. Do you think I wanted to be Chosen?" His confused look was sufficient answer. "Do you know what my life is like? Constantly working, constantly at risk, surrounded by Protectors, not out of desire but out of need? Betrothed to a man who is nearly as old as my father? Betrothed not to one I love, but to one who will, hopefully, help produce heirs that will pass muster as Chosen?" She turned back to Krys. "I, too, am familiar with the stories you have read. I, too, would choose to be wed to someone I love. But it is not to be. I have been Chosen, and I have a duty. I will not fail in my duty to the Empire any more than you will."

Focusing on Val, she asked, "You chose to die for me. Why?"

His thoughts turned inward, settling on the demanding eyes of Mr. Wyzcha, Sir Jarl. "I didn't," he answered finally. "Not for you."

She sat back, awaiting the rest of his answer.

"He might have been my uncle, but Sir Jarl has been more like a father to me since I left the orphanage. He called on me to do something special, something for him. That was the call I answered."

"I know. I'm only surprised that you know, as well." She turned to Krys. "Our Knights put the needs of Empire before personal needs, and Sir Jarl was no exception. Val did the same when he answered that call. He didn't do it for me, he did it, ultimately, for the Empire. For the very idea of Empire.

"Krys, we cannot know at this moment what your talents will become. If you are what I think you are, the Empire calls on you to serve. *I* call on you to serve. Will you?"

"How can I answer?" Krys asked in consternation. "Two days ago I was in an orphanage. Now you're asking me to stand beside you as you rule the Empire, or will rule it someday."

"Val chose."

Krys looked at Val, her gaze softening. "You *did* choose. I hardly know you, but already I would follow you anywhere. I feel like I'm in a fairy tale."

"Maybe we are," Val murmured. "But I think we're looking too far down the road. All we really want to do at the moment is go to school."

"Will you stay with me?"

"I will for as long as I can. I'm not sure we're following the same path."

Daughter stood up and came around the table to place arms about both of their shoulders. "We are, each of us, tools. But we're people, too. I will never forget that. Each of us is called, and each of us answers that call in our own way. I was not a child when I was called. You are still children, and I will not permit you to make choices of that magnitude yet. I do ask that you consider my request about Rrestriss. You have nothing to lose, and much, much to gain. Later, if you are needed, I will call. By then you will be adults, and you will be free to choose. Is that fair enough?"

Val fondled the money key in his pocket, then slowly let it slide away. He removed his hand and shamelessly placed it behind Daughter's back. He gave her a hug, knowing it was probably not part of the dinner etiquette, or part of any etiquette at all. She tightened her grip about his shoulders and kissed his forehead. Then she leaned over Krys and did the same. Krys looked startled, then a delighted look came into her eyes. "I *am* in a fairy tale," she said.

Later, as they were leaving, Krys turned to Daughter, her young eyes suddenly older. "You will find your knight in shining armor, Ellandra of the Chosen."

Daughter's hand went to her throat, and for the first time since they'd met, Val sensed her uncertainty. "You know my name?"

"Yes, My Lady."

"No one knows my name. Daughter is a title bestowed long ago. It is my name now."

"Yes, My Lady."

"Is that the Seer talking, or the fairy tales talking?"

"Can it be both?"

"Is it?"

"Yes, My Lady. It was just a feeling that came to me when you said you were betrothed, but it was a strong feeling. I sensed great happiness, but more, I sensed fulfillment."

"Will we . . .?" she whispered, suddenly vulnerable.

"You will both have to choose. Would you want it otherwise?"

Chapter Forty-seven

Krys led Val down the corridor and entered her new stateroom. Val could only shake his head at the luxurious quarters, wondering who had been forced out to make room for him and Krys. But it wasn't his problem. Such things were the domain of Daughter. He sat at a small table with a workstation considering his day. Krys was not only his sister, she had some special gift that truly enthralled Daughter. And he had gone into the net! What a momentous day. The net was enough all by itself, but his sister! Though they'd missed all the early years together, he sensed the love that flowed from her to him, and he reveled in it. A sister! And she wanted to stay with him. Life was suddenly too wonderful. Tomorrow he would go Outside. Would he pass muster, as Daughter put it? He knew he would. There was no question in his mind on that score.

He was suddenly hungry. Dinner had not been fun, and he'd not had the opportunity to eat everything. He considered room service, but he was, technically, a crewmember now. He would not push the bounds of his relationship with Daughter or Captain Jzazbe.

>Hey, partner, wasn't that you with me in the net today?<
>Yea. Pretty cool, huh?<
>Have you forgotten what we did in there?<

>I hope not.<

>Well, I'm hungry, too. Did we or did we not learn how to work the auto-chef?<

>Hey, you're right!< Without further ado, he headed for the lounge.

When he finally got to bed that night, he tucked Krys under her covers before stretching out on his own bed to stare at her.

Her gaze met his. "Don't leave me, Val."

"I won't." He raised himself on one elbow. "I'm 5397867A. You're 5397867B. I guess that means I was born first. I'm your big brother, and I'm not going anywhere without you."

He and Krys breakfasted together the next morning in the lounge. He would have preferred eating in the crew mess, but he somehow knew he wasn't allowed there. Without Daughter's presence, the meal was much more relaxed, though both of them concentrated on doing things Daughter's way.

"You seem distracted, Val," Krys finally said.

"I suppose I am. I have a test to take today."

"A test!"

"I'm going Outside. They tell me I might not adapt. Most don't. Can you do your magic on me and tell me if it will go okay?"

"It's not that simple, Val. Besides, you don't want simple answers. It's not your way."

She was right. Besides, what if she said he'd fail?

He rose from the central shaft at nine o'clock sharp, and Captain Jzazbe was waiting for him. Another senior officer stood beside him.

"It's protocol to report a few minutes early, Mister Val."

"Yes, sir."

Jzazbe spoke to the other officer. "You have the conn, Commander." He rose from his seat and motioned for Val to take the same workstation as the day before, but this time Jzazbe sat down in the seat beside him.

He stared at Val for a time before saying, "There are several ways to go about introducing you to the Outside. At the Academy they normally engage you in pilot duties for several weeks, letting you sense the emptiness that surrounds us in pieces, a little at a time. You're too busy to focus on much of anything but the ship. I'm prepared to do it that way if you'd prefer."

Val frowned. "What's the alternative, sir?"

Jzazbe's lips pursed. "There's only one way to really know if you're cut out for this. We call it 'walking the ship.'"

"We actually go outside?" Val asked with a gulp. He hadn't been thinking along those lines.

"No. We do it all through the net. We don't put on space suits, and your body stays right here. But Val, you know how realistic the net is. Your mind will be telling you that you're out in space, and your vision will be telling you that you're out in space. It's incredibly realistic and, to most, overwhelming. On the surface it's a test of your ability to operate a ship in space, but at a more fundamental level it's a test of your ability to control your mind. To master the experience, your mind must be stronger than your senses. Your mind is the key. You have to be capable of remembering it's a virtual experience, that your body is not at risk, that it is still here on the bridge. Most can't do that."

"You have."

"I have, but that doesn't mean I like it. In fact, I don't like it."

"Has everyone else here done it?"

"Yes, but we serve the Royal Family and our standards are high. It's not so on every ship within the fleet. All pilots, navigators, and captains have to do it, but they're just a small percentage of the officer cadre."

"I want to know if I can be a star pilot, sir."

"I know you do, and you've taken well to the net. I think you're up to it."

"Then let's do it."

Jzazbe sighed. This was clearly not an event high on his list. "Very well. Join the net. I'll meet you there."

Val's eyes widened. "You're going with me?"

"I will not send you out there alone."

Val's gaze stayed locked on Jzazbe as he lowered the helmet to his head. Jzazbe reached out and lowered his visor, and Val was in the net. There was no delay this time.

"Welcome back," the AI said. "Would you like to review what we did yesterday before going Outside?"

"No. I haven't forgotten."

Jzazbe joined moments later. "Take us to the top hatch, Val. The one just forward of the top turret."

Val didn't hesitate. With just a thought, they raced through the net to the hatch.

"I'll go first," Jzazbe informed him. "Follow when you're ready." He climbed up a ladder and placed his hand on the hatch controls, then turned back to Val. "Remember, we're in a virtual world – it's all simulation." Val nodded, and Jzazbe activated the control. The hatch irised open, and Jzazbe climbed out in a crouch and disappeared from view.

Val stared at the opening, then he stared out past the opening. He'd expected inky blackness, but even through the small opening of the hatch, stars littered the view. He knew his body should be exploding, then freezing in the vacuum, and a chill shook his body, but it was just momentary. He turned to Artmis.

>Ready?<

>Uh, my father was not fond of this, and neither am I. You first.<

>Okay. Stay here if you want.<

>I'll be right behind you. It's my test, too.<

Val tucked his crutch under a shoulder and placed both hands on the ladder. He climbed, his view expanding little by little as he drew closer to the hatch. When his head poked all the way out of the hatch, he sucked in a breath. Sharp points of cold light stared back at him wherever he looked, their infinite numbers suddenly filling him with an understanding of the uncompromising vastness of Outside.

For just a moment, he felt like the abyss would suck him in. A shiver shook his body from head to toe.

He twisted this way and that, his mouth hanging open to study, to let his mind absorb the feelings coming from his senses, the feelings he must accept if he was ever to call this place home.

Starlight varied in intensity and concentration. Occasional areas of near blackness might be due to a lack stars, or they might be nebulae with higher concentrations of dust that hid the stars within. He didn't know, but he knew he would know one day.

He closed his eyes and let his mind continue seeing the stars, feeling the light, not the dark. When he opened his eyes again, nearby space was empty and dark as he knew it would be, but his view was not dark. A grin lit his face. There were so many stars that he could not make out the familiar constellations of his home, and so much color! In his mind, stars had always been twinkling pinpoints of white light, but now! Yellows and reds and blues all stared back at him.

Excitement filled him, akin to the feelings he experienced every time a ship landed or took off. This place of unfathomable beauty was their real home, not the space port. This place could become his real home, too.

He turned to take in more of the view, then discovered Captain Jzazbe squatting down beside him.

"Please tell me that's not a grin," Jzazbe said in amazement.

"Sorry, sir. I guess it is. This is peculiar, standing in space without a space suit. I know I'm not really here, but it feels like the real thing. I like it."

"Not so fast, Mister. You're not done yet. The idea is that you come all the way out, remember?"

"Oh, right." Val climbed another rung, then suddenly found it impossible to move his foot to the next. His grin faded.

Jzazbe knew the feeling and leaned toward him. "Take my hand, lad."

Val stared at him. "I thought I'd feel like I was falling out here, but I don't. It's more like I'll get whisked away if I don't hold onto something."

"It's different for each person. For me, it's the blackness, despite the stars. Use your mind, Val. Remember, this is an exercise of the mind. There's no wind up here."

Val took the outstretched hand. He instantly felt more secure and climbed the rest of the way. When his foot and crutch were planted on the outside of the ship, he stood slowly to face Jzazbe.

"Well done, Val." Jzazbe reached out both hands and turned him, keeping a hand on each shoulder. They stood side by side staring out at the breathtaking view.

"Care to take a stroll?" Jzazbe offered.

"Yes, sir. Uh, just a second." Val turned back to the hatch and reached a hand out to Artmis. "Come out, my friend. The view is worth it."

Artmis struggled mightily, a grim set to his mouth as he first lifted one foot from the ladder, then the other. Val took both of his hands to help him to his feet. Artmis held tightly to Val, but he forced himself to look about.

>It is breathtaking, but I'd as soon be done with this.<

On the net, Artmis' thoughts were as clear to Jzazbe as they were to Val, and he sensed Artmis' distaste. "Take your time. When you're ready, we'll take a stroll."

Val held Artmis as they followed Captain Jzazbe. They circled the gun turret, then angled off toward the edge of the ship and walked along the circumference. After a time Artmis relaxed his hold on Val, though he kept to the inside of their stroll.

"Any problems?" Jzazbe asked.

"No, sir," Val replied.

"I'm managing, sir," Artmis said, "but I know what's next. It will be harder."

"You're doing well, very well. Val, the grin is inappropriate," he added, not sharing Val's amazement at what they were doing.

"Yes, sir," Val said, but the grin soon found its way back.

"I wish I could share your enjoyment, Val. For me, this is always a challenge."

"How many times have you done it?"

"Four times. Once as a cadet, and several times as an instructor."

"You taught at an Academy, sir?"

"I did, for five years. It was good duty, but I prefer a line position."

"I guess you got one. There can't be many who can claim to be Daughter's captain."

"No, not many, and the importance of her work makes it doubly satisfying. We have one more thing to do here, if you're up to it. It's not a requirement, it's more an act of pride among us spacers than anything else, but you've come this far. I want you to take it the rest of the way if you can."

"What is it?"

"We transition to the other side of the ship."

Val considered the meaning of the words, then looked hard at Captain Jzazbe. "You're joking, sir."

"No, but like I said, it's not a requirement. I'll go first. You two follow if you can. Remember, this is an exercise of the mind, nothing more."

Val gulped. "More like an exercise of will, sir."

"That, too," Jzazbe replied grimly. He sat down near the edge of the ship, then rolled over on his stomach with his feet toward the edge of the ship. Slowly, carefully, he edged his way outward to his waist. His legs and feet clung to the curved edge of the ship, and he inched further until his body was spread eagled on the edge. He disappeared out of sight, but not out of mind. As always when in the net, Val and Artmis sensed the thoughts of others who were also in the net, and Jzazbe's personal struggle as he inched his way across the curve, then onto the other side of the ship, could not be hidden.

It didn't take long. Jzazbe never let himself stop moving. "I'm over," he said. "Are you ready, Val?"

"I am, sir."

"Wait," Artmis demanded. "I'm next. I'm not trying to prove anything to anybody. Val, you're going to hold me as long as you can. Sir, I'd appreciate you taking hold of my feet when you can."

"I will, Artmis. Remember, this is just an exercise of the mind."

"My mind is telling me it's real even though I know it's not. Here I come."

Artmis followed Jzazbe's example and inched his way out. Val held to his hand as long as he could, but their fingers eventually lost touch, and for Artmis it was an eternity before he felt Jzazbe's hand on his foot. As soon as he did, he gasped in relief and hurried the rest of the way.

"I'm over," he announced proudly to Val. "Come on! It's not that hard."

Val, sat on the edge of the ship and looked out to the stars, alone and considering. The whole purpose of the exercise was to test his mind, not his body. He stood and turned, taking in the vast, breathtaking wholeness of the place he wanted to call home. He would be a starship pilot, of that he had no doubt now. He had passed his test, and nothing would hold him back. This, then, was the place he would call his home, this place between the stars, this place of mostly nothingness, but with those so very important points of light to which he would bring ships someday. This was his new home. He respected it, but he would not fear it.

He understood the test now. It was, truly, an exercise of the mind. Its purpose was not to see if you could go outside to fix a broken ship. Heck, there wasn't anything out here to fix that he could see. The test was constructed to determine if you could sustain sanity in the vast gulfs between the stars. And more, it was a test of will. To pass, you had to choose to pass. You had to damp down the instincts that were hollering at you, you had to set aside the natural fright. Fleet officers would face threats, and they had to control their fear. This was one way of determining if they could.

He knew it was impossible to be out here in space without a suit. Heck, he wasn't even cold any more, and his chest kept rising and falling as if he was really breathing even though there was no air. When he thought about the fright, it was there, very real, very strong, and at the fundamental level of instinct.

He stared at the edge of the ship, studied his feelings, examined them, and brought them under control. He damped down the fear, forced himself to see through it, and suddenly he sensed the awsome magnitude of the task before him. He savored the feeling for a time.

"Ship, you've created a sense of gravity around the whole ship, correct? It doesn't matter where I stand, I'll still feel like the surface of the ship is down?"

"I know what you're thinking, Val. So, too, do the others. You are correct."

Captain Jzazbe interjected. "Val, our purpose here is not to impress others, it is only to test ourselves. It is your own mind your are testing, not mine."

"Understood, sir. This is a test I assign myself." He stood, and his fear remained under control. He knew he was right, that his mind was right. He crutched toward the edge of the ship fully upright and continued crutching across the curved edge of the ship until he had come all the way around to face Jzazbe and Artmis.

He approached Jzazbe and saluted, the grin no longer on his face. What he had just done was not the foolish prank of a child, it was more like a test of manhood, and his mind had been equal to the task.

"Well done, Val," Jzazbe said as he saluted back. "That's a first, and something I'd never considered. I think I'll give it a try myself."

"We're not out here to impress others, sir," Val said, turning Jzazbe's words back to him.

"Indeed, we are not. I'm going to do it, and it is not an act of showmanship any more than was yours. Actually, I believe your method might be easier than my own. Wait here."

Jzazbe stepped to the edge of the ship, then just kept walking, his body always at right angles to the surface of the ship. He disappeared from view, but he returned shortly.

"Amazing. It works! By the way, have you looked up from this side of the ship?"

Val turned around and looked up. He gasped. Directly overhead was a bright, elongated ellipse of light. He knew without being told that he was looking toward the center of the galaxy. The galaxy was truly a disc. He'd seen it from the ground, but never in such majestic glory. And . . . that was where his future lie. He would traverse a portion of that great ellipse during whatever years lay ahead of him, and he would do so in the uniform of an imperial officer. His leg suddenly felt weak. Jzazbe joined him on one side, and Artmis joined him on the other.

They stayed that way, holding to each other for a long time. Jzazbe pointed out stars that he knew, some of them important sector headquarters of the Empire. He called on the AI to show the other ships of the squadron, and dim outlines of several showed clearly among the stars. None of them was close by, so no details could be discerned. Planets, those on this side of the sun, were highlighted, and of course the sun was clearly visible, though they were far enough out in the system that they could only see it as a star brighter than the rest.

"Seen enough?" Jzazbe finally asked.

"Yes, sir, for this visit, but I'd like to return," Val answered.

"I've seen enough," Artmis answered without hesitation.

"Okay. Time's up. Ship, bring us back."

"Uh, sir, would it be okay if we climbed back in by ourselves?"

"Why?"

"Uh, it just seems like the whole thing would be more complete. I know this is just an exercise of the mind, but I'd like to come back in on my own."

"I understand. I have things to do. Why don't you two stay out here for a while. Come in when you're ready."

"Are we late for dinner?"

"I don't know. Don't worry. Daughter is willing to wait when it's appropriate." He stood up, and Val stood up with him.

Val reached for Jzazbe's shoulder and touched it lightly. It was probably a major breach of etiquette, but he didn't care. "Sir, thank you. I shall never forget this day."

Jzazbe took Val's other shoulder and faced him. "Nor I. It has been my great honor to go through this important test with you. I ask that you remember my part in this, for you might have the opportunity to repeat it with someone else one day."

"I will remember, sir."

Jzazbe disappeared, and Val sat down beside Artmis again. They looked at each other, then both punched the other lightly on the shoulder. Big grins lit their faces.

* * * * *

Val and Artmis returned to the bridge. Before disconnecting, Val focused on the AI. "Thank you," he said.

"You're welcome, Val. You're done for today. I'll see you tomorrow morning."

When he removed his helmet, he discovered Daughter, Otis, and Krys in attendance on the bridge. Daughter greeted him, but more formally in front of the crew. "So, Mister Val. It appears you will, indeed, have the opportunity to become a star pilot."

He went to her and knelt down on his only knee, his crutch acting as his missing leg. "I like it out here, My Lady."

"Stand up, Val. Captain Jzazbe has something for you."

Val rose and turned to Captain Jzazbe. "Congratulations," he heard as if from far away. "You're wearing a spacer's uniform, and it's time to add some rank to it." Jzazbe stepped forward to pin emblems to each side of Val's collar. "As ship's Captain, I name you Cadet Val for the duration of this voyage. Congratulations."

Val stepped back and saluted Jzazbe. "I'm honored, sir. Title or not, thank you for the opportunity you've given me."

"You're a member of the crew now, cadet. You have no official status, but from here on out you'll stand a watch just like the rest of us. When other assignments don't interfere, I should add."

"I can eat in the crew's mess now, sir?"

"You're no longer a one-legged beggar, Val, and you never will be again. It's the only place you can eat, unless the ship's owner invites you to dine with her. Your sister is hereby invited to join you in crew's mess, as well."

"Aye, aye, sir," Val said, saluting him again.

Jzazbe put an arm around his shoulders and pulled him to the side. "We don't salute on the bridge, cadet," he said quietly.

"I understand, sir. I'll never forget the opportunity you've given me."

"I know you won't."

Daughter stepped forward to join them. "I feel like I've missed out on something important. Too bad the Chosen are not suited to flying ships – it's something I'll never be able to share with you. But Val, I know how much this means to you, and I'm pleased to share the event with you. You are one of the lucky ones: you have what it takes to fly a starship, and now you know it. I personally believe there is more within you than just flying ships, but for the moment that is enough. We're all proud of you."

Val didn't know what to do, so he kneeled before her with his head down. She gave him a moment to gather himself, then lifted his chin.

"Stand, Cadet Val, and be recognized."

He stood, and Krys was the first to throw her arms around him in delight.

* * * * *

Val's training wasn't over – it had just begun. And he didn't have many opportunities to eat in the crew's mess. Daughter, always busy, seemed to enjoy the breaks from her duties to be with Val and Krys. And she found that she enjoyed teaching them deportment. Her own training on such matters had begun almost at birth, and she really had to think about things that had become second nature to her.

Val remained on a four hour watch – he had too many other things on his schedule to permit an eight hour watch. *Resolve* carried a full complement of courses, and even a few teachers. After all, it was common practice among the fleet for children to accompany their parents on long voyages. He and Krys spent hours together every day on their pads and in classes designed to improve their language skills, and Daughter assigned basic classes on history, mathematics, science, and art. Doctor Storvo supervised daily physical exercise classes for everyone on the ship, and Val and Krys were no exception to the requirement.

Borg provided personal weapons training, training that Otis demanded of everyone in Daughter's retinue. Val and Krys were so far behind in this area that most of their weapons training was in the form of personal tutoring. Val's missing leg made for some interesting moments, but Borg taught Val to use his crutch as a weapon. A difficult process with only one leg, balance was always an issue, but Val persevered and became quite handy with the crutch as a weapon.

Krys had no interest in firing blasters, but she persevered, actually scoring reasonably well when she forced herself not to flinch, which wasn't very often. As for the personal defense training, she found it impossible to strike hard enough to actually hurt someone, hence she often found herself on the receiving end of bruises.

Val took to the training with gusto, knowing it was another step along the way to officer training. His aim with a blaster quickly reached an acceptable level, and Borg transitioned him between a number of different weapons and training scenarios that left Val breathless but beaming.

Daughter participated in the training, though not frequently. She didn't need training, only proficiency. She had spent a lifetime honing her skills, and neither Val or Krys was willing to take her on.

He and Krys toured the squadron, as much for the squadron's benefit as their own. Crewmembers wanted to meet the one who had saved all their jobs, and the two were well received. Krys had a lot less interest in the ships than did Val, but she genuinely enjoyed meeting so many new people.

Captain Jzazbe gave considerable thought to the training Val received in the net. There was little doubt in his mind that Val would one day become a fleet officer, and the Academy would teach him everything he needed to know, but Academy training focused on ship handling, navigation, weapons, and leadership, not the intimate details of shipboard systems. Those details were left to specialist crewmembers who were supervised by officers. Jzazbe considered it a weakness in the Academy curriculum. Most young officers struggled mightily during their early years as they learned the intimate details of shipboard systems, and some never did learn.

Val would learn how ships worked, and he would learn from the bottom up rather than from the top down. His time on *Resolve* would focus on the ship, not command of the ship.

Jzazbe worked out a detailed program with the ship's AI. He gave Val a few days of fun flying the ship, but then Val was put to work. Every system on the ship was studied in depth during the ensuing months, and Val spent many hours with the ship's chief engineer inspecting and repairing things.

He dutifully learned systems, processes, and procedures, but what most intrigued him was the ship's AI. Val spent every available minute working with the AI to learn how it did its job, and it wasn't long before he figured out how to find his way around the net without the assistance of the AI. It was a slow process, a challenging and difficult job that few ever bothered to learn. After all, ship's AI's never failed, but Val reveled in the challenge.

Chapter Forty-eight

Months passed. Krys and Val stayed with the ship through three stops, spending port time investigating worlds new to them. They were always accompanied by a crewmember, and whenever possible, Otis detailed one of the Great Cats to shadow them without their knowledge.

Basaggit was their fourth new world. Though they had some knowledge of Daughter's purpose on Basaggit, they were in no way involved in her efforts. A full week passed during which Krys and Val became quite familiar with the port and its immediate surroundings.

This was their last day in port. Daughter would announce her findings later in the day, then *Resolve* would depart. Krys, Val, and Ensign Vorgaskia headed out on foot, planning to enjoy lunch at a local establishment. They made their way through the crowded port terminal to the sidewalk out front and stood in a short queue for a skimmer. While they waited, Krys felt uneasy for some reason, and her eyes roved the crowd. Far down the sidewalk to her right, her gaze settled on several wooden boxes stacked by the curb outside the baggage claim area. She blinked, then stiffened for a moment as her eyes glazed over. When she came back to herself, she blinked again, then reached for Val's arm.

"Those boxes are all parts of a gun, a very long gun," she whispered into his ear.

His eyes searched and settled on the boxes. "What? How can you know what's inside them?"

"I don't know. I was looking at them, then I saw the gun all assembled on a roof somewhere."

"Uh . . . you mean you had a vision?" he asked guardedly.

She looked into his eyes. "I guess I'd have to call it that. There's no question in my mind, Val. It's a gun, and I think it has something to do with our purpose here."

Val stared at her, then at the boxes, then his eyes took in the other bystanders while he considered. Three Drambda, each with four strong arms and hands, loitered near the boxes. Clearly, they were porters. Beyond them, near the far corner of the building, he spotted a Corvold leaning against the wall. Its leathery-skinned head was stationary, but its eyes moved constantly, studying everyone on the sidewalk. Val knew that not all Corvolds were bad, three of them had died trying to warn Sir Jarl of the intended assassination on Hespra III, but he also knew it was the Corvolds who had carried out the attempt against Daughter.

He took Krys' arm and turned her away. He focused on Ensign Vorgaskia. "Sir, it might turn out to be nothing, but Krys just learned of a potential threat to Daughter."

Vorgaskia's expression suddenly hardened. "What are you talking about? We just got here."

"Don't turn around, sir. We're under observation by a Corvold. There are some boxes down the way that are parts of a gun. Krys said it will be a very long gun once it is assembled. It might be intended for a sniper."

Vorgaskia focused on Krys. "What makes you so sure?"

"You'll have to trust me, Ensign. How I know is classified as an Imperial Secret, but I speak true."

"We're going back to the ship," Vorgaskia announced grimly.

Just then a freight hauler settled into position beside the boxes. "No, we're not," Val said, brooking no argument. "You are, Krys. Let Captain Jzazbe know what's going on, and make sure he notifies Otis." To Vorgaskia, he said, "You're going to follow the guns. Take our skimmer, but don't follow too close. You don't want them knowing you're following. Got it?"

"I'm not leaving you. You know my orders, Cadet."

"Sir, your orders place Daughter first, always. The Corvolds tried to kill her once, and maybe they're trying again. Can you take that chance? Now get going. It's better if you leave before they do. My suggestion is that you go up high and keep an eye on them from above rather than trying to follow them. Hurry, sir."

"What about you?"

"I'm going to see where the Corvold goes. I think he's part of this. If I'm wrong, you'll know where the gun ends up, and you can notify the ship. Trust me, sir. I'll be careful."

Vorgaskia's lips compressed. He stared at Val, then nodded and boarded the skimmer. It whooshed into the sky, and Val paid it no more heed.

"Get going, Krys. I'm counting on you to convince Jzazbe."

She squeezed his arm, then turned and disappeared inside the terminal building.

Val turned away from the shipment of boxes and the Corvold, suspecting that if the Corvold really was a lookout, he would stay in the area for a few extra minutes before following the boxes. A hundred meters down the road leading from the port, a beggar squatted on a blanket. Val approached him, coins exchanged hands, then the beggar handed his coat to Val and sauntered off. Val drew the filthy cloak about himself and pulled the hood over his head, removed his boot, and rolled his pant leg up as high as it would go. He then settled down on the blanket with his cup in his hand.

>I need a little help here, Artmis.<

>*We* need a little help here. I'll do what I can, but you're far too clean to pass as a beggar.<

Val rubbed dirt into his hands and leg. When he started on his face, he cried out. >Ouch! What have you done to me?<

>You're soon going to have nasty sores on both cheeks and your chin. Anyone looking at you will not see your face, they'll just focus on the sores. I promise you, no one is going to want to be close to you once they see them.<

A few minutes later, the Corvold passed Val at a brisk pace, paying him no heed. Val gave him some distance, then picked up his blanket and crutched off between two buildings. As soon as he was out of sight of the Corvold, he raced ahead a few buildings, then waited. Soon enough, the Corvold passed by, clearly headed into town. A short time later, the Corvold entered crowded streets, and Val was able to follow him directly. No one, including the Corvold, thought about beggars with anything other than disdain and indifference.

The Corvold entered a seedy restaurant, and Val suddenly had a dilemma. What if the Corvold left by a back entrance? He hurriedly crutched by the establishment and rounded the next corner, then crutched past the alleyway and huddled on his blanket inside a recessed doorway. He had a view of the alley in both directions and a view of the main street in one direction. If the Corvold came back out the front and retraced his steps, Val would lose him.

He didn't have long to wait. The Corvold came out the back door, looked in both directions, then walked away from Val. He turned left at the first corner. Val moved down the side street, still one block away from the Corvold, and lay down against the building on his blanket. He, too, was an expert at checking for tails. He suspected the Corvold would double back through the alley to see if anyone was tailing him.

He was right. The Corvold returned to the alley and crossed one street away from Val. Val picked up his blanket and moved to the corner just in time to see the Corvold turn back toward the main street two blocks ahead of him. Val went back into his stealth mode on the main street and had no trouble keeping the Corvold in sight.

This process repeated itself twice more, then the Corvold turned down another main street, eventually entering a block of old buildings that, according to a sign, were soon to be razed, to be replaced by new buildings. He turned into a doorway guarded by another Corvold and entered a tall building that had once been an apartment complex.

Val checked out the back of the building, but all the doors were locked. He desperately wanted to get inside, but it was broad daylight and the only entrance was guarded. He and Artmis considered for a time, then settled on a plan. Acting as if every step was a struggle, Val crutched up to the guard.

"Hold it, you. What do you think you're doing?" the guard demanded.

"This is my home, sir." Val mumbled. "What are *you* doing here?"

"None of your business. Get out of here."

"But I live here. I have a permit from the owner."

"No one lives here. Show me the permit."

"I don't *carry* it, sir. It's a private agreement between the owner and myself. I pay him weekly for the space."

"Where is this space?"

"Near the back of the building on this floor. Follow me and I'll show you."

"I'm not going anywhere. You'll have to wait until later. Go away."

"Sir, I won't bother you."

"Come back in an hour and you can go in." The Corvold looked hard at Val's face hidden within the hood, then stepped away quickly. "You're disgusting. Go away."

"An hour? I'll just wait over here then, sir." Val moved down the street some ten meters and set his blanket on the sidewalk, then settled himself shakily, but he was thinking hard. He had a timeline. Whatever was taking place here would be over in an hour. Actually, it would probably be over a lot sooner. Val had no idea how long it took to assemble a weapon, but it probably wasn't very long.

Just then, Ensign Vorgaskia rounded the corner, followed closely by another Corvold who held a blaster on him.

"Found this guy snooping around. Look at his uniform. I think he's a cop."

Vorgaskia had removed his ensign pins, and there was no other identification on him, so Val didn't think they could trace him back to Daughter. If they did, he didn't know what would happen.

"Who are you?" the first Corvold asked.

"I *am* a cop, an undercover military cop. I've traced a stolen shipment to somewhere around here. Have you seen any wooden crates going into any of these buildings?" He turned to the second Corvold. "Put your weapon away. You know the penalty for threatening the police."

The Corvolds stared at each other for a time, then the guard made a decision. "Take him inside. You know what to do."

"Hey, wait!" Vorgaskia demanded. "Surely you're not going to kidnap a policeman."

The blaster moved toward the door, indicating just exactly that. The moment it moved, Vorgaskia lunged, taking the blaster in both hands and turning it aside. He swept a foot out, dropping the guard, but he could not pull the weapon from the guards fierce grip. The first Corvold pulled out a miniblaster, and Val knew he had to act. Without rising, he flicked the field adjustment on his stunner and aimed it at all three men. When he pushed the button, all three fell to the ground unconscious.

He rose and quickly moved to them, taking both blasters and settling them in the voluminous pockets of his cloak. He readjusted his stunner to a narrow beam and stunned both Corvolds again, just for good measure, then dragged Vorgaskia back around the nearest corner. At least he was out of sight of anyone coming or going through the door. He crutched back to his blanket and returned with it to Vorgaskia, covering him up to make him look like a sleeping beggar. It was the best he could do on short notice, and he no longer needed the blanket for his own disguise.

He entered the building cautiously, not having any idea what to expect. There were no more guards nearby, though he suspected there would be some on the roof. That's where Krys said the weapon would be placed.

The air in the building was stale and stiflingly hot. Val wanted to remove his cloak, but he wasn't ready to give it up – he might have further need of it, and both hands were occupied. One held the stunner and the other held his crutch.

A stairway beckoned to him as soon as he entered, but Val decided that was too obvious. He moved to the far left side of the building and took the stairway there. It was a long climb, a very long climb. He reached the top with the muscles in his leg quaking and had to sit for a time massaging them.

He opened the door to the roof just a crack and waited for his eyes to adjust to the bright light, then inched out onto the roof, his eyes darting everywhere. A maze of machinery and equipment restricted his view, but the machines offered concealment as well. He moved carefully between and around them, looking always for movement.

He found it. One guard stood near the doorway at the top of the central stairs. Val edged back and away, always keeping a machine between himself and the guard. He worked his way to the far edge of the roof and peered around a massive machine, checking both directions. It was clear to his left, but he had to think about what he was seeing to the right. A large tarp was in place, and he couldn't see what was beneath it, but sticking out just slightly toward the edge of the roof was the muzzle of a serious looking gun. Val followed the track of the muzzle, and about a mile away was the governor's palace. That's where Daughter would deliver her findings.

He stepped back in consternation. Not again! He didn't want to go through this again. But what else could he do? There was no one to stop these guys but him.

He had a little time. He wasn't going to go rushing off to certain death this time. He settled down to think. He had two blasters and a stunner. He didn't want to use a blaster if he could help it. He couldn't be certain what was going down here, and what if he chose wrong? What if these guys were part of the local police force providing security for Daughter? The evidence indicated otherwise, but there was a small chance he was wrong. He pulled out his stunner and looked at it. He was too far away for a wide-field shot. He adjusted it to a narrow beam, then poked his head around the structure for another look.

Suddenly, a hard, gnarled hand grasped his face from behind and pulled him back. He cried out, but the hand muffled his cry. He raised the stunner to fire blindly behind himself, but an arm reached out and held his fist tightly. He stared at the arm. It was covered in light brown fur. He relaxed, and as soon as he did, the hand over his mouth relaxed and he could turn. It was Borg, the Great Cat.

Borg's lips lifted in a leer of greeting, and his horrible breath washed over Val, but Val didn't care. In fact, he welcomed the smell.

Borg's lips closed. He placed a hand on Val's head and pressed down lightly, indicating that Val was to remain in place and out of sight. Then the Great Cat was gone without a sound.

Val started shaking, so relieved was he. Borg was an expert, and these Corvolds didn't stand a chance. More important, Borg had every legal right to act as he saw fit to protect Daughter, so Val was not going to have to shoot anyone and maybe face jail as a result.

He kept the stunner in one hand and the full size blaster in the other, just in case, and waited. Before long, he heard shooting far off in the distance. It wasn't Borg, it was too far away. He believed it was coming from the vicinity of the governor's palace, but who would be foolish enough to attack there? If security there was anything like what he'd seen on Hespra III, hundreds of police and Imperial Marines guarded the place.

Then he froze with awareness. The Corvolds probably learned on Hespra III that *Resolve* would show up at the slightest hint of danger. Daughter would be whisked to the roof and be exposed for a brief moment as she boarded the ship. He peered around the corner and sure enough, the tip of the great gun was angled in that direction. He discerned no movement of the gun, and that made sense. It was probably already sighted in.

Minutes later, *Resolve* appeared and hove to just above the roof of the palace. The ramp opened, and Val knew Daughter would appear any moment.

What was Borg doing? He had not seen or heard the Great Cat in some minutes, and he didn't want to do anything that would foil Borg's plan, whatever that plan was. But he couldn't let the gun fire either.

He waited another moment, then made a decision. He didn't want to shoot anyone, but he could shoot the gun itself. He moved out from the machine, exposing himself, and took careful aim with the blaster. The sound of his firing would spoil whatever plan Borg had, but Val couldn't not act. He pulled the trigger.

Blast! The shot struck the gun and deflected it. Val was pretty sure it damaged the gun, as well. A muffled scream sounded from whomever was sighting in the gun, then pandemonium broke loose. The tarp flew back, and three Corvolds emerged with drawn weapons. Val moved back out of sight, believing that Borg had them covered, then he remembered the guard at the door. He crutched back in that direction, keeping close to the machinery for cover to find the guard out cold. Borg had dealt with him.

Val, feeling less threatened, crutched over to the unconscious guard and peered around a metal structure at the gun. Borg had disarmed the three Corvolds and was directing them toward the door.

Two more doors burst open, one on each end of the roof, and two Corvolds leaped out from each one onto the roof with weapons drawn, but Borg could not see them.

Val yelled, "Four more on the roof!"

Borg growled at his three prisoners. "Call them off, or all of you die."

All three Corvolds started yelling, but the four attackers continued racing toward the damaged gun. Did they even know there was a Great Cat here? Surely not, or they, too, would have surrendered.

Borg fired at the first to appear, and he was not using a stunner. Val, taking the hint, fired at the two coming from his right and downed both of them. Borg took the last one, then turned calmly back to his prisoners.

"Are there any more?"

One spoke for the three. "Ten of us in total."

"Then they are all accounted for. I hope for your sake that you are not lying."

He turned to Val. "Lie down where you are, and discard your weapons. Others will be here soon, and I don't want you injured in the confusion."

Val did as ordered, though he kept his weapons within easy reach, and he still had his crutch as a last resort. Imperial Marines swarmed out of the doors, and there was, to Val, a lot of confusion for a while. Local police arrived and demanded explanations, but Borg just gave them a quick briefing, then he and Val left. He would give them the details later.

It was a long way down the stairs. Just before reaching street level, Val suddenly felt weak. He settled down on a step with his back against the wall, his eyes glazed.

"What is it?" Borg asked.

Val didn't answer, just looked straight ahead with glazed eyes. Borg touched his shoulder. "Are you injured?"

"No." He looked up to the Great Cat and said softly, "I killed today."

Borg nodded and stepped back. There was nothing he could say so he remained silent, leaving Val alone to deal with his feelings. Artmis, too, remained silent.

Val felt numb. His mind kept reliving the dying moments of the two Corvolds he had shot. He was aware of nothing else, just the ending of those two lives, the once living flesh bursting from their bodies as the blaster bolts struck, weapons flying away, and the bodies collapsing to the roof, all because of the choice he had made. Unconsciously, he rubbed his hands together, trying to clean them, but nothing would wash the stain of killing from his body or his mind. He would have to live with it forever. Killing for whatever reason was a bad thing, a bad thing. He desperately wished he'd used the stunner instead.

After a time, he lifted his head to Borg. "How do you do it?"

Borg stared back at him before answering, then growled. "It is not a thing lightly done, my friend. Never let it be so. It is one thing to kill to eat, it is quite another to kill for a cause. Always, always, it is the last resort. Come, we should return to the ship. They will be anxious."

Val stood up, though his strength had fled. He made his way slowly to the street, then looked up and down the street as if seeing it for the very first time. It was like a new day had dawned for him, and he was not sure he liked it.

Vehicles and creatures of every description packed the street, though he did not see any Corvolds among them. He turned left toward the port, and Borg fell in beside him. As they rounded the first corner, Val stopped in astonishment. To all appearances, there lay a beggar sound asleep through all the hubbub. He crutched over to Ensign Vorgaskia and removed the filthy blanket.

Borg noted the uniform immediately and sniffed the body. "He is not dead."

"No. I stunned him. They were going to kill him, so I stunned all of them. It was the only way to save him."

Borg reached out and turned Val's face to him. "Today you have killed, but you also saved a life, maybe many lives. Do not focus only on the killing."

"I take it Daughter is okay?"

"She was never in any danger. The moment Otis received Krys' report, he moved the meeting to another location."

Val was confused. "Then why all this? Why did *Resolve* show up?"

"Had we been able to contact you, we would have recalled you and let the local authorities deal with this. As it was, you could not be reached, and we had no way of knowing your plan, so we could only support you. We let the Corvolds believe nothing had changed, even though it had. Ensign Vorgaskia made a brief handshake with the network which allowed us to locate him, then you. Once we had a location, we could act, and we did. What happened to your communicator?"

Val stared at the Great Cat with wide eyes. "This was all for *me*?"

"It was, though it has served the authorities well. There is now no question about what these Corvolds were up to. Prior to them firing at me, the evidence was all circumstantial."

Val stared at the Great Cat aghast. Daughter's security had ended up protecting him, not her. He knew suddenly that he had erred, erred gravely. His look was all the Great Cat needed.

"Do not sell yourself short, Val. You are part of our team, and we do not abandon our team members. What happened to your communicator?"

Val shook his head in dismay, answering absently, "I turned it off. I didn't want it chirping at the wrong time. Beggars don't usually carry communicators."

Borg pushed back the hood and studied Val's face. "You're injured."

"No, just part of the disguise. As a beggar, I can go most places unobserved. It served me well today, though I wish I had not turned off the communicator. Artmis will fix me up as soon as he can."

"I think you can discard the cloak now. It has served its purpose."

"No. I'll return it to its owner. Let's get Ensign Vorgaskia picked up."

"I've already called for a ride. He can go with us."

"Uh, do you mind if I walk? I'm not ready to face her yet, or anyone else for that matter. Especially Otis."

"As you wish."

* * * * *

He'd never seen Daughter so mad. The moment he entered her

quarters, she came from behind her desk, her eyes as threatening as the business end of a blaster.

"Don't you *ever* do anything like that again," she vented. "What were you thinking? I have all these ships and sailors here to protect me, and you take it on your own shoulders . . ." She stopped inches in front of him, suddenly aware that a lost, dirty, smelly, and forlorn young man stood before her. "Val?" she asked softly.

He hung his head. "I'm sorry, My Lady."

She lifted his chin. "Sorry for what?"

"For leading Ensign Vorgaskia and Borg into danger. And . . . I killed two men today."

"Oh, I see." She gathered him in her arms and held him, sensing if not seeing the tears running down his face. She knew he wouldn't want her to see the tears. "I'm so, so sorry." Then to herself she mumbled, "What have I done? He's far too young to be a part of this. I should have seen that sooner."

"No, My Lady," his muffled voice sounded. "We're not too young. Just don't send us away. Please. Not yet."

She kissed his head and squeezed him tighter.

* * * * *

Basaggit was two days behind them when Daughter called Val to her quarters. When he arrived, he found Krys, Otis, and Captain Jzazbe in attendance. Daughter sat behind her desk, and Otis sat beside the desk with his tail curled around his feet. Jzazbe stood off to the side, and Krys sat on the edge of a chair, her eyes hooded.

Otis spoke first. "You know you erred back on Basaggit."

"I do, Sir."

"In what ways did you err?"

Everyone he held most dear to him was in this room, and he was about to receive the worst chewing out of his life. He felt the blood rushing to his face, but he knew he had failed Otis, and in failing Otis, he had failed Daughter. Whatever punishment he had coming, he deserved. He squared his shoulders and lifted his chin,

"Lots of ways, sir, but most important, I failed you. I failed to heed the advice you gave me when I first came aboard *Resolve.*"

"And that was . . .?"

"I failed to use all the resources at my disposal, just as I did with the crystals on Hespra III. Then, I acted alone in spite of you and your team of Protectors. On Basaggit I not only had the resources represented by you and your team, I had the full resources of Captain Jzazbe and the squadron, the local police, and Daughter. Time was short, and I chose to act without consulting any of you, and there was time to do so."

"Why didn't you?"

Val's gaze dropped to the deck, but a moment later it lifted back to Otis. "At the time, it felt right, sir. Krys notified Captain Jzazbe who notified you and Daughter, so I knew Daughter would be safe, but I wanted to make certain. I had the skills to follow the Corvold, and I believed the situation would be manageable."

"What if there had been other Corvolds, other weapons?"

"Exactly, sir. My focus was too small."

"Again."

"Yes, sir."

Otis stared at Val for a long while. He turned to Daughter and a look full of meaning passed between the two of them, her eyes glittering in triumph. His muzzle swung back to Val, then he rose and padded toward Val, circling him, then coming to a stop with his muzzle inches away from Val's face. Their gazes locked.

"I am not easily pleased, but your words please me, young man. Tell me, what would you do differently now?"

"The sole purpose of everyone here, including me, is to ensure the safety of Daughter. My focus should have been that, and only that. Catching the Corvolds was important, but it paled in comparison to Daughter's safety."

"Precisely." Otis turned away, growling low in his throat as he prowled the room.

Val had never seen the Great Cat so agitated, and he continued staring straight ahead, fearful of what might come.

Otis padded back into his field of view. "Listen carefully, Val. Do not misunderstand my words. To survive on Hespra III, you developed a survival mechanism that depended solely on your own abilities. That must change. To lead in the manner of a fleet officer, you must learn to command others, to use them as your resources. You must force yourself to overcome this serious shortcoming if you want to succeed. Understood?"

"Yes, sir."

"And that brings us to my responsibilities. I, too, am responsible for Daughter's safety. I use all of my resources to ensure success. In this particular case, my need was not just to thwart this attack, it was to prevent future attacks by the Corvolds, attacks that might have come without forewarning." He looked to Krys, his gaze softening, then his gaze hardened again and he turned back to Val. His lips lifted, displaying a feral leer. "That need has been met. The Corvold survivors have directly implicated the senior Corvold leadership, and the Empire is now empowered to intervene. I do not believe we will have a repeat performance by the Corvolds."

Val squirmed, remembering the meeting so long ago between Sir Jarl and the Corvolds. "They're not all bad, sir."

Daughter spoke up. "I have not forgotten that it was the warning from a few heroic Corvolds that resulted in my ultimate rescue. Our response will be balanced, but the Corvold leadership will suffer. In time, it will be restored from within, but that is not your concern."

Val nodded, knowing he was out of his depth here.

Otis didn't give him long to squirm. "You're a loner, Val, and it's something you have to change, but know this: we Protectors are loners, too. We've learned to use all our resources, but at heart, we, too, are loners. We always trust our instincts. Your instincts told you to go after the Corvold, to search out and deal with the threat. It was the wrong thing for you to do, but it was also the best thing to do. The operation you set up and carried out to prevent another assassination attempt was simple and effective. It would have brought honor even to my Protectors."

Otis brought a fist to his chest. "I salute you, Val. You have twice answered the call of duty, a duty to which you have not even sworn the appropriate oath. You are a Protector of the first rank, and you are a credit to this fleet and the Empire we all serve."

Val stared at him, his jaw hanging open, speechless. Had he heard right? Had Otis just forgiven him?

Otis lowered his hand and sat, his gaze locked on Val's. "I know what you're thinking, young man. No, I have not forgiven you. You must learn to lead others, not just yourself. But I honor you, as well."

Val didn't know it, focused as he was on Otis, but Daughter looked to Jzazbe and nodded.

Jzazbe waited until he sensed Val had digested Otis' words, then he spoke. "Cadet Val, look at me." Val turned to him, his commanding officer.

"Three things define the best fleet officers," Jzazbe said: "intellect, leadership, and knowledge of their job. Intellect is something you either have or don't have, and you have it. We've been giving you knowledge, and we'll continue to do so as long as you're on this ship, but there's no way we're prepared to teach you leadership. Still, you showed leadership in setting up your operation to save Daughter, including convincing a reluctant ensign to follow your orders. Time was short, but you developed a plan and you assigned duties. That took quick, accurate thinking, which falls under the category of intellect and leadership in my book.

"In terms of knowledge, you used knowledge none of us have and never will have. You used what you knew and chose to become a beggar again, the perfect disguise for the operation you set up. You encountered difficulties, and you chose rightly. In choosing rightly, I include here your saving the life of a fellow crewmember.

"You *are* going to the Academy, Val. We're going to do something now that will ensure that you either excel or fail. We're going to make your job there harder, a lot harder."

Val gulped, confused. "Sir?"

"Rarely does a commissioned officer go through the Academy. Commissioning comes after the Academy. As a commissioned officer, you're going to attract a lot more attention than you'll want, you're going to get the hardest jobs, and you will no doubt frequently regret what I am about to do here. These great reasons to the contrary, I invite you to take the oath. Will you?"

"Sir?" He turned to Daughter. "My Lady?"

Daughter stood up and came around her desk to face Val. "This is between you and Captain Jzazbe. I am not in favor of this, you're far too young, but I know the full measure of its meaning to you. I suspect you know the commissioning words by heart. Will you say them?"

"I, Cadet Val . . ."

"Not to me, Val. Raise your right hand and face Captain Jzazbe."

Val turned to Jzazbe with his hand raised, palm out. "I swear allegiance to the throne. I swear . . ."

He had it word for word, of course. When he was done, Jzazbe removed two pins from a pocket. "Cadet Val, I hereby award this field commission to you and welcome you to the ranks of Empire officers." He removed Val's cadet pins and replaced them with the pins of a real officer, an ensign.

Jzazbe stood back and saluted Val, and Val returned the salute, then reached out a shaking hand to Jzazbe.

"Is this real, sir?"

"It's real, Ensign Val. You are officially an Empire officer. This is such a rare occurrence that it automatically qualifies you for entrance to an Academy of your choice. It does not, however, guarantee graduation. Understood?"

Val gulped, grateful for his crutch. His knee felt weak. "I

understand, sir. Thank you, sir."

"We're not done yet, Val," he heard from far away.

He turned to Daughter, though his mind had not yet fully digested Jzazbe's words.

Daughter's hand was held out before him. "Do you recognize these?" she asked. In the palm of her hand rested two rings of tiny, glistening stars.

Val blinked as he focused on her words. "Uh, they're part of everyone's insignia of rank, My Lady."

"Not everyone's, Val. The stars symbolize the Crown. They are awarded only to those who directly serve the Royal Family. They are worn beside your rank. Whatever rank you ever attain, you will always have the privilege of wearing the crowns, which are awarded only to the Queen's Own. I don't know if the Academy will let you wear your rank of ensign, but they will never prohibit you from displaying the crown. I hope you do so with pride. You will certainly do so with my blessing."

She attached the pins to both sides of his collar and stepped back, saying, "I hereby recognize you, Val, as a fleet ensign in the Queen's Own."

Val didn't know what to do, so he kneeled before her with his head down. She gave him a moment to gather himself, then lifted his chin.

"Stand, Ensign Val and be recognized."

He stood, and Krys threw her arms around him in delight. "I'm so proud of you," she whispered in his ear.

Captain Jzazbe was next. Val didn't know whether to salute him or what. Jzazbe just stuck out his hand and they shook. "I'm proud to have you as a member of the Queen's Own," he said. "I hope it doesn't complicate things too much for you at the Academy. Competition there is fierce and you'll be singled out by your peers and your instructors, but I happen to think you're up to it. Your duties here will remain unchanged for the present."

"Uh, what about Ensign Vorgaskia? Is he in trouble?"

"He is not. He had a difficult decision to make, and he chose well. Daughter's safety always comes first. It's what the Queen's Own are all about. A commendation is already in his file, and a promotion is not far away."

Daughter dismissed Jzazbe, then it was just the four of them. She took a seat and motioned for Val and Krys to sit on the couch before her.

"Rrestriss has agreed to accept both of you as students. The choice is yours. What do you say?"

Krys stared at her with eyes that suddenly spilled tears. "I'm not ready to leave you yet. This is the only home I have ever known, and I like it here."

Daughter's gaze softened. "Nor am I ready for you to leave. You two brighten my every day . . . well, when I'm not frightened to death for you," she added, glancing at Val. "There's no hurry to leave, only to make the decision. Once made, it will take time to change my schedule. If you go, I want to drop you off. I want to personally introduce you to a people I cherish."

Krys looked stricken. When her lower lip began trembling, Val put an arm around her shoulders.

"I have to go, Krys," he said softly. He reached out a hand and turned her chin to him. "You don't."

"I won't leave you, and I want an education."

His lips tightened. "You won't be with me when I go to the Academy. You know that. You could get an education right here. You're already getting an education here. And think about her need," he said, pointing his chin toward Daughter. "Seer or not, your knowing the purpose of that gun probably saved her life. Your being here might be the best thing for both of you."

Krys opened her mouth to speak, but no words came out. Daughter stepped into the breach. "The education you get here will never compare with what you will learn from the Rress, my dear. There is simply no comparison. I need you to go."

Krys jumped to her feet, angry. "No, Mother. I'm not ready . . ." She stared at Daughter in horror, then collapsed to one knee, her head bowed deeply. "I'm sorry, My Lady. I didn't mean . . ." She stopped speaking, not certain what she wanted to say.

Daughter's attention suddenly focused on Krys, her mind shifting from school on Rrestriss to the waif of a girl before her. Krys had called her 'Mother.' An accidental slip, yes, but the relationship Krys called into being with that one simple word had come from the heart. With a warm look in her eyes, she went to Krys and pulled her to her feet, her arms going around the anxious young woman in an embrace.

"You honor me, child, more than words can ever say. You've never known a mother, and I've never known a child of my own, but I will forever cherish what you just gave me. In my mind, during the past months you've both become my family. I *am* your mother at the moment. I will be your mother for as long as you will let me."

"Is forever too long?" Krys sobbed into her shoulder.

Tears flowed from both sets of eyes, copiously. "May I call you daughter?" Daughter asked softly into Krys' ear.

Krys squeezed harder. "I love you, Mother. Proper or not, I love you. I can't leave."

Daughter lifted her eyes to Val. "How about you, Val? Are we one happy family here?"

He, too, had risen to his feet, but he stood frozen in place. "My Lady, I'm an Empire officer in service to you."

"Oh, don't be so full of yourself. Come here and give me a hug."

He stared at the two of them. What he saw called to him like nothing else ever had. When Krys reached an arm out to him, he went to them with his arms around both. "I *am* part of a family. I have a mother and a sister. Whoever would have thought . . ."

Chapter Forty-nine

Resolve landed on Lianli. The problem Daughter had come to resolve was another dual claim issue, but this time one of the claimants was the district governor himself. Lianli was scheduled for colonization, an issue always high on governors' lists of things to accomplish during their tenure. The world had no sentient races, and its ecology was perfect for colonization, but a mining company had discovered huge, valuable deposits of a rare metal used in the manufacture of space ship hulls. The deposits were easily accessible and a successful test dig, a mile long strip mine, had already been completed by automated machines. If free to spread, the mines would, in time, cover a significant portion of the planet. That was unacceptable on a world planned for colonization.

Normally the sector governor would decide claims of this nature, and he had done so, but so valuable was the metal that the mining company had appealed the decision to the Queen. Both parties argued a legitimate claim to strategic Empire need, and it was up to Daughter to settle the matter.

Testings by Daughter were not anticipated this time. She hoped to find compromise and had several ideas in mind, including the fact that the metal was not going anywhere and would be available for later generations to mine. She was leaning in that direction, but she had to hear arguments from both sides, and she had no doubt that both sides would argue hard.

She decided to see the world for herself, so the meeting was held on Lianli instead of the district headquarters.

Resolve landed at a spaceport that was just an unimproved field. This world was still in the raw exploration stage. Daughter's meeting was scheduled for mid-day local time, and Captain Jzazbe, always thoughtful of Daughter's needs, adjusted his arrival time so that shipboard time would be the same as local time. Daughter would not be at a disadvantage from lack of sleep, though the other participants might be, depending on how long they'd been on the planet. The governor's representative had traveled far for this meeting, and she suspected the senior mining representative had done the same.

Krys and Val had been cleared to venture out on the surface, and though there was little to do or see, both looked forward to experiencing a primitive world unspoiled, as yet, by civilization.

Krys stepped from the ramp to the ground. The moment both feet touched the ground, she stiffened. Val, right beside her, had seen this before, and his focus became just her. She didn't stay in the trance long, and when she came out of it, she was in a hurry.

"Back to the ship, Val. We have a job to do."

"Uh . . . what job?"

"We've been called to a meeting. I'm not certain where, but it's not far."

"You're taking the ship? You must be kidding."

"I'm not kidding. I have some preparations to make. Will you advise Captain Jzazbe that we're leaving as soon as Daughter returns?"

"No! She's not done here yet. What's this all about? Where are we going?"

"Not off planet. We're going to a field, just an ordinary field in the wilderness."

"Krys, I can't order Captain Jzazbe."

She bit her lip. "No, you can't. Just tell him to make preparations. We'll wait for Daughter to return. She'll agree, Val. Tell him that. Now go! I have a lot to do."

He gave her a questioning look. "Have you had a vision?"

"Sort of. More of a calling."

He went to Jzazbe expecting argument, but Jzazbe took him seriously. "We're always ready to go at a moment's notice, Ensign. Is Daughter in danger?"

"I don't think so, sir. It's something else, something very

different. Thank you, sir."

He bolted from the bridge and returned to Krys. She wasn't in their room, so he went to Daughter's quarters. Krys was just entering with her arms full of clothing.

"Those look suspiciously like something from the orphanage," he challenged.

"They are. I gave the ship my shift for a sample, so they're all the same, just different sizes."

"I'll just wear my uniform."

"No, you won't. My instructions were to wear only clothing made of natural fibers. We will not carry weapons or communicators or anything else of Empire manufacture."

"Otis will never go for it."

"He has to abide by my rules this time. He and Mother both."

"*Your* rules?"

She stared at him, but there was no uncertainty in her look. "I don't know who's rules they are, but we're going."

Daughter was tired when she got back. The meeting had not gone well, and she was not in the mood for Val and Krys at the moment.

"What is it?" she asked as soon as she noticed them. Her eyes narrowed. "You're dressed oddly."

Krys stood. "I have a similar garment for you, Mother. I'm sorry, but your day is not done. We've been called to another meeting."

"Not today. I've heard enough for one day. I'm taking a nice long bath."

"This is not optional, Mother. We've been called to a meeting. I don't know why or by whom, but we are to go to a barren field not too far from here and wait. The call is strong. You cannot dismiss it."

Daughter took a step back. "You've had another vision?"

"Not like any vision I've ever had before, but yes. You have to wear this," she said, holding out a plain shift.

Daughter changed swiftly and they went to the bridge. Jzazbe was ready, but he didn't know where to go. Krys pointed her arm, and he had the pilot lift the ship and fly in the direction she pointed. He brought the outside view to a forward screen, and Krys peered intently.

Suddenly, she pointed. "There. That field near the tree line. Do not land, Captain. The ship is not to touch the ground. Just lower the ramp and we'll step off." She turned to Daughter. "Val and I will go first. I'll call for Otis next – he has to assure himself of your safety, then he'll call you. The rest of the Protectors will have to remain at a distance, but they can be nearby." She turned to Otis. "I'm sorry, but it has to be this way."

"Who are we going to meet, and why? I don't want you and Val going out alone."

"I can't say who, and I can't say why, but I know there is no threat here today." She turned to Daughter. "Nothing artificial is to touch the ground. We three are dressed in simple gowns made of natural fibers, and we'll go barefoot. Otis and his men are already barefoot." She looked at the weapons belt strapped to his body. "It would be better if you left that behind."

He growled low in his throat. "You ask too much, child."

"It is not me asking. I'm following instructions."

"And you don't know whose instructions."

"I don't. You once spoke to me of dreams, of how your people believe in dreams and spirits and demons. Otis, had this been your dream, you would go, and you would comply with the instructions without hesitation. I sense rightness here, and you would, too."

Otis looked into her eyes. What he sensed in those eyes was not the adolescent demand of a timid young girl whom Daughter called Seer, it was the look of the woman she might someday become. Her eyes did not demand, they commanded.

His great head nodded respectfully. "As you wish."

* * * * *

Krys and Val stepped from the ship's ramp to a field that stretched all the way to the tree line. She took his hand, and the two of them moved toward the trees some 100 meters distant.

Krys studied Val as he crutched beside her. "You seem to be struggling," she noted.

He grimaced. "I've grown, and the crutch is a little short. It's worse on this soft surface. I wish I'd replaced it before leaving Hespra III."

"I'm sure we could make you a new one."

He nodded. "I will, but I like this one. It has just the right indentation for my hand, and I'm used to its balance. I might see if the Chief can make an extension. Most likely, he'll show me how to do it myself. It's how we do things, but I'm afraid it will be unbalanced. We'll see."

They covered half the distance, then Krys just settled to the ground facing the trees. Val settled beside her and stared across the field at the trees, his crutch ready in his hand in case of trouble.

The trees were dead, just limbs and dried leaves, though here and there the bright green of new leaves peeked through the brown. The trunks were massive. Ten men standing with outstretched arms would not reach around them.

He focused all his senses, reaching out for anything. He felt a gentle breeze coming from his right, but it carried no clues. He sniffed, and the smells spoke of nature, not the comfortable smells of the city, and they were unfamiliar to him. His eyes roved, but the only motion he detected was a slight waving of tree branches. He listened, but he only heard the occasional twittering of birds amidst the rustle of leaves in the trees. The very absence of sound bothered him, and he focused his hearing more sharply, to no avail. He tasted, but all he sensed was the dryness of the dusty field. He felt the ground with his hand, but his hand only touched dirt and grass.

His vision was his best armor, and it was the first to detect change. He saw motion near the tree line, but it was too low to see clearly. He raised his crutch to stand for a better look, but Krys stopped him.

"Remain seated, Val."

The motion was slow, and it took a long time for him to make out what was coming, then he gasped. A line of five tree limbs approached them, each some four feet in length. Gnarled wood formed the body of each, a body festooned with short branches to form arms and legs and . . . more branches. Each branch grew dried, brown leaves, including four long legs that sprouted their own short branches and leaves. A longer, gnarled branch formed a neck tipped with a large, vertically held leaf, more or less triangular. The large leaf had to be a head, though no eyes, ears, or mouth were apparent. There was nothing of beauty, just a dead, brown leaf, almost transparent. Small ribbed veins spread from the main rib to the very edges of the leaf. There was no room for a brain in the thin head, at least he didn't think there was room, but these creatures clearly moved under their own power. Val knew that these perfectly camouflaged creatures would be invisible in the dead-looking forest, whether high up in trees or as dead branches fallen to the ground.

Krys looked back toward the ship. All six Protectors had spread out around her, Val, and the leaf creatures. They were ready, but they held as the creatures approached. Daughter stood on the ramp, ready to step off when called. Krys nodded her head, pleased.

The creatures stopped side by side before Val and Krys. One reached out to Val's crutch and took it into its hands. It backed away and scratched a shallow depression in the ground, then bent forward with one hand to the depression. A clear liquid leaked from its fingers, almost as if it was urinating, and the depression filled with the moisture. The bottom of Val's crutch went into the liquid, then the creature began running its hands up and down the smooth, dried wood of the crutch. Soon, the crutch lost its rigidity, became supple, then Val stopped watching: two of the creatures had reached a hand out, one to him and one to Krys.

The fingers on the end of the hand resembled branches, and along each finger more tiny branches stuck out, ending in leaves, but the tips of the fingers looked soft and round. Krys reached up with one hand to let each of her fingers touch the tips of the fingers on the proffered hand. The moment she did, a warm smile lit her face.

Val followed her example, touching a fingertip to each of the fingers held out before him. He was suddenly filled with a sense of peace, of harmony with the world around him, with himself, and with this creature of leaves. He felt the love this creature held for all things living and not living, and he knew he was included.

His awareness grew, and he suddenly sensed Krys and the creature she touched. He knew her thoughts, felt her happiness and her completeness, and from the creature of leaves she touched, he sensed the bond between all of these creatures, their oneness with everything around them, including the sky above, the dried grasses and dirt of the field he and Krys sat upon, the forest of trees before them, the wonderful stream running through that forest, and the rest of the leaf people in the forest. He felt the awareness of thousands, then millions of similar creatures among the trees, all united through the bond he was now a part of. He closed his eyes, savoring the perfectness of the world through these creatures' senses.

Krys turned her head and beckoned to Otis. He came and sat beside Val, lifting his hand to the third creature in the line. The moment those fingers touched, Val sensed Otis, almost as if they were on the net in the ship, but this was far more complete. He sensed the savagery Otis always held in check just below the surface, but he sensed so much more, as well. He sensed instinct, strong instinct, and he sensed strength and duty and honor. He sensed an awareness of self within the surroundings, each person and thing in high relief, perfectly positioned with reality. He sensed the love Otis held for Daughter, and to his surprise, he sensed the love Otis held for him and Krys. Otis sensed him and Krys, then he sensed the rest of the creatures and their thoughts, and he reveled in a peace and harmony never felt by him before this day. He savored, and as he savored he relaxed as much as it was possible for a

Great Cat to relax.

At a thought from one of the creatures, Otis turned his head and beckoned Daughter to join them. His eyes lifted to the rest of his team and he spoke. "There is no threat here. More will come. You are to let them approach without restriction. Believe me as you believe in the spirits of your ancestors."

Daughter joined them, and Val instantly sensed her hesitation. This mind link was akin to what she did during a Testing, and the results of Testings had to remain private. A complete melding of her mind with others would be against all tradition.

The leaf creature before Krys spoke to Daughter. "You need not fear, child. We will not break a trust. Let yourself go. Feel the love we hold for you."

Daughter, alone of the four, hesitated. She sensed the feelings this creature held for her and for all, but she was a Chosen, and the Chosen must know. She released the one whose fingers she touched. Val felt the release as a physical break, and a piece of the aura dissipated.

Daughter went to the leaf creature before Krys. He seemed to be in charge. She lifted both hands to his leaf head and stared hard into the face of the leaf before her.

More words found their way to his mind. "Oh, you are a bold one. *You would Test me?* Test away, my dear, but beware, you might learn more than you wish."

Her hands shook, but she kept them in place. What happened between the two, Val would never know, nor would any of the others, but Daughter held to her Test for a long time. Then, still holding her hands to the face, she knelt on both knees before it with her head bowed, tears cascading from her eyes. She spoke just loud enough for Val, Krys, and Otis to hear: "I know truth as I have never known it before. In all whom I have Tested, no matter how wonderful the person, and I include myself, there is always a dark side. In you I find only light. There is no dark. This Chosen has Tested you and finds you True."

She removed her hands from the leaf creature and turned to the Protectors waiting behind. "Whatever takes place here today, you are to hold. We are among friends and will not be harmed in any way. There is no coercion here. I say this as Chosen." She returned to her original place and touched her fingers to the leaf creature before her.

Communicating with these creatures did not need words. Thoughts and feelings pervaded, and they were all that mattered. The four visitors soon found themselves among the trees, and they understood. Each of the individual leaf people was just one small part of a whole, but the whole was much more inclusive than they imagined. Their thoughts flew across the world, joining with millions and billions of individual leaf people. They never lost sense of individuals, but, too, they sensed the greater oneness of the individuals as they became the Whole. The Whole carried them across the world, their beautiful world, the world with which they were one, then the four visitors found themselves on the border of the strip mine.

The thoughts of the Whole focused on the great scar in the ground. The four visitors learned that the leaf people congregated and grew along the very courses of metal and minerals being mined by the newcomers to their world. The homes of millions of leaf people had gone away here, scraped away without pity. The very concept saddened the four, but for Otis the vision was one of horror, and he literally cried out for the lost trees. His own people had gone through a similar culling two thousand years ago, and they had nearly succumbed.

Daughter reached out mentally to him, enveloping him with understanding and compassion. "It will not happen again, my friend. We will stop it now, just as we stopped it then. We thought this world held no sentient life, but we were wrong. This world is already settled. We will designate it as an emerging world, and no one will be allowed to come here."

They were suddenly back in the field where they had started. The creature standing before Krys let all of them know that this was not the purpose of the meeting. The awful scar upon the surface of this world was but a scratch compared to what was coming. He carried their thoughts with him on a journey, first to the sky, then beyond the sky and into space. A beautiful world hung below them, a jewel, but his thoughts did not stop there. He took them further, to several neighboring stars where they sensed the feelings of all the many beings living on worlds circling those stars. When they got over their surprise, he took them further, out into the Empire where they felt the life forces of so, so many. He carried them through the Empire, then beyond, and everywhere they went, they sensed life, life in many forms but life that was always the same. Birth, living, loving, creating new life, guiding the young, dying: all these things were experienced by all living creatures, and it was right.

They circled the galaxy in their thoughts, never far from life, then they went further. First a neighboring galaxy, then galaxies farther away and farther away yet. Everywhere, life differed, but what those lives sought remained the same. Living came first, but equally important, life everywhere sought love, to be loved and to love in return. Love was the fountain of life, and from it everything else flowed.

They turned back, but as they drew closer to the boundary of their Empire, they sensed change. They still sensed life, but that life was not healthy. Love was diminished, unfocused as survival became the foundation of life's purpose.

Sadness filled the thoughts of their tour guide, and they found themselves back in the field they had once considered barren. Now, they knew this place in its fullness as part of something so much more. They sensed each other again and exchanged looks of amazement and wonder.

Deep growls sounded from around them, from the Protectors, and they looked up to see the trees disintegrating. Millions of leaf creatures were abandoning their perches, crawling down to the ground. Soon, the trees were bare and a vast swarm of leaf creatures made their way toward the small group. Dust rose from the swarm and a soft shushing sounded as the many, many feet rustled through the tall grass.

Otis turned to his men. "Hold. There is no threat."

It took a while, but the four were eventually surrounded by a living sea of the leaf creatures. Each of the creatures was in contact with each other, and as such they were the Whole. The four from the ship, still linked to the leaf creatures through their fingertips, sensed this and were not afraid.

Part Three – You Are Called

Chapter Fifty

Aboard Beta IV, Val was nearly done with his story. One meal had been served in the Queen's quarters, and it was nearly time for the next. His story had been long, longer than he'd intended, but Mike and Reba deserved to know all of it. People's lives had changed in the clearing on Lianli that day, or perhaps become more complete depending on your perspective. In any case, Mike and Reba were now a part of that completeness.

Everyone had been sitting for hours. Val now stood, his primary focus his First Knight. "There we were, surrounded by thousands of leaf creatures. We had no idea what their purpose was, but we soon found out. They called six individuals to duties that remained unexplained. In calling us, they also Named us.

"I'll tell you who they called, but first I want to tell you the parting words of the leaf creature who stood before Krys. He seemed to be in charge, though I believe he simply represented the rest of his people to us. I have studied his words at length, and I held to them during my long incarceration aboard this vessel.

"He said, *'We do not have all answers. The future is not preordained. Many paths, many outcomes are possible. Choices are yours to make, and the consequences of those choices are yours to shoulder.'"*

"You speak of heavy burdens, Val."

"*He* spoke of heavy burdens, Sire, but he left us with the means to shoulder them. The exact words of his gift are the following: '*Listen to your heart, always. If you do, you will know what is right. You will never be asked to do more.'"*

The Queen, Otis, and Val had spent years considering those words. Val let silence fill the Queen's quarters for a little while as Mike and Reba's thoughts went internal.

"Before leaving us that day, Sire, he left us with one more gift: '*Other Great Ones await your call, for they, too, are called, and they, too, listen with their hearts. You will know them for who they are.'"*

Mike stared at him for a long time. He turned to look at Reba and found, for the first time ever, tears coursing down her cheeks. Val, too, noticed, and he went to her with a handkerchief and wiped at the tears.

"Your story is beautiful, all of it," she said to him. "I wish I could have been there with you. I almost feel like I was."

He smiled fondly at her. "Maybe you were, My Lady, if only in spirit, for you are called."

"Me?"

"Yes, you. Let me say the words again: '*Other Great Ones await your call, for they, too, are called, and they, too, listen with their hearts. You will know them for who they are.'* I knew the moment I saw you in the net aboard *Resolve*, and I have known every moment since. I call you in the name of the leaf people, Reba."

Ellie spoke. "I know your heart, Reba. It is true, and I, too, call you in their name. Just as we were called, you are called to stop this horror that is spreading through our Empire."

Reba's hand went to Val's hand on her shoulder. She pulled his hand away and took it in both of her own. Her shining eyes remained locked on Val's. "I hear your call, Val, and I accept."

Still holding that hand, she turned to Ellie. "I hear your call as well, Your Majesty, and I accept."

Mike's gaze moved between them. The hairs on the back of his head stood up. "Such a calling is not a kindness," he said softly.

Otis padded up to him. He didn't sit this time, he put his face right into Mike's face. "It is not a kindness, Sire. There are no assurances we will prevail, and there are no assurances we will survive the process. You made a commitment to me once back on Earth, a commitment you fought against for a time. What convinced you to side with us that day?"

Mike squirmed, suddenly uncomfortable in front of his friends. That had been a very private moment for him, a very private decision. "Does it matter? We got the job done. Isn't that what's important?"

Otis stayed in his face. "What convinced you, Sire?"

"Well . . . actually . . . it was you. You said I couldn't not agree, and you were right."

"And why couldn't you not agree?"

"Otis, there were billions, maybe trillions of people out there counting on us. What's one person when it comes to that?"

"They're still out there, Sire, and they're still calling. We're not done yet. We're not here because of the leaf people. We're not here because of our positions in the Empire. We are here because we listen to our hearts, and they speak true."

"Ellie speaks true. The rest of us are not bound by her constraints."

"But our hearts speak true to ourselves, Sire. Yours, mine, Her Majesty's, Val's, Reba's, and others yet to be called. You cannot deny that."

"Nor can I prove it."

"You don't have to prove it. That's what the leaf people gave us. They gave us the means to trust within our small group. All of us have accepted the call of our people. We'd be here giving everything that we are even without the leaf people's intervention. What they have given us is the means to trust each other and to know that each other speaks true."

"You speak of a higher calling, even higher than the call Ellie made when she knighted me. Am I to serve two masters?"

Otis stepped back a step, his head angled in a question. *"To what do you think she called you, Sire?* Don't you get it? Do you think she didn't know?"

The two stared at each other for a long time, their thoughts coming to the same place. "Refuse if you can," Otis said softly, his eyes never blinking.

"You know I can't."

Otis nodded. "In the days to come, I suspect that each of us will at some points regret our decision. For me it was never a choice, but if it was, I would choose no different. It is who I am."

Ellie went to Otis and put her arms around him. "It is who you are, my friend. In all our years together, I have never seen you waver from that."

"Nor have I seen you waver, Your Majesty. There have been, and there will continue to be times when the wind forces us to lean a little."

"There will, but within our small group we will be true. Val, why don't you finish your story?"

Val nodded. "We're almost done. There we were, sitting in a dry, dusty field surrounded by thousands of leaf people. All of them were in contact with each other, and as such they were the Whole. Through their representatives with whom we still maintained contact we sensed all this and were not afraid.

"Krys became the focus of the head leaf creature. He spoke to her, though his thoughts carried to the minds of all. He said, *'You are our Messenger. Your struggle will be mighty. When your need is greatest, the Guide will find you. Give all that you are, for you are more than you know. I call both of you.'*

"I know what you're going to ask, Sire. We don't know who the Guide is."

Mike's lips thinned. "Where is she?"

"I don't know."

"We should find her. She's important."

"She might be better equipped to find us, Sire."

He nodded with pursed lips. "Indeed. I was mentioned in one of her visions, and I don't like the feeling it gives me. Now, maybe it's starting to make more sense."

"I'm glad to hear that, Sire. Artmis and I were called that day, as well."

"And your title was what?"

"Let me finish with the others, Sire. Otis was next. What did he say to you, Otis?"

"His exact words were, *'The Protector. You heed the call of past generations, but future generations now call upon you. Protect well, my friend, for they are counting on you. Hear their call, for it is mine as well.'*"

Val nodded. "The Queen, who was Daughter at the time, was the last in line. What were his words for you, Mother?"

She looked at him, but since Val already knew what she was about to say, she turned her focus to Mike. "He seemed to study me for a time, then suddenly his thoughts hardened. He spoke almost angrily. *'Mother of future generations. You test for truth, but who tests the tester?'* Then just as suddenly, his thoughts softened, and I almost felt like he was holding me in his arms, comforting me like a father would a daughter. He said, *'The answer lies in your people. Do not fail them. Heed their call, for you are called as no other Chosen before you has been called.'"*

Mike stared at her as she spoke. When she was done, he continued staring, blinking from time to time.

"Frightening words, are they not?" she asked. "Who am I to be called at this time, at this place, to have the hopes of future generations dependent on me?"

He shook his head. He had no answer.

She stood and came to him. He, too, stood. She reached her arms around him and pressed her body to his. "His words give me strength, Michael. I have accepted his call, and I accept the call of my people."

She released one arm from around his waist and turned to the others. "I am the Last of the Chosen. Hear me well: until a Chosen stands free in the Palace, I will not yield so long as there is breath in my body."

Reba took a step forward and went to one knee, her head bowed. "I stand with you, My Queen."

Val, Otis, and Jessie followed her example, though none needed to speak the words. Reba had spoken for all of them.

Mike loosened his grip around Ellie to follow their example, but she held tight to his waist, reaching a hand up to caress his face. "Never you, Michael, for you are the Knight."

"You mean First Knight."

"That, too." She studied his eyes for a time, then turned to the others. "Rise, all of you. Never kneel before me again. Instead, stand with me. Stand united with me."

Reba, Val, and Otis stood and came to her. Arms reached out, joining one to the other, not just in unity of purpose but in friendship.

Ellie stared solemnly at them. "If ever a Queen had a more intimate circle of advisors, I do not know of her. Thank you."

They broke for dinner. When they returned to the Queen's quarters, all showed the stress of a long day, but their day was not yet done.

Mike took the same chair he'd had all that day and decided to move the meeting along. "You're the last, Val. You still haven't told us what the Leaf Creature said to you."

"Almost, Sire, but six were called that day." He nodded to Ellie.

Ellie stood, then simply kneeled on both knees before Mike, taking his only available hand in hers. "The Leaf Creature told me to heed the call of my people, for I was called as no other Chosen before me had been called." She paused, then said softly, "He wasn't done, Michael. He said, and these are his exact words, *'The Knight will stand with you. Lean on him, love him if you will, but hear him well, for he holds the keys. Your Talents are nothing without the keys.'"*

Mike leaned away from her. The whole room fell silent, all eyes on him. He looked around at those eyes, eyes whose futures were, if he was, indeed, the Knight, dependent on him.

He knew her words should make him proud, even puffed up, but they did not. Nor did her words make him feel small. Instead, they felt right to him. Almost as if something that had been missing since the very beginning, since the Chessori spaceship fell from the skies that night, fell into place. A feeling of rightness washed through him. Suddenly, he knew his place was here, and it was the right place for him. He sat up straighter.

"You are the Knight," Ellie said softly.

He stared into her eyes and nodded. "I am. I have no keys."

"Not true. You've already shown us the way many times. There are more keys, I'm certain. You'll just have to find them."

It was just the two of them for the moment. He reached out and caressed her face. She leaned into his hand, but their gazes did not waver.

"It's in my nature to tell you that you have the wrong man," he said softly, intimately, "but you don't. Don't ask me how I know, because I can't tell you, but I know it's true. I'm the Knight." He looked briefly away from her to the ceiling. "I almost feel like he's here right now," he mumbled.

"Who's here, Michael?"

"The Leaf Man."

Tears filled Ellie's eyes. She had known for a long time that he was the Knight, but she had feared that her words would be difficult for him, maybe even destroy him. She should have known better.

"Maybe he is," she said softly. "Welcome to my world, finally."

"I'm a man from an emerging world, Ellie. I can't do this on my own, even if I find these keys, whatever they are."

"You won't have to. You'll have all of us in this room standing with you, and one in particular." She stood up and left his side. "Val, it's time to finish your story."

Mike, too, stood, his gaze on Val, demanding this time.

Val sensed the demand and responded, "In a moment, Sire. The Leaf Man, as you call him, said to me, *'Be strong and whole so that others will find their way. You have already shown that one leg is sufficient to carry the burden of duty, but what lies beyond duty?'"*

Mike's brow furrowed. "An interesting question. Do you know the answer?"

I didn't at the time, but I do now."

Mike blinked a few times as he considered. "And what is it that lies beyond duty, Val?"

"Duty focuses on self. Beyond self lies everyone and everything else. Different people might use different words, but for me, what lies beyond duty is Honor."

Mike considered for a long time before nodding. "And your title?"

Val ignored the question. "Had you been there, Sire, you would never need proof of the story I have told here today. Nevertheless, I stand before you as living proof. When the leaf creatures left us, I had trouble standing up to return to the ship. You see, they'd taken my crutch.

"As I told you at the beginning of this story, one of them had dug a hole and filled it with liquid from his own body, then he placed my crutch in the hole and started massaging the crutch. When I last saw it, the wood had turned supple. The leaf creature continued working on the crutch while we were otherwise occupied."

Mike's eyes misted. "No way . . ."

"Yes, way. The other Protectors later verified the facts. When the leaf people left us and we stood up, I discovered that I had two legs. The leaf creature had turned my crutch into a new leg."

Mike stared at him in wonder. Ellie came to his side and touched his arm. "I was there, Michael. Val speaks true."

Mike's head began swimming all of a sudden. Jake did whatever Riders do and he recovered, but Ellie noticed and reached out a hand to steady him. He didn't respond: his full attention was on Val. "What title were you given, Val?"

"I was named the Right Arm."

* * * * *

All of these things were known to Ellie, Val, and Otis, but for Mike and Reba it was all new. Both sat in silence for a time deep in contemplation. Ellie gave them time, but not a lot of time.

"That meeting took place almost thirteen years ago. Three of us here have had years to consider the implications of that day. You and Reba have not. You will, but not right now.

"Today we have focused on the past. Tomorrow we turn our attention to what lies in the future. Today I have formed my Inner Circle. At the moment, it is the five of us. Every Queen before me has relied on the advice of her Inner Circle, as will I. Within my Inner Circle titles are dropped. I expect each of you to speak freely and true, whether the words are welcome or not." She focused on Val. "You call me Mother, and I shall always cherish the name. Do you know my real name?"

"I do, Your Majesty. Krys spoke it long ago."

She nodded. "My name is Ellandra of the Chosen, but Mike has shortened it to Ellie, just as Rebecca has been shortened to Reba. I like it. Within my Inner Circle, I am addressed as Ellie. Understood?"

"Your Majesty, calling you Mother in private is one thing. What you ask is something altogether different. In my wildest imaginings, I had never thought I would be in a position to offer you counsel."

"I've always known you would. I told you all those years ago that I would not hesitate to call you to my side. The time has come."

"I serve at your command, Your Majesty," Val said. "I'm honored more than you will ever know."

"I doubt it. I saw something special in you when you were just a boy with one leg and a crutch, when I taught you how to eat properly and how to conduct yourself in a manner suited to royalty. I loved you then, and I love you now. I won't have to teach you how to be a Knight; you've been one all your life, but you're much more than a Knight to me, Val. You're family. There will be other Knights, but you hold a special place in my heart, as do Mike, Jake, Reba, Artmis, and Otis."

She stood up and took his hands. "All your life prior to this day has been preparation for what is to come. The Empire is counting on each of us in this room to give all that we are. We cannot fail." She took his head in her hands and kissed him on the mouth, then she gave him a hug. "As Ellie, I say welcome aboard, Val. You, too, Artmis."

"I *am* welcome here, but there's one who's missing."

"We'll find her, Val. Our family will be complete one day." She hugged him again. "This is your Naming day. Kneel before me if you will."

She placed her hands on Val's head, saying, "Lieutenant Val, like the Phoenix you rose by your own determination from the ashes of poverty. Upon your commissioning you swore an oath of allegiance to the Royal Family, an oath to which you remained true. In reward, I now ask for even greater sacrifice in my name. Artmis, you have shared the trials, tribulations, and commitment of the past thirteen years. Will you each swear fealty to my Crown?"

Despite all the words he'd spoken in this room today, Val found himself unable to utter a word. He remembered back to the time on Hespra III when he'd held Sir Jarl in his arms, a man who had truly been a Great One of Empire. And now he, Val, was being asked to fill those shoes.

His Queen looked down at him with glistening eyes, knowing exactly what this moment meant to him. She brushed a stray lock from his forehead and said softly, "Say yes, Val."

"Yes," he croaked.

"I take that for a yes. Stand, please." Poor Val couldn't get up. Mike and Reba had to help him. Ellie reached into a pocket and produced two Knight's Pins. "You wore these very Pins once before. Do you recognize them?"

A look of wonder crossed his face. "They're the ones?"

"They are. I have kept them all these years, knowing they would one day be yours. The last time you wore them you were impersonating a dead Knight. I'm certain Sir Jarl, if he was alive today, would be pleased for you to wear them again. Will you?"

Otis let out a growl of satisfaction. He, too, had waited many years for this occasion.

Val straightened. "I will, Your Majesty."

Ellie explained to Mike and Reba that the Pins were smaller versions of the First Knight's pendant worn by Mike and made of the same rare gem. Eyes still twinkling, she met Mike's gaze from over Val's shoulder as she removed his lieutenant's insignia. She activated the jewels and locking mechanisms by placing her own and Val's hands over the Pins, then attached both Pins to his collar, one on each side.

As she pinned them in place, she said, "With these tokens, I knight thee, Sir Val and Sir Artmis, Knights of the Realm. Your word is my command on all worlds of the Empire." She kissed him on both cheeks, then had to help steady him as his eyes glazed over again.

"And now it's your turn, Reba. Will you kneel before me?"

Reba smiled. She knew precisely what was going on. "I will, Your Majesty, but it's not necessary. I'm just happy to be here. Let me rise through the ranks as is proper."

"What's proper is that I surround myself with capable individuals in whom I place complete trust. You've been called, Reba. We've been mind-linked on the net, something no Queen has ever done. I know you for who you are, and I choose you. This is not as much a reward as it is a demand for even greater sacrifice in my name. Kneel before me, if you will."

"I wish my father could be here," Reba said softly. Tears sprung to Ellie's eyes again, and Reba knew exactly what was going through her mind. Ellie had no remaining family. She embraced Ellie as her own eyes filled.

"We're your family now," Reba said softly.

Ellie stood back with a smile. "You're my sister, and I say that with happiness in my heart."

Reba knelt, and Ellie placed her hands on Reba's head. "Do you, Rebecca Morrison, swear fealty to my Crown?"

"I do, Your Majesty," she replied strongly.

"Please rise." She took two more Knight's Pins from a pocket, activated them, and pinned them to Reba's collar, saying, "With these tokens I knight thee, Lady Rebecca, Knight of the Realm. Your word is my command on all worlds of the Empire."

She kissed Reba on both cheeks, then passed her to Mike for a congratulatory hug. Val was next in line beside Mike. Still dazed, he blushed as he kissed Reba on the cheek, lingering perhaps a little longer than necessary.

Ellie found Mike staring at her, then his eyes moved to Otis and his eyebrows rose in an unspoken question. Ellie sighed and looked warmly at Otis. He nodded his head, and she turned back to Mike, though she spoke to all of them.

"I asked Otis long ago to kneel before me. He refused. He told me his focus was only me, and Knights are required to focus on more. I asked him again shortly after our meeting with the leaf people and he agreed. Like us, he was tasked by them to look to the future. I have never seen him show his Pins, but he has been a Knight for many years."

Jessie didn't just growl, she roared, startling everyone. Ellie turned to her in surprise, but Jessie held her head high. "No one knows, even on Brodor, Your Majesty. He is the first of our people to wear the Pins." She bowed to Ellie, then she bowed to Otis.

"Yes. Well!" Ellie clapped her hands together. "This has been a day of deep reflection for all of us. We're done with official business, and I invite each of you to remain here or to spend time in private reflection, all except Reba." She looked fondly to Reba. "You will be otherwise engaged."

Reba smiled. "What do you have in mind for me, My Queen?"

"Ask Mike, my dear."

Reba turned to Mike with an expectant look.

He smiled. "As Knights, I expect we'll be tasked with things beyond normal expectations, and we'll need all the help we can get. Jake has a gift for you that you might find helpful."

"You mean . . .?"

"Yes. He's created a new Rider. His offspring has chosen you."

Her mouth quivered. "Oh, Jake," she breathed.

Tears of happiness fell unabashedly from Ellie's eyes as Mike approached Reba. She had only witnessed a transfer on one other occasion, and that occasion had not been a happy one. This one was.

Reba was dressed in a standard one-piece coverall. Mike looked at it for a moment and frowned. "Uh, there has to be skin to skin contact, Reba."

She didn't hesitate. "Close your eyes, Mike. You too, Val," she said, casting a mischievous glance in his direction. Val turned his back to her immediately. Mike heard the seals on her coveralls part, then her hands guided his to rest on her hips. The transfer needed only a few minutes, but they were long minutes. Mike felt nothing as the Rider left his body for hers.

>Okay, Mike. It's done. What a relief.<

"It's done," Mike said as he removed his hands from her bare hips.

"I think I'd better help here," Ellie said. "Give me a second to get her closed up."

When Mike opened his eyes again, Reba was just standing still with her eyes closed. Mike laid a hand on Val's shoulder and turned him around to watch.

"Hi, yourself," Reba said aloud. "Do you have a name?" Moments later, "We'll work on it together." She just stood there without awareness of the others in the room.

"Okay, looks like she's out of it," Mike said. "Jake tells me she'll probably want a few days to herself. Val, do you know where her room is?" he asked as he took Reba's arm in his.

"I do. May I help?"

He took her other arm and the two left Ellie's quarters without even saying goodbye, but a smile remained on her face and her heart was filled with happiness. A new chapter was about to open in their lives, and though she still sensed great danger, she had the beginnings of a wonderful team by her side to help her through those dark times. More important, she had friends by her side, friends whom she loved and friends who loved her for herself, not her position.

Yes, her heart was filled with happiness.

Chapter Fifty-one

Krys waited on the bridge as *Rappor* exited hyperspace on the outskirts of Orion III. In the net, Stven, M'Sada, and Tarn studied sensors and decided things looked normal within the system.

"Continue inbound, but keep an eye out. We don't know if they've figured out who we are yet," Stven ordered.

"If we're not marked yet, we will be soon. I'll keep an eye out," M'Sada replied.

Stven told the gunners to stand down, then he exited the net. He turned, mindful of brushing anyone off their feet with his tail. Krys waited anxiously, and Kross waited beside her. Tarn removed his helmet and lounged back in his seat.

"All normal, My Lady. We're continuing inbound," Stven reported to her.

"Our ship will soon become an item of interest to the Rebels," Kross stated, "if it hasn't already. We won't be able to use it much longer. We should give consideration to a change at Orion III."

"Depending on how the meeting goes on Orion III with Admiral Korban, we might be able to borrow one from him," Tarn spoke up. "If subsequent meetings go well, we might be able to switch to a different ship at each stop."

Kross growled. Clearly, he liked the idea.

Krys was not so certain. "Admiral Chandrajuski set this up as a civilian operation for a good reason. What if things don't go so well at one of our stops? As Imperial officers, you'd be bound by whatever orders were given us by senior commanders. What if I just buy us a new ship, another civilian ship?"

"That takes time, a lot of time, and I'd rather not give up the modifications Chandrajuski made to *Rappor,*" Stven said.

"What if we change the name of the ship?" Tarn asked.

"Can we?" Stven asked in surprise. "The name is hard-wired into the beacon."

"I have no idea."

Gortlan, the engineer, was called. When asked, he considered for a time. "The beacon cannot be changed without changing the AI, and the ship has to be completely powered down to do that. Provided we had access to another AI, we could do so in port, but what good would that do? As soon as we left, they'd have our new ID."

"Admiral Chandrajuski hinted that civilian ships are sometimes used in clandestine operations," Krys said. "Could those ships have a means of changing their beacons?"

Gortlan shook his head. "No way. I can visit the military port at Orion III and ask around, but if there was such a thing, I think I'd have heard."

"What if I hire a trader?" she asked. That brought surprised looks from everyone.

"We'd be subject to the whims of their crew. You wouldn't even need us anymore," Tarn said with a worried look.

"We're not splitting up, but it remains an option," she declared.

It would take three weeks to reach Orion III. Normal shipboard duties continued, including serious personal weapons training under the tutelage of the three Great Cats. Her message would not always be well received. That day had not yet come, but it would eventually, perhaps even here on Orion III. When it did, the three Great Cats and six crewmembers wouldn't stand much of a chance, but Kross insisted on maximum performance. The Great Cats were famous for refusing to give up under any circumstances. Orion III would not likely be a problem – Admiral Korban's loyalty was beyond reproach – but like everyone else, he did not know one of the Chosen had survived the coup. It was possible he had gone over to the Rebels simply because there was no one else in charge.

Half a year had gone by since leaving Rrestriss, and visits to

Mitala I, Rega VIII, and Strdx III, each taking about two months, had gone well. Senator Truax had left the ship at their first stop, and they had no idea of his present whereabouts. Krys had visited the Sector Commanders and the governors, and her message had been well received. She had attempted visions with each, but she had seen nothing.

She continued her daily exercise and meditation periods, and Tarn usually joined her. During the past months, he'd become more limber than at any time during his life, and he liked the feeling. He was less fond of the time spent meditating, and he was frequently gone by the time Krys completed hers, but she was working on him and he was getting better.

The approach to Orion III was not without incident. Stven, examining the many ships within the system, discovered two Chessori traders emerging from hyper a couple of weeks behind them. A small puff of noxious gas escaped from each nostril, bringing shouts of anguish from the others on the bridge. M'Sada was forced to withdraw from the net. He raced from the bridge, his two upper hands preening his long antennae furiously.

Stven ignored the commotion as he considered. Both Chessori were simple traders, but he was leery of all Chessori. They had learned of the terrible mind weapon at Rrestriss, but they had encountered no Chessori since then, and he was not anxious to experience its effect himself.

He called Krys to the bridge. "There are two Chessori traders a couple of weeks behind us. We'll have to limit our time on Orion III. I'd like to be away before they get anywhere close."

She bit her lip, then nodded. "We'll be as quick as we can."

They landed on the civilian side of the port. Kross and Sheeb accompanied Krys and Tarn while Gortlan headed off on his own for the military side of the port. He would ask around to see if anyone knew how to change beacon codes.

Getting in to see Admiral Korban was not an easy process. Krys did not want to resort to using the locket that identified her as a Friend, so Tarn presented the computer chip with the message from Chandrajuski, though he did not allow anyone to read it. They eventually reached Korban's outer office where they were stopped by a commander. He agreed to deliver the chip to Korban, but he would not let them pass.

Kross, the Great Cat, spoke. "Commander, we are here on Imperial business. I demand access to the admiral."

So respected were the Great Cats that they were shown into Korban's office without delay.

Korban rose from behind his desk, displeasure showing on his face. That displeasure increased when Kross closed the door, but when Krys held the locket out for his inspection, his features softened.

"A Friend of the Royal Family," he said, a hand rubbing his chin as he contemplated. "I'm not sure these things have meaning any more, but I will honor anyone who presents one. What can I do for you?"

"I'm here to convince you that the meaning of the lockets is not changed," Krys responded. She held out the chip from Chandrajuski. "A mutual friend asks that you read this."

Admiral Korban scanned the message, then sat down to read it carefully. When he was done, his gaze rose to meet hers. "You carry a message. What is the message?"

"May I ask first, sir, if you're aboard with Struthers? Does he count you as one of his own?"

"Considering the contents of this message and its source, your question surprises me. I hope you know the answer."

"I must hear it from you," Krys demanded.

Korban's lips thinned. "Very well. I have not joined with the new regime, nor will I. Chandrajuski may count me as an ally."

"And may the Empire?"

"The Empire is dead, young lady."

"It is not, sir. That is the gist of my message."

"All the Chosen are dead."

"Not true, sir. One lives."

Korban's gaze left hers and drifted, his thoughts deep. Krys waited patiently until she saw his eyes focus on her again.

She knew the question he would ask. "It's Daughter, sir."

"This is critical, young lady. The whole Empire believes that all the Chosen are dead, including me."

"Consider your source, Admiral," Kross demanded from across the office. "None other than Struthers, I suspect. Have you ever known one of my species to speak wrongly of the Royal Family?"

"You'd lie through your teeth if that's what it took to protect them, but it would serve no purpose if they no longer existed. Where is she? The last I heard, she was away on a treaty mission to the Chessori."

"The mission was a failure, Admiral," Krys stated. "I believe it was a trap set for her by Struthers, but she escaped, and she lives."

"Where is she?"

"I cannot say."

He swept to his feet, leaning across his desk toward her, fire in his eyes. "Cannot, or will not?"

"Cannot. I can tell you that she is not yet out of danger. She won't be as long as Struthers is in control, but she lives. Through her, the Realm lives, as well."

"Give me proof."

"I cannot. Will not Admiral Chandrajuski's letter suffice?"

He stepped from behind the desk. "I'll have to confirm its contents, but the presence of a Great Cat in combination with the letter compels me to act in accordance with his wishes. Quite frankly, if true, your message empowers me."

"Admiral Chandrajuski's feelings, as well. He's organizing something to help her restore the throne. Would you care to join his team?"

"It's not his team. It's the Queen's team."

"Queen! You mean Daughter's team, sir."

"No. If she is, indeed, the last of the Chosen, she is Queen."

"Just like that? Doesn't the Imperial Senate need to confirm her or something?"

"It does not. The Queen is dead. The law requires a Queen. If Daughter is the last of the Chosen, she is Queen. Confirmation by the Imperial Senate is only a courtesy to them and a means for the Empire to engage in pomp and ceremony. It is not a requirement. Now, what is Chandrajuski organizing? What does he need of me?"

"We left before a plan was finalized. I leave it to you to contact him. In the meantime, his message is that things may get very difficult in the coming months, particularly for you top commanders. He wants you to remain in command for as long as you possibly can to preserve assets the Queen will need. He counsels a holding action if necessary. Do you know what that means?"

A hand rose back to his jaw as he considered. "I'm already doing that, but without a plan, holding actions usually fail. My own plan is weak. I hope his is stronger. He and I will exchange messages. Until then, I'll keep my forces in readiness."

"If you reach the point where you can no longer hold, you are to retreat with as many assets as you can pull together."

"That makes sense. Is a meeting place arranged?"

"You have a person, not a place. Admiral Buskin is in charge of whatever assets come his way."

"Buskin, eh? I know him, and I approve, but I have to know where he is."

"That's the difficult part, sir," Tarn said. "The more people who know, the more chance there is of word leaking to the Rebels.

Chandrajuski does not even know where Buskin will be hiding out. Instead of you contacting him, he'll contact you from time to time."

"It's risky. What if I have to leave in a hurry?"

"Then leave. We'll give you a set of coordinates where, hopefully, a messenger will be waiting, provided Struthers has not discovered him. We are visiting others with this same message, and I'm certain you could name many on our list. As a last resort you can contact one of them and a way will ultimately be found to lead you to Buskin."

"The plan is full of holes, but that might actually be to our advantage for the time being." He considered the three visitors, then said, "I appreciate the risks you take in delivering Chandrajuski's message. I'll confer with him as soon as I can. Until I learn otherwise, count me in. Is there anything else?"

"There is," Tarn said. "We come as civilians, but we're a military crew on special assignment. We believe our ship is known to our enemies. We'd like to change our beacon if that's possible. Admiral Chandrajuski hinted at certain things that might be in place for clandestine missions. Would the ability to change a ship's beacon in space be one of them?"

"That would be illegal."

"Yes, sir. But is there a means? The message we carry, as you agree, is critical."

Korban settled back into his chair. "You ask too much. Can you offer any more proof that you are who you say you are?"

Krys spoke. "A Friend presented her credentials, Admiral. She travels in the presence of a Great Cat, and she carries a message of hope. We have a Queen, and I ask for your support in her name. Do you expect to get a better offer somewhere else?"

Korban paled. "You speak in her name?"

Krys stood her ground, knowing she had overstepped her authority, but knowing, too, that her actions were necessary.

"In this, I speak in her name, sir."

"You lay your life on the line, young lady."

"Every day. So, too, does my crew. The beacon?"

"A method exists, but the process is not easy, and it can only work with a military AI."

"We have a military AI."

Korban's eyebrows lifted. "Chandrajuski doesn't miss much, does he."

Tarn spoke up. "He didn't give us the means to change our beacon, sir. I don't think he expected us to have the problem, at least not this early in our mission."

"What problem?"

"The Chessori. We believe they're searching for us, possibly on behalf of the Rebels. They may be in league with each other."

Korban frowned. "They're just traders."

"Not so, sir. I personally observed 15 Chessori ships destroy three Empire heavy squadrons without retaliation. Our guys never got a shot off."

"Not possible," Korban snapped.

"What do you really know about them, sir?"

Korban considered. "Actually, very little. They seem timid. From all reports, they're well-behaved."

"All a ruse, sir. For the first time in the history of Empire, we are up against a mind weapon, a mind weapon that disables anyone within its range. The crewmembers in those squadrons were as good as any, but against the mind weapon they were completely helpless."

Tarn leaned toward Korban, choosing his words with care. This message needed to be clearly understood. "Sir, the Chessori are as much your enemy as the Rebels. I beg you to heed this warning."

Korban stayed in Tarn's face. "What is the range of this mind weapon? You've clearly seen it in action, yet you survived."

"It's range is unknown. We observed its use from afar."

"How do we combat it?"

"We have a plan, sir, but the plan is in its infancy, and I cannot divulge its nature. It will be revealed to you when we know more. Until then, I counsel in the strongest possible terms: avoid the Chessori, and under no circumstances engage them. The weapon is devastating in its effectiveness, and you are powerless against it. So are we. It's why we need to change our beacon."

"Why don't I assign you to a squadron?"

Krys stepped to Tarn's side. "Chandrajuski considered all this before we left Centauri III. Squadrons are just as powerless against the Chessori mind weapon as we are. It was his belief that one civilian ship might have more success."

"I'll need to talk with him. I'm on board with you for the moment, but I'm still not fully convinced. If all is as you say, his plan is a good beginning. His plan for retreat is excellent."

"And for that reason, I might have a final message to deliver. But this message, once it's out of the box, cannot be rescinded. May I have a few minutes to consider, Admiral?"

"You may. Your message has given me hope, and that's a

precious gift."

Krys gave Tarn a hard look, then went to a couch and settled into her meditation position. Korban started to say something, but Tarn held up a hand for silence. He gave her a full ten minutes, an excruciatingly long period of time for Korban and himself. Korban clearly did not understand, and he grew more and more angry as the minutes passed. Finally, Tarn said softly, "Will you take her hand, sir?"

Korban looked a question to him, but Tarn just stood his ground. Taking care not to disturb what was clearly a state of trance, Korban went to Krys and took her hand, placing it between both of his own.

Her eyes flew open. It took her a moment to remember where she was, then a smile split her face from side to side, and tears welled in her eyes. She looked to Tarn, first in triumph, then in supreme happiness.

"What did you see, Krys?"

She replied to Korban instead. "You will receive a visitor sometime in the future. I cannot say when. He is a Knight of the Realm."

Korban stepped away from her in surprise. "Who, exactly, are you?"

"I am the Queen's Seer," she replied.

Korban's lips thinned, confusion clear in his expression.

Krys gave him time to consider, then said, "My existence is an Imperial Secret, Admiral. The list of those who know about me is very small. Do you understand?"

He blinked, then blinked again. "No, I don't understand at all. I've heard tales, but you're telling me they're true?"

"I cannot speak for tales, but I am true. When you confer with Admiral Chandrajuski, will you give him a message from me?"

"Of course."

"Please tell him that my vision was of a Knight of the Realm presenting his credentials to you. Tell him the Knight's Pin was open."

A roar escaped from Kross, then silence filled the room as each considered her words. The Pins could only be opened by a true Knight, and for the Pin to open, the Chosen who had activated it had to be alive.

Korban broke the silence. "Whose image . . . ?" he started to ask, then his communicator buzzed. He picked it up, listened, then said, "I'm okay. Everything's fine in here. Just a little excitement from the kitty." He placed the communicator down, his eyes on Krys.

"The image was of Daughter," she answered.

"Then she must be alive. She really is Queen."

"I speak true, Admiral. Since this is a vision of the future, not only is she alive today, but she will be alive when this Knight arrives.

And there's more. Words came with the vision, as they sometimes do:

To fight is to fail. Leadership prevails. Sixty-eight thirteen tests resolve. Give all that you are.

Korban backed away, blinking. "What kind of words are those?"

"The words of my visions always come in the form of a riddle, sir. It's our job to decipher the riddle."

"Humph. My job is to fight when necessary. You're telling me I'm going to fail?"

"You're also a leader, sir. It appears that your leadership might be more successful than your fighting. Considering that the Chessori are your enemy, it's probably true."

"It is possible for the smarter commander to win even if he holds the weaker hand. What's this 68-13?" He thought for a while, then said, "If I'm not to fight, I'll have to acknowledge a weak hand and join up with Buskin." He held out his hands in defeat. "So there goes Chandrajuski's plan to hold. I'm disappointed. I do not want to give in to the Rebels."

She nodded her head. "I understand, sir, but wait. I don't think we're done yet." She turned to Tarn.

He was looking down at the floor, his brow furrowed. He lifted his gaze to her. "You said a number. It was sixty-eight thirteen. Do you mean six thousand eight hundred thirteen?"

"Not exactly. They were two separate numbers. One number was 68, the other 13."

Tarn thought for a time, then went to the Admiral's bookshelf. He pulled a thick tome from a shelf and plopped down on a chair with the manual on his lap. He paged through it, could not find what he wanted, and frowned in disgust. He hefted the book and returned it to its place.

His eyes searched for another, but Admiral Korban interrupted. "I see where you're going with this, Lieutenant. It's in the Standing Operations Orders. I think you're looking for Section 68, Paragraph 13. I'm familiar with it."

Tarn nodded and pulled out his personal pad, unfolded it, and started pushing keys. When he found what he was looking for, he paled. His gaze rose to meet Korban's.

"I see why it asks for all that you are, sir."

Korban nodded grimly and turned to Krys. "That particular order deals with the self destruction of a ship. Under certain conditions the captain of a small ship might choose to lose his ship before it is, for example, boarded by pirates, or perhaps on course to crash into a populated area." Korban's attitude of superiority evaporated. "I've never heard of it being done."

Tarn focused back on Krys. "Is there anything more you can tell me about what you saw?"

"Just a Knight holding out a Pin to Admiral Korban."

"Can you tell me where they were?"

She closed her eyes. "I believe they were right here in this office," she said.

Tarn turned away, thinking deeply. Krys saw his head nodding side to side, as if a puzzle was coming together in his mind.

He nodded once more, then turned back to her and Korban, his manner confident. "Sir, if ever there was a call to hold, this is it."

Korban directed a piercing look toward him. "It's clear that I'm not to fight, and I cannot hold forever. You should know that Orion Sector already has a new governor, one assigned by Struthers. The day will come when I either stand against him or retreat. If I don't fight, what alternative do I have besides retreat if I'm to conserve resources for the Queen?"

"I believe the first two phrases go together, sir. *To fight is to fail. Leadership prevails.* I believe the word fighting refers to weapons, sir. There are other ways to fight, and in your case I believe your fight will be a holding action. I believe your battle will be a battle of wits, not a battle of weapons."

"I'm not certain I agree."

"Then don't agree, but keep in mind that whenever this Knight shows up, you are still in this very office. You will have held at least that long. Once the Knight arrives, he'll have orders that are beyond reproach, whatever they are. Until then, your focus is to lead."

"And Section 68, Paragraph 13?"

"You say its applicability is to small ships. I would raise the bar, sir."

"You mean it applies to large ships? I can foresee no conditions under which the rule would apply."

"Nor could the writers of the Operations Order, sir, but they were not in the midst of a coup. It might well apply under some conditions we cannot foresee. My guess is that you will know when the time comes. But sir, you might not have raised the bar high enough."

"What? You think it should apply to *all* of my ships?"

Tarn spoke softly. "It might apply to your whole sector."

Korban aged before their very eyes. "I'm to make such a decision?"

"I'm sorry, sir, but it looks that way. In my opinion this is a call to hold, and I believe it foretells a terrible ordeal for you personally."

"If it comes true."

Tarn sat down and leaned toward Korban. "Sir, the Knight will verify everything. I'm certain. Until then, you will carry the seed of uncertainty, and that seed could grow into something more, something bad. I wish I could lighten the burden, but this vision, in my opinion, offers little in terms of a way out for you."

Korban leaned back, a grim set to his lips, but he remained silent for the moment, and Tarn continued.

"It's reasonable for you to question, sir. In fact, it's your duty to question, and that includes what has gone on here today. It might help if I enlighten you further concerning the Queen's Seer. I've been with her for a year now. She's had a number of visions, and I am alive today because of one of them."

Korban raised an eyebrow, but Tarn ignored the implied question.

"I'm not the issue, sir. Her visions, or more important, the focus of her visions is what matters. Each and every one of her visions has focused on the coup. She forecast the coup twelve years before it happened, though even she did not understand the meaning of the vision. She forecast the coup again shortly before it happened and still didn't understand. Since then she's had visions of others including Daughter, me, Chandrajuski, and now you. Sir, I have personal knowledge of at least three of her visions coming to pass."

"Why me, and why now?"

"A good question, sir. I ask myself the same thing every day. Why am I still alive?"

Tarn shook his head, wishing he knew the answer. "I can't tell you how or why these visions occur, but each appears focused on restoring the Queen to the throne. You, personally, have been singled out, for what I don't know, but I believe you hold a position of great importance to the restoration of the throne."

Korban continued to stare at him. Tarn had already said more than, by rights, he should, but he felt compelled to continue. He locked gazes with the admiral. "I'm just a lieutenant, sir," he said. "Truth be told, I'm really just an ensign that Admiral Chandrajuski promoted for this mission. I am in no position to be counseling senior admirals, but I have had some success with interpreting these visions. I ask your permission to be blunt."

Korban continued leaning back in his chair as he looked from

Tarn to Krys, then back to Tarn again. "I'm not certain where I stand with any of this, Lieutenant, but your argument has so far held together. Say what you must."

"Sir, the very presence of Krys in this office directs specific attention to you and to Orion Sector. Your battle will be one of wits, not of weapons. How you will fight this battle I do not know, but you will lead Orion Sector for the Queen. In accepting the call, you also accept the fact that the demands on you personally will be terrible, so terrible that section 68, paragraph 13 will be invoked in some manner."

Korban stared back at Tarn, his face a mask set in stone. He did not want to hear these words, yet in a way they called to him as no others ever had.

"You will receive a visit from a Knight of the Realm some day in the future," Tarn continued. "That visit is, in effect, a visit from the Queen herself. Once the Knight comes, you will be certain. Until then, you have only Krys' word that all this is true.

"Sir, as a sector commander you are bound by an oath given directly to the Queen. I believe that debt is now called in. Some will abandon their sectors, but I believe that you, sir, are tasked with holding. Your holding might be categorized more as an ordeal, but your actions are crucially important to the Queen. We're all counting on you, sir."

Krys stared proudly at Tarn. She had wondered about his place in all of this. His performance in Chandrajuski's office had left little doubt, but now all doubt was erased. From the few simple words of a riddle and her brief vision of a Knight, he had concocted a plan that would direct the efforts of an entire sector.

She shifted her focus to Korban and sensed his wavering. "You still doubt, Admiral," she said.

"I do, but not as much as I should. I sense a rightness within both of you."

"Then we are nearly done. I have only one more piece of information for you. Lieutenant Lukes does not know the source of my visions, but I do."

Tarn whirled on her in shock. She reached a hand up to his face and caressed. "We'll rectify that, and soon."

She turned back to Korban. "Admiral Chandrajuski received a vision even more frightening than yours. He found himself in the midst of a horrible dilemma. I am going to tell you what I told him. The words I am about to say are not my own, but I cannot reveal their source. The words are a gift from someone wise beyond our comprehension, someone who knew what was coming."

Korban rose slowly from his seat, simultaneously eager and hesitant to hear what Krys was about to say.

"He spoke of heavy burdens, sir, but he left us with the means to shoulder them. He told us that we are to listen to our hearts, always. If we do, we will know what is right, and we will never be asked to do more."

Korban stared at her, this waif of a woman who's words, if true, would change his life, direct his life in ways none of them could foresee.

"I know what you're thinking, sir. In Admiral Chandrajuski's words, those are the words of a woman, not a fighter."

She cocked her head to the side in a question, a very personal question. "Let me ask you, does your heart not hear my words? Can you tell me you don't feel rightness in what has transpired here today?"

A low, continuous growl sounded within Kross' throat. When Krys turned to him, he shook his head as if to clear it. He looked into her eyes and gruffly cleared his throat.

She reached out and touched the fur of his neck. "I wish you had been there, my friend. Otis was, and he was called. So, too, was Daughter."

Krys turned back to Korban. "Sir, Daughter was there when these words were spoken. I speak in her name when I tell you to trust in your heart. Listen to your heart, Admiral. What you find there will be true."

* * * * *

The moment they stepped out of the building, Krys grabbed Tarn and pulled him into an embrace, jumping up and down as she held to him. "I'm so happy!" she cried.

He held tight and swung her around, then set her down and pushed her out to arms length. "And I'm happy for you. The Knight's Pin was open. That confirms everything! Not only that, you actually had another vision at a time of your own choosing."

"Tarn, we have a Queen! I feel so strong all of a sudden. But there's more." He looked a question at her, and she beamed. "I saw the Knight. It was Val."

He stepped back in awe. "Your boyfriend is a *Knight?*"

She blinked, a look of disbelief on her face. "*Boyfriend?*"

"We're talking about Val here, the Val from your orphanage, right?"

She reached out a shaking hand to his face. "How long have we been together now?"

"About a year."

"And in all that time you haven't known? Oh, Tarn, I've been unfair. I just realized there's so much you don't know, and it's not right. I'm sorry.

"Like what?"

She dropped her hand from his face and stepped away, then turned in a circle as she searched for guidance.

"There's so much. Do you know you're one of only six people who were called by name to save the Empire?"

Kross growled deep in his throat, and she whirled to face the Great Cat. "I'm surprised you don't know. Otis has not shared his story with the brotherhood?"

Kross' silent stare was all the answer she needed.

Softly, knowing they were in a very public place, she asked, "He, too, was there. Did you know he's been Knighted?"

A savage roar filled the space before Korban's headquarters, echoing across the lawns and through the trees. Everyone stopped to stare, but Kross didn't care. He paced before her, his energy barely controlled.

"It's true, Kross. I thought you knew."

"He is the first of my people."

"I think I knew that. He will probably not be the last." She turned back to Tarn. "Val is a Knight. At least, according to this vision, he will be one eventually. For all these years he's tried to emulate the vision he carried of Sir Jarl, the Knight who died bringing me and him to Daughter's attention. Daughter knew how he felt about Sir Jarl; his Knighting must have been a special moment for both of them. He's now one of the great ones of Empire, a position he could only imagine."

"Uh, I think you're right up there with him, Krys."

"No. I haven't *done* anything, I just *am.*"

Staring into her eyes, he said "I won't let you sell yourself short, my friend."

"Nor will I," Kross broke into their world, a world that had for the moment become just the two of them. "I will never forget today. You truly are who you say you are, My Lady."

Her eyes flashed as she corrected him. "I'm not My Lady."

"You are to me. You occupy a special place in Daughter's world, and probably in her heart. You do in mine as well. I'm honored to serve you, and I'm honored to call you My Lady. Now, we must be away from here."

She took Tarn's arm and headed back in the direction of the ship. "Our crew must know the story of me, Val, Daughter, and Otis. They deserve to know. I'm only sorry I didn't tell you all sooner."

She stopped and pulled Tarn around to face her. "You have to know this right now, Tarn. Out of all the Empire, six people were named that day. I'll give you the details later. When the naming took place, we didn't know what it was for, but now we do. We have been called to lead the effort to restore peace across the Empire. Maybe even beyond the Empire if my sense is right. You were one of the six. I was told that in my hour of need the Guide would find me. You are the Guide, Tarn."

He balked. "I'm just a lieutenant, Krys. Just an ensign, really."

"Call yourself what you will, but your position surmounts rank, just as mine does. You are the Guide. For all these years I believed you were to be my guide, but I see now that I was wrong. You're *their* guide, Tarn. I'm the Messenger, and you provide guidance to whomever my vision is directed. Can you believe me?"

They really did need to get out of this public place. He took her arm and turned her toward the spaceport, suddenly seeming to stand taller.

"Actually, I do believe you. I can't say why, I just know you're right. I *am* the Guide. I hesitate to ask, but whose company am I in?"

"Mine; the Queen; the Knight, whoever he is; Otis; and my brother Val."

* * * * *

Gortlan was locked in a meeting with a Senior Chief somewhere on the military side of the port, and the meeting was expected to last all day. Since they had to wait for him, Kross requested a few hours for himself. Krys didn't question him, she just encouraged him to do whatever it was he had to do.

It took Kross a while, but he eventually located another Great Cat, one whom he knew slightly. When speaking among their own kind, they used their true names, not their working names. True names could not be pronounced by humans.

"Greetings, Sgujkdsla. I have information. It is Imperial in nature."

"Greetings, Pytgbvlw. You should see Bxpturzgb."

Kross blinked. "He's here?"

He's here, and he'll be out soon. We're a team of three."

Kross was pleased to hear the name Bxpturzgb. Kross was a

Guardian, but Bxpturzgb was one of the elite Protectors who had served with Otis for a time. He would know Daughter well, and he might know Krys. He waited patiently until two Great Cats emerged from a building with a human. He did not recognize the human. Sgujkdsla indicated all clear to Bxpturzgb, then joined him, a decidedly abnormal behavior during Protection duties. A few words were exchanged, then Bxpturzgb left the small group to join Kross.

Standard greetings were exchanged, then the two Great Cats sauntered down the boulevard, passersby giving them a wide berth. "It's an Imperial matter, sir. We should talk in private."

Bxpturzgb led him to a nearby alley and turned into it. "Speak," he commanded.

"Daughter lives, sir."

Bxpturzgb's ears twitched, about all the emotion one ever saw from a Protector. "She's here?" he asked softly.

"No. Her location is unknown. I protect a Friend who seeks her."

"How do you know?"

"The Friend is the Seer. She has made certain predictions."

The ears twitched again. "The Seer! There is only one."

"That is her claim."

"Take me to her."

"Your contract, sir?"

"As you say, this is an Imperial matter. Our client will have to manage with one less. Does Brodor know?"

"I sent a message four months ago. They should know by now, but there have been more developments. Have you received a recall?"

"I wouldn't be here if I had."

"There will be a general recall. We're needed on another project. I can speak more openly if we go to my ship."

"And I must see Krys."

The two Great Cats padded into the ship where they found Krys and Tarn in the midst of their exercises. She looked at the new addition, peered hard, and stopped what she was doing. "Borg?" she asked.

"At your service, old friend."

She came to him and wrapped her arms around his great neck in a hug. He suffered her ministrations patiently, as cats do on occasion. When she released him, he sat back on his haunches, his method of standing at attention.

She stepped away, looked at Kross, then back to Borg. "I'm looking for her, but I have not found her yet. I know she lives. Until I find her, we are on a mission to tell others that there is a Queen."

"What others?"

"We have a list of senior military officers. Senator Truax is pursuing a similar agenda with certain senators."

"Kross tells me there is a general recall of Guardians. Why?"

She briefed him fully, with Kross interjecting items of special interest when appropriate. When they were done, Borg simply turned and left. He was back three hours later with two additional Great Cats. The cats met in private, and when they emerged, three left, including Sheeb.

Krys stopped them. "Sheeb, are you leaving?"

"I am, My Lady. It has been my greatest honor to serve you."

"But . . .?"

"The decision is made, and it serves you best. Borg will stay with you. I am needed on Brodor to share my experience of the Chessori with others."

She knew it was not her place to overrule Borg. This was his decision, and she had no place in it. "Farewell, friend, and thank you."

Sheeb nodded and turned away.

Gortlan returned late that night, and they were away. Stven's first concern after departure was to check on the two Chessori traders that had trailed them on their way to Orion III. They were still a full week out, and he felt comfortable with the spacing between them. He set his course directly away from theirs.

A week later, two more Chessori traders materialized on the screens directly ahead of them. M'Sada was in the net at the time, and he called Stven immediately from a deep sleep. They studied the presentation, then chose the obvious solution. They turned hard away from the Chessori in front of them. A short time later the Chessori turned to intercept them. Behind them, the two Chessori inbound to Orion III turned to bypass the planet and head toward them, as well.

M'Sada fine-tuned their course to put as much distance as he could between both sets of Chessori while Stven considered options. When the final computations were displayed, his options evaporated. The inbound Chessori would intercept them about a day before the two trailing Chessori, and both would join with *Rappor* long before a safe jump point was reached. He'd been trapped.

Stven and M'Sada left the net to confer. "We could head directly for the incoming set." Stven mused. "We'd be by them in a flash."

"Not if they take control of our minds."

"We could program the ship to keep going no matter what other orders it received."

"It might work," M'Sada said. "Let's keep it as an option.

There's another. A few years ago, I was with a squadron chasing a lone smuggler. He didn't have a chance, but he jumped before we reached him."

"We can't jump. We're too far inside the system."

"So was he."

"Did he make it?"

"I'll never know. We had no means of following. He was actually farther in than we'll be. We'll at least be in the outer system. Maybe we ought to play with the AI for a while."

"You know it won't let us jump that early."

"Let's get Gortlan up here. Maybe he'll have an idea."

Gortlan pondered the problem while M'Sada did his best to coax potential solutions from the AI. It couldn't execute the solutions, but it could set up and display them.

"You know it's risky, right?" Gortlan said to Stven.

"So is anything else we've come up with."

Gortlan's lips thinned in displeasure. "What I learned back on Orion IV might come in handy here. You're not going to like the process of changing the beacon. We have to get out where no one can see us and shut down the AI."

"Shut it down! Out in the middle of nowhere?"

"Yes, sir. Not for long, but it has to be complete. I'll insert some new programming before we shut down. When we re-boot, the new beacon code will be accessed instead of the old one. It's simple on the surface, but the process can be ugly."

Stven had to ask, but he was certain he didn't want to hear the answer. "How ugly?"

"Without an AI, there's nothing monitoring all the other computers. Strange things have been reported, from weightlessness to lights out. It's not done often, so it's not an exact science. Crews that might have to use it get extra training in monitoring systems while the AI is out."

"Is there still a net?"

"Yes, but no one to drive it."

"We can still maneuver the ship? And jump?"

"You can, but only manually. Computing jumps manually takes a lot of time, and if we come out near a star or something, we're in big trouble. Think hard on this, sir."

"If we do this, do we do the whole thing? Insert the new beacon code and all?"

"Depends on how far the jump takes us. When we reboot, we'll be sending out the new code. You want to do it where no one will know."

"So we'll need two jumps just to be certain. You can reboot after the second jump. Are you up to speed on the process?"

Gortlan nodded, a grim expression on his face. "To tell you the truth, sir, it's against everything I've ever learned as an engineer. It scares the crap out of me."

"Me, too."

Stven went back into the net where he joined M'Sada in his calculations. "Do them carefully, my friend. You're going to have to make the next one manually," he said.

"Manually! Carefully? I have no idea what the AI is doing. Computing a jump this far inside a system is completely beyond me. I feel like a pupae."

They waited as long as they could, but they had no idea of the range of the Chessori mind weapon. The closest Chessori were two days away when Stven called Gortlan. "Ready?"

"As I'll ever be. You have to start it. Only I can finish it. It's a safeguard."

"Ready, M'Sada?"

"Go for it. We're on track. I'll execute in half an hour."

To the AI, he issued two simple commands. "MANUAL OVERRIDE."

"MANUAL OVERRIDE ACCEPTED BUT NOT RECOMMENDED."

"SHUTDOWN."

There was no further communication from the AI. It took him a while as he floundered around in a net that had suddenly lost its brain, but he found M'Sada. "Need any help?"

"Nope. Just keep the net functioning. I need to hit the jump point precisely. And watch your breathing. This is not a good time to get excited."

"Okay. I'm going to check on the rest of the ship while you do the flying." He began the laborious process, almost like swimming, as he transitioned through the net, checking on the most important subsystems. First came the power plant. Without it they had no hope. All indications were satisfactory. He stayed for a while to make sure, then went to Life Support. He discovered all the circulation fans dead and got them going again. Atmosphere quickly came back to normal. Please don't fart now, he told himself. He really needed M'Sada at the controls, and the poor guy just couldn't suffer the pain it caused him. He went back to the power plant, it was okay, then he went to weapons. Tarn was holding the gunnery net together, and the gunners did not have to go to manual control. He checked shields, and they were fully charged and ready.

"Counting down," M'Sada called.

Stven swam back to the bridge to keep an eye on the jump. The jump point was reached, and M'Sada executed. Now they just had to wait. The jump would not be long, so he stayed.

The jump ended. "Where are we?" M'Sada demanded frantically as he looked for anything nearby that they might hit.

"I'm looking! I'm looking!"

Their frantic efforts were unnecessary – they had not come out of the jump near anything that would kill them. This time. The next time might be different.

Stven mentally relaxed and joined M'Sada in a search for other ships, but they had reached interstellar space and were alone.

"Okay to fart now?" he asked with a chuckle.

"No! I'm not leaving. You'll screw up my settings. I'm working on the next jump."

They jumped again some four hours later. By then Stven was exhausted from holding the net together. "I never really appreciated what the AI does for us," he said.

"Let's just hope the whole thing comes back. I'm going to set up another jump just in case it doesn't. Why don't you start running some tests on the AI?"

"Gortlan's doing that. I'll help with the jump."

When the AI finally finished rebooting, it came back fully, and they set course for their next stop. After the next jump, they both took a time-out. Stven looked at M'Sada. "We need some training, buddy. I don't want to go cold into that again."

M'Sada was busy preening his long antennae. "I found it interesting."

"Sure. You got to do the easy part, the flying. I had to take care of the ship."

"Let's go find out how good a job you did."

Krys and Tarn were in the galley, almost finished cleaning up. "What happened?" Stven asked in alarm.

Krys just kept working. Tarn struggled to hide his laughter as he helped her. "Looks like the auto-chef was preparing a banquet for a hundred. At least we can get around now. Krys was locked in her room until just a little while ago."

Stven's neck drooped. "*Lots* more practice," he mumbled.

Chapter Fifty-two

Commodore Elotch M'Dama absently preened his whiskers with his upper hands. An Empire squadron commander, he was assigned to Aldebaran Sector where he reported to Admiral Seeton.

He was a Schect. His bulbous, multifaceted eyes gave him a 360 degree view of the room so he didn't need to face the two humans, but he had learned that humans were more comfortable speaking to him if they felt he was looking at them directly.

Across a low table, Admiral Seeton and Governor Veswicki sat in comfortable chairs in the admiral's office. M'Dama's body did not suit itself well to chairs.

"Refreshments?" Seeton asked him out of courtesy. A smile glinted in his eyes; they knew each other well. M'Dama returned the smile in his own way, with a few clicks of his sharp, serrated mandibles. It was well known that humans could not tolerate the eating habits of the Schect.

"I believe I'll pass on that, sir," he replied.

"Very well. We'll get down to business then. I don't believe you've met Governor Veswicki?"

"I have not, sir. It's a pleasure to meet you, Governor."

"The pleasure is mine, Commodore. You come with high

recommendation."

"And your reputation precedes you, Governor. Or should I call you Admiral?"

"A good question, Commodore. As you probably know, I'm not exactly welcome in my old sector. I don't recognize Struthers' authority to remove me from office, so I'm still the legitimate governor of Triton Sector, but it will be a long time before I return, if ever. At the moment, I wear the uniform when it suits my needs, and I play the politician when appropriate. My presence here in Aldebaran Sector is strictly unofficial."

"I understand, sir. You wage your battles on many fronts, all of them unofficial. You know I'm behind you or else I wouldn't be here."

"You know we're resisting the Rebel takeover?"

"I've heard rumors, very quiet rumors. I'm glad to hear it from you personally, sir."

"Supporting me places you in grave danger."

M'Dama bowed. "I stand by my oath, Governor. Need I say more?"

"No. We, too, stand by our oaths. Where our principles will take us is not clear at this time, but we begin with resisting the Rebels. We've established a plan, and you are part of that plan."

M'Dama bowed again. "Your words please me, sir. I will help in any way that I can."

"These are unusual times, Commodore, and we have an unusual mission for you. The goal we are working toward may be a little more comprehensive than you've heard. We're not just organizing here in Aldebaran Sector, we've made considerable headway in other sectors, as well. We're keeping a low profile for the moment, though I fear we'll be forced to show our hand in the next year or two.

"Our focus at the moment, and yours, is Orion Sector. We believe it is among our list of supporters, but we're getting conflicting reports from there. Admiral Korban, Sector Commander on Orion III, is well known to Admiral Seeton and myself, and we have strong reason to believe he's on our side, but the last two courier ships we sent to him have not returned. We're going to send a stronger force to ensure success."

"So you'd like my squadron to pay him a visit?"

"We would, but not directly. We want to get a feel for what's going on in Korban's sector, not just at his headquarters. We're thinking that some stops along the way might be beneficial. We'd like you to test the waters in a couple of outlying systems. Depending on how that goes, you might decide to return here directly, or you might decide it's appropriate to continue on and pay a visit to Korban. We'd really like you to meet with him, but only if you believe he's of the right persuasion. Do you understand my meaning?"

If staring had been possible for M'Dama, he might have stared at Veswicki. Instead, he rose up from the floor to pace on eight hands while his upper hands continued a refreshing preening. He finished with his whiskers and moved on to his antennae. Old smells had to be removed to make room for the new, and it was a never-ending process. His multifaceted eyes continued taking in everything in the room. When he turned back to Veswicki, he said, "This sounds more political than military."

"Normally I would agree, but in view of the two missing couriers, strength will be key. No one would be foolish enough to take on a full squadron, so there shouldn't be any fighting, but there might very well be some posturing."

"Against our own men?"

"If they are our own. I no longer classify the Rebels as our own."

"Is it possible that Korban joined with the Rebels?"

"I consider that extremely unlikely. However, it is not at all unlikely that he is no longer the Sector Commander. He might even be dead. If so, who's in control? We need to know."

"Has he sent any of his own couriers to you?"

"If he has, they have not gotten through. In our last communication with him, he informed us that he's in serious trouble. The new governor of Orion Sector has made inroads in the outlying districts, though not on Orion III itself. Korban is too strong there, but he cannot hold out for an unlimited time."

"What exactly do you want from me?"

"We want, first, to find out if Korban is in control of his sector. Second, if he is, we need to find out if he needs our assistance. We're prepared to reassign a number of our own squadrons to him, squadrons we know are loyal, but clearly, we don't want to send them if that means we're just turning them over to the Rebels. You might discover other needs, as well."

"Have you constructed a cover story for my presence in Orion Sector?"

"We have," Seeton responded. "Smuggling is on the increase since the fall of the Empire. We've received reports of some serious operations out of Algnada, and the perpetrators may have expanded into Orion Sector. They're not anywhere near Orion III, but it would not be out of the ordinary for you to officially request assistance from Sector

Headquarters there if you've tracked them into the sector."

"Is this a real group?"

"It is. We have no hard evidence that they're moving into Orion Sector, but they could be."

"I like it, sir. It's a completely natural cover. I have a couple of acquaintances out that way, fleet officers whose judgment I trust. One is, at last report, on Bvest, and the other is on Krandt. Those districts are close enough to Algnada to be reasonable stops for my squadron."

Seeton pulled up a holographic image from the table before him and made inquiries. The three worlds were, indeed, in reasonable proximity to each other. He turned to Veswicki and received a nod of acceptance.

"Very well," Seeton said. "Your official orders are to track the movements of these smugglers. We'll send over a file with everything we have on them so you'll be briefed. Just know that your real job is to get a feel for what's going on in Orion Sector. It's vital that we know if Korban continues to speak for the sector. Orion Sector is of great importance to our plans. We don't want to lose it to the Rebels."

* * * * *

Commodore M'Dama's squadron lifted from Aldebaran I three days later and set course for Bvest. M'Dama gave thought to his orders as his upper hands idly preened his whiskers and worked their way back to the two long antennae extending from his head. The Empire was in turmoil, and turmoil spelled uncertainty. The loss of the two couriers sent to Orion III had him more concerned than he'd let on to Seeton and Veswicki. Was the loss of those ships a harbinger of things to come? Was civil war on the horizon? He suspected it was, and he suspected they thought so, as well. Why else would they need a full squadron to gather information?

If it came to civil war, he knew he could not side with the Rebels. In the absence of Empire his oath was void, but his principles had not changed. The way the Rebels had come into power was wrong, and he would resist them in any way he could.

M'Dama concluded that his squadron might encounter resistance, but what kind of resistance? Was he capable of taking up arms against other Empire ships, ships that might be manned by crews he'd served with during his long career? Might it come down to Empire fleets engaging each other? The thought sickened him, but it also forced him to focus on his beliefs. He could not take a stand against the Rebels by himself: to do so would place him on the same level as the Rebels. But Governor Veswicki had inferred that a new government was being formed to resist the Rebels. Knowing Admiral Seeton as well as he did, and knowing the reputation Governor Veswicki had built during his many years in Fleet Command, he believed the new government would have as its foundation the principles of the old Empire. He would not be acting alone if he was acting in support of their efforts.

His body rested comfortably on a custom-made platform on the bridge of the cruiser. His normal duty station was in the Operations Center, the nerve center of the squadron, but his preferred place was on the bridge. He was a spaceman at heart, and he never tired of the details of navigating the stars.

His upper hands had completed their work on his antennae and moved back to the short whiskers of his face while he considered. Seeton might be doing Governor Veswicki's bidding, but the choice of squadron commander had been Seeton's, and that choice had been based on more than just military skills. He had chosen a commander who might face grievous decisions during the coming months, and M'Dama's beliefs were well-known to him and in line with his own.

There had never been a case of Empire squadron fighting Empire squadron, not in all the long history of the Empire. There weren't even tactics for doing so. Fleets and squadrons, if facing each other one-on-one, would be evenly matched. After all, they'd gone to the same schools. The outcome would depend on the abilities of the individual leaders of those men and ships. Was that one of the reasons Seeton had chosen him?

Probably. M'Dama's skills as a tactician were legendary, and he could say that with deserved pride. But equally important, M'Dama could be counted on to choose wisely and without hesitation.

His upper hands stopped their grooming: he had reached a decision. His duty was clear. He would not seek confrontation, but his squadron would be prepared to uphold the principles of Empire if it was called to do so. It was back to battle school for him and his men. They would have to get creative if such a battle between evenly matched opponents ever materialized, but the creativity had to come before the battle, not during the battle. The simulators aboard his ships would get a hard workout on this voyage.

He called his operations staff together. Several meetings later, he brought all ships' captains aboard the cruiser for discussion. To his surprise, he did not encounter resistance. Most had already considered the idea. No one knew what was going to happen to the Empire, but everyone suspected it would come down to civil war, and not on a small scale.

They began with what they knew, and they expanded on that knowledge to develop tactics against an opposing squadron of equal firepower. Two things became evident during the practice encounters: quickness of commitment, and a willingness to engage with his own cruiser immediately.

Cruisers usually stood off from a battle, committing the smaller escort ships first and engaging its larger guns from a distance only when necessary. Against the usual adversaries, small groups of smugglers, a cruiser's firepower was never needed.

But against a full squadron, M'Dama quickly learned that the cruiser was key to the outcome. A squadron that was not ready, that had not fully committed to battle, would suffer immediate losses, and those early losses could be magnified by the awesome firepower of his cruiser. He could then concentrate the full firepower of his squadron against the enemy cruiser. He believed most squadron commanders would not be well prepared to conduct a battle on this scale.

Nor did he kid himself. The losses, no matter who won, would be devastating to both sides.

Well, that was the mission Seeton had set him on. It might not come to pass, and he desperately hoped it would not, but the reality of the two missing couriers was never far from his thoughts.

* * * * *

The visit to Bvest was enlightening. An old friend from the academy, Commander Agoda, had aged beyond belief. And he had been demoted from captain to commander.

"Failure to swear allegiance," he said quietly over refreshments at a local pub.

"Allegiance to whom?" M'Dama asked.

"The new order. What else?"

"The Rebels have reached into fleet command?"

"They have here. I hear it's not so everywhere."

"Can you give me numbers? Has Orion Sector gone over to the Rebels?"

"I don't think so. I can't give you numbers – I don't know them. We have a new admiral here who has definitely sided with the Rebels. I hear he was recently promoted to that rank by the governor, then assigned here."

"By the governor! It's Korban's job to assign admirals."

"It is. Scuttlebutt has it that Korban's hanging on by a thread and has had to make compromises with the governor. He's choosing his battles, fighting those he can win and compromising on those he can't. The governor is new, too."

"We just got a new governor in Aldebaran Sector, as well. I don't think he's made any headway at all against Seeton. It's probably just a matter of time, though. The politicians hold all the power in the long run."

"Well, I can only say that Korban is fighting a holding action. To what end, I don't know. Look what's happened here, and we're just on the fringes, not in the thick of things. Maybe that's why he gave in to the governor in our case. I would imagine he's in a pretty tough spot. How do you fight the politicians? We've sworn to do their bidding."

"We have, but only if we recognize their legitimacy. Seeton doesn't, nor do I. It's pretty obvious where you stand."

"I'll quit before I go against everything I've ever stood for, and I'm not alone. We keep hoping someone will provide the leadership we need to pull us together. We're basically powerless right now, and it's getting worse."

"Would you like to leave? I've got room for you in my squadron."

"I'd love to, but the answer is no. Besides the fact that my family is here, I'm not ready to quit. I'll hang in here until the bitter end. Can you give me any encouragement?"

"Nothing specific, but you can tell people you trust that you are not forgotten. A lot of us have refused to capitulate. I believe the day will come when you will have the opportunity to turn the tables. I personally would not want to be your new admiral. I think his tenure will be short."

Agoda smiled. "That's what I wanted to hear. We'll be ready to assist whoever it is that opposes these tyrants. Unless, of course, they're tyrants themselves."

"They're not. Like you, they stand by their oaths. What that means in the absence of Empire I don't know, but they're the good guys. I can't say more."

Others from his squadron returned with similar stories. Things were bleak here on Bvest.

M'Dama set sail for his next stop, Krandt, with a heavy heart. He realized now that Seeton had been sheltering his men from the new Rebel politicians, and his respect for the man rose to a new level. To the fleet in Aldebaran Sector, little had changed since the coup. He now had a much better idea of what Seeton was up against, and he wondered at the skills it took to deal with the new government without capitulating.

He prepared a message drone to Seeton and launched it just before his second jump through hyperspace. Shortly after that jump, he was called to the bridge.

Captain Stning greeted him with a frown, motioning him over to one of the boards. "Sir, I think we're being followed."

"Followed! Through hyperspace? Not possible."

"My thoughts exactly, sir. But look at this," Stning said pointing to the board. "This is immediately after our first jump. We were preparing to launch the drone when we discovered another ship on our long range scanner. I chalked it up to pure coincidence, but here it is again after our last jump." The picture on the board changed to the current time. Indeed, a ship held station far behind them.

"What ship is it?" M'Dama asked.

"It's too far away to say. Nor can I say if it's the same ship we saw before, but it's gone beyond coincidence at this point."

"Agreed. Have you hailed him?"

"Yes. There's no response."

"Hmm. Perhaps we should pay him a visit."

"I'd like that very much," Captain Stning replied.

"Very well. You'll have orders from the Operations Center momentarily." M'Dama pulled a communicator from his belt and issued orders to his staff. When he was done, he turned back to Stning, his upper hands preening his whiskers in thought. "Was the ship there before we launched the drone?"

"No, sir. It showed up just as we jumped."

"Did you happen to notice if the drone made its first jump?"

"No, sir. We didn't wait around long enough."

"Hmm. I think we'll prepare another drone. I'll be in the Operations Center, Captain."

The squadron turned about and headed toward the nearby ship. It, too, turned about and away from them, keeping its distance from them constant. Even at full speed they were not able to close the distance.

M'Dama's whiskers were getting the full treatment by then. "Come about and resume course to Krandt," he ordered. We'll see if he follows. To an aide, he added, "Prepare another drone for Admiral Seeton. We'll launch this one the moment we drop from hyper and see what happens. Set it to jump as soon as it can."

The jump went as planned. The drone launched just as the trailing ship appeared. It changed its course to intercept the drone, and the squadron changed its course to intercept, as well.

The mystery ship had two choices now: it could break off its attack on the drone and continue shadowing the squadron, or it could go after the drone and risk the squadron catching up to it. The three ships gradually drew closer to each other, then the drone winked out of existence. It had jumped long before the mystery ship reached it.

The moment the drone disappeared, the interloper headed away from the squadron at top speed. There was no chance of catching it. M'Dama called off the intercept and turned his ships back toward Krandt.

Captain Stning called M'Dama to the bridge. "We got closer this time, sir. We still can't identify the ship, but it's a Chessori trader."

"Chessori! Are you certain?"

"Absolutely certain, sir."

M'Dama altered course away from Krandt after two more jumps, but the Chessori trader remained on their tail. No one had a clue how the Chessori was tracking them through hyperspace, but there was no doubt now that it was, indeed, tracking them.

* * * * *

The meetings on Krandt went much differently than they had on Bvest. M'Dama, after meeting an old shipmate, was quickly escorted to the admiral's office. Admiral Dgoffs, he discovered, was still very much aligned with the old Empire. Efforts were underway to undermine that loyalty, but those efforts had been rebuffed. He had refused to stand down when his replacement arrived. That replacement had been sent packing on the first commercial ship available, and the destination was far from Orion III. It would be months before he returned to Orion III with the news. What would happen then was anyone's guess, but Dgoffs believed the Rebels would go after softer targets before setting their sights on him. The clock was ticking, but he would never submit to Rebel domination.

"Do you have word of Admiral Korban?" M'Dama asked.

"I do. I returned from a meeting with him just before this new admiral showed up."

"Can you tell me how things are going on Orion III?"

"I cannot, unless you can provide some proof of whose side you're on."

"So sides are being taken here, too?"

Dgoffs nodded. "They are. Where do you stand?"

M'Dama hesitated, then committed. "I stand against Struthers. I can tell you that something is being organized to fight the Rebels, but I am not free to divulge details."

"What is your interest in Korban?"

M'Dama's whiskers began getting another workout. "I can't say. We, too, cannot afford to trust anyone."

Slamming his fist on his desk, the admiral growled, "A fine state of affairs. Our forces are reduced to individuals commanding loyalty only to themselves. We must find a way to resurrect the old structure."

"The old structure had its basis in politics, as will any future structure." M'Dama replied.

"Too true. But it won't be these Rebels, not in my district, and not in a lot of others. Korban's hand is yet strong, but it weakens by the day. I can say no more. I suggest you pay him a personal visit."

"I may do just that," M'Dama replied. "I might be speaking out of turn, sir, but your actions and words give me hope. The future structure you seek is under formation. Its success depends entirely on others like you who hold firm."

Dgoff's gaze narrowed. "Who's in charge?"

"I can't say, sir. I can say, however, that you will be pleased."

"Humph. I hope you're right. You can tell whoever it is that I can be counted on to hold true to the old Empire beliefs. That will tell him whether I'm in or out."

"You'll be in, sir. Tell me, have you heard anything about a Chessori ability to track ships through hyperspace?"

Dgoffs spoke the Chessori name as an expletive. "Chessori! They're trying to weasel their way into everything. I've received orders from the governor to allow 'observers' aboard my warships. I haven't refused the order, not yet, but I haven't found any Chessori that meet my qualifications either. And I won't. What's this about tracking through hyperspace? It's completely new to me."

"Me, too, but we were followed from Bvest, matched jump for jump. And the Chessori did its best to take out our messenger drones."

Dgoffs leaned back in his chair, his eyes slits. He remained silent for a time. When he spoke, it was softly. "These Chessori are bad news, Commodore. I'm beginning to wonder if they're in cahoots with the Rebels."

M'Dama's whiskers began a new, refreshing preening. After a time, he said, "To what end? What benefit would they be to the Rebels? They're just traders."

Dgoffs peered through slitted eyes as he replied, "So they say.

What do we really know about them? You tell me they tracked you through hyper. What else can they do?"

M'Dama had no reply.

"I need to pay another visit to Korban," Dgoffs said, "but I dare not leave right now. If you're off to see him, please inform him of our conversation. I know he's under the same pressure to allow Chessori among his crews."

"I really can't say where I'm headed, sir," M'Dama said.

"Doesn't matter. I can read between the lines."

"After turning out your replacement, I think you may need to be careful about visits to Orion III. I know of at least two other couriers that vanished on their way to Korban."

"Hmm. Give my regards to him when you see him. *If* you see him," the admiral said as he rose from his chair.

"I shall endeavor to do so, sir."

Another messenger drone was prepared during the voyage out-system with a synopsis of everything M'Dama had learned from Dgoffs and the other contacts his men had made. This time M'Dama decided to launch the drone before his first jump, and he followed it until it winked out of existence. Only then did he set course for Orion III.

Shortly after the first jump, a full squadron of Empire ships appeared on his screens. He considered briefly, then ordered another drone launched.

"What message do you want to send?" Captain Stning asked.

"No message. Just launch the drone as quickly as you can, and make sure its trajectory is not too far from this approaching squadron. Give it plenty of time before it jumps. I want to see what happens."

The drone was launched, and a fighter from the approaching squadron dispatched it before it reached its jump point. M'Dama set off for his command center, setting his battle plans in motion on the way. When he arrived, he opened a communications link to the approaching squadron.

"Identify yourself," he demanded.

The picture of a large human, one of the giant N'Ninwa, formed on the communicator. "Admiral Jsbaki here. Would you be so kind as to pull over for a chat?"

"I don't think so," M'Dama replied. "Why did you take out my drone?"

"Orders, you know. Let's see . . . you're a commodore, right? That means I outrank you. I'm ordering you to pay me a courtesy call. Just you."

"I don't think so, sir," M'Dama replied.

"Then I shall, regretfully, have to ask you to turn your command over to me."

"A squadron commander cannot give such an order, sir."

"I'm giving you an order, Commodore. If you force my hand, I will have to demand your surrender."

"You're an Empire squadron. How can you ask for the surrender of another Empire squadron?"

"Well, it seems your political affiliations are in question. Come on over and we can chat about it."

M'Dama's whiskers were not getting their usual workout. He was entirely calm, though deeply disappointed. "I think I'll just leave," he said.

"You know that won't work. You can't hide from us."

"Are you prepared to fight?"

"If I must," Admiral Jsbaki replied.

"I will not condone Empire ships fighting each other," M'Dama announced in as disappointing a voice as he could construct. "I'll come about while I consider your orders. Will you join me aboard my ship?"

"No, but I think I'll let our squadrons merge. That way you won't get too frisky."

"Very well. I'll get back to you later," M'Dama replied as he broke the communications link. Then he began issuing orders. His squadron held its formation for the time being while he studied the opposing fleet's trajectories. The two squadrons approached each other, his own support ships spreading out just enough to provide safe spacing for Jsbaki's ships as they mingled with his own. It was a strange feeling – he had never seen two squadrons merge before. Squadrons always maintained their own integrity. Jsbaki could not have made his intentions more clear. M'Dama wondered how prepared Jsbaki and his men were to engage him. Was this posturing, or were they planning to open fire before he did?

As he had anticipated, Jsbaki held his cruiser in reserve. Each ship in M'Dama's squadron was assigned a target. M'Dama briefly considered the legal implications of his ships firing the first shot without warning, but he quickly dismissed the idea. Jsbaki's demand for surrender was, in essence, all the declaration of war he needed.

The squadrons merged, and he gave the order. Guns on the ships of his squadron opened up on their targets. His frigate took out three enemy fighters in seconds, then joined him to focus on Jsbaki's frigate. M'Dama opened up with twelve batteries, and his frigate brought all its guns into action. Jsbaki's frigate never had a chance and went dead in space within just a few minutes. The fact that it didn't simply explode spoke volumes about the hardness of these large capital ships.

The enemy fighters responded more quickly than the capital ships, but only five remained after the opening salvo. M'Dama paired up his fighters against Jsbaki's fighters with two-to-one odds, and he and his frigate turned to engage Jsbaki's cruiser which was just entering the fray.

To the best of M'Dama's knowledge, two cruisers had never before been locked in mortal combat. He had the upper hand as a result of his earlier preparations, but killing a cruiser was a difficult and lengthy process. His gunners had predetermined targets, and they were effective, but plans rarely held together after the first shot was fired. Both cruisers moved sprightly despite their bulk, and targets did not remain in the crosshairs for long.

His own cruiser took a direct hit on a main battery. The whole ship shook with the resultant explosion. Worse, the shields failed in that area. Captain Stning adroitly maneuvered the massive ship to protect the area from Jsbaki's guns. Between M'Dama's cruiser and his frigate, Jsbaki lost five of his twelve batteries in a short period, and he was forced to defend himself against two capital ships at the same time with his remaining seven batteries. When M'Dama ordered his cruiser and frigate to concentrate on just one side of the ship, the weakened side, Jsbaki had only two batteries with which he could return fire. He rolled his ship, of course, to bring the other batteries into action, but by then he'd lost one more battery.

M'Dama lost another main battery, and one weapons control center was lost in the ensuing blast which again shook the whole ship. Other control centers picked up the load. So far, he had not lost a single ship, though each of them had suffered significant damage. Jsbaki's fighters were giving as good as they received, but against two-to-one odds, they had little chance. It wasn't long before they were gone, and M'Dama ordered his fighters to support his frigate which had suffered badly but was still operational. He had never seen fighting so intense. In less than an hour Jsbaki's cruiser began having difficulty maneuvering, then it stopped maneuvering at all. It went dead in space.

M'Dama's staff let out a cheer. They had done it!

Jsbaki appeared on the communicator. The nonchalant attitude was no longer in evidence.

"Are you prepared to surrender?" M'Dama demanded.

"No. I just wanted to say that you put up a valiant effort. Congratulations on a job well done. I'll say farewell now."

His visage disappeared from the screen. Moments later everyone in both fleets suffered the horror of the Chessori mind weapon, the first time for all of them. M'Dama's body fell to the floor, spasming out of control. All coherent thought ceased. The agony lasted for hours as Jsbaki's Chessori counterparts on the cruiser pounded away at him. The end, when it finally came, was a blessing.

Chapter Fifty-three

Beta IV, with the Queen aboard, dropped from hyperspace and her bridge screens filled quickly with information. One planet, indeed the only planet circling the bright yellow sun ahead, held center stage. The system bustled with civilian ship activity. As yet, the bridge crew detected no hostile response.

The planet hung in space like a jewel, perfectly suited for colonization except for one thing: it was so far off the space lanes that no one wanted to come here. Located on the very fringes of the galaxy, its night skies were hideously dark, devoid of stars except for a dim, narrow band in the direction of the galactic core. In every other respect, the planet bordered on ideal. A molten planetary core and three moons ensured an abundance of seismic activity. Very tall mountain ranges and small tides were the result. Heavy metals and minerals lay within easy reach. The planet had virtually no axial tilt, consequently temperatures varied little at any given location. A large portion of the planet basked in pleasant, temperate conditions, making Parsons' World a farmer's dream come true. With abundant sources of energy and good planning to prevent the planet from becoming mired in industrial wastes and pollution, Parsons' World provided a perfect environment in almost all ways, lacking only one thing: neighbors.

Parsons' World: comfortable, desirable, naturally wealthy in resources, lacking nothing except neighbors. Parsons' World: a den of thieves, making it a world no one else wanted, a world that didn't want anyone else, yet a world strangely key to the Queen's plans for restoring the throne.

Its location was perfect for its original settlers, a right-wing religious group that had balked at paying Empire duties and taxes. Parsons' World's self-righteous ideals had, over the millennia, metamorphosed. Its religion became its economics. The Parsons' World economic model, proudly based on beating the Empire at its own game, called for elusive, cunning, and fine-honed management of shady activities, activities defined by everyone else in the Empire as criminal.

Serge Parsons, the latest in a long succession of Parsons and an old adversary of Admiral Norris Jons, would not likely welcome their arrival, and the tattered remains of the small squadron did not have to wait long to find out. The communications screen filled with a creature made out of yellow, at least that was Mike's initial reaction. When he got over his surprise he made out an alien face feathered in bright yellow, with matching eyes, beak, crest, and ears, even a yellow tongue. The only non-yellow features were tiny black pupils within the yellow eyes. Its voice, surprisingly deep and mellow, greeted them without the slightest indication of warmth.

"Cruiser *Beta IV*, state your intentions."

"Private communication for Serge Parsons," Admiral Jons stated calmly.

"Standby."

A new face, that of a middle-aged human with brown hair, widely spaced, commanding brown eyes, and a pointed beard showing the first signs of gray, filled the screen almost immediately. "To whom do I owe the pleasure?" he asked, without humor or welcome. "Show yourself."

Jons nodded to the communications officer, and the video link energized. A grim smile appeared on Serge Parsons' face as his brow furrowed in thought. "Jons, my favorite Fleet troublemaker." Peering more closely, he added, "Why, you've been promoted! Congratulations, Admiral. What's on your agenda today? What have I done to risk your ire this time?"

"We need a tightbeam conversation, Serge. Can you arrange it on your end?"

"That's a military tool, Norris. You know that. I wouldn't have any idea how to do such a thing."

"Serge, I'm not here to threaten you. Just do it."

Parsons searched Jons' eyes for a time. "I'd feel a little better if you'd shed some of that *delta v*. Looks to me like you're bent on getting here in a hurry."

"I am in a hurry. I'll shed a little *v* if it will make you feel better. Heck, I'll even swing the conn over a few degrees, but I don't want to waste a lot of time. Get back to me as soon as you can."

It took the communications officer and the ground controllers ten minutes to set up the link. When Serge Parsons returned, he was seated behind a desk in a comfortably appointed office.

"Okay, Norris. You have my undivided attention, but don't think things aren't hopping down here."

"How secure are we?" Jons queried.

Parsons' eyes narrowed. "What's going on, Norris? Nothing's absolutely secure, you know that." He paused, then added carefully, thoughtfully, "We're probably more secure than you realize. We have a few tricks you haven't figured out yet. You didn't get rid of much *delta v* by the way. You'd better talk fast."

"Do you know about the coup?"

"Of course. You know I have excellent intelligence." His eyes narrowed. "Not you, too, Norris. Don't tell me you've switched sides. I won't believe you."

"Would you believe me if I said I'm requesting asylum?"

"Hmm . . . that's a twist." He ran a hand through his hair and rubbed the back of his neck while considering. "Parsons' World is not in the business of offering asylum to Imperial squadrons. And, no, it doesn't fit. I don't see you giving up, Norris. Your coming here will just attract a lot of unwanted attention. Go somewhere else."

Jons gave out an exasperated sigh. "It's not for me, Serge. It's for my passengers. I'm just the delivery boy. We can't discuss this over the comm. I'll guarantee safe passage if you'll come up for a meeting."

"Not a chance, Norris. I might be willing to offer safe passage for one ship to come down. A small ship."

"Serge, that won't do. These are special circumstances. I give you my word that I'm not here to fight."

"Sorry. We have too much history behind us, you and I, and not all of it honorable."

Ellandra of the Chosen stepped into the video pickup, her gaze locking onto Parsons.' His face drained of color. He rose slowly from his chair as if a great weight had suddenly been placed on his shoulders. "I see . . ."

The connection broke. Jons broke his end of the transmission, as well. Moments later Serge Parsons' visage appeared on the screen, indicating the tightbeam transmission had been terminated.

"I'm coming out to meet you, but I won't come aboard. You have my personal guarantee that anyone who boards my ship will be returned safely. That squadron of yours will have to remain out-system. That's the best I can do." He broke the connection.

Jons turned to the others. "Can't say I'm surprised. Our coming to the planet with a cruiser is a risk he's unwilling to take. I would probably do the same in his shoes. Do we call it off?"

Mike broke the silence. "We need to do this. We also have to think about the Queen's safety. What . . ."

Ellie interrupted. "Mike, there's still Alexis. She can remain here to ensure the line of Chosen continues if something happens to me. Serge Parsons is a businessman. We must negotiate with him, but only I can determine if he is a true scoundrel or a man of honor."

Admiral Jons cleared his throat and said, "Based on our values, he's a scoundrel, Your Majesty, but from his point of view, he's not. He has a personal code of honor to which I believe he remains true. As for his associates, I can't speak for them. I believe you can trust his personal guarantee of safety."

"Then it's settled."

* * * * *

Ellie, Mike, Reba, Val, Otis, Jessie, and Admiral Jons were escorted to Serge Parsons' office aboard his ship. They found him sitting at a personal command center in his office engrossed in the net, probably ensuring they kept their end of the bargain. He kept them waiting for a time, then lifted the helmet from his head and rose, stepping out from behind his desk to approach the Queen. He did not kneel.

"Welcome, Your Majesty," he stated with pursed lips. "Your ships appear to be moving off."

"As promised, my fleet will not threaten you provided you keep your end of the agreement."

"Huh! Some agreement! Never thought I'd see the day . . . Would you care for refreshments, or would you like to get down to business?"

Admiral Jons introduced the group, then spoke for all of them. "Serge, we'd like to propose, well, heck, it's pretty obvious why we're here. We need help."

Serge leaned back to sit on the edge of his desk. Crossing his arms, he said, "I'm a simple man. You know how I operate. What's in it for me?"

Ellie spoke up. "Perhaps legitimacy, Mr. Parsons? I may be able to work something out along those lines."

"Legitimacy! What would I want with legitimacy?" he asked, perplexed. "That would take all the challenge and profit out of it." Looking closely at Ellie, he said, "I do not seek, nor do I need, legitimacy, Your Majesty. My business is not at all hindered by your fleets' best efforts to shut me down. You'll have to do better than that."

"What is it you seek, Mr. Parsons?"

"An open-ended offer like that?" He thought for a time, then rose to face her. "This coup is bad for business. For the moment, things are in turmoil and the pickings are easy, but the long-term prospects are bleak. No one will be able to hold all this together. I'm already adding more armaments to my ships for their own protection. Before you know it, piracy will be rife. Every planet's going to have to protect itself, and interstellar trade, including my own, is going to drop off to nothing. It'll be too risky. I like avoiding duties and taxes, but I'm no pirate. I want things to go back to the way they were."

"You're not a pirate?" Mike asked, surprised.

"Of course not!" Serge replied. "Where's the long-term profit in that? Hasn't Norris told you what I do?"

"I think inferences were made, but nothing specific."

"Care to do the honors, Norris?"

"Serge, even I don't know everything you're tied up in. Illegal ship modifications and smuggling are what I've gone after you for. I suspect weapons manufacturing and distribution, drug smuggling, hiring criminals. For all I know you've sunk to slavery, assassination, transporting mercenary armies, and who knows what else."

"And you came here in spite of those beliefs?" Serge asked incredulously. "Maybe I'm working for the other side. Have you thought of that?"

"Are you?" Ellie asked sharply.

"No, Your Majesty, I am not. Nor do I condone assassination or slavery. Any drugs I carry have antidotes and are used by those who choose their own fates. As to the rest, we have standards here. Any of my people caught operating outside our standards have everything they own confiscated and are not allowed to return."

"Honor among thieves, eh?" Ellie scoffed.

"There you have it, Your Majesty," Serge answered proudly.

"I'm a thief, but only in the eyes of the Empire. In my little fiefdom, we stick to the Code. Your Empire can afford it," he added, amusement showing in his eyes.

Ellie walked up to him. "Perhaps with a little modification of the Code to fit our present reality, we can forge a temporary alliance."

"I repeat, what's in it for me?"

"Is a return to the status quo adequate?" Ellie responded immediately.

"What's it going to cost?"

"Lots, maybe all that you have. Perhaps even more. The only thing I can promise is that in return you will get plenty of that 'challenge' you crave." She stood her ground before him, adding, "By your own words, you admit that your success is based on the success of the Empire. Like it or not, that makes you a part of the Empire. I am your Queen, Mr. Parsons. I require your help, and I am asking for your help."

"Humph," he grumbled. "I'll not fall into that trap so easily. I may be willing to help in small ways, but my personal fortune would not dent the resources you're up against."

She smiled. "Then we'll just have to use it wisely, won't we."

"What is it you need?"

She grimaced and turned away from him, pacing, her hands clutched behind her. "I plan to attack the problem on two distinct levels: political and military. A political solution is, and will remain, our highest priority. My military forces will help provide the means for us to get our political message out.

"I rule the Empire, Mr. Parsons. To rule in the manner of the Chosen is to serve. I will continue to serve with every fiber of my being. I would welcome the opportunity to give up that responsibility, but I cannot and will not do so until our legitimate political process makes that demand of me. The Rebel leadership has led everyone to believe the line of Chosen is ended, that there is no hope of restoring the Empire as it was. My job is really quite simple, at least on the surface. I have to prove to the Imperial Senate that the line of Chosen is not ended. After that, the Senate can choose whatever form of leadership it so desires, as it has always chosen. It is the very reason my line is referred to as 'Chosen.' As much as I might wish it otherwise, I believe the royal family will have the requisite popular support.

"So, we need a strong, loyal military to keep these Rebels in check while we pursue the more fundamental track to permanent resolution in the political arena. One cannot happen without the other. I will not stop this coup militarily, I am not willing to subject the general populace to all-out civil war, but I cannot rebuild the necessary political foundation without a strong military force behind me.

"We start with the military side of things. That force is almost nonexistent right now. It will need a leader which I will supply, and it will need a secure base of operations, something you may be able to help us with until it gets on its feet. We might also take advantage of some of those unusual ship modifications Admiral Jons referred to."

Mike went to Ellie's side. He met Parsons' gaze squarely. "There you have the gist of our plan, Mr. Parsons. We need to flesh it out with intelligence, we need a base, a few ship repairs, and help getting around for a while. Beyond that, we can't say at the moment, but there will be more."

"Call me Serge, all of you," he said to Mike, Ellie, and turning to encompass the rest as his head nodded. "As strange as it may seem, and I find this very strange indeed, we seek the same ends. You're right, Your Majesty," he said turning back to her, "when you say that in the long term Parsons' World needs the Empire. A year ago I would not have agreed with you, but now . . . now I believe we're on the same team. Perhaps only for the moment, but we're on the same team."

Turning to Mike, he asked, "What happened to your arm, First Knight?"

Mike grimaced as he looked down at the arm strapped across his body. "A little run in with the Chessori, I'm afraid."

"Ah, yes. The Chessori," Serge mumbled as he looked away, troubled. His eyes rose back to Mike's. "They're in it up to their missing eyebrows. And they're cutting into my business. I'm hearing rumors about a disgusting psi weapon they've designed. Can you tell me if these rumors are true?"

"Too true, I'm afraid, though we suspect the weapon may be inbred. Do you have any information to the contrary?"

"Inbred, eh? Interesting." Serge thought for a moment. "No, only rumors. But if I can get my hands on one of them, and I'm working on it, we'll soon find out. I've dealt with the Chessori. I don't think they're all bad. They're excellent traders," he added grimly.

"We need information on the coup, Serge. How good is your intelligence? Do you know who's behind it, how extensively they've taken over?"

Serge turned to Ellie. "You don't know?"

"We know very little. We suspect a lot. I was away at the time, trying to work out a treaty with the Chessori. I have not yet returned to the Palace. What can you tell us?"

"Two squadrons escorted you on that mission. Are the nine ships out there all that have returned?" Serge asked, worry in his voice.

Ellie rose to stand before him. "It's time for me to determine your true loyalties, Mr. Parsons. Will you submit to a Test?"

"I will definitely not submit," he said, taking a step back and holding out a hand to ward her off. "We may be on the same team temporarily, but I, too, have state secrets to protect."

"My gift can be controlled, Serge. I give you my word that I will not probe. I only wish to determine the truth of the words you speak. Without agreement on this we'll be forced to leave. You'll have to decide how to deal with any future governments on your own. I do not offer a second opportunity for this." She folded her arms as she awaited his response.

"I've sworn an oath to never submit to your probe, Your Majesty. It's against our Code."

"I'm not Testing you under duress, Serge. I am not interrogating you, and Admiral Jons has not captured you, but I must determine the truth of you as it relates to me. Nothing more. Each of the others in this room has been through this and will vouch, I am certain, for the fact that I never, ever, reveal to others what I discover without their permission."

"I believe in two-way deals. How can I be certain of your words?"

"Is thousands of years of precedent not adequate?"

He turned away from her and thought long and hard before reaching a personal decision. When he turned back to her, gone was the light, devil-may-care attitude. He spoke softly. "These are unusual times and the stakes are the very highest. Many will be forced to make personal choices."

He smiled a sad smile. "Indeed, your very presence aboard this vessel means that our old world is gone, perhaps forever. Whatever happens, my people will have a new order to contend with. Parsons' World may not survive the coming conflict, certainly not in the style we now enjoy, if the Rebels succeed in their efforts. But more fundamental, my forefathers would insist we choose that which is right over that which is convenient. I will do my best to see that Parsons' World does so.

"For me personally, what you intend is right. For our mutual benefit, I hereby pledge my personal support to you along with my very considerable resources. I will see this through to its end with you. As for Parsons' World, my people will have to speak for themselves. I believe I can swing things in your favor, but the task will not be easy, nor will it happen overnight or in secrecy. Initially, the help I offer will be limited.

You may proceed with your Touch."

He sat down on the edge of his desk, and Ellie placed both of her hands around his head. She entered his mind, as only a Chosen could, and did her thing. Mike wasn't certain, but he thought he detected a momentary look of surprise on her face. When she was done, she dropped her hands from his head to his shoulders, leaned toward him, and said softly, "Thank you, Serge. You speak true."

Poor Serge was still shaking his head to clear it as she stepped away.

"You have pledged your support, and I accept that pledge, but only after you understand the full depth of my plight." His eyes rose to meet hers, and she added, "Truth is a two-way street, Serge. You deserve to know. I set out with two squadrons and nearly five thousand people. Of those, one damaged ship, four people, and one Rider survived. Admiral Jons, his ships, and three of the four Knights here were not part of the treaty mission. They have each endured staggering risks to keep me alive. The ships of Admiral Jons squadron, each of them severely damaged and understaffed, are the extent of my forces at the moment."

Serge continued to shake his head. "Did I hear right? Only five made it back?"

"If you call this 'back,' yes, five people made it back. In my mind, we have not and will not have made it back until we stand free in the Palace."

Serge was stunned. "What happened?"

"Soon after our arrival on Dorwall, we experienced the mind weapon of the Chessori for the first time. My Protectors, led by Sir Otis, got us off the planet, but none of the other ships made it. We escaped with only one ship, and almost everyone on the ship had been killed. We picked up Sir Mike and Lady Reba at our first stop and we fought off more Chessori, but a Rebel squadron was waiting for us as soon as we made it off-planet."

"Don't tell me you took on a whole squadron."

"No, we didn't. We jumped."

Serge, startled and deeply troubled, walked back to his desk and leaned against it, his back to the rest of the room and his shoulders slumped in defeat. "The Empire has fast ships, Your Majesty?" he demanded.

"What's a fast ship?"

He turned quickly, a furious look on his face. "The Chosen cannot lie. Answer me!"

She raised an eyebrow. "Tell me what a fast ship is."

"A ship that can make jumps inside a system."

"I've never heard of such a thing, Serge." She turned to Jons with a questioning look.

Jons, too, looked surprised, then thoughtful. His eyes rose to the ceiling as he recalled various encounters with Serge's traders, traders that he believed were smugglers.

"Is that how you're doing it?" he asked softly.

Serge's shoulders slumped again, and he walked around his desk to sit in his chair, his eyes shifting between Jons and Mike. "How else could you jump so close to the primary star? No AI in existence would let you."

"We had a pretty sharp Artificial Intelligence," Mike answered, sensing that more was going on in the room than he understood. "It was more like a person, and I named it George. He calculated the least dangerous jump, then died so that I could execute the jump manually."

Serge rubbed his face with both hands. "This is getting out of control. What you describe is impossible, First Knight. There's no way you brought that ship clear across the galaxy, without an AI."

"It was that or die. It took a year, Serge."

"A year," Serge spat out, not believing him.

Mike nodded. "During part of the voyage we also had to fight off more Chessori. They tracked us through hyperspace, and we had some difficulty losing it."

"Wait a minute. Are you saying you were tracked through hyperspace?"

"We were definitely tracked, though we believe the tracker read our jump commands just prior to the jump while we were in normal space. We tested the idea, and I'm confident that we were right. We believe a tracker mechanism was installed in the ship prior to its departure for Dorwall."

"Humph. How did you get away?"

"I'll tell you if you'll tell us more about these fast ships you're referring to."

Serge's lips pursed and he changed the subject. "So how did Jons get involved?"

Ellie spoke. "Sir Mike brought us to Gamma VI, and we were again attacked by Rebels and Chessori. I announced my presence, and Admiral Jons' squadron is what remains after a mutiny culled Rebels from loyal Empire crewmembers. The fighting was terrible, as you can imagine, and the squadron is not operational."

"You test my imagination, Your Majesty."

"The story is true. I vouch for it as a Chosen."

Serge leaned back in his chair and looked at Mike. "You really brought that ship through multiple jumps *manually*?"

"No. *We* brought it through manually. All of us."

"You said your injuries were the result of the Chessori."

Ellie intervened. "Jons' squadron was riddled with Chessori observers. The failure of the treaty mission and the coup go hand in hand, Serge. It was all a set-up, a set-up that we blindly walked into. The Rebels and Chessori are clearly in league with each other."

"Jeez, I never put the two together quite like that," he said, stunned. "You know that Struthers is behind the coup, don't you?"

"Struthers! Mother's First Knight? Impossible!"

"Sadly not, Your Highness. Admiral Juster is his right hand man."

"My brother? Are you mad?" she yelled, a look of horror on her face. She swayed on her feet, then collapsed.

* * * * *

Serge's ship arrived at Parsons' World a week later, but his first stop was not at a spaceport. At Ellie's request, Serge brought the ship down in an uninhabited wasteland far from civilization. The Great Cats set up a perimeter, then Ellie and Mike walked out into the desert.

The sun was just rising as Serge watched Ellie and Mike walk away from the ship. A hundred meters from the ship, Ellie took Mike by the shoulders, and together they sank to their knees facing each other. To Serge's astonishment, Ellie reached both hands to the ground and scooped up a handful of dirt. Mike, too, reached to the ground with his one hand and grasped a handful of dirt. They faced each other and raised their hands to the level of their chins, then slowly let the dirt trickle through their fingers until their hands were empty. Then they did it again, and once again. No words were exchanged that Serge could see or hear. When they were done, Ellie helped Mike to his feet and they returned arm in arm to the ship. The ship lifted and turned towards Serge's home, and he never discovered the purpose of this strange event.

Chapter Fifty-four

A long, fat freighter lifted sluggishly from Parsons' World, headed out-system with Val and Reba aboard.

Two days later, a similar ship followed with four Great Cats and a team of men and women hand-picked by Serge Parsons.

A full week passed before a fast scout carrying Ellie, Mike, and the rest of their delegation shot up from Parsons' World going for all it was worth, chased by a number of heavily armed traders. The scout outran its pursuers, matched courses with *Beta IV,* and was taken aboard. The squadron turned and fled. A few shots were exchanged with the pursuing ships, all from long range, but they had no hope against the *Beta IV* and eventually turned back.

Weeks later, *Beta IV* and her escorts jumped, disappearing from the system. They would rendezvous with yet a third Parsons' World trader in deep space where Ellie and Mike would transfer to the trader. As far as most of Parsons' World knew, the special visitors had outstayed their welcome there. It was a simple deception, but Serge Parsons needed time to convince other leaders on Parsons' World that joining with the Queen was in their best interests. His commitment to the Queen would remain closely held for as long as it could.

To Mike, the whole operation marked a turning point in his

experience – it was but the first of the castle intrigues that he feared would become commonplace in his life.

Chapter Fifty-five

Ten weeks later *Beta IV* and her escorts dropped out of hyperspace on the fringes of Centauri III, Sector Headquarters of Admiral Chandrajuski. Centauri Sector was huge, extending roughly in a pie shape from heavily traveled lanes close to Triton Sector all the way out to the border, an area of continuing exploration.

Chosen partly for its central location within the sector, Centauri III had been developed over the centuries into a purely governmental world, a center for sector administration. As with any center of government, it had sprouted developed areas settled by wealthy bureaucrats, lobbyists, and administrators, and it had sprouted nearby areas of hangers-on, the less than affluent cast-offs of every society, and every level of society in between. A prime sector, Serge's intelligence indicated the Rebels had taken over Centauri III.

Admiral Chandrajuski, unbeknownst to himself, was the individual chosen by Ellie to rebuild her military forces.

After dropping from hyper, *Beta IV* completed the identification process with ground controllers and was cleared in without delay, just one small group of many, many other ships transiting the system. When queried about their mission, the communications officer on *Beta IV* requested he speak with Admiral Chandrajuski immediately via secure link. This produced quite a delay. The duty officer eventually came on to inform them that Chandrajuski was not available.

Aboard one of Serge's sluggish freighters on the outskirts of the system, Ellie stepped up to a communicator to play her part. Her voice and video were relayed to *Beta IV*, then on to the planet, making it appear as if she was on *Beta IV*.

"Centauri III Control, I am Daughter. Do you recognize me?"

The duty officer gulped and looked at something off-screen. "Your voice identification is verified. I am at your command, Your Majesty."

"I will speak with Admiral Chandrajuski. See that he is informed."

"Yes, Your Majesty. Immediately."

Immediately turned into two hours. When Chandrajuski appeared, Mike was floored. Without having given the matter conscious thought, he'd expected a human. Well, Chandrajuski wasn't even remotely human. A bright green triangular head on the end of a long neck appeared on the communications screen, a head whose only remotely human feature might be its eyes. Those eyes reminded Mike of Albert Einstein – wise, concerned, and bright with intelligence.

"Your Majesty! What a relief to see you," he said in a deep, mellow voice. "Are you well?"

"As well as can be expected. Please ask those in attendance with you to lock-in the secure channel, then leave."

"At once," he replied. The communications officer aboard *Beta IV* made the appropriate adjustments as directed and cleared her to continue.

"What of the Empire and my family?" she demanded.

Chandrajuski closed his eyes as he searched for the right words. "Daughter . . . Your Majesty . . . I am so sorry. You must know what has happened."

"I know a little, enough to frighten me. I've heard that the Palace was decimated."

"The buildings stand, but all within are gone," he stated sadly. "The Chosen must carry on with you at its head. You are Queen."

"Queen of what?" she demanded. "Is there anything left of my realm?"

"We have many things to discuss. I am so glad you came to me instead of anywhere else. Here you will be safe. Ellandra . . . Ellandra, there is so much to discuss, then plans must be made. I will prepare for your arrival. I can have a few things ready for you when we meet in private, including a staff that I think you will find helpful. Does that meet your approval?"

"Thank you, Admiral. Until then."

She signed off and reached for the nearest seat with a shaking hand. Her eyes had sunk inside dark circles. When she looked up at Mike, she reached for his hand and squeezed hard.

"Our worst fears have come true. They're waiting for us. He is not in command."

"You're certain?" he asked.

"Yes. Did you catch the queues, or have you forgotten what I taught you?"

"Hardly. Jake won't let me. I caught the use of your first name. That's bad."

"Using it twice is very bad," she informed him. "We'll have to activate our alternate plan. I knew this wouldn't be easy, but deep inside I had hoped we might run into a little good luck for a change. The only other thing of consequence he said was about a staff. We might find some help among them."

Beta IV continued inbound. Soon, though, a fleet of Empire ships dropped out of hyperspace nearby and changed trajectory to close with her. *Beta IV* waited as long as she could, then turned away from the planet, set up a jump, and disappeared from all screens. The pursuing ships followed, though after a few more jumps they would lose the tracker signal from the cruiser. Parsons' World technicians had located the device and left instructions on its removal. After its removal, *Beta IV* and her attending ships would be free to head to their new base for refitting.

Mike contacted Val and Reba and cleared them in. They hit atmosphere on the night side of the planet with Reba flying *Joline* at the captain's invitation. Chosen personally by Serge, Captain Palmetier knew the situation with the Queen and was an active supporter.

Reba had been enchanted upon entering *Joline's* net, though Val had been shocked and angered at the nature of the ship. *Joline* was a trader, long, fat, and ugly. The underside of the ship was flat to permit as much surface area as possible to contact the ground upon landing. Numerous cargo bays made up most of her interior. Appearing slow and ungainly, just a typical freighter, this ship was not what she seemed. She could outrun most Empire military ships, though she had never needed to. She could also defend herself like an angry hornet, but again she had never needed to. If her crew ever let a situation deteriorate to that point, they had failed in their covert jobs.

But most enchanting to Reba was her net, her equivalent of George. Unlike *Beta IV's* net that Reba had trained on, a net developed by the Empire and essentially devoid of personality, *Joline* was delightful and, like George, she craved friends, though she was not limited to keeping her friends safe as George had been. In fact, unless overridden, her programming required her to prevent forced boarding by Empire troops at any cost. Serge Parsons' secrets were not to be discovered by the Empire.

Joline was smart, much smarter than George had been. She'd been created on Shipyard, a secret planet maintained by Parsons' World, a world even farther out beyond the border. Focused on research, development, and manufacturing, Shipyard was Parsons' World's most jealously guarded secret.

Joline packed refinements developed on Shipyard that Val had never heard of, including a well-refined technique for making micro jumps, allowing her to jump with great accuracy much closer to planets than could other ships, almost right into atmosphere if desired. Ships with her drive were referred to as 'fast ships' by the crews who flew them. She also carried a ship's beacon that could be altered at will or simply turned off. The ship's log built into the beacon was a complete fabrication, as well. Val was aghast at this unbelievable breach of protocol. No wonder, he thought in frustration, Jons had never been able to get the goods on Parsons' World. The technology on this ship far outclassed anything he'd seen in the Fleet. Considering their present predicament, though, his eyes lit up at the possibilities.

Joline and her crew were smugglers. They were very, very good, and they were very, very proud. They never used *Joline's* special capabilities when under Empire perusal, but they did frequently use her secrets to avoid that perusal. By turning off her beacon and using the fast ship drive, she could sneak into most any planet unobserved. She couldn't use a spaceport under those circumstances, but she didn't need all the fancy facilities and landing aids used by other ships. She simply dealt directly with suppliers and end users wherever they might be.

Reba, bouncing with excitement as she made her first landfall as pilot, knew that *Joline* looked like just another meteor as she entered atmosphere. *Joline* offered suggestions and encouragement, but she remained out of the control circuits for Reba's training. In spite of its ungainly appearance, there was little sensation within the ship of its fiery path through the night sky. Reba held true to her course until picking up the automated tracking beam from the spaceport, then she carefully guided the ship down the beam, settling into her assigned berth with barely a tremor.

The crew spent hours unloading the ship, then engaged in the time honored tradition of all sailors–a visit portside for a brief return to civilization before heading out on another multi-month assignment. Reba's eyes filled with new wonders at every turn as she and Val strode purposely down the main avenue. The area bordering the spaceport felt like a frontier city, full of life and color, raucous. Skimmers, personal vehicles held aloft by antigravity generators, raced here and there, barely clearing the heads of pedestrians who strolled along, seemingly unconcerned. Val had to continually keep Reba from ducking and flinching as the skimmers whooshed overhead. He did not want her to attract undue attention by advertising her newness to Empire life, but in the end that proved to be the least of the challenges she presented.

>I'm surprised it's so boisterous,< Reba said to Celine, her Rider.

>Are ports on Earth so different?<

>Depends. I guess a lot of them are as crusty, but there's a lot more energy here than I've seen in most ports on Earth. This is a sector headquarters for the Empire. I had expected things to be clean and orderly.<

>They're as clean and orderly as the inhabitants want them to be,< Celine replied. >I find it vibrant and exciting.<

>It's all of that. I hope you don't mind that I'm being a little hard on Val. It's all in fun.<

>Fun for you, my dear, but I'm not so sure it's fun for him. He looks worried.<

>But it forces him to hold my arm, and I won't do anything stupid that might endanger the mission.<

>I know you won't. Want me to tone down the hormones?<

>Definitely not. I don't get opportunities like this. He doesn't have a chance against the two of us.<

Reba, relatively new to having a Rider aboard, was only just getting a feel for Celine's feelings, but she definitely sensed her shaking her non-existent head.

Aliens of every imaginable description, many dressed in colorful attire, walked or waddled or slithered on their appointed errands. The standard bars and houses of ill repute lined both sides of the avenue, hawkers strutted their wares on street corners and in front of shops, and the mix of smells emanating from various establishments was almost overpowering at times. Reba, doing her best to look bored, was, in reality, practically hovering over the ground with excitement. This was her second new planet, but she'd seen little of Parsons' World. Val kept her arm in his, one moment keeping her from bouncing with excitement and the next keeping her from ducking beneath a speeding skimmer. He kept up a running commentary on their surroundings as they walked.

Several blocks from the spaceport, Val and Reba separated from their crew and slid into a bar fronting the avenue. It turned out to be, essentially, a worn out refuge for spacers down on their luck. It was perfect. They were on their own now and had to make certain they weren't observed. Over the next few hours and several bars later, Val was reasonably confident they were not being followed.

He flagged down a public skimmer, and they headed across the city to meet with one of Serge's men. The 'man' turned out to be a creature standing three feet tall with an equally long tail. It reminded Reba of a platypus with a tail, and it acted the part as well, seeming like a fish out of water. Black downy fur covered its body. Its head had a short, flat beak, light green in color, and the short legs ended in fingers with webbing between the light green digits. It spoke Galactic High Standard with a noticeable lisp. Val seemed unsurprised at meeting the creature, but Reba struggled to hold back laughter.

>What is it?< she asked Celine.

>A Plankid. And yes, it prefers a water environment. Its home probably has a large pool or tub surrounded by vegetation.<

In spite of its ungainly appearance, the creature worked for Serge and was highly respected as a spy. It had no interest in their mission or with introductions, nor did it offer a name, but it had the proper password. It flagged down another skimmer and took them to a tall apartment building, directing the skimmer to a private landing at the top of the building. Two floors had been rented, including the penthouse, and standard groupings of furnishings for heterogeneous alien dwellers and guests were already in place. Their small group would not need all 23 units, but the group did need privacy.

"Serge doesn't mess around, does he?" Reba commented after their inspection. "I thought we were on a budget," she added, looking askance at the creature.

"Serge's activities do not come cheap," it replied, "but his returns are generally acceptable. I have rented the property for one planetary year, and I have remained within my budget. If that is all, you have no further need of my services. Goodbye."

"I guess we just pick rooms, Val," Reba said as she picked up her travel bag.

He flopped down on a couch. "I'm exhausted. Must be all the

training I'm giving you. That was a nice approach, by the way."

A bright smile lit her face. "Thanks! I may get the hang of starships yet. I'm not ready to do it without your help, though."

"Yes, you are, and you know it. Do you have something nice to change into? I'd like to take you out to dinner."

She blinked, sobering. "Uh . . . that sounds suspiciously like a date. Are you asking me out?"

Val looked a little uncertain of himself, something she rarely saw. "I don't know how things are done on Earth, but where I come from this is how we start relationships." He lifted his chin to her defiantly, daring her to refuse. "Yes, I'm asking you out on a date, Reba. We've been together for months, but this is the first opportunity I've had to have your undivided attention without others around. Will you accompany me?"

"Starting a relationship, huh?" she responded with a glimmer in her eyes. She moved to stand before him, then simply sat on his lap and rested her arms around his neck, her eyes inches from his. "If you think this relationship is just getting started, buster, you're even more dense than Mike was."

Val looked startled, then a grin lit up his face. He put his arms around her and pulled her into an embrace.

"We have work to do, you know," she said after a time.

"No, we don't. My body doesn't even know what day it is, let alone what time zone we're in. Aren't you exhausted?"

"I was. I'm not any more. Does your offer still stand?"

"It does. I've made a reservation at the best restaurant in town."

"How did you do that? And how do you know the best restaurant?" she asked, leaning away from him.

"Serge has connections."

"Serge! You mean he helped you plan this?"

"Maybe a little. Are you still on for dinner?"

"You bet, Sir Val. The offer is made, and I accept. Give me a few minutes," she said, jumping up and heading off to a nearby bedroom.

Val chose the room next to hers and heard her shower running while he changed. He was waiting for her when she came out. Dressed in a floor length green dress that clung to her body, he could only stare.

"Where did you get that dress?" he wondered aloud.

"Like you said, Serge has connections," she replied with her dazzling smile, taking his arm and leading him to the lift. "Come on, I'm hungry. I have a feeling this will be a memorable evening."

* * * * *

Others began arriving three days later. First came four large
crates delivered to the apartments. Reba and Val had been waiting
anxiously for them and unloaded them as quickly as they could. Four
Guardians crawled out from a grim incarceration. During the next
several weeks, fifteen more individuals, all handpicked by Serge, arrived
and went to work gathering intelligence on Chandrajuski's situation.

Mike, Ellie, Otis, and Jessie arrived last. Discussions, even
arguments, had ensued concerning Ellie's participation on Centauri III,
but she had pulled rank and prevailed. Only she could recruit Admiral
Chandrajuski, and then only after the use of her Talents. Mike could
recruit, and his badge of office would suffice for identification, but he
could not Test. Too much was at stake to permit mistakes at this point.
She used the argument that Alexis was in a safe place, hence her
succession was assured. She and Mike arrived as wealthy merchants,
their Great Cats always at their sides.

Chandrajuski was under house arrest at his estate on the outskirts
of town. An Admiral Vorst, a human, had replaced him and had culled
through the headquarters staff, dismissing or imprisoning those he felt
were not loyal to the Rebel cause. The new regime was well established
at the highest levels in Centauri Sector and was slowly extending its
tentacles into lower levels.

Along with the report on Chandrajuski's whereabouts came
frightening news. His estate was guarded by three gleasons, the most
fearsome creatures known in the galaxy. Otis and Jessie growled long
and deep at this news.

"It's a trap," Otis stated emphatically to Ellie. "This is the worst
possible news. Struthers is using Chandrajuski as bait to catch you."

"What does it mean, Otis?" demanded Mike.

"It means, Sire, that we may not be able to spring the admiral. Is
there anyone else suitable for his position, Your Majesty?"

"There's always someone else, Otis, but I really want him. And
we're here. Time is a precious commodity, and we have months invested
in this."

"Time is not precious if we fail."

"No, not if we fail. We will not fail. Gleasons are not known for
their intelligence. You'll have to outsmart them."

"Your Majesty, I repeat, it's a trap. Chandrajuski is bait; you are
the prize."

"What makes these gleasons so bad?" asked Mike.

Otis turned to him. "They are pure terrors, Sire. Their death-dealing skills even surpass those of Protectors. They're extremely difficult to find, let alone kill. They are humanoid, but their bodies change color to blend into the surroundings, making them virtually invisible. They have two of almost everything: two sets of arms, two nervous systems, and two circulatory systems. They have only one head, but each side of the brain can function independently if necessary."

He paused to let Mike consider, then added softly, "It gets worse, Sire. They mind link among their own kind. What one knows, the other two will know instantly, if indeed there are only three of them guarding the admiral. To make matters worse, they are without scruples. Their world never accepted the Empire, nor was the Empire ever able to civilize them. In the end, the Empire gave up trying. Their world was placed off limits, and they were prevented from leaving. I have never known them to work for anyone. Struthers has pulled off a major coup if he has their assistance."

"You really hate them, don't you."

"I fear them, Mike. Remember the story I told you about how the Empire saved my people?"

"I do."

"It was from the gleasons we were saved, and even with the Empire's help it was a near thing."

"They must have some weaknesses," Mike demanded.

"My ancestors discovered a few minor weaknesses, but these are very, very dangerous creatures, Mike."

"How do you fight them if you can't see them?"

"Exactly. Great battles are remembered in songs handed down from one generation to another. From these songs I know that when severely wounded the gleasons lose their ability to change color to match their surroundings. They lose their invisibility."

Mike frowned. "But you have to see them to wound them."

Otis nodded. "The only other weaknesses I know of are that the gleasons have a strong body odor and they have poor vision. To compensate for the poor vision they see into the infrared, meaning they sense body heat in the dark."

Mike frowned. "So let's think it through," he said. "We have to meet twice with Chandrajuski. He has directed us to some member of his staff, but who that person is has been impossible to determine. He, or it, is very deeply hidden. We must get that one name from him. Following that, we have to extract him. Those are the only two contacts we have to make with him. We have to do it under the very noses of the Rebels and the gleasons, both of whom are expecting us."

He turned to Ellie. "We're asking too much."

"It must be done, Michael. I need someone to restore my military forces. We'll have the same problem with whomever we seek. The list of candidates for this job is not long and Struthers knows them as well as I do, perhaps even better. He was, after all, Mother's First Knight."

Silence descended upon the room. Otis said what was on everyone's mind. "You are Queen, and you are the Last of the Chosen. You are their target."

She turned to him with fire in her eyes. "Then give me an alternative."

The two stared at each other, long years of friendship and love warring with the calls of Empire each had accepted so long ago.

Ellie broke the silence, her eyes betraying the love she felt for her Protector of so many years. She said softly, "When the leaf people left us in that field on Lianli, you asked, 'We are called, but to what?' I answered that I did not know, but we were a part of something bigger than ourselves and that the burden would be heavy. We now know what that burden includes, my friend. I said it then, and I say it again now, we will stand together or fall together."

A great chill wracked the body of the Great Cat. He shook his head to rid himself of the sensation and said equally softly, "The Chosen have no purpose if there is no Empire. I cannot promise a successful outcome, but I will give you all that I am, Your Majesty."

* * * * *

One of them had to meet with Admiral Chandrajuski. Ellie not only needed to let him know a plan was being prepared, she needed a name from him, someone he trusted as a contact. Serge's spy was called upon to help. Within a few days, Mike, Val, and Reba found themselves working for a cleaning company.

Jake had finished with Mike's arm and the cast was gone, but his use of the arm was limited. He exercised it daily, but it was still weak. He wasn't the only one on the work crews with disabilities, but it held him back. Reba's quality of work was equal to Val's, but her looks got in the way: the shift leaders felt threatened by her. Consequently, she found herself on the receiving end of the worst jobs. After two long weeks of hard, unending work, Val was finally selected to work on the crew servicing Chandrajuski's home.

Chandrajuski's property sprawled over ten acres, surrounded by a force-fence visible only by tall posts along its perimeter. Within the perimeter, the land was a natural escarpment of high grass and scattered trees, far from the city.

The home's single floor was unusual, but no more unusual than the home's occupants. A high dome on the west end of the building was the primary living area for Chandrajuski and his family, permitting the growth of forest-like plants throughout its five-story interior. The cleaners were not ordinarily responsible for the forest area of the home, only the more public parts on the east end that were used for entertainment and meetings with outsiders.

Val, as the newest member of the cleaning crew, was assigned to cleaning bathrooms.

As he worked, he felt himself under observation. Turning quickly, he saw the flash of a bright green tail retreating from the doorway. A short time later he heard a low chittering conversation. Without turning, he said, "Come here, little ones. I would meet you."

Three miniature versions of Chandrajuski appeared hesitantly, vying for position in the hallway outside the bathroom, then freezing in place. Had Mike been there, he would have said they reminded him of praying mantises, though they stood two feet tall. Bright green, they balanced on four extremely long and thin legs partially folded as if poised to flee. Two long arms, powerful looking, ended in hands with fingers and two opposing thumbs, hands that seemed to be held at the ready for instant fighting. Everything about them was green, tinged here and there with yellow. Their heads, perched at the end of long and powerful necks, were triangular and hairless. Their chests, very deep, were the only non-delicate looking part of their bodies. But like Chandrajuski, their resemblance to insects ended the moment one looked into their eyes. Large, dark eyes full of intelligence and curiosity peered back at Val.

They watched and waited, poised to flee, looking like a good wind would blow them away. Val turned back to his work as he talked. "Welcome, little ones. Do you have names?" More chittering. "Do you understand my speech?" asked Val.

One boldly stepped closer, speaking in a high singsong voice, "We understand your speech, sir."

"Who are you, then?"

"I am known as Grimmatis, sir. We are of the Children."

"You are the admiral's children? Is he here?"

"Always, now."

"May I speak with him?"

"Not unless you have an appointment."

"I have no appointment, but I know he wants to speak with me. Can you keep a secret?"

"We are Gamordians, sir. Of course we can keep a secret."

"I must speak with him secretly. No one can know. Is that possible?"

"We know, so it is not possible."

Val's eyes rose to the ceiling. "I meant no one else can know. I must speak either with him or with your mother."

"Mother supervises. She will come if needed."

"It must be a secret."

The three children scampered away. Later, as he prepared to move on to the next bathroom an adult Gamordian blocked his way, completely filling the doorway to the hall.

"I am Chandra Chandrajuski. I would inspect your work," she stated with authority.

Val stood back and motioned her into the bathroom. She stuck her head in the door, blocking the hallway with her body. Her gaze swept the room once, missing nothing.

"The mirror is streaked. Will you fix that?" she asked, pointing at an invisible blemish.

Val grabbed his cleaning equipment and went to work as he whispered. "Your husband and I must talk. Can you arrange it?"

"You are part of the cleaning staff. How can you be so presumptuous?" she asked softly.

Val reached into a pocket and withdrew one of his Knight's Pins. "Take this to him. He will understand."

She took the Pin in her hand without expression and looked directly into his eyes. She clearly recognized the significance of the Pin. "The rest of your work appears to be satisfactory. Thank you for your efforts on our behalf," she said, then backed away.

She caught up to him an hour later. "Come with me, please," she ordered.

Val followed while she searched for the supervisor to request assistance in the living quarters. The supervisor huffed a little but acquiesced. Val followed Chandra through a doorway into the domed part of the home and stopped in wonder. Bright green, incredibly healthy looking trees grew everywhere, trees whose trunks rose delicately but quite high before branching out to create a canopy under which he could see to the far side of the room. A strong, pleasant aroma of the forest filled his head. An adult Gamordian, probably the admiral, was raking dead leaves into piles across the room.

"I would ask your assistance with disposing of this mess," the Gamordian called.

"Of course, sir."

The admiral handed him a rake with both hands, one hand sliding into Val's to return the Pin. "Where did you come by that token?" he asked quietly as he returned to work.

"I'm certain you know, sir. It is not a relic of the old regime."

"You are young for the position."

"As is the source," Val responded as he worked. "I need a name from you."

"How is it you came to your cleaning job?" the admiral asked more loudly as he worked. "Do you like cleaning, or is your position temporary?"

"I work to feed myself, sir, any way that I can. I have no loftier ambition, but the work I do usually pleases my supervisors."

"Then you make enough money to survive, I take it."

"Barely. Tips are always appreciated, sir."

"Yes, I suppose they are. I miss my work. Do you know who I am?"

"I believe you were the Sector Commander before the change, sir."

"I was, and now I'm wasting away. I miss the responsibility, and I miss my staff, my personal assistant, Jeffers, especially. He only rarely comes to see me anymore, and then only on business for the Rebels. Do you have word of the Empire?" he asked innocently.

"No, sir. Such things are above me. What do I care if change comes? It makes no difference to me."

"Short-term, possibly not," grumbled the admiral. "Come, I'll show you where to dispose of the refuse."

Chandrajuski led the way to a door that led to the outside. "There are other entrances, but this one will do for now," the admiral stated as they worked.

"It did not appear to be locked," Val noted absently.

"There is no need. None of our doors are locked. There is nothing here of value to me except my family, and we are guarded by beasts more hideous than you can imagine. Do not think of coming back to steal from me. You would not succeed."

"I am no thief, sir. Though I am a lowly servant, I have honor."

"I applaud your honor, young man." Chandrajuski led them outside, each carrying a side of a blanket filled to overflowing with dead leaves. As they walked, they scattered the leaves through the brush.

Chandrajuski said softly, "I believe we can speak more freely now. Tell me the Queen is not here."

"She's determined to free you. She has work for you," Val mumbled, not looking at the admiral.

"Her death has been foretold, as was this meeting with you. She must leave."

Val clutched the blanket fiercely. Chandrajuski had used the word 'foretold.' It spoke clearly of visions. Had his twin sister, Krys, been to see him? She'd lived here, and he'd searched for her only to discover that she'd perished along with a fleet of Chandrajuski's ships. "Are you speaking of my sister? She's dead."

"All a ruse. She's out on assignment. Do not look for her here."

Val's heart skipped a beat. She was all the family he had, and they were very close. He continued spreading leaves as he considered the admiral's words.

Chandrajuski did not give him much time. "Others can fill my shoes, but not hers. She *must* leave."

Val pursed his lips in agreement. If Ellie's death had been foretold by Krys, she must, indeed, get away from here. "It will not be easy to convince," he stated softly. "Can you tell me more?"

"Only the words that came in the vision. '*Easy to leave, hard to remain. The man of dirt comes to one in shadow. She will fall to the unseen, but Death is not forever.*'"

Val continued spreading the dead leaves as he considered. "Always riddles. This one seems fairly clear, at least part of it. Krys must be getting better. I'll relay the message, Admiral."

They headed back inside. Before parting, Chandrajuski added, "These guards are a hideous bunch. I've been doing some research on the Empire's activities to subjugate them and have come up with some interesting information. We were not completely unsuccessful against them."

"I can't imagine the Empire failing at anything, sir."

"Let us hope so, young man." Very softly, he added, "Sire."

* * * * *

Ellie was not pleased when she heard of the vision. Too much time had been taken on this project already, and she was not anxious to start over. Besides, she really wanted Chandrajuski at her side.

"Krys' visions are difficult to interpret, almost impossible. The word 'she' could refer to anyone," she stated firmly.

"Come on, Ellie," Mike scoffed.

She turned to him with her hands on her hips. "Her visions don't come with a date-time stamp. We don't even know if the vision applies to this situation. Suppose we leave in search of someone else. Anyone we find to replace Chandrajuski will probably be in the same predicament, and the words of the vision would apply equally then."

"You could leave, right now. The rest of us can see this through."

"And if I leave, will that be the action that causes the vision to come true? Do you want me to die far out in space, all alone?"

He turned away with a grimace. He didn't like these visions, didn't like the very idea of them.

Ellie approached him and reached a hand up to his cheek, caressing. "The words included, *'Death is not forever.'*"

He took her hand and looked into her eyes. "Where I come from, death is forever. There's no getting around it. Can the outcomes of her visions be changed?"

"I don't know, Michael." She turned to Val. "Do you know?"

He shook his head. "Surely you won't take the chance?"

"What else can I do? What if the vision applies to whatever alternative path I choose? What if, because I panic and run off somewhere else, that's what causes it to happen? Maybe if I stay here the path of the vision is changed and I'll not die. Or maybe the first words of the vision, *easy to leave, hard to remain* apply to me, not Chandrajuski. Or maybe they apply to both of us."

She looked hard at Val. "I'll not die willingly nor easily, but if I am to die, I want to be with Mike and the rest of you when I do. Give me a better solution."

They couldn't. Mike felt like they were caught up in a catch-22. They were damned if they did and damned if they didn't. He was not willing to risk Ellie, and he was ready to leave immediately, but he couldn't say that would change the outcome of the vision.

She turned back to him. "We'll just have to plan well." She put her arms around him. "I've just found you, and I'm not leaving."

"By the way," she said later when it was just the two of them, "I see you've been mentioned in another vision."

"It's like you and I are tied together somehow. It's unsettling, to say the least. I wish it would stop."

She smiled. "We are tied together, my love, by some power higher than the both of us. Our futures *are* linked. Are you ready to make it official?"

He blinked. Had he heard right? Had the Queen of All Space, as he thought of her, just proposed to him? He went internal. >What's she talking about, Jake?<

>I think you perceive correctly, Mike. Why don't you ask her?<

>No way! I'm just Mike Carver, Earthman. I'm just here by accident, and she's *Queen,* Jake.<

>You're Mike Carver, First Knight, my friend. I don't think she chose you for that position because you were the only one around. You're very much a part of her Empire now, and I know you like being here. *Everyone* knows the two of you are in love.<

He turned to Ellie and pulled her into an embrace. "In all the months we've had together, we've never had a moment of privacy. I love you, but I want to prove it to you. I want to court you if this Empire of yours will let me. Have you ever been courted?"

"No, not until I met you. Isn't that what we've been doing this past year?"

"Well . . . it's been a pretty strange courtship, and there's lots more to it."

She leaned back from him with a contented smile on her face. "I figured you'd say something like that. Know this, Michael: I like this courting. I love you and my heart is home. You'll come around one day. My Empire will not stop this 'courting,' nor will I. In the meantime, know it's your Empire, as well."

"Then let's get you out of here. I'm not ready for you to die, nor as First Knight am I ready for the last of the Chosen to die."

She closed her eyes and sighed, returning to his embrace. "The last of the Chosen cannot die, Michael. The Empire is counting on us to change the outcome of the vision, and with this advance knowledge it might be possible to do so."

He wished he had a better plan, but he didn't. "I love you, Princess, no matter what happens."

"I know."

* * * * *

A meeting with Captain Jeffers proved difficult to set up. Besides the fact that he was busy, he rarely left the base, even living there. His only relaxation came during meals at the Officers Club. Val ambushed him there.

"Excuse me, sir," Val said as he stood at attention beside Jeffers' table, where Jeffers was enjoying a meal with three other senior officers.

"Lieutenant?" Jeffers queried in irritation. "Can't you see I'm having dinner?"

"An urgent dispatch, sir. Sorry to bother you. Please sign here, and I'll disappear."

"Wait. I might need to send a response."

As Jeffers began opening the package, Val glanced anxiously at the others sitting around the table. "Uh, sir, I was told it is for your eyes only," he risked.

Jeffers looked up at him in annoyance. "These are always 'eyes only,' Lieutenant." Jeffers looked into the envelope and withdrew a piece of paper. He studied it briefly, looked thoughtful, then looked up at Val. "I'll need to think about a response. Wait outside. I'll join you in a few minutes."

"Yes, sir." Val turned on his heel and marched away as if on a mission.

Jeffers and his three companions emerged from the club half an hour later. "I have transportation, sir," Val offered, "but there's only room for you."

"We have our own transportation. Why don't you come with us instead?"

Sweat broke out on Val's forehead. Was he headed into capture and interrogation? "Of course, sir. After you, sir."

Minutes later they pulled up before a poorly lit row of small offices near the flight line. Jeffers unlocked the door to an end unit and led the way in. As soon as the door closed, he turned to Val. "Where did you get this?" he asked, holding out the Knight's Pin.

Val turned to take in the other officers who were now holding blasters pointed at him. "I must know with whom I am speaking, Captain Jeffers."

"Lieutenant, your life is on the line here. Answer the question. You may speak freely before these others."

"I may speak freely of Chandrajuski? He sent me to you." Jeffers looked worriedly to the other officers.

"To whom do you report, Lieutenant?"

"The Pin is mine. The answer lies inside."

"Show me."

Val passed his hand over the Pin, and it sprung open. Ellie's countenance shone forth. When Jeffers lowered his gaze to the Pin, he paled.

"Sire," Jeffers stated as he returned the pin to Val, "we are at your command."

"I am Lieutenant Val for as long as I am on this world, Captain."

"Of course, Sire. What is your command? You may speak freely. This room is safe."

"Chandrajuski gave me your name. He did not give any others."

"Let me speak plainly, Sire. His loyalty to the Empire has never been questioned by the Rebels. Our loyalty is a secret, a well-protected secret. Each of us in this room is loyal to our oaths. We will never submit to tyranny, but the Rebels trust us."

"Hand me your weapons, all of you," Val commanded.

The three officers hesitated, understandably. Val nodded his head. "Consider, gentlemen: if my purpose here is to reveal your true beliefs to your new governor, you are already lost to your cause."

They sensed the truth in his words. They handed the weapons over one by one. Val raised a communicator to his mouth, spoke one word, then turned out the lights and opened the door. Two Great Cats immediately sprang into the gloom, followed shortly thereafter by two hooded figures. The door closed and the lights came back on. The shorter of the two figures reached up and pulled away a hood to reveal the Queen's face.

Jeffers and his associates immediately bent to one knee before her. "Arise, my heroes," she commanded. "I would be introduced."

Captain Jeffers introduced the others: Admiral Hortle of Fleet Command, his assistant Captain Jonders, and Admiral Tonga, chief of Survey and Intelligence.

"Who leads among you?" Ellie asked.

"Chandrajuski, Your Majesty," replied Captain Jeffers. A knowing smile lit her face.

Admiral Tonga spoke up. "These are unusual times, Your Majesty. Though we three outrank Captain Jeffers, we report to him. He leads the underground for Chandrajuski. Though unorthodox, the process works."

She removed her cloak, as did Mike. The officers saluted him, then shook hands as Ellie introduced him.

"Your Majesty," Jeffers said turning to her, "It's incredibly dangerous for you to be here. We must address whatever issues you have, then get you out of here."

"First things first, Captain. We deal with the highest matters of state. I must assure myself of your loyalties. Will you submit?"

"With honor, Your Majesty," Jeffers replied.

Ellie Tested all four and found none wanting. She was pleased and let them know it. "You have remained true to your oaths," she said. "There is no higher honor among civilizations. Now, to work. My purpose in coming here is to release Admiral Chandrajuski from his imprisonment. We can make room for you and any others you choose. Will you assist me in this venture?"

"Your Highness," Jeffers pleaded, "Chandrajuski's replacement, Admiral Vorst, is expecting just such an attempt. I have ingratiated myself into his confidence and in so doing have managed to retain my position, much to our advantage. I believe I am privy to most, if not all, of his plans. We will have only one opportunity."

The meeting lasted an hour, after which Jeffers called a halt. "Your Majesty, I must protect my cover, or this is all for naught. We four will be missed if we remain any longer. You have the outlines of a plan. We can complete the details later."

"Yes, our time is up. I will leave you with a special communicator to arrange future meetings. It is not of Empire manufacture and cannot be overheard by anyone outside our small group."

"No, Your Majesty. I cannot risk its discovery. We have a network set up for just this sort of thing. If Sir Val is willing to act as intermediary, we'll stay in contact through him."

Ellie bit her lip while contemplating. She turned to Mike for guidance and received a nod, then to Otis who also nodded his agreement. A meeting point for Val was set up for the next day, and they all departed as surreptitiously as possible.

Otis, after deep reflection, decided to lead their efforts against the gleasons personally. Though his first responsibility was to protect Ellie, he concluded that the greatest risk to her was the gleasons, and he was the most skilled warrior among the Great Cats. He went off planet to do the research suggested by Chandrajuski in his meeting with Val. He would not provide the slightest opportunity to the enemy to send tracers after him as he searched the world net here on Centauri III. His search would take place elsewhere.

He returned weeks later, but he had learned nothing of value from the Empire's efforts against the gleasons two thousand years previous. His own people had done most of the fighting and were the only experts. Otis knew that a serious injury always resulted in the gleasons' bodies returning to their natural color, a dark green. If he and the other cats could find the gleasons and wound them, they could then deal with them in a normal fashion. Finding them would be his first priority.

"Wouldn't it be better to take them out from long range?" Mike asked. "Surely we can get the right weapons for you."

"We already have them, Sire. We'll take them out from a distance if we can find them, but we'll make plans to cover all contingencies. I have only two cats to go up against each gleason. I would assign more if I had them. I cannot stress how utterly devastating these creatures are."

The Great Cats huddled together for a time, then all but Otis left. They would have three days to study the area around Chandrajuski's home, during which time they would attempt to pinpoint the locations of the gleasons and keep them in sight. The extraction of Chandrajuski would occur on the fourth day. The plan was set in motion without delay.

* * * * *

Admiral Tonga, Chief of Intelligence for Centauri Sector but secretly one of Chandrajuski's key followers, reported excitedly to Vorst, the new Sector Commander. His agents had intercepted information that the Queen was on Centauri III. She was planning to rescue Chandrajuski that very evening.

"Hmm," Vorst smiled grimly. "You have a plan?"

"The gleasons will deal with them, I'm certain, but I can put together a reaction force just to be certain. And we won't need Chandrajuski any more after tonight. He can be taken care of, as well."

Vorst thought for a time before speaking. "Does she know of the gleasons?"

"Not if she's planning to enter the premises, sir. We believe she has only a handful of men. No one would be so foolish if they knew of the gleasons."

"I've been waiting a long time for this," Vorst said as he rubbed his hands together in anticipation. "Inform the gleasons they are to let the new arrivals into the house. They are not to let them leave the grounds alive. Jeffers will take responsibility for the reaction force. I want you to stay here and follow the action. And inform Jeffers I will accompany him."

"Very well, sir, though I would very much like to lead tonight."

"No. Your job is intelligence, not operations. You'll stay behind, keeping the big picture in mind and keeping me informed of any problems that might develop. We cannot underestimate the Queen. I expect she'll have backup plans and a reserve force prepared to assist her if necessary. I want every man called up, all posts active."

Tonga replied with his own grim smile. "Might I suggest just the opposite, sir? Let me keep my best men in place and put appropriate ships on alert, but otherwise keep our staffing to a minimum. I would very much like to mislead them."

"A good idea. Work it out with Jeffers. Just do not underestimate her. And she may have diversions planned to distract us. Do not let us become distracted, Admiral. No matter what else happens, we have only one mission tonight. Our focus is only the Queen. Understood?"

"We will keep our focus on the Queen, sir."

Chapter Fifty-six

Krys and Tarn both spent time in the net working with Stven on the skills needed to manage the ship without a net. They had visited four more worlds in the eight months since Orion III, and they had changed the beacon after each one. The work was challenging at first, then it just became monotonous. The Great Cats declined to help, reminding them that it was impossible for anyone else to be in the net with them.

When they came out of hyper, Aldebaran I lay dead ahead. So, too, did a large number of Chessori traders. Stven looked at M'Sada who was again doing the driving. "What do you think?"

"They can't possibly know who we are."

"Agreed. Let's just act normal and continue inbound."

"Okay, unless one of them turns toward us."

No threats materialized, and they landed three weeks later. This time, instead of going directly to Admiral Seeton, the fleet commander they were to call upon, Krys, Tarn, and Trist, the third Great Cat, checked into a local hotel. They partied that night, doing their best to act the part of rich kids. They left the hotel at mid-morning the following day in search of Seeton.

They were careful, knowing that Seeton was not the senior admiral on Aldebaran I. When Tarn claimed to be a personal friend of the admiral's, doors opened, and Trist's presence added credence to his story.

When they were shown into Seeton's office, he came from behind his desk but did not offer a greeting. Unlike a lot of the senior commanders they had met, Seeton was not a large man. He was spare, of average height, and he sported a goatee. His gaze was stern and unrelenting.

"Who are you?" he demanded.

"Not who we appear to be, sir," Tarn answered. "We come from Admiral Chandrajuski."

"I wondered if it was something like that. Few civilians seek me out, and I knew you were not friends of mine. He's been sacked, you know."

"Sir?" Tarn blurted out, looking sharply to Krys. Her lips trembled, but her eyes remained dry. From her earlier vision of him, she knew his road would be difficult. Would he hold, as she believed the vision called for him to do?

"I only just received word. I'm sorry," Seeton added.

"Has he left?" she asked.

"He's been placed under arrest by the new governor," Seeton growled.

"New governor!" Tarn blurted out again.

"I'm afraid so. We have a new governor here, as well."

"What happened to the old one?" Krys asked softly.

"He's dead. Struthers isn't taking no for an answer."

Her eyes opened wide in alarm. She started to speak, but Tarn cut her off. "So you support Struthers now, sir?"

Seeton stared at him. "Why do you ask?"

"Do you?"

"We're done here. It's time for you to leave."

Trist growled low in her throat. "Answer the question, Admiral," she demanded.

His gaze settled on her as he considered. "To you, I will answer. Never. Never will I support the man or his Rebel cause. Don't ask me who I now answer to because I don't know, but it's not him or our new governor. I think it's time you told me who you are."

Krys reached behind her neck and carefully unclasped the locket, then handed it to Seeton. He examined it, then moved to the doorway. "It's okay," he said calmly to the staff members milling about. Weapons appeared from various places and went back into drawers. He closed the door and turned to Krys. "Who are you?" he asked, as if nothing untoward had happened.

"I am many things, but I am first a messenger. I carry a dispatch from Admiral Chandrajuski." She handed him the chip and waited while he inserted it into his work station and read the letter. When he turned to her, he was brief. "What is your message?"

"The Empire is not bereft of legitimate leadership," she said. "We have a Queen, and she is very much alive."

Seeton's hand shook slightly as it passed across his forehead. "I would so like to believe you," he breathed. "Have you proof?"

"Are a Friend's word, the word of Admiral Chandrajuski, and the presence of a Great Cat not enough?"

"It's a good beginning, but it's not enough. Do you appreciate the impact those few words have on . . ." His eyes rose to the ceiling, then searched the room. "Well, everything! Everything we stand for, and everything that happens from this moment forward?"

"We do, sir. The old system is not dead, and it's up to you and others like you to keep it alive. She's counting on you."

"You've seen her?"

"Not in the manner you wish for, but I promise you, the Queen lives."

He suddenly seemed to deflate. "Surely you've seen the pictures."

"Not all the Chosen were at the Palace, sir."

"All are reported dead."

"Reported by whom?"

His eyes narrowed. "Of course! Of course he would make such a claim. He had to." He paused in thought for a moment, then said, "There is another who must hear this."

"There are many others who *will* hear it, Admiral. Our list is long."

"I mean here. Now."

Krys turned to Tarn with alarm in her eyes. This was not part of the plan.

"Who is it, Admiral?" Tarn asked harshly. "What you do with our message after we deliver it is up to you, but our words are only for you. Our presence here cannot become known."

"If his name is not on your list, your list is incomplete. If I tell you his name and you fail to convince me of your story, you will not leave this office with your freedom." He looked to the Great Cat. "That includes you."

Trist just stared back at him with that imperturbable look cats seem to have stored up for just such occasions. As Seeton considered her, he knew she was not in the least concerned with threats from him.

Nor was Krys. "What is the name, Admiral."

He hesitated, then said, "Signio Veswicki."

Trist spoke instantly. "Bring him, Admiral."

Seeton stepped from the office. As soon as he did, two sets of worried eyes turned on the Great Cat.

"He's right," Trist said. "If his name is not on the list, it should be. I don't doubt for a moment that it is on Senator Truax's list."

"Who is he?" Krys asked.

"Governor of Triton Sector. I suspect he's out of a job at the moment."

"His loyalty is not in question?"

"I assure you, it is not. I'll add that he was a senior member of Fleet Command before he was Named governor."

"He's an admiral, then?" Tarn asked.

"Before he retired, he was a very senior admiral. When the Queen learns he is alive, she will call him to her side. I have heard rumors that Struthers is searching hard for him. He is an ally, Krys, an important ally. You may speak freely with him, of that I am certain."

A stooped old man with a cane and considerable facial hair was ushered into the office. Seeton closed the door and began introductions, then hesitated. "I don't believe you gave me your names," he said in surprise.

Tarn did the honors. "Lieutenant Tarn Lukes, Ms. Krys, and the Great Cat Trist." And you are. . .?" he asked, turning to the old man.

"Who I am does not matter." The old man turned to Seeton. "What's this all about, Harry?"

"Perhaps you should be seated first, old man?" Seeton asked, the corners of his mouth curling up into a tight smile. He turned to Krys. "Meet Governor Signio Veswicki, governor of Triton Sector."

The old man instantly straightened up. The cane, rather than a support, suddenly looked like a weapon in his hands. "Harry?" he said with a dangerous look.

"They're couriers from Chandrajuski. Their message, if true, changes all our plans."

Veswicki turned to them, his eyes studying them intently. He did not have to ask. Krys simply said, "We have a Queen, Governor. She is very much alive."

He just stared at her, then at Tarn and Trist, then at Seeton. "I happen to know that she died," he said softly, menacingly.

Krys did not flinch. "Daughter lives. She is now Queen."

He might have discounted Krys' words, but he would not discount the words of a Great Cat. His eyes went to Trist.

"It's true, Governor. Daughter lives. She is now our Queen," she said.

"You've seen her?"

"I have not. This one has," she said, indicating Krys.

"Since the Palace fell?"

"I have, Governor."

He studied her for a time, then removed the beard, mustache, and the colored lenses in his eyes. The face of an aging, trim man emerged. She could easily see this man dressed in a uniform rather than the rumpled civilian suit he now wore. As he stood erect, even the suit seemed to unrumple. With a look into his eyes, Krys sensed a true leader standing before her, one of those rare individuals whom anyone would follow.

"Where is she?" he asked, his forehead creased in a demand.

"I don't know at the moment. When I last saw her, she was in mortal danger. I have good reason to believe she survived that particular trial."

Veswicki stared at her for a time. "You set our hopes up, then dash them?"

"I do not. I sense loyalty to the realm in both of you. It's time for you to know the full story. Will you sit? It's a long story."

Both chose to stand, but by the time she had finished her story, both were sitting.

"Gods, Harry! Do you know what this means?" Veswicki asked.

"I do, Signio. Our plan can be modified to fit. And I can't wait to arrest the new governor and my boss."

"In time. Not yet."

"No, not yet, but instead of hesitation, we can move with confidence, knowing our path is right."

Veswicki looked to Krys. "We cannot find it within our hearts to abrogate everything we have ever stood for, and that's what it takes to join with Struthers. We've been putting a plan together to organize a few sectors against him. We've already made contacts, but we move with hesitation because in a way it means we've gone rogue.

"Our system of Empire governance places the politicians above the military, but to act as we've planned requires the military to supplant the politicians for a time, and possibly for a long time. Worse, no matter which course we choose, that of Struthers or that of martial law, our models predict failure in the end. Enduring peace requires a charismatic, benevolent leader. Only the Chosen have been able to fill those shoes. And now . . . now all our efforts will lead to the restoration of that which is right. For the gift you have given us today, we will forever be in your debt."

"It's a long road ahead of us, Governor," Krys said.

"And the single most important thing we can do is to locate and protect the Last of the Chosen. Nothing takes precedence over that. I would encourage you to focus your energies in that direction."

"Trust me, Admiral, I have tried, and I am trying. Until I succeed, I will continue on the mission assigned to me by Admiral Chandrajuski."

"You know he's imprisoned?"

"We just learned. I'm saddened, but it doesn't change anything."

"It does not. Your message must get out, and you deliver it powerfully. But we should look to managing our resources. Chandrajuski did not know of our activities here. We've already made some headway, possibly in places a visit from you is no longer needed. We can take your message, and our delivery will have equal impact because of who we are. Let's face it. Knowing Chandrajuski, your list is long. If you were to visit every name on the list, it would take years, maybe centuries. We will have to act within the next two years. With some minor disruptions to Struthers' efforts, we might have three years. No more than that."

"Why such a short time?"

"It's quite simple really. When Struthers next convenes the Imperial Senate, and if the existence of a surviving Chosen is not universally accepted, he will be installed as the leader of the Empire. He'll be the legal ruler then, Krys. We'll legally be the Rebels."

"In that case, it sounds to me like Senator Truax's efforts are more important than ours."

"In the long run they are, and I'm going to have to give serious thought to how I can supplement his efforts. I just learned that we still have a Queen, and it's changed everything. I'll flesh out these preliminary thoughts over the next few days, but here's the important thing: Struthers only gets one shot at it. If he loses the vote, he's either out, or he'll have to disband the Senate. In the short term, certain actions can force him to delay that Senate meeting. Certain other military actions might even force him to disband the Senate, which as strange as it might sound is to our benefit. Everything we do must be aimed at preventing the Senate from legitimizing his government, even if it means we have no Senate for a while. Do you see where I'm going with this?"

"I do, sir."

He turned to Seeton. "Harry, with Chandrajuski out of the picture, she's lost her support base. Are you willing to pick it up?"

Seeton looked at Krys. "Are you willing to let me pick it up?"

"I am, sir."

He nodded, and Veswicki continued. "Will you share your list with me?"

She squirmed in her seat. That list had become all important, and Chandrajuski had warned her not to trust anyone. She looked to Tarn for advice.

He nodded his head. "These are good people, Krys. I know you sense that. We have to trust someone."

She turned back to Veswicki and nodded. "I don't have it with me."

"I'm glad to hear that."

"It includes plans and methods for retreat, Governor. Chandrajuski believes that some commanders will not be able to hold their positions of power. Before they are replaced, he's asking them to escape with all the resources they can muster. He's provided a leader to gather them up."

Veswicki's eyes sparkled. "A masterful stroke! Not only does he augment our forces, he denies those assets to Struthers. Of course, with him imprisoned the whole plan is compromised, but we can develop a new one." He looked to Seeton.

"I'll get my staff working on it, Signio."

Trist growled. "This has direct impact on the welfare of my principal, and potentially the Queen. Your staff is a source of compromise, Admiral. Perhaps you should develop it yourself."

"Wise words, Trist. Since the coup, and since the arrival of Governor Veswicki, I've made changes to my staff. They are all of the right persuasion. Trust me, I've been thorough. All our lives, theirs included, are at stake here."

Trist dipped her head in acknowledgement.

Veswicki rose from his seat and went to Krys, squatting down before her as she sat in a chair. "Admiral Chandrajuski is a friend of mine, as well," he said. "You must accept the fact that he will not be allowed to live."

She leaned toward him, their faces separated only by inches. "I have strong reason to believe he'll survive."

Veswicki rose, and she rose with him. "How do you know?"

She looked briefly at Tarn, then turned back to Veswicki. "I had a vision in which he was alive. I believe the Queen will seek him out, regardless of the difficulties."

Veswicki's eyes looked to the ceiling in thought. "She might go to him. He's one I would put on a very short list."

"Are you on that list?"

"I would be if she knew where I was, but my location is a secret. I'm the number one enemy of Struthers right now, and he's searching for me with great diligence."

"I would say you're number two at the moment," she said, her lips pressed together grimly.

Veswicki's eyebrows raised. "I do believe you're right, young lady. Your news changes everything. Will you stay for a few days while we consider adjustments to the plan?"

"I will, sir. The plan is flexible; we expected change."

A new plan was produced, and Krys' part in it remained unchanged, but Veswicki was going to direct considerable resources to assisting Senator Truax. In his mind, the political side of things held equal importance to Krys' activities.

"What are your plans for helping him?" she asked.

Veswicki looked at her kindly. "Do you really want to know?"

She considered his words. "I'd like to know. He's a close friend, but I see where you're going with this. It's probably best that I don't know. Am I done here?"

"We've made an adjustment or two to your list, and I'll be contacting certain individuals on that list. They've been marked, so don't waste your time with them. Yes, I think we're done."

"Before leaving, I'd like to attempt a vision with each of you. Will you allow me to try? It doesn't often work," she added with downcast eyes.

Veswicki and Seeton looked at each other in surprise. The looks of surprise soon changed to looks of hesitation.

"I share in your hesitation, sirs," she said. "The choice is yours, of course. One admiral chose against just before going into battle. He knew he could not effectively lead his forces if I foretold his doom. Three squadrons were lost as a result of that choice, though I cannot honestly say I could have produced a vision that would have swayed him. Admiral Chandrajuski faced the same difficult choice, but he agreed. I believe that what he learned during that vision will be a source of strength to him during his present difficulties. I believe, further, that the consequences of his choice will benefit our new Queen in her efforts to restore the throne."

"Who can say no to that?" Seeton said. Veswicki, too, nodded his head in acquiescence, though his reluctance showed.

She looked to Tarn. "It doesn't matter who goes first."

He nodded his head, and she tucked her legs beneath her on the chair, settling into her meditation position.

Governor Veswicki was the first to take her hand. Instead of her eyes flying open, this time a smile lit her face. She opened her eyes and nodded to him, then closed them again, though the smile remained for some time. When it was well and truly gone, Tarn motioned to Seeton. He, too, took her hand. This time she did not smile. She opened her eyes with a sober expression. He stepped back, suddenly afraid.

She remained comfortably in her meditation position and addressed both of them. "When I See, it is always something in the future. Sometimes my visions are accompanied by words, always in the form of a riddle. My vision of you, Admiral Seeton, consists only of words. They are the following:

Many demands. There are battles, and there are great battles. Two follows one. Rule two wins.

Seeton's gaze was locked on hers, but his eyes blinked repeatedly, his thoughts clearly on the words of her vision. He licked lips that had gone dry while he considered. "Do you know what they mean?" he asked her.

"I never do. It's up to us to solve the riddle. *Many demands* seems simple enough, particularly if battles are being waged. The business with battles also seems straight-forward, though these riddles never are. The rest is unclear to me."

"My thoughts exactly. The words are simple, but what do they mean? Of course two follows one, and who knows what Rule two is?" He turned to Veswicki. "Do you know?"

Veswicki shook his head. "Almost, but I can't quite grasp it." He shook his head again. "The meaning eludes me. We'll have to think on this."

Krys looked over at Tarn who was sitting almost at attention in his chair, ignored through most of the meeting by these senior officers as their thoughts dealt with matters of such great import. Through all the many hours she and Tarn had spent together, she knew him well, and her thoughts, of late, rarely strayed far from him, but she had never seen him look quite this way. His brow was furrowed, and his eyes seemed glazed as he looked straight ahead, almost as if he was in a trance. She untangled her legs and went to him, crouching down before him. She touched his knee, and his gaze lost its glazed look to settle on her own.

"Tarn?" she asked.

He smiled kindly at her and covered her hand with his own. "You've done well, My Lady."

Her face lit up. "You know what it means?"

"I might. A pattern is clear. I can't say if it's the right pattern." He looked at Veswicki, then Seeton. "If I'm right, sir, she's given you what every admiral has ever hoped for – a crystal ball focused on a campaign. I hesitate to tell you, because if I'm wrong, it could mislead you into disaster."

"Son, experts will study this message after you're long gone. I've never been a great one with riddles. I prefer clarity. Tell me what you think."

"The message is in four parts. None of the parts, by themselves, means much, but if you put them together they form a pattern, and maybe a strategic plan. Let me present a scenario. A battle is brewing. Your resources are limited, they always are, and as a commander, you're pulled in many different directions as you place these resources. Pretty standard warfare, isn't it, sir?"

"It's textbook."

"Okay, so the battle's shaping up, and your resources are committed. You might have losses, but that's okay as long as you win, right?"

"To a point."

"That's the crux of the message, sir. Two follows one. I don't think the phrase stands alone. I think it applies to the phrase before it."

Veswicki's eyes widened. So, too, did Seeton's a moment later, and a grin lit his face as he considered the repercussions. "A second, larger battle follows the first. If I've overcommitted to the first battle, I might not have sufficient resources for the second. It fits!" he said, smacking a fist into his other open hand. Gods, what a boon!"

"There's the last part, sir."

"Yes. *Rule two wins.* You said all parts of the message form a plan, but what is rule two?"

"It's pretty basic, sir. To win a battle, ideally a commander would want several things. After superior intellect and adequate resources, what would you most want?"

"A location for the battle so I could set my resources."

"And that's where Rule two comes in. Remember the mantra, sir? It was the first thing forced on you at the Academy."

"I do. A sailor's duty comes first, preservation of self comes second . . ." He stopped talking as he considered the words. "How does this relate to location?" he mumbled. He looked to Tarn. "To win, I must save myself?"

"Maybe not just yourself, sir. Maybe your command. To win, you must save your command. I believe the second major battle might take place right here."

Seeton looked to Veswicki with a look of awe on his face. They stared at each other, then at Tarn, and finally at Krys who continued to stare at Tarn in wonder. She placed a hand on Tarn's cheek, and for a moment it was just the two of them in the room again. Then she turned to Veswicki.

"Yours was a vision, Governor. There were no words." With some difficulty he forced his mind back to the matter at hand and nodded. "Will you describe the First Knight, please?"

"Struthers?"

"Yes."

"Human, late middle-age, tall and authoritative, balding. Since he carries a Rider, the balding is something he chose."

She nodded. "In my vision you sat across a table from two men. There may have been others in the room, I can't say. One of the men was a Knight. He's my brother." She glanced at Tarn with a look of triumph. "The other was a tall, dark man. A full head of black hair, black eyebrows, the dark stubble of a beard, black eyes, and a craggy face. His hand . . . it was a hard hand accustomed to hard labor . . . was just retracting from a medallion attached to a gold chain that lay on the table. The medallion was open, and the new Queen's countenance shone forth."

"A First Knight's medallion?" Veswicki asked.

"I believe so, though I've never seen one. That is not the most significant issue. The medallion was open, gentlemen. Do you understand the significance of that?"

Veswicki's gaze never moved from hers. "She is alive whenever this meeting takes place. Because it's a vision, you believe the meeting takes place in the future, not the past."

"Precisely. Had the meeting already taken place, you would know, wouldn't you sir."

She turned to Tarn. "I think we're done here."

"Almost, My Lady."

Veswicki blinked, then took a step back. "My Lady?"

Krys turned a stern expression on Tarn. He ignored her as he addressed Veswicki and Seeton. "Some are born with the title, and some earn it. I believe she has earned it."

Veswicki looked at him in amazement, still shaken from the revelations he had been part of in this small room. But he turned to Krys and bowed. "He's right, My Lady."

Seeton, too, bowed. "We shall be forever grateful for what you have brought us. You have carried your gauntlet to us, and it is now our turn to carry it the rest of the way. We will not disappoint you, My Lady."

"I am but the Queen's Seer," she stated emphatically. "It is her we serve, no one else."

"But we can honor, My Lady, and we do." He turned to Tarn. "You had another issue, Lieutenant?"

"I do, sir. On our approach to Aldebaran I, we noticed quite a few Chessori ships, more than we've seen in any other system. What is their purpose here?"

"They're just traders," Seeton answered. "Why do you ask?"

"Because they are our enemy, and yours. Their presence here causes me great concern for you. We have not told you everything." He looked at Krys. She nodded her head, and he continued. "We told you Daughter's trade mission to Dorwall was a failure. The reason it was a failure is that the Chessori destroyed it."

"Lieutenant, she was escorted by two heavy squadrons," Veswicki reminded him.

"And I personally observed their remains with my own eyes."

"Surely you jest, Lieutenant."

"No, sir. Admiral Chandrajuski dispatched three heavy squadrons to go to her rescue when confronted with a vision from Krys. She and I watched from afar as the three squadrons, 42 ships, approached 15 Chessori defenders. A few shots were fired, then the guns of our squadrons went dead. The Chessori destroyed all 42 ships without suffering counterattack."

As his story unfolded, their eyes filled with alarm. "We know how they did it," he added. Veswicki and Seeton stood, and Tarn rose with them. "They have a weapon of some kind that affects the mind. The mind weapon completely incapacitates everyone within its range except for the Great Cats. They succumb, but through sheer willpower they continue to function."

The two admirals could do little but stare at him. In all the history of Empire there had never been a weapon that affected the mind.

"I cannot speak to the capabilities of individual traders, sirs," Tarn continued, "but Chessori military ships brought three full squadrons to their knees without firing a shot, and we have firsthand knowledge of a single trader attempting to do the same to us. He was taken out by Great Cats, but without the cats the squadron would have succumbed. We were again chased by four Chessori traders as we left Orion Sector. We never came within firing range, but in our opinion, had we come close enough to them, we'd be dead now. I believe that four Chessori ships might have overcome even the cats. The Rebels are our enemy, but so too are the Chessori. We have surmised that they might even be working together. The mind weapon of the Chessori must be considered in your plans, sirs. Admiral Buskin is working on a plan to counter the mind weapon, but it is not yet ready."

Tarn turned to Krys. "We've done everything we came here to do. It's time to go." He took her arm and led her and Trist from the room. *Rappor* lifted an hour later.

Chapter Fifty-seven

Otis peered at the late afternoon sun as he loped across the tree-studded grassland, his gait effortless and silent. Shadows lengthened in the lowering sun, turning the shadows of trees into long-armed giants reaching toward something unseen in the east, seemingly changing shape as the tall grass undulated in the breeze. He knew what the shadows reached for: the eons old call to battle that presaged the coming struggle.

The gleasons did not know about the presence of him and his brothers and sisters, but they didn't need to know. They were that good. He had never personally encountered a gleason, but he knew the songs and believed the gleasons to be evil incarnate. Not much on imagination and not much on prescience, Otis nevertheless felt his soul shudder as if a demon had floated across his grave.

The People believed in spirits good and bad, angels and demons, reality and the supernatural. They were, after all, still quite primitive at heart. Though they functioned well in the most modern of societies, age old beliefs still lurked in the hearts of the modern Guardian and Protector. Beneath the façade of civilized behavior imposed by their chosen purpose within Empire lay simple, ancient beliefs honed by generation upon generation of survivors. For the People, change came slowly. The traits most treasured among them remained strength, perfect reflexes, and the mental agility necessary to survive, all bounded by personal integrity. These traits had sustained them over the millennia.

Today all that would be tested. Today the demons might prevail. He and his team would use every skill in their considerable repertoire to take the demons down, but their success was not a sure thing.

Jessie and the rest of the cats had been running surveillance on the gleasons for three days and nights. They had remained outside the perimeter surrounding Chandrajuski's home, a perimeter outlined by tall poles. The poles projected an invisible sensory field that detected motion, heat, sound, and life force itself. The cats knew how to get around the system which had been designed and built by the Empire prior to the coup, but it was not an easy or sure thing. The slightest wrong move would send a warning to the gleasons guarding the property.

Jessie had the equipment, and it was her job to circumvent the barrier. The other cats would maintain their surveillance of the three gleasons. A number of plans had been discussed before the teams moved into position. The plan he selected would depend on what those surveillance teams discovered. How hard was it to keep the gleasons in sight? Would it be possible to surprise them? What weapons did they have? What were their patrol patterns, their eating and sleeping patterns?

Otis slowed and lowered his belly to the ground as he neared Chandrajuski's property. He stopped and paused to look, listen, and smell. All seemed well. He resumed his forward progress, though much more slowly now. He sensed Jessie before he saw her, and he moved cautiously ahead, emitting a very low growl to alert her of his presence. He did not want to instigate a battle out here by mistake. Her ears twitched; she had heard and acknowledged his signal.

She briefed him on her team's findings. Two of the gleasons were under observation at present, one on each side of the property. The whereabouts of the third was unknown, but they believed it was sleeping.

Otis looked around uneasily, his hackles lifting in alarm. Could it be out here studying them at this very moment? The demon floated across his grave again. The gleasons were not smart, but they were cunning. The creature could very easily have circled around behind them. Jessie had reason to believe it had not, but the creatures were virtually invisible when they chose to be, and the breeze was coming from the direction of the house. A gleason outside their position would be undetectable, but they would be detectable to it.

Her plan called for four cats to act as two-man sniper teams. She and Otis would take out the first gleason. They would have to do it slowly to ensure it had time to get a mental message off to its partners, but they absolutely had to kill it before its partners arrived. Two other cats would take out the second gleason. She and Otis would remain in the vicinity of their first kill, drawing the remaining gleason to them. Two cats would be placed strategically to defend them with sniper shots from a distance, and they would be joined by the other two if time permitted.

Otis did not like the plan: it did not play to the strongest abilities of the Great Cats. They were at their best as individuals, using their intelligence, great strength, and quick reflexes to best their opponents. But one on one, the cats were no match against the gleasons. Close-in personal combat was to be avoided if possible. Against the gleasons' four hands, each finger tipped with a sharp claw, finding an opening would be pure luck. Otis never depended on pure luck. The goal was to bring as many weapons to bear on each gleason as possible, preferably from a distance and preferably on all the gleasons at the same time. That would not be possible today unless the third gleason could be located, but knowing the whereabouts of even two was an advantage he had not counted upon.

Though he did not like Jessie's plan, he knew it was the best plan. The two of them would be bait, and that was appropriate. Of the six cats, they were the two most experienced. Three hours remained before the Queen and her party would arrive. It was time to move into position.

Jessie went to work on the fence, working carefully with delicate tools and projectors to modify the field between two posts, bending and lifting the field to provide a narrow band beneath that was free of sensors. The work took a full hour. She and Otis squirmed carefully and silently through the cleared section, then moved even more carefully into the killing zone. The other cats followed, handing off surveillance one at a time.

Jessie, intimately familiar with the lay of the land, led while Otis kept a ten foot interval behind her. Both moved with all the stealth bred into their race, their very lives and the success of the Queen's mission in their hands. If they failed, the Queen failed.

Having never seen a gleason, Otis was not sure what to expect, but when the gleason finally came into view, he knew it immediately. He caught a shimmer beneath a tree as the creature moved, and he instantly froze, then lowered his belly to the ground. A smell registered on his senses, and though he had never smelled a gleason, he knew instantly that it was the smell of his prey. Oily and obnoxious, the smell sickened. His hackles rose up, his jowls rose in a silent roar, and he felt the ancient

blood lust rise. His deadly skills were ready: the hunt was on. Calm and
focused, he felt as if his whole life had been preparation for this one
fight.

Jessie signaled to the other pair of cats that she and Otis had
their prey in sight. The two cats moved off to set up a sniping position
while the team from the other side of the compound kept the second
gleason in view. They settled in to await the arrival of the rest of the
Queen's party, moving as the gleason moved, never letting it out of their
sight.

Ellie, her Knights, and the rest of their contingent arrived. The
moment they set foot into Chandrajuski's home, Jessie gave her signal
and fired at the gleason in her sights. Two quick shots took off a leg and
an arm. She and Otis moved in instantly as the creature went down
silently, its ability to change color gone. It was now a dark green, a color
that blended well into the shadow cast by the tree above it. In spite of its
terrible wound, each remaining hand held a weapon. Two blasters and a
knife were ready.

Otis rose and loosed off another shot, hitting the gleason in the
torso and throwing it backward. The gleason arose instantly and fired a
blaster, but Otis had flattened himself to the ground. The shot narrowly
missed. Jessie finished the creature off, then both of them raced to its
side to make sure the job was done.

The other gleason under observation melted into the tall grass
the moment its partner was shot. It's reflexes were simply incredible.
The two cats aiming at it never got off a shot. They moved out silently,
grimly determined, using all their senses to track their prey. The gleason
had disappeared in the direction of Otis and Jessie. The cats followed at a
run, their bellies scraping the ground. One cat exposed itself to draw fire,
but nothing happened. He raced a few meters, then raised up again. The
gleason materialized beside it, sinking a knife into its ribs. The cat
dropped, soon to die. The second cat got off a shot, creating a huge hole
in the side of the gleason's torso. It turned two blasters on the cat and
fired both. The cat was hit. One front leg disappeared, and it instantly
lowered itself to the ground. The gleason disappeared into the grass.

The cat, despite the terrible wound, moved in the direction of
Otis and Jessie, knowing that was where the gleason was headed. He
intercepted the gleason just before it reached them and let out a howl as
he fired his blaster. The gleason responded instantly. A poisoned knife
flashed into the side of the cat, and he fell. The sniper and spotter reacted
instantly, firing repeatedly and killing the gleason. As if rehearsed, the
third gleason appeared at their side, killing both snipers with blaster

shots.

Otis and Jessie were on their own. Two gleasons were dead, but the third was fully functional. They split up in the direction of the last gleason as it faded into the grass. Otis fired repeatedly into the grass in an effort to distract the creature, and Jessie followed suit, throwing several grenades in a spread pattern. In self defense, the gleason returned fire. Otis and Jessie fired repeatedly at the area the shots came from. Amazingly, one of the shots struck home. A scream rent the gathering twilight as the gleason lowered itself to the ground. Jessie was on it in an instant, followed closely by Otis. Her teeth bit into the gleason's neck, its most vulnerable spot, while her feet and hands tried to fight off the gleason's weapons. Its feet tore at her body as she bit deeper in an effort to sever its spinal cord.

The cicada sound suddenly erupted. The muscles in all the combatants screamed in protest, and Jessie and the gleason fell apart. The gleason recovered first, though it, too, was slowed greatly by the Chessori mind weapon. It reached out with a knife toward Jessie, but Otis leaped to her aid, catching the arm. He and the gleason rolled across the ground. Another knife appeared and sliced through the back of Otis' leg, severing a main tendon. They separated, and Jessie was ready. She fired two quick shots, but the gleason was already moving. One shot struck the gleason in the torso, and the other took off an arm. The gleason fired back, but Jessie had moved and the shot missed.

Moving erratically under the effect of the Chessori mind weapon and its wounds, it vanished into the high grass trailing blood. The cats pursued, Otis following as quickly as he could on three legs, but they could not track the beast at a full run. Tracking took time, time they did not have.

The rescue party in the house had to be warned. Otis and Jessie broke off and raced for the house. Their mission had failed. Their only concern now was to protect the Queen. Two of the three gleasons were dead, one was severely, possibly mortally wounded, but free. Its first priority would be the Queen. They would have to finish the job inside.

Chapter Fifty-eight

A darkened air car landed a quarter mile away from the guardhouse. Four figures emerged, including Mike and Val. Reba would stay beside the Queen this night. The four figures silently worked their way to the guardhouse and knocked on the door, knowing they were under observation. When the door opened, they burst in with weapons ready, but Jeffers had placed his men well. The guards all held their hands in the air.

A guard spoke. "The password is '*durgadskri*.'" Mike, Val, and the other two relaxed slightly as weapons were collected. Mike entered the viewing room from which the guards kept constant watch on the Gamordians and was sorely tempted to destroy it, but he had been warned that to do so would alert headquarters. A similar display there repeated everything this one observed.

"Remain here until the recall is sounded," Mike reminded the guards. "And don't waste any time getting to the assembly point if you want to go with us."

"Very well, sir. Uh, could you fire at the wall a bit, just to make it look like we tried to resist you? Just in case all does not go well?"

"We can do better than that. Don't take this personally." He and Val stunned each of the guards with weapons set to minimum. The guards would only be out for a few minutes, but residual effects would still be present if they were interrogated later.

Val whispered into his communicator. They were joined by five more darkened flitters and drove up to the house. They entered and quickly searched the house, then gathered in the forest room where Chandrajuski and his wife were held under gunpoint.

"What is this?" Chandrajuski demanded.

Ellie removed her hood, ordering all weapons lowered as she did so. Chandrajuski and his wife lowered their back legs and heads in a bow with eyes closed, their expressions impossible to interpret as anything but pleased. "Your Majesty, you honor us," Chandrajuski said simply.

"It's good to see you again, Admiral. May I call upon your services?"

"Chandra and I are at your service as always. I am so sorry about events."

"As am I. The throne will be restored. You will lead my forces."

"I am at your command, Your Majesty. To what forces do you refer?"

She smiled grimly. "Those you see are all we have at present. It's not an easy task I set for you, but we can discuss that later. For the moment, it's time to be away."

"Please complete your Testing then, Your Majesty."

Ellie took his head between her two hands and did her eye thing on him. It was very brief, and a look of relief washed across her face as she released him. "A ship will be here momentarily. We can move outside," she said.

"Not so fast, Your Majesty," came a triumphant voice from behind them. The room quickly filled with guards led by Jeffers himself, followed closely by Admiral Vorst who strutted to the front of his men, blaster in hand.

He and the Queen locked gazes for a time. "You've led a grand hunt, Your Majesty. You must have known you could not prevail with such a small force."

"Vorst. Why am I not surprised?" she stated distastefully. "What could possibly be in this for you? No one will give you the power you so crave."

"Careful, Your Majesty. You are perilously close to divulging that which you learned only through your Touch."

"It does not take the Touch to know you, Vorst."

"Well, as you can see, I now have command of a full sector. That's more than your mother would ever have granted."

"You will not hold it. You're not up to it."

Anger lit his face. "I've laid a trap, and you fell into it, something no one else has managed to do. I have demonstrated my worth. Now, drop your weapons."

"Never," replied the Queen. "And mine is pointed right at your heart. You will be the first to die."

"Vorst," spoke Chandrajuski, "order your men to lower their weapons immediately. You will not receive a second request." Vorst sneered at Chandrajuski, who simply said, "Children!"

The branches above their heads shook as many, many small Gamordians reached down with stunners pointed at the Rebels.

"Only stunners, Admiral?" Vorst asked confidently.

"I would not harm my own men, Vorst."

Vorst turned to discover his own men's weapons pointed at him. He blanched, but he turned back to Chandrajuski with his chin lifted. As he spoke, his arm lifted into the air. "I had anticipated as much."

Immediately a strong cicada sound erupted. Everyone, including the Gamordian children perched in the trees, fell to the floor writhing in pain, though a few staggered about with their hands over their ears, equally out of control. Only Mike and Reba remained standing. They both focused on three Chessori standing in the background, and their blasters made quick work of the three. The cicada sound stopped abruptly, and Mike and Reba quickly moved within the Rebel forces to disarm everyone except Jeffers. Though Jeffers vouched for his men, there was no need to take chances.

Mike went to Ellie as the people on the floor began recovering. She got to her feet with his assistance and clung to him. Just then, Otis burst into the room running on three legs, Jessie beside him with great rents in the flesh along her flanks.

"One lives!" Otis yelled as he and Jessie closed in on Ellie. From the back of the room, a dark figure rose briefly and let fly a knife directly at Ellie. Otis leaped from the floor, his blaster speaking and striking the gleason as the knife entered his own chest. The dark figure rose again and let fly another knife. Mike and Reba fired at the creature, each shot striking squarely to fling the creature backwards. Jessie launched herself to intercept the blade, but it was a perfect throw and she was not in time. The blade buried itself in Ellie's heart.

The Last of the Chosen collapsed to the floor, dead.

A Note From the Author

This author has been threatened with bodily harm (figuratively) because of the cliff-hangar ending, and you readers are right.

My apologies to all of you. Sorry! I'm new to this, and though I write a good story, I still have a lot to learn about writing. I hope you will bear with me.

Rather than force you to buy the next book just to keep from going insane, I am giving you a look at the first chapter of Book Two in the series. The full book is available for purchase, but here is a sample, included with your purchase of _**Last of the Chosen.**_

My readers have taught me that a book is like a contract between the writer and the reader. The reader is owed a good experience, and there should be a reasonable amount of closure at the end of the book, even if it is clear that there is more to follow.

I listen to your comments, and I thank you for them. There will be no more cliff-hangar endings in my writing.

Turn the page to sample Book Two of the Spirit of Empire series.

Spirit of Empire: Book Two

Knights of
the Chosen

Lawrence P. White

Knights of the

Chosen

Chapter One

The gleason struck so quickly that only a few in the great forest room of Chandrajuski's home knew it was even there. Most were still shaking off the terrible effects of the Chessori mind weapon. The three Chessori lay dead, killed by Mike and Reba, but Otis, Ellie's Protector, lay dying with a knife in his side. Ellie, the Last of the Chosen, collapsed with a knife in her heart, dead before she reached the floor.

Jessie, Mike's Protector and the only remaining Great Cat, leaped to the back of the room, firing repeatedly at the gleason to make certain it was dead.

Mike fell to the floor with Ellie, cushioning her. "Guard us!" he yelled to the room at large. Without waiting for a response, he went internal.

>Jake, I need you. She needs you.<

Jake knew exactly what he meant. >It's not done like this, Mike. You're my host.<

>We're her First Knight, Jake. Find a way. You are her only chance.<

Ellie's death had come so suddenly that Jake was at a loss, completely unprepared for what Mike asked of him. He had never considered living anywhere but within Mike. Riders always committed to a host and remained with them forever. The thought of leaving Mike devastated him. He wanted to fission a new Rider instead, but he knew his Queen did not have time.

>I'll try. Give me a minute, then remove the knife.<

Mike closed his hands around Ellie's neck, providing skin-to-skin contact for Jake, feeling for a pulse as he did so. There was no pulse at all. He closed his eyes, oblivious to all other activity within the room, feeling intently, waiting for a pulse. Still nothing. He waited the full minute, then pulled the knife from her chest and immediately went back to feeling for a pulse.

After a time, he thought he felt a faint pressure. The pressure gradually increased until he was certain there was a pulse, though it remained weak.

"Thank you, Jake," he whispered and was momentarily surprised that there was no response. But there could be no response. Jake was no longer a part of him.

His attention widened to take in his surroundings. All eyes were on him and Ellie. Vorst, the replacement Sector Commander, lay bound hand and foot. Jessie crouched beside Otis who was unconscious. "Is he . . . ?" Mike struggled to ask.

"Not yet," she growled in response. "But it will not be long. The knives are almost certainly poisoned."

Mike turned to Reba who stood at the ready, her blaster trying to cover the whole room.

"Jake has gone to Ellie. It seems to be working."

Her eyes closed as she went internal to her Rider. When her lips thinned and she holstered her blaster, Mike knew the two of them had reached agreement. She went to Otis and laid her hands on him. After a time, she removed the knife from his side.

She turned back to Mike, the sparkle that was always evident in her eyes gone. "Let's get out of here."

Jeffers, the leader of Chandrajuski's underground, spoke into a communicator, then ordered everyone outside to the assembly point. One of Serge's freighters was just settling to the ground. As they struggled to get Ellie and Otis aboard, the freighter was struck by fire from above. It quickly responded with its own weapons, but it could not move until the ramp closed. Its upper shields glowed from hits, and dissipating energy streaming from the shields struck several of Jeffers' men. There was no hope for them.

Jeffers boarded and quickly ran for the bridge. When he arrived, the ship was just lifting. Captain Palmetier, though busy, immediately lifted his visor and raised a blaster toward him.

Jeffers raised his hands, shouting, "I'm on your side." He set his own blaster on the floor and slid it toward Palmetier, then submitted as two crewmen pinned his arms to his sides. A glance at the screens showed a full squadron of fighters engaging the freighter.

A loud, "Time to boogie, Jer," came over the speakers as another freighter appeared on the screens headed directly into the fray, its weapons firing nonstop. Serge Parsons had come in person.

"On the way, boss," replied Palmetier curtly. He slid his visor back over his face to cover a grin.

Moments later, a cruiser came into view from over the horizon, moving fast.

"That one's on our side," yelled Jeffers. "So are a couple of others. Be careful who you shoot at. Get me into the net so I can help."

The two crewmen were uncertain until Sir Val showed up. "Let us both into the net," he ordered.

It didn't take long before they cleared the fighters and headed for space. In fact, by the time they reached space, there wasn't a single Rebel fighter left. The Rebel command ship, a cruiser, broke off its pursuit when Jeffers' friendly squadron approached. When two more squadrons of Jeffers' ships came over the horizon, it was no contest. The Rebel cruiser retreated.

They reached the edge of space, but they did not have to wait three weeks to jump as did Jeffers' ships. Use of the micro jumping capability might give away a closely held secret, but Ellie's life hung in the balance. *Joline's* beacon went silent, and it was likely the Rebels would not even see the ship amidst all the confusion. As Palmetier prepared jump computations for the first micro jump, Val contacted Serge and gave him a set of coordinates, explaining to him that three heavy squadrons loyal to Chandrajuski and the Queen would head for that point in space. Admiral Chandrajuski wanted those ships, but none of them knew the location of the Queen's secret base.

Serge balked until apprised of the Queen's condition, then grimly advised Val that he'd take care of it.

Joline's sickbay carried no life support tanks, only a medic and basic supplies. Jake and Celine, the two Riders, had their work cut out for them.

From his own experience Mike knew that, at the very least, food was essential to their survival. The healing process used by Riders consumed large amounts energy. The medic attached two IV's to each of them and pushed all the nourishment she could into the comatose bodies.

Her principle concern for her patients was not the physical damage caused by the knives – the Riders seemed to have that problem well in hand. Her greater concern was whether the Riders could cope with whatever poison had been on the blades. She took blood samples, then had to wait while a computer worked on the samples.

Mike remained by Ellie's side. She couldn't hear him, but he believed his presence might somehow help. She and Otis each contracted high fevers despite their Riders' best efforts.

The computer only partially resolved the issue of the poison. It was there, and its molecular structure had been analyzed, but it matched no known compound. The medic made an educated guess that it was from the home world of the gleasons. Any wrong attempts to treat it might make Jake and Celine's jobs harder.

It didn't take Mike long to make the logical connections. He called Captain Palmetier.

"You carried Otis on his research mission to study the gleasons. Do you have his notes?"

"I do."

"There might be some mention of poisons used by the gleasons. Can you get everyone you can to review the records for us?"

"We'll get on it immediately."

It took a while, but Val and Reba eventually showed up with printouts in hand. "We have a number of possibilities, Mike," Val advised. "We've discarded most of them as being so lethal that they kill instantly. Neither Ellie or Otis would still be alive if they had been used. We're down to three that are a little slower acting but just as deadly."

They showed the printouts to the medic who studied them intently. She then went to work on her computer.

"Of the three, I can synthesize antidotes for two," she announced after some study. "An antidote for the third is unknown. I cannot say which of the remaining two is most likely. I'm going to take samples for testing."

"How long will the testing take?" Mike asked wearily.

The medic worked while she talked, taking new samples of blood from Ellie and Otis and placing those samples on a number of test dishes. "A day or two, minimum. I have to let the growths get started, but I can work on making both antidotes while that's going on. Then we test the antidotes on the test growths. Another few hours to a day or so."

"Let me know the minute you have the antidotes ready," Mike

ordered. "It doesn't look to me like we have days. They're burning up with fever."

The antidotes were ready in a few hours. Mike pushed the medic as hard as he could. "Is there any sign of growth yet in the test samples?"

"Only microscopic. Not enough to test."

"You have lots of samples. Test a few right now."

The medic did as ordered, but she was not happy about it. "The tests results will not be valid, Sire."

"I know. You can run complete tests on the other samples later."

Mike then reached both hands down inside Ellie's hospital gown, placing both hands flat against her stomach. With his eyes closed, he willed his thoughts to Jake. "Come on, Jake. Come to me," he whispered.

It didn't take long for Jake to sense his presence. Though he couldn't feel anything, Mike *felt* Jake's presence.

>Hello, Man,< he heard faintly, as if from far away.

>Hi, Jake.<

>I'm too busy for idle chatter. I don't think we're going to make it this time.<

>Yes you are, and I'm going to help. I need you to pass me a sample of the poison.<

>You already have samples.<

>No, Jake. I need you to pass a sample into my body. We don't know which antidote to use. We'll test one of them on me.<

He felt Jake's presence strengthen in him. He had Jake's complete attention for the moment. More, he sensed Jake's suffering. The poison was clearly killing him as well as Ellie.

>Not a good idea, Mike. This is a bad one.<

>I know, and from the looks of things, you can't save her by yourself. Please let me help, for both of your sakes.<

>You understand that if I lose her, I am lost as well?<

>I kind of guessed that.<

>Okay, here you go. This stuff hurts.<

>Make it a strong sample, Jake. If we guess wrong, if we use the wrong antidote, it will kill both of you.<

>Okay. I have to go. See you on the other side.<

Mike felt Jake's presence withdraw. He pulled his hands from Ellie and turned to the medic who was staring at him with a shocked expression.

"Any results yet?" he asked.

"No, Sire. I just started the test. *What were you doing?*"

"Communicating with her Rider. The poison is in me now, and it's already working. You'd better get another bed ready."

The medic's eyes rose to the ceiling. With a frown, she bustled Mike off to a bed. Reba started to chew Mike out, but Val put his arm around her waist and leaned toward her ear.

"You know it's the right thing to do. I'd do it for you in a heartbeat. In fact, I'm surprised I didn't think of it myself. He's doing it for her, not just for the Empire."

"Of course he is. My god, it could all fall apart right here," she breathed.

"No. One Heir remains, if she proves to have the Touch. I'm staying the course. Will you?"

"I choose to stay with you no matter what course we follow," she whispered into his ear.

Mike's body arched. He groaned, "Someone better make a decision."

The medic turned frightened eyes to him. "It's too soon, Sire. I can't be certain."

Chandrajuski's long, jointed legs inched his bright green body farther into sick bay, the wise old eyes of the giant praying mantis swinging toward the medic until they were on a level with her own. Speaking like a father rather than the queen's senior military commander, he said, "You must decide, child. If you choose wrong, it will not be held against you. We understand."

She returned to her test dishes, taking samples and placing them under a microscope for visual inspection. The computers had so far been inconclusive. Switching samples back and forth, still peering into the eyepiece, she eventually said, "I believe it is most likely this one, but I can't be certain."

"Then the decision is made," Chandrajuski said to her. "Administer the antidote. If this one fails, we will administer the other to Otis."

Twenty minutes later Mike stirred, then opened his eyes. Chandrajuski took charge, turning to the medic. "Were both knives poisoned with the same chemical?"

"Yes."

"Administer the antidote to both of them, at once."

Both Ellie and Otis' fevers broke hours later. Both remained in a coma as the Riders did their work, but the immediate danger had passed.

Mike was able to leave his bed the following day, though he remained weak. He found Jessie sitting by Ellie's side, her tail curled around her feet, her body wrapped in massive bandages.

"How are they doing?"

"About the same. No worse. The poison damaged multiple organs. They're beyond help from the medic, but she believes the Riders have a chance. They both need tanks, but the ship doesn't carry a tank."

"You've been here a while, haven't you?"

"I have my responsibilities. I will answer to Otis when he recovers."

"Can't you share the job with the other cats?"

"What others?"

"You mean . . ." He paused, suddenly aware that the rest of the Great Cats were missing. They must have perished in their battle against the gleasons.

"I'm sorry. I didn't know." After a time, he asked, "Were any of them special to you?"

"All of them were special to me. We were team members."

"Why don't you take a break, get some rest. I'll stay."

"You couldn't protect her from a feather right now."

"Neither could you."

"You'd be surprised, Sire."

"Okay, I'll get Val or Reba to relieve you. Will that be acceptable?"

"Bring both of them, and be certain they're armed. We cannot guarantee the loyalty of the crew. She is not to be left unguarded, even for a moment."

Notes From the Author

If you liked the book, or even if you did not like the book, I am asking you to take a moment to write a review on Amazon.com. Writing reviews on Amazon is easy, just one or two sentences is adequate, and they are important to authors and readers alike.

* * * * *

Writing is a very personal business. I'm always trying to improve, and I welcome any feedback you would like to give. Check out my web site:

www.spiritofempire.com

On that website you will find a link to my books and a link to my private email. I enjoy hearing from my readers, whether the comments are positive or negative. I will do my very best to respond to every email.

The third book in the series, _Voice of the Chosen_, is planned for release around Christmas 2011. I will do my best, but I make no promises. Both the release date and the title are subject to change.

It's been a lot of fun to write this series. I hope you have enjoyed reading it as much as I have enjoyed writing it. Please, Please, Please, send in those reviews, and don't hesitate to email me.

About the Author

Born in 1950, I have been a pilot all of my working life and a writer for most of that time. I flew over 600 combat missions in Vietnam and have since traveled over most of the Earth flying private jets. About half of my career has been in management positions.

If ever there was a case of life experience informing what a writer writes, I am that case. I have met people from all walks of life and from all over our wonderful planet, and I have liked almost all of them. It is only a small stretch for me to imagine liking aliens.

I encourage your feedback. Feel free to check out my website and send an email.

Email: larry@spiritofempire.com

Website: www.spiritofempire.com

Made in the USA
Lexington, KY
09 November 2011